THE THIRD RUTH RENDELL OMNIBUS

By the same author

To Fear a Painted Devil
Vanity Dies Hard
The Secret House of Death
One Across, Two Down
A Demon in My View
A Judgement in Stone
Make Death Love Me
The Lake of Darkness
Master of the Moor
The Killing Doll
The Tree of Hands
Live Flesh
Talking to Strange Men
The Bridesmaid
Going Wrong
The Crocodile Bird

Chief Inspector Wexford novels

From Doon with Death
A New Lease of Death
Wolf to the Slaughter
The Best Man to Die
A Guilty Thing Surprised
No More Dying Then
Murder Being Once Done
Some Lie and Some Die
Shake Hands for Ever
A Sleeping Life
Put On by Cunning
The Speaker of Mandarin
An Unkindness of Ravens
The Veiled One
Kissing the Gunner's Daughter

Short Stories

The Fallen Curtain
Means of Evil
The Fever Tree
The New Girl Friend
The Copper Peacock

Omnibuses

Collected Short Stories
Wexford: An Omnibus
The Second Wexford Omnibus
The Third Wexford Omnibus
The Fourth Wexford Omnibus
The Fifth Wexford Omnibus
Ruth Rendell Omnibus
The Second Ruth Rendell Omnibus

Novella

Heartstones

Non-fiction

Ruth Rendell's Suffolk

THE THIRD RUTH RENDELL OMNIBUS

One Across Two Down
Make Death Love Me
The Lake of Darkness

Ruth Rendell

HUTCHINSON
London

This Omnibus edition first published in 1994 by Hutchinson

One Across Two Down
First published in 1971 by Hutchinson

Make Death Love Me
First published in 1979 by Hutchinson

The Lake of Darkness
First published in 1980 by Hutchinson

1 3 5 7 9 10 8 6 4 2

Random House (UK) Ltd
20 Vauxhall Bridge Road, London SW1V 2SA

Random House Australia (Pty) Ltd
20 Alfred Street, Milsons Point, Sydney, NSW 2061, Australia

Random House New Zealand Ltd
18 Poland Road, Glenfield, Auckland 10, New Zealand

Random House South Africa (Pty) Ltd
PO Box 337, Bergvlei, 2012, South Africa

A CIP catalogue for this book is available from the British Library

ISBN: 0 09 178249 X

Set in Plantin type
Typeset by Pure Tech Corporation, Pondicherry, India
Printed and bound in Great Britain by
Mackays of Chatham PLC, Chatham, Kent

Contents

ONE ACROSS TWO DOWN

For my son.

Come into the garden, Maud,
  For the black bat, night, has flown,
Come into the garden, Maud,
  I am here at the gate alone,

Alfred, Lord Tennyson

Contents

PART ONE
Blank Puzzle

1

Vera Manning was very tired. She was too tired even to answer her mother back when Maud told her to hurry up with getting the tea.

'There's no need to sulk,' said Maud.

'I'm not sulking, Mother. I'm tired.'

'Of course you are. That goes without saying. Anyone can see you're worn out with that job of yours. Now if Stanley had the gumption to get himself a good position and brought a decent wage home you wouldn't have to work. I never heard of such a thing, a woman of your age, coming up to the change, on her feet all day in a dry cleaner's. I've said it before and I'll say it again, if Stanley was a man at all . . .'

'All right, Mother,' said Vera. 'Let's give it a rest, shall we?'

But Maud, who scarcely ever stopped talking when there was anyone to listen to her and who talked to herself when she was alone, got out of her chair and, taking her stick, limped after Vera into the kitchen. Perching herself with some difficulty – she was a large heavily built woman – on a stool, she surveyed the room with a distaste which was partly sincere and partly assumed for her daughter's benefit. It was clean but shabby, unchanged since the days when people expected to see a ganglion of water pipes protruding all over the walls and a dresser and built-in plaster copper requisite fitments. Presently, when the scornful glance had set the scene for fresh propaganda, Maud drew a deep breath and began again.

'I've scraped and saved all my life just so that there'd be something for you when I'm gone. D'you know what Ethel Carpenter said to me? Maud, she said, why don't you give it to Vee while she's young enough to enjoy it?'

Her back to Maud, Vera was cutting meat pie in slices and shelling hard-boiled eggs. 'It's a funny thing, Mother,' she said, 'the way I'm an old woman one minute and a young one the next, whichever happens to suit your book.'

Maud ignored this. 'Why don't you give it to Vee now, she said. Oh no, I said. Oh no, it wouldn't be giving it to her, I said, it'd be giving it to that no-good husband of hers. If he got his hands on my money, I said, he'd never do another hand's turn as long as he lived.'

'Move over a bit, would you, Mother? I can't get at the kettle.'

Shifting an inch or two, Maud patted her thick grey curls with a lady's idle white hand. 'No,' she said, 'while I've got breath in my body my savings are staying where they are, invested in good stock. That way maybe Stanley'll come to his senses. When you have a nervous breakdown, and that's the way you're heading, my girl, maybe he'll pull his socks up and get a job fit for a man, not a teenager. That's the way I see it and that's what I said to Ethel in my last letter.'

'Would you like to sit up now, Mother? It's ready.'

Vera helped her mother into a chair at the dining room table and hooked her stick over the back of it. Maud tucked a napkin into the neckline of her blue silk dress and helped herself to a plateful of pork pie, eggs, green salad and mashed potato. Before starting on it, she swallowed two white tablets and washed them down with strong sweet tea. Then she lifted her knife and fork with a sigh of sensual pleasure. Maud enjoyed her food. The only time she was silent was when she was eating or asleep. As she was starting on her second piece of pie, the back door slammed and her son-in-law came in.

Stanley Manning nodded to his wife and gave a sort of grunt. His mother-in-law, who had temporarily stopped eating to fix him with a cold condemning eye, he ignored. The first thing he did after throwing his coat over the back of a chair was to turn on the television.

'Had a good day?' said Vera.

'Been up to my eyes in it since nine this morning.' Stanley sat down, facing the television, and waited for Vera to pour him a cup of tea. 'I'm whacked out, I can tell you. It's no joke being out in the open all day long in weather like this. To tell you the truth, I don't know how long I can keep on with it.'

Maud sniffed. 'Ethel Carpenter didn't believe me when I told her what you did for a living, if you can call it a living. A petrol pump attendant! She said that's what her landlady's son does in his holidays from college. Eighteen he is, just a student doing it for pin money.'

'Ethel Carpenter can keep her nose out of my business, the old bag.'

'Don't you use language like that about my friend!'

'Oh, pack it up, do,' said Vera. 'I thought you were going to watch the film.'

If Stanley and Maud were in accord over one thing it was their fondness for old films and now, having exchanged venomous glances, they settled down among the tea things to watch Jeanette Macdonald in *The Girl of the Golden West*. Vera, a little revived with two hot cups of tea, sighed thankfully and began clearing the table. Altercation would break out again, she knew, at eight o'clock when Stanley's favourite quiz programme conflicted with Maud's favourite serial. She dreaded Tuesday and Thursday evenings. Of course it was only natural that Stanley, with his passion for puzzles, should want to watch the quizzes that took place on those nights; and natural that Maud, in common with five million other middle-aged and elderly women, should long for the next development in the complicated lives of the residents of *Augusta Alley*. But why couldn't they come to an amicable arrangement like reasonable people? Because they weren't reasonable people, she thought, as she began the washing-up. For her part, she couldn't care less about the television and sometimes she hoped the cathode ray tube would break or a valve go or something. Certainly the way things were they wouldn't be able to afford to get it seen to.

Jeanette Macdonald was singing Ave Maria when she got back to the living room and Maud was accompanying her in a sentimental cracked soprano. Vera prayed for the song to end before Stanley did something violent like bringing Maud's stick down on the table with a thunderous crash, as he had done only the week before. But this time he contented himself with low mutterings and Vera leant her head against a cushion and closed her eyes.

Four years Mother's been here, she thought, four long years of unbroken hell. Why had she been so stupid and so impulsive as to agree to it in the first place? It wasn't as if Maud was ill or even really disabled. She'd made a marvellous recovery from that stroke. There was nothing wrong with her but for a weakness in the left leg and a little quirk to her mouth. She was as capable of looking after herself as any woman of seventy-four. But it was no use harking back now. The thing was done, Maud's house sold and all her furniture, and she and Stanley had got her till the day she died.

Maud's petulant angry wail started her out of her half-doze and made her sit up with a jerk.

'What are you turning over to ITV for? I've been looking forward to my *Augusta Alley* all day. We don't want that kids' stuff, a lot of schoolkids answering silly questions.'

'Who pays the licence, I'd like to know?' said Stanley.

'I pay my share. Every week I turn my pension over to Vee. Ten shillings is the most I ever keep for my bits and pieces.'

Stanley made no reply. He moved his chair closer to the set and got out pencil and paper.

'All day long I was looking forward to my serial,' said Maud.

'Never mind, Mother,' said Vera, trying to infuse a little cheerfulness into her tired voice. 'Why don't you watch *Oak Valley Farm* in the afternoons when we're at work? That's a nice serial, all about country people.'

'I have my sleep in the afternoons, that's why not. I'm not upsetting my routine.'

Maud lapsed into a moody silence, but if she wasn't to be allowed to watch her programme she had no intention of allowing Stanley uninterrupted enjoyment of his. After about five minutes, during which Stanley scribbled excitedly on his pad, she began tapping her stick rhythmically against the fender. It sounded as if she was trying to work out the timing of a hymn tune. 'Dear Lord and Father of Mankind,' Vera thought it was, and presently Maud confirmed this by humming the melody very softly.

Stanley stood it for about thirty seconds and then he said, 'Shut up, will you?'

Maud gave a lugubrious sigh. 'They played that hymn at your grandfather's funeral, Vera.'

'I don't care if they played it at Queen Victoria's bloody wedding,' said Stanley. 'We don't want to hear it now, so do as I say and shut up. There, now you've made me miss the score.'

'I'm sure I'm very sorry,' said Maud with heavy sarcasm. 'I know you don't want me here, Stanley, you've made that very plain. You'd do anything to get rid of me, wouldn't you? Grease the stairs or give me an overdose?'

'Maybe I would at that. There's many a true word spoken in jest.'

'You hear what he says, Vera? You heard him say it.'

'He doesn't mean it, Mother.'

'Just because I'm old and helpless and sometimes I hark back to the old days when I was happy.'

Stanley leapt to his feet and the pencil bounced on to the floor.

'Will you shut up or do I have to make you?'

'Don't you raise your voice to me, Stanley Manning!' Maud, satisfied that she had ruined Stanley's quiz, rose and, turning to Vera with great dignity, said in the voice of one mortally wounded, 'I shall go to bed now, Vera, and leave you and your husband in peace. Perhaps it wouldn't be expecting too much if I was to ask you to make my Horlicks and bring it up when I'm in bed?'

'Of course I will, Mother. I always do.'

'There's no need to say "always" like that. I'd rather go without than have it done in a grudging spirit.'

Maud wandered round the room, picking up her knitting from one chair, her glasses from another, her book from the sideboard. She could have got all these things by walking behind Stanley, but she didn't. She walked between him and the television set.

'Mustn't forget my glass of water,' she said, and added as if she was boasting of some highly laudable principle, as salutary to the body as it was demanding of strength of character, 'I've slept with a glass of water beside my bed ever since I was a little mite. Never missed one. I couldn't sleep without my glass of water.'

She fetched it herself, leaving a little trail of drips from the over-full glass behind her. They heard her stick tapping against the treads as she mounted the stairs.

Stanley switched off the television and, without a word to his wife, opened the *Second Bumper Book of Advanced Crosswords*. Like an overworked animal, worn out with repetitive tedious labour, her mind empty of everything but the desire for sleep, Vera stared at him in silence. Then she went into the kitchen, made the Horlicks and carried it upstairs.

*

Sixty-one, Lanchester Road, Croughton, in the northern suburbs of London, was a two-storeyed red brick house, at the end of a terrace, and built in 1906. There was a large back garden, and between the living room bay and the front fence a strip of grass five feet by fifteen.

The hall was a passage with a mosaic floor of red and white tiles, and downstairs there were two living rooms and a tiny kitchen, as well as an outside lavatory and a cupboard for coal. The stairs ran straight up without a bend to the landing from which opened four doors, one to the bathroom and three to the bedrooms. The smallest of these was big enough to accommodate only a single bed, dressing table and curtained off area for clothes. Vera called it the spare room.

She and Stanley shared the large double bedroom at the front of the house and Maud slept in the back. She was sitting up in bed, the picture of health in her hand-knitted angora bedjacket. But for the thirty or so metal curlers clipped into her hair, she might well have entered for and won a glamorous grandmother contest.

Perhaps the bottles and jars of patent and prescribed medicaments on the bedside table had something to do with the preservation, indeed the rejuvenation, of her mother, Vera thought, as she handed Maud the mug of Horlicks. There were enough of them. Anti-coagulants, diuretics, tranquillizers, sleep inducers, and vitamin concentrates.

'Thank you, dear. My electric blanket won't come on. It needs servicing.'

Turning away from her draggled and exhausted reflection in Maud's dressing table mirror, Vera said she would see to it tomorrow.

'That's right, and while you do you can ask them to look at my radio. And get me another ounce of this pink wool, will you?' Maud sipped her Horlicks. 'Sit down, Vee. I want to talk to you where *he* can't hear.'

'Can't it wait till tomorrow, Mother?'

'No, it can't. Tomorrow might be too late. Did you hear what he said to me about doing me in if he had the chance?'

'Oh Mother, you don't really think he meant it?'

Maud said calmly, 'Stanley hates me, not that it isn't mutual. Now you listen to what I've got to say.'

Vera knew what was coming. She heard it with slight variations once or twice a week. 'I'm not leaving Stan, and that's that. I've told you over and over again. I'm not leaving him.'

Maud finished her Horlicks and said in a cajoling tone, 'Just think what a life we could have together, Vee, you and me. I've got money enough for both of us. I'm telling you in confidence, I'm a wealthy woman by anyone's standards. You wouldn't have to lift a finger. We'd have a nice new house. I saw in the paper they're building some lovely bungalows out Chigwell way. I could buy one of them bungalows outright.'

'If you want to give me some of your money, Mother, you can give it to me. I shan't argue. God knows, there's plenty we need in this house.'

'Stanley Manning isn't getting a penny of my money,' said Maud. She took her teeth out and placed them in a glass; then she gave Vera a gummy wheedling smile. 'You're all I've got, Vee. What's mine is yours, you know that. You don't want to share it with him. What's he ever done for you? He's a crook and a jailbird.'

Vera controlled herself with difficulty.

'Stanley has been to prison once and once only, Mother, as you very well know. And that was when he was eighteen. It's downright cruel calling him a jailbird.'

'He may have been to prison just the once, but how many times would he have been back there if all those people he works for hadn't been soft as butter? You know as well as I do he's been sacked twice for helping himself out of the till.'

Getting to her feet, Vera said, 'I'm tired, Mother. I want to go to bed and I'm not staying here if all you can do is abuse my husband.'

'Ah, Vee . . .' Maud put out a hand and managed to make her wrist quiver as she did so. 'Vee, don't be cross with me. I had such high hopes for you and look at you now, a poor old drudge tied to a man who doesn't care whether you live or die. It's true, Vee, you know it is.' Vera let her hand rest limply in her mother's and Maud squeezed it tenderly. 'We could have a lovely house, dear. We'd have fitted carpets and central heating and a woman in to clean every day. You're still young. You could learn to drive and

I'd buy you a car. We could go for holidays. We could go abroad if you like.'

'I married Stanley,' said Vera, 'and you always taught me marriage is for keeps.'

'Vee, I've never told you how much I've got. If I tell you, you won't tell Stanley, will you?' Vera didn't say anything, and Maud, though seventy-four and for many years married herself, hadn't yet learnt that it is no good telling secrets to a married person if you want them to remain secrets. For, no matter how shaky the marriage and how incompatible the partners, a wife will always confide other people's confessions in her husband and a husband in his wife. 'My money's mounted up through the years. I've got twenty thousand pounds in the bank, Vera. What d'you think of that?'

Vera felt the colour drain out of her face. It was a shock. Never in her wildest dreams had she supposed her mother to have half that amount, and she was sure it had never occurred to Stanley either.

'It's a lot of money,' she said quietly.

'Now don't you tell him. If he knew what I was worth he'd start thinking up ways to get rid of me.'

'Please, Mother, don't start that all over again. If anyone heard you they'd think you were going daft in the head. They would.'

'Well, they can't hear me. I'll say good night now, dear. We'll talk about it again tomorrow.'

'Good night, Mother,' said Vera.

She didn't think any more about what her mother had said on the lines of taking her away from Stanley. She had heard it all before. Nor was she very much concerned that Maud suspected Stanley of murderous inclinations. Her mother was old and the old get strange ideas into their heads. It was silly and fantastic but it wasn't worth worrying about.

But she did wonder what Stanley would say when – and that would have to be when she was less tired – she told him how much money Maud had in the bank. Twenty thousand! It was a fortune. Still thinking about it, and thinking how even one twentieth part of it would improve the house and make her lot so much lighter, Vera stripped off her clothes and rolled exhausted into bed.

2

Maud was an old woman with dangerously high blood pressure and one cerebral thrombosis behind her, but she wasn't affected in her mind. The ideas she had that her son-in-law might kill her if he got the chance weren't the fruit of senile maunderings but notions of human behaviour formed by Maud in her impressionable teens.

She had gone into service at the age of fourteen and much of the talk in the kitchen and the servants' hall had dealt with unscrupulous persons whom her fellow servants suspected of murder or the intention of murder for gain. Cook often insisted that the valet in the big house across the square would poison his master as soon as the time was ripe merely for the sake of the hundred pounds promised to him in the old man's will, while the butler countered this with horrible tales of greedy heirs in the great families that had employed him. Maud listened to all this with the same receptive ear and the same gullibility as she listened to the vicar's sermons on Sundays.

It seemed that from the butler down to the tweeny, no servant was without a relative who at some time or another had not considered popping arsenic in a rich aunt's tea. A favourite phrase in the servants' hall, on the lines of Eliza Doolittle's statement, was:

'It's my belief the old man done her in.'

And it was Maud's sincere belief that Stanley Manning would do her in if he got the chance. Enlightening Vera as to the extent of her fortune had been a temptation she hadn't been able to resist, but when she awoke on the following morning she wondered if she had been unwise. Vera would very likely tell Stanley and there was nothing she, Maud, could do about it.

Nothing, that is, to silence Vera. Much could perhaps be done to show Stanley that, though he might kill her, he wouldn't profit from his iniquities. With these things uppermost in her mind, Maud ate the breakfast Vera brought to her in bed and, when her daughter and son-in-law had left for work, got up, dressed and left the house. With the aid of her stick she walked the half-mile to the bus stop and went down into town to consult a solicitor whose name she had found in Stanley's trade directory. She could easily have bought her own wool and seen to the servicing of her electric blanket at the same time and saved Vera's feet, but she didn't see why she should put herself out for Vera when the silly girl was being so obstinate.

Back in the house by twelve Maud ate heartily of the cold ham, salad, bread and butter and apple crumble pie Vera had left her for her lunch and then settled down to write her weekly letter to her best friend, Ethel Carpenter. Like most of the letters she had written to Ethel since she came to live in Lanchester Road, it dealt largely with the idleness, ill manners, bad temper and general uselessness of Stanley Manning.

There was no one, Maud thought, whom she could trust like she could trust Ethel. Even Vera, blindly devoted to that good-for-nothing, couldn't be relied on like Ethel who had no husband, no children and no axe to grind. Poor Ethel had only her landlady, owner of the house in Brixton where she occupied one room, and Maud herself.

Ah, you valued a friend when you'd been through what she and Ethel had been through together, thought Maud as she laid down her pen. How long ago was it they'd first met? Fifty-four years? Fifty-five? No, it was just fifty-four. She was twenty and the under housemaid and Ethel, little, innocent seventeen-year-old Ethel, the kitchen maid at that sharp-tongued cook's beck and call.

Maud was walking out with George Kinaway, the chauffeur, and they were going to get married as soon as their ship came in. She had always been a saver, had Maud, and whether the ship came in or not they'd have enough to get married on by the time she was thirty. Meanwhile there were those delicious quiet walks with George on Clapham Common on Sundays and the little garnet engagement ring she wore round her neck on a bit of ribbon, for it wouldn't have done at all to have it on her finger when she did out the grates.

She had George and something to look forward to but Ethel had nothing. No one knew Ethel even had a follower of her own or had ever spoken to a man, bar George and the butler, until her trouble came on her and Madam turned her out of the house in disgrace. Ethel's aunt took her in and everyone treated her like dirt except Maud and George. They weren't above going to see her at the aunt's house on their evenings off, and when the child came it was George who persuaded the aunt to bring it up and George who contributed a few shillings every week to its maintenance.

'Though we can ill afford it,' said Maud. 'Now if she'd only stop being a little fool and tell me who the father is . . .'

'She'll never do that,' said George. 'She's too proud.'

'Well, they do say that pride goeth before a fall and Ethel's taken her fall all right. It's our duty to stick by her. We must never lose touch with Ethel, dear.'

'If you say so, dear,' said George, and he got Madam to take Ethel back just as if she were a good girl without a stain on her character.

Those were the hard days, Maud thought, leaning back her head and closing her eyes. Twelve pounds a year she got until the Great War came and made people buck up their ideas. Even when the master raised her wages it was hard going to get a home together and in the end it was George's good looks and nice manners that gave them their start. Not that there had ever been anything wrong between him and Madam – the very idea! – but when she died George was in her will, and with the two hundred and fifty he got and what Maud had saved they'd bought a nice little business down by the Oval.

Ethel always came to them for her holidays and when Vera was born Ethel was her godmother. It was the least she could do for Ethel, Maud confided in George, seeing that she'd been deprived of her own daughter and wasn't likely ever to get a husband of her own, second-hand goods as she was.

What with George's charm and Maud's hard work the shop prospered and soon they could think themselves comfortably off. Vera was sent to a very select private school and when she left at the late (almost unheard-of) age of sixteen, Maud wouldn't let her get a job or serve in the shop. Her daughter was going to be a lady and in time she'd marry a nice gentlemanly man, a bank clerk or someone in business – Maud never told people her husband kept a shop. She always said he was 'in business' – and have a house of her own. Meanwhile she gave Vera all the money she wanted within reason for clothes and once a year they all went down to Brayminster-on-Sea – dear old Bray, as they called it – and stayed at a very genteel boarding house with a view of the sea. Sometimes Ethel went with them and she was just as pleased as they when her goddaughter found favour in the sight of the boarding house keeper's nephew, James Horton.

James had the very job Maud envisaged as most desirable in a son-in-law. He worked in the Brayminster branch of Barclay's Bank, and when during the winter months he occasionally came up to London and took Vera on the river or to a theatre matinée, Maud smiled on him and began discussing with George what they could do for the young couple when they fixed the day. A deposit on a house and two hundred for furniture was Ethel Carpenter's recommendation and Maud thought this not unreasonable.

Four years older than Vera, James had been a petty officer in the Royal Navy during the war. He had a nice little sum on deposit at the bank, was a dutiful son and a churchgoer. Nothing could be more suitable.

Maud had old-fashioned ideas and thought young people should only be allowed to know each other if they had been properly introduced or if their parents were old friends. It was with horror, therefore, that she learned from Mrs Campbell, the wife of the fishmonger down the road, that Vera had been seen about in the company of the young barman at the Coach and Horses whom, Mrs Campbell alleged, she had met at a dance.

It was all George's fault, Maud told Ethel. If she had had her way, Vera would never have been allowed to go to that dance. She had tried to put her foot down but for once George had asserted himself and said there was no harm in Vera going with a girl friend and what could be more respectable than the Young Conservatives' annual ball?

'I'm sure I don't know what James will say when he hears about it,' Maud said to Vera.

'I don't care what he says. I'm sick of James, he's so boring. Always on about going to bed early and getting up early and saving money and keeping oneself to oneself. Stanley says you're only young once and you might as well enjoy yourself. He says money's there to spend.'

'I daresay he does when it's someone else's. A barman! My daughter sneaking out with a barman!' Although she sometimes permitted George to enjoy a quiet pint in the Bunch of Grapes on Friday nights, Maud had never in her life set foot in a public house. 'Anyway, it's got to stop, Vee. You can tell him your mother and father won't allow it.'

'I'm twenty-two,' said Vera, who, though her father's daughter in looks and generally in temperament, had inherited a spark of her mother's spirit. 'You can't stop me. You're always on about me getting married but how can I get married when I never meet any men? Girls can't meet men when they don't go out to work.'

'You met James,' said Maud.

Afterwards she wasn't sure which was the worst moment of her life, the time when Mrs Campbell told her Stanley Manning had served two years for robbery with violence or the time when Vera said she was in love with Stanley and wanted to marry him.

'Don't you dare talk of marrying that criminal!' Maud screamed. 'You'll marry him over my dead body. I'll kill myself first. I'll put my head in the gas oven. And I'll see to it you won't get a penny of my money.'

The trouble was she couldn't stop Vera meeting him. For a time nothing more was said about marriage or even an engagement but Vera and Stanley went on seeing each other and Maud nearly worried herself into a nervous breakdown. For the life of her, she couldn't see what Vera saw in him.

In all her life she had only known one man she could fancy sharing her bed with and by this yardstick she measured all men. George Kinaway was six feet tall with classic Anglo-Saxon good looks apart from his weak chin, while Stanley was a little man, no taller than Vera. His hair was already thinning and always looked greasy. He had a nut-brown face that Maud prophesied would wrinkle early and shifty black eyes that never looked straight at you. Well aware of who wore the trousers in the Kinaway household, he smiled ingratiatingly at Maud if ever he met her in the street, greeting her with an oily, 'Good morning, Mrs

Kinaway, lovely morning,' and shaking his head sadly when she marched past him in cold silence.

She wouldn't have him in the shop or the flat above it and she consoled herself in the knowledge that Stanley worked in his bar every evening. The main disadvantage of Vera not having a job was that she was at liberty to meet Stanley during the day, and barmen work peculiar hours, being free for most of the morning and half the afternoon. But Maud thought that 'anything wrong', by which she meant sexual intercourse, only ever took place between ten and midnight – this belief was based on her own experience, although in her case she regarded it as right and proper – and it was during those two hours that Stanley was most busily occupied. It was with horror and near-incredulity, therefore, that she learnt from a weeping Vera that she was over two months pregnant.

'Poor Ethel all over again,' sobbed Maud. 'That such a disgraceful thing should happen to my own child!'

But, foolish and wicked as Vera had been, she mustn't be allowed to suffer as Ethel had suffered. Vera should have her husband and her house and a decent home for her baby. Vera should be married.

Instead of the big wedding Maud had dreamed of, Vera and Stanley were married quietly with only a dozen close relatives and friends as guests and they went straight off home to the little terraced house in Lanchester Road, Croughton. There was little Maud could do to humiliate Stanley but she had seen to it that, when she and George put up the money for the house, the deeds were in Vera's name and Stanley was made to understand that every penny must be paid back.

They had been married three weeks when Vera had a miscarriage.

'Oh my God,' said Maud at the hospital bedside, 'why ever were we so hasty? Your father said we should wait a bit and he was right.'

'What do you mean?'

'Three weeks we should have waited . . .'

'I've lost my baby,' said Vera, sitting up in bed, 'and now you'd like to take my husband away from me.'

When she was well again, Vera took a job for the first time in her life to pay back the money she owed her parents.

For Maud was adamant. She didn't mind giving Vera a cheque now and then to buy herself a dress or taking her out and giving her a slap-up lunch, but Stanley Manning wasn't getting his hooks on her money. He must pull up his socks, make a decent living and then Maud would think again. . . .

As soon as she realized this would happen, she set out to get Vera away from him, a plan which was far more tenable now she actually lived in the same house with her daughter. She pursued it in two ways: by showing her how difficult her present life was, making it even more difficult and maintaining an atmosphere of strife; and by holding out the inducements of an alternative existence, a life of ease and peace and plenty.

So far she had met with little success. Vera had always been stubborn. Her mother's daughter, Maud thought lovingly. The little bribes and the enticing pictures she had painted of life without Stanley hadn't made a chink in Vera's armour. Never mind. The time had come to put the squeeze on. It hadn't escaped Maud's notice that Vera had turned quite pale at the mention of that twenty thousand pounds. She'd be thinking about that now while she stood in that dreadful place, shoving re-texed, moth-proofed coats into polythene bags. And tonight Maud would play her trump card.

Thinking about it and the effect it would have made her sigh contentedly as she laid her head back against the pillows and switched on the second bar of the electric fire with her good foot. Vera would realize that she meant business and Stanley . . . Well, Stanley would see it was useless getting any ideas about helping his mother-in-law out of this world.

Funny, really. Stanley wanted to get rid of her and she meant to get rid of Stanley. But she was going to get in first. She had him by the short hairs. Maud smiled, closed her eyes and fell at once into deep sleep.

3

Of the fifty motorists who pulled in for petrol at the Superjuce garage that day only five got service from Stanley. He didn't even hear the hooters and the shouts of the half-dozen out of the other forty-five who bothered to wait. He sat with his back to them in his little glass booth, dreaming of the twenty thousand pounds Maud had in the bank and which Vera had told him about at breakfast.

When George Kinaway had died, Stanley had waited excitedly for the contents of the will to be made known to him. He could hardly believe his ears when Vera told him there was no will, for everything had been in her mother's name. Impatient like most people of his kind, he prepared for another long bitter wait and his temper grew sourer.

The tobacconist's had been given up and Maud had retired to luxury in a small but sumptuous detached house at Eltham. Stanley never went there – he wasn't invited – and he showed no sympathy when Vera, lunched and cosseted by her mother, returned home from a day at Eltham full of anecdotes about Maud's high blood pressure. Through the years this was Stanley's only consolation and, being a man of more than average intelligence who could have excelled at any of several well-paid careers if he had only put his mind to it (if he had had a chance, was the way he put it), he set out to study the whole subject of blood pressure and hardening of the arteries. At that time he was working as a factory nightwatchman. No one ever tried to break into the factory, which was on its last legs and contained nothing worth stealing, so Stanley whiled away the long hours very pleasantly in reading medical books he got out of the public library.

It was therefore no surprise to him when he arrived home one morning to be greeted by Vera with the news that her mother had had a cerebral thrombosis.

While pulling long faces and being unusually kind to his wife, Stanley began calculating his inheritance. There ought to be at least eight thousand from the sale of Maud's house as well as a tidy sum in the bank. The first thing he'd buy would be a large car just to put the neighbours' noses out of joint.

Then Maud got better.

Stanley, hope springing eternal, agreed that she should come and live with them in Lanchester Road. The extra work, after all, would fall on Vera and if the eight thousand didn't immediately fall into his lap, there was bound to be a shareout. No one, in Stanley's view, parked themselves on a relative without paying their way, and if Maud was sticky, he would drop her a gentle but unmistakable hint.

Two days after she arrived, Maud explained her intentions. With the exception of ten shillings a week, her whole pension would be handed over to Vera, but her capital remained where it was, comfortably invested. 'I never heard such a diabolical bloody liberty,' said Stanley.

'Her pension pays for her food, Stan.'

'And what about her lodgings? What about the work she makes?'

'She's my mother,' said Vera.

The time had come to put that phrase into the past tense. Not murder, of course, not actual murder. Since he had knocked that old woman on the head and taken her handbag when he was eighteen, Stanley had never laid violent hands on anyone and when he read of murder in the newspapers he was as shocked as Vera and as vociferous as Maud in demanding the return of the death penalty. As in the case of that shot police constable, for instance, PC Chappell who had died trying to stop thugs breaking into Croughton post office last month. No, murder was something he wouldn't ever consider. An accident was what he had in mind. Some sort of carelessness with the gas or a mix-up over all those pills and tablets Maud took.

A scheme for gassing Maud taking shape in his mind, Stanley walked into the house whistling cheerfully. He didn't kiss Vera but he said hallo to her and patted her shoulder as he went to switch on the television.

Thinking now of her days as numbered, Stanley had been prepared to unbend a little with Maud. But as soon as he saw her, sitting up straight at the table and already on her second helping of eggs and chips, her face red with determination and ill temper, he girded himself for battle.

'Had a busy day, Ma?'

'Busier than yours, I daresay,' said Maud. 'I had a chat over the fence with Mrs Blackmore this afternoon and she said her husband went to get his petrol at your garage but he couldn't get no service. He could see you, though, and he reckoned you were asleep.'

Stanley glared at her. 'I don't want you gossiping over the fence any more, is that clear? Walking all over my garden and trampling down the plants.'

'It's not your garden, it's Vera's.'

She could scarcely have said anything more irritating to Stanley. Brought up in the country, on the borders of Essex and Suffolk where his father had a smallholding, he had loved gardening all his life and he called it his only relaxation, forgetting for the time his crosswords and his medical books. But this passion of his was out of character – gardening is generally associated with the mild, the civilized and the law-abiding – and Maud refused to take it seriously. She liked to think of Stanley as among the outcast, the utterly lost, while gardening was one of the pastimes she had respected all her life. So she would watch him tending his heather garden or watering his gladioli and then, when he came in to wash his hands, tell him not to forget that the garden, along with the rest of the property, was Vera's and Vera could sell it over his head whenever the fancy took her.

Now, pleased that her retort had needled Stanley, she turned to Vera and asked if she remembered to get her skein of wool.

'It went right out of my head, Mother. I *am* sorry.'

'That puts paid to my knitting for tonight then,' said Maud sourly. 'If I'd known I'd have got it myself when I was in town.'

'What were you doing in town?'

'I went,' said Maud, shouting above the television, 'to see my solicitor.'

'Since when have you had a solicitor?' said Stanley.

'Since this morning, Mr Clever. A poor old widow in my position needs a solicitor to protect her. He was very nice to me, I can tell you, a real gentleman. Great comfort he gave me. I told him I'll be able to sleep in my bed now.'

'I don't know what you're on about,' said Stanley uneasily, and he added, 'For God's sake someone turn that TV down,' as if Vera or her mother and not he had switched it on. 'That's better. Now we can hear ourselves speak. Right, what's all this about?'

'My will. I made my will this morning and I got the solicitor to put it the way I want it. If Vera and me were living alone it'd be a different thing. All I've got is coming to her, I don't know how many times I've told you. But you listen, this is what I've done. If I die of a stroke you get the lot but if I die of anything else it all goes to Ethel Carpenter. And now you know.'

Vera dropped her fork. 'I don't know at all, Mother. I don't know what any of that's supposed to mean.'

'It's clear enough,' said Maud. 'So just think about it.'

She gave them a grim smile and, hobbling rapidly to the television, turned up the volume.

'That,' said Stanley in bed that night, 'is the biggest bloody insult I've ever had said to me. Insinuating I'd put her out of the way! I reckon she's going cracked.'

'If it's true,' said Vera.

'It doesn't matter a damn whether it's *true*. Maybe she went and maybe she didn't, and maybe the solicitor put that in and maybe he never did. Whichever way you like to look at it, she's got us by the short hairs.'

'No, she hasn't, love. It's not as if we'd have dreamt of harming her. Of course she'll die of a stroke. What hurts is that Mother should even think of such a thing.'

'And if she doesn't die of a stroke, what then?'

'I don't believe any solicitor'd put that in a will.' Vera sighed heavily and turned over. 'I must go to sleep now. I'm dead tired.'

On the whole, Stanley thought Vera was right and no solicitor would have agreed to Maud's condition. It probably wasn't legal. But if Maud said it was and there was no one with the knowledge to argue . . .

Vera worked all day Saturdays and Stanley and Maud were left alone together. On fine Saturdays Stanley spent hours in the garden and when it rained he went to the pictures.

March had been mild and the almond tree was already in flower. Daffodils were in bud but the ericas in his heather garden were just past their prime. It was time to nourish them with a bale of peat, for the soil of Croughton was London clay. Stanley fetched a new sackful from the shed, scattered peat around the established plants and dug a trench. This would be filled with peat for the new plants he had ordered.

Although he objected to Maud's gossiping over the fence with Mrs Blackmore at number 59 or Mrs Macdonald at number 63, Stanley wasn't averse to breaking off from his digging for an occasional chat. Today, when Mrs Blackmore came out to peg a couple of shirts on her line, he would have liked nothing better than to have catalogued, as was his usual habit, Maud's latest solecisms and insults, but this would no longer do. He must establish himself in his neighbours' estimation as a tolerant and even affectionate son-in-law.

'She's all right,' he said in answer to Mrs Blackmore's enquiry. 'As well as can be expected.'

'I always say to John, Mrs Kinaway's wonderful really when you think what she's been through.'

Mrs Blackmore was a tiny birdlike woman who always wore her dyed blonde hair tied up in two bunches like a little girl, although in other respects she seemed resigned to middle age. Her eyes were sharp and bright and she had the disconcerting habit of staring hard into the eyes of anyone with whom she happened to be talking. Stanley met those eyes boldly now, doing his best not to blink.

'You can't help admiring her,' he said with a little smiling shake of his head.

'I know you really feel that.' Mrs Blackmore was somewhat taken aback and temporarily her eyes wavered. 'Has she seen the doctor lately?'

'Old Dr Blake retired and she won't have anything to do with the new one. She says he's too young.'

'Dr Moxley? He's thirty-five if he's a day. Still, I daresay that seems young to her.'

'You have to respect their funny ways, the old folk,' said Stanley piously. Their eyes engaged in a hard tug-of-war which Stanley won. Mrs Blackmore dropped her gaze and, muttering something about getting the lunch, went into the house.

Stanley's own meal was of necessity a cold one. He and Maud ate in silence and afterwards, while Stanley sat down with the *Daily Telegraph* crossword, his mother-in-law prepared to have her rest.

When she was alone she simply sat in an armchair and dozed with her head against one of the wings, but on Saturdays, with Stanley in the room, she made a considerable fuss. First she gathered up every available cushion, making a point of pulling out the one behind Stanley's head, and arranged them very slowly all over the head and foot of the sofa. Then she made her way upstairs, tapping her stick and humming, to return with an armful of blankets. The weight of the blankets made her breath laboured and she gave vent to groans. At last, having taken off her glasses and her shoes, she heaved herself up on to the sofa, pulled the blankets over her and lay gasping.

Her son-in-law took absolutely no notice of any of this. He filled in his crossword, smiling sometimes at the ingenuity of the man who had set it, and occasionally mouthing the words of a clue. When Maud could stand his indifference no longer, she said acidly:

'In my young days a gentleman took pride in helping an old lady.'

'I'm no gentleman,' said Stanley. 'You have to have money to be a gentleman.'

'Oh, no, you don't. Gentlemen are born, let me tell you. You'd be uncouth no matter what money you'd got.'

'You could do with being a bit more couth yourself,' said Stanley and, having triumphantly silenced his mother-in-law, he filled in 28 across, which completed his puzzle.

Maud closed her eyes and set her mouth in a grim line. Doodling on the edge of his paper, Stanley watched her speculatively until those crinkled compressed lips relaxed, the hand which gripped the blanket went limp, and he knew she was asleep. Then, folding his paper, he tip-toed out of the room and made his way to Maud's bedroom.

She had evidently spent the greater part of the morning writing to Ethel Carpenter, for the finished letter lay exposed on her bedside table. Stanley sat down on the edge of the bed to read it.

He had always suspected that he and his doings formed one of the favourite topics of the old women's discussions, but he had never supposed that Maud would devote three and a half sides of paper to nothing but a denigration of his character. He was outraged and he was also bitterly hurt. It was a favour he was doing Maud, after all, letting her live in his house, and the ingratitude implicit in this letter made his blood boil.

Frowning angrily, he read through what Maud had to say about his laziness and his ill manners. She had even had the effrontery to tell Ethel that he had borrowed a fiver from Vera the day before which, Maud declared, he intended to put on a horse for the National. This had been Stanley's purpose but now he told himself he had wanted it to buy more peat and young heather plants. The old bitch! The evil-tongued old bitch! What was this next bit?

'Of course poor Vee will never see her money again,' Maud had written. 'He will see to that. She works like a slave but she wouldn't have a rag for her back, bar what I give her. Still, it is only a matter of time now before I shall get her away from him. She is too loyal to say yes Mother I'll come, knowing no doubt what a scene *he* would make and perhaps even strike her. I wouldn't put anything past him, my dear. The other day I told her I would buy her whatever she liked to name on condition she would leave him and the tears came into her poor eyes. It went to my heart, I can tell you, seeing my only child in distress. But I tell myself I am being cruel only to be kind and she will thank me on her bended knees when she is rid of him at last and living with me in the lovely house I mean to buy her. I have got my eye on one I saw in an advertisement in the Sunday paper, a lovely place just built in Chigwell, and when Vee has her afternoon off I am thinking of hiring a car to take us both out to look at it. Without *him* of course. . . .'

Stanley nearly tore the letter up, he was so angry. Until then he had no idea of Maud's plans, for Vera had been afraid to tell him about them, although he had guessed there was something afoot. If I'd only got money, he raged, I'd sue the old bitch for what-d'you-call-it? – enticement. That's what I'd do, have her up in court for trying to take a man's lawful wife away from him.

He sat staring moodily at the letter, suddenly aware of the great danger he was in. Without Vera, he had no hope of ever getting his hands on that twenty thousand. It would be the bread-line for him all the rest of his life while Vera lived in luxury. My God, he thought, even the house, the very roof over his head, belonged to her. And what a beanfeast those two would have, hired cars, perhaps even a car of their own, a modern house in snooty Chigwell, clothes, holidays, every convenience. The whole idea was unbearable to contemplate and suddenly he was seized with the urgency of what he must do and reminded too of his original purpose in coming up to Maud's room.

Leaving the letter as he had found it, he turned his attention to the three containers of pills which stood under the bedlamp. Those pale blue capsules were sleep-inducing; they didn't interest him. Next came the yellow vitamin things which, Stanley was sure, were responsible for Maud's vitality and kept her tongue in sprightly working order. Nevertheless, he wouldn't mess about with them. There were the ones he wanted, the tiny anti-coagulant tablets called Mollanoid of which Maud took six a day and which, Stanley supposed, kept her blood from clotting as it coursed through those brittle arteries. He took one from the carton and folded it inside his handkerchief.

She was still asleep when he came downstairs and, generously, he would have let her have her rest without interruption on any other Saturday. But now, with the memory of the libellous letter uppermost in his mind, he switched on the television for *Sports Round-Up* and took a bitter pleasure in seeing her jerk awake.

Stanley wasn't allowed to leave his glass booth between nine and five, although he often did so and for this truancy had several times been threatened with the sack. But the chemist on the other side of the street would be closed when he knocked off and he couldn't afford to wait until the following Saturday before buying the substitute tablets he required.

He waited until one o'clock, the slackest time of the day, and then he sneaked across the road. But instead of one of the girls being behind the counter, the pharmacist himself was on duty and showed such an interest in all this fumbling among the bottles and boxes that Stanley thought it wiser to try Boots, although it was a quarter of a mile away.

There he found all the goods on display on self-service stands and he was able to study a variety of white pills without being observed. All the aspirin and codeine and phenacetin tablets were too big and the only thing he could find approximating in size to Maud's anti-coagulants were a saccharine compound for the use of slimmers.

These he thought would do. The tablets looked exactly like the one he had appropriated. He tried a single tablet on his tongue and it was very sweet, but Maud always swallowed her tablets down quickly in a sweet drink and very likely the taste would be disguised.

'D'you mind not eating the goods before you've paid for them?' said a girl assistant pertly.

'If you're accusing me of stealing I want to see the manager.'

'All right, all right. There's no need to shout. That'll be five and six, please.'

'And bloody daylight robbery,' said Stanley. But he bought a phial of Shu-go-Sub and ran all the way back to the garage.

Three cars were drawn up by the pumps and Stanley's boss, holding the petrol nozzle delicately and furiously as far as possible from the lapels of his immaculate suit, was doing his best to serve the first customer. Stanley went into the booth and watched him through the glass. Presently, when the cars had gone, his boss lurched into the booth, rubbing his oily hands.

'I've had about enough of this as I can stand, Manning,' he said. 'God knows how much custom we'd have lost if some enterprising motorist hadn't phoned me to ask what the hell was going on. I said I wouldn't tell you again and I won't. You can have your cards and get out on Friday.'

'It'll be a pleasure,' said Stanley. 'I was going, anyway, before this dump goes bust.'

The loss of his job didn't particularly dismay him. He was used to losing jobs and he enjoyed the freedom of several weeks out of work, during which he would draw ample untaxed unemployment benefit. Telling Vera, though, was something he didn't much look forward to and he was determined to prevent Maud finding out. That would be nice, something to cheer a man up, having his misfortunes shouted over the garden fences and sent winging in choice virulent phrases down over the river to Ethel Carpenter in Brixton.

But perhaps Maud wouldn't be able to gossip or write letters much longer. Stanley fingered the phial in his pocket. She often said it was only her tablets that kept her alive and maybe it wouldn't be more than a few days when her system reacted violently to a concentration of saccharine instead of its usual anti-coagulant intake.

Stanley walked home slowly, stopping outside the Jaguar showrooms to eye speculatively a dark red E-type.

4

'These tablets,' said Maud, 'have a very funny taste. Sweetish. You're sure they made up the prescription right, Vee?'

'It's your regular prescription, Mother. The one old Dr Blake wrote out before he retired. I took it to the chemist like I always do.' Vera picked up the carton and looked at it just to make sure Maud wasn't taking vitamins or diuretics by mistake. No, it was the Mollanoid all right. *Mrs M. Kinaway*, the label said, *two to be taken three times a day*, and there was the little smear the chemist's thumb had made because he hadn't waited for the ink to dry before handing it to her. 'If you've got any doubts,' she said, 'why don't you let me make you an appointment with Dr Moxley? They say he's ever so nice.'

'I don't want him. I don't want young boys messing me about.' Maud sipped her breakfast tea and swallowed her second tablet. 'I daresay I've made the tea too sweet, that's what it is. Anyway, they're not doing me any harm, whatever's in them. To tell you the truth, I feel better than I have done for months, not so tired. There's the postman now. Run down like a good girl and see if there's anything from your Auntie Ethel.'

The telephone bill and a letter with the Brixton postmark. Vera decided she wouldn't open the bill until she got home. All right, that was being an ostrich, but why not? Ostriches might stick their faces in the sand but they did all right, galloping about in Australia or wherever it was and they didn't get old before their time. I wouldn't mind being an ostrich or anything, come to that, thought Vera, as long as it was a change from being me.

She grabbed her coat from the hook in the hall and trailed up the stairs again, buttoning it as she went. Maud was up, sitting on the side of her bed buffing her fingernails with a silver-backed polisher.

'It's only ten to,' said Maud. 'You can spare the time to hear what Auntie Ethel has to say. You never know what news she's got.'

What news did she ever have? Vera didn't want to chance being late just to hear that Ethel Carpenter's cyclamen had got five flowers on it or her landlady's little niece had the measles. But she waited just the same, tapping her feet impatiently. Anything to keep the peace, she thought, anything to put Mother in a good mood.

'What d'you think?' said Maud. 'Auntie Ethel's going to move. She's giving up her room and getting one near here. Listen to this: "I heard of a nice room going in Green Lanes just half a mile from you, dear, and popped over to see it on Saturday." Why didn't she call, I wonder? Oh, here it is, she says – yes, she says, "I would have looked you up but it seemed a shame to disturb you." Ethel always was considerate.'

'I must go, Mother.'

'Wait just one minute . . . "I wouldn't want to come when Vee was out and you say she works on Saturdays." Etcetera, etcetera. Oh, listen, Vee. "My landlady has got a student to take my room from April 10th, a Friday, and as she has been so good to me and I don't want to put her out, and Mrs Paterson in Green Lanes can't take me till the Monday, I was wondering if Vee could put me up for that weekend. It would be such a treat to see you and Vee and have a nice long chat about old times." I'll write back and say yes, shall I?'

'I don't know, Mother.' Vera sighed and gave a hopeless shrug. 'What will Stanley say? I wouldn't want you and Auntie Ethel getting at him all the time.'

'It's your house,' said Maud.

'That sort of thing now. That's the very thing I mean. I'll have to think about it. I must *go*.'

'I'll have to let her know soon,' Maud called after her. 'You put your foot down. Stanley'll have to lump it.'

He was bound to have heard that, she thought, lying in bed in the next room as he no doubt was. The prospect of the ensuing battle excited her and she felt a surge of well-being comparable to that she used to feel long ago on Sunday morning when she was looking forward to her weekly walk with George.

It was wrong, of course, to *enjoy* quarrelling. George would have told her to keep the peace at any price. But George had never lived in the same house as Stanley Manning and if he had done he would have approved of her tactics. He would have seen the importance of rescuing Vera.

Maud went over to the dressing table and took her framed photograph of George out of a drawer. The slight sentimentality which the sight of it aroused in her was mixed with that exasperation she had so often felt for her husband when he was alive. Without a doubt she missed him and, if he could have been resurrected, would have welcomed him back, but still she had to admit that in some ways he had been a drag on her, too weak, too scrupulous and much too inclined to let things drift. Ethel, now, was a different person altogether. Ethel had had to fight for things all her life just as she had.

Maud put the photograph away. Nothing could have pleased her more than the news contained in the letter. With Ethel just down the road, and very likely popping in every day, the conquest of Vera would be accomplished in a matter of weeks. Ethel had such a grasp of things, such bustling strength. She would talk to Vera and when Vera saw that an outsider, an uninvolved observer, agreed with her mother, she would surrender and bow to circumstances with all George's resignation.

Stanley would be left alone. It made Maud almost chuckle aloud to think of him dependent only on what he could earn for himself, cooking his own meals and sinking into the squalor which Maud felt was his natural habitat. Not that he would be allowed to occupy this house. He must find himself a room somewhere. But all that could be gone into once Vera was out of his influence. And then perhaps they could settle Ethel in here. Life had treated Ethel badly and it would be such a joy to give her a home of her own at last and see her smiling, maybe even weeping, with gratitude. Maud's heart swelled, full of the pleasure of philanthropy.

The unemployment benefit which the Labour Exchange paid out to Stanley was a good deal in excess of the sum he had mentioned to Vera. He needed the surplus for himself, for he was spending a fortune on Shu-go-Sub as well as a fair amount on almost daily visits to the pictures to get out of Maud's way. Hoping to see a considerable decline in her health by this time, he was bitterly disappointed to notice that rather than enfeebled, she seemed actually stronger, more vital looking and younger than before he had begun emptying Shu-go-Sub tubes into the Mollanoid carton. If only she would exert herself more, go for walks or carry heavy weights. Letter-writing wasn't likely to raise her blood pressure.

Entering the house that evening after a pleasant three hours watching a double horror bill, he was sure there was something going on. Those two were hatching a plot between them, perhaps the very thing he most dreaded, the enticement of Vera. They had stopped talking the minute he walked in the back door and Vera looked as if she had been crying.

'I've been tramping the streets since one,' he said, 'looking for work.'

'Work's not easy to come by when you've no qualifications,' said Maud. 'Can't they find you anything down at the Labour?'

Stanley took the cup of tea Vera handed him and shook his head gloomily.

'Something will turn up, dear.'

'Doesn't matter to him one way or the other, does it?' said Maud. 'He's got someone to keep him. Have you given Vee that money you owe her?'

Since he had been substituting saccharine for Maud's tablets, Stanley had moderated his attitude to her, calling her 'Ma' and giving in over the television programmes, much as it went against the grain. But now self-control snapped.

'You mind your own business, Maud Kinaway. That's a private matter between me and my wife.'

'What concerns Vera concerns me. That's her money that she earned. Haven't you ever heard of the Married Women's Property Act? Eighteen-seventy-something that went through Parliament. More than a hundred years a woman's had a right to her own money.'

'I suppose you were sitting in the Ladies' Gallery when it was passed,' said Stanley.

The blood rushed into Maud's face. 'Are you going to sit there and let him speak to me like that, Vera?'

Vera wasn't sitting at all, but scuttling between the living room and the kitchen with plates of sausages and mashed potato. 'I'm so used,' she said not quite truthfully, 'to hearing you two bicker that it goes right over my head. Come and sit down, do. We want to be finished and cleared away before *Augusta Alley* comes on.'

Prickly and resentful, Maud and Stanley sat down. Neither of them had done a stroke of work all day and their stored-up energy showed in their eyes and the zest with which they both fell on their food. Vera picked at a sausage and left half her mashed potato. It was no good, she hadn't any appetite these days and she began to wonder if Maud hadn't been right when she said she was heading for a nervous breakdown. Sleep didn't refresh her and she was as tired in the mornings as when she went to bed. Having Auntie Ethel here for a long weekend wouldn't help either, as Maud would want a great fuss made over her best friend's entertainment, a clean cloth on the table every day, homemade cakes and then, of course, there would be the spare room to get ready.

Maud must have read her thoughts or else she hadn't been thinking of anything else all day, for she said as she spooned up a second helping of potato, 'Have you told Stanley yet?'

'I haven't had a chance, have I? I only got in half an hour ago.'

'Told me what?' said Stanley.

Maud swallowed two tablets and made a face. 'We're having my friend Ethel Carpenter to stay here.'

'You what?' Stanley was much relieved, in fact, to hear that was all it was, for he had expected an announcement of Vera's imminent departure. But now that the greater evil was at least temporarily postponed, the lesser seemed outrageous and he got up, flinging back his chair, drawing himself up to his full height of five foot five.

'Only for two or three days,' said Vera.

'*Only*. Only two or three days. Here am I, up to my neck in trouble, no job, no peace in my own home, and you tell me I've got to have that old cow . . .'

'Don't you dare! Don't you dare use that foul language in my presence!' Maud was on her feet as well now, clutching her stick. 'Ethel's coming here and that's that. Vera and me, we've made up our minds. And you can't stop us. Vera could have you evicted tomorrow if she liked, turned out in the street with just the clothes you stand up in.'

'And I,' said Stanley, thrusting his face close up to hers, 'could have you put in an old folks' home. I don't have to have you here, nobody can make me.'

'Criminal!' Maud shouted. 'Jailbird! Pig!'

'Two can play at that game, Maud Kinaway. Mean old hag! Poisonous bitch!'

'Lazy no-good wastrel!'

Watching them from the end of the table, Vera thought that any minute they would come to blows. She felt quite calm. If they did strike each other, if they killed each other, she thought she would feel just the same, just as enervated, disembodied and empty of everything but a cold despair. With a dignity neither of them had ever seen in her before, she got up and said in a steady emotionless voice of a High Court judge:

'Be quiet and sit down.' They stopped and turned to look at her. 'Thank you. It's quite a change for either of you to do anything I ask. Now I've got something to say to you. Either you learn to live together like decent people . . .' Maud tapped her stick. 'Shut up, Mother. As I said, either you behave yourselves in future or I'm going.' Vera turned away from the flash of triumph in Maud's eyes. 'No, Mother, not with you, and not off somewhere with Stanley either. I shall go away by myself. This house doesn't mean a thing to me. I can earn my own living. God knows, I've had to do it long enough. So there you are. One more row and I pack my bags. I mean it.'

'You wouldn't walk out on me, Vee?' Stanley whined.

'Oh, yes, I would. You don't love me. If I hadn't got a wage coming in and – and what I'll get from Mother one day, I wouldn't see you for dust. And you don't love me either, Mother. You just love power and playing God and being possessive. All your life you've got your own way but for the once and you can't bear it that once somebody beat you at your own game.'

Vera paused for breath and stared into the two flabbergasted faces. 'Yes, I've shaken you both, haven't I? Well, don't forget what I said. One more row and off I go. And another thing. We'll have Auntie Ethel here but not because you want her, Mother. Because I do. She's my godmother and I'm fond of her and, as you're always pointing out, *this is my house*. Now we'll have the television on. *Augusta Alley*, and you can watch it in peace, Mother, Stanley won't disturb you. He knows I mean what I say.'

After that she went out into the kitchen and, although she had won and silenced them, although they were now sitting sullenly in front of the screen, she laid her head on the table and began to sob. Her strength wasn't like Maud's, constant, implacable, insensitive, but intermittent and brief as her father's had been. She doubted whether she had enough of it to make good her threat.

Presently, when she had stopped crying, she washed the tea things and went upstairs. There, in front of her dressing table, she had a good hard look at herself in the glass. Crying hadn't helped. Of course, her face wasn't usually as blotchy and patched with red, but the wrinkles were always there and the brown bruise shadows under her eyes, and the coarse white hairs among the sandy ones, dull pepper-coloured hair that had once been red-gold.

It was understandable that Stanley no longer loved her, that he only kissed her now during the act of love and sometimes not even then. There came into her mind the memory of those afternoons they had spent in the country, London's country of commons and heaths, before they were married and when she had conceived the child that died before it could be born. It seemed like another life, and the man and the woman who had ached for each other, and had clung together gasping in the long grass under the trees, other people.

Strange how important passion was to the young. Beside it, suitability and prudence and security went for nothing. How she and Stanley had laughed at James Horton with his bank account and his church membership and his modest ambition. He'd be a bank manager now, she thought, living in a fine house and married to a handsome woman in her early forties, while she and Stanley . . . She had wasted her life. If James saw her now he wouldn't recognize her. Miserably she stared at her own worn and undesirable reflection.

Downstairs, Maud and Stanley watched *Augusta Alley*, the old woman with a triumph that showed on her face in a perpetual smug smile, her son-in-law impassively, biding his time.

5

Everyone has his escape, his panacea, drugs, drink, tobacco, or, more cheaply and innocently, the steady and almost mechanical habit of reading light fiction. Stanley liked a drink and a smoke when he could afford them and he had always been a reader, but the true and constant consolation of his life came from doing crossword puzzles.

Almost every paperback issue of crossword books as well as the fuller and fatter annuals reposed in his bedroom bookcase along with a much-thumbed copy of *Chambers Twentieth Century Dictionary*. But the white squares in these books had long been filled in and, in any case, the solving of the problems afforded him less pleasure than completing a fresh puzzle each day, one which arrived virgin white on the back page of the *Daily Telegraph* and which, if the answers eluded him, could only be solved by waiting, sometimes almost breathlessly, for the following morning's issue.

He had been doing the *Telegraph* puzzle every day for twenty years and now there was no longer any question of not finishing it. He always finished it and always got it right. Once, some years back, he had found it necessary, like most crossword enthusiasts, to abandon the puzzle when it was half-completed and take it up some hours later to find that the elusive clues had clarified during the interim. But even this small frustration had passed away. He would sit down with the paper – he never bothered to read the news – and generally every clue had been solved twenty minutes later. Then an immense satisfaction bathed Stanley. Self-esteem washed away his pressing problems, every worry was buried, sublimated in those interlocking words.

It was no sorrow to him that his wife and his mother-in-law showed not the slightest interest in this hobby of his.

He preferred it that way. Nothing can be more irksome, more maddening, to the amateur of crosswords than the well-meaning idiot who, anxious to show off his etymological knowledge, demands from his armchair to be told how many letters in fifteen down or what makes you think four across is yelp and not bark.

Stanley had never forgotten George Kinaway's efforts in this direction, his feebly hearty, 'Haven't you finished that puzzle yet?' and his groping determination to supply straightforward answers to clues whose fascination lay in their almost lunatic subtlety. How to explain to such a fool as he that 'One who is willing' (nine letters, five blanks, T, three blanks) is obviously Testatrix and not Volunteer? Or that 'One way or the other, he is tops in the Moslem world' (three letters) is the palindrome Aga and not Bey?

No, those women knew their limitations. They thought it was a silly kid's game – or said they did because it was all Greek to them – but at least they didn't interfere. And these days Stanley needed his puzzles more than ever. The one high spot in his day was the half-hour, perhaps at lunch-time, perhaps in the evening, when he could escape from his worries and, suddenly far away from Vera and her mother, lose himself in the intricacies of words and plays upon words.

The rest of the time, God knew, he had trouble enough. He saw very clearly that matters had come to a head, to a straight battle between Maud and himself. On his side he had youth, comparative youth, at any rate, but he couldn't see that he had much else. The dice were heavily loaded in Maud's favour. She wanted to get Vera away from him and it was hard to see how, in time, she could fail. Stanley couldn't understand how she hadn't already succeeded. If he had been in Vera's place, if his mother had come to him with bribes and offers of money and ease, he would have been off like a shot. Stanley felt quite sick when he thought of his fate if Maud were allowed to win. Why, the chances were that pair of bitches wouldn't even let him keep this house.

And now Maud had an ally rushing to her support. If that letter he had read was a typical example of the sort of effusions Maud sent weekly to Ethel Carpenter, her friend would arrive armed against him. He shuddered when he thought of Ethel taking Vera aside, whispering to her in corners, putting Maud's case far more forcefully than Maud could herself, because Ethel would appear as a detached observer, an impartial outsider, seeing the pros and cons without emotional involvement. There was nothing he could do about it. Ethel would come, put in three days' forceful persuasion, and, if that wasn't enough to do the trick, would be just around the corner, dropping in two or three times a week, ready with arguments, wearing away Vera's opposition until, at last, beaten down by the pair of them, she would give in.

There was nothing he could do about it – except get rid of Maud first.

But the failure of the Shu-go-Sub had shaken Stanley badly. He read and re-read all his medical books and when he had digested every word reached the conclusion that there are basically no rules as to the incidence of strokes. Maud had had one; she might have another tomorrow; she might never have another. Worry could induce one, but, on the other hand, it might not. And what worries did Maud have? Anti-coagulants might prevent one. Ease and quiet might prevent one. No one could say for sure that the absence of anti-coagulants and a life of anxiety would cause one. Stanley reflected disgustedly that what doctors didn't know about cerebral thrombosis would fill more volumes than their knowledge. They couldn't even tell you when one was going to occur.

Then there was the question of the will. Stanley was almost certain that Maud couldn't have got any solicitor to agree to that condition. Why, she might quite accidentally fall under a bus. In that case was Vera not to inherit? No, it was an impossible, lunatic condition, but how was he to find out for sure whether or not it had been made? Of course, there was nothing to stop him walking into any solicitor's office and asking straight out. And then, if Maud died, accidentally or by his hand, you could be damn sure the first thing to happen would be that solicitor shooting his mouth off to the police. Clever Maud, Maud with the balance swinging down and throbbing heavily in her favour.

If only he could think of something. It was April now and in a week's time Ethel Carpenter would be here. Once let her arrive and he could say goodbye to everything he had ever hoped for, and look forward to a miserable poverty-stricken old age.

Meanwhile, Stanley continued to substitute Shu-go-Sub for Mollanoid, destroying the anti-coagulants as Vera fetched them on prescription from the chemist and dropping the saccharine into the labelled bottle while Maud was asleep. But it was a forlorn hope. Without his crossword puzzles, he sometimes thought he would go utterly to pieces.

'We can't let your Auntie Ethel sleep in that room as it is,' Maud said. 'We'll have to get a new bedspread for one thing, and some sheets and towels.'

'Well, don't look at me, Mother,' said Vera. 'I've just had the phone bill to pay.'

'I wasn't intending you to pay for them, dear,' Maud said hastily. 'You get them and I'll give you a cheque.' She smiled ingratiatingly at her daughter and stirred herself to clear the table. The last thing she wanted at the moment was to antagonize Vera. Suppose she had really meant what she said and would be wicked enough to run away and leave her with Stanley? She would have to cook Stanley's meals and wait on him. 'We'd better both have new dresses, too. When you have your afternoon off we'll go down to Lucette's and choose something really smart.'

'Anyone would think it was the Queen coming,' said Stanley.

Maud ignored him. 'I'm getting quite excited. I think I'll have that girl in to give me a home perm and you must have your hair set in your lunch hour. And we'll need some flowers for Auntie's room. Auntie Ethel loves flowers.'

She settled down contentedly with her knitting, repeating silently the words she had written to Ethel Carpenter that morning. '. . . You mustn't be too upset by the state of this house, dear. It's a poor old place and a crying shame that Vee should have had to live in it so long but we shall soon see some changes. When I see you I'll show you some of the details of new houses estate agents have sent me. The one I have my eye on has a fully fitted Wrighton kitchen and luxury sunken bath. Quite a change from the old days!! And I've been wondering if you would like to move in here.

Of course, I would have it painted throughout for you and a sink unit put in. We can talk about it when you come. I know I can rely on you to help me in bringing Vee round to my point of view . . .' Maud smiled and saw that Stanley had caught her smile. He frowned blackly. If only he knew!

'Time for *Augusta Alley*,' she said confidently.

Stanley didn't say a word. He threw down his completed puzzle, flung open the french windows and went into the darkening garden.

'We've got some old tab coming here,' said Stanley to Mr Blackmore. 'Pal of my ma-in-law's. They couldn't make more fuss if it were royalty.'

'I daresay Mrs Kinaway doesn't see all that many people.' Blackmore stuck his ladder against the house wall and mounted it, carrying with him brush and paint pot.

'Excitement's no good to her.' Stanley stuck his fork in the soil. 'Going on the way she is she'll have another one of those strokes.'

'I sincerely hope not.'

'Hmm,' said Stanley and turned away to concentrate on his trench. He had ordered a fresh bale of peat and it ought to arrive in a day or two. The next thing was to wheedle the money for some of that new variety of majenta heather out of Vera. If she had any. God knew how much she and the old girl together had blued on entertaining Ethel Carpenter.

For once, however, she'd done some of the work herself. Light work, of course, the kind of thing the ladies who had employed her wouldn't have been above undertaking. Stanley drew in his breath in an angry hiss when he looked at his ruined display of daffodils, every other one snapped off, not even cut, to make a fancy flower arrangement in Ethel Carpenter's bedroom.

The room itself had been transformed. Anxious about the sudden dissipation of his inheritance, Stanley had looked on gloomily while Maud wrote out cheques, one for Lucette's where her dress and Vera's had come from, one for all the special food they had got in and another for the draper's who had sent up a pair of lemon nylon sheets, two matching frilled pillowcases and a pair of black and lemon towels. But it was Vera, of course, who had washed all the paintwork and turned the mattress and starched the little lace mats Maud wanted to see on Ethel's dressing table.

The depredation of his daffodil bed so depressed Stanley that he gave up gardening at eleven and trailed despondently into the house. He didn't go into the dining room. Maud was in there, having her hair permed by the dispirited young housewife who went out hairdressing to help make ends meet. The door was shut but that didn't prevent a nasty smell of ammonia and rotten eggs from seeping into the rest of the house.

The second post had come, the one that brought local or near-local letters. A fortnight before Stanley had written to the editor of a national newspaper offering his services as a crossword puzzle setter, a job which he felt would really suit him and give outlet to his creative talents. But the editor hadn't replied and Stanley had almost given up hope. He picked up the letters from the mat and contemplated them gloomily. Nothing for him as usual. Just the gas bill and a long envelope addressed to Maud.

It wasn't stuck down. Stanley took it into the kitchen and wondered who could be writing to Maud and typing the address. Possibly her solicitor.

From the other side of the thin dividing wall he heard Maud say, 'If that's the last curler in, dear, why don't you pop into the kitchen and make us a nice cup of coffee?' He grabbed the letter and took it upstairs.

In the privacy of his bedroom, his crossword annuals around him, he slid the single folded sheet out of the envelope. It wasn't from a solicitor. It wasn't a letter as such at all. Growing suddenly cold, Stanley read:

64, Rosebank Close, Chigwell, Essex

> This desirable bungalow property, freehold and overlooking the Green Belt, is moderately priced at £7,600, and comprises a magnificent through lounge with York stone fireplace, two double bedrooms, luxurious air-conditioned kitchen with waste disposal unit, spacious bathroom and separate W.C. Details are as follows:

Stanley didn't read the details. He had seen enough. Maud must be very confident if she had reached the stage of actually approaching estate agents. Like the commander of an army, she had decided on her strategy and was marching ahead, overthrowing everything that obstructed her path. While he . . . he and his poor forces were falling back on every hand, their weapons impotent, their pathetic outflanking movement ineffective. Soon he would be driven into what sanctuary he could find for himself. And it wasn't going to be any St Helena but a furnished room or even – horror of horrors! – a working men's hostel.

Here, at least, was one desirable property she would never get her hands on. Stanley put a match to the paper and burnt it in the grate. But destroying it afforded him small pleasure. It was about as satisfying as burning the dispatch that tells the defeated general the battle is over, his forces scattered and capitulation inevitable. As in such a case, another dispatch will come. The destruction of the news does nothing to impair the fact of defeat.

He went downstairs and indulged himself in the only comfort left to him. But the crossword puzzle was completed in fifteen minutes and Stanley found that these days he was no longer able to derive his old pleasure from digesting and appreciating the clues after they were solved, from chuckling silently over such witty efforts as: 'Nutcracker Suite' – Tchaikovsky's interpretation of shelling, or 'Wisdom Tooth' – Root cause of biting wit? Nevertheless he repeated them slowly to himself and the very repetition of the words soothed him. He rested his elbows on the kitchen table and whispered over and over again: 'Underwear for barristers' – briefs: 'Does this book tell of a terrible Tsar at Plymouth?' – *Ivanhoe*. A pity they didn't put two in every day instead of only one, he thought with a sigh. Maybe he'd write to them and suggest it. But what would be the use? They wouldn't answer. Nothing went his way these days.

The hairdresser girl was off now. He heard the front door close. Maud came out into the kitchen, her iron-grey hair in large fat curls all over her head. The curls reminded Stanley of those cushion-shaped pot scourers one buys in packets. They had the same hard, metallic and durable look. But he said nothing, only giving her a dismal stare.

Since Vera's threatening outburst they had been wary of each other in the evenings, distant rather than polite, scarcely ever provocative. But during the day war had been maintained with as much vitriol as ever and Stanley expected her to pull the paper away from him with some such accompanying insult as: 'Why don't you take your lazy self out somewhere?' but Maud merely said, 'She's made a nice job of my hair, hasn't she? I wouldn't want Ethel to think I'd let myself go.'

Half a dozen apt and rude retorts came to Stanley's lips. He was deciding which one of them would have the most stinging effect, bring the blood rushing to Maud's face and spark off a bitter interchange, when, staring sourly at her, he saw it would be of no use. Maud hadn't made that innocent remark about her hair because she was weakening or softening with age or because it was a nice sunny day. She wasn't trying to establish a truce. She had spoken as she had because warfare was no longer necessary. Why bother to swat a fly when you have only to open a window and drive it outside? She had won and she knew it.

Speechless, Stanley watched her open the larder door and view with a blank, perhaps very faintly amused, expression the cold pie Vera had left for their lunch.

6

When Stanley was out of work, it was unusual for either him or Maud to appear downstairs before nine-thirty in the morning. Indeed, Maud often remained in her room until eleven, manicuring her nails, tidying her dressing table and her shelf of medicaments, writing another instalment of her weekly letter to Ethel Carpenter. But on Friday, April 10th, the morning of Ethel's arrival – E-Day, as Stanley called it bitterly – both astonished Vera by appearing at the breakfast table.

Each had awakened early, Stanley because the gloom and actual dread occasioned by the imminence of Ethel's coming had made dozing in bed impossible, and Maud because she was too excited to sleep.

Taking her place at the table and filling her plate liberally with cornflakes, Maud thought how wonderfully and suddenly those two had begun to dance to her piping. It was a good fortnight since Stanley had spoken an insolent word to her. Defeat was implicit in every line of his body, hunched up as it was, elbows on the table, dull eyes staring disconsolately out into the garden. And as for Vera . . . Maud had hardly been able to stop herself from shouting with triumph at Vera's face when she had seen all those new towels and sheets arrive at the house, her wistful wonder at the blue and white spotted dress, a model, Maud had made her buy. One word from Auntie Ethel and she would yield utterly. Of course she would; it wasn't human nature to do otherwise.

'One egg or two, Mother?' Vera called from the kitchen.

Maud sighed with satisfaction. Her quick ears noted that Vera's voice had lost that querulous, martyred tone which used to annoy her so much. It was now reserved for Stanley.

'Two, please, dear.' Maud swallowed her two tablets, washing them down with a big gulp of tea. Really strong and sweet it was, the way she liked it. Sugar was what she needed to keep her strength up for the long day ahead, sugar and plenty of protein.

Vera bustled in with the plate of eggs and bacon, stopping to saw off a thick slice of bread for Maud. Stanley sipped his tea slowly like an invalid.

'Try and get home early, won't you, Vee?'

'I'll see if I can make it by five. You said Auntie Ethel wouldn't be here till five, didn't you?'

Maud nodded complacently.

She went to work with a will as soon as Vera had gone, scouring the thin carpets with Vera's old vacuum cleaner, waxing the hall floor and lastly preparing the feast which was to gladden Ethel's heart. It was years since she had done a stroke of housework and in former days she would rather have seen the place turn into a slum about her than let Stanley Manning see her lift a duster. But now it no longer mattered. Stanley wandered about from room to room, watching her and saying nothing. Maud didn't care. She hummed her favourite old hymn tunes under her breath as she worked ('Lead us, Heavenly Father, Lead us' and 'Love Divine, All Loves Excelling'), just as she used to do all those years ago in the big house before the master and mistress were up.

They had lunch at twelve.

'I'll clear away and do the dishes,' she said when they had finished their cold rice pudding. 'It wouldn't do to have Ethel come and find the place in a mess.'

'I don't know why you and Vee can't act more natural.'

'Cleanliness,' said Maud, taking advantage of Vera's absence to have a prohibited dig at him, '*is* natural to some people.' She rushed around, wiping surfaces, her limp hardly noticeable. 'I shall put on my new dress and get myself all ready and then I'll have a lay-down on my bed.'

'What's wrong with the couch in there?' Stanley cocked a thumb towards the dining room.

'That room is all tidied up ready for tea, and I can't go in the lounge on account of that's where we're going to receive Ethel.'

'My God,' said Stanley.

'Please don't blaspheme.' She waited for the spirited rejoinder and when it didn't come, said sharply, 'And you needn't go messing the place up. We don't want them crossword puzzles of yours laying about.'

Stanley rose to that one but only with a shadow of his former verve. 'You needn't worry about me. I'm going to take my lazy no-good self out. Maybe you'd like me to stay away the whole weekend.' Maud sniffed. She rinsed her hands, dried them and moved majestically towards the door. Stanley tried a feeble parting shot. 'Mind you don't oversleep. God knows what would happen if *Miss* Carpenter had to hang about waiting on the step.'

'I'm a very light sleeper,' Maud said gaily. 'The least little thing wakes me.'

Life wasn't going to be worth living for the next few days. Those women would be screaming at him morning, noon and night to wipe his feet and wash his hands and run around after Ethel Carpenter till he couldn't call his soul his own. She would go, of course, on Sunday or Monday, but only round the corner to Green Lanes, and how many times a week would he find her back here again, her feet under his table?

That in itself was a sufficiently gloomy prospect, Stanley thought, leaning forward on the table, his head in his hands. He could at a pinch put up with that, but one day he'd walk in from the pictures or from work – he'd have to get a job if only to get out of this house – to find the lot of them gone and a note on the table with a Chigwell phone number on it and a short request for him to find other accommodation.

Once let Ethel arrive and the eventual outcome was inevitable. Stanley glanced up at the old kitchen clock. Half past one. Three and a half hours and she would be here.

He wandered into the dining room to find himself a more comfortable chair but it was chilly in there and the excessive neatness had about it an almost funereal air. The laid and spread table was covered by a second cloth, as white as snow. Indeed, the whole arrangement, stiff and frigid-looking, gave the impression of a hillocky landscape blanketed by crisp fresh snow. Stanley approached the table and lifted the cloth, then pulled it away entirely.

In the centre of the table stood a pillar of red salmon, still keeping the cylindrical shape of the can from which it had come, and surrounded by circles of cucumber and radishes cut to look like flowers. This dish was flanked by one of beetroot swimming in vinegar, another of potato salad and a third of cole slaw. Three cut loaves of different varieties awaited Maud's attention when her guest arrived. The butter, standing in two glass dishes, had been cut about and decorated with a fork. Next Stanley saw a cold roast chicken with a large canned tongue beside it, and on the perimeter of the table three large cakes, two iced and bound with paper frills and one Dundee. Chocolate biscuits and ginger nuts had been arranged in patterns on a doily and there were half a dozen little glass dishes containing fish paste, honey, lemon curd and three kinds of jam.

All that fuss, Stanley thought, for an old woman who was no better than a common servant. Sausages or fish fingers were good enough for him. So this was the way they meant to live once they'd got all their sneaking underhand plans fixed up? He dropped the cloth back and wondered what to do with himself for the rest of the afternoon. He couldn't go out, except into the garden, for he hadn't a penny to bless himself with.

Then he remembered he'd seen Vera drop some loose change into the pocket of her raincoat the night before. She hadn't worn that coat this morning because the early part of the day had been bright and summery. Stanley went upstairs and opened his wife's wardrobe. Hoping for a windfall of five bob or so which would take him to the pictures, he felt in the pockets, but both were empty. He swore softly.

It had begun to rain, a light drizzle. Vera would get wet and serve her damn well right. Five past two. The whole grey empty afternoon stretched before him with an old women's tea party at the end of it. Might as well be dead, he thought, throwing himself on the bed.

He lay there, his hands behind his head, miserably contemplating the cracked and pock-marked ceiling which a fly traversed with slow determination like a single astronaut crossing the bleak surface of the moon. The *Telegraph* was on the bedside table where he had left it that morning, and he picked it up. He didn't intend to do the puzzle – that he was saving to alleviate the deeper gloom of the coming evening – but looked instead at the deaths column which ran parallel to the crossword clues.

How different his life would be if between the announcements of the departure of Keyes, Harold, and Konrad, Franz Wilhelm, there only appeared Kinaway, Maud, beloved wife of the late George Kinaway and dear mother of Vera. . . . He scanned the column unhappily. Talk about three score and ten being man's allotted span! Why, to find a man or woman dying in their late eighties was commonplace, and Stanley counted three well over ninety. Maud might easily live another twenty years. In twenty years' time he'd be sixty-five. God, it didn't bear thinking of . . .

Stanley was aroused from his dismal reverie by the front doorbell ringing. Only the girl come to read the gas meter, he supposed. Let her ring. By now Maud was snoring so loudly that he could hear her through the wall. So much for all that rubbish about being a light sleeper and hearing every sound.

She had over-tired herself with all that unaccustomed work. A tiny shred of hope returned as Stanley wondered if the work and the excitement had perhaps been too much for her. All that polishing and bending down and reaching up . . .

The bell rang again.

It could be his new bale of peat arriving. Stanley got off the bed. The rain had stopped. He poked his head out of the window and, seeing no seedsman's van parked in the street, was about to withdraw it when a stout figure backed out to the path from under the overhanging canopy of the porch.

Stanley hadn't seen Ethel Carpenter since his wedding but he had no doubt that this was she. The frizzy hair under the scarlet felt helmet she wore was greyish white now instead of greyish brown but otherwise she seemed unchanged.

She waved her umbrella at him and called out, 'It's Stanley, isn't it? I thought for a minute there was nobody in.'

Stanley made no reply to this. He banged down the window, cursing. His first thought was to go into the next room, and shake Maud till she woke up, but that would put Maud into a furious temper which she would assuage by abusing him violently in the presence of this fat old woman in the red hat. Better perhaps to let Ethel Carpenter in himself. Two or three hours chatting alone with her was Stanley's idea of hell on earth, but on the other hand he might use the time profitably to put in some propaganda work.

On the way down, he peered in at Maud but she was still snoring with her mouth open. He trailed downstairs and opened the front door.

'I thought you were never coming,' said Ethel.

'Bit early, aren't you? We didn't expect you till five.'

'My landlady's new lodger came in a bit before time, so I thought I might as well be on my way. I know Maud'll be sleeping, so you needn't wake her up. Well, aren't you going to ask me in?'

Stanley shrugged. This old woman had an even more shrewish and shrill manner than Maud and he could see he was in for a fine time. Ethel Carpenter trotted past him into the hall, leaving her two suitcases on the doorstep. Treating me like a bloody porter, thought Stanley, going to pick them up. God, they weighed a ton! What had she got in them? Gold bars?

'Heavy, aren't they? I reckon I've nearly broke my back lugging them all the way from the station. I'm not supposed to carry weights, not with my blood pressure, but seeing as you haven't got no car and couldn't put yourself out to meet me, I didn't have much option.'

Stanley dumped the cases on the gleaming mosaic floor. 'I was going to meet you,' he lied. 'Only you were coming at five.'

'Well, we needn't have a ding-dong about it. By all accounts, you're fond of a row. There, I'm coming over dizzy again. The room's just going round and round.'

Ethel Carpenter put one hand up to her head and made her way somewhat less briskly than before into the seldom used front room Vera and Maud called the lounge.

'I had a couple of dizzy spells on my way here,' she said, adding proudly, 'My blood pressure was two hundred and fifty last time I saw my doctor.'

Another one, thought Stanley. Another one moaning about something no one could prove and using it to get out of doing a hand's turn. For his part, he was beginning to believe, despite all his reading, that there was no such thing as blood pressure.

'Don't you want to take your things off?' he said gloomily. Get her upstairs and maybe Maud would wake up. He saw that any anti-Maud propaganda he might have in mind would fall on stony ground. 'D'you want to see your room?'

'May as well.' Ethel took her hand from her head and shook herself. 'The giddiness has passed off. Well, that's a relief. I'll have my cases up at the same time. Lead on, Macduff.'

Stanley struggled up the stairs after her. Anybody would think by the weight of them that she was coming for a fortnight. Maybe she was . . . Christ, he thought.

In the spare room Ethel took off her hat and coat and laid them on the bed. Then she unpinned her scarf to stand revealed in a wool dress of brilliant kingfisher blue. She was about Maud's build but fatter and much redder in the face. She surveyed the room and sniffed the daffodils.

'I've been to this house before,' she said. 'There, you didn't know that, did you? I came with Maud and George when they were thinking of buying it for Vee.' Stanley clenched his teeth at this reminder, certainly intentionally made, of the true ownership of the house. 'I thought you'd have bettered yourself by now.'

'What's wrong with it? It suits me.'

'Tastes differ, I daresay.' Ethel patted her hair. 'I'll just have a peep at Maud and then we'll go down again, shall we? We don't want to wake her up.'

Grimly resigning himself to fate, Stanley said, 'You won't wake her. It'd take a bomb falling to wake *her*. She sleeps her three hours out.'

A sentimental smile on her face, Ethel gazed at her friend. Then, closing the door, she resumed a more truculent and severe expression.

'That's no way to talk about Vee's mother. Everything you've got you owe to her. I knew you'd be here when I came, being as you're on the dole, and I thought we might have a little talk, you and me.'

'You did, did you? What about?'

'I don't want to stand about on the landing. The giddiness is coming over me again. We'll go downstairs.'

'It strikes me,' said Stanley, 'you'd be better lying down if you feel queer. I've got to go out, anyway. I've got things to see to.'

Once in the lounge she sank heavily into the chair and lay back in silence, her breath coming in rough gasps. Stanley watched her, convinced she was putting on a show for his benefit. No doubt, she thought she'd get a cup of tea out of him this way.

Presently she sighed and, opening her large black handbag, took out a lace handkerchief with which she dabbed at her face. For the time she seemed to have forgotten her plan to take him to task, for when she spoke her voice was mild and shaky and her attention caught by a framed photograph of Vera and Stanley which stood on the marble mantelpiece. It had been taken at their wedding and Vera, deriving no pleasure from looking at it, usually kept it in a drawer. But Maud, determined to brighten up this gloomy room, had got it out again along with a pair of green glass vases, a Toby jug and a statuette of a nude maiden, all of which were wedding presents.

'I've got that picture myself,' said Ethel. 'It stands by my bed. Or stood, I should say, seeing that it's packed in the trunk I'm having sent on with all my other little bits.'

'Sent on to Green Lanes?' asked Stanley hopefully.

'That's it. Fifty-two Green Lanes, to Mrs Paterson's.' She stared at the picture. 'No, I don't reckon that's the same one. My one's got the bridesmaids in, if I remember rightly. Let's have a closer look.'

As soon as she got to her feet she became dizzy again. Although it went against the grain with him, Stanley got up to give her his arm. But Ethel made a little movement of independence, a gesture of waving him away. She took a step forward and, as she did so, her face contorted and she gave a hollow groan, an almost animal sound, the like of which Stanley had never heard before from a human being.

This time he started forward, both arms outstretched, but Ethel Carpenter, groaning again, staggered and fell heavily to the floor before he could catch her.

'My Christ,' said Stanley, dropping to his knees.

He took her wrist and felt for a pulse. The hand sank limply into his. Then he tried her heart. Her eyes were wide open and staring. Stanley got up. He had no doubt at all that she was dead.

It was twenty-five to three.

Stanley's first thought was to go for Mrs Blackmore. He knocked at the front door of number 59 but there was no one in. There was no need to knock at Mrs Macdonald's. Underneath the figures 63 a note had been pinned: 'Gone to shops. Back 3.30.' The street was deserted.

Back in the house a thought struck him. Who but he knew that Ethel Carpenter had ever arrived? And immediately this idea was followed by another, terrible, daring, wonderful and audacious.

Maud would sleep till four at least. He looked dispassionately at the body of Ethel Carpenter, speculatively, calculatingly, without pity. There was no doubt she had died of a stroke. She had overdone it. Her blood pressure had been dangerously high and carrying those cases three-quarters of a mile had been the last straw. It was cruelly unfair. No one profited by her death, no one would be a scrap the happier, while Maud who had so much to leave behind her . . .

And of a stroke too, the one death Maud had to have if he was ever going to get his hands on that twenty thousand. Why couldn't it have been Maud lying there? Stanley clenched his hands. Why not do it? Why not? He had a good hour and a half.

Suppose it didn't work out? Suppose they rumbled him? There wasn't much they could do to him if one of them, Maud or Vera or some nosy neighbour, came in while he was in the middle of his arrangements. They might put him inside for a bit. But a couple of months in jail was better than the life he lived. And if it came off, if the hour and a half went well, he'd be rich and free and happy!

In his last term at school, when he was fifteen, Stanley had taken part in the school play. None of the boys had understood what it was all about; nor, come to that, had the audience. Stanley had forgotten all about it until now when some lines from it came back to him, returning not just as rubbish he had had to learn by heart, regardless of their meaning, but as highly significant advice, relevant to his own dilemma.

> There is a tide in the affairs of men
> Which, taken at the flood, leads on to fortune.
> Neglected, all the voyage of their lives
> Is lost in shallows and in miseries.
> On such a full sea are we now afloat
> And we must take the current while it serves
> Or lose our ventures.

If ever a man was afloat on a full sea it was Stanley Manning. These iambic pentameters, hitherto meaningless, had come into his mind as a direct command. If he had been a religious man, he would have thought them from God.

The telephone was in the lounge where Ethel Carpenter lay. He ran upstairs two at a time to make sure Maud was still asleep and then he shut himself in the lounge, drew a deep breath and dialled the number of Dr Moxley's surgery. Ten to one the doctor wouldn't be in and they'd tell him to phone for an ambulance and then it would be all over.

But Dr Moxley was in, his last afternoon patient just gone. So far, so good, thought Stanley, trembling. The receptionist put him through and presently the doctor spoke.

'I'll come now before I make any of my calls. Mr Manning, you said? Sixty-one Lanchester Road? Who is it you think has died?'

'My mother-in-law,' said Stanley firmly. 'My wife's mother, Mrs Maud Kinaway.'

PART TWO
Across

7

When he put the phone down Stanley was shaking all over. He'd have to take the next step before the doctor came and his courage almost failed him. There was a half bottle of brandy, nearly full, in the sideboard and Stanley, sick and shivering, got it out and drank deep. It wouldn't matter if Dr Moxley smelt it on his breath as it was only natural for a man to want a drink when his mother-in-law had fallen down dead in front of him.

Vee would have to see the body, *a* body. That meant he'd have to be careful about how he did it. God, he *couldn't* do it! He hadn't the strength, his hands weren't steady enough to swat a fly, let alone . . . But if Maud were to come down while the doctor was there . . .

Stanley drank some more brandy and wiped his mouth. He went out into the still passage and listened. Maud's snores throbbed through the house with the regularity of a great heart beating. Stanley's own had begun to pound.

The doorbell rang and he nearly fainted from the shock.

Dr Moxley couldn't have got there already. It wasn't humanly possible. Christ, suppose it was Vee forgotten her key? He staggered to the door. This way he'd have a stroke himself . . .

'Afternoon, sir. One bale of peat as ordered.'

It was in a green plastic sack. Stanley looked from it to the man and back again, speechless with relief.

'You all right, mate? You look a bit under the weather.'

'I'm all right,' Stanley mumbled.

'Well, you know best. It's all paid for. Shall I shove it in your shed?'

'I'll do that. Thanks very much.'

Dragging the sack through the side entrance, Stanley heard Mrs Blackmore pass along the other side of the fence. He ducked his head. When he heard her door slam he tipped the peat out on to the shed floor and covered it with the empty sack.

Seeing two other people circumstanced very much like himself, the delivery man who lived, he knew, in a poky council flat, and Mrs Blackmore, a tired drudge with a chronic inability to manage on her housekeeping, brought Stanley back to reality and hard fact. He must do it now, vacillate no longer. If he had been as familiar with Hamlet as he was with Julius Caesar, he would have told himself that his earlier hesitation, his moment of scruples, was only the native hue of resolution sicklied o'er with the pale cast of thought.

He closed the front door behind him and mounted the stairs, holding his hands clenched in front of him. Maud was quiet now. God, suppose she was up, dressed, ready to come down . . . ? Outside her door he knelt down and looked through the keyhole. She was still asleep.

It seemed to Stanley that never in his life had he been aware of such silence, the traffic in the street lulled, no birds singing, his own heart suspending its beats until the deed was done. The silence, heavy and unnatural, was like that which is said to precede an earthquake. It frightened him. He wanted to shout aloud and break it or hear, even in the distance, a human voice. He and Maud might be alone in an empty depopulated world.

The hinges of the door had been oiled a week before because Maud complained that they squeaked, and it opened without a sound. He went to the bed and stood looking down at her. She slept like a contented child. His thoughts were so violent, so screwed to courage, that he felt they must communicate themselves to her and wake her up. He drew a deep breath and put out his hands to seize the pillow from under her head.

Dr Moxley didn't ring the bell. He used the knocker and it made a tumultuous metallic clatter through the house. Maud turned over, sighing, as if she knew she had been reprieved. For a moment, watching her, Stanley thought it was all up with him. His plan had failed. But still she slept and still her hand hung limp over the side of the bed. Holding his hand to his chest, as if he feared his lurching, actually painful, heart would burst through his rib cage, Stanley went down to admit the doctor.

He was a boyish-looking man with a shock of black hair, a stethoscope hanging round his neck.

'Where is she?'

'In here,' said Stanley, his voice throaty. 'I thought it better not to move her.'

'Really? I'm not a policeman, you know.'

Stanley didn't like that at all. He was beginning to feel sick. He shuffled into the room after the doctor, aware that his face was covered in sweat.

Dr Moxley knelt down on the floor. He examined the body of Ethel Carpenter and felt the back of her neck.

'My mother-in-law,' said Stanley, 'had a stroke four years back and . . .'

'I know all that. I looked up Dr Blake's notes before I came out. Help me to lift her on to the couch.'

Together they got the body on to the couch and Dr Moxley closed her eyes.

'Have you something to cover her with? A sheet?'

Stanley couldn't bear another moment's delay.

'Was it a stroke, Doctor?'

'Er – yes. A cerebral thrombosis. Seventy-four, wasn't she?'

Stanley nodded. Ethel Carpenter, he remembered, had been a bit younger than that, three or four years younger. But doctors couldn't tell, could they? They couldn't tell that precisely. Apparently they couldn't.

Now the doctor was doing what Stanley had longed for, getting a small pad out of his briefcase and a pen from his breast pocket.

'What about that sheet, then?'

'I'll get it,' Stanley mumbled.

'While you're doing that I'll write out the death certificate for you.'

The sheets were kept in the linen cupboard in the bathroom. Stanley pulled one out, but, before he could go downstairs again the sickness overcame him, accompanied by a fresh outbreak of sweat, and he vomited into the washbasin.

The first thing he saw when he came back into the lounge was Ethel Carpenter's ringless left hand dropping from the couch. Christ, she was supposed to be a married woman . . . The doctor had his back to her and was writing busily. Stanley unfolded the sheet and draped it over the body, tucking the hand into its folds.

'That's right,' said Dr Moxley more pleasantly. 'This is an unfortunate business for you, Mr Manning. Where's your wife?'

'At work.' Give me the certificate, Stanley prayed. For God's sake, give it to me and go.

'Just as well. You must tell yourselves that she'd had a long life, and certainly it was a quick and probably painless death.'

'We can't any of us go on for ever, can we?' said Stanley.

'Now you'll need these.' Dr Moxley handed him two sealed envelopes. 'One is for the undertaker and the other you must take with you when you go to register the death. You follow all that?'

Stanley wanted to say, I'm not stupid because I don't talk la-di-da like you, but instead he simply nodded and put the envelopes on the mantelpiece. Dr Moxley gave a last inscrutable glance at the sheeted body and strode out, his stethoscope swinging. At the front door he stopped and said, 'Oh, just one thing . . .'

His voice was terribly loud, ringing as if he were addressing an audience instead of just one man. A cold shiver ran through Stanley, for the doctor's expression was suddenly thoughtful. He looked like a man who has recalled some vital step he has omitted to take. Holding the door ajar, he said, 'I didn't ask whether you wanted burial or cremation.'

Was that all? Stanley hadn't thought of it either. He wished he dared ask the doctor to keep his voice down. In a tone so low that it was almost a whisper, he said, 'Cremation. That was her wish. Definitely cremation.' Burn Ethel, destroy her utterly, and then there could never be any questions. 'Why d'you want to know?' he asked.

'In cases of cremation,' said Dr Moxley, 'two doctors are required to certify death. It's the law. Leave it to me. I imagine you'll be having Wood's the undertakers and I'll ask my partner . . .'

'Dr Blake?' Stanley said before he could stop himself.

'Dr Blake has retired from practice,' said Moxley a shade coldly. He gave Stanley a penetrating look, reminiscent of Mrs Blackmore, and then he banged out of the house, crashing the front door.

Enough to wake the dead, Stanley thought. It was a quarter to four. Time enough to get on to the undertakers when he had hidden Ethel's body and dealt with Maud . . . The corpse under the sheet might get by a doctor who had never seen Maud before, but it wouldn't get by Vera. Vera must see Maud and, needless to say, she must see Maud dead.

He pulled back the sheet and rolled it up. Then he put his hands under Ethel Carpenter's arms and dragged her half on to the floor. He was a small thin man and her weight was almost too much for him. He stood up, gasping, and his eye lighted on the black handbag which stood beside the chair she had been sitting in. That would have to be hidden too.

He opened the bag and a wave of something sweet and sickly tickled his nostrils. The scent came from a half-empty packet of violet cachous. Stanley vaguely remembered seeing these things, sweets used as breath fresheners, in glass bottles in sweetshops before the war when he had been a boy. Sometimes his mother used to buy them at the village shop or when they went into Bures for a day out. He thought they had long elapsed into disuse along with aniseed balls and Edinburgh rock and now their scent, assailing him unexpectedly, brought back his old home to him, the green river Stour where he had fished for loaches and Miller's Thumbs, the village between a fold in the shallow hills, an ancient peace.

He took out a violet cachou and held it between finger and thumb. A powerful perfume of violets and strong sugar came to him and he held it to his nose. Seventeen he'd been when he'd run away from them all, his parents, his brothers, the river and the fishing. Off to make his fortune, he'd told them, sick with envy and resentment of his two brothers, one halfway through a good apprenticeship, the other off to college. I'll be back, he'd said, and I'll be worth more than the lot of you. But he never had gone back and the last time he'd seen his father was at the Old Bailey where they'd sent for him to be present at his son's trial.

Things were different now. That fortune had taken nearly thirty years to make but now it was almost made. Just one more little step to take . . . And when he'd got the money, maybe next week, he'd go up to Bures in his car and surprise them all. 'How about a spot of fishing?' he'd say to his brother, the master printer, and he'd bring out his shining new tackle. 'Put it away,' he'd say to his brother, the secondary school teacher, when he felt in his pocket for a handful of silver. The resentment would be theirs then when his mother took him about to the neighbours boasting of her most successful son . . .

Stanley put the cachou back in the packet and the vision dimmed. The only other thing of interest in the bag was a fairly thick wad of pound notes, bound with an elastic band. Ethel's savings, he supposed, money to pay her new landlady advance rent.

No need to destroy those with their dead owner.

He was counting the notes when he heard a very faint sound above him, a stair creaking. His fantasies had temporarily calmed him but now the sweat started again all over his face. He took a step backwards to stand trembling like a small animal guarding its kill in the face of a larger advancing predator.

The door opened and Maud came in, leaning on her stick.

8

Maud screamed.

She didn't stop to argue with Stanley or question him. What she saw before her told her exactly what had happened. For twenty years she had been expecting her son-in-law to repeat the violence for which he had been sent to prison. It had been an elderly woman then; it was an elderly woman now. As before, Stanley had attacked an old woman for her money but this time he had gone further and had killed her.

She raised her stick and advanced upon him. Stanley dropped the wad of notes and backed against the open piano. His hands, crashing down on the keys, struck a deep resounding chord. Maud made for his face, but Stanley ducked and the blow caught him agonizingly between his neck and his shoulder blade. He fell to his knees but staggered up again almost at once and hurled one of the green glass vases at her.

It struck the wall behind Maud's head and sent a shower of emerald slivers spraying across the room.

'I'll kill you for this!' Maud screamed. 'I'll kill you with my own hands!'

Stanley looked around for more missiles, edging between the couch and the piano, but before he could snatch up the second vase, Maud struck him again, this time on the top of the head, and caught him as he staggered with a series of violent blows to the body. For a moment the room went black and he saw shapes whirling against this blackness, red squares and triangles and cascading stars.

Maud would beat him to death. Horror and rage had given her an unexpected strength. Sobbing now, crouched in a corner, he turned his shoulder to receive the coming blow and as it struck him he seized the tip of the stick.

It struggled in his grasp like something alive. Stanley pulled himself up on it, hand over hand. He was stronger than she, for he was male and thirty years younger, and he pulled himself to his feet until he was face to face with Maud.

Still they didn't speak. There was nothing to say. They had said it all in those four years and now all that was left was a crystallization of mutual loathing. It throbbed in Maud's breathless grunts and in Stanley's hiss. Once again they might have been alone in the world or outside the world, on some unpeopled unfurnished plane where there was no emotion but hatred and no instinct but self-preservation.

For each of them there was one desire, possession of the stick, and they concentrated on it in a savage, but for some moments equal, tug-of-war. Stanley, seeming to retreat from a very slightly advantageous position, kicked hard at Maud's shins and with a cry she let the stick fall and rattle on the floor.

Stanley picked it up and hurled it across the room. He made a leap for her throat, seizing her neck in both hands. Maud gave a hoarse gasp. As Stanley's hard fingers dug into her carotid artery, she kneed him in the groin. They both cried out simultaneously, Stanley sobbing with pain, and fell apart.

He jerked back on his heels, ready to spring again, but Maud was enfeebled without the stick she had depended on for years. Her arms flailing, she had nothing to break her fall, and as she toppled her head struck the jutting edge of the marble mantelpiece.

Stanley crept over to her on all fours and looked down, his heart drumming, at the consummation of all his wishes.

Vera didn't cry or even speak at all when he broke the news to her but her face went very white. She nodded her head, accepting, as he told her how Maud had been in the lounge, just standing by the mantelpiece and looking at the wedding photograph, when suddenly she had felt bad, touched her forehead and fallen to the floor.

'It was bound to happen sooner or later,' he ended.

'I'll go up and see her,' said Vera.

'As long as it won't upset you.' He had expected this, after all, and had provided for it. He followed her up the stairs.

Vera cried a little when she saw Maud.

'She looks very peaceful.'

'I thought that myself,' Stanley said eagerly. 'She's at peace now, I thought.'

They spoke in whispers as if Maud could hear them.

'I wish you'd rung me at the shop.'

'I didn't see any point in upsetting you. It wasn't as if there was anything you could do.'

'I wish I'd been here.' Vera bent over and kissed Maud's cold forehead.

'Come on,' said Stanley. 'I'll make you a cup of tea.'

He wanted to get her out of here as quickly as possible. The curtains were drawn and the room dim, only a wan filtered light playing on Maud's features and the medicine store by the bed. But let Vera shift that pillow an inch and she'd see the gash on Maud's head under the grey curls.

'I suppose I ought to watch by the bed all night.'

'You what?' said Stanley, alarmed, forgetting to whisper. 'I never heard such rubbish.'

'It used to be the custom. Poor Mother. She loved me really. She meant things for the best. The doctor said it was another stroke?'

Stanley nodded. 'Come on down, Vee. You can't do any good hanging about in here.'

He made a pot of tea. Vera watched him, murmuring the

same things over and over again as recently bereaved people do, how unbelievable it was but really only to be expected; how we must all die but still death came as a shock; how glad she was that her mother had had a peaceful end.

'Let's go into the other room. It's cold out here.'

'All right,' said Stanley. As soon as she saw the table she'd remember and start asking questions, but he was ready for her. He picked up their two cups and followed her.

'My God,' said Vera, opening the dining room door, 'Auntie Ethel! I forgot all about Auntie Ethel.' She looked at her watch and sat down heavily. 'It's nearly six. She's late. She was coming at five. Not like Auntie Ethel to be late.'

'I don't reckon she'll come now.'

'Of course she'll come. She wrote and said definitely she was coming. Oh, Stan, I'll have to break it to her. She'll take it hard, she was ever so fond of Mother.'

'Maybe she won't come.'

'What's the good of saying that?' said Vera. 'She's late, that's all. I couldn't eat a thing, could you?'

Stanley was famished. The mingled scents of the salmon and the chicken were working on his salivary glands and he felt sick with hunger, but he shook his head, putting on a maudlin expression.

As well as hungry, he felt utterly exhausted and he couldn't relax until he was out of danger. Vera had seen her mother and hadn't been suspicious; there was no reason why she should go into the spare room where the body of Ethel Carpenter lay under the bed, concealed by the overhanging bedspread. So far so good.

'I can't think what's happened to Auntie,' said Vera fretfully. 'D'you think I ought to ring her landlady in Brixton?'

'She's not on the phone.'

'No, but I could get on to the café on the corner and ask them to take a message.'

'I wouldn't worry,' said Stanley. 'You've got enough on your plate without bothering about Ethel Carpenter.'

'No harm in waiting a bit longer, I suppose. What time are the undertakers coming in the morning?'

'Half ten.'

'I'll have to ring Doris and say I shan't be in to work. Though God knows how they'll manage with the other girl away on holiday.'

Stanley almost choked over his tea. 'I can see to the undertakers, Vee. You don't want to be here when they come.'

'I don't want to . . . But my own mother, Stan!'

'If you want to go in, you go in. You leave everything to me.'

Further discussion was prevented by the doorbell ringing. Vera came back with Mrs Blackmore who, though Stanley had imparted the news to no one, was by this time in full possession of the facts. Perhaps the doctor's doorstep speech had been overheard by her. Whatever her source, she had, she told Vera, already passed on what she called the 'sad tidings' to Mrs Macdonald and various other cronies in the neighbourhood. So confident was she of her intuition in matters of this kind that she had not thought it necessary to wait for confirmation. A black coat thrown hastily over her floral overall, she announced that she had come to pay her last respects to Mrs Kinaway. In other words, she wanted to view the body.

'Only yesterday I was having such a lovely talk with her over the fence,' she said. 'Well, we're all cut down like flowers, aren't we?'

Distastefully eyeing Mrs Blackmore's inquisitive rabbity face and her bunched hair, Stanley reflected that the only flower she reminded him of was the deadly nightshade. Still, better let them all come and gawp at Maud now than sneak in on her substitute at the undertakers. A watchful guardian of the dead, ready to intercept any tender hand which might try to smooth back Maud's hair, he went upstairs with the two women.

Five minutes after Mrs Blackmore, loudly declaring her willingness to do 'anything I can, dear. Don't hesitate to ask,' had gone, both Macdonalds arrived with a bunch of violets for Vera.

'Sweet violets for mourning,' said Mrs Macdonald sentimentally. Their scent reminded Stanley of Ethel Carpenter's handbag. 'We don't want to see her, Mrs Manning. We want to remember her as she was.'

After that Vera and Stanley were left alone. It unnerved Stanley to realize that his wife was waiting for Ethel Carpenter but he could do nothing about that. Presently, without a word, Vera took away the cutlery that had been laid for her mother.

'You'd better eat something,' she said.

At ten o'clock when Ethel Carpenter still hadn't come, she cleared the table and they went to bed. She had a last look at Maud from the doorway but she didn't go in again. They put the light out and lay side by side, not touching, each wide awake.

Vera fell asleep first. Every nerve in Stanley's body was tingling. What was he going to do if Vera didn't go to work in the morning? He'd have to make her go out. Perhaps he could get her to go and register the death . . . That wouldn't leave him much time for all he had to do.

Soon after midnight he too slept and immediately, or so it seemed to him, began to dream. He was walking by the river, going home, and he had walked all the way from London like a tramp, his possessions in a bundle on his back. It seemed that he had been walking for years, but he was nearly there now. Soon he would reach the point where the river described a great meander and at this point his village would come into view, the church spire first and then the trees and the houses. He could see them now and he quickened his pace. For all his apparent poverty, the pack on his back and his worn-out shoes, he knew they would be glad to see him and welcome him home with congratulations and tears of joy.

The sun was coming up, for it was very early morning, and Stanley struck across the meadow, soaking his trousers in dew up to his knees. In the village no one was up yet. But his mother would be up. She had always been an early riser. The cottage door opened when he pushed it and he went in calling her.

He heard her coming down the stairs and went to the foot of them, looking up. His mother came down. She had grown old and she used a stick. First he saw her legs and her skirt, for the stairs had become long and steep in his long absence, and at last he saw her face. He started back, crying something aloud. It wasn't his mother's face, but Maud's, waxen yellow, the teeth bared, blood running from a wound in her scalp. . . .

He awoke screaming, only the screams came out as a

strangled groan. It took him several minutes to reorientate himself, to realize it had been a dream and that Maud was dead. After that he couldn't sleep again. He got up and walked about the house, looking first in on Maud and then into the spare room. The daffodils Maud had picked for Ethel gleamed whitely at him in the thin moonlight.

He went downstairs where he felt it was safe to put a light on. The house smelt of food, tinned fish and cold meats which wouldn't keep long because there was nothing to preserve them. Now that he had come to himself and the dream was fading, he was struck by a sudden anxiety that he had failed to take some important step. He had forgotten to do something but he couldn't think what that something was. He sat down and put his head in his hands.

Then he remembered. Nothing so very important after all. For the first time in twenty years he had passed a day without doing his crossword puzzle.

He found the *Daily Telegraph* and a ballpoint pen. The sight of the virgin puzzle sent a little thrill of pleasure through him. Funny how just looking at the empty puzzle frame, the exquisitely symmetrical mosaic, brought him peace and steadied his shaking hands. He must have done thousands of them, he thought. Six a week times fifty-two times twenty. God, that was three thousand, seven hundred and forty-four puzzles, not counting all the ones in his crossword paperbacks and annuals.

Stanley picked up the pen.

One across: 'Calf-love may decide one to take this German language course' (two words, six, eight). Stanley pondered only for a moment before filling in 'Wiener Schnitzel'. His body relaxed as if it was immersed in a warm bath and he smiled.

9

The alarm went off at seven.

Vera was out of bed and halfway to the bathroom before she remembered. She came back, wondering whether there was any point in waking Stanley, but he was awake and staring wide-eyed at the ceiling.

'I'm up now,' she said. 'I may as well go to work.'

'I should. It'll take your mind off things.'

But he couldn't be sure she really would, she dithered and hesitated so much, until he saw her actually going down the path. As soon as she was out of sight he fetched in the empty peat sack and took it upstairs. Better remove Maud's wedding ring and slip it on Ethel's finger. Funny, the way it made him feel so squeamish. He was glad he hadn't eaten the eggs and bacon Vera had offered him for breakfast.

Ethel had a ring of her own which she wore on the little finger of her right hand. His own hands shaking, Stanley pulled it off. It was an odd little ring, a thin circle of gold with two clasped hands, tiny gold hands, where there might have been a stone. Stanley put it on Maud's finger and then he bundled her body into the sack.

There was no one about in the Blackmores' garden – they lay in bed till all hours on Saturdays and their bedroom was in the front. Gasping with the weight of it, Stanley dragged the sack across the narrow strip of concrete outside the back door and humped it into the shed. Next Ethel's suitcases. They were of the expanding kind and not fully expanded, although they were so heavy. Stanley opened the lighter of the two and crammed in Ethel's coat and hat and the umbrella which, to his relief, he found was of the telescopic variety. He lugged them downstairs and put them in the shed beside the sack. Nobody but he ever went to the shed but, just to be on the safe side, he shovelled peat all over the sack and the cases. Anyone going in and just giving things a cursory glance would think Stanley Manning had a ton of peat in there instead of a couple of hundredweight.

Things were going well.

By half past nine he had got Ethel lying where Maud had been, on the back room bed, covered by a sheet. It would be a nice touch, he thought, and one likely to impress the undertakers if the corpse they came for had flowers by it so he fetched the vase of daffodils and put it among Maud's pills.

On the dot of ten the undertakers arrived and, having

given Stanley a form to fill in, applying for permission to cremate, took away the body of Ethel Carpenter.

When she had registered Maud's death during her lunch hour, Vera telephoned the Brixton café next door to Ethel's former landlady.

'I'm ever so sorry to bother you. My dad was in business and I know you're busy, but could you ask Mrs Huntley to ring me back?'

It was ten minutes before the phone rang and when it did Vera was filling in time by placing newly cleaned blankets into polythene bags.

'I just wondered,' she said to Mrs Huntley, 'if Miss Carpenter's still with you. She never turned up at our place yesterday.'

'Never turned up? She left here – let's see – it would have been about twenty to one. She had her two cases with her and she left a trunk for me to send on to her new address in Green Lanes, 52, Green Lanes, Croughton. The men came for it just now.'

Vera had to sit down, she felt so weak at the knees.

'Did she say anything about coming to us?'

'The last thing she said to me was they won't be expecting me so early, Mrs Huntley, but I may as well go. Mr Manning's bound to be in, she said, and I can have a chat with him. She said she'd take it slow on account of her cases being so heavy.'

'Did you say *twenty to one*?'

'Might have been a quarter to,' said Mrs Huntley.

'Then she should have been here by two!'

'Maybe she changed her mind. Maybe she went straight to Green Lanes after all.'

'I suppose she must have done,' said Vera.

But it wasn't like Ethel. To arrange to come to stay, arrange it by letter, putting everyone out, and then just not turn up would be a churlish way to behave. And Ethel, though sometimes sharp and malicious and difficult, wasn't churlish or unpunctual or casual at all. She belonged to the old school. Vera couldn't understand it.

At five, when things were slack and the High Street shops emptying, Vera left the cleaners in charge of Doris, her assistant, and caught the bus that went down Green Lanes.

Number 52 was a much nicer house than her own in Lanchester Road. Although semi-detached, it had a double front with imposing gables, a big front garden that was mostly elaborate rockery and a half-timbered garage. A thin middle-aged woman came to the door with a boy and a girl tagging along behind her who might have been either her children or her grandchildren.

'Won't you come in?' she said when Vera had introduced herself.

'I mustn't. My husband will worry if I'm late.' Stanley had never worried in the past when she was late but he had been so nice to her since Maud died, so considerate, that the possibility didn't seem so fantastic as it might have been once. 'I only wanted to know if Miss Carpenter was here.'

'I'm not expecting her till Monday,' said Mrs Paterson in a breathless harassed voice. 'Monday she said definitely. I couldn't cope with anything extra *now*.' The hall behind her was cluttered with toys and from the depths of the house came sounds suggestive of a hungry bitch with a litter of puppies. 'My daughter's had to go into hospital and left the children with me, and my dog's just whelped . . . really, if I'd known there was going to be all this trouble, I wouldn't have considered letting the room at all.'

Vera looked at her helplessly. 'I thought she must be here,' she said. 'She's disappeared.'

'I expect she'll turn up,' said Mrs Paterson. 'Well, if you won't come in, perhaps you'll excuse me while I go and get all this lot fed.'

Stanley was waiting on the doorstep for her, the anxious husband she had never quite believed in even when she was talking to Mrs Paterson.

'Where have you been? I was worried about you.'

Vera took off her coat. That he should have worried about her brought her such intense pleasure that it was all she could do not to throw her arms around him.

'The undertakers came,' he said. 'I've fixed up the cremation for Thursday. We'll have to get cracking asking all the family along. Leave getting the tea for a bit. I've got a form here I want you to sign.' Completing it had been interesting but somewhat frightening as well. Stanley had not much cared for that bit where the applicant was asked if he had any reason to suspect foul play or negligence. Nor had he enjoyed telephoning Dr Moxley to ask for the name of the second certifying doctor, although it had been a relief when Moxley had called him back to say all was done and that the other doctor was some character called Diplock. Blake's name hadn't been mentioned.

'Just sign here,' he said, putting the pen into Vera's hand.

Vera signed.

'Oh, Stan, you've been so marvellous in all this. I can't tell you what a comfort you've been, taking everything off my hands.'

'That's O.K.,' said Stanley.

'Now the only real worry I've got is Auntie Ethel.' Briefly Vera told him about her phone call and her visit to Mrs Paterson. 'D'you think we ought to go to the police?'

Every scrap of colour left Stanley's face. '*Police*?'

'Stan, I'll have to. She may be lying dead somewhere.'

Stanley couldn't speak properly. He cleared his throat. 'The police aren't interested when women go missing.'

'That's only when it's young girls, when it's women who may have gone off with men. Auntie Ethel's seventy.'

'Yeah. I can see that.' Stanley thought quickly, wishing he didn't have to think at all. And now, just when everything was going so well . . . 'Look, don't you do anything till Monday. Wait and see if she turns up at Mrs Paterson's. Then if you don't hear from her we'll get on to the police. Right?'

'Right,' said Vera doubtfully.

All day long John Blackmore had been stuck on a ladder outside his back door painting his house. As soon as he had gone in for tea Vera had come home. Stanley peeped into his shed, noting that the pile of peat was just as he had left it. He locked the door and put the key in his trousers pocket. Then he went over to the heather garden where the deep trench was still unfilled. In the cool May twilight the heathers stood brilliant white against the soft chestnut-coloured peat. White heather, he thought, white heather for luck.

The following day, Sunday, was bright and hot. Vera got the piece of beef topside out of the larder and sniffed it. Just on the turn again. It was always the same. Every hot week-end the Sunday joint was high before she could cook it and she had to soak it in salt water to try and take away the sweetish foetid taint.

'You'll be able to buy a fridge now,' said Stanley. He could see she didn't quite know what reply to make to this. Casually he gave her arm a light pat. Tears came into Vera's eyes. 'I'll just walk up the road and get myself a paper,' he said. 'I miss the crossword on Sundays.'

It was years since he had felt so happy and light-hearted. Everything had gone perfectly. And what had he done wrong? Nothing. It would have been unpleasant if he had actually had to – well, smother Maud, but that hadn't been necessary. Maud had died through her own fault. Now all that remained to stop any awkward questions being asked was to pay a visit to Mrs Paterson.

He jumped on the Green Lanes bus. It stopped right outside the house and within minutes Stanley was smiling ingratiatingly at Mrs Paterson whom he quickly summed up as a tired grandma, a busy woman who would be only too glad to have one of her problems taken off her shoulders.

'Name of Smith,' he said. A dog was howling and he raised his voice to a shout. 'Miss Ethel Carpenter asked me to call.'

'Oh, yes?' Over her shoulder, Mrs Paterson bellowed, 'Shut the dog in the garden, Gary. I can't hear myself speak. There was a lady here,' she said to Stanley, 'asking after her.'

'Well, it's like this. She's stopping with me. I've got this room going, you see, and she looked at it last week. Couldn't make up her mind between this place and mine.'

'These old dears!' said Mrs Paterson, clearly relieved.

'Yeah. It's good of you to take it this way. Fact is, she came round Friday afternoon and said she'd settled for my place, after all. I reckon she didn't like to tell you herself.' With some reluctance, Stanley felt in his pocket for the wad of notes he had taken from Ethel's handbag. 'She wouldn't want you to be out of pocket. She reckoned five quid would make it all right.'

'You don't want to bother,' said Mrs Paterson, taking the notes just the same. 'I'm not sorry things have turned out this way, I can tell you. Now I can let my grandson have her room.'

'There'll be a trunk coming,' said Stanley. 'Being sent on

it is. I'll call round for that.' Was she going to ask for his address? She wasn't.

'You can leave that to me. I'll take it in. It was good of you to come.'

'My pleasure,' said Stanley.

He bought a paper from the kiosk on the corner and by the time the bus got to the top end of Lanchester Road he had done half the clues in his head. 'Frank takes a well-known stage part.' Candida, thought Stanley, wishing he had brought a pen with him. Marvellous, really. Whatever would they think of next? Good training for the mind, crossword puzzles. He marched up the path whistling.

10

Throughout that Sunday John Blackmore stood on his ladder, painting the side of his house, and every time Stanley put his nose outside the back door, Blackmore acknowledged him with a wave of his brush or a remark to the effect that it was all right for some. It was still light at eight and Blackmore was still painting.

'Don't you worry about me if I'm late home tomorrow,' said Vera as they went to bed. 'I'm going straight round to Mrs Paterson when I've finished work to see if Auntie Ethel's turned up.'

'Sometime,' said Stanley casually, 'I suppose we'd better have a word with your mother's solicitor.'

'That can wait until after the funeral.'

'Oh, sure. Sure it can,' said Stanley.

He slept well that night and when he got up Vera had gone. Everything was clean and tidy downstairs and Vera had left his breakfast on a tray as usual, cornflakes poured out for him, milk already in his teacup and water in the kettle. Blackmore's car was gone; he had left for work. Stanley felt considerable relief. He was beginning to be afraid his neighbour might be taking his summer holiday and intended to devote an unbroken fortnight to house painting.

Mrs Blackmore's Monday wash was flapping on the line, but she was still coming and going with pegs and odds and ends of small linen, adjusting the clothes prop and disentangling sheets which had wound themselves round the line in the stiff breeze.

'Lovely drying day!'

'Uh-huh,' said Stanley.

'Things are getting back to normal with you, I daresay. Mrs Manning bearing up all right?'

Stanley nodded, trying not to look at the shed.

'Well, I'll get these last few bits out and then I'm off to my sister's.'

Feeling more cheerful, Stanley pottered about the garden. He pulled a couple of groundsel plants and a sow thistle out of the rose bed but he wasn't in the mood for weeding this morning and his attention kept wandering back to the heather bed with its blanket of peat and the yawning trench in the middle of it. Mrs Blackmore's voice made him jump.

'What are you going to put in that great hole?'

A light sweat broke out on Stanley's forehead.

'I'm going to fill it up with peat. I'm putting a whole sack of peat in there.'

'That's what I said it was for,' said Mrs Blackmore. 'John and me, we noticed it, you see, and John said . . .' She giggled embarrassedly and bit her lip. 'Well, never mind what he said. I wondered if you were going to bury some new potatoes in a tin. They say if you do that you have them all fresh for Christmas.'

'It's for peat,' said Stanley doggedly. He knew what Blackmore had said all right. He could just picture the two of them gossiping and sniggering and Blackmore saying, 'Maybe that's for Mrs Kinaway, save him paying out for the funeral.'

He moved over in the direction of the Macdonalds' garden. Mrs Macdonald, whose husband had a better job than Blackmore, was hanging her wash on a metal whirl-line with plastic strings. She, too, glanced up in happy anticipation of a chat, but Stanley only nodded to her.

The two women began shouting amicably to one another across his intervening lawn. Stanley went back into the house and did the crossword puzzle.

In the end, by a stroke of luck, the two women set off out together. From his vantage point behind the piano in the lounge, Stanley watched Mrs Macdonald come out of her own house with her basket on wheels and wait at Mrs Blackmore's gate. The Blackmores' door closed with a crash and then Mrs Blackmore, dressed for a day out in a summery pink coat and floral hat, trotted up to her friend and whispered something to her. They both looked hard at Stanley's house. Blackening my character again, he thought. He watched them move off towards the bus stop.

When they were out of sight, he went upstairs and, from the bedroom that had been Maud's, scanned the surrounding gardens. Everywhere washing waved and bellied and streamed in the wind. The linen was brilliant white, whiter and tidier than the ragged clouds which tossed above the tossing lines, and all this eddying whiteness had an almost hypnotic effect on Stanley so that he felt he could stand there for ever, staring himself to sleep. His limbs seemed weighted down by a great reluctance for the task ahead of him. So far everything had been done secretly and covertly. Now he must do something in the open air, publicly (although he couldn't see a soul in all those gardens who might observe him), and perhaps what he was about to do was the first truly illegal and punishable thing. But it must be done, and now, before Mrs Macdonald returned from shopping.

Both his neighbours' houses were empty. Stanley was sure of that. The Blackmores had no children and the Macdonalds' two teenagers were at school. It was unnerving, though, to have to start work with that blank bedroom window of the Macdonalds' staring down at him. Who did those Macdonalds think they were, anyway, having an extension built on the back of their house, jutting right out and overlooking his garden? He'd have had the law on them for that, infringing his right to ancient lights or whatever it was, only he'd never been able to afford a solicitor . . . Damn that sightless, closed, uncurtained window! There's no one at home, no one at home, he assured himself as he unlocked the shed and scraped away peat with his hands.

The wind blew the light feathery stuff about, powdering Stanley's clothes and hands with brown dust. He lugged the suitcases out first and, having peeped out cautiously to make sure he was still unobserved, dragged them towards the trench and lowered them in. They took up more room than he had bargained for, leaving only about a foot to accommodate the sack which contained Maud's body.

Maud's body . . . Up till then Stanley had felt a little weary, a little mesmerized, and considerably apprehensive, but he hadn't felt sick. Now a lump of nausea came up into his throat. He kicked some peat over the suitcases and breathed deeply. The nausea receded slightly.

Screwing himself to a pitch of determination, Stanley went back into the shed and grasped the neck of the sack. His fingers, slippery now with sweat, slid about on the thick green plastic. No one watching him would imagine that sack contained anything as soft and amorphous as peat. But no one *was* watching him. He was observed only by a bird which sat on the spiraea branch and by the black, pupilless eye of the Macdonalds' window.

If only it was quiet . . . The thrashing linen made slapping, cracking sounds as it filled with air and the wind drove the air out of it. Stanley was surrounded by a chorus of busy disembodied noise, but the linen didn't seem disembodied to him. Rather it was as if he was attended and observed by a crowd of crackling idiots, white watchers that cackled and sniggered at each fresh move he made.

Cocooned in gleaming slippery green, Maud's body slithered and bumped over the concrete. Stanley had to drag it, for it was too heavy for him to lift. A dead weight, he thought, a dead weight . . . He mustn't be sick.

Pushing the body into the cavity above the cases was the worst part of all. He had thought he would be able to avoid actually touching Maud, but now he couldn't. Her dead flesh felt icy and stiff through the cold damp folds of plastic. Stanley heard himself give a sob of horror. The top of the sack lay almost level with the surrounding earth. Stanley crouched over it, pressing at it with his hands. He didn't think he had the strength to get up, but he managed it at last, staggering. With heavy hands from which the sweat streamed just as if they had been dipped in water, he got his shovel and filled a bucket time after time with peat.

When the operation was completed, the resulting heap looked just what it was – a grave. He began levelling the soil which abutted on to it, pulling heather fronds and flowers above the dusty brown mass, until finally the sickness overcame him. He lay spreadeagled face-downwards on the ground and retched.

'Whatever's the matter, Mr Manning? Are you all right?'

It sounded to Stanley as if Mrs Macdonald must be standing right behind him. He jerked up, half-rolling on to the peat heap. She was ten yards away, staring curiously at him from the other side of the fence, the washing on her whirl-line streaming out and crackling as the metal shaft squeaked. Ghosts on a crazy roundabout, Stanley thought wildly.

'I came back from shopping and I saw you lying on the ground. Whatever came over you?'

He muttered, 'Something disagreed with me . . .' and then, his face and hands streaked with peat dust, he lurched unsteadily into the house.

When Vera came away from Mrs Paterson's, she felt as if a load had been lifted from her shoulders. But her relief was mixed with annoyance. How could Auntie Ethel be so inconsiderate? To write to Maud promising to come for the weekend, even to fix a definite time of arrival, and then just not turn up; worse even, to take Mrs Paterson's room only to throw her over for someone else. Well, she was very lucky, Vera thought, in encountering someone as tolerant and easy-going as Mrs Paterson. Not many landladies would take that sort of treatment and be content with a mere five pounds as recompense. It was a pity, though, that she hadn't had the presence of mind to ask this Mr Smith for his address.

Still, if Ethel was going to behave in this cavalier way, they were well rid of her. Let her make a fuss because no one told her Maud was dead or asked her to the funeral. How was anyone supposed to get in touch with her when she hid herself in this stupid mysterious way?

As Vera was unlatching her front gate, Mrs Macdonald came out.

'Has your husband got over his bad turn?'

'Bad turn?'

'Oh, haven't you seen him yet? I never meant to upset you, really I didn't.'

'Just tell me what's happened, Mrs Macdonald.'

'Well, nothing really. Only when I got in from the shops

this morning there was poor Mr Manning laying, actually laying, on the ground out among those heather plants of his. Been sick, he had.'

'But what was it?'

'Something that disagreed with him, he said. My boy Michael was home from school with a sore throat and he said he'd been watching Mr Manning at his gardening, watching him through the back bedroom window, and he saw him collapse.'

Vera hurried indoors, expecting to see Stanley prone on the sofa, but he was sitting in a chair, intent on his crossword annual, and he had his usual healthy, though sallow, colour. Better say nothing of what she had heard. Stanley hated being spied on by the neighbours. Instead she told him of her interview with Mrs Paterson.

'I said it'd be all right,' said Stanley.

'I know, dear. I've been very silly. The best thing will be to forget all about Auntie Ethel and her nonsense. Could you eat a bit of steak?'

'Uh-huh,' said Stanley, taking no further notice of her. Vera sighed. Of course he'd been under a strain, what with Mother dying like that before his eyes, but if only he would sometimes, just sometimes, speak nicely to her or thank her for what she did for him or show by a glance or a smile that he still loved her. Perhaps you couldn't expect it after twenty years. Vera ate her meal in silence. There was a lot she would have liked to discuss with her husband but you cannot have much of a conversation with a man whose face is concealed behind a large book. She cleared the table, Stanley moving impatiently but not looking up while she removed his plate, and then she went up to the room that had been Maud's.

She sat down in front of the dressing table, but before she opened the drawer where Maud had kept her papers she caught a glimpse of herself in the glass and sighed afresh at her reflection. It wasn't only lack of money but lack of time . . . She wondered apprehensively what Stanley would say if she spoke to him of giving up her job. Then, averting her eyes, she opened the middle drawer and lifted its contents out on to the bed.

On top was a bundle of letters from Ethel Carpenter. Beneath these Maud's cheque book, her birth certificate, her marriage lines, Vera's own certificate of baptism. How painful it all was, a job that had to be done and as quickly as possible. The light was fading fast now and the room growing dim, but the papers in her hands still showed white with the last brilliant whiteness that comes before dark.

Here was a letter from a firm of solicitors: Finbow and Craig, of High Street, Croughton. 'Dear madam, An appointment has been made for you with our Mr Finbow to discuss the question of your testamentory dispositions . . .' After the funeral, Vera decided, she too would make an appointment with Mr Finbow.

Next, sandwiched among the papers, she found a flat jewel box full of little brooches and chains and souvenir trinkets. There was nothing she really fancied for herself – perhaps she might keep that cameo pendant with the picture of Mother and Dad inside it – and most of it could be given away to the relatives coming on Thursday.

Vera came next to Maud's red leather photograph album. On the first page was her parents' wedding picture, George tall and awkward in his hired morning coat, Maud in a knee-length dress of white crêpe-de-Chine, clutching his arm determinedly. Then there were photographs of herself as a baby. Maud had put captions to them all in careful copperplate: Vera aged one; Vera takes her first steps; then, when she was older, a child of five or six: Vera gets to know her Auntie Ethel; Vera on the sands at Brayminster-on-Sea.

'Dear old Bray!' That was the heading written across the next double page. Maud had always called the seaside resort that, loving it and making it her own. Dear old Bray! On a postcard photograph, taken by a beach photographer, Ethel Carpenter in 1938 hat and Macclesfield silk dress walked along the sands, holding the hand of ten-year-old Vera. Maud wore sunglasses in the next snapshot and George had a handkerchief with knots in its four corners on his balding head to protect it from the sun.

More and more snaps of Bray . . . 1946 and the war over. Vera grown up now, a pretty eighteen with long curls and a crimson mouth that looked black and shiny in the snap. Two years later the New Look. Little cotton jacket with a peplum, long skirt with a flare at the hem. Had she really worn shoes with ankle straps and heels four inches high? James Horton holding her hand, whispering something to her in the sunshine, the bright sea behind them. James Horton. Suppose it had been he downstairs, he her husband who had been ill and whom she had tended, would he have smiled and thanked her and held up his face for a kiss?

There was no picture of Stanley in the album, not even a wedding photograph. Vera closed it because it was too dark now to see any more. She bent her head and wept softly, the tears rolling on to the old red leather binding.

'What are you doing up here in the dark?'

She turned as Stanley came into the room and, thinking she heard in his voice a tiny hint of tenderness or concern, she reached for his hand and held it against her cheek.

11

Standing with bowed head between George Kinaway's brother Walter and Maud's sister Louisa, Stanley watched the coffin slowly drawn away from behind the gilt screen towards the waiting fire. The vicar exhorted them to pray for the last time and while Vera wept quietly, Stanley looked down even further, studying his shoes.

'Nothing from Ethel Carpenter, I see,' said Aunt Louisa when they were outside in the paved courtyard looking at the flowers. 'I must say I expected to see her here. These are from Uncle Tom and me, Stanley. Wreaths are so dear these days and they all go to waste, don't they? So we thought a sheath would be nice.'

'Sheaf,' said Stanley coldly. It was just like those Macdonalds to send an enormous great cross of lilies. Done on purpose to make the relatives' flowers look mean, he had no doubt.

They got into the hired cars and went back to Lanchester Road. It was all Stanley could do to keep his temper at the sight of Mrs Blackmore getting stuck into the sherry and the ham sandwiches. They hadn't even had the decency to send flowers either. With a long pious face he brushed off Mrs Blackmore's attempts to find out how much Maud had left but as soon as they had all gone he telephoned Finbow and Craig.

'It seems a bit soon,' said Vera when he told her an appointment had been made for the following day.

'Tomorrow or next week, what's the odds?'

'I'll be glad to get it over. It was a nice funeral.'

'Lovely,' said Stanley with sincerity. He couldn't, in fact, recall any clan gathering he had ever enjoyed so much. If only he hadn't got to solve the problem of collecting that trunk . . .

'You know, love,' Vera said, 'it's years since we had a holiday. When we've got everything settled, why don't we go down to dear old Bray for a week?'

'You go,' said Stanley. 'I've got business to see to.'

'You mean you've got a job?'

'Something in the offing.'

Stanley looked away coldly. He didn't care for that wistful encouraging look Vera had given him. A job indeed. She couldn't think big, that was her trouble. He poured himself the dregs of the sherry and began to think about Pilbeam.

In telling his wife he had a job in the offing Stanley hadn't been strictly truthful. It was not in the offing, it was in the bag but it was also nothing to be proud of. He had only taken it because it allowed him more or less unrestricted use of a van.

A florist in Croughton Old Village wanted a driver and delivery man and on the day before the funeral Stanley had walked down to the Old Village, the vestigial remains of a hamlet that had been there before London spread across the green fields, applied for the job and was told to start on the following Monday.

Delighted with the way things were working out for him, he wandered across the village green and, sitting down on the steps of the war memorial (Dulce et decorum est pro patria mori), lit a cigarette.

There is perhaps no more pleasant occupation for a man whose expectations have almost come to fruition than that of speculating what he will do with the money when he gets it. His thoughts toyed happily with visions of cars, clothes, abundant liquor and the general appurtenances of making a splash, but Stanley was under no illusion that he could live for the rest of his life on twenty thousand pounds. He was too big a man now to consider working for anyone else, unless it was as a setter of crossword puzzles. That might come later as a sideline. First, he thought, he would rather like to go into business and what he saw before him as he crossed the road and stepped on to the pavement gave him the idea that it might be profitable and consistent with his new dignity as a man of private means to keep a shop. After all, dreary old George Kinaway had made a good thing out of it, a very good thing, and what George Kinaway could do he could do standing on his head.

In front of him was a row of shops with crazily sagging Tudor gables above them and a row of aged trees to give them an old-world expensive look. There was a chi-chi-looking art place with abstract paintings in its window, a dolly girls' boutique, a treasure house of Indian jewellery and between this and a place selling old books a vacant shop, its door boarded up and a notice over its window: *These desirable premises to let.*

Standing with his nose pressed against the dirty finger-marked glass of the shop window was a short stout man. Still whistling, Stanley too stopped and stared inside at a dim dusty interior cluttered with cardboard boxes. The other man gave a heavy sigh.

'Lovely day,' said Stanley cheerfully.

'Is it?' His companion turned to face him and Stanley saw a snub-nosed baby face topped by sparse colourless hair. He was smoking a cigarette he had obviously rolled himself and as he raised his hand to his mouth Stanley noticed that the top of the forefinger was missing and this finger ended in a blob of calloused flesh instead of a nail. It reminded him of a chipolata sausage. 'All right for some, I daresay.' Stanley grinned. 'What's with you, friend? Won the pools, have you?'

'As good as,' said Stanley modestly.

The other man was silent for a moment. Then he said somewhat lugubriously, 'I'm a joiner by trade, a joiner and cabinet maker. Thirty years I've been in the trade and then the firm goes bust.'

'Hard cheese.'

'This place . . .' He banged on the glass. 'This place could be a little goldmine in the right hands.'

'What sort of a goldmine?' Stanley asked cautiously.

'Antiques.' The other man bit off the dental with a short sharp explosion and a spot of saliva struck Stanley's cheek. 'What I don't know about the antique . . .' Spit, splutter, bite . . . 'business you could write down on a postage stamp.' He backed away from Stanley slightly and assumed the attitude of an orator. 'It's like this,' he said. 'You buy up a couple of chairs, genuine Hepplewhite, say, and make – or I make – a dozen more, incorporating bits of the genuine two in each chair. D'you get the picture? Then you can sell the lot as Hepplewhite. Who's to know? It'd take a top expert, I can tell you. Or a table. An inlaid table top, circa 1810 – put legs on it, Bob's your uncle.'

'Where d'you get the table top?'

'Knocking. Going on the knock. Up Barnet way and further out, Much Hadham and the villages. Some of those old girls have got treasure trove hidden away in their lofts.'

'Who'd buy it?'

'You're joking. There's not an antique shop in Croughton as yet, but there's folks with so much lolly they don't know what to do with it. Antiques are the thing. Didn't you know? All you need is capital.'

'I might be able to lay my hands on some capital,' said Stanley carefully.

The snub nose wrinkled. 'Come and have a drink, my old love. Name of Pilbeam, Harry Pilbeam.'

'Stanley Manning.'

Pilbeam bought the first round and they discussed it. When it came to Stanley's turn he excused himself, saying he had to see a man, but they arranged to meet on the following Wednesday when Stanley said he would have more idea of how the land lay.

He didn't want to waste his money on Pilbeam yet, and whisky was a diabolical price these days. Of course, he'd still got most of the money he'd taken from Ethel Carpenter's handbag but he was reluctant to break into that.

Alone in the house the morning after the funeral, he took the notes out of his pocket and looked at them. They smelt strongly of violet cachous. Compared with what was coming to him, they were a drop in the ocean. The smell slightly disquieted him and he knew the wisest thing would be to burn them but he couldn't bring himself actually to destroy money. No harm could come of keeping them for a week or so. He went upstairs and from the bedroom bookcase took out the crossword annual of 1954. Then he distributed Ethel's money evenly among its pages before replacing it in the bookcase.

At this moment, he thought, looking at the old metal alarm clock, Vera would be at the solicitor's. He had almost made up his mind to enter into partnership with Harry Pilbeam but it would be nicer if he could go to the Lock-keeper's Arms next Wednesday a rich man instead of just an heir apparent.

'Your mother's will is quite straightforward, Mrs Manning,' said Mr Finbow. 'I don't understand what you mean about a condition.'

Vera didn't know how to put it. It sounded so strange.

She floundered. 'My mother . . . Er, my mother said she'd altered her will – well, way back in March. She said her money would only come to me if – oh, dear, it does sound so awful – if she died of a stroke and not anything else.'

Mr Finbow's eyebrows went up at that as Vera had known they would. 'There was nothing like that. Mrs Kinaway made her will on March 14th and, as far as I know, that was the only will she ever made.'

'Oh, I see. She must have been – well, joking, I suppose. She really led us to believe . . . It was rather awful.'

'Such a condition would have been most irregular, Mrs Manning, and hardly legally binding.' What must he think of her? Vera wondered. That Maud had gone in terror of her life while she lived with her only daughter? It was cruel of Maud to have exposed her to such embarrassment.

'Anyway, I have the will here,' said Mr Finbow. He opened a drawer in his cabinet and withdrew an envelope. 'All the late Mrs Kinaway's estate passes unconditionally to you as her sole heir. Indeed, there was no real need for her to have made a will under the circumstances, except that it avoids intestacy problems, probate and so on. Had you predeceased her, the estate was to have been divided equally between Mrs Louisa Bliss, her sister, and Miss Ethel

Carpenter. The property amounts to – let me see – approximately twenty-two thousand pounds, at present mostly invested in stock.'

'When can I . . . ?'

'Quite soon, Mrs Manning. In a week or two. If you wish the stock to be sold, I will personally hand you a cheque. Of course, should you require any cash at present, a hundred or two can easily be made available to you.'

'No, thank you,' said Vera.

'A week or two?' said Stanley thoughtfully when she got home. 'Just what I thought, all plain sailing.' He smiled wryly to himself when he thought how Maud had fooled them, or half-fooled them, over that condition. Not that it mattered. Taken all in all, things were working out beautifully.

12

The van was a green one, plain on one side and painted with a wreath of roses on the other. Stanley parked it at the kerb, the plain side towards Mrs Paterson's house, and tossing the bouquets of flowers on to the van floor so that they wouldn't be visible through the window, knocked at the front door.

As soon as Mrs Paterson opened the door, he saw the trunk behind her in the hall.

'Oh, Mr Smith, I'd just about given you up.'

'Couldn't make it before,' said Stanley.

'Would you like my son-in-law to give you a hand with it?'

And see the flowers he was supposed to be delivering?

'I'll manage,' said Stanley. The heavy weights he had to carry these days! He'd rupture himself at this rate.

'Here, why don't you put it on my grandson's pushchair and wheel it out?'

To Stanley's relief she didn't come down the path with him as he trundled the wobbly trunk out to the van. Nor did she seem sufficiently curious about him as to ask his address or keep the door open after he had started the van.

He drove the van down the narrow cobbled lane that led from the Old Village into Croughton High Street and parked it half on the pavement and half in the street. Then, making sure no one was watching him, he clambered into the back of the van and contemplated Ethel Carpenter's trunk.

It was made of wood and painted black. Stanley thought it must be very old, probably the 'box' Ethel had taken with her from situation to situation when she was in service. Of course, it *would* be locked. He wasn't at all anxious to dispose of it without making himself aware of its contents, so he got a hammer and a wrench out of the van's tool kit and got to work on the lock.

After about ten minutes' straining and hammering the lock finally gave. Stanley lifted the lid and looked inside. On top of the winter clothes was a cardboard box made to contain writing paper. It still contained writing paper only this paper had been written on. His eyes narrowing, Stanley read the letters Maud had written to her best friend. As he had suspected, they were full of derogatory allusions to himself. Fine thing if they fell into the wrong hands. The best thing would be to burn them. Stanley rolled them up and stuffed them in his pocket.

There didn't seem much else of any interest apart from a wedding photograph of himself and Vera and one of George Kinaway. Someone had written on the back of it, *This and your ring, all I have of you.* Stanley put it in his pocket with the letters and then he looked to see if any of the clothes were marked with Ethel's name. They weren't but, rummaging among camphor-smelling wool, his hand encountered something hard and cold.

The bottom of the trunk contained several small parcels wrapped in tissue paper. The cold thing his hand had touched was the elbow of a china figurine protruding from the paper. He unwrapped it and saw a shepherdess with a crook and a black lamb. Tearing off paper excitedly, he brought to light next a carriage clock, a pot-pourri bowl and a silver cream jug. With a thoughtful backward glance at the vacant shop, Stanley wrapped all these things in the *Daily Telegraph*.

The canal banks were shored up with walls of yellow brick beneath which the duller yellow water flowed sluggishly. A couple of barges waited at the lock gates and a woman was walking a corgi along the towpath. Two children were at play in the garden of the lock-keeper's house and Stanley quickly realized he had no opportunity of disposing of the trunk at present.

He drove back to the shop and gave a fictitious order to the florist to have a bouquet of spring flowers made up for delivery to the other side of Croughton at 10 p.m. The florist grumbled a good deal but cheered up when Stanley said he would take the flowers himself. Stanley didn't want any bills sent out to people who didn't exist and he decided reluctantly to pay for the order himself with what remained of his dole money.

While he had his tea he left the van parked outside the house with the trunk still in it but he brought the newspaper parcel indoors. He hid Ethel Carpenter's treasures in the back of his wardrobe and burnt the letters and the photograph in the bedroom fire grate.

It had been raining intermittently all day but now the rain fell heavily, drumming against the windows. Vera drew the curtains, put the light on and fetched writing paper and envelopes. Then she sat down and stared helplessly at the paper. What a fool she was! All day long she'd been thinking about this holiday of hers without ever considering how to set about finding an hotel in Brayminster. How did you find out about hotels, anyway? Vera had never stayed in one.

This, she reflected miserably, was something everyone knew about, everyone but her. Her life had been hard but it had also been sheltered and now she realized that, though forty-two years old, she couldn't begin to do any of the things other people seemed to take in their stride. Suppose I had to book a restaurant for a dinner or buy theatre tickets or make a plane reservation or buy a car, she thought. I wouldn't know how to set about it. I'm like a child.

Other people had guidebooks and holiday brochures. You wrote to the address or rang them up. Vera knew she would never have the courage to telephone an hotel. Oh, it was all hopeless, she was too tired and too old to learn now.

Unless . . . of course! Why hadn't she thought of it before? She knew one boarding house in Bray, Mrs Horton's in Seaview Crescent.

It was more than twenty years since she had last stayed there. Mrs Horton had seemed old to her then but probably she had really been younger than Vera was now. That meant she'd be under sixty. Certainly James wouldn't still be living with his aunt, so she needn't be afraid of running into him, of seeing his face fall at the sight of the change in her. But James would have moved far away . . .

More at ease than she had been all day, Vera began to write her letter.

The rain had driven much of the traffic off the roads but Stanley drove on doggedly, the wheels of the van sending fountains spraying over the pavements. He kept to a snail's pace, though, for the windscreen wipers were inadequate to deal with the torrents that poured down the glass and he could hardly see.

A deluge, he thought, that's what it is. A nice word for a crossword puzzle. How would you set about making up a clue for it? 'A pull in the river causes this flood'? Not bad that. 'Lug in Dee,' he said aloud, as if explaining to some novice. Now that would be a job he'd really like, setting crosswords, and maybe, after the business had got going and he had ample time on his hands, he would be able to get himself such a job, for money talked and influenced and opened doors. With money you could do anything.

This was just the weather he would have ordered if he'd had any choice in the matter. You'd think the end of the world was coming the way everybody was shut up indoors. He drove slowly up the approach road to the lock and saw that the windows in the lockkeeper's house were curtained. The rain, though savage enough close to, had the appearance in the distance of a thick swirling mist.

No silly old bags giving their dogs an airing tonight. Two empty barges were moored this side of the lock, their hulls rapidly filling with water. The canal had already begun to rise. Its yellow frothing waters seemed to reach up and meet the rain which crashed on to it like a quivering sheet of steel.

Stanley had never seen the canal quite like this before. Usually, at any rate by day, it was busy with barges and kids fishing and the eternal procession of dog walkers. And, although it wound among fields of a sort, litter-covered waste ground really, dotted about with sick-looking trees, it was a hideous mockery of what a waterway should be. Instead of woods and unspoilt countryside, all you could see were the slummy backs of two or three converging suburbs, half-built factories, and tumbled warehouses.

But tonight the rain obscured all this. No houses were discernible in clear silhouette, only lights visible in clusters and separated from each other by the black unlit masses of factory buildings. And suddenly, because of the rain and the sparse scattered lights, the whole place took on an almost rural aspect so that Stanley was again reminded strongly of his old home where, as you walked along the river bank at night, a mist rose thickly from the water and the villages could be seen as knots of light gleaming between the shallow folded hills.

A faint nostalgia took hold of him, a nostalgia that was mixed with irritation as he drove very slowly along the tow-path, wincing each time his tyres sank into ruts filled with muddy water.

When he was well out of sight of the lock-keeper's house he switched off his own feeble sidelights and drove on for a few yards in darkness, very conscious of the canal – briefly and foolishly he had thought of it for a moment as the river – lapping and gurgling to the left of him. Now if it *had* been his river, there'd be a bend here where you had to turn sharply to the left. When you got along a few yards the hills divided and you could see the village lights winking over there. Well, this wasn't the Stour but Croughton Canal and now was no time for fantasies of that sort. A fine thing if he and the van went into the water with Ethel's trunk.

When he had reversed it almost to the brink, he opened the van's rear doors. Cursing the blinding rain, he clambered over the driver's seat and began to shove the trunk from behind. It slid slowly along the rubber mat. Stanley grabbed the bouquet of flowers and tossed them on to the passenger seat. Another final heave . . . He pushed, bracing his feet against the dashboard.

Suddenly the trunk shot out, bounced once on the canal wall and fell into the water with a tremendous splash. Kneeling between the open doors, Stanley started back on to his heels, but the water broke against him in a huge wave, drenching him from head to foot. He swore luridly.

Great eddies wheeled away across the canal. Too wet now to bother with a raincoat, Stanley crouched on the parapet of the wall and looked down into the depths. Then, rolling up his soaked sleeves, he thrust his arm into the water. But he couldn't touch the top of the trunk, although he reached down as far as he could without actually toppling in. Right, he thought, getting up, another job jobbed.

After she had sent the letter Vera thought she had been rather silly. Twenty years was a long time and Mrs Horton would have moved away. But in the middle of the week a letter arrived with the Brayminster postmark. When she had allowed herself to hope at all, Vera had looked forward to a long chatty letter full of reminiscences and news, but Mrs Horton wrote formally, simply saying she would be pleased to see Mrs Manning and would reserve a nice room for her with a view of the sea.

The price quoted was well within Vera's means. She would have her holiday money and the small bonus the dry cleaners gave their manageresses in the summer. Nor was there any need to worry about Stanley, who had settled down quite marvellously in his new job and would have his own wages to live on while she was away.

'You won't be here to collect the cheque from Finbow and Craig,' he grumbled when she told him her holiday was fixed.

'Mr Finbow said a week or two, dear, and two weeks will only just be up when I get back.' She smiled lovingly at him, remembering the beautiful and totally unexpected gift of flowers he had brought her that wet night when he had had to work late. If only he was coming with her . . .

'I'll drive you to the station in the morning if you like.'

'That's sweet of you, dear.'

'The week after you come back I'll have my own car.'

'Whatever you like, Stan, and I'll have an automatic washer, I think, and a fridge.'

'There's no need to go mad,' said Stanley coldly, and he pencilled in the word which completed his crossword, 'onyx'. 'Only a pound left out and with ten to come it's turned to stone.'

'I only hope you'll be all right on your own.'

'I'll be fine,' said Stanley.

13

Alone in the house, Stanley took stock of his life, congratulating himself on his excellent management. Nothing had gone wrong. Maud was safely buried and the heathers were beginning to flourish on her grave. Perhaps in a few months' time he'd have a garage built just on that spot. He'd need somewhere to keep his Jaguar. Ethel Carpenter was a handful of grey ashes, or rather an urnful, the mere powdery contents of a casket now reposing on the lounge mantelpiece between the wedding photograph and the nude statuette. Her trunk and clothes were at the bottom of the canal, the *objets d'art* which he had retrieved stowed in his wardrobe and waiting to be sold over the counter as soon as he and Pilbeam had opened their shop.

He had met Pilbeam as arranged and they had celebrated their new partnership in the Lockkeeper's Arms. Pilbeam had been less affable when Stanley had admitted his capital was at present tied up but Stanley thought he had been able to allay his doubts. Once Vera had returned and Finbow come up with the loot, a matter of ten days or so, he would be able to show Pilbeam concrete proof of his affluence.

Yes, things had gone admirably.

Stanley went down to the Old Village, told the florist that the job didn't suit him, after all, and, turning a deaf ear to the reproaches and indeed abuse which ensued, collected his week's money. He walked across the green and smoked a cigarette, sitting on the steps of the war memorial and gazing in the direction of the shop which would soon be his. His vivid imagination presented it to him not as it now was but as it would be when Gothic gilt lettering ornamented the blank space above the window, when the door was a mullioned affair with a chased brass knob, the window full of apparently authentic collector's pieces and the interior thronged with customers all desperate to part with their money.

Life was glorious.

He went into the Lockkeeper's off-licence and bought himself a half-bottle of whisky and six cans of beer. Then, armed with the materials for a liquid lunch, he returned home where he settled himself on the dining room sofa, a spot for four years sacrosanct and reserved to Maud.

Stanley poured himself a tumbler of whisky and raised it at the framed photograph of her mother Vera had hung on the wall. 'Absent friends!' he said. He smiled and switched on the television for *Sports Round-Up*, recalling how in the past he had almost always had to miss it because the noise disturbed Maud's afternoon rest.

Vera only had one case and she meant to go from the station to Mrs Horton's by bus. The bus came and it was a single-decker green one, not very different from the buses she and James used to travel in down to the sea. They hadn't changed the sea-front at all. There was the old bandstand, the pretty little pier, there the cliffs where thrift grew and the orange daisies with the long Latin name Vera could never remember.

She couldn't see a single amusement arcade or fish and chip shop but the old stall selling rock and candy floss was still there and she saw a child go up to it with a bucket and spade, a fair-haired child who might have been herself all those many years ago.

Vera got off at the bottom of Seaview Crescent, feeling she must be in a dream. It wasn't possible that progress and the current mad craze for pulling things down and putting new things up had passed Brayminster by. It wasn't possible but it had happened. It was a Saturday afternoon in summer on the South Coast and there was no canned music, no screaming mobs, no coach parties and no strings of exhausted donkeys carrying screaming children along the sands. Vera listened to the quiet. In the copper beech tree which still stood in the garden of the big house on the corner a bird was singing. She was at the seaside in the

South of England in June and the only sound was a singing bird.

She walked slowly up the street and rang the bell of Crescent Guest House and when Mrs Horton herself opened the door, Vera was almost too moved to speak. Inside, the house looked the same. Vera looked wonderingly at the beach ball and the spade a child had left by the umbrella stand, just where she had left hers.

'Brings back the past a bit, doesn't it?' said Mrs Horton kindly. 'You look all in. Would you like to go up to your room and have a lie-down?'

'I'm not tired,' said Vera, smiling. 'I was just thinking how nothing's changed.'

'We don't like changes in Bray.'

'No, but how do you avoid them? I mean, everywhere else has changed utterly since the war.'

Mrs Horton led the way upstairs. 'Well, down here, you see, we like to keep ourselves to ourselves. We're a bit like Frinton in Essex. Other places want the money, but we don't care so much about that. We don't let the coach parties in and our preservation society sees to it that the place doesn't get all built up. And we've got a good council. I hope things stay this way.'

'So do I,' said Vera as Mrs Horton showed her into the room Maud and George used to share.

'Your mother was so fond of this room. How is your mother, Mrs Manning?'

'Dead,' said Vera.

'Oh dear, I'm sorry to hear that.' Mrs Horton looked searchingly at Vera and then she said, before she went downstairs, 'You have had a bad time, one loss after another.'

Stanley lay on the sofa all Saturday afternoon. He wasn't used to whisky and it made him sleep heavily. The phone ringing awakened him but before he could get to it it had stopped. Ten minutes later it rang again. Pilbeam. Would Stanley meet him for what he called a short snort in the Lockkeeper's Arms at eight and discuss business? Stanley said he would and had Pilbeam phoned him before?

'Not me, my old love. Maybe it was your stockbroker.'

Well, suppose it had been? The solicitor, that is, to say the money had come through. But he wouldn't be working on a Saturday, would he? Stanley considered calling the number of Finbow and Craig but then thought better of it. Early days yet.

He opened a can of beans for his tea and he was making himself a piece of toast to go with them when the phone rang again. Vera, he supposed, to tell him she'd arrived safely, just as if he'd be worrying himself in case the train had crashed.

He gave the number and it was a girl's voice he heard.

'Mr Manning? Mr Stanley Manning?'

Finbow's secretary. Bound to be. 'Speaking,' Stanley said smoothly.

'You won't know me, Mr Manning. My name's Caroline Snow. I was given your phone number by a Mrs Huntley.'

Mrs Huntley? Mrs Huntley? Where had he heard that name before? In some unpleasant connection, he was sure. Stanley felt a very faint disquiet, nothing amounting to a shiver, but a kind of sense of coming events casting their shadows before them. He cleared his throat. 'What were you wanting?'

'Well, to talk to you or your wife, actually. I'm making some enquiries about a Miss Ethel Carpenter.'

Stanley lowered himself gingerly into the chair Ethel Carpenter had occupied a few minutes before her death. His mind was curiously blank and he found himself temporarily unable to speak.

The girl's voice said, 'Could I come over and see you? Would you be very kind and let me come tomorrow evening?'

A faint squeak that Stanley hardly recognized as coming from himself said, 'No, but . . . Look, what exactly . . . ?'

'Then may I come at eight? That's marvellous. I'll be over at eight and I'll explain everything. Thank you *so* much.'

'Look, don't ring off. I mean, could you give me some idea . . . ?' The phone clicked and went dead in his hand.

He found that he was trembling very much as he had done when, sitting in this very chair, he had held the receiver in his hand after Dr Moxley had promised to come. Then he had been at the height, the very zenith, of his troubles, but now they were all over. Or were they? He found that the palms of his hands were sweating and he wiped them on the knees of his trousers.

This was trouble from the least expected quarter. The beauty of making use of Ethel Carpenter in his plan had been her solitary state, her lack of any friends in the world but Maud and the extreme unlikelihood of anyone ever enquiring about her. This was the last thing he had anticipated. He went back into the dining room and finished off the whisky, but he had no appetite for his beans and he dropped the can into the pedal bin.

The whisky comforted him a little but it also made him feel slightly sick. Suppose that girl had been a policewoman? Unlikely. She sounded young, nervous and eager. Who the hell could she be, this Caroline Snow? She didn't sound more than twenty-five, if that. Not one of Mrs Huntley's friends or she wouldn't have said 'a Mrs Huntley' like that. Some child, now grown up, whose family Ethel had worked for?

That would be it. He wished he had bothered to listen when Maud had told all those interminable stories about where Ethel had worked and whom she had worked for and the names of their kids. But he hadn't and it was too late now. Still, the more he thought about it the more likely it appeared that this was who she was, some upper-class little madam looking up her old nanny. In London on holiday from the provinces, no doubt, and taking it into her head to go and be patronizing to the family retainer. Mrs Huntley would simply have told her the Mannings were Ethel's friends and their house the best place to root her out. In that case, why hadn't Mrs Huntley sent her along to Green Lanes?

There would be, no doubt, a perfectly simple explanation. Feeling a good deal better, Stanley decided to tell her Ethel was lodging with some people called Smith but that he didn't know where they lived. A girl like that, spoilt and used to having everything done for her, would soon get fed-up. He belched loudly, looked around for his crossword and then remembered he had already done it.

Still rather queasy, Stanley made his way down to the Lock-keeper's Arms at eight o'clock. He took a single pound note with him for, since Vera wasn't about to borrow from, he'd have to make his pay last him a week.

Pilbeam was already there and he looked as if he had been drinking steadily for several hours. The whisky he was putting away had put him in an aggressive, prickly mood.

'Your round, I think,' he said to Stanley. Evidently he had a long memory. Reluctantly Stanley bought two double whiskies.

'Well, old man, when can I expect the first instalment?'

'The what?' said Stanley, his mind still on Caroline Snow.

'Don't give me that,' said Pilbeam loudly. 'You heard. The first instalment of this capital of yours we hear so much about.'

'There's been a hold-up at my solicitor's.'

'Well, you'd better get twisting your solicitor's arm, then, hadn't you?'

'It's coming. A week or two and we'll be able to get started.'

'O.K. But remember I'm an impatient man. I've got the lease and I had to touch the missus for the lolly. She'll want it back and quick, make no mistake about that.'

'I won't,' said Stanley feebly, and then more firmly, 'Your round, I reckon.'

'We'll drink to a glorious future,' said Pilbeam more amiably and he fetched two more whiskies.

'By the way,' said Stanley, remembering Caroline Snow who might be a policewoman and might have a search warrant or something, 'by the way, I've got a few bits to show you, pieces we might flog.'

'That's my boy. What sort of bits?'

'A carriage clock and some china stuff.'

'Where are they?'

'Back at my place.'

'I tell you what,' said Pilbeam. 'Why don't you and me go back there now and give the stuff the once-over? Your wife there, is she?'

'My wife's away.'

'No kidding? You nip round the Off, Stan old boy, and get us a bottle of Haig and we'll make an evening of it.'

Stanley had to tell him he hadn't got any money and Pilbeam, his bad temper returning, said in a very nasty tone that he'd buy it just this once but Stanley would have to stump up his share when they got to Lanchester Road.

Still in an ill humour, Pilbeam hardly spoke until they were inside the house and then he said he wasn't impressed by Stanley's domestic arrangements.

'Don't do yourself very well, do you?' Pilbeam looked scornfully at the worn carpet and Vera's framed photographs. 'No wonder you've capital. You haven't spent much on this place.'

'I'll get the stuff I told you about. It's upstairs.'

'You do that, old man. And while you're about it, I'll relieve you of twenty-six and nine.'

'That's upstairs too,' Stanley muttered.

There was no help for it. He'd have to use a couple of Ethel's notes. Stanley opened the crossword annual for 1954 and took two from between the pages. Then he got the parcels out of his wardrobe and went back to Pilbeam who was already drinking whisky from one of Vera's sherry glasses.

'Funny pong they've got about them,' he said sniffing the notes. 'Where've you kept them? In a tin of talcum powder? Right old miser you are, Stan.' He pocketed the notes but he didn't produce any change.

'Are you going to have a dekko at these, then?'

Pilbeam examined the shepherdess, the bowl, the jug and the clock, sniffed and pronounced them saleable but of no great value. Then he put his feet up on the sofa and, without waiting for an invitation, told Stanley the story of his life.

It made an interesting narrative, full as it was of accounts of Pilbeam's brushes with the law, his escapades with women and the fortunes he had nearly made. But Stanley found his attention wandering constantly back to Caroline Snow. Who was she? What was she going to ask him? Would she come alone? Stanley drank for comfort until his head was thick and fuddled and when Pilbeam reached a point in his story where he had nearly married an heiress old enough to be his mother, he nodded off into a jumpy stupor.

The last thing he remembered that night was Pilbeam getting up and saying, 'I'll give you a ring in a day or two.'

'No good,' Stanley murmured thickly, 'before next week.'

'You leave that to me, Stan old boy. I'll twist your arm so as you know how to twist your stockbroker's.'

It was noon the next day before Stanley came down after a night spent stretched on his bed, fully clothed. Pilbeam had left all Ethel's property behind, but he had taken the bottle and Stanley's change.

Unused to heavy drinking, Stanley had a blinding headache. He felt as if there was someone standing inside his head, pressing with all his force against the bony walls of his prison in a splitting effort to get out.

The sight of the food made him give a slow, painful retch. Tentatively, he peeled the paper from the joint of beef Vera had left him and which he had forgotten to leave, soaking in salt water, on the tiled larder shelf the night before. It was on the turn, not exactly high but too far gone to eat when you felt as queasy as he did. He tipped it into the bin to join the beans. Well, he didn't feel up to eating anything, anyway. Instead he took two aspirins and wandered out into the garden.

Suddenly, for the first time since he got up, he was aware that it was a very hot day, blindingly, oppressively hot for the time of year, the kind of day that makes weather records and gives rise to newspaper articles about people faint from the heat and the tar melting on the roads. The garden was virtually without shade. Never a sun worshipper, Stanley gave a malevolent glare over the fence to where the Macdonalds sat, eating their Sunday lunch under a striped awning. Some people didn't know what to do with their money, he thought, eyeing their new garden furniture with scorn and Mrs Macdonald's bikini with disgust. She was forty-five if she was a day and she ought to know better, she with a son of fifteen. The boy, who was wearing nothing but a pair of swimming trunks, glared back at Stanley and Stanley went indoors.

The dining room, shut up since the night before, its french windows beaten on by the sun since seven, was as hot as a furnace and it stank of Pilbeam's cigars. Stanley retched again and staggered into the cooler kitchen. He might have taken a chair out on to the concrete into the shade by the back door but he didn't want to be overlooked by John Blackmore who, still painting his house, was perched on his ladder.

Presently he made himself a cup of tea and took it

upstairs. He lay on the rumpled bed, sweating profusely, but he couldn't relax. In seven hours' time he was going to have to deal with Caroline Snow.

His feelings about the coming interview were considerably less sanguine than they had been on the previous evening. It was difficult to understand how a few words on the telephone and the revelation of certain aspects of Pilbeam's character could have drawn so sudden and so dark a cloud across his happiness. Only hours, not years, had passed since he had sat without a care in the world on the steps of the war memorial.

At last he fell into an uneasy sleep and dreamed that he could hear Maud snoring through the wall. It was only the Blackmores' lawn mower, he discovered when he awoke, but the notion that his subconscious was translating commonplace sounds into aural hallucinations of his late mother-in-law upset him. That was the first dream he had had of her since the night of her death.

The sun had moved round to the front of the house and penetrated the thick curtains, suffusing the bedroom with hot glowing light. All Stanley's clothes seemed to be sticking to him. When it was nearly six he got up and put on a clean shirt. He went downstairs and re-wrapped Ethel's bowl and jug and clock and china and pushed them inside the side-board.

He hadn't had a thing to eat all day but the very thought of food made him queasy again. Maybe he'd go out, go for a bus ride or see what was on at the pictures. Then Caroline Snow would find an empty house and serve her right. But Stanley knew he wouldn't go. To postpone for another day or even days finding out who Caroline Snow was and what she wanted would be unbearable.

At half past seven he found he had started to pace up and down. It was cooler now but not very much and he kept the french windows shut. The Macdonalds were still outside, still laughing and playing with a beach ball and exchanging badinage with John Blackmore on his ladder as if, because they hadn't a care in the world, they thought no one else should have either. Stanley forced himself to sit down. A muscle in the corner of his mouth had started to twitch and jump.

Suppose she brought her husband with her? Or Mrs

Huntley or – God forbid – a policeman? She'd be at the station by now, he thought, looking at his watch, just about to catch the bus up. Ten minutes and she'd be here. Stanley went upstairs and looked out of all the windows which gave on to the street. It was deserted, but for one brave spirit washing his car down. That'll be me in a week or two, Stanley told himself for comfort, me with my Jaguar and my van parked side by side. By that time Caroline Snow would be in the past, a bad dream . . .

What could they do to him, anyway? What could anyone do? Ethel Carpenter was a handful of ashes in an urn and he'd yet to learn any clever sod could analyse ashes and find out whose they were. In any case, he hadn't laid a finger on her. Was it his fault she'd fallen down dead in his lounge? He'd given her a damn good funeral, far better than she'd have had if that Mrs Huntley had found her dead in her own room. Really, he'd done her a service. Very dignified that cremation had been and in the best of taste. The way he worried you'd think he was a murderer or something.

Five past eight. Stanley found that his heart had begun to grow very gradually lighter as the crucial hour passed by. He went downstairs and opened the french windows. The Macdonalds were packing up their furniture and their stupid toys. Stanley felt almost sufficiently well and relaxed to mow the lawn. He muttered something in reply to Blackmore's greeting and got the mower out of the shed. Up and down the lawn twice, the shorn grass spraying into the box. Perhaps it would be just as well to pop indoors and check she hadn't turned up, after all.

Stanley ran quietly up the stairs, leaving a trail of grass cuttings behind him. His bedroom windows showed him a deserted street. Even the car washer had finished and gone in. A beautiful, calm evening. Not normally a man to derive peace and tranquillity from communing with nature, Stanley now felt that nothing bad could happen on such a serene and tender night. The sky was a cloudless pastel violet, the shadows long and still. How beautiful his lawn would look when close-cut, its edges trimmed with the long shears.

Almost placid now, he returned to it.

The mower cut smoothly in long clean sweeps and Stanley

worked evenly and methodically, for he liked his lawn to have a neat ribbed look like a piece of corded velvet or a very expert sample of knitting. The heather garden was in shadow now, sleeping under its quilt of peat and mowings. Up and down, up and down . . . Twenty-five past eight. What a fool he had been to get into a state!

He came down towards the house, pushing the machine. What the hell was Blackmore up to, making signs to him?

'There's someone at your door, mate.'

Stanley's mouth dried.

'What?'

'A young lady ringing your doorbell.'

'O.K., O.K.,' said Stanley. His palms were running with sweat. He wiped them on his trousers and went into the dining room. The whole house seemed to reverberate with the vibration of the bell. Momentarily, Stanley put his damp hands over his ears. Why shouldn't he just go upstairs and keep his ears covered until she had gone? But Blackmore had seen her, Blackmore would tell her where he was . . .

'Oh, Christ!' Stanley moaned. 'All right, all right,' he said, 'I'm coming.'

The ringing stopped. He opened the door.

'Mr Manning? Oh, good evening. I'm Caroline Snow. I'm so sorry I'm late. I had a job finding your house.'

Stanley gaped at her. For a moment his terror had left him. It wasn't fear which made him speechless. He had seen such creatures as she before, of course, seen them on television in the Miss World contests or the covers of the magazines Vera sometimes bought, even sometimes seen near copies of them driving up to the pumps at the Superjuce garage. But no one like this had ever until now rung the bell at 61, Lanchester Road.

'Isn't it hot? May I come in? Oh, thank you so much. I'm afraid I'm being a terrible nuisance.'

'That's all right,' Stanley mumbled.

He followed her into the dining room. Even from behind she looked nearly as good as from in front. Her long pale blonde hair covered her shoulders in a thick gold veil. Stanley didn't think he had ever seen such a straight back or such legs, legs which were so long and smooth and exquisite that it was almost painful to look at them.

When she was in the room and had turned to face him he wondered how he could ever have thought her back view was as nice. Her skin was tanned a smooth, even and satiny brown, much darker than her hair. Swedish or something, Stanley thought feebly. His eyes met sea-green eyes, as cool and calm as northern waters, and a wave of perfume floated over him so that he felt slightly faint.

'Can I get you a cup of tea?' he said.

'That would be great.'

He went into the kitchen and put the kettle on. It wasn't just the beauty of that face that had made him stare at her. He stared because he felt it wasn't entirely unfamiliar to him. Somewhere he had seen it, or a face very like it though somehow changed and spoiled, in the recent past. In a film? In the paper? He couldn't remember.

'First I'd better explain,' said Caroline Snow when he went back to her, 'why I've come.'

'Well, I did wonder,' said Stanley.

'Naturally you did. But I didn't feel I could talk about something so – well, personal and private on the phone. Did you know your kettle's boiling?'

Stanley got up and went out to turn it off. He meant to go on being tactful and polite but when he came back he found himself blurting out involuntarily, 'Who are you?'

She smiled. 'Yes, well, that's the embarrassing part. I may as well tell you and get it over. I'm Ethel Carpenter's granddaughter.'

14

'You can't be,' Stanley said. 'She wasn't ever married.'

'I know, but she had a baby at seventeen just the same.'

Stanley, who had held his mouth open ever since Caroline Snow's revelation, now closed it, swallowing some air. At last he said, 'Now you mention it, I did know. My wife must have told me.'

Caroline Snow said, 'I think I'd better tell you the whole story.'

'O.K.,' said Stanley, resigning himself. Having got so far, he'd better know the worst. 'I'll get the tea.' Her grand-daughter, he thought miserably as he poured on the boiling water. Almost as bad as a policewoman.

She smiled at him. Stanley thought she looked less pretty when she smiled, for her teeth were uneven. She also looked much more like Ethel Carpenter and now Stanley knew whose face hers had reminded him of.

'Let's have it, then,' he said.

'My people live in Gloucester,' Caroline Snow began, 'but I'm at training college in London. I'm training to be a teacher and I'm in my second year. Well, we had to do a special study this term, Greek myths or genealogy, and I chose genealogy.' Stanley looked at her suspiciously. He knew quite well what genealogy was, for his passion for crossword puzzles had given him a large vocabulary and, in any case, he was fond of words. But he couldn't see what genealogy had to do with teaching kids to read and write and he wondered if Caroline Snow was lying. 'Honestly, I'd have chosen the myths if I'd known what I was letting myself in for. Our lecturer wanted us all to make family trees, one for the paternal side and another for the maternal. You do follow what I mean?'

'Of course I do,' said Stanley, offended. 'I'm not ignorant.'

'I didn't mean that. Only it's a bit complicated. Well, doing Dad's tree was easy because all his people came from a village outside Gloucester and I got hold of the parish records and everything. I got that all finished by half-term. Then I came to Mummy's. She was very shy about it, didn't want to give me any help at all, which isn't a bit like Mummy. She's a marvellous person, absolutely terrific. You'd adore her.'

'I daresay,' said Stanley. When was she going to come to the point? The last thing he wanted was to hear about marvellous adorable Mummy whom he was sure he'd loathe at sight.

Caroline Snow crossed her long legs and lit a cigarette. Gimlet-eyed, Stanley watched the packet returned to her handbag with mounting rage. 'Anyway, to cut a long story short, I rather nagged Mummy about it all and then she told me. She said she was illegitimate. I'd always understood her parents were dead and that's why she'd been brought up in an orphanage, but she said she'd just told me that. The truth is her mother's still alive and she never knew who her father was. Well, at last I got it all out of her.

'Her mother was Ethel Carpenter, a housemaid who'd had her when she was only seventeen. My mother was brought up by Ethel's aunt until she was seven and then the aunt got married and the new uncle sent Mummy to this orphanage. Wasn't it awful? Mummy never saw her own mother and for years the only member of her family she did see was a cousin who came to visit her. He was Ethel's cousin actually and he was very kind to Mummy.

'Well, Mummy had brains, thank goodness, and went to training college – the same one as I'm at actually – and when she was teaching in a school in Gloucester she met Dad and married him and they lived happily ever after. It's rather a terrible story, though, isn't it?'

'Yeah.' Stanley watched her stub out her cigarette. 'I don't see where you come into it,' he said.

'I've had my grandmother on my conscience,' said Caroline Snow. 'I felt so bad about her, you see. Mummy's never wanted to meet her. I suppose she thought it would be too heartbreaking for them both. But now I've come so far I've just got to find her. Think what it would mean to her, Mr Manning, a poor lonely old woman suddenly finding she'd got a whole family of her own.'

Stanley could well understand Mummy's feelings, although most of his sympathy went to Mr Snow. That'd be a fine thing, he thought, having the good luck to marry an orphan and then getting an old mother-in-law thrust on you when you were middle-aged. Probably have to part out with money for her too. If I were in his shoes, Stanley said to himself, I'd smack that girl's bottom for her. Interfering little bitch of a do-gooder.

'I'd give the whole idea up if I were you,' he said aloud. 'It stands to reason, if she'd wanted a family she'd have hunted all you lot up long ago.' It was, he thought, a good line to take, charitable to the unfortunate Mr Snow as well as opening up a let-out for himself. He warmed to it. 'She won't want to be reminded of her past, will she? The disgrace and all? Oh, no, you give it up. I reckon your dad'd say the same. It's always a mistake, stirring things up. Let sleeping dogs lie is what I say.'

'I'm afraid I disagree with you,' Caroline Snow said stiffly. 'You must read the papers. You know what a terrible problem we have in this country with the old people, how lonely some of them are and how friendless. I'd never forgive myself if I gave up now.' She smiled, giving him an indulgent look. 'Anyway, you don't really mean it. Mrs Huntley told me you'd had your own mother-in-law living with you for years and having to be looked after. You didn't abandon her, now did you? And now she's dead you've got nothing to reproach yourself with. Well, I don't want to reproach myself either.'

This little speech temporarily took Stanley's breath away. He gaped at her, frowning. Her zeal and her innocence were beyond his understanding. He cleared his throat. 'How did you get on to Mrs Huntley?'

Serene again, Caroline Snow said, 'The cousin who used to visit Mummy in the orphanage is still alive, although he's a very old man. I went to see him first and he said he'd lost touch with my grandmother but he knew her last place had been with some people called Kilbride. I found them and they told me she had a room with a Mrs Huntley.'

'And she put you on to us?'

'Well, she said you'd know where my grandmother was, on account of she and Mrs Kinaway being such close friends. And she said my grandmother had been coming to stay here with you but she'd changed her mind and now she's got lodgings in Croughton with a Mrs Paterson but she'd forgotten the address. I thought – I thought if you could just give me that address I'd go round now and introduce myself and . . . Oh, I feel so nervous and excited! I'm quite sick with nerves. Just imagine, Mr Manning, what she'll think when she sees me. I'm going to tell her she'll never be alone again. We've got quite a big house in Gloucester and I want Daddy to turn the attics into a flat for her. I want to take her home myself and show her her new home and just see her face.'

I'd like to see Daddy's, thought Stanley. Poor sod. It was one thing for this silly little piece, arranging people's lives for them. She wouldn't be there to listen to Ethel banging on the floor with her stick and demanding meals at all hours and monopolizing the TV. She'd be living it up in London at her college. That poor devil, he thought with indignation. It was his, Stanley's, duty to prevent anything like that happening, his bounden duty . . . He was so outraged that for a moment he had forgotten the impossibility of Snow's house ever being invaded by a mother-in-law. Then, suddenly, he remembered. Ethel was dead, all that remained of her some fifteen feet away from them in an urn on the mantelpiece. It didn't matter where Caroline Snow went or where she looked, for Ethel had vanished from the face of the earth.

'Mrs Paterson's address is fifty-two, Green Lanes,' he said, 'but I don't think you'll find her there. My wife said she'd found somewhere new.'

Caroline Snow wrote down the address. 'Thank you so much,' she said fervently. 'I'm sure I'll be able to trace her now. But wasn't it odd her telling Mrs Huntley she was coming here and then suddenly changing her mind?'

Stanley frowned. 'When you've had as much experience of old people as I have,' he said with feeling, 'you won't be surprised by any of the funny things they do.'

She got up, first looking at him in rather a woebegone way, her ardour perhaps a little dampened, and then eyed herself critically in the mirror. 'I wonder if I look at all like her? I'm the image of Mummy and Mummy's supposed to look like her.'

'Yeah, you do a bit,' said Stanley.

Caroline Snow swung round to face him. 'Then, you do know her? You have seen her?'

Stanley could have bitten his tongue out.

'She was at my wedding,' he muttered.

'Oh, I see.' She picked up her bag and Stanley saw her to the door. 'I'll let you know how I get on,' she said.

From the bedroom window Stanley watched her hurrying along in the direction of Green Lanes. Somewhere he had once read that most of the things one has worried about have never happened. How true that was! When the girl had disappeared from view he finished mowing the lawn in the half-light, whistling an old tune which he later realized had been Tennyson's *Maud*.

Vera was enjoying her holiday. She had met some nice people, a married couple about her own age and who were also staying at Mrs Horton's. They insisted on taking her about with them in their car, along the coast to Beachy Head and inland to Arundel Castle, and they laughed and asked Vera if she thought they were on their honeymoon when she demurred and suggested she was intruding. They wanted her to share their table but Vera wouldn't do that. She ate alone, sitting in the window and watching holiday-makers coming up from the beach, and she enjoyed her food, relishing every scrap because she hadn't had to cook it herself.

There was only one thing that troubled her and that was neither her new friends, the Goodwins, nor Mrs Horton had once asked about Stanley, where he was and why he hadn't come with her. Vera felt rather piqued. She couldn't help thinking that, in the early days of her marriage, when Maud had still come to Bray for holidays, she had poisoned Mrs Horton's mind against Stanley. I shan't mention him, if that's the way they want it, Vera said to herself. She felt no pressing need to talk about him. Now he was far away, she found she hardly thought about him and this made her so guilty that she sent him a postcard every day.

At a loss to know how to amuse herself one wet afternoon, Mrs Goodwin took Vera up to her bedroom where she washed and set her hair, made up her face, and, while Vera was waiting for the set to dry, turned the hem of Vera's blue and white spotted dress up two inches.

'You've got very nice legs. Why not show them off?'

'At my age?' said Vera.

'Life begins at forty, my dear. You'll look ten years younger, anyway, when I've finished with you.'

Vera did. She stared in wonderment and unease at her new self, at the bouffant golden-brown hair, the pale blue eyelids and the pink mouth Mrs Goodwin had created with a lipbrush. The dress barely reached her knees. Feeling half-naked she went down to dinner and hid herself in her alcove away from the other diners.

She was waiting for Mrs Horton's maid to bring her second course, when a man came into the dining room and wandered about, evidently looking for someone. Vera watched his reflection in the window. She was so busy staring at this that she nearly jumped out of her skin when a hand touched her shoulder. She turned and looked upwards, flushing slightly.

He was a stranger, quite unfamiliar to her, a man of fifty perhaps with a rather haggard face, fair hair gone pepper and salt, a long lean man with an anxious, even forbidding, look. Vera half-rose. She must have done something wrong. Forgotten to pay for her deck chair perhaps . . .

'I'm sorry . . .' she hesitated, stammering. 'What – er . . . ?'

He smiled at her and it made him look much younger.

'Hallo, Vee.'

'I don't think . . . I don't know you, do I?'

'You used to know me. I know I've changed. You haven't, not very much. I'd have recognized you anywhere. May I sit down?'

'Oh, yes, of course.'

He pulled up a chair, offered her a cigarette. Vera shook her head.

'My aunt told me you were here. I meant to come yesterday but, I don't know . . . I suppose I was shy. It's been so long. How are you?'

Confidence came to Vera and a poise she didn't know she possessed.

'I'm very well, thank you, James. It's good to see you.'

'Oh, Vee, you don't know how glad I am to see you,' said James Horton.

15

Gradually, as the week went on, Stanley's small panic receded. For the first few evenings he sat close to the phone, the crossword puzzle on his knees, expecting a call from Caroline Snow. But no call came. In fact nothing came from the world outside at all but daily postcards from Vera. She wrote that she was having a wonderful time, meeting new people, going out and about with them every day. Stanley felt very bitter towards her and resentful.

As soon as she got back she could go down to that Finbow and get Maud's money out of him. It was downright diabolical, solicitors hanging on to other people's rightful inheritances for weeks on end.

'How's your head, Stan?' said Pilbeam when he phoned on Thursday.

'There's nothing wrong with my head,' said Stanley.

'Bet there was Sunday morning. One sniff of a barmaid's apron and you're out like a light.'

'I told you,' said Stanley, 'it was no good ringing me this week. I'll have the money on Tuesday like I said.'

'You never did, in point of fact, me old love. But let it pass. Tuesday, you said?'

'That's a promise.'

'I sure am glad to hear that, Stan. I've been out knocking today – got a lend of a van – and some of the things I've picked up'll make you hair curl.' It was a funny thing about Pilbeam, Stanley thought. The mere sound of the man's voice brought him vividly before one, snub nose, sausage-like finger and all. 'How about a snifter in the Lockkeeper's tomorrow night, so as I can get a clearer picture of the state of your finances?'

Stanley was obliged to agree. Pilbeam would get a clear picture of his finances all right when he turned up in the Lockkeeper's with all he had left of last Friday's pay, ten bob.

The whole Macdonald family and the two Blackmores were outside the Macdonalds' gate, admiring Fred Macdonald's new car, when Stanley left the house to keep his appointment. He would have marched past them without a word but the Macdonald boy, Michael, barred his way, holding both arms outstretched.

'Look what my dad's just brought home, Mr Manning.'

'Very nice,' said Stanley, but still they wouldn't let him get away. Macdonald got out of the car and invited Stanley to take his place and examine the arrangements for the automatic gear change. Unable to think of an excuse, Stanley got sulkily into the car and contemplated the control panel.

'No more wearing my left foot out on the clutch in a traffic jam,' said Macdonald jubilantly. 'Comfortable, isn't she? I've only got one complaint. When I sink into that I'll fall asleep behind the wheel.'

The women were nattering nineteen to the dozen, scuttling around the car and pointing out the mirror-like gloss on its bodywork, the vast capacity of its boot and the workmanship of its chrome. Mrs Macdonald was swollen with pride. Wait till they see my Jag, Stanley thought, after this tin can. Then they'll laugh on the other side of their faces.

'The mirror adjusts at the touch of a finger,' said Macdonald, thrusting his head through the window.

Stanley put it to the test. He moved the mirror an inch down and glanced into it. Then he stared harder, going hot all over. From the High Street end of Lanchester Road Caroline Snow was walking along the pavement in the direction of his house. She wore large round sunglasses with mauve lenses and a skirt several inches shorter than the one she had worn on Sunday. Stanley looked down, twiddling knobs and pulling small levers. One of these operated the windscreen washers and a fountain of water gushed across the glass.

'Here, here,' said Mrs Macdonald. 'Mind what you're doing, I shall have to get a leather to that.' She frowned spitefully at Stanley and pulled the car door open. 'Anyway, you're wanted. There's someone come to call on you.'

Stanley got out very slowly, not looking behind him. Macdonald slapped him on the shoulder. 'When the cat's away the mice will play, eh, old man? Very good taste you've got, if I may say so.'

'I don't know what you're talking about,' Stanley muttered. Six faces confronted him, the children's inquisitive, the women's indignant, the men's frankly prurient. John Blackmore gave a crooked grin and then he slowly winked. 'Excuse me,' Stanley said. 'Got to go in.'

He scuttled up the path to where Caroline Snow stood waiting for him on the doorstep. Behind him he heard Mrs Blackmore say, 'Well, really! How disgusting!'

'I just had to come and see you again, Mr Manning. I do hope it's not inconvenient?'

The air in the house smelt stale. Stanley flung open the french windows. The girl followed him.

'Perhaps we could sit in the garden? It's so hot, isn't it? And your garden's lovely.'

'I haven't got time for any sitting about,' said Stanley

hurriedly. He looked at his watch. 'I've got an appointment at half past six.'

'I've really come to you,' the girl said, taking no notice of all this, 'because – well, you were very kind to me on Sunday and you're really the only responsible man I can talk to. You see, I've relied on Daddy all my life but Daddy's such a long way away.'

Let me be your father, Stanley thought eagerly, forgetting for the moment all about his date with Pilbeam. 'What exactly d'you want me to do, Miss Snow?'

'I went to see Mrs Paterson,' Caroline Snow said earnestly, 'and she said Miss – er, my grandmother had got a room with a Mr Smith but she doesn't know his address. Now college comes down on Tuesday and I have to go home so I wondered . . . My grandmother's bound to come and see you and your wife sometime, isn't she? I thought if you'd be kind enough to tell her about me if she does and – well, write to me, I could look her up when I get back to London.'

'Yeah, I could do that,' Stanley said slowly. Of course he could. He could tell her he'd seen Ethel and Ethel had moved again or even that Ethel didn't want to make contact with her relatives. Suddenly he was inspired. Making his voice sound as confident as he could and infusing into it a hint of the paternal, he said, 'Why don't you ask your father's advice? Have you told him anything of all this?'

'Well, no . . . As far as Mummy and he know, I just wanted my grandmother's name for this family tree.'

Wonderful. Just what he'd hoped for. He could just imagine Snow's horror when he heard of this search for his mother-in-law and his relief when he learned she wasn't to be found. 'Your dad's a man of experience. He'll know what's the best thing to do.' He will, Stanley thought, if he's in his right mind. 'He might feel rather hurt if you went over his head like this. She is his mother-in-law after all. He might not . . .'

'Oh, but Daddy's a marvellous person. He's got a terrific social conscience. He couldn't bear to think . . .'

'Can you be quite sure of that, Miss Snow?' Stanley leaned earnestly towards her. 'Certainly your father'll want to know all the details you've told me, but isn't it likely he'll want to do any further investigating himself? Besides, he and your mother may feel your grandmother's got a right to privacy, if that's what she wants, and it seems she does want it. No, he wouldn't like it at all if you put people's backs up and got the police on a wild goose chase.'

'I wonder if you're right?' Caroline Snow looked nearly convinced. 'You've put things in a different perspective for me, Mr Manning. Actually, I've just remembered something. Once, years ago when I was quite young, a gipsy came to our door when Mummy was out and I gave her some clothes and made her a cup of tea and when Daddy heard about it he was *furious*. He said the state should look after people like that. He'd got quite enough supporting his own family.'

The man with the terrific social conscience! Stanley almost laughed aloud.

'Of course, it's not really a parallel case, but it does make me think I ought to ask Daddy before I go any further.' She got up. 'You've really been very kind, Mr Manning. I'm sure you've given me the right advice. I won't do another thing before I've asked Daddy.' She held out her hand. 'I'm afraid I've made you late for your appointment.'

'Better late than never,' Stanley said cheerfully. 'I'll walk with you. It's on my way.'

They left the house together. John Blackmore, who was trimming his hedge, favoured Stanley with another wink. Stanley talked about the weather and the car he was going to buy and the business he was going into to take the girl's mind off Ethel Carpenter.

'I wonder now why I got this idea something terrible might have happened to her? I suppose it was because Mrs Huntley said she was carrying fifty pounds on her.'

'She'll be living it up on that without a care in the world,' Stanley said reassuringly.

Caroline Snow smiled at him and in that smile he saw Ethel grinning up at him and waving her umbrella. She gave him the address of her father's house and they parted cordially.

That, Stanley thought, was the last he would ever see or hear of her. He walked to the Lockkeeper's Arms because he couldn't afford the bus fare. The little shop was still boarded up but the agent's placard had been taken away.

Pilbeam wasn't alone but surrounded by a circle of friends, all of whom seemed extravagantly big men. He didn't introduce any of them to Stanley but moved away from them without a word. For some indefinable reason this made Stanley uneasy.

Without asking Pilbeam's preferences – he knew them – Stanley bought two halves of bitter and, floundering in a mass of prevarication, set about giving his new partner a picture of his finances.

Pilbeam said only, 'Next week, me old love. First thing next week.'

Some of Vera's ideas about James Horton had been right and some wrong. He was manager of Barclay's Brayminster branch; he was well-off, for he had inherited money both from his father and his uncle; he did live in a nice house. But he wasn't married to a woman in her handsome early forties and he hadn't a family of teenage children. His wife had died of cancer five years before, leaving him with one son, now at university.

'A lonely life, James,' Vera said on her last evening as she and James sat in the cocktail lounge of the Metropole Hotel.

'It gets lonely sometimes.'

'You never thought of marrying again?'

'Not until lately,' said James. 'You know, Vee, you haven't told me a thing about yourself. We've been out together every night – oh, mostly with the Goodwins, I know – but all the time I've seemed to do nothing but talk of my life and I haven't given you a chance to tell me about yours. I'm afraid I've been very self-centred.'

'Oh, no. I've been so interested.'

'I suppose it's living alone that makes one want to talk. But your life must have been as lonely as mine.'

'What makes you say that?' Vera looked at him, puzzled.

'Aren't we almost in the same boat, Vee? I a widower and you a widow, you childless and I . . .'

'James,' Vera said loudly, 'whatever made you think I was a widow?'

He turned rather pale and stammered, 'But my aunt said . . . You came down here alone and you never . . .'

'I'm afraid Mrs Horton's got it wrong. I'm not a widow.

My husband just couldn't get time off from work. Oh dear, now I begin to see a lot of things I didn't understand.'

'You mean you live with your husband? You and your husband . . .'

'Of course. I'm going home to him tomorrow.'

'I see,' said James Horton. 'I've been rather foolish and obtuse.'

16

All Vera's cards were on the mantelpiece but not displayed. They were tucked in a stack behind a vase. Stanley hadn't asked her if she had enjoyed herself and she was very hurt.

'How's the job?' she asked quietly.

'I've resigned, if you must know. I'm going into the antique business. There's pots of money to be made out of antiques and we're taking a shop in the Old Village. Me and my partner, that is.'

'Your partner?' said Vera. 'What partner? Who is he, Stan? Where did you meet him?'

Vera looked so aghast that it would hardly have made matters worse to tell her he had met Pilbeam in the street and founded the partnership in a pub. But Stanley was one of those men who never tell their wives the truth if a lie will serve instead. 'He was put in touch by a mutual friend,' he said vaguely. 'A client of mine at the Superjuce gave him my name.' He knew Vera wouldn't believe him but at the moment he hardly cared. He shifted his eyes sullenly. Two hours before she came home he had telephoned Finbow and Craig only to be told by a secretary that Mr Finbow had a matter he wanted to discuss urgently with Mrs Manning and a letter on the subject would reach her on Monday morning. Another hold-up. God knew what Pilbeam would say if the money wasn't forthcoming in the Lockkeeper's on Tuesday night.

Vera said astutely, 'Has this man got any capital?'

'Be your age,' said Stanley. 'He's rolling. Would I get involved with him if he hadn't?'

'I don't know what you'd do, Stan. But I reckon you're a child when it comes to business. I know more about business than you do. Promise me you won't do anything silly.'

Stanley didn't answer her. He couldn't get that letter out of his mind and the more he thought about it the more he felt the tiny muscles around his eyes twitching. On Sunday night he slept badly, being visited by troubling dreams of Maud. In one of them he and she were discussing the contents of her will and Maud told him she wasn't finished with him yet, that Mr Finbow's letter would be concerned with a clause in that will designed to upset any business schemes he might have.

He was therefore less indignant than he might otherwise have been when Vera brought him a cup of tea and read aloud to him:

'Dear Mrs Manning,

'With regard to your inheritance from the late Mrs Maud Kinaway, I have been in touch with the firm of stockbrokers acting for the late Mrs Kinaway. Owing to the recent fall in the stock market, I feel it my duty to inform you that I consider it inadvisable to sell the stock in which your late mother's moneys are invested, at the present time. I am, however, reliably advised that the market is once more rising and that it would be expedient to retain these stocks for a further few weeks.

'No doubt, you will wish to discuss this whole question with me as soon as possible. I should like to stress that should you desire this stock to be sold forthwith, I will naturally proceed to instruct your late mother's stockbroker accordingly. Perhaps you could arrange to call at my office early this week.

'I remain,
'Yours sincerely,
'Charles H. Finbow.'

'I just hope he's on the level,' Stanley said gloomily, 'and not playing ducks and drakes with our money. You can tell him to sell that stock right away.'

'Don't be silly, dear,' Vera said mildly. 'Mr Finbow's only acting in our interests. He means that if he sold those shares now he'd get hundreds less than if we waited a few weeks.'

Stanley sat up, choking over his tea. 'You what? We've got to have that money. God knows, we've waited long enough.' He felt quite sick with horror. Imagine Pilbeam's face if he was asked to wait weeks. The whole enterprise would go up the spout. 'You'll go there today,' he spluttered, 'in your lunch hour and I'm coming with you.'

'I can't, Stan. Doris is off and I can't get away for lunch.'

'If you won't, Vee, I will.' Stanley threw back the covers. 'I'll go down there alone and get that money if I have to knock his teeth in.'

'I'll see what I can do,' Vera sighed.

Alone in the house, Stanley paced up and down, sweating. In the pub on Friday he had confidently promised Pilbeam money to buy a van, money for decorating and furnishing the shop and enough ready cash to stock it. Finbow would have to cough up. His eye fluttered painfully and to calm himself he sat down and did the crossword puzzle.

He was just filling in 26 across, 'Last Post' eight letters, four and four, 'Ultimate mail before leaving the field', when the doorbell rang on a sharp peremptory note.

Stanley never answered a doorbell naturally and innocently as other people do. He always debated whether it was wise to answer it at all. Now he crept into the front room and peeped through the curtains. Pilbeam stood on the doorstep with a large heavily built man who looked no more than twenty-eight and who was recognizable as one of those henchmen who had moved silently away from Pilbeam in the pub on Friday.

Stanley let the curtain fall, but not before Pilbeam's eyes had met his. There was no help for it. The door would have to be answered. He opened it and Pilbeam put his foot inside and on to the mat like a pushing salesman.

He didn't introduce his companion. Stanley didn't expect him to. They all knew why the friend had come. There was no need for hypocritical formalities.

'I told you Tuesday,' Stanley said.

'I know, old man, but what's a day one way or the other? We all realize the big lolly's coming tomorrow. What I want is fifty on account now.'

They came in. Stanley couldn't stop them.

'I haven't got fifty,' he said, very conscious of the friend's size and youth.

'Thirty, then,' said Pilbeam. 'It's in your own interest, Stan. Me and my mate have got our eye on a couple of *famille rose* vases. It'd be a sin to let them go.'

'I'll see,' said Stanley feebly. The friend's mammoth shoulder was nudging his. 'Sit down. Make yourselves at home. The money's upstairs.'

He scuttled up the stairs and made for the bookcase. Leafing thirty notes from the pages of the crossword annual, he became aware of a step behind him and then that Pilbeam was standing in the doorway, watching the operation with interest and a certain bewilderment.

'So that's your little safe deposit, is it? By gum, it stinks of violets.'

Speechless, Stanley handed over the thirty pounds. There were now only thirteen notes left in the annual.

'This is my husband,' Vera said when they were admitted to Mr Finbow's office. It wasn't an introduction she had often had to make. She and Stanley hadn't lived in a world where many introductions were called for. But whenever she had to say those words she was conscious of a little creeping feeling of shame, a feeling which was even more intense today as she glanced at Stanley and noticed the belligerent set of his chin and the calculating suspicious gleam in his eye. 'He wanted to come with me.'

'How do you do, Mr Manning?' said Mr Finbow. 'Won't you both sit down. Now then, I think my letter explained the situation, but if you'd like any further details I'd be glad to give them.'

Stanley said, 'We would. That's why we're here.'

Mr Finbow raised his eyebrows slightly and turned his attention pointedly in Vera's direction. 'The position is this, Mrs Manning. The money your late mother bequeathed to you is principally invested in two stocks, Euro-American Tobacco and Universal Incorporated Tin. Both very sound investments, as safe, if I may say so, as houses. You are, however, no doubt aware of the effect on the stock market of the recent Arab-Israel crisis.'

He paused, perhaps for some comprehending response from Vera. But Vera, although vaguely aware that there had been a lot on television about the Middle East during April and May, had been too involved with personal crises to pay much attention, and she could only give a rather helpless nod.

'I am told,' said Mr Finbow, 'that to sell at this juncture would result in a loss of several hundred pounds, owing to the considerable fall in prices.'

Vera nodded again. 'But these – er, investments, they'll get back to what they were before?'

'I am assured they will. You see, Mrs Manning, the two companies I've mentioned are vast world-wide concerns which generally maintain their shares at a steady level. There's absolutely no question of any long-term deterioration in their value. The point is that the current price is temporarily unsatisfactory. In other words, any knowledgeable person would tell you it would be unwise to sell at present. But wait, say, six weeks and we should see a considerable improvement in . . .'

'Six weeks!' Stanley interrupted. 'What about the interest? What's happening to all that?'

'As I have just explained,' the solicitor said less patiently, 'the price is currently reduced. The price of each individual share is lowered but your wife's income is unaltered as there has been no change in the dividend policies of the companies.'

'O.K., O.K.,' said Stanley. 'So you say. But how do we know there won't be more of these crises? You can keep us hanging on like this month after month. It's our money you're playing with.'

'I *beg* your pardon?'

'Well, isn't it? My wife told you to sell. Weeks ago that was. And now, because you've been hanging about, there's not so much money there as what you said at first. Seems plain enough to me.'

Mr Finbow got up out of his chair and, turning his back on Stanley, addressed Vera in a cold courteous voice. 'If you're dissatisfied, Mrs Manning, perhaps you would prefer to find another firm of solicitors to act for you?'

Red with shame, afraid to look at Stanley, Vera stammered, 'Oh, no. No, you mustn't think that. I don't think my husband quite . . .'

'I understand all right,' said Stanley, not at all put out.

'Not that any of that matters a damn. We said we wanted you to sell and we do. You can sell the lot right now, this afternoon. It's our money and that's what we want. Right?'

For a moment Mr Finbow looked as if he would have a seizure. Then he said very icily, 'I am not a stall-holder in a street market. I am a solicitor and a senior partner in a firm of unblemished reputation. Never – never have I been spoken to in those terms before in my own office.' Momentarily he closed his eyes as if in pain. Stiffly, he addressed Vera. 'May I have your instructions, Mrs Manning?'

Vera looked down. Her hands were trembling in her lap. 'I'm sorry, Mr Finbow. Really, I'm very sorry.' She raised her eyes miserably. 'Of course, you must do whatever's best. We're not in actual need of the money. It's just – just that there were one or two things . . .'

Mr Finbow said quickly and slightly more sympathetically, 'There are several insurance policies also which matured at your mother's death. If it was a question of, say, five hundred pounds, I will be happy to give you a cheque for that immediately.'

'Five hundred pounds would do very nicely,' said Vera more happily. She waited, her head turned away from Stanley, while Mr Finbow drew the cheque. 'And please don't do anything about selling those shares until you and the stockbroker think it's right.'

'Very well,' said Mr Finbow, shaking hands with her and behaving as if Stanley wasn't there. 'May I say I think you've been very wise, Mrs Manning. Good afternoon.'

'Oh, Stan, how could you?' Vera said as they went downstairs. 'I don't know what Mr Finbow must have thought of you.'

'Blow that for a lark. He can think what he likes, pompous old bastard. Now, if you'll just write your name on the back of that cheque I'll take it along to Barclay's and open an account. Here'll do, on that table. You'd better get back to the shop or you'll be late.'

Vera stopped, but she didn't open her handbag. 'I don't have to be back till two. I thought I'd miss lunch today and go and look at some fridges in the Electricity Board.'

'Good idea. Get cracking, then.' Stanley held out his hand expectantly.

'When I said "look at", I meant buy. You know I've been longing to get a fridge. I can't buy one without any money and I shan't have any money till I get a cheque book. We'll both go to the bank first. Don't you think it would be nicer to have a joint account?'

'Nicer', in Stanley's mind, was hardly the word. He saw, however, that under the circumstances it was inevitable and they entered the Croughton branch of Barclay's together.

The manager wasn't in the least like James Horton to look at, being short and stout, but he reminded Vera of James perhaps because like James he was a manager of another branch of James's bank. She hadn't thought much about James since her return but now he came vividly to her mind, a gentle, courteous and thoughtful man, and she couldn't help contrasting his civilized behaviour with Stanley's conduct at Finbow and Craig.

'There you are, Mrs Manning,' said the chief clerk, bending over the manager's desk. 'Your cheque book, and Mr Manning's too. And a paying-in book for each of you. Naturally, we'll send you cheque books with your names printed on them as soon as they come through.'

The manager showed them to the door.

'That,' said Stanley, 'is what I call a gentleman.'

He had deciphered the last clue in the crossword puzzle ('Golden Spaniel' – 'The marksman's 9-carat companion') when Vera came in, pink with excitement.

'I've bought it, dear, a lovely refrigerator with a place to keep salads. And, oh, I know it's very extravagant but I've bought an automatic washer, too. They're sending both of them up tomorrow.'

'What did all that lot cost?' said Stanley, replacing the cap on his pen.

'Just on a hundred. Having all that money went to my head, I suppose. But I've made up my mind, I shan't touch another penny until the rest comes through from Mr Finbow.'

'It's your money,' said Stanley graciously. 'It's you your mum left it to, after all.'

'You mustn't say that, darling. It's ours. I want you to buy yourself a new suit and any little thing you fancy. You've got your own cheque book now.'

Stanley put his hand in his pocket and fingered it, the crisp green book, hard and as yet untouched in its plastic folder. Very generous of Vee really, to look at it in that light, giving him *carte blanche* as it were. He would have dipped lavishly into the account, anyway, but it was nice getting permission first.

The washing machine and the refrigerator arrived at nine-thirty the following day. Stanley was still in bed, and getting up to let the men in put him in a bad temper. Then he reflected that it was Tuesday, a good day for him in two ways. He was going to keep Pilbeam happy and Caroline Snow was off to Gloucester. At one o'clock he put the wireless on for the news, thinking wistfully how one problem would be off his mind for ever if the Paddington-Gloucester train crashed. It was amazing what a lot of trains did crash these days. Rail travel was getting as dangerous as going in aircraft. But the news was all about the negotiations taking place to quieten down the Middle Eastern ferment and trains weren't mentioned.

Vera was too occupied playing with her new kitchen toys to enquire closely into his reasons for going out at a quarter to eight. He told her casually that he had a business appointment without adding that it was to take place in a pub, a venue which rather detracted from the respectable air with which Stanley wanted his new venture imbued.

Pilbeam was already there. He always was already there.

'Sorry about yesterday's little *contretemps*, Stan, but needs must when the devil drives. I got the vases and some *very* pleasing Georgian silver. Time you came down to the shop and looked over the loot. Now, about this van. A mate of mine's offered me a smart little job. It's ours tomorrow if we fancy it and only two hundred and fifty quid.'

'I reckon I can find that,' Stanley said.

'Well, I should hope so, old man. After your promises, I really should hope so. I've the wife to pay back, you know, and if we're off to Barnet in our van tomorrow . . .'

'Leave it to me,' said Stanley.

They bought the van in the morning. Stanley gave Pilbeam's friend a cheque for it and drew another to cash. The van wasn't his idea of a smart little job, being battered about the bumpers and chipped on the bodywork, but it started first go and carried them as far as Croughton Old Village.

Pilbeam didn't say much on the journey and Stanley supposed he was sulking. But when he pulled up outside the shop he realized he'd been wrong. Far from sulking, Pilbeam had been silent from suppressed excitement and now, as he got out, he said proudly:

'Well, old man, what d'you think? Surprise, surprise, eh? You can see I haven't been idle.'

Stanley could hardly believe his eyes. When he'd last seen the shop the bow window had been cracked and dirty and the doorway boarded up. Now the window was repaired and every pane highly polished, affording a delectable view of the treasures within. Above it, expertly lettered in gilt, was the name *The Old Village Shop*, and there was more gilt lettering on the door, a glass and wrought iron affair with a curly brass handle.

Pilbeam unlocked it and let him in.

Inside the walls were papered in a Regency stripe and the floor was carpeted in dark red. On an oval table stood a pair of candelabra and a big glass rose bowl. Wide-eyed, Stanley tip-toed about, looking at hunting prints and Crown Derby plates and unidentifiable pieces of bric-à-brac. What he saw cheered him enormously, for he had begun to lose faith in Pilbeam. The man's arrival on the previous day to extort money from him by violence if necessary had shaken him, and the knocked-about old van had been almost the last straw. Now, gazing around him at polished wood and gleaming china, he felt his faith renewed.

'Who did all this decorating, then?' he asked.

'Couple of mates of mine.' Pilbeam seemed to have dozens of friends. 'I got them to do a rush job as a special favour. Like it?'

'It's grand,' said Stanley.

'I told them to send the bill to you. That all right?'

'Oh, sure,' Stanley said less comfortably. 'About what sort of . . . er, figure will it be?'

'Say fifty, old man. About fifty. That won't break you, eh? Then there's the carpet. Lovely drop of Wilton that is, as you can see. But I don't reckon you'll get the bill for that before the autumn. Open tomorrow, shall we?'

'Why not?'

They celebrated with a drink at the Lockkeeper's Arms and then they took the van up north into the villages of Hertfordshire. At the houses they called on Pilbeam did the talking. He seemed to like best the shabbier among the ancient houses and those occupied by a lone middle-aged or elderly woman whose husband was away at work.

His method was to ask this housewife if she had any old china or silver and mostly she had. While she was up in the loft turning it out, Pilbeam had a quick glance round at her furnishings, and when she came down again he bought everything she showed him, paying good prices until she was bemused by the sudden influx of cash given in exchange for what she thought of as rubbish. Just as they were leaving Pilbeam would offer her ten or twenty pounds for the piece he had had his eye on all the time, a wing chair or a writing desk, and in her greed and delight she usually agreed to his offer. Pilbeam took the attitude that he didn't really want this particular piece, he was doing her a favour in taking it off her hands.

'I'll give you twenty, lady,' he would say, 'but it'll cost me the same again to do it up, then I can sell it for forty-five. You see, I'm being completely honest with you. I'm in this for a profit.'

'But I could have it done up and make the profit myself.'

'I said it'd cost *me* twenty to do it up. That's not the price a cabinet maker'd charge you. More like thirty or forty.'

'Well, *you* know,' the woman would say. 'I'm sick of it, anyway. I'm glad of the chance to get rid of it. The last lot of stuff I cleared out I had to pay them to take it away.'

The cash for these transactions came out of Stanley's pocket.

'It's not falling on stony ground, old boy,' said Pilbeam. 'Now, if you could just let me have twenty-five for the wife, we'll call it a day, shall we?'

Stanley had to write a cheque for Mrs Pilbeam. He had no cash left. 'Just make it out to H. Pilbeam,' said her husband. 'Hilda's her name, the old battleaxe.'

Well, he'd got through the four hundred remaining in the bank all right, Stanley thought. The decorators would have to wait. Still, he wouldn't have to part out with any more for a bit and Vera had said she wouldn't touch another penny. In any case, by the end of the week he'd take his first money out of the business.

The next day he took Ethel Carpenter's ornaments with him to the Old Village Shop and arranged them tastefully on the oval table.

17

It was no good Stanley going out with the van. He wouldn't know, as Pilbeam put it, a Meissen vase from a baby's chamber pot, so while his partner plundered drawing rooms, Stanley stayed behind to mind the shop. The price of everything was marked on its base or one of its legs and Pilbeam said not to drop at all, not to haggle. They could take it or leave it.

They left it. Stanley made only one sale on his first day and that was a silver teaspoon, sold to a putative godmother for fifteen bob. He went home rather crestfallen to find a tightlipped red-eyed Vera who answered him in monosyllables when he told her about his day.

'What's got into you?'

'You know very well what's got into me.'

'No I don't. You were all right this morning.' Surely she couldn't have found out about the money he'd had? His cheque book was safe in his own pocket. 'I'm not a thought reader.'

Vera sat down, picked at her food and burst into tears.

'For God's sake!' said Stanley. 'What's wrong with you?'

'You are. You're what's wrong with me, you having your girls in this house while I was away.' She lifted to him red eyes full of bitter reproach. 'How could you, Stan?'

'Girls?' said Stanley. 'What the hell are you on about? I never had any girls here. You must be round the twist.'

'Well, girl, then. One girl, if that makes it any better. The whole neighbourhood's talking about it. They're all laughing at me, the lot of them. They always say the wife's the last to know, don't they?'

Caroline Snow. Damn her, she was a jinx, an evil genius if ever there was one. Trouble after trouble she was making for him.

'I suppose Mrs Macdonald told you,' he said.

'As a matter of fact, it was Mrs Blackmore, but they all know. They're all talking about it. How this tall blonde girl came here on Sunday, the day after you'd got me out of the way, and then how she was back again on the Friday. Stayed for hours, Mrs Blackmore said, and she saw you go off down the road together.'

'I can explain,' said Stanley classically. 'She's – she's a girl me and my partner are thinking of taking on to do the books. I had to interview her, didn't I?'

'I don't know. But if that's true, why did you say no one came here when I was away? Those were your words, not mine, I didn't ask you. Nobody came here, you said.'

'I forgot.'

'Nobody ever comes here,' Vera said wearily. 'We haven't got any friends, or hadn't you noticed? Nobody but the neighbours come in here for years on end, but that girl came and you forgot to tell me. You *forgot*. How d'you think I feel? What am I supposed to think?'

'You ought to believe me,' said Stanley. 'Me, not the neighbours, bloody gossiping mob. I'm telling you the truth, Vee.'

'Are you? You wouldn't know the truth if you saw it, Stan. Lies or truth, it's all the same to you. Suppose I ring up this Pilbeam, this partner of yours, and ask him if you're engaging a girl to do your books?'

'He's not on the phone,' Stanley muttered. Christ, he'd have to prime Pilbeam in the morning just in case she made good her threat. 'I reckon you ought to trust me, Vee.'

'Why? Have you ever given me any reason to trust you the whole of our married life?'

That night Vera slept in the bed she had got ready for Ethel Carpenter.

As the weeks went on the shop did better. Because their funds were exhausted Pilbeam served in the shop on Thursday and Friday and his presence made a difference to their sales. Stanley could see he was a good and relentless salesman with a fine line in persuasive talk. He sold the oval table and the four chairs which each had a fragment of Hepplewhite concealed about them as genuine unblemished Hepplewhite to a woman who claimed her house was furnished throughout with Swedish white wood, and the candelabra as a present for a teenage tearaway. Pilbeam said he could sell central heating to tribesmen in Equatorial Africa and Stanley believed him. But when he asked for his cut out of their week's takings, Pilbeam said they mustn't touch a penny for a long time yet. All their cash was needed for buying in.

Stanley went home empty-handed.

His relations with Vera had improved but they weren't restored to normal. Feeling relaxed and happier one evening, he'd rested his arm lightly round her shoulders while she was standing by the cooker, but she'd flinched away from him as if his arm was red hot.

'Isn't it time we let bygones be bygones?' he said.

'Do you swear that girl was nothing to you, just a girl after a job? Will you swear you never touched her?'

'I can't stand the sight of her,' Stanley said truthfully, and after that Vera was nicer to him, asking about the business and planning what they'd do with the money when it came, but sometimes when they were watching television or he was at work on a crossword, he'd look up and catch her staring at him in a strange way. Then she would drop her eyes in silence.

She was beginning to look forward to the arrival of the money now and while Stanley did the *Telegraph* puzzle she begged the city page from him and studied the markets, well satisfied that from day to day Euro-American Tobacco and International Tin showed steady improvement. Maud would have wanted her to have the money, she thought, wanted her above all to have the things that money would buy. She had had one of those snapshots of Maud enlarged and hung on the dining room wall and now when she looked at it she often reflected how sensible and perceptive Maud had been, seeing Stanley from the first for what he was. Money wouldn't improve her daughter's marriage, Maud had always known that, but it would make her life as an individual rather than as a wife easier. It was something to be miserable in comfort.

It was nice now to sit at the table while Stanley was

engrossed in his puzzle and write out cheques for the gas bill and the electricity instead of having to empty one of the tins she kept in the kitchen dresser and take the money all in coins down to the showrooms. Marvellous just to write eight pounds, nine and three and sign it without having to wonder whether you couldn't make it less next time by turning the light out every time you left a room . . .

That week Stanley took ten pounds home with him.

'It could be five times that, me old love,' said Pilbeam, 'only we need all the capital we've got for fresh stock. The fact is we're hamstrung till you cough up.'

And Stanley, who had been doubtful about his partner right until the time the shop opened, now saw that every forecast Pilbeam had made was true. He *did* know what he was talking about; he *was* an expert in the antique business. The whole thing was the gold-mine he had promised, a quarry of rich ores which could only be dug out and converted into coin when a sizeable capital sum was invested in it. The terrible thing was that his capital, his own legitimate capital, was invested elsewhere in footling tin and tobacco, untouchable until Finbow gave the word.

His nerves were in a bad way. His hands didn't shake and he no longer had those attacks of sick fainting but something even more upsetting had happened to him. The twitch in his eye had become permanent.

The twitching had come on again when Vera had questioned him about the girl's visits. Then it had been in the muscles of his right eye. His eyelid jumped up and down especially when he was tired. Stanley went into the public library and looked up his symptoms in the medical dictionary he had first consulted when he had had designs on Maud. The dictionary said the twitching was commonly known as 'live flesh' and was brought about by tiredness and worry but usually stopped after a short time. If it didn't it might be more serious, an early sign, in fact, of some disease of the central nervous system.

What, anyway, was a short time? Hours, days, weeks? There was no sign of this twitch abating and he'd had it for a fortnight now. The only time it stopped was when he was doing a crossword. The trouble with that as therapy was that he could now do the puzzle in ten minutes. Perhaps a better idea would be to begin at the other end, as it were, and make up crosswords himself.

Two or three years before he had tried doing this but there was no peace with Maud always there in the evenings and he had given it up. Now it was different. Sitting in the shop, whiling away time between customers, he sketched out crossword frames on the pad Pilbeam and he used for their bills. Sometimes Pilbeam was out on the knock, sometimes tapping away in the little workshop at the back. His eye was obedient and still while he invented clues and slotted in the words, for the task was a challenge to his mental powers. It occupied him, often to the exclusion of all else, and he found himself devoting whole hours together to the problem of finding a word to fit blank, R,O,G, blank, blank, S, blank, blank, before finally coming up with prognosis.

It was becoming something of an obsession, but Stanley knew it would go, just as the twitching would go, when the money came. Then he'd attend to the shop with real vigour, knowing that Pilbeam wouldn't appear from the back every few minutes to make nasty cracks about people who couldn't honour their obligations. Meanwhile, his crosswords were harmless enough and they kept his mind off the money and his eye from twitching.

Nearly a month had passed after opening the joint account when a letter came from the bank. Stanley had already gone to work, muttering under his breath E, blank, G, H, blank, and quite unable as he had been for three days now to find a word to fit this five-letter puzzle. He passed the postman but he was too involved with this apparently insoluble cypher even to suppose he might at last be bringing news from Finbow and Craig.

The envelope was addressed to Mr and Mrs Manning and Vera hesitated before opening it on her own but at last she did and a shiver of disbelief ran through her.

'Dear Mr and Mrs Manning,

'I am sorry to have to inform you that your joint current account is overdrawn to the sum of £35. I feel sure that you will wish to rectify this matter as soon as possible and am confident of receiving a remittance to cover the outstanding amount within the next few days.

'Yours sincerely,
'Arthur Frazer (Manager).'

But it couldn't be! She had only drawn cheques for the refrigerator and the washer and to pay the fuel bills. The account stood at five hundred pounds when opened and there ought to be at least three hundred and seventy there now. She had told Stanley to buy himself a suit, but he hadn't. Could it be a mistake? Oh, it must be. Did banks make mistakes? Everyone did sometimes, so banks must too.

Again Vera was aware of her ignorance of so many of those matters the average person takes in his stride. Perhaps she had written one of those cheques wrongly, put in an extra nought. But wouldn't the gas or the electricity people be honest about it? Or would they just hang on to what they'd got like Stanley had once when a greengrocer had handed him change for a five and not the single pound note he'd given him?

Worse than that, could the bank prosecute her? Somewhere she remembered hearing that it was an offence, actually against the law, to write cheques that couldn't be honoured. If only there was someone she could turn to, someone she could ask.

Maud would have known. Vera looked desperately at the photograph of her mother on the wall. Maud had been a good businesswoman, a marvellous manager, as sharp as any accountant, but Maud was dead. There was only Doris at the shop or Mrs Blackmore or Mrs Macdonald. Vera didn't want any of these women knowing her business. It was bad enough their discussing her married life and Stanley's deceit among themselves.

She didn't know anyone else, unless . . . Well, why not? James had said he was her friend. 'Don't let's lose touch now, Vera,' he'd said. Of course, that was before she'd told him her husband was alive and living with her, and they *had* lost touch. Not a word had passed between them since she came back from Bray.

But if she didn't ask James, what was she going to do? Lose three hundred and seventy pounds? More than that, because she was overdrawn by another thirty-five.

Almost distraught, Vera telephoned the dry-cleaner's and told Doris she wouldn't be in. She didn't feel well, she said truthfully. There was no point in hesitating any longer, pacing up and down and rereading that letter. Vera got out her address book and then she dialled the long string of numbers that would put her directly through to Brayminster.

The bank wasn't open yet and James was free. He seemed very pleased to hear Vera's voice, not sad or disillusioned as he had been at their last encounter.

'You're not putting me out at all, Vee. Of course I'll give you any advice I can.'

Rather haltingly and with many apologies for troubling him, Vera explained.

'I see. What does your husband say?'

It never occurred to Vera to get in touch with Stanley.

'I haven't told him yet.'

There was a short silence at the other end of the line. Then James said, 'It's a joint account, you say?'

'Yes, but Stanley doesn't need money. He's in business, he's doing well.'

Why did James suddenly sound so sympathetic, so gentle?

'I really think you should speak to your husband, Vee. But I'll tell you what I'll do. I've met Mr Frazer once or twice and I'll give him a ring now and say you're a friend of mine and that you'll be in to see him at eleven. Will that be all right? You'll have time to get in touch with your husband first.'

'You're awfully kind, James.'

'I'd do anything for you, Vee. You know that. Would you like me to lend you thirty-five pounds just to tide you over?'

'I couldn't think of it,' Vera said vehemently. 'No, please, I didn't want to speak to you for that.'

'You're welcome if you need it. Now, Vee, don't *worry*. The bank has honoured these cheques so there's no question of their being returned to drawer or anything of that sort. Mr Frazer will be quite understanding. Just ask him to give you a statement and show you the cheques that have passed through your account. D'you understand?'

'Yes, of course.'

'Good. Nobody is going to lecture you or threaten you in

any way. I suppose as a bank manager I shouldn't say this, but thousands upon thousands of people are overdrawn every month and they don't turn a hair. I only wish they would. Get in touch with me tomorrow, will you?'

'I wouldn't think of it,' said Vera.

James said calmly, 'Then I'll phone you. Yes, I will. It's been lovely talking to you, Vee. Give me that pleasure again tomorrow.'

Vera felt a good deal better and very pleased that she had plucked up the courage to talk to James. But she wouldn't be able to see Stanley before she went into the bank. He had told her he'd be out in the van till noon.

She made up her face carefully in the way Mrs Goodwin had taught her and put on the blue and white spotted dress. By five to eleven she was in a waiting room at the bank and after a few minutes Mr Frazer himself put his head round the door and invited her into his office. His manner was quite pleasant and cordial.

'I had a call from your friend, Mr Horton,' he said. 'But you mustn't ever be afraid to come and see me, Mrs Manning.'

Vera blushed hotly. What a fool they must both think her!

'Perhaps you'd like to see your statement,' said Mr Frazer.

While it was being fetched he chatted easily about the weather and about Brayminster where he had once spent a holiday. Vera could only answer him in monosyllables. She felt anything but at ease. The bank had a serious air about it and she suddenly wondered if she was on the threshold of something immensely serious in a personal sense to herself.

The statement was brought in by a girl clerk. Mr Frazer sent her away and then he passed the statement with its batch of cheques enclosed over to Vera. He lit a cigarette but Vera shook her head when he offered one to her.

It was the first time she had ever seen a bank statement and she didn't understand it. Bewildered, she picked up the top cheque, expecting to find it as incomprehensible as the statement, and then she saw her own handwriting. It was the one she had sent to the Gas Board. I suppose they pay it into their bank, she thought, and the money's marked to their credit there and then it somehow gets to my bank and they subtract the money from what I've got. Straightforward, really.

Back to the statement. The Gas Board had their money all right but only because the bank had paid, not because she had the money. She hadn't had any money before she'd written that cheque. She blushed again.

Here was her cheque for the refrigerator and the washer and another one to the electricity people. Vera turned up the last but one. She drew her breath sharply. Verity Vehicles, she read, two hundred and fifty pounds, £250.0.0, Stanley G. Manning. There was one more. To cash, £150. Stanley G. Manning.

'My husband,' she stammered. 'I'd forgotten . . . He did say . . . Oh, dear, I'm so sorry . . .'

'Well, we like to think we don't make many mistakes, Mrs Manning.'

'I'm the one who made the mistake,' Vera said and the words suddenly meant far more than just an apology for extravagance. 'I'll try to pay it back – well, next week. I don't know how but I'll try.'

'My dear Mrs Manning, we're not bloodsuckers. You mustn't be so upset. As long as you've managed to straighten matters out by the end of the month . . .'

'You're very kind,' said Vera. Everyone was very kind, very understanding, bending over backwards to help her because – because they pitied her so. And, of course, they knew what had happened. James had guessed from the start. Mr Frazer had seen through her clumsy little covering up tactics. They all knew she was married to a man she couldn't trust an inch.

As soon as he saw Vera's face, Stanley realized he was in trouble again. This time he wasn't going to put up with being ignored, more or less sent to Coventry. He flung his coat over the back of a chair, scowled at Maud's picture on the wall – she might as well be still alive for all the good her death had done him – and said:

'I suppose those interfering women have been giving you a few more details about my so-called girl friend.'

'I haven't seen Mrs Blackmore or Mrs Macdonald today.'

'What is it, then?'

Vera poured herself a cup of tea and sipped it in silence. Silence, thought Stanley. 'Permission is possibly quiet. Anagram on 'license' . . . God, he'd have to control himself, not keep seeing every word as part of a crossword puzzle. For the first time in their married life Vera had helped herself to a cup of tea without pouring one for him.

'What's up with you?' he said, his nerves on edge.

Vera turned round. She looked old and ugly, deep shadows ringing her eyes, deep lines scored from nose to mouth. 'I may as well have it out,' she said. 'I've been to the bank this morning. I had a letter from the manager.'

'Oh, that.'

'Yes, that. Is that all you can say?'

'Look, Vee, you said I could have some of the money. You said, buy yourself anything you want.'

'I said a suit or any little thing you wanted. I didn't say draw out four hundred pounds. Stan, I don't mind you having the money. But couldn't you have told me? You wanted it for the business, didn't you? Couldn't you have just said? Did you have to make me look a fool in front of the bank manager and nearly worry myself to death?'

'You said you wouldn't write any more cheques. How was I to know you'd start paying bills?' Why was she staring at him like that? Her eyes were fixed on him so that he had to look away.

'What's wrong with your eye?' she said coldly.

'Nothing. The muscles keep jumping, that's all. It's my nerves.'

Silence again. Then Vera said, 'We can't go on like this, can we? God knows, I didn't want Mother to die, but when she was dead, I thought – I thought things would be better. I thought we'd have a proper marriage like other people. It hasn't worked that way, has it?'

'I don't know what you're on about,' said Stanley, edging his way into the dining room. He sat down on the sofa and began doodling on a sheet of paper. Vera followed him. 'Look, I'm sorry about the money, but there's no need to make a song and dance about it. I can easily get it back out of the business.'

'Can you, Stan? We haven't seen much out of the business yet, have we? Come to that, I don't even know there is a business. You haven't taken me to the shop or introduced me to Mr Pilbeam or . . .'

'Do me a favour,' said Stanley huffily. His eye was opening and shutting like an umbrella. 'Can't you take my word for it?'

Vera laughed. 'Take your word? Stan, you can't be serious. I can't take your word for anything. You just say the first thing that comes into your head. Truth or lies, it's all the same to you. I don't think you know the difference any more. And, Stan, I can't bear it. I can't bear to be left in the dark and humiliated and deceived just because doing that to me is easier for you than telling the truth. I'd – I'd rather be dead or not with you.'

Stanley hadn't paid much attention to all this. Vera's remark about his eye had affected him more than all her analysis of his shortcomings. Drawing a crossword puzzle frame and inserting a couple of words, he had heard nothing since then but her last sentence. It leapt at him like a red warning light.

Alarmed, he said, 'What d'you mean, not with me?'

'When people reach the stage we've reached, they separate, don't they?'

'Now, look, Vee, don't you talk like that. You're my wife. And all this – well, it's six of one and half a dozen of the other. If I keep you in the dark it's on account of the way you nag me. A man can't stand nagging.' Can't stand, either, having no control over his own face. Stanley covered up his eye and felt the lid jerk against his hand. 'You're my wife, like I said, and have been for twenty years. There's a good time coming, Vee, I promise you. We'll both be in clover by the end of the year and . . .'

She stared at him even harder.

'Do you love me?'

What a question! What a thing to ask a man when he was tired and worried and maybe on the verge of Parkinson's Disease. 'Of course I do,' Stanley muttered.

Her face softened and she took his hand. Stanley dropped his pencil reluctantly and laid his other hand on her shoulder. His eye was aching. For a long time Vera said nothing. She held his hand tightly and then, without letting it go, sat down beside him. Stanley fidgeted nervously.

'We'll have to make a fresh start,' Vera said suddenly.

He sighed with relief. A fresh start. 'Beginning again with a new jump?' Surreptitiously he felt among the cushions for his pencil. That S could be the S in business, the word going down. 'After public transport I'm on a Scottish loch . . .'

'Yes, we'll have to start again,' Vera said. 'We'll both have to make an effort, Stan, but that won't be so hard now we've got all this money coming to us.'

Stanley smiled at her, his eye quite normal.

'We'll sell this house and buy a new one and we'll scrap all this old furniture. Mother would have liked to see us in a modern house.' That 'us', Stanley thought, was a mere courtesy. Maud would have liked to see *him* in a modern concentration camp. 'And we'll have proper holidays together and a car. I'll promise never to nag you again if you'll promise to be open with me. But I have to trust you, Stan. You do see that?'

'I'll never tell another lie to you, Vee, as long as I live.'

She stared at him, wishing she could believe what he said, that at last he was being sincere. Stanley returned her gaze glassily. He had thought of his word. E, blank, G,H, blank. Eight, of course, the only English word surely to fit that particular combination. And all day long he'd been wondering if he could alter the H to O – change the word across from phone to Poona – and make 18 down ergot. Triumphantly Stanley wrote in 'eight' and beside it, 'One over it is too many drinks'.

18

The bill came in from the decorators and someone had written across the top of it: 'Prompt settlement will be appreciated'. They would have to take their appreciation elsewhere. Stanley didn't at all appreciate the demand for £175, instead of the fifty Pilbeam had spoken of so confidently. Vera and he, making their fresh start, sat side by side on the sofa, studying the market. Euro-American Tobacco had dropped a couple of points overnight. Stanley's eye fluttered lightly, then began a rhythmic blinking.

'You want to put some more money into the business, don't you, Stan? I only hope it'll be safe.'

'You said you wouldn't nag me,' said Stanley. He reached for the sheet of paper on which he was composing a larger and more ambitious crossword. Nag would fit into that three-letter space, he thought. Nag, nag, nag. How about, 'The horse may pester'? Yes, that would do. Nag meant 'horse' and 'pester' . . .

'I don't mean to nag. But have you formed a sort of company or a partnership? Have you had it done legally, Stan?'

'I trust my partner and he trusts me,' said Stanley. 'Pity I can't say the same for my wife.' He printed in 'nag' and then tacked 'wife' on to the W in 'window'. Wife: 'If in two compass points find a spouse'. Vera was looking at his eye now, although the twitching had stopped.

'Don't you think you ought to see the doctor about that tic you've got?' she said.

James was as good as his word. He phoned Vera at home and, getting no reply, phoned the cleaner's.

'Well, Vee, I said he wouldn't eat you, didn't I? What was it all about, a simple mistake on someone's part?'

'My husband forgot to tell me he'd written rather a large cheque.' Loyally, Vera lied, 'He's put it all back out of his business.'

'That's fine.' James didn't sound as if he thought it was fine at all. He sounded as if he didn't believe her, a notion which was confirmed when he said, 'Vee, if you're ever worried about anything, you'll get in touch with me, won't you?'

'I've got Stanley,' Vera said.

'Yes, of course. I hadn't forgotten. But there might be a time when . . . Good-bye, Vera. Take care of yourself.'

It was time she did, Vera thought, time she took care of herself. Really, it was ridiculous for a woman in her financial position, or prospective financial position, to keep on working in a cleaner's. She handed a customer two newly cleaned pairs of trousers and then she sat down to write her resignation as manageress of the Croughton Laundry.

Thursday. Her afternoon off. Vera left the shop at one and called in at the nearest estate agent's. He would be pleased to handle the selling of the house, he said. What kind of a figure had she thought of asking? Vera hadn't thought about it at all, but the estate agent knew the type of house and suggested four thousand, five hundred pounds. He promised to come to Lanchester Road during the afternoon and look the place over.

Vera made herself some scrambled eggs for lunch and finished up the chocolate mousse they could now keep overnight because they had the refrigerator. It was unlikely the estate agent would get there before three and that would give her an hour to make things look a bit shipshape upstairs.

Before the house was sold she'd have to make an effort and clear out Maud's room properly, all those clothes that Aunt Louisa didn't want, all those papers and the bottles and jars whose contents had kept Maud alive for four years.

After the funeral Vera had shut them up in one of the dressing table drawers. She opened it now and contemplated Maud's various medicines, anti-coagulants, diuretics, mineral salts, vitamins, sleeping tablets and tranquillizers. I wonder if the chemist would take them back? Vera thought. It seemed a wicked waste just to throw them away.

Now for the clothes. She was packing them into an old bolster case when the doorbell rang. Vera was expecting the estate agent and she was surprised to see a young woman on the doorstep.

'Good afternoon. I'm collecting for the Chappell Fund.'

Vera thought she said 'chapel fund' and was about to say she was Church of England when she remembered the young policeman who had been shot during the Croughton post office raid. She opened her purse.

'Thank you so much. Actually, we're trying to get a thousand pounds collected privately for Mrs Chappell and some of us are getting up a few stalls at the Police Sports next week. If you do happen to have . . .'

'Would you like some cast-off clothing?' Vera asked. 'My mother died recently and all her clothes were good. Nobody wants them now and I'd be glad if you'd take them off me.'

The young woman looked delighted, so Vera went upstairs, fetched the bolster and handed it to her.

'These were your mother's, you say?'

'That's right. I've no use for them, really.'

'Thank you very much. You've been a great help.'

The only thing that worried Stanley now was the money. Once get his hands on that and life would be serene. It was obvious he was never going to hear another word from Caroline Snow.

Relishing the picture, he imagined her bursting into her home in Gloucester and pouring out the whole story to Snow, tired, poor devil, after a hard day's work toiling to keep women in luxury. Probably Snow was watching the box or even doing a crossword. In his mind's eye, Stanley saw the man's face fall when he heard how he was expected first to find a mother-in-law he had never before considered as a serious menace and then welcome her to his hearth and home.

'We must find her, mustn't we, Daddy? You're so marvellous in a crisis. I knew you'd know what to do.'

Stanley chuckled at this piece of silent mimicry. And what would Snow say?

'You leave it to me, darling.' Soothing tone, brain sorting it all out like a computer. 'I'd like to talk it over with your mother when we're alone.'

Shift to scene with marvellous Mummy, tête-à-tête, lights dimmed, Caroline off somewhere with dog or boy friend.

'She's such an impetuous child, dear.'

'Yes, I know. But I can't destroy her faith in me, can I?'

'She adores you so, darling. I must say for my part I don't exactly relish a reunion with a mother I haven't seen for forty years.'

'There's no question of that. Nothing would induce me to pal up with the old lady and have her here. Good heavens, I'm not a glutton for punishment . . .'

'Why not just say you've got in touch with the police, dear? Say they're making enquiries. Caroline will have forgotten the whole thing when she's been home a week.'

'Of course she will. You're so marvellous, darling.'

Stanley laughed uproariously at this invented cameo of the set-up and dialogue *chez* Snow. He could almost see them sitting there among their refined middle-class G-plan furniture. It was a pity he had to keep it to himself and couldn't tell anyone about it. He wiped his eyes and when he had stopped laughing his eye began to twitch ferociously.

He was trying to hold the eyelid steady, seeing if he could control it by an effort of will, when Pilbeam walked into the shop, holding a plastic bag full of horse brasses.

'You want to get that eye of yours seen to, old man. I had an aunt with the same trouble, St. Vitus's Dance.'

'What happened to her?'

Pilbeam tipped the horse brasses on to the floor and sat down. 'She got to jerking all over. It was embarrassing being with her.' He scratched his nose with the nailless finger. 'Why don't you go and see the quack? I can cope here.'

The group practice whose list he was on held an afternoon surgery three times a week. His worry over getting his hands on his inheritance had long since driven any apprehension over the part he had played in Maud's death from Stanley's mind, so, after waiting forty minutes, he walked more or less serenely into the surgery where Dr Moxley sat behind his desk.

'What seems to be the trouble?'

The swine might take the trouble to look at me, Stanley thought sourly. He explained about his eye and as he spoke it fluttered obligingly.

'They call it "live flesh".'

'They do, do they? And who might "they" be?'

'A medical book.'

'Oh, dear, I wish you lay people wouldn't be always poking about in medical books. You only frighten yourselves. I suppose you thought you'd got muscular dystrophy.'

'Well, have I?'

'I shouldn't think so,' said Dr Moxley, laughing breezily. 'Been worrying about something, have you?'

'I've got a lot on my mind, yes.'

'Stop worrying, then, and your twitch'll stop.' Just like that, Stanley thought indignantly. As if telling someone not to worry would stop them. Bloody doctors, they were all the same. He took the prescription for a sedative and was halfway to the door when Dr Moxley said, 'How's your wife? Getting over Mrs Kinaway's death all right?'

What business was it of his? Stanley muttered something about Vera being all right. The doctor, a past master, Stanley thought, at switching moods, smiled and said genially, 'I ran into old Dr Blake the other day. He was quite upset to hear Mrs Kinaway had died. Surprised, too. He said he'd seen her in the street only a couple of days before and she looked very fit.'

Stanley was speechless. The scare over Caroline Snow, now past, had been bad enough. The last thing he had anticipated was that questions might be asked at this late date about Maud. Why, it was weeks and weeks . . .

'He couldn't understand Mrs Kinaway having another stroke when she was on Mollanoid.' Moxley gave an innocent yet somehow sinister smile. 'Still, these things happen. Dr Blake's very conscientious. I advised him not to give it another thought.'

Stanley walked out in a daze. Who would have thought Maud's old doctor would still be hanging about the neighbourhood? Probably it meant nothing. He had enough troubles without bothering about that.

To get his prescription made up Stanley went into the same chemist's he had been to when buying Shu-go-Sub and suddenly he remembered that two and a half tubes of saccharine tablets still remained in Maud's Mollanoid cartons. The first thing he'd do when he got home was get hold of those tablets and burn them just in case Moxley and the conscientious Blake were planning to make a swoop on the house to investigate.

'What's happened to all your mother's stuff?' he asked Vera.

'All gone. I've been having a turn-out. The estate agent said we could get a better price if the place was smartened up so I thought I'd do some decorating.'

Decorating was a dirty word to Stanley. Sourly he watched Vera come down the steps, wipe her brush and put the lid on the distemper tin. Distemper was a good word for a puzzle and he couldn't remember ever doing one in which it had been used. Distemper: 'Paint prescribed for the dog's disease'. Very good.

'You've thrown everything out?' he asked casually.

'Everything but her clothes. Someone came round collecting for the police.'

Stanley felt the sweat break out on his upper lip. 'The *what*?'

'Whatever's the matter? You're jerking all over.'

Stanley clenched his hands. Even they were jumping. He couldn't speak.

'Well, not the police really, dear.' Vera was sorry she had put it that way. Stanley had always been afraid of the police. 'They were collecting for that policeman's widow, Mrs Chappell, and they were so pleased when I gave them Mother's clothes. Stan, dear, let me make you a cup of tea. You're overwrought, you're worrying about your eye. Come along. You can do your crossword while I'm making the tea.'

'I've done it.'

'Then make one up. You know you like doing that.'

Still jumping and shivering, Stanley tried to sketch a crossword frame. He wrote in 'distemper' and then 'policewoman' going down from the P. Perhaps the woman had come on an innocent errand; perhaps Moxley had meant nothing sinister. But suppose instead Moxley had dropped a hint or two to the police and they had sent this woman round because . . . What could they find out from Maud's clothes? Perhaps there was some substance present in a person's sweat when they had high blood pressure or when they were taking saccharine or weren't taking Mollanoid. For all Stanley knew, Moxley might be an expert in forensics. He wrote 'forensics' in, going down from the R in distemper.

They might go round all the chemists and find that a man answering his description had bought a lot of saccharine . . . Then they'd dig Maud up. The gash on her head might be gone by now. They'd analyse the contents of her stomach and find Shu-go-Sub, masses of it. But no Mollanoid. Maud hadn't taken any since early March.

His eye winked, half-blinding him, so that he couldn't see the words he had printed across the white squares.

PART THREE
Down

19

It was high summer now, a fine, beautiful summer. Hot day succeeded hot day and this sameness was reflected in the Mannings' life. Nothing changed for the better – or, Stanley comforted himself, for the worse either. The police showed no further interest in him and he hadn't been back to Dr Moxley, although his eye still twitched. He couldn't stop worrying about the money.

Letters went back and forth between Vera and Mr Finbow but there was no hint in anything the solicitor wrote that it would now be prudent to sell those tin and tobacco shares. Vera refused firmly though kindly to sell them against Mr Finbow's advice or to ask for another advance, even though Stanley had shown her the reminder which had come from Pilbeam's decorators with 'please settle outstanding payment at once' scrawled across it. Pilbeam made Stanley's life a misery with his nagging about the shop's need for more capital.

A 'For Sale' board had been put up outside the house. No one came to view it. It lacked, the agent told Vera, certain amenities which these days were indispensable.

'We might have a garage built,' said Vera. 'Only it would mean sacrificing your heather garden.'

'Doesn't matter,' said Stanley. A garage would keep Maud hidden for ever. On the other hand, how much unearthing would the builders have to do to lay foundations?

'I'll see about it, then, and I'll carry on with my decorating. We ought to get an offer soon. The agent says sales are booming.'

'Dare say it to the goose in front of the vase for a big bang . . .'

'What did you say, dear?'

'A clue in my crossword. Booming. Dare say it to . . . Oh, never mind.'

'You don't seem to think about anything but crosswords these days,' said Vera.

It was true. Puzzles, inventing them and solving them, had become an obsession with him. He even did them secretly in the shop while Pilbeam was out, so that when his partner came back his head was full of floating words and puns and anagrams, and when Pilbeam started afresh on his demands, as he did every day, he could turn a vague, half-deaf ear.

'Remember that old bag we flogged the Georgian table to?' Pilbeam would say. 'She wants to do her whole flat over in period. With me working day and night and you coming up with the cash to buy in, we could make five hundred on this deal alone.' Or, 'We're hamstrung, Stan. It makes me weep the opportunities we're missing.' And always he ended up with, 'We've got to have that money. Now, Stan, not in the sweet by-and-by.'

Stanley was too much in awe of Pilbeam to do more than placate him with soothing promises. He saved his rage for Vera.

'I tell you, I've got to have that money for the business. It's ours but we can't touch it. We're as poor now as when your bloody old mother was still alive. The business'll go bust if I don't have the money. Can't you get that into your head?'

Vera flinched away from him, afraid of his greed and the wild light in his eyes. His face twitched dreadfully when he was angry. But she was most frightened when instead of answering her properly he replied with some meaningless conundrum.

One day towards the end of July Vera started work on the small spare bedroom and as she was turning out she came upon Maud's collection of pills which she had put in here while she was painting her mother's room. It seemed wasteful to discard them all, especially as one of the little plastic cartons hadn't been opened and the other was only half empty. There would be no harm in asking the chemist about them while she was out shopping.

As she left the house she encountered the builders bringing in bags of cement and a concrete mixer.

'No need to wait in for us, lady,' said the foreman. 'We shan't make a start on your garage till next week, what with this strike at the brickworks. You won't mind us leaving our gear in readiness, will you?'

Vera said she wouldn't. She went straight into the chemist's and asked if it would be all right to return the carton of tablets as none of them had been used.

The pharmacist smiled. 'Sorry, madam, we don't do that. We advise our customers to throw away all unused drugs. To be on the safe side, you see.' He removed the cap and looked at the contents of the carton.

'They're called Mollanoid, I believe.'

Pharmacists, like doctors, prefer lay people to be in utter ignorance of such esoteric matters. This one was no exception. He frowned at Vera. Then he took out a single tablet, looked closely at it and said:

'What makes you think these tablets are Mollanoid?'

Vera said rather tartly, 'You made up the doctor's prescription and you wrote Mollanoid on the label. My mother always took Mollanoid for her blood pressure.'

'Certainly I made up the presciption and *wrote* the label, but these are not the tablets I put in the carton. Mollanoid is what we call an anti-coagulant, in other words it helps prevent the formation of clots in the bloodstream. As I say, these aren't Mollanoid.'

'What are they, then?'

The pharmacist sniffed the tablet he was holding and put it to his tongue. 'Some compound of saccharine, I imagine.'

'*Saccharine*?'

'The stuff slimmers use to sweeten tea and coffee,' the pharmacist said in the tone of one addressing a retarded child.

Vera shrugged. Rather confused and puzzled, she finished her shopping. Was it possible that the pharmacist himself had made a mistake in his dispensing and the carton had always contained saccharine? It seemed unlikely but more probable than that Maud had been secretly taking saccharine. If that had been the case, what had she done with the Mollanoid? Certainly she wouldn't have stopped taking them. She depended on them utterly as a lifeline and often said that but for them she would have had a second stroke.

Choosing a cheap but pretty wallpaper and deciding on a colour scheme distracted Vera's mind but, for all that, she decided to mention the matter to Stanley when he came in. He was rather late and as soon as Vera saw him she knew he was in no state to be interested in other people's medical problems.

'My eye's killing me,' he said.

For the first time in their married life he had left his dinner, lamb chops, chips and peas, untouched, and Vera, who formerly would have been anxious and solicitous, hardened her heart. If she told him to go to the doctor again he would only snap at her. She couldn't talk to him, they had no real communication any more. Often these days she thought of James Horton who was sympathetic and gentle and with whom it was possible to have conversation.

'What's the matter with you now?' she asked at last, trying to keep her tone patient.

'Nothing,' said Stanley. 'Nothing. Leave me alone.'

His eye blinked and squeezed shut as if fingers inside his head were squeezing it. The something that was doing the squeezing seemed to laugh at him and at the success of its tricks which he couldn't combat. But that something must be himself, mustn't it? God, he thought, he'd go off his rocker at this rate.

Vera was watching him like a hawk. He couldn't tell her that he was trembling and twitching and off his food because he was terribly frightened, because something had happened that day to reduce him to a far worse state than he had been in when the Chappell Fund woman had called or even when he had first seen Maud fall to her death. His teeth were chattering with fear and he ground them tightly together as if he had lockjaw.

That afternoon, while he was out in the van, a policeman had called at the Old Village Shop.

He had been to Hatfield to relieve an old woman of an eighteenth-century commode for approximately a fifth of its true value, and driving back had tried to calm his pulsating eye by finishing off an imaginary crossword. Stanley could now invent and complete crosswords in his head just as some people can play chess without a board. He drove the van into the yard at the back of the shop, murmuring under his breath, Purchase: 'An almost pure hunt for this buy', when he saw a uniformed policeman leave the shop and cross to a waiting car. His eye moved like a pump, jerked and closed.

'What was that copper doing here?' he asked Pilbeam in a strangled thin voice.

'Just checking on the stock, old man.' Pilbeam stroked the side of his nose with the nailless sausage-like finger. He often did this but now Stanley couldn't bear to see it. It made him feel sick. 'They often do that,' Pilbeam said. 'In case we're harbouring stolen goods in all innocence.'

'They've never done it before. Did he ask for me?'

'You, old boy? Why would he ask for you?' Pilbeam smiled blandly. Stanley was sure he was lying. He was always up to something when he stared you candidly in the eye like that. 'Been a good day, me old love. I reckon we can each take ten quid home with us tonight.'

'I see that china and silver of mine went.'

'A lady from Texas, she had them. Crazy about anything English, she was. I reckon she'd have paid anything I'd asked.' Pilbeam laid his hand on Stanley's sleeve, the finger stump just touching the bare skin at the wrist. His eyes weren't frank and friendly any more. 'I promised my old woman I'd pay her back next week. Money, Stan, loot, lolly. My patience, as the old ex-Führer put it, is getting exhausted.'

Stanley wanted to ask him more about the policeman's visit but he didn't dare. He desperately wanted to believe Pilbeam. Surely if the policeman had wanted to talk to him he would have called at Lanchester Road. Perhaps he had called and found no one in.

If he'd been right and somehow or other they'd analysed Maud's clothes, if Moxley had been shooting his mouth off, if Vera had boasted to all the neighbours about the garage they were going to have built . . . Suppose, all these weeks, the police and the doctors had been building up a case against him from hints and hearsay . . . He was afraid to go home, but he had nowhere else to go. All the evening he could sense Vera had something she wanted to tell him but was too sulky or too subtle to come out with it. Maybe the police had been getting at her too.

He couldn't sleep that night. Every muscle was twitching now and the remedy seemed almost worse than the disease. He began to wish he'd never done a crossword in his life, so compulsive was this need to keep inventing clues, to slot words across, fit others down. All that night and Saturday night he had a chequer-board pattern in front of his eyes.

He felt he was on the edge of a nervous collapse.

Vera couldn't stay in the same bed with him when he twitched like that. He slept on Sunday night, from sheer exhaustion, she guessed, and his whole body rippled galvanically in sleep. In the small hours she made tea but she didn't wake him. Instead she took her own tea into the spare room.

She switched on the light, stepped over paint pots and got into the spare bed. As soon as she saw Maud's pills all her bewilderment came back to her. She reached for the half-empty carton of Mollanoid, the ones Maud had been taking right up to her death, and removed the lid.

I wonder, she thought, if Mother planned to stop taking sugar because Dr Blake told her she should lose weight? Perhaps she had bought saccharine and had used a Mollanoid carton to keep it in.

It was beginning to get light. Vera could hear a thrush singing in the Blackmores' laburnum. The meaningless and not really musical trill depressed her. She felt very cold and she pulled the bed covers up to her chin.

But as she prepared to settle down and snatch a couple of hours' sleep, her eye fell once more on the carton she had opened. Mollanoid. Of course they were Mollanoid. They looked exactly like the tablets Maud had been taking three times a day, every day, for four years. But they also looked exactly like the ones she had taken to the chemist on the previous morning. Again Vera sat up.

Maud hadn't touched those, hadn't taken a single one of them. These, on the other hand, were three-quarters used, and the carton which contained them had stood by Maud's plate at her last breakfast. Vera knew that. In the increasing light she noticed the smear on the label the chemist had made, handing her the carton before the ink had quite dried. And casting her mind back to that breakfast – would she ever forget it or forget Maud's elation? – she recalled her mother's taking two of the tablets just after spooning sugar plentifully into her tea.

Her heart began to pound. Slowly, as if she were a forensic expert about to test poison at some risk to himself, she picked out one of the tablets and rested it on her tongue.

For a moment there was no taste. Vera's heart quietened. Then, because she had to know, she pressed the tip of her tongue with the tablet on it against the roof of her mouth. Immediately a rich sickly sweetness spread across the surface of her tongue and seeped between her teeth.

She spat the tablet into her saucer and then lay face downwards, numb and very cold.

It was ten when Stanley woke up. He stared at the clock and was out of bed and half across the room before he remembered. This was the day he was going to the doctor's. He'd told Pilbeam he wouldn't be in before lunch.

Just thinking the word doctor started his eye twitching again. He cursed, put on his dressing gown and went into Maud's room to see if the builders had started work yet. It was imperative to keep an eye on them in case they got too enthusiastic and began digging the earth they were to cover. But the garden was empty and the concrete mixer idle.

It wasn't like Vera not to bring him a cup of tea. Perhaps she hadn't wanted to disturb him. Poor old Vee. She wasn't much to look at any more and, God knew, she'd always been as dull as ditchwater, but a man could do worse. No breakfast tray either. Come to that, no Vera. The house stank of paint. Stanley felt the beginnings of a headache. He'd missed Moxley's morning surgery but there was another one at two and he'd go to that. Everywhere was clean and tidy. Obviously, Vera had cleaned the place and gone out shopping.

He mooched back to the kitchen, his eye opening and shutting in a series of painful winks. She hadn't even left the cornflakes out for him. He got the packet out of the larder, poured out a dishful and looked around for the *Telegraph*. Might as well do the puzzle. There was no question any more whether he could do it or not or even whether he could do it at a single sitting. The only amusement it still afforded Stanley was seeing if he could beat his record of seven minutes.

The newspaper was folded up, lying on top of the refrigerator. Stanley picked it up and saw that underneath it was a letter poking half out of its envelope. The envelope was addressed to Vera but that had never deterred him before and it didn't deter him now. He pulled it out with shaking fingers and read it.

The money had come through.

Mr Finbow would expect Vera at her earliest convenience and would hand her a cheque.

Stanley rubbed his eyes. Not because they were twitching but because tears were running down his face.

20

Years and years he had waited for this moment. Ever since he'd first set eyes on Maud and heard how well heeled she was, he'd dreamed of today, now or long ago, now or in time to come, the shining hour when it would all be his. Twenty-two thousand pounds.

His eye hadn't twitched once since he had read that letter. He also now saw clearly that in imputing sinister motives to a harmless housewife collecting for a sale and a policeman on routine duty he had been letting his imagination run away with him. Money cured all ills, mental and physical. No doctors for him. Instead he would take a bus down to the Old Village.

Pilbeam was in the shop, polishing a brass warming pan. 'You're early,' he said morosely. 'What did the quack say?'

Stanley sat down on the piecrust table. He felt like a tycoon. Laconically he said, 'I've got a thousand quid for you. I may as well write a cheque for the decorators at the same time and you can give it to them. There'll be loads more next week if we need it. We're laughing now, boy. No more worries. No more struggling on a shoestring.'

'You won't regret it, Stan. I'll promise you you won't regret it. My God, we knew what we were doing when we started this little lark!' Pilbeam slapped him on the back and pocketed the cheques. 'Now, I'll tell you what. We'll go down to the Lockkeeper's and we'll split a bottle of Scotch and then I'll treat you to a slap-up lunch.'

Not quite half a bottle, but four double whiskies on an empty stomach, followed by a heavy meal of steak, fried potatoes, french beans, carrots, mushrooms, raspberry pie and cream, sent Stanley reeling towards Lanchester Road at half past two. He badly wanted to burst into song as he made his way unsteadily along the respectable streets of dull little villas, but to be arrested on this glorious golden day, one of the happiest days of his life, would be a disastrous anticlimax.

The sky which, when he first got up, had been overcast had cleared while they were in the Lockkeeper's and now it was very hot. One of the hottest days of the year, Stanley thought, immensely gratified that the weather matched his mood. He passed the Jaguar show-rooms and wondered whether it would be possible to buy a car that very afternoon. That scarlet Mark Ten, for instance. He didn't see why not. It wasn't as if he was after some little mass-produced job like Macdonald's tin can which lesser mortals, miserable wage-earners, had to wait for months for. He must sober up. Have a cup of tea perhaps and then he'd buy the car and take Vera for a ride in it. Maybe they'd go out Epping Forest way and have a meal in a country pub.

These pleasant fancies sliding across the surface of his fuddled brain, he marched into the kitchen and called, 'Vera, where are you?'

There was no answer. Sulking, he thought, because I didn't hang about to tell her what the doctor said. Doctor! The last thing he needed.

He could hear her moving about upstairs. Probably she was toiling away painting that bedroom. Well, she'd have to buck her ideas up, expand her horizons. People with his sort of money didn't do their own decorating. He moved carefully into the hall. Better on the whole not to let her see he'd been drinking.

He called her name again and this time he heard a door close and her face appeared over the banisters. For a woman who had just come into twenty thousand pounds, she didn't look very happy.

'I thought you'd gone in to work,' she said.

'The doctor said I was to take the day off. Come down here. I want to talk to you.'

He heard her say something that sounded like, 'I want to talk to you, too,' and then she came slowly down the stairs. She was wearing the blue and white spotted dress and she hadn't any paint on her hands. A sudden slight chill took the edge off his joy. What a moody, difficult woman she was! Just like her to find something to nag about on this day of days. He knew she was going to nag. He could see it in the droop of her mouth and in her cold eyes.

'Did you get the money?' he said heartily. 'I couldn't help seeing old Finbow's letter. At last, eh?'

She was going to say she hadn't got it. She'd asked Finbow to hang on to it, re-invest it, something diabolical. Christ, she couldn't have!

'You *did* get the money?'

'Oh yes, I got it.' He'd never heard quite that tone in her voice before, that chilling despair.

'And paid it into the bank? What's up, then, love? Isn't this what we've been waiting for, planning for?'

'Don't call me love,' said Vera. 'I'm not your love. You mean you've been planning for, don't you? But you haven't planned well enough. You should have disposed of your saccharine tablets after you'd killed my mother.'

Momentarily Stanley thought that this couldn't be real. He'd drunk too much and passed out and that bloody awful puzzle dream was starting again. But we always know when we are awake that we cannot be dreaming even though when actually dreaming we feel all this may be real, and Stanley, after the first sensation of nightmare unreality, had no need to pinch himself. Vera *had* said what she'd said. They were in the kitchen at 61, Lanchester Road and both were wide awake. She *had* said it, but he asked her to repeat it just the same.

'What did you say?'

'You said for two pins you'd kill her and she said you would and, God forgive me, I didn't believe either of you. Not until I found what was in those medicine cartons.'

There is a great difference between anticipating the worst, dreading, dreaming and living in imagination through the worst, and the worst itself. Stanley had visualized this happening, or something like this, over and over again, although usually his accuser had been a doctor or a policeman, but he found that all these preparations and rehearsals did nothing to mitigate the shock of the reality. He felt as if he had been hit on the head with something heavy but not heavy enough to bring blissful unconsciousness.

In a feeble trembling voice he said what he had planned to say when 'they' started asking, 'I didn't kill her, Vee. Just taking saccharine didn't kill her.'

'She died of a stroke, didn't she? *Didn't she?* Isn't that what she had while I was out? You know it is. Dr Moxley came and said she'd died of a stroke.'

'She'd have had that stroke, anyway,' Stanley muttered.

'How do you know? Have you got medical degrees? You know very well you wanted her to die, so you took away her tablets and put saccharine in the carton and she died. You murdered her. You murdered her just as much as if you'd shot her.'

Vera went out of the kitchen and slammed the door behind her. Alone, Stanley felt his heart pounding against his ribs. Why hadn't he had the sense to burn those bloody saccharines after Maud had died? And how had Vera found out? That hardly mattered now. He put his head into the sink and drank straight from the cold water tap. Then he went upstairs.

She was in their bedroom, throwing clothes into a couple of suitcases. He fumbled in his mind, trying to find the words. At last he said, 'You wouldn't go to the police about this, would you, Vee?'

She didn't answer. Her hands went on folding mechanically, slipping sheets of paper between the clothes, tucking in a pair of rolled-up stockings. He stared at her stupidly and suddenly the meaning of what she was doing came home to him.

'Are you off somewhere, then?'

She nodded. There were little beads of sweat on her upper lip. It was a very hot day.

Stanley managed a hint of sarcastic bravado. 'May I ask where?'

'I'll tell you whether you ask or not.' Vera marched into the bathroom and came back with her spongebag. 'I'm leaving you,' she said. 'It's all over for us, Stanley. It was over years ago really. I could take you treating me like a servant and having that girl here and living off my money, but I can't stay with a man who murdered my mother.'

'*I did not murder your mother,*' he shouted. 'I never murdered anyone. Anyone'd think you liked having her here. Christ, you wanted her out of the way as much as I did.'

'She was my mother,' Vera said. 'I loved her in spite of her faults. I couldn't live with you, Stanley, even if I managed to forget what you've done. You see, I can't stand you near me. Not now. Not any more. After what I found out last night, you make me feel sick just being in the same room with me. You're really wicked, you're evil. No, please don't come near me.' She moved away as he came towards her and he could see that she was trembling. 'Mother always wanted me to leave you and now I'm going to. Funny, isn't it? It was what she wanted and now she's getting what she wanted but not until after she's dead. I suppose you could say she's won at last.'

Stanley's head was splitting. 'Don't be so stupid,' he said.

'You've always thought me stupid, haven't you? I know I'm not brainy, but I can read, and once I read somewhere that people mustn't be allowed to profit from their crimes. I can't think of anything worse than letting you have any of Mother's money when it was you that killed her. So I'm sorry, I didn't mean to lead you on and then let you down. Up till this morning I meant the money to be yours as much as mine, more yours than mine if you wanted it. But I've hardened myself now.' Vera closed the lid of one of the suitcases and looked at him. 'Mother left it to me and I'm keeping it.'

'You can't!' Stanley shouted, one triumph left to him. 'You can't keep it. That bank account's a joint account. I can draw the lot out tomorrow if I like and, by God, I will!'

Vera said quietly, 'I didn't pay it into the joint account. That account was more or less closed, anyway, thanks to you overdrawing on it. I opened a new one this morning, a private account for me only.'

21

Vera picked up the cases and carried them downstairs.

Stanley remained sitting on the bed, the hot sun striking the back of his neck through the closed windows. Again he was aware of a sense of unreality, of nightmare. Nightmare. He said the word over and over to himself. Nightmare,

nightmare, nightmare . . . 'Nasty dream of nocturnal charger?' Christ, not that again!

His left eye had begun opening and shutting involuntarily, tic, tic, tic. Stanley swore and clenched his hands. He listened. She was moving about downstairs. She hadn't gone yet. He'd have to talk to her, make her see reason.

She was standing in front of the dining room mirror, applying lipstick.

It is hard to say nice things to someone you hate. Stanley hated Vera at that moment far more than he had ever hated Maud. But the things had to be said. Most men will say anything for twenty-two thousand pounds.

'You've been the only woman in my life, Vee. Twenty years I've been devoted to you. I've taken everything for your sake, your parents insulting me and then your mother moving in here. I'm a middle-aged man now. I'll go to pieces without you.'

'No, you won't. You've always been in pieces. Having me here never made you pull yourself together yet. God knows, I tried, and now I'm sick of trying.'

He began to plead. He would have gone down on his knees but he was afraid she'd walk away and leave him there on all-fours like an animal. 'Vee,' he said, pulling at her sleeve, 'Vee, you know I'm making a go of this business, but I have to have a bit of capital.' It was the wrong thing to say. He could tell that from the look on her face, the contempt. Like a really distraught loving husband, he moaned at her, 'Vee, you're all I've got in the world.'

'Let's call a spade a spade,' said Vera. 'My money's all you've got in the world.' She pulled on a pair of navy-blue gloves and sat down on an upright chair as if she were waiting for something or someone. 'I've thought about that,' she said. 'I've thought and thought about it all. And I've decided it wouldn't be right to leave you without anything.' She gave a heavy sigh. 'You're so hopeless, Stan. Everything you touch turns out a mess except crossword puzzles. You've never held a job down yet and you on't hold this one. But I wouldn't like to think of you penniless and without a roof over your head, so I'm going to let you have this house. You can keep it or sell it, do what you like. If you're silly enough to sell it and hand the money over to that Pilbeam – well, that's your business.'

'Christ,' said Stanley, 'thanks for bloody nothing.' She was going to give him this house! She was taking everything that was his and leaving him this end-of-a-terrace slum. And suddenly what she was doing and that she meant it came fully home to him. Vee, his wife, the one person he was sure he could keep under his thumb and manipulate and get round and persuade that black was white, Vee was selling him down the river. He said wildly, 'You don't think I'm going to let you get away with it, do you? Let you go just like that?'

'You haven't got much choice,' Vera said quietly, and suddenly there was a sharp knock on the door. 'That'll be the driver of the car I've hired.'

She bent down to pick up her cases. Stupefied, Stanley would have liked to kill her. As she lifted her face, he struck her hard with the flat of his hand, first on one cheek, then the other. She made a whimpering sound and tears began to flow over the marks his hand had made but she didn't speak to him again.

After the car had gone he wept too. He walked about the room, crying, and then he sat down and pounded the sofa arm with his fists. He wanted to scream and break things but he was afraid the neighbours would hear him.

Crying had exacerbated the twitch in his left eye. It continued to water and pulsate after he had stopped crying. He tried holding the lid still in two fingers but it went on moving in spite of this as if it wasn't part of his body at all but a trapped fluttering insect with a life of its own.

He had lost the money. *He had lost it, all of it.* And now, his face working terrifyingly and uncontrollably, he realized amid the turmoil of his thoughts that for almost the whole of his adult life the acquiring of that money had been his goal, its possession the dawning of a golden age. At first he had thought of it in terms of only a thousand or two, then eight or nine, finally twenty with a bonus of two added. But always it had been there, a half-concealed yet shimmering crock at the end of a rainbow. To possess it he had stayed with Vera, put up with Maud and, he told himself, never bothered to carve out a career. He had wasted his life.

He thought of it all but not calmly and panic kept returning by fits and starts, making him catch his breath in loud rasping gasps. At last he knew the true meaning of living in the present. Everything behind him was waste and bitterness while ahead there was nothing. Worse than nothing, for now that Vera knew of his attempt on Maud's life and the police had somehow been alerted, now that Pilbeam would have to know that all his vaunted capital amounted to just the roof over his head, how could he even contemplate the passing of another hour, another minute?

He stared at the clock, watching, though not of course actually seeing, the hands move. That was what his life had been, a slow, indiscernible disintegration towards the present utter collapse. And each moment, apparently leaving the situation unchanged, was in reality leading him inexorably towards the end, something which, though inconceivable, must be even worse than the present horror.

A little death would make the unbearable present pass. With jumping, twitching hand he felt in his pocket. Eight pounds remained out of the ten he had brought home on Friday. The pubs wouldn't yet be open but the wine shop in the High Street would. He staggered into the kitchen and rinsed his face at the sink.

Outside it was even hotter than indoors but the feel of fresh air made him flinch. Walking was difficult. He moved like an old man or like one who had long been confined to bed after a bad illness. There were only a few people about and none of them took any notice of him and yet he felt that the streets were full of eyes, unseen spies watching his every movement. In the wine shop it was all he could do to find his voice. Speaking to another human being, an ordinary reasonably contented person, was grotesque. His voice came out high and weak and he couldn't keep his hands from his face, as if by continually wiping it, smoothing the muscles, he could still those convulsive movements.

The assistant, however, was accustomed to alcoholics. His own face was perfectly smooth and controlled as he took the five pounds from Stanley for two bottles of Teacher's and another pound for cigarettes.

Back at the house he drank a tumblerful of the whisky, but without enjoying it. Instead of making him feel euphoric, it merely deadened feeling. He took one of the bottles and a packet of cigarettes upstairs with him and lay on the bed, wishing in a blurred, fuddled way that it was winter and not nearly midsummer so that the dark might come early. Stanley found he didn't like the light. It was too revealing.

Words came unbidden into his mind and he lay on his back splitting them and anagrammatizing them and evolving clues. He found he was saying the words and the clues out loud, slurring them in a thick voice. But the twitch, temporarily, was gone. He went on talking to himself for some time, occasionally reaching for the bottle and then growing irritable because the drink was making him forget how to spell and lose the thread of words in black spirals which had begun to twist before his eyes.

A whole night of deep sleep, total oblivion, was what he needed, but instead he awoke at nine with a headache that was like an iron hand clamped above his eyebrows. It was still light.

The dream he had just had was still vividly with him. It hadn't been what one could call a nasty dream, not in the sense of being actually frightening or painful, and yet it belonged nevertheless in the category of the worst kind of dreams a human being can have. When we are unhappy we are not made more so by nightmares of that unhappiness; our misery is rather intensified when we dream of that happy time which preceded it and of people, now hateful or antagonistic, behaving towards us with their former affability.

Such had been Stanley's recent experience. He had dreamed he was back in the Old Village Shop distributing largesse to Pilbeam and had seen again Pilbeam's joy. Now, wide awake, he realized that four hours before, thinking he had reached the depths, he had underestimated his situation. Not only had he been robbed of his expectations and left penniless; he had also given his partner a cheque for a thousand pounds and another, to be handed to the decorator, for one hundred and seventy-five. Both those cheques would bounce, for the money was all Vera's, stashed away in a private account.

There seemed no reason to get up. He might as well lie there till lunchtime. Somewhere he could hear running water, or thought he could. The night had been so full of dreams, dream visions and dream sounds, that it was hard to sort out imagination from reality.

He had forgotten to wind the clock and its hands pointed to ten past six. It must be hours later than that. Pilbeam would wonder why he hadn't come in but Stanley was afraid to telephone Pilbeam.

His head was tender and throbbing all over. At the moment he wasn't twitching and he didn't dare think about it in case thinking started it up again. He lay staring at the ceiling and wondering whether there was any point in going down to fetch the *Telegraph*, when a sharp bang at the front door jolted him into sitting up and cursing. Immediately he thought of the police, then of Pilbeam. Could it be his partner, come already to say the cheques were no good?

He rolled out of bed and looked through the crack in the curtains, but from there he couldn't see under the porch canopy. Although there was no lorry in the street, it occurred to him that his visitor might be one of the builders. Whoever it was knocked again.

His mouth tasted foul. He slid his feet into his shoes and went downstairs without lacing them. Then he opened the door cautiously. His caller was Mrs Blackmore.

'I didn't get you out of bed, then?' Presumably she inferred this from the fact that he was still wearing his day clothes, although these were rumpled and creased. 'I just popped in to tell you the pipe from your tank's overflowing.'

'O.K. Thanks.' He didn't want to talk to her and began to close the door.

She was back on the path by now but she turned and said, 'I saw Mrs Manning go off yesterday.'

Stanley glowered at her.

'She looked proper upset, I thought. The tears was streaming down her face. Have you had another death in your family?'

'No, we haven't.'

'I thought you must have. I said to John, whatever's happened to upset Mrs Manning like that?'

He opened the door wider. 'If you must know she's left me, walked out on me. I slapped her face for her and that's why she'd turned on the waterworks.'

That wives sometimes leave their husbands and husbands strike their wives was no news to Mrs Blackmore. Speculating about such occurrences had for years formed the main subject of her garden fence chats, but no protagonist in one of these domestic dramas had ever before spoken to her of his role so baldly and with such barefaced effrontery. Rendered speechless, she stared at him.

'That,' said Stanley, 'will give you something to sharpen your fangs on when you get nattering with old Mother Macdonald.'

'*How dare you speak to me like that!*'

'Dare? Oh, I dare all right.' Savouring every luscious word, Stanley let fly at her a string of choice epithets, finishing with, 'Lazy, fat-arsed bitch!'

'We'll see,' said Mrs Blackmore, 'what my husband has to say about this. He's years younger than you, you creep, and hasn't ruined his health boozing. Ugh, I can smell it on your breath from here.'

'You would, the length of your nose,' said Stanley and he banged the door so hard that a piece of plaster fell off the ceiling. The battle had done him good. He hadn't had a real ding-dong like that with anyone since Maud died.

Maud . . . Better not think about her or he'd be back on the bottle. He wouldn't, he'd never think of her again unless – unless the police made him. His eye was still twitching but he was getting used to it, 'adapting' himself, as some quack of Moxley's ilk would put it. One thing, the police hadn't come yet. Would they search the house before they started on the garden? Stanley decided that probably they would. Not that there was anything for them to find, as Vera was sure to have taken that carton of Shu-go-Sub away with her. May as well check, though . . .

He went into the room where Vera had spent her last night in Lanchester Road. The carton with the little ink smear on the label was still beside the bed. Stanley could hardly believe his eyes. What a fool Vera was! Without that no one could prove a thing. The police wouldn't even get a warrant to dig up the garden.

Stanley took the cap off the carton and flushed the tablets down the lavatory. Then he ran the basin and the bath taps. Often this simple manoeuvre had the effect of freeing the jammed ballcock and making it rise as it should do as the water came in from the main. He listened. The outfall pipe had stopped overflowing.

The phone bell made him jump, but he didn't consider not answering it. Letting it ring and then wondering for hours afterwards who it had been would be far worse. He picked up the receiver. It was Pilbeam and Stanley swallowed hard, feeling cold again.

But Pilbeam didn't sound angry. 'Still under the weather old boy?' he asked.

'I feel rotten,' Stanley mumbled.

'Bit of a hypochondriac you are, me old love. You don't want to dwell on these things. Still, I'm easy. Take the rest of the week off, if you like. I'll pop round to see you sometime, shall I?'

'O.K.,' Stanley said. He didn't want Pilbeam popping round but there was nothing he could do about it.

Just the same, the call had put new heart into him, that and his discovery and the destruction of the tablets. Maybe those cheques wouldn't bounce. That man Frazer, the bank manager, was a good guy, a real gentleman. He mightn't like it but surely he'd pay up. What was a mere £1,175 to him? Probably that private account business was just a polite sop to silly women like Vera. He and she were still man and wife, after all; Frazer had seen them together and given them a cheque book each. Those two cheques would come in and Frazer wouldn't think twice about them. He'd pay up and then perhaps he'd write to Stanley and caution him not to be too free with writing cheques. Absurd, really, how low he'd let himself get yesterday. Panic and shock, he supposed. Very likely Vera would come back, asking for his forgiveness.

There was someone knocking at the door again. John Blackmore, come to do battle on his wife's behalf. The fool ought to know better, ought to thank his stars someone with more guts than he had had put his wife in her place at last.

Stanley had no intention of answering the door. He listened calmly to the repeated hammering on the knocker and then he watched Blackmore return to his own house. When he went downstairs again he found a scribbled note on the mat:

'You have got it coming to you using language like that to my wife. You came from a slum and are turning this street into one. Don't think you can get away with insulting women.

'J. Blackmore.'

This note made Stanley laugh quite a lot. Slum indeed! His father's cottage was no slum. He thought once more of the green East Anglian countryside, but no longer of going back there as a conquering hero. Go back, yes, but as the prodigal son, to home and peace and forgiving love . . .

Through the kitchen window he could see that water was again beginning to stream from the outfall pipe. It looked as if he would have to go up into the loft. Vera had always seen to things of this kind but Stanley had acquired, mostly from her accounts, a smattering of the basic principles of plumbing. He fetched the steps from where she had left them, mounted them and pushed up the trapdoor. It was dusty up there and pitch black. He went back for a torch.

This was the first time he had ever been in the loft and he was surprised to find it so big, so quiet and so dark. Vera had said you must stand on the crossbeams and not between them in case you put your foot through the plaster, and Stanley did this, encountering on his way to the tank, the skeleton of a dead bird lying in its own feathers. It must have come in under the eaves and been unable to find its way out. Stanley wondered how long it had been there and how long it took for newly dead flesh to rot away and leave only bones behind.

He lifted off the tarpaulin which covered the tank and plunged his arm into the water. The ball on the end of its hinged arm was some nine inches down. He raised it and heard the cocks close with a soft thump.

Having washed his hands in a dribble of water – he didn't want the ballcock to stick again – he fetched the paper and took it back to bed with him to do the crossword. As if he were a real invalid, he slept most of the day away and during the afternoon, dozing lightly, he several times thought he heard someone at the door. But he didn't go down to answer it and when he finally left the bedroom at half past six there was no one about and the builders' equipment hadn't been moved. By now he was light-headed with hunger so he ate some bread and jam. This place, he thought, is more like Victoria station in the rush hour than a private house. There was someone at the door again. Blackmore. He'd heard a car draw up. Adrenalin poured into Stanley's blood. If he wanted a fight he could have it. But first better make sure it was Blackmore.

Once more he stationed himself at the window, one eye to the division between the curtains. There was a car there all right but it wasn't Blackmore's old jalopy. Stanley waited, gazing down. The man retreated from the porch. He was tall and dark and in his middle thirties. Stanley didn't know him but he had seen him about, mostly going in and out of Croughton police station.

Christ, he thought, Vera hasn't wasted much time.

Stanley prayed the policeman would go back to his car but instead he made for the side entrance, going out of his watcher's line of vision. Quaking, Stanley crept into Maud's room. From there he watched the policeman walk slowly round the lawn. He by-passed the heather garden but stopped in front of the cement mixer. Then he walked round it, rather as a man may walk round an isolated statue in an exhibition, looking it up and down with a thoughtful and puzzled expression. Then he gave his attention to the cement sacks, one of which he kicked so that the paper ripped and a thin stream of grey dust trickled out.

Back in his own bedroom, Stanley stood as still as he could, which wasn't very still as his whole body was twitching and quivering with fear. It was a job to bring the front garden into focus, particularly as his eyelids weren't under control. At last he got a blurred image of the policeman going back to his car. But instead of getting into it, he unlatched the Blackmores' gate and walked up their path.

Stanley had reached a stage of fear when no stimulant could help him. If he drank whisky he knew he would throw it up. His thoughts raced incoherently. The Blackmores would pass on everything they knew of his relations with Maud. Mrs Macdonald would tell of finding him prone on the earth after filling in the trench he'd prepared in advance. Flushing away those tablets wouldn't help him, for there had been at least one other carton, now no doubt handed over to the police by Vera. That would be enough for them to get a warrant and dig and find Maud, bones maybe among her outer coverings like the bird in the loft.

The loft! He could hide in the loft. It wouldn't matter

then if they broke down the doors to get in. He'd be safe up there. The steps were still where he had left them under the trapdoor. Cigarettes in one pocket, bottle in the other, he went up the steps and hoisted himself on to a beam. Then, looking down, he knew it wouldn't work. Even if he closed the trap, they'd see the steps.

Unless he could pull the steps up after him.

Stanley lay down flat, bracing his feet against the galvanized wall of the tank. At first, when he grasped the steps, he thought he'd never do it, but he thought of the policeman and renewed fear brought strength. Dragging them straight up was no use. He'd have to use a sort of lever principle. Who was it said, 'Give me something to stand on and a long enough pole and I will move the earth?' Well, he was only trying to move a pair of steps. Use the edge of the trap as a fulcrum, ease them slowly towards him, then pull them down to rest on the joists. Careful . . . Mustn't make a mark on the plaster. He felt as if his lungs would burst and he grunted thickly. But it was done.

When he was shut in he kept his torch on for a while but he didn't need light and he found he could listen better in the dark. With the extinction of light he felt something that was almost peace. There was no sound but a tiny lapping in the tank.

Sitting there in the dark, he felt the twitches beginning again like spirit fingers plucking at his eyelids, his knee, and delicately, with the gentleness of a caress, across the skin of his belly. Stanley found that he was crying. He only knew it because the fingers holding his cigarette encountered tears.

He wiped them away on his sleeve and then, although he couldn't see them, he spoke silently the name of every object in the loft: joist, beams, bottle, matches, stepladder, storage tank. Clues formed themselves expertly. 'Storage tank', eleven letters, seven and four. 'It holds water but rots up with age on the armoured vehicle.' 'Stepladder': 'Snake spelt wrong at first for a means of climbing.'

Oh God, he thought, he must be going mad, sitting in the dark in a loft, setting clues for puzzles that would never be solved, and he rested his cheek against the cold metal in despair.

PART FOUR
Last Word

22

When Stanley came down from the loft the whole neighbourhood was asleep, not a light showing anywhere. He rolled into his unmade bed, certain he wouldn't sleep, but he did and very heavily until past nine in the morning. Fumbling his way downstairs, still in his soiled and sweaty clothes, he found a letter on the front doormat.

It was from Vera and headed with the address of that boarding house at Brayminster.

'Stanley,

'After what you did you will probably think I have changed my mind about the house. Don't worry, you can still have it. I promise you can and I am putting it in writing as I don't suppose you would take my word. I am staying here until I find somewhere else to live. Please don't try to find me. I have been told I could ask for police protection if you did and then get a court order. I never want to see you again.

'Vera.'

Cursing, Stanley screwed it up. It more or less proved she'd been to the police, the bitch. Who else would have told her about getting court orders? Better keep the letter, though. Carefully he smoothed out the creases. Once he got out of this mess, he'd sell the house all right. Get four thousand for it and put the lot in the business. Maybe in the long run he'd make as much money that way as if he'd had Maud's money and when he did he'd take care Vera got to know about it.

After another meal of bread and jam, he had a bath and put on clean clothes, and, as he had foreseen, the pipe started overflowing again. By this time he had become an expert in getting quickly in and out of the loft and he could manage it without getting too dirty. Stanley passed a reasonably serene day, lying on the sofa, gently sipping whisky and drawing, on the plain side of a sheet of wallpaper, an enormous crossword, eighteen inches square.

Pilbeam came round about eight. Having first checked that this wasn't another representative of the law, set on his trail by Vera, Stanley let his friend in. Together they finished the whisky.

'You look a bit rough, old man.' Pilbeam studied him with the disinterested and unsympathetic curiosity of a biologist looking at a liver fluke through a microscope. 'You've lost weight. That must be trying, that eye.'

'The doctor,' Stanley said, 'says it'll just pass off.'

'Or you'll pass on, eh?' Pilbeam laughed uproariously at his joke. 'Not before we've made our packet, I trust.'

Stanley thought quickly. 'Would you have any objection if I took a bit of time off? I'm thinking of going away, maybe down to the South Coast to join my wife.'

'Why not?' said Pilbeam. 'I may go away myself. We can close the shop for a week or two. One way of whetting our customers' appetites. Well, I must be on my way. All right if I have twenty of your classy fags off you? I haven't got a bean on me but we're more or less one flesh, aren't we, like it says in the marriage service?'

Pilbeam laughed loudly all the way up the path.

The cheque was all right, then. He'd given it to Pilbeam on Monday and today it was Thursday, so it must be all right. And in the morning he would go away. Not to Vera but to his mother and father. I'm going home, Stanley thought. Even if I have to hitch all the way, even if I arrive penniless on the doorstep, I'm going home. But he cried himself to sleep, weeping weakly into the dirty pillow.

Early on Friday morning, when Vera was told that she was urgently needed at Croughton police station, she went to catch the first train, but Mrs Horton had alerted James and he was waiting for her in his car. They reached Croughton by ten-thirty.

Pilbeam had already been with the police for two hours by then.

She passed him coming out as she was taken into the superintendent's office but neither knew the other. There were a great many people coming and going whom Vera didn't know but who she suspected were connected with the case against her husband. She avoided Mrs Blackmore's sharp eye and the curious fascinated gaze of young Michael Macdonald. The superintendent questioned her closely for an hour before he let her go back to James and weep in his arms.

Stanley awoke with a splitting headache. Another hot day. Still, better to stand by the roadside in sweltering heat than pouring rain. His reflection in the mirror showed him a seedy, nearly elderly man with a pronounced and very apparent tic. Maybe his appearance would arouse pity in the heart of those arrogant bastards of motorists from whom he hoped to cadge lifts.

He bundled up a spare pair of trousers and the two clean shirts he had left and stuffed them into a suitcase. It was nearly noon. God, how deeply he slept these days! He was sitting on the bed, combing his hair, when he heard a car draw up. Blackmore home for lunch. Without getting up, he shifted along the bed and put his eye to the crack between the curtains.

All the blood receded from the muscles of his face. He crushed the comb in his hands and a bunch of teeth came off into his palm. A police car was parked outside. As well as the man who had been there before, there were three others. One of them opened the boot and took out a couple of spades. The others marched up the path towards his front door.

Stanley climbed up the steps, clutching his suitcase. At the moment his hand touched the trapdoor he heard his callers hammer on the front door. He gave a violent shiver. Almost as soon as the hammering stopped the doorbell rang. Someone was keeping his finger on the button. Stanley clambered through the square aperture, lay across the joists and hauled on the steps. Afterwards he didn't know how he'd managed to lever the steps up without dropping them to ricochet over the banisters, or how he had lifted them at all, his whole body was jumping so violently. But he did lift them and, almost by a miracle, succeeded in laying them soundlessly down beside him. He wiped his hands on his trousers to avoid making marks on the outer surface of the door, and then he dropped it into its frame.

When it was done he rolled on to his back and lay in the dark, murmuring over and over, 'Oh, Christ, Christ, Christ . . .'

Stanley pressed his ear to a very thin crack, more a join than a crack, between the boards of the door and listened. Yes, he could hear something now, the sound of someone forcing open the back door. He heard the lock give and the footsteps in the kitchen. How much of his movements could they hear? Would even the most minute shifting on the old joists send a great reverberation to those on the ground floor?

They were coming up the stairs.

The wood creaked under his ear and then someone spoke.

'I reckon he's gone, Ted. Pilbeam said he'd do a bunk and Pilbeam wouldn't lie to us. We've got too much on him.'

Judas, thought Stanley, bloody double-crossing Judas, with his 'me old love' and his Stan this and Stan that. Footsteps moved across the landing. Into the bathroom, Stanley thought.

Ted's voice said: 'They've started digging, sir. There's quite a crowd in the Macdonalds' garden. Shall I put up screens?'

'They'd have to be sky-hooks, wouldn't they?'

They stopped talking and Stanley heard 'Sir' – an inspector? A chief inspector? A superintendent? – moving about in the bedrooms. Ted went downstairs.

So they knew now. Stanley held his body as still as he could, clenching his hands. They knew. Vera had told them and Blake had put his spoke in and somehow or other Moxley had supported them. In a minute they would scrape away the peat and find Maud's body.

No one would hear him now if he struck a match. They weren't looking for him, anyway, they said so, but searching the house for evidence of how he had killed Maud. Without getting up, he felt for the box, took out a match and struck it in front of his face. The flame sent strange long shadows like clasping and unclasping fingers rippling across the beams and up into the roof. He looked at his watch. He thought that hours and hours had passed but it was only twelve-thirty. Would they go away when they had found what they had come to find, or would they leave a man in the house? He could do nothing about it but continue to lie between the joists, walled in by wood as if he were already in his own coffin.

Stanley had no idea how much time passed before 'Sir' and his assistants returned to the landing. Again it seemed like many hours. His limbs ached and every few seconds sharp burning pains stabbed his knees, his shoulders and the joints of his arms. He wanted to scream and scream to let the fear out of him, for he was like a man possessed of a devil which could only be released in a scream. He clasped his hand over his mouth to stop the screaming devil leaving him and tearing down through the floor to those below.

Someone slammed the back door.

Feet, many feet, tramping up the stairs, sent vibrations through his body. There was about eight feet, he thought, between the landing floor and the ceiling and he was perhaps a foot above the ceiling. That meant 'Sir's' head might be only three feet away from his. He pressed his mouth against raw splintery wood to muffle his ragged gasping breath.

'Thirteen quid in pound notes, sir,' someone said. 'They were between the pages of this annual.'

For a second the words were meaningless. They were nothing like those he had expected. Why didn't they speak of Maud? Maud, Maud, he mouthed into the wood. She must be lying down there now amid the ruins of his garden, bones in her own feathers.

'Sir's' voice broke up the fantasy and Stanley felt his body stiffen. 'They smell of violets like the inside of that handbag.'

'And the thirty Harry Pilbeam handed over to us, sir.'

'Yes. I never thought I'd say thank God for Harry Pilbeam. But he knows which side his bread is buttered, that lad. Shop his own wife for a quid if she hadn't divorced him ten years back. When I told him we were on to his little game, faking antiques and selling them for the genuine article, he couldn't wait to get back in good with us by passing over the carriage clock and that piece of china.'

Someone laughed.

'I must say it's given me some satisfaction to know that he conned Manning properly. The moron's actually handed Pilbeam – Pilbeam, I ask you! – nearly two thousand quid all told. God knows where he got it from.'

'What had Pilbeam in mind, d'you know?'

'Bleed him for as much as he could get and then do a bunk's my guess.'

Silence fell. Stanley lay as still as a corpse, letting the words flow and pass over him. He didn't understand. What were they doing there? What were they hoping for? They had dug but they hadn't found Maud. Why not? A tiny thrill of hope touched him. Was it possible that they hadn't been looking for Maud at all but for stolen goods, something that Pilbeam had put them on to?

From a long way away a voice came. Unidentifiable, the words a jumble of sound. They were in Maud's room now, now moving back to the landing. The muzzy sound cleared into distinguishable words like a picture coming into focus.

'That'll have been the mother-in-law's room, Ted.'

'What's happened to her, then? Gone off with the wife?'

'No, no. The old woman's dead. Died of a stroke round about the time Manning . . .'

Again the voices swam away into a jumble and the footfalls receded. Stanley had been holding his breath. Now he let it out carefully. His heart was hammering. It was true, they hadn't found Maud. They hadn't found anything but a handful of pound notes. He was hiding in vain. They only wanted to question him about Pilbeam. And he'd tell them, everything they wanted to hear and more besides. An eye for an eye . . . Revenge on Pilbeam would be sweet indeed. They had nothing on him, nothing. By a miracle they had guessed nothing, found nothing, and they thought Maud had died a natural death.

He moved his right hand and brought it in silence across to the handle on the inside of the trapdoor. The cramped fingers closed over the handle and then Stanley hesitated. If he came down now they'd think he had something to hide. Better let them go, let them leave the house, then come down and tell them what they wanted of his own volition. 'Sir' and his assistants were directly underneath him again now and someone was descending the stairs. They were leaving. Once more Stanley held his breath.

More than anything in the world now he wanted one of them to speak the words that would tell him he was free, cleared of any suspicion, just a fool who had allowed himself to be taken for a ride by a con man. The briefest sentence would do it. 'We only need Manning for a witness' or

'I reckon Manning's paid enough already for trusting Pilbeam.' They must say it. He could almost hear them saying it.

The footsteps went down the stairs.

Ted said, 'I suppose we'll have to get Mrs Huntley for the identification, sir,' and 'Sir' said softly and slowly, 'There's not much doubt, though, that this is the body of Miss Ethel Carpenter.'

23

'You poor dear,' said Mrs Huntley. In the police station waiting room she moved her chair closer to Vera's and touched her hand. 'It's far worse for you than any of us.'

'At least I didn't have to identify her. That must have been awful.'

Mrs Huntley shuddered. 'But for the little ring, I wouldn't have known her. She'd been in the ground for . . . Oh, I can't bear to speak of it.'

'He – my own husband – he killed her for fifty pounds. They found the wound on her head where he struck her. If there's any comfort for me at all, it's that Mother never knew. I'll tell you something I won't ever tell anyone else . . .' Vera paused, thinking that there was one other person she might tell, one person to whom in time she might tell everything. 'I thought,' she said softly, 'I thought he'd killed Mother for her money, but now I know that was wrong. There's a mystery there that'll never be cleared up. You see, if he'd killed Mother, he wouldn't have needed that fifty pounds. Thank God Mother never knew anything about it.'

'There were a good many things poor Mrs Kinaway never knew,' said Mrs Huntley thoughtfully. 'Like who was the father of Miss Carpenter's child. She told me one day when she was feeling low. You know now, don't you?'

'I guessed. I guessed as soon as I saw that girl this morning. She must be my niece. If Mother had ever met that girl, and she would have if . . .' Vera half-rose as Caroline Snow came into the room. In spite of the shock of it all and the horror, she smiled, gazing at the face which might have been her own twenty years ago.

'This is my father,' said Caroline Snow. 'He helped me. He went to the police when we couldn't find her. Daddy is absolutely marvellous. He promised that when we found her she could come and live with us, but we didn't find her. Well, not until . . .'

The man's eyes met Vera's. He looked kind, patient, capable of great endurance. He was her brother-in-law. She had a whole family now.

'I'm sorry, I'm sorry,' was all she could say.

'It wasn't your fault.' His blue eyes flashed. 'Mrs Manning, you're all alone. Come and stay with us. Please say you will.'

'One day I'd like to,' said Vera. 'One day when this is all past and gone.' And meet my sister, she thought. 'But I have somewhere to go to, somewhere and someone.'

The police wouldn't let her go yet. They questioned her and questioned her as to where Stanley might be but Vera couldn't help them. She could only shake her head helplessly. There were so many people in the police station, so many faces, Mrs Paterson, Mrs Macdonald and her son, an important key witness, Mrs Blackmore, the man who delivered peat, and they all reminded her of that old unhappy life in Lanchester Road. She wanted only one person and at last they let her go out to the car where he was waiting for her.

'One day,' he said, echoing her own words, 'when this is all past and gone, you'll get a divorce and . . .'

'Oh, James, you know I will. It's what I want more than anything in the world.'

Stanley stayed in the loft until his watch told him it was ten o'clock. He used his last match to see the time, but it was pain rather than the loss of light that drove him down. His body ached intolerably in every joint and he would have come down in any circumstances, even if, he told himself, the house had still been full of policemen.

Very clearly now he saw the trap he had made for himself. He had murdered no one but the body he had hidden had died by violence; by burying Ethel's cases and Ethel's ring with it, by using Ethel's money, he had irrevocably branded himself as a killer and a thief. There was his record too, the record which showed he was capable of such an act. No use now to ask for an examination of the real body of Ethel. By his own desire that body was reduced to ashes, a fine soft powder, delicate and evanescent, far more elusive of analysis than the cobwebby dust which now clung to his clothes and his skin.

Standing on the landing in the shadowy gloom of the summer night, Stanley tried to brush this dust off his clothes until the air was filled with soot-smelling clouds. He wanted to cleanse himself of it entirely, for he felt that it was Ethel who clung to him, enveloping him in ashy vapour. For months Maud had haunted him, appearing in dreams, but Maud was gone now for ever. He seemed to feel Ethel standing beside him as she had stood on the day of her death, listening to Maud's snores, about to admonish him as she was admonishing him now. He shivered and whimpered in the dusk, brushing Ethel off him, wiping her off his face with shaking hands.

His own body had a smell of death about it. Afraid to use water and set the pipe overflowing again, he made his way down the stairs. His limbs were gradually losing their stiffness and their pain. Life was returning to them and with it fear. He had to get away.

The house was full of creaks and whispers. In the dark Stanley bumped into furniture, knocking the telephone off its hook so that it buzzed at him and made him whimper abuse at it. Ethel was in here too, the very essence of Ethel, waiting quietly for him on the mantelpiece. The room was full of greenish sickly light from the single street lamp outside. He took hold of the urn in fingers which shook and twitched and threw it on the floor so that grey powdery Ethel streamed across the carpet. And then he had to go, run, escape, leave the house and Ethel in possession of it.

Nobody followed him. No one had been waiting for him. He ran, his heart pounding, until he was far from Lanchester Road, across the High Street and into the hinterland of winding, criss-crossing roads where everyone went to bed early and nearly all the lights were out. Then he had to stop running, stand and hold his aching chest until he could breathe normally again.

Just to be out of that house, to be free of it and not pursued, brought him a tiny shred of something like hope. If he could get hold of some money and some means of transport . . . Then he could go home to Bures and his river. They wouldn't look for him there because Vera would tell them how he didn't get on with his parents and had run away and never wrote. He leant against a wall, bracing himself, trying to get his thoughts into some sort of coherent order, trying to make his brain work realistically, calmly. I'm going home, he said, going home, and then, shuffling at first, then moving faster, he turned his steps in the direction of the Old Village.

The shop was in utter darkness. Steadier and saner now that he was doing something purposeful, Stanley made his way round the back, checked that the van was there and unlocked the back door. Thank God, he said to himself, he always carried the shop key and the van key in his jacket pocket. In his absence, Pilbeam had got rid of nearly all their stock and, apart from a few hideous and probably unsaleable pieces, the place was empty. Pale light from a metal-bracketed antique street lamp filtered waterily across a huge mahogany table and lay in pools on the floor.

A couple of cars passed in the street and one stopped outside, but it wasn't a police car. Stanley looked at it vaguely across the shadows and the flowing citron-coloured light and then he opened the till. It contained twenty pounds in notes and just short of another five in silver. He was transferring them to his pocket when he heard footsteps coming round the back. There was nothing to hide behind but a pair of maroon velvet curtains Pilbeam called portières and which he had rigged up on one of the walls. For a moment Stanley's body refused to obey him, he was so frightened and so dreadfully weary of being frightened and hunted, but at last somehow he got behind the curtains and flattened himself against the wall.

The back door opened and he heard Pilbeam's voice.

'That's funny, me old love, I could have sworn I locked that door.'

'Did you leave anything in the till?'

'You must be half cut, Dave. That's what we've come for, isn't it? Should be near enough thirty quid.'

Stanley trembled. He couldn't see anything but he felt their presence in the room where he was. Who was Dave? The huge man Pilbeam had brought round with him to Lanchester Road? He heard the till open with a squeak like an untuned violin string. Pilbeam said, 'Christ, it's empty!'

'Manning,' said Dave.

'How could it be? They'll have him behind bars.'

Dave said, 'You think?' and ripped aside the lefthand portière. Leadenly, Stanley lifted his head and looked at them. 'Turn out your pockets,' Dave said sharply.

A little courage returned to Stanley. There is always a little left in reserve right up to the end.

'Why the hell should I?' he said in a thin high voice. 'I've a right to it after what he's had out of me.'

Dave's shadow was black and elongated, the shadow of a gorilla with pendulous hands. He didn't move.

Pilbeam said, 'Oh, no, Stan, old man. You haven't got a right to nothing. You never had nothing, did you? It's easy giving away what's not your own.'

Stanley edged behind the table. Nobody stopped him. 'What's that supposed to mean?' he said.

'Cheques that bounce, Stan, that's what it means. I don't think you've ever been properly introduced to my friend, Dave. Let me do the honours. This is Stan, my partner, Dave old boy. Dave, Stan, is the – er – managing director of the firm that did some of our decorating.'

Stanley's mouth went dry. He cleared his throat but still he had no voice.

'What d'you expect me to do?' Dave said. 'Shake hands with him? Shake hands with that dirty little murderer?'

'You can shake hands with him in a minute,' said Pilbeam. 'I promise you you shall and I will too. First I'd like to tell my friend Stanley that both his cheques, mine and Dave's, came back yesterday marked Refer to Drawer. Now I might overlook a thing like that, old man, being as we're old mates, but Dave . . . Well, Dave's different. He doesn't like sweating his guts out and then being made a monkey of.'

Stanley's voice came out as a squeak, then grew more powerful. 'You shopped me,' he said. 'You bleeding copper's nark. You did dirt on me behind my back. Nothing but lies you've told me. You haven't got a wife, haven't had a wife for ten years. You . . .'

His voice faltered. Pilbeam was looking at him almost gently, his eyes mild, his mouth twitching at the corners. Even his voice was indulgent, kindly, when he said, 'Let's shake hands with him now, Dave, shall we?'

Stanley ducked, then overturned the table with a crash so that it made a barricade between him and the other two men. Dave kicked it, planting his foot in the centre of its glossy top. It skidded back until its legs struck the wall and Stanley was penned in a wooden cage.

They came for him, one on each side. Stanley thought of how he had fought with Maud, centuries, aeons ago. He felt behind him for a vase or something metal to throw but all the shelves had been emptied. He cringed, arms over his head. Dave pulled him out, holding him by a handful of his jacket.

When he was in the middle of the shop, Dave held him, locking his arms and, as he kicked and wriggled, Pilbeam caught him under the jaw with his fist. Stanley sobbed and kicked out. For that he got a kick on the shin from Dave, a kick which made him scream and stagger.

In wordless dance, the three men edged round the overturned table, Stanley hoping for a chance to grab its legs and send the heavy mass of wood toppling to crush Dave's feet. But he was limping and shafts of pain travelled from his shin up through his body. When he was back against the wall again he cringed back cunningly to make them think he was done for, and as Pilbeam advanced slowly upon him, Stanley twisted suddenly and grabbed the velvet portières. There was a scrunch of wood as the rail which held them came apart from the wall. Stanley hurled the heavy mass at his assailants and for a moment they were enveloped in velvet.

Right at the back of the shop now, within feet of the door, Stanley found a weapon, a nine-inch-long monkey wrench Pilbeam had left under the till counter. As Dave emerged, struggling and cursing, Stanley threw the wrench as hard as he could. It missed Dave's head and struck him in the chest, just beneath the collar bone. Dave howled with pain. He flung himself on Stanley as Stanley reached the door and was struggling with the handle.

For perhaps fifteen seconds the two men grappled

together. Dave was much taller than Stanley but he was impeded by the pain in his chest and even then Stanley might have got away but for the intervention of Pilbeam who, creeping along the floor, suddenly grabbed Stanley's legs from behind and threw him face downwards.

Dave picked him up, held him while Pilbeam pummelled his face and then, holding him by the shoulders, banged his head repetitively against the wall. Stanley's knees sagged and he dropped, groaning, into the pile of velvet.

When he came to he thought he had gone blind. One of his eyes refused to open at all, and with the other he could see only implacable blackness. He put his hand up to his face and it came away wet. With blood or with tears? He didn't know because he couldn't see. His fingers tasted salty.

Then gradually something took vague dark shape before him. It was the table, set up on its legs again. Stanley sobbed with relief because he wasn't blind. The place was so dark only because the street lamp had gone out.

The velvet he was lying on was soft and warm, a tender gentle nest like a woman's lap. He wanted to bury himself in it, wrap it round his tired body and all the hundred places that ached and throbbed. But he couldn't do that because he was going home. The green Stour was waiting for him, the fields that were silver with horse beans and emerald with sugar beet.

He sat up in the darkness. The place he was in seemed to be a sort of shop without any goods for sale. What was he doing there? Why had he come and where from? He couldn't remember. He knew only that he had passed through a time of great terror and pain and violence.

Had he always trembled and jumped like this, as if he had an incurable disease? It didn't matter much now. The beckoning of the river was more urgent than anything. He must get to the river and lie on its banks and wash away the tears and the blood.

Vaguely he thought that someone was after him but he didn't know who his pursuers were. Attendants in a hospital perhaps? He had run away from a hospital and fallen among thieves. When he stood up he rocked badly and walking was difficult. But he persevered, shuffling, his arms outstretched to fumble his way along by feel. Outside somewhere he thought there was a car and it was his car because he had an ignition key in his pocket. He found the car – in fact, he bumped into it – and opened the door with his key.

When he was sitting in the car he switched on the light and looked at his face in the mirror. It was black and bruised and there was dried blood on it. Over his left eye was a cut and under the cut the eye jerked open and shut.

'My name is George Carpenter,' he said to the stranger in the mirror, 'and I live at . . .' He couldn't remember where he lived. Then he tried to recall something – anything – out of the past, but all he could see was women's faces, angry and threatening, swimming up out of the darkness. Everything else had gone. No, not quite . . . His own identity, he hadn't lost that. His name was George Carpenter and he had been a setter of crossword puzzles, but he had become very ill and had had to give it up. The illness was in his brain or his nerves and that was why he twitched so much.

An unhappy life, a life of terrible frustration. The details of it had gone beyond recall. He didn't want to remember them. When he was a boy he had been happy, fishing in the river for Miller's Thumbs and loaches. The Miller's Thumbs had faces like coelacanths. They were fish left over from another age when there were no men in the world. Stanley found he liked to think of that time; it eased the pressure in his head.

Loach was a funny name. Useful if you were setting a puzzle and had to fit a word into L, blank, A, blank, H. 'Loach: For this fish the Chinese pronounces another.' He turned the ignition key and started the van.

Stanley had been driving for so long that by now he drove quite mechanically, as if the van were not something he had to operate but an extension of his own body. He had no more need to think about driving than he had to think about walking when he moved across a room. The streets he drove through seemed familiar but still he couldn't place them. On the bridge by the lock-keeper's house he stopped and looked down into the canal. He wasn't far from home, then, for here was the Stour, lying limpid between its green willows, his green river, cold and deep and rich with fish. It wasn't green now but black and ripple-free, a metallic gleam on its flat surface.

Soon the dawn would come and then the river would go

bright as if its green came, not from the awakening sky, but from some hidden inner source of colour. And people would appear from those black unlighted houses whose outlines he could just see cutting into the horizon and walk in the fields as the morning mist rose and spread and pearled the grass.

There was a white police car on the other side of the bridge, a stationary car with its headlights full on but trained away from him. A speed trap, he thought, although there were no cars but his to trap. They must be waiting for someone, some runaway villain they were hunting.

They would have no chance to trap him, for he wasn't going their way. He was going to take the tow path and drive slowly along it until the dawn came and then, when the river became a dazzling green, lie on the bank and bathe his hurt face in the water.

The surface of the path was hard and bumpy like ridged rock. Each time the van shuddered a spasm of fresh pain made him wince. Soon he would stop and rest. The dawn was coming up ahead of him, the black sky shredding apart to disclose the thin pale colour behind it. Bures and the Constable villages lay before him. He could see the shape of them now in a crenellated horizon.

Stanley switched off his lights, and in the distance he saw another car following him. They must be coming, he thought, to warn him off the river. Someone had fishing rights here and he'd be poaching. When had he ever cared for anyone else's rights?

They wouldn't be able to see him now his lights were off. He knew his river better than they did. Every bend in it, every willow on its banks was as familiar to him as a solved crossword.

Once he was home and safe he'd start doing crosswords again, bigger and better ones, he'd be the world's champion crossword puzzler. Even now, weak and trembling as he was, he could still make up puzzles. He found he had forgotten the words that made up his own name, but that didn't matter, not while he had his skill, his art. 'Undertake the fishing gear': 'Tackle'. 'Sport a leg in fruity surroundings': 'Fishing', 'Undertake . . .' Stanley shivered. There was some reason why he couldn't find a clue for that word, that ugly word which had dealings with death. He drove faster, the van's suspension groaning, but his mind was calmer, he was almost happy. Words were the meaning of existence, the panacea for all agony.

'Panacea': 'Cure is a utensil with a twisted card'. 'Agony': 'The non-Jew mixes with an atrocious pain'. He could do it as well as ever.

There was a bend ahead at this point. Very soon the bank veered to the left, following the river's meander, and when you could see his village, just a black blot it would be on the grey fields, you had to brake and turn to the nearside. 'Meander' – a beautiful word. 'I and a small hesitation combine to make the river twist.' Or, better perhaps, 'Dear men', (anag. seven letters) or how about 'Though mean and red, the river has a curve in it'?

Stanley's body ached and his eyes glazed with weariness. He was afraid he might fall asleep at the wheel, so he shook himself and forced his eyes to stare hard ahead. Then, suddenly, he saw his village. It was floating in a grey mist, peaceful, beckoning. Now, at this point, the river meandered.

'The winding river,' he heard himself whisper, anagrammatizing, 'is a dream need.' He groaned aloud with pain and longing and then he pulled the wheel feebly to follow the way the path should go.

The van slid and sagged, running out of control, but gradually and slowly. Stanley's hands slipped weakly from the wheel. It was all right now, he was home. No more running, no more driving. He was home, cruising gently downhill to where his village loomed in front of him.

And the dawn was coming, rising bright and green and many-coloured like a rainbow, pouring in through the van's open windows with a vast crunching roar. Stanley wondered why he was screaming, fighting against the wet dawn, when he was home at last.

The police car screeched to a halt on the canal bank. Two men got out, running, slamming doors behind them, but by the time they reached the shored-up edge the water was almost calm again with nothing to show where the van had gone down but dull yellow ripples spreading outwards in wide concentric rings. The dawn showed muddy red over the warehouses and the first few drops of rain began to fall.

MAKE DEATH LOVE ME

To David Blass with love

In writing this novel, I needed help on some aspects of banking and on firearms. By a lucky chance for me, John Ashard was able to advise me on both. I am very grateful to him.

R.R

1

Three thousand pounds lay on the desk in front of him. It was in thirty wads, mostly of fivers. He had taken it out of the safe when Joyce went off for lunch and spread it out to look at it, as he had been doing most days lately. He never took out more than three thousand, though there was twice that in the safe, because he had calculated that three thousand would be just the right sum to buy him one year's freedom.

With the kind of breathless excitement many people feel about sex – or so he supposed, he never had himself – he looked at the money and turned it over and handled it. Gently he handled it, and then roughly as if it belonged to him and he had lots more. He put two wads into each of his trouser pockets and walked up and down the little office. He got out his wallet with his own two pounds in it, and put in forty and folded it again and appreciated its new thickness. After that he counted out thirty-five pounds into an imaginary hand and mouthed, thirty-three, thirty-four, thirty-five, into an imaginary face, and knew he had gone too far in fantasy with that one as he felt himself blush.

For he didn't intend to steal the money. If three thousand pounds goes missing from a sub-branch in which there is only the clerk-in-charge (by courtesy, the manager) and a girl cashier, and the girl is there and the clerk isn't, the Anglian-Victoria Bank will not have far to look for the culprit. Loyalty to the bank didn't stop him taking it, but fear of being found out did. Anyway, he wasn't going to get away or be free, he knew that. He might be only thirty-eight, but his thirty-eight was somehow much older than other people's thirty-eights. It was too old for running away.

He always stopped the fantasy when he blushed. The rush of shame told him he had overstepped the bounds, and this always happened when he had got himself playing a part in some dumb show or even actually said aloud things like, That was the deposit, I'll send you the balance of five thousand, nine hundred in the morning. He stopped and thought what a state he had got himself into and how, with this absurd indulgence, he was even now breaking one of the bank's sacred rules. For he shouldn't be able to open the safe on his own, he shouldn't know Joyce's combination and she shouldn't know his. He felt guilty most of the time in Joyce's presence because she was as honest as the day, and had only told him the B List combination (he was on the A) when he glibly told her the rule was made to be broken and no one ever thought twice about breaking it.

He heard her let herself in by the back way, and he put the money in a drawer. Joyce wouldn't go to the safe because there was five hundred pounds in her till and few customers came into the Anglian-Victoria at Childon on a Wednesday afternoon. All twelve shops closed at one and didn't open again till nine-thirty in the morning.

Joyce called him Mr Groombridge instead of Alan. She did this because she was twenty and he was thirty-eight. The intention was not to show respect, which would never have occurred to her, but to make plain the enormous gulf of years which yawned between them. She was one of those people who see a positive achievement in being young, as if youth were a plum job which they have got hold of on their own initiative. But she was kind to her elders, in a tolerant way.

'It's lovely out, Mr Groombridge. It's like spring.'

'It is spring,' said Alan.

'You know what I mean.' Joyce always said that if anyone attempted to point out that she spoke in clichés. 'Shall I make you a coffee?'

'No thanks, Joyce. Better open the doors. It's just on two.'

The branch closed for lunch. There wasn't enough custom to warrant its staying open. Joyce unlocked the heavy oak outer door and the inner glass door, turned the sign which said *Till Closed* to the other side which said *Miss J. M. Culver*, and went back to Alan. From his office, with the door ajar, you could see anyone who came in. Joyce had very long legs and a very large bust, but otherwise was nothing special to look at. She perched on the edge of the desk and began telling Alan about the lunch she had just had with her boy friend in the Childon Arms, and what the boy friend had said and about not having enough money to get married on.

'We should have to go in with Mum, and it's not right, is it, two women in a kitchen? Their ways aren't our ways, you can't get away from the generation gap. How old were you when you got married, Mr Groombridge?'

He would have liked to say twenty-two or even twenty-four, but he couldn't because she knew Christopher was grown-up. And, God knew, he didn't want to make himself out older than he was. He told the truth, with shame. 'Eighteen.'

'Now I think that's too young for a man. It's one thing for a girl but the man ought to be older. There are responsibilities to be faced up to in marriage. A man isn't mature at eighteen.'

'Most men are never mature.'

'You know what I mean,' said Joyce. The outer door opened and she left him to his thoughts and the letter from Mrs Marjorie Perkins, asking for a hundred pounds to be transferred from her deposit to her current account.

Joyce knew everyone who banked with them by his or her name. She chatted pleasantly with Mr Butler and then with Mrs Surridge. Alan opened the drawer and looked at the three thousand pounds. He could easily live for a year on that. He could have a room of his own and make friends of his own and buy books and records and go to theatres and eat when he liked and stay up all night if he wanted to. For a year. And then? When he could hear Joyce talking to Mr Wolford, the Childon butcher, about inflation, and how he must notice the difference from when he was young – he was about thirty-five – he took the money into the little room between his office and the back door where the safe was. Both combinations, the one he ought to know and the one he oughtn't, were in his head. He spun the dials and the door opened and he put the money away, along with the other three thousand, the rest being in the tills.

There came to him, as always, a sense of loss. He couldn't have the money, of course, it would never be his, but he felt bereft when it was once again out of his hands.

He was like a lover whose girl has gone from his arms to her own bed. Presently Pam phoned. She always did about this time to ask him what time he would be home – he was invariably home at the same time – to collect the groceries or Jillian from school. Joyce thought it was lovely, his wife phoning him every day 'after all these years'.

A few more people came into the bank. Alan went out there and turned the sign over the other till to *Mr A. J. Groombridge* and took a cheque from someone he vaguely recognized called, according to the cheque, P. Richardson.

'How would you like the money?'

'Five green ones and three portraits of the Duke of Wellington,' said P. Richardson, a wag.

Alan smiled as he was expected to. He would have liked to hit him over the head with the calculating machine, and now he remembered that last time P. Richardson had been in he had replied to that question by asking for Deutschmarks.

No more shopkeepers today. They had all banked their takings and gone home. Joyce closed the doors at three-thirty, and the two of them balanced their tills and put the money back in the safe, and did all the other small meticulous tasks necessary for the honour and repute of the second smallest branch of the Anglian-Victoria in the British Isles. Joyce and he hung their coats in the cupboard in his office. Joyce put hers on and he put his on and Joyce put on more mascara, the only make-up she ever wore.

'The evenings are drawing out,' said Joyce.

He parked his car in a sort of courtyard, surrounded by Suffolk flint walls, at the bank's rear. It was a pretty place with winter jasmine showing in great blazes of yellow over the top of the walls, and the bank was pretty too, being housed in a slicked-up L-shaped Tudor cottage. His car was not particularly pretty since it was a G registration Morris Eleven Hundred with a broken wing mirror he couldn't afford to replace. He lived three miles away on a ten-year-old estate of houses, and the drive down country lanes took him only a few minutes.

The estate was called Fitton's Piece after a Marian Martyr who had been burnt in a field there in 1555. The Reverend Thomas Fitton would have been beatified if he had belonged to the other side, but all he got as an unremitting Protestant was fifty red boxes named after him. The houses in the four streets which composed the estate (Tudor Way, Martyr's Mead, Fitton Close and – the builder ran out of inspiration – Hillcrest) had pantiled roofs and large flat windows and chimneys that were for effect, not use. All their occupants had bought their trees and shrubs from the same very conservative garden centre in Stantwich and swapped cuttings and seedlings, so that everyone had Lawson's cypress and a laburnum and a kanzan, and most people a big clump of pampas grass. This gave the place a curious look of homogeneity and, because there were no boundary fences, as if the houses were not private homes but dwellings for the staff of some great demesne.

Alan had bought his house at the end of not very hilly Hillcrest on a mortgage granted by the bank. The interest on this loan was low and fixed, and when he thought about his life one of the few things he considered he had to be thankful for was that he paid two-and-a-half per cent and not eleven like other people.

His car had to remain on the drive because the garage, described as integral and taking up half the ground floor, had been converted into a bed-sit for Pam's father. Pam came out and took the groceries. She was a pretty woman of thirty-seven who had had a job for only one year of her life and had lived in a country village for the whole of it. She wore a lot of make-up on her lips and silvery-blue stuff on her eyes. Every couple of hours she would disappear to apply a fresh layer of lipstick because when she was a girl it had been the fashion always to have shiny pink lips. On a shelf in the kitchen she kept a hand mirror and lipstick and pressed powder and a pot of eyeshadow. Her hair was permed. She wore skirts which came exactly to her knees, and her engagement ring above her wedding ring, and usually a charm bracelet. She looked about forty-five.

She asked Alan if he had had a good day, and he said he had and what about her? She said, all right, and talked about the awful cost of living while she unpacked cornflakes and tins of soup. Pam usually talked about the cost of living for about a quarter of an hour after he got home. He went out into the garden to put off seeing his father-in-law for as long as possible, and looked at the snowdrops and the little red tulips which were exquisitely beautiful at this violet hour, and they gave him a strange little pain in his heart. He yearned after them, but for what? It was as if he were in love which he had never been. The trouble was that he had read too many books of a romantic or poetical nature, and often he wished he hadn't.

It got too cold to stay out there, so he went into the living room and sat down and read the paper. He didn't want to, but it was the sort of thing men did in the evenings. Sometimes he thought he had begotten his children because that also was the sort of thing men did in the evenings.

After a while his father-in-law came in from his bed-sit. His name was Wilfred Summitt, and Alan and Pam called him Pop, and Christopher and Jillian called him Grandpop. Alan hated him more than any human being he had ever known and hoped he would soon die, but this was unlikely as he was only sixty-six and very healthy.

Pop said, 'Good evening to you,' as if there were about fifteen other people there he didn't know well enough to address. Alan said hallo without looking up and Pop sat down. Presently Pop punched his fist into the back of the paper to make Alan lower it.

'You all right then, are you?' Like the Psalmist, Wilfred Summitt was given to parallelism, so he said the same thing twice more, slightly re-phrasing it each time. 'Doing OK, are you? Everything hunky-dory, is it?'

'Mmm,' said Alan, going back to the *Stantwich Evening Press*.

'That's good. That's what I like to hear. Anything in the paper, is there?'

Alan didn't say anything. Pop came very close and read the back page. Turning his fat body almost to right angles, he read the stop press. His sight was magnificent. He said he saw there had been another one of those bank robberies, another cashier murdered, and there would be more, mark his words, up and down the country, all over the place, see if he wasn't right, and all because they knew they could get away with it on account of knowing they wouldn't get hanged.

'It's getting like Chicago, it's getting like in America,' said Pop. 'I used to think working in a bank was a safe job, Pam used to think it was, but it's a different story now, isn't it? Makes me nervous you working in a bank, gets on my nerves. Something could happen to you any day, any old time you could get yourself shot like that chap in Glasgow, and then what's going to happen to Pam? That's what I think to myself, what's going to happen to Pam?'

Alan said his branch was much too small for bank robbers to bother with.

'That's a comfort, that's my one consolation. I say to myself when I get nervy, I say to myself, good thing he never got promotion, good thing he never got on in his job. Better safe than sorry is my motto, better a quiet life with your own folks than risking your neck for a big wage packet.'

Alan would have liked a drink. He knew, mainly from books and television, that quite a lot of people come home to a couple of drinks before their evening meal. Drinks the Groombridges had. In the sideboard was a full bottle of whisky, an almost full bottle of gin, and a very large full bottle of Bristol Cream sherry which Christopher had bought duty-free on the way back from a package tour to Switzerland. These drinks, however, were for other people. They were for those married couples whom the Groombridges invited in for an evening, one set at a time and roughly once a fortnight. He wondered what Pam and Pop would say if he got up and poured himself a huge whisky, which was what he would have liked to do. Wondering was pretty well as far as he ever got about anything.

Pam came in and said supper was ready. They sat down to eat it in a corner of the kitchen that was called the dining recess. They had liver and bacon and reconstituted potato and brussels sprouts and queen of puddings. Christopher came in when they were half-way through. He worked for an estate agent who paid him as much as the Anglian-Victoria paid his father, and he gave his mother five pounds a week for his board and lodging. Alan thought this was ridiculous because Christopher was always rolling in money, but when he protested to Pam she got hysterical and said it was wicked taking anything at all from one's children. Christopher had beautiful trendy suits for work and well-cut trendy denim for the weekends, and several nights a week he took the girl he said was his fiancée to a drinking club in Stantwich called the Agape, which its patrons pronounced Agayp.

Jillian didn't come in. Pam explained that she had stayed at school for the dramatic society and had gone back with Sharon for tea. This, Alan was certain, was not so. She was somewhere with a boy. He was an observant person and Pam was not, and from various things he had heard and noticed he knew that, though only fifteen, Jillian was not a virgin and hadn't been for some time. Of course he also knew that as a responsible parent he ought to discuss this with Pam and try to stop Jillian or just get her on the pill. He was sure she was promiscuous and that the whole thing ought not just to be ignored, but he couldn't discuss anything with Pam. She and Pop and Jillian had only two moods, apathy and anger. Pam would fly into a rage if he told her, and if he insisted, which he couldn't imagine doing, she would scream at Jillian and take her to a doctor to be examined for an intact hymen or pregnancy or venereal disease, or the lot for all he knew.

In spite of Christopher's arrant selfishness and bad manners, Alan liked him much better than he liked Jillian. Christopher was good-looking and successful and, besides that, he was his ally against Wilfred Summitt. If anyone could make Pop leave it would be Christopher. Having helped himself to liver, he started in on his grandfather with that savage and, in fact, indefensible teasing which he did defend on the grounds that it was 'all done in fun'.

'Been living it up today, have you, Grandpop? Been taking Mrs Rogers round the boozer? You'll get yourself talked about, you will. You know what they're like round here, yak-yak-yak all day long.' Pop was a teetotaller, and his acquaintance with Mrs Rogers extended to no more than having once chatted with her in the street about the political situation, an encounter witnessed by his grandson. 'She's got a husband, you know, and a copper at that,' said Christopher, all smiles. 'What are you going to say when he finds out you've been feeling her up behind the village hall? Officer, I had drink taken and the woman tempted me.'

'You want to wash your filthy mouth out with soap,' Pop shouted.

Christopher said sorrowfully, smiling no more, that it was a pity some people couldn't take a joke and he hoped he wouldn't lose his sense of humour no matter how old he got.

'Are you going to let your son insult me, Pamela?'

'I think that's quite enough, Chris,' said Pam.

Pam washed the dishes and Alan dried them. It was for some reason understood that neither Christopher nor Pop should ever wash or dry dishes. They were in the living room, watching a girl rock singer on television. The volume was turned up to its fullest extent because Wilfred Summitt was slightly deaf. He hated rock and indeed all music except Vera Lynn and ballads like 'Blue Room' and 'Tip-toe Through the Tulips', and he said the girl was an indecent trollop who wanted her behind smacked, but when the television was on he wanted to hear it just the same. He had a large colour set of his own, brand new, in his own room, but it was plain that tonight he intended to sit with them and watch theirs.

'The next programme's unsuitable for children, it says here,' said Christopher. 'Unsuitable for people in their first or second childhoods. You'd better go off beddy-byes, Grandpop.'

'I'm not demeaning myself to reply to you, pig. I'm not lowering myself.'

'Only my fun,' said Christopher.

When the film had begun Alan quietly opened his book. The only chance he got to read was while they were watching television because Pam and Pop said it was unsociable to read in company. The television was on every evening all the evening, so he got plenty of chances. The book was Yeats: *The Winding Stair and Other Poems*.

2

Jillian Groombridge hung around for nearly two hours outside an amusement arcade in Clacton, waiting for John Purford to turn up. When it got to eight and he hadn't come, she had to get the train back to Stantwich and then the Stoke Mill bus. John, who had a souped-up aged Singer, would have driven her home, and she was more annoyed at having to spend her pocket money on fares than at being stood up.

They had met only once before and that had been on the previous Sunday. Jillian had picked him up by a fruit machine. She got him starting to drive her back at nine because she had to be in by half-past ten, and this made him think there wouldn't be anything doing. He was wrong. Jillian being Jillian, there was plenty doing: the whole thing in fact on the back seat of the Singer down a quiet pitch-dark country lane. Afterwards he had been quite surprised and not a little discomfited to hear from her that she was the daughter of a bank manager and lived at Fitton's Piece. He said, for he was the son of a farm labourer, that she was a cut above him, and she said it was only a tin-pot little bank sub-branch, the Anglian-Victoria in Childon. They kept no more than seven thousand in the safe, and there was only her dad there and a girl, and they even closed for lunch, which would show him how tin-pot it was.

John had dropped her off at Stoke Mill at the point where Tudor Way debouched from the village street, and said maybe they could see each other again and how about Wednesday? But when he had left her and was on his way back to his parents' home outside Colchester, he began having second thoughts. She was pretty enough, but she was a bit too easy for his taste, and he doubted whether she was the seventeen she said she was. Very likely she was under the age of consent. That amused him, that term, because if anyone had done any consenting it was he. So when Tuesday came and his mother said, if he hadn't got anything planned for the next evening she and his father would like to go round to his Aunt Elsie's if he'd sit in with his little brother, aged eight, he said yes and saw it as a let-out.

On the morning of the day he was supposed to have his date with Jillian he drove a truckload of bookcases and record player tables up to London, and he was having a cup of tea and a sandwich in a café off the North Circular Road when Marty Foster came in. John hadn't seen Marty Foster since nine years ago when they had both left their Colchester primary school, and he wouldn't have known him under all that beard and fuzzy hair. But Marty knew him. He sat down at his table, and with him was a tall fair-haired guy Marty said was called Nigel.

'What's with you then,' said Marty, 'after all these years?'

John said how he had this friend who was a cabinet-maker and they had gone into business together and were doing nicely, thank you, mustn't grumble, better than they'd hoped, as a matter of fact. Hard work, though, it was all go, and he'd be glad of a break next week. This motoring mag he took was running a trip, chartering a plane and all, to Daytona for the International Motor-cycle Racing, with a sight-seeing tour to follow. Three weeks in sunny Florida wouldn't do him any harm, he reckoned, though it was a bit pricey.

'I should be so lucky,' said Marty, and it turned out he hadn't had a job for six months, and he and Nigel were living on the Social Security. 'If you can call it living,' said Marty, and Nigel said, 'There's no point in working, anyway. They take it all off you in tax and whatever. I guess those guys who did the bank in Glasgow got the right idea.'

'Right,' said Marty.

'No tax on that sort of bread,' said Nigel. 'No god-damned superann. and NHI.'

John shrugged. 'It wouldn't be worth going inside for,' he said. 'Those Glasgow blokes, they only got away with twenty thousand and there were four of them. Take that branch of the Anglian-Victoria in Childon – you know Childon, Marty – they don't keep any more than seven thou. in the safe there. If a couple of villains broke in there, they'd only get three-and-a-half apiece *and* they'd have to deal with the manager and the girl.'

'You seem to know a lot about it.'

He had impressed them, he knew, with his job and his comparative affluence. Now he couldn't resist impressing them further. 'I know the manager's daughter, we're pretty close, as a matter of fact. Jillian Groombridge, she's called, lives in one of those modern houses at Stoke Mill.'

Marty did look impressed, though Nigel didn't. Marty said, 'Pity banks don't close for lunch. You take a branch like that one, and Groombridge or the girl went off to eat, well, you'd be laughing then, it'd be in the bag.'

'Be your age,' said Nigel. 'If they left the doors open and the safe unlocked, you'd be laughing. If they said, Come in and welcome, your need is greater than ours, you'd be laughing. The point is, banks don't close for lunch.'

John couldn't help laughing himself. 'The Childon one does,' he said, and then he thought all this had gone far enough. Speculating about what might be, and if only, and if this happened and that and the other, was a sort of disease that kept people like Marty and Nigel where they were, while not doing it had got him where he was. Better find honest work, he thought, though he didn't, of course, say this aloud. Instead he got on to asking Marty about this one and that one they had been at school with, and told Marty what news he had of their old schoolfellows, until his second cup of tea was drunk up and it was time to start the drive back.

The hypothetical couple of villains John had referred to had been facing him across the table.

Marty Foster also was the son of an agricultural labourer. For a year after he left school he worked in a paintbrush factory. Then his mother left his father and went off with a lorry driver. Things got so uncomfortable at home that Marty too moved out and got a room in Stantwich. He got a job driving a van for a cut-price electrical goods shop and then a job trundling trolleys full of peat and pot plants about in a garden centre. It was the same one that supplied Fitton's Piece with its pampas grass. When he was sacked from that for telling a customer who complained because the garden centre wouldn't deliver horse manure, that if he wanted his shit he could fetch it himself, he moved up to London and into a squat in Kilburn Park. While employed in packing up parcels for an Oxford Street store, he met Nigel Thaxby. By then he was renting a room with a kitchen in a back street in Cricklewood, his aim being to stop working and go on the Social Security.

Nigel Thaxby, like Marty, was twenty-one. He was the son and only child of a doctor who was in general practice in Elstree. Nigel had been to a very minor public school because his father wanted him brought up as a gentleman but didn't want to pay high fees. The staff had third-class honours or pass degrees and generally no teachers' training certificates, and the classroom furniture was blackened and broken and, in fact, straight Dotheboys Hall. In spite of living from term to term on scrag-end stew and rotten potatoes and mushed peas and white bread, Nigel grew up tall and handsome. By the time excessive cramming and his father's threats and his mother's tears had squeezed him into the University of Kent, he was over six feet tall with blond hair and blue eyes and the features of Michelangelo's David. At Canterbury something snapped in Nigel. He did no work. He got it into his head that if he did do any work and eventually got a degree, the chances were he wouldn't get a job. And if he did get one all that would come out of it was a house like his parents' and a marriage like his parents' and a new car every four years and maybe a child to cram full of useless knowledge and pointless aspirations. So he walked out of the university before the authorities could ask his father to take him away.

Nigel came to London and lived in a sort of commune. The house had some years before been allocated by the Royal Borough of Kensington and Chelsea to a quartet of young people on the grounds that it was being used as a centre for group therapy. So it had been for some time, but the young people quarrelled with each other and split up, leaving behind various hangers-on who took the padding off the walls of the therapy room and gave up the vegetarian regime, and brought in boy friends and girl friends and sometimes children they had had by previous marriages or liaisons. There was continuous coming and going, people drifted in for a week or a month and out again, contributing to the rent or not, as the case might be. Nigel got in on it because he knew someone who lived there and who was also a reject of the University of Kent.

At first he wasn't well up in the workings of the Social Security system and he thought he had to have a job. So he also packed up parcels. Marty Foster put him wise to a lot of useful things, though Nigel knew he was cleverer than Marty. One of the things Marty put him wise to was that it was foolish to pack up parcels when one could get one's rent paid and a bit left over for doing nothing. At the time they met John Purford in Neasden, Marty was living in

Cricklewood and Nigel was sometimes living in Cricklewood with Marty and sometimes in the Kensington commune, and they were both vaguely and sporadically considering a life of crime.

'Like your friend said, it wouldn't be worth the hassle,' said Nigel. 'Not for seven grand.'

'Yeah, but look at it this way, you've got to begin on a small scale,' said Marty. 'It'd be a sort of way of learning. All we got to do is rip off a vehicle. I can do that easy. I got keys that'll fit any Ford Escort, you know that.'

Nigel thought about it.

'Can you get a shooter?' he said.

'I got one.' Marty enjoyed the expression of astonishment on Nigel's face. It was seldom that he could impress him. But he was shrewd enough to put prudence before vanity, and he said carefully, 'Even an expert wouldn't know the difference.'

'You mean it's not for real?'

'A gun's a gun, isn't it?' And Marty added with, for him, rare philosophical insight, 'It's not what it does, it's what people'll think it'll do that matters.'

Slowly Nigel nodded his head. 'It can't be bad. Look, if you're really into this, there's no grief in going up this Childon dump tomorrow and casing the joint.'

Nigel had a curious manner of speech. It was the result of careful study in an attempt to be different. His accent was mid-Atlantic, rather like that of a commercial radio announcer. People who didn't know any better sometimes took him for an American. He had rejected, when he remembered to do so, the cultured English of his youth and adopted speech patterns which were a mixture of the slang spoken by the superannuated hippies, now hopelessly out of date, in the commune, and catch phrases picked up from old films seen on TV. Nigel wasn't at all sophisticated really, though Marty thought he was. Marty's father talked Suffolk, but his mother had been a cockney. Mostly he talked cockney himself, with the flat vowels of East Anglia creeping in, and sometimes he had that distinctive Suffolk habit of using the demonstrative pronoun 'that' for 'it'.

Seeing that Marty was serious or 'really into' an attempt

on the Childon bank, Nigel went off to Elstree, making sure to choose a time when his father was in his surgery, and got a loan of twenty pounds off his mother. Mrs Thaxby cried and said he was breaking his parents' hearts, but he persuaded her into the belief that the money was for his train fare to Newcastle where he had a job in line. An hour later – it was Thursday and the last day of February – he and Marty caught the train to Stantwich and then the bus to Childon which got them there by noon.

They began their survey by walking along the lane at the back of the Anglian-Victoria sub-branch. They saw the gap in the flint walls that led to the little yard, and in the yard they saw Alan Groombridge's car. One one side of the yard was what looked like a disused barn and on the other a small apple orchard. Marty, on his own, walked round to the front. The nearest of the twelve shops was a good hundred yards away. Opposite the bank was a Methodist chapel and next to that nothing but fields. Marty went into the bank.

The girl at the till labelled Miss J. M. Culver was weighing coin into little plastic bags and chatting to the customer about what lovely weather they were having. The other till was opened and marked Mr A. J. Groombridge, and though there was no one behind it, Marty went and stood there, looking at the little office an open door disclosed. In that office a man was bending over the desk. Marty wondered where the safe was. Through that office, presumably, behind that other, closed, door. There was no upstairs. Once there had been, but the original ceiling had been removed and now the inside of the steeply sloping roof could be seen, painted white and with its beams exposed and stripped. Marty decided he had seen as much as he was likely to and was about to turn away, when the man in the office seemed at last to be aware of him. He straightened up, turned round, came out to the metal grille, and he did this without really looking at Marty at all. Nor did he look at him when he murmured a good morning, but kept his eyes on the counter top. Marty had to think of something to say so he asked for twenty five-pence pieces for a pound note, wanted them for parking meters, he said, and Groombridge counted them out, first pushing them across the counter in two stacks, then thinking better of this and slipping them into a little bag like the ones the girl had been using. Marty said thanks and took the bag of coins and left.

He was dying for a drink and tried to get Nigel to go with him into the Childon Arms. But Nigel wasn't having any.

'You can have a drink in Stantwich,' he said. 'We don't want all the locals giving us the once-over.'

So they hung about until five to one. Then Nigel went into the bank, timing his arrival for a minute to. A middle-aged woman came out and Nigel went in. The girl was alone. She looked at him and spoke to him quite politely but also indifferently, and Nigel was aware of a certain indignation, a resentment, at seeing no admiration register on her large plain face. He said he wanted to open an account, and the girl said the manager was just going out to lunch and would he call back at two?

She followed him to the door and locked it behind him. In the lane at the back he met Marty who was quite excited because he had seen Alan Groombridge come out of the back door of the bank and drive away in his car.

'I reckon they go out alternate days. That means the bird'll go out tomorrow and he'll go out Monday. We'll do the job on Monday.'

Nigel nodded, thinking of that girl all alone, of how easy it would be. There seemed nothing more to do. They caught the bus back to Stantwich where Marty spent the twenty five-pences on whisky and then set about wheedling some of Mrs Thaxby's loan out of Nigel.

3

Fiction had taught Alan Groombridge that there is such a thing as being in love. Some say that this, indirectly, is how everyone gets to know about it. Alan had read that it had been invented in the middle ages by someone called Chrétien de Troyes, and that this constituted a change in human nature.

He had never experienced it himself. And when he considered it, he didn't know anyone else who had either. Not any of those couples, the Heyshams and the Kitsons and the Maynards, who came in to drink the duty-free Bristol Cream. Not Wilfred Summitt or Constable Rogers or Mrs Surridge or P. Richardson. He knew that because he was sure that if it was a change in human nature their natures would have been changed by it. And they had not been. They were as dull as he and as unredeemed.

With Pam there had never been any question of being in love. She was the girl he took to a couple of dances in Stantwich, and one evening took more irrevocably in a field on the way home. It was the first time for both of them. It had been quite enjoyable, though nothing special, and he hadn't intended to repeat it. In that field Christopher was conceived. Everyone took it for granted he and Pam would marry before she began to 'show', and he had never thought to protest. He accepted it as his lot in life to marry Pam and have a child and keep at a steady job. Pam wanted an engagement ring, though they were never really engaged, so he bought her one with twenty-five pounds borrowed from his father.

Christopher was born, and four years later Pam said they ought to 'go in for' another baby. At that time Alan had not yet begun to notice words and what they mean and how they should be used and how badly most people use them, so he had not thought that phrase funny. When he was older and had read a lot, he looked back on that time and wondered what it would be like to be married to someone who knew it was funny too and to whom he could say it as a tender ribaldry; to whom he could say as he began to make love with that purpose in view, that now he was going in for a baby. If he had said it to Pam in those circumstances she would have slapped his face.

When they had two children they never went out in the evenings. They couldn't have afforded to even if they had known anyone who would baby-sit for nothing. Wilfred Summitt's wife was alive then, but both Mr and Mrs Summitt believed, like Joyce, that young married people should face up to their responsibilities, which meant never enjoying themselves and never leaving their children in the care of anyone else. Alan began to read. He had never read much before he was married because his father had said it was a waste of time in someone who was going to work with figures. In his mid-twenties he joined the public library in Stantwich and read every thriller and detective story and adventure book he could lay his hands on. In this way he lived vicariously quite happily. But around his thirtieth birthday something rather peculiar happened.

He read a thriller in which a piece of poetry was quoted. Until then he had despised poetry as above his head and something which people wrote and read to 'show off'. But he liked this poem, which was Shakespeare's sonnet about fortune and men's eyes, and lines from it kept going round and round in his head. The next time he went to the library he got Shakespeare's Sonnets out and he liked them, which made him read more poetry and, gradually, the greater novels that people call (for some unapparent reason) classics, and plays and more verse, and books that critics had written about books – and he was a lost man. For his wits were sharpened, his powers of perception heightened, and he became discontented with his lot. In this world there were other things apart from Pam and the children and the bank and the Heyshams and the Kitsons, and shopping on Saturdays and watching television and taking a caravan in the Isle of Wight for the summer holidays. Unless all these authors were liars, there was an inner life and an outer experience, an infinite number of things to be seen and done, and there was passion.

He had come late in life to the heady intoxication of literature and it had poisoned him for what he had.

It was adolescent to want to be in love, but he wanted to be. He wanted to live on his own too, and go and look at things and explore and discover and understand. All these things were equally impracticable for a married man with children and a father-in-law and a job in the Anglian-Victoria Bank. And to fall in love would be immoral, especially if he did anything about it. Besides, there was no one to fall in love with.

He imagined going round to the Heyshams' one Saturday morning and finding Wendy alone, and suddenly, although, like the people in the Somerset Maugham story, they had known and not much liked each other for years, they fell violently in love. They were stricken with love as Lancelot and Guinevere were for each other, or Tristram and Isolde. He had even considered Joyce for this role. How if she were to come into his office after they had closed, and he were to take her in his arms and . . . He knew he couldn't. Mostly he just imagined a girl, slender with long black hair, who made an appointment to see him about an overdraft. They exchanged one glance and immediately they both knew they were irrevocably bound to each other.

It would never happen to him. It didn't seem to happen to anyone much any more. Those magazines Pam read were full of articles telling women how to have orgasms and men how to make them have them, but never was there one telling people how to find and be in love.

Sometimes he felt that the possession of the three thousand pounds would enable him, among other things, to be in love. He took it out and handled it again on Thursday, resolving that that would be the last time. He would be firm about his obsession and about that other one too. After this week there would be no more reading of Yeats and Forster and Conrad, those seducers of a man's mind, but memoirs and biography as suitable to a practical working bank manager.

Alan Groombridge wondered about and thought and fantasized about a lot of odd and unexpected things. But, apart from playing with banknotes which didn't belong to him, he only did one thing that was unconventional.

The Anglian-Victoria had no objection to its Childon staff leaving the branch at lunchtime, providing all the money was in the safe and the doors locked. But, in fact, they were never both absent at the same time. Joyce stayed in on Mondays and Thursdays when her Stephen wasn't working in Childon and there was no one with whom to go to the Childon Arms. On those days she took sandwiches to the bank with her. Alan took sandwiches with him every day because he couldn't afford to eat out. But on Monday and Thursday lunchtimes he did leave the bank, though only Joyce knew of this and even she didn't know where he went. He drove off, and in winter ate his sandwiches in the car in a lay-by, in the spring and summer in a field. He did this to secure for himself two hours a week of peace and total solitude.

That Friday, 1 March, Joyce went as usual to the Childon Arms with Stephen for a ploughman's lunch and a half of lager, and Alan stuck to his resolve of not taking the three thousand pounds out of the safe. Friday was their busiest day and that helped to keep temptation at bay.

The weekend began with shopping in Stantwich. He went into the library where he got out the memoirs of a playwright (ease it off gradually) and a history book. Pam didn't bother to look at these. Years ago she had told him he was a real book-worm, and it couldn't be good for his eyes which he needed to keep in good condition in a job like his. They had sausages and tinned peaches for lunch, just the two of them and Wilfred Summitt. Christopher never came in for lunch on Saturdays. He got up at ten, polished his car, perquisite of the estate agents, and took the seventeen-year-old trainee hairdresser he called his fiancée to London where he spent a lot of money on gin and tonics, prawn cocktails and steak, circle seats in cinemas, long-playing records and odds and ends like *Playboy* magazine and bottles of wine and after-shave and cassettes. Jillian sometimes came in when she had nothing better to do. This Saturday she had something better to do, though what it was she hadn't bothered to inform her parents.

In the afternoon Alan pulled weeds out of the garden, Pam turned up the hem of an evening skirt and Wilfred Summitt took a nap. The nap freshened him up, and while they were having tea, which was sardines and lettuce and bread and butter and madeira cake, he said he had seen a newsflash on television and the Glasgow bank robbers had been caught.

'What we want here is the electric chair.'

'Something like that,' said Pam.

'What we want is the army to take over this country. See a bit of discipline then, we would. The army to take over, under the Queen of course, under Her Majesty, and some general at the head of it. Some big pot who means business. The Forces, that's the thing. We knew what discipline was when I was in the Forces.' Pop always spoke of his time at Catterick Camp in the nineteen-forties as 'being in the Forces' as if he had been in the navy and air force and marines as well. 'Flog 'em, is what I say. Give 'em something to remember across their backsides.' He paused and swigged tea. 'What's wrong with the cat?' he said, so that anyone coming in at that moment, Alan thought, would have supposed him to be enquiring after the health of the family pet.

Alan went back into the garden. Passing the window of Pop's bed-sit, he noticed that the gas fire was full on. Pop kept his gas fire on all day and, no doubt, half the night from September till May whether he was in his room or not. Pam had told him about it very politely, but he only said his circulation was bad because he had hardening of the arteries. He contributed nothing to the gas bill or the electricity bill either, and Pam said it wasn't fair to ask anything from an old man who only had his pension. Alan dared to say, How about the ten thousand he got from selling his own house? That, said Pam, was for a rainy day.

Back in the house, having put the garden tools away, he found his daughter. His reading had taught him that the young got on better with the old than with the middle-aged, but that didn't seem to be so in the case of his children and Pop. Here, as perhaps in other respects, the authors had been wrong.

Jillian ignored Pop, never speaking to him at all, and Pam, though sometimes flaring and raving at her while Jillian flared and raved back, was generally too frightened of her to reprove her when reproof was called for. On the face of it, mother and daughter had a good relationship, always chatting to each other about clothes and things they had read in magazines, and when they went shopping together they always linked arms. But there was no real communication. Jillian was a subtle little hypocrite, Alan thought, who ingratiated herself with Pam by presenting her with the kind of image Pam would think a fifteen-year-old girl ought to have. He was sure that most of the extra-domestic activities she told her mother she went in for were pure invention, but they were all of the right kind: dramatic society, dressmaking class, evenings spent with Sharon whose mother was a teacher and who was alleged to be helping Jillian with her French homework. Jillian always got home by ten-thirty because she knew her mother thought sexual intercourse invariably took place after ten-thirty.

She said she came home on the last bus, which sometimes she did, though not alone, and Alan had once seen her get off the pillion of a boy's motor-bike at the end of Martyr's Mead.

He wondered why she bothered with deception, for if she had confessed to what she really did Pam could have done little about it. She would only have screamed threats while Jillian screamed threats back. They were afraid of each other, and Alan thought their relationship so sick as to be sinister. Among the things he wondered about was when Jillian would get married and how much she would expect him to fork out for her wedding. Probably it would be within the next couple of years, as she would very likely get pregnant quite soon, but she would want a big white wedding with all her friends there and a dance afterwards in a discothèque.

Pop had given up speaking to her. He knew he wouldn't get an answer. He was trying to watch television, but she had got between him and the set and was sitting on the floor drying her hair with a very noisy hair dryer. Alan could bring himself to feel sorry for Pop while Jillian was in the house. Fortunately she often wasn't, for when she was she ruled them all, a selfish bad-tempered little tyrant.

'You haven't forgotten we're going to the Heyshams' for the evening, have you?' said Pam.

Alan had, but the question really meant he was to dress up. They were not invited to a meal. No one at Fitton's Piece gave dinner parties, and 'for the evening' meant two glasses of sherry or whisky and water each, followed by coffee. But etiquette, presumably formulated by the women, demanded a change of costume. Dick Heysham, who was quite a nice man, wouldn't have cared at all if Alan had turned up in old trousers and a sweater and would have liked to dress that way himself, but Pam said a sports jacket must be worn and when his old one got too shabby she made him buy a new one. To make this possible, she had for weeks denied herself small luxuries, her fortnightly hair-do, her fortnightly trip to Stantwich to have lunch in a café with her sister, the cigarettes of which she smoked five a day, until the twenty-six pounds had been garnered. It was all horrible and stupid, an insane way to live. He resigned himself to it, as he did to most things, for the sake of peace. Yet he knew that what he got was not peace.

Jillian, unasked, said that she was going with Sharon to play Scrabble at the house of a girl called Bridget. Alan thought it very handy for her that Bridget lived in a cottage in Stoke Mill which had no phone.

'Be back by ten-thirty, won't you, dear?' said Pam.

'Of course I will. I always am.'

Jillian smiled so sweetly through her hair that Pam dared to suggest she move away out of Pop's line of vision.

'Why can't he go and watch his own TV?' said Jillian.

No one answered her. Pam went off to have a bath and came back with the long skirt on and a frilly blouse and lacquer on her hair and her lips pink and shiny. Then Alan shaved and got into a clean shirt and the sports jacket. They both looked much younger dressed like that, and smart and happy. The Heyshams lived in Tudor Way so they walked there. Something inside him cried aloud to tell her that he was sorry, that he pitied her from his soul, poor pathetic woman who had lived her whole life cycle by the age at which many only just begin to think of settling down. He couldn't do it, they had no common language. Besides, was he not as poor and pathetic himself? What would she have replied if he had said what he would have liked to say? Look at us, what are we doing, dressed up like this, visiting like this people we don't even care for, to talk about nothing, to tell face-saving lies? For what, for what?

At the Heyshams' the hosts and guests divided themselves into two groups. The men talked to each other and the women to each other. The men talked about work, their cars, the political situation and the cost of living. The women talked about their children, their houses and the cost of living. After they had been there about an hour Pam went to the bathroom and came back with more lipstick on.

By ten-fifteen they were all bored stiff. But Alan and Pam had to stay for another three-quarters of an hour or the Heyshams would think they had been bored or had quarrelled before they came out or were worried about one of their children. At exactly two minutes to eleven Pam said:

'Whatever time is it?'

She said 'whatever' because that implied it must be very late, while a simple 'What time is it?' might indicate that for her the time was passing slowly.

'Just on eleven,' said Alan.

'Good heavens, I'd no idea it was as late as that. We *must* go.'

The Cinderella Complex, its deadline shifted an hour back, operated all over Fitton's Piece. Evenings ended at eleven. Yet there was no reason why they should go home at eleven, no reason why they shouldn't stay out all night, for no one would miss them or, probably, even notice they were not there, and without harming a soul, they could have stayed in bed the following day till noon. But they left at eleven and got home at five past. Pop had gone to his bed-sit, Jillian was in the bath. Where Christopher was was anybody's guess. It was unlikely he would come in before one or two. That didn't worry Pam.

'It's different with boys,' he had heard her say to Gwen Maynard. 'You don't have to bother about boys in the same way. I insist on my daughter being in by half-past ten and she always is.'

Jillian had left a ring of dirty soap round the bath and wet towels on the floor. She was playing punk rock in her bedroom, and Alan longed for the courage to switch the electricity off at the main. They lay in bed, the room bright with moonlight, both pretending they couldn't hear the throbbing and the thumps. At last the noise stopped because, presumably, the second side of the second LP had come to an end and Jillian had fallen asleep.

A deep silence. There came into his head, he didn't know why, a memory of that episode in Malory when Lancelot is in bed with the queen and he hears the fourteen knights come to the door.

'Madam, is there any armour in your chamber that I might cover my poor body withal?'

Would he ever have such panache? Such proud courage? Would it ever be called for? Pam's eyes were wide open. She was staring at the moonlight patterns on the ceiling. He decided he had better make love to her. He hadn't done so for a fortnight, and it was Saturday night. Down in Stoke Mill the church clock struck one. To make sure it would work, Alan fantasized hard about the black-haired girl coming into the bank to order lire for a holiday in Portofino. What Pam fantasized about he didn't know, but he was sure she fantasized. It gave him a funny feeling to think about that, though he didn't dare think of it now, the idea of the fantasy people in the bed, so that it wasn't really he making love with Pam but the black-haired girl making love with the man who came to read the meter. The front door banged as Christopher let himself in. His feet thumped up the stairs. Madam, is there any armour in your chamber . . . ?

His poor body finished its work and Pam sighed. It was the last time he was ever to make love to her, and had he known it he would probably have taken greater pains.

4

Marty Foster's room in Cricklewood was at the top of the house, three floors up. It was quite big, as such rooms go, with a kitchen opening out of it, two sash windows looking out on to the street, and a third window in the kitchen. Marty hadn't been able to open any of these windows since he had been there, but he hadn't tried very hard. He slept on a double mattress on the floor. There was also a couch in the room and a gate-leg table marked with white rings and cigarette burns, and a couple of rickety Edwardian dining chairs, and a carpet with pink roses and coffee stains on it, and brown cotton curtains at the windows. When you drew these curtains clouds of dust blew out of them like smoke. In the kitchen was a gas stove and a sink and another gate-leg table and a bookcase used as a food store. Nobody had cleaned the place for several years.

The house was semi-detached, end of a terrace. An Irish girl had one of the rooms next to Marty's, the one that overlooked the side entrance, and the other had for years been occupied by a deaf old man named Green. There was a lavatory between the Irish girl's room and the head of the stairs. Half a dozen steps led down to a bathroom which the top-floor tenants shared, and then the main flight went on down to the first floor where a red-haired girl and the man she called her 'fella' had a flat, and the ground floor that was inhabited by an out-all-day couple that no one ever saw. Outside the bathroom door was a pay phone.

On Saturday Marty went down to this phone and got on to a car-hire place in South London called Relyacar Rentals, the idea of stealing a vehicle having been abandoned. Could they let him have a small van, say a mini-van, at nine on Monday morning? They could. They must have his name, please, and would he bring his driving licence with him? Marty gave the name on the licence he was holding in his hand. It had been issued to one Graham Francis Coleman of Wallington in Surrey, was valid until the year 2020, and Marty had helped himself to it out of the pocket of a jacket its owner had left on the rear seat of an Allegro in a cinema car park. Marty had known it would come in useful one day. Next he phoned the Kensington commune and asked Nigel about money. Nigel had only about six pounds of his mother's loan left and his Social Security Giro wasn't due till Wednesday, but he'd do his best.

Nigel had learnt the sense of always telling everyone the same lie, so he announced to his indifferent listeners that he was going off to Newcastle for a couple of weeks. No one said, Have a good time or Send us a card or anything like that. That wasn't their way. One of the girls said, In that case he wouldn't mind if her Samantha had his room, would he? Nigel saw his opportunity and said she'd pay the rent then, wouldn't she? A listless argument ensued, the upshot of which was that no one was violently opposed to his taking ten pounds out of the tin where they kept the rent and light and heat money so long as he put it back by the end of the month.

With sixteen pounds in his pocket, Nigel packed most of his possessions into a rucksack he borrowed from Samantha's mother and a suitcase he had long ago borrowed from his own, and set off by bus for Cricklewood. The house where Marty lived was in a street between Chichele Road and Cricklewood Broadway, and it had an air of slightly down-at-heel respectability. In the summer the big spreading trees, limes and planes and chestnuts, made the place damp and shady and even rather mysterious, but now they were just naked trees that looked as if they had never been in leaf and never would be. There was a church opposite that Nigel had never seen anyone attend, and on the street corner a launderette, a paper shop and a grocery and delicatessen store. He rang Marty's bell, which was the top one, and Marty came down to let him in.

Marty smelt of the cheap wine he had been drinking, the dregs of which with their inky sediment were in a cup on the kitchen table. Wine, or whisky when he could afford it, was his habitual daily beverage. He drank it to quench his thirst as other people drink tea or water. One of the reasons he wanted money was for the unlimited indulgence of this craving of his. Marty hated having to drink sparingly, knowing there wasn't another bottle in the kitchen waiting for him to open as soon as this one was finished.

He swallowed what remained in the cup and then brought out from under a pile of clothes on the mattress an object which he put into Nigel's hands. It was a small, though heavy, pistol, the barrel about six inches long. Nigel put his finger to the trigger and tried to squeeze it. The trigger moved but not much.

'Do me a favour,' said Marty, 'and don't point that weapon at me. Suppose it was loaded?'

'You'd have to be a right cretin, wouldn't you?' Nigel turned the gun over and looked at it. 'There's German writing on the side. Carl Walther, Modell PPK Cal 9 mm kurz. Then it says *Made in W. Germany*.' The temptation to hold forth was too much for him. 'You can buy these things in cycle shops, I've seen them. They're called non-firing replica guns and they use them in movies. Cost a bomb too. Where'd you get the bread for a shooter like this?'

Marty wasn't going to tell him about the insurance policy his mother had taken out for him years ago and which had matured. He said only, 'Give it here,' took the gun back and looked at the pair of black stockings Nigel was holding out for his inspection.

These Nigel had found in a pile of dirty washing on the floor of the commune bathroom. They were the property of a girl called Sarah who sometimes wore them for sexy effect. 'Timing,' said Nigel, 'is of the essence. We get to the bank just before one. We leave the van in the lane at the back. When the polone comes to lock up, Groombridge'll be due to split. We put the stockings over our faces and rush the polone and lock the doors after us.'

'Call her a girl, can't you? You're not a poove.'

Nigel went red. The shot had gone home. He wasn't homosexual – he wasn't yet sure if he was sexual at all and he was unhappy about it – but the real point was that Marty had caught him out using a bit of slang which he hadn't known was queers' cant. He said sullenly, 'We get her to open the safe and then we tie her up so she can't call the fuzz.' A thought struck him. 'Did you get the gloves?'

Marty had forgotten and Nigel let him have it for that, glad to be once more in the ascendant. 'Christ,' he said, 'and that finger of yours is more of a giveaway than any goddamned prints.'

Neither affronted nor hurt, Marty glanced at his right hand and admitted with a shrug that Nigel was right. The forefinger wasn't exactly repulsive to look at or grotesque but it wasn't a pretty sight either. And it was uniquely Marty's. He had sliced the top off it on an electric mower at the garden centre – a fraction nearer and he'd have lost half his hand, as the manager had never tired of pointing out. The finger was now about a quarter of an inch shorter than the one on the other hand and the nail, when it grew again, was warped and puckered to the shape of a walnut kernel.

'Get two pairs of gloves Monday morning when you get the van,' snapped Nigel, 'and when you've got them go and have your hair and your beard cut off.'

Marty made a fuss about that, but the fuss was really to cover his fear. The idea of making changes in his appearance brought home to him the reality of what they were about to do. He was considerably afraid and beginning to get cold feet. It didn't occur to him that Nigel might be just as afraid, and they blustered and brazened it out to each other that evening and the next day. Both were secretly aware that they had insufficiently 'cased' the Childon sub-branch of the Anglian-Victoria, that their only experience of robbery came from books and films, and that they knew very little about the bank's security system. But nothing would have made either of them admit it. The trouble was, they didn't like each other. Marty had befriended Nigel because he was flattered that a doctor's son who had been to college wanted to know him, and Nigel had linked up with Marty because he needed someone even weaker than himself to bully and impress. But among these thieves there was no honour. Each might have said of the other, He's my best friend and I hate him.

That weekend the thought uppermost in Nigel's mind was that he must take charge and run the show as befitted a member of the élite and a descendant of generations of army officers and medical personages, though he affected to despise those forbears of his, and show this peasant what leadership was. The thought uppermost in Marty's, apart from his growing fear, was that with his practical know-how he must astound this upper-class creep. He got a pound out of Nigel on Sunday to buy himself a bottle of Sicilian wine, and wished he had the self-control to save half for Monday morning when he would need Dutch courage.

On Sunday night Joyce Culver steamed and pressed the evening dress she intended to wear on the following evening. Alan Groombridge broke his resolution and re-read *The Playboy of the Western World* while his family, with the exception of Jillian, watched a television documentary about wildlife in the Galapagos Islands. Jillian was in the cinema in Stantwich with a thirty-five-year-old cosmetics salesman who had promised to get her home by ten-thirty and who doubted, not yet knowing Jillian, that there would be anything doing on the way.

John Purford, with fifty other car and motor-cycle fanatics, was taking off from Gatwick in a charter aircraft bound for New York and thence for Daytona, Florida.

5

The fine weather broke during the night, and on Monday morning, 4 March, instead of frost silvering the lawns of Fitton's Piece, heavy rain was falling. It was so dark in the dining recess that at breakfast the Groombridges had to have the unearthly, morgue-style, lymph-blue strip light on. Wilfred Summitt elaborated on his idea of an army takeover with a reintroduction of capital punishment, an end to Social Security benefits and an enforced exodus of all immigrants. Christopher, who didn't have to be at work till ten, had lit a cigarette between courses (cereal and eggs and bacon) and was sniping back at him with the constitution of his own Utopia, euthanasia for all over sixty and a sexual free-for-all for everyone under thirty. Jillian was combing her hair over a plate of cornflakes while she and Pam argued as to whether it was possible to put blonde streaks in one's hair at home, Pam averring that this was a job for a professional. They all made a lot of irritable humourless noise, and Alan wondered how he would feel if the police came into the bank at ten and told him a gas main had exploded and killed all his family five minutes after he left. Probably he would be a little sorry about Pam and Christopher.

He left the sandwiches in the car because it was his day for going out. Along with her coat, Joyce had hung an evening dress in the cupboard. It was her parents' silver wedding day, and she and Stephen were going straight from work to a drinks party and dinner at the Toll House Hotel.

'You'll be having your silver wedding in a few years, Mr Groombridge,' said Joyce. 'What'll you give your wife? My mother wanted a silver fox but Dad said, if you don't watch out, my girl, all you'll get is a silver*fish*, meaning one of those creepy-crawlies. We had to laugh. He's ever so funny, my dad. He gave her a lovely bracelet, one of those chased ones.'

Alan couldn't imagine how one bracelet could be more chaste than another, but he didn't ask. The bank was always busy on a Monday morning. P. Richardson was the first customer. He asked for two portraits of Florence Nightingale and sneered at Alan who didn't immediately guess he meant ten-pound notes.

Marty showed Graham Coleman's driving licence to the girl at Relyacar Rentals in Croydon and gave his age as twenty-four. She said she'd like a ten-pound deposit, please, they'd settle up tomorrow when they knew what mileage he'd done, and if he brought the van back after six would he leave it in the square and put the keys through Relyacar's letter box?

Marty handed over the money and said yes to everything. The mini-van was white and clean and, from the registration, only a year old. He drove it a few miles, parking outside a barber's shop where he had his hair and beard cut off and his chin and upper lip closely shaved. He hadn't really seen his own face for three years and he had forgotten what a small chin he had and what hollow cheeks. Depilation didn't improve his appearance, though the barber insisted it did. At any rate, the Relyacar girl wouldn't know him again. His own mother wouldn't.

There was something else he had to do or buy, but he couldn't remember what it was, so he drove back to pick up Nigel. He went over Battersea Bridge and up through Kensington and Kensal Rise and Willesden to Cricklewood where Nigel was waiting for him in Chichele Road.

'Christ,' said Nigel, 'you look a real freak. You look like one of those Hare Krishna guys.'

Marty was a good driver. He had driven for his living while Nigel's experience consisted only in taking out his father's automatic Triumph, and he had never driven a car with an ordinary manual gear shift. Nor did he know London particularly well, but that didn't stop him ordering Marty to take the North Circular Road. Marty had already decided to do so. Still, he wasn't going to be pushed around, not he, and to show off his knowledge he went by a much longer and tortuous route over Hampstead Heath and through Highgate and Tottenham and Walthamstow. Thus it was well after eleven before they were out of London and reaching Brentwood.

When they were on the Chelmsford bypass, Nigel said, 'The shooter's OK and you've got your stocking. We can stuff the bread in this carrier. Let's have a look at the gloves.'

Marty swore. 'I knew there was something.'

Nigel was about to lay into him when he realized that all this time Marty had been driving the van with ungloved hands, and that he too had put his ungloved hands on the doors and the dashboard shelf and the window catches, so all he said was, 'We'll have to stop in Colchester and get gloves and we'll have to wipe this vehicle over inside.'

'We can't stop,' said Marty. 'It's half-eleven now.'

'We have to, you stupid bastard. It wouldn't be half-eleven if you hadn't taken us all round the houses.'

It is twenty-three miles from Chelmsford to Colchester, and Marty made it in twenty minutes, somewhat to the distress of the mini-van's engine. But there is virtually no on-street parking in Colchester whose narrow twisty streets evince its reputation as England's oldest recorded town. They had to go into a multi-storey car park, up to the third level, and then hunt for Woolworth's.

When the gloves were bought, woollen ones because cash was running short, they found they had nothing with which to wipe the interior of the van. Neither of them had handkerchiefs, so Nigel took off one of his socks. The rain, of which there had been no sign in London, was lashing down.

'It's twenty past twelve,' said Marty. 'We'll never make it. We'd better do it Wednesday instead.'

'Look, little brain,' Nigel shouted, 'don't give me a hard time, d'you mind? How can we do it Wednesday? What're we going to use for bread? Just drive the bugger and don't give me grief all the goddamned time.'

The narrower roads to Childon did not admit of driving at seventy miles an hour, but Marty, his hands in green knitted gloves, did make it. They put the van in the lane behind the bank, up against the flint wall. Nigel got out and came cautiously to the gap in the wall, and there he was rewarded.

A middle-aged man, thin, paunchy, with greased-down hair, came out of the back door and got into the car that stood on the forecourt.

Half an hour before, Mrs Burroughs had come into the bank with a cheque drawn on the account of a firm of solicitors for twelve thousand pounds. She didn't explain its source but her manner was more high-handed than usual. Alan supposed it was a legacy and advised her not to put it in her deposit account but to open a new account under the Anglian-Victoria Treasure Trove scheme which gave a higher rate of interest. Mrs Burroughs said offendedly that she couldn't possibly do that without consulting her husband. She would phone him at his office and come back at two.

The idea of Mrs Burroughs, who lived in a huge house outside Childon and had a Scimitar car and a mink coat, acquiring still more wealth, depressed him so much that he broke his new rule and took the three thousand out of the safe while Joyce was busy talking about the price of beef with Mr Wolford. Strange to think, as he often did, that it was only paper, only pictures of the Queen and a dead Prime Minister and a sort of super-nurse, but that it could do so much, buy so much, buy happiness and freedom and peace and silence. He tore one of the portraits of Florence Nightingale in half just to see what it felt like to do that, and then he had to mend it with Sellotape.

He heard Mr Wolford go. There was no one else in the bank now and it was nearly ten to one. Joyce might easily come into his office, so he put the money into a drawer and went out to the lavatory where there was a washbasin to wash the money dirt off his hands. It looked like more rain was coming, but he'd go out just the same, maybe up to Childon Fen where the first primroses would be coming out and the windflowers.

Joyce was tidying up her till.

'Mr Groombridge, is this all right? Mr Wolford filled in the counterfoil and did the carbon for the bank copy. I don't know why I never saw it. Shall I give him a ring?'

Alan looked at the slip from the paying-in book. 'No, that's OK. So long as it's come out clear and it has. I'm off to lunch now, Joyce.'

'Don't get wet,' said Joyce. 'It's going to pour. It's come over ever so black.'

He wondered if she speculated as to where he went. She couldn't suppose he took the car just to the Childon Arms. But perhaps she didn't notice whether he took the car or not. He walked out to it now, the back door locking automatically behind him, and got into the driving seat – and remembered that the three thousand pounds was still in his desk drawer.

She wouldn't open the drawer. But the thought of it there and not in the safe where it should have been, would spoil for him all the peace and seclusion of Childon Fen. After all, she knew his combination, if she still remembered it, just as he knew hers. Better put it away. He went back and into his office, pushed to but didn't quite close the door into the bank, and softly opened the drawer.

While he was doing so, at precisely one o'clock, Joyce came out from behind the metal grille, crossed the floor of the bank and came face to face with Marty Foster and Nigel Thaxby. They were between the open oak door and the closed glass door and each was trying to pull a black nylon stocking over his head. They hadn't dared do this before they got into the porch, they had never rehearsed the procedure, and the stockings were wet because the threatening rain had come in a violent cascade during their progress from the van to the bank.

Joyce didn't scream. She let out a sort of hoarse shout and leapt for the glass door and the key that would lock it.

Nigel would have turned and run then, for the stocking was only pulled grotesquely over his head like a cap, but Marty dropped his stocking and charged at the door, bursting it open so that Joyce stumbled back. He seized her and put his hand over her mouth and jammed the gun into her side and told her to shut up or she was dead.

Nigel followed him in quite slowly. Already he was thinking, she's seen our faces, she's seen us. But he closed the oak door behind him and locked and bolted it. He closed and locked the glass door and walked up and stood in front of Joyce. Marty took his hand from her mouth but kept the gun where it was. She looked at them in silence, and her face was very pale. She looked at them as if she were studying what they looked like.

From the office Alan Groombridge heard Joyce shout and he heard Marty's threat. He knew at once what was happening and he remembered, on a catch of breath, that conversation with Wilfred Summitt last Wednesday. His hands tightened on the bundle of notes, the three thousand pounds.

The Anglian-Victoria directed its staff to put up no resistance. If they could they were to depress with their feet one of the alarm buttons. The alarms were on a direct line to Stantwich police station where they set in motion a flashing light alert system. If they couldn't reach an alarm, and in

Joyce's case it was perhaps impossible, they were to comply with the demands of the intruders. There was an alarm button under each till and another under Alan's desk. He backed his right foot and put his heel to it, held his heel above it, and heard a voice say:

'We know you're on your own. We saw the manager go out.'

Where had he heard that voice before, that curious and ugly mixture of cockney and Suffolk? He was sure he had heard it and recently. It was a very memorable voice because the combination of broad flat vowels with slurred or dropped consonants was so unusual. Had he heard it in the bank? Out shopping? Then the sense of the words struck him and he edged his foot forward again. They thought he was out, they must have seen him get into his car. Now he could depress the alarm without their having the faintest idea he had done so, and thereby, if he was very clever, save three thousand of the bank's money. Maybe save all of it once he'd remembered who that strange voice belonged to.

'Let's see what's in the tills, doll.'

A different voice, with a disc jockey's intonation. He heard the tills opened. His foot went back again, feeling for the button embedded in the carpet. From outside there came a clatter of coin. A thousand, give or take a little, would be in those tills. He lifted his heel. It was all very well, that plan of his, but suppose he did save the three thousand, suppose he stuffed it in the clothes cupboard before they came in, how was he going to explain to the bank that he had been able to do so?

He couldn't hear a sound from Joyce. He lowered his heel, raised it again.

'Now the safe,' the Suffolk or Suffolk-cockney voice said.

To reach it they must pass through the office. He couldn't press the alarm, not just like that, not without thinking things out. There was no legitimate reason why he should have been in his office with three thousand pounds in his hands. And he couldn't say he'd opened the safe and taken it out when he heard them come in because he wasn't supposed to know Joyce's combination. And if he'd been able to save three, why not five?

Any minute now and they would come into the office.

They would stuff the notes and the coin – if they bothered with the coin – into their bag and then come straight through here. He pulled open the door of the cupboard and flattened himself against its back behind Joyce's evening dress, the hem of which touched the floor. Madam, is there any armour in your chamber that I might cover my poor body withal . . . ?

He had scarcely pulled the door closed after him when he heard Joyce cry out.

'Don't! Don't touch me!' And there was a clatter as of something kicked across the floor.

Lancelot's words reminded him of the questions he had asked himself on Saturday night. Would he ever have such panache, such proud courage? Now was the time. She was only twenty. She was a girl. Never mind the bank's suspicions, never mind now what anyone thought. His first duty was to rescue Joyce or at least stand with her and support her. He fumbled through the folds of the dress to open the door. He wasn't afraid. With a vague wry amusement, he thought that he wasn't afraid because he didn't mind if they killed him, he had nothing to live for. Perhaps all his life with its boredom, its pain and its futility, had simply been designed to lead up to this moment, meeting death on a wet afternoon for seven thousand pounds.

He would leave the money in the cupboard – he had thrust it into the pockets of his raincoat which hung beside Joyce's dress – and go out and face them. They wouldn't think of looking in his raincoat, and later he'd think up an explanation for the bank. If there was a later. The important thing now was to go out to them, and this might even create a diversion in which Joyce could escape.

But before he touched the door, something very curious happened. He felt into the pockets to make sure none of the notes was sticking out and against his hands the money felt alive, pulsating almost, or as if it were a chemical that reacted at the contact with flesh. Energy seemed to come from it, rays of power, that travelled, tingling, up his arms. There were sounds out there. They had got the safe open. He heard rustling noises and thumps and voices arguing, and yet he did not hear them. He was aware only of the money alive between and around his fingers. He gasped and clenched his hands, for he knew then that he could not leave the money. It was his. By his daily involvement with it, he had made it his and he could not leave it.

Someone had come into the office. The drawers of his desk were pulled out and emptied on to the floor. He stood rigid with his hands in the coat pockets, and the cupboard door was flung open.

He could see nothing through the dark folds of the dress. He held his breath. The door closed again and Joyce swore at them. Never had he thought he would hear Joyce use that word, but he honoured her for it. She screamed and then she made no more sound. The only sound was the steady roar of rain drumming on the pantiled roof, and then, after a while, the noise of a car or van engine starting up.

He waited. One of them had come back. The strange voice was grumbling and muttering out there, but not for long. The back door slammed. Had they gone? He could only be sure by coming out. Loosening his hold on the money, he thought he would have to go out, he couldn't stay in that cupboard for the rest of his life. And Joyce must be somewhere out there, bound and gagged probably. He would explain to her that when he had heard them enter the bank he had taken as much money as he had time to save out of the safe. She would think him a coward, but that didn't matter because he knew he hadn't been a coward, he had been something else he couldn't analyse. It was a wrench, painful almost, to withdraw his hands from his pockets, but he did withdraw them, and he pushed open the door and stepped out.

The desk drawers were on the floor and their contents spilt. Joyce wasn't in the office or in the room where the safe was. The door of the safe was open and it was empty. They must have left her in the main part of the bank. He hesitated. He wiped his forehead on which sweat was standing. Something had happened to him in that cupboard, he thought, he had gone mad, mentally he had broken down. The idea came to him that perhaps it was the life he led which at last had broken him. He went on being mad. He took the money out of his coat pockets and laid it in the safe. He went to the back door and opened it quietly, looking out at the teeming rain and his car standing in the dancing, rain-pounded puddles. Then he slammed the door quite hard as if he had just come in, and he walked quite lightly and innocently through to where Joyce must be lying.

She wasn't there. The tills were pulled out. He looked in the lavatory. She wasn't there either. While he was in the cupboard, hesitating, she must have gone off to get help. Without her coat, which was also in the cupboard, but you don't think of rain at a time like that. Over and over to himself he said, I was out at lunch, I came back, I didn't know what had happened, I was out at lunch . . .

Why had she gone instead of pressing one of the alarm buttons? He couldn't think of a reason. The clock above the currency exchange rate board told him it was twenty-five past one and the date 4 March. He had gone out to lunch, he had come back and found the safe open, half the money gone, Joyce gone . . . What would be the natural thing to do? Give the alarm, of course.

He returned to his office and searched with his foot under the desk for the button. It was covered by an upturned drawer. Kneeling down, he lifted up the drawer and found under it a shoe. It was one of the blue shoes with the instep straps Joyce had been wearing that morning. Joyce wouldn't have gone out into the rain, gone running out without one of her shoes. He stood still, looking at the high-heeled, very shiny, patent leather dark blue shoe.

Joyce hadn't gone for help. They had taken her with them.

As a hostage? Or because she had seen their faces? People like that didn't have to have a reason. Did any people have to have a reason? Had he had one for staying in that cupboard? If he had come out they would have taken him too.

Press the button now. He had been out at lunch, had come back to find the safe open and Joyce gone. Strange that they had left three thousand pounds, but he hadn't been there, he couldn't be expected to explain it. If he had been there, they would have taken him too because he too would have seen their faces. He looked at his watch. Nearly twenty to two. Give the alarm now, and there would still be time to put up road blocks, they couldn't have got far in twenty minutes and in this rain.

The phone began to ring.

It made him jump, but it would only be Pam. It rang and rang and still he didn't lift the receiver. The ringing brought into his mind a picture as bright and clear as something on colour television, but more real. Fitton's Piece and his house and Pam in it at the phone, Pop at the table in the dining recess, drinking tea, Jillian coming home soon and Christopher. The television. The punk rock. The doors banging. The sports jacket, the army takeover, the gas bill. He let the phone ring and ring, and after twenty rings – he counted them – it stopped. But because it had rung his madness had intensified and concentrated into a hard nucleus, an appalling and wonderful decision.

His mind was not capable of reasoning, of seeing flaws or hazards or discrepancies. His body worked for him, putting itself into his raincoat, stuffing the three thousand pounds into his pockets, propelling itself out into the rain and into his car. If he had been there they would have taken him with them too. He started the car, and the clear arcs made on the windscreen by the wipers showed him freedom.

6

They took Joyce with them because she had seen their faces. She had opened the safe when they told her to, though at first she said she could only work one of the dials. But when Marty put the gun in her ribs and started counting up to ten, she came out with the other combination. As soon as the lock gave, Nigel tied a stocking round her eyes, and when she cried out he tied the other one round her mouth, making her clench her teeth on it. In a drawer they found a length of clothes-line Alan had bought to tie down the boot lid of his car but had never used, and with this they tied Joyce's hands and feet. Standing over her, Marty looked at Nigel and Nigel looked at him and nodded. Without a word, they picked her up and carried her to the back door.

Nigel opened it and saw the Morris Eleven Hundred in the yard. He didn't say anything. It was Marty who said,

'Christ!' But the car was empty and the yard was deserted. Rain was falling in a thick cataract. Nigel rolled the plastic carrier round the money and thrust it inside his jacket.

'Where the hell's Groombridge?' whispered Marty.

Nigel shook his head. They splashed through the teeming rain, carrying Joyce out to the van, and dropped her on the floor in the back.

'Give me the gun,' said Nigel. His teeth were chattering and the water was streaming out of his hair down his face.

Marty gave him the gun and got into the driver's seat with the money on his lap in the carrier bag. Nigel went back into the bank. He stumbled through the rooms, looking for Alan Groombridge. He meant to look for Joyce's shoe too, but it was more than he could take, all of it was too much, and he stumbled out again, the door slamming behind him with a noise like a gunshot.

Marty had turned the van. Nigel got in beside him and grabbed the bag of money and Marty drove off down the first narrow side road they came to, the windscreen wipers sweeping off the water in jets. They were both breathing fast and noisily.

'A sodding four grand,' Marty gasped out. 'All that grief for four grand.'

'For Christ's sake, shut up about it. Don't talk about it in front of her. You don't have to talk at all. Just drive.'

Down a deep lane with steep hedges. Joyce began to drum her feet on the metal floor of the van, thud, clack, thud, clack, because she had only one shoe on.

'Shut that racket,' said Nigel, turning and pushing the gun at her between the gap in the seats. Thud, clack, thud . . . His fingers were wet with rain and sweat.

At that moment they came face to face, head on, with a red Vauxhall going towards Childon. Marty stopped just in time and the Vauxhall stopped. The Vauxhall was being driven by a man not much older than themselves, and he had an older woman beside him. There was no room to pass. Joyce began to thrash about, banging the foot with the shoe on it, clack, clack, clack, and thumping her other foot, thud, thud, and making choking noises.

'Christ,' said Marty. 'Christ!'

Nigel pushed his arm through between the seats right up

to his shoulder. He didn't dare climb over, not with those people looking, the two enquiring faces revealed so sharply each time the wipers arced. He was so frightened he hardly knew what he was saying.

With the gun against her hip, he said on a tremulous hiss: 'You think I wouldn't use it? You think I haven't used it? Know why I went back in there? Groombridge was there and I shot him dead.'

'Sweet Jesus,' said Marty.

The Vauxhall was backing now, slowly, to where the lane widened in a little bulge. Marty eased the van forward, hunched on the wheel, his face set.

'I'll kill those two in the car as well,' said Nigel, beside himself with fear.

'Shut up, will you? Shut up.'

Marty moved past the car with two or three inches to spare, and brought up his right hand in a shaky salute. The Vauxhall went off and Marty said, 'I must have been out of my head bringing you on this. Who d'you think you are? Bonnie and Clyde?'

Nigel swore at him. This reversal of roles was unbearable, but enough to shock him out of his panic. 'You realize we have to get shot of this vehicle? You realize that? Thanks to you bringing us down a goddamned six-foot-wide footpath. Because that guy'll be in Childon in ten minutes and the fuzz'll be there, and the first thing he'll do is tell them about us passing him. Won't he? Won't he? So have you got any ideas?'

'Like what?'

'Like rip off a car,' said Nigel. 'Like in the next five minutes. If you don't want to spend the best years of your life inside, little brain.'

Mrs Burroughs phoned her husband at his office in Stantwich and asked him if he thought it would be all right for her to put Aunt Jean's money in the Anglian-Victoria Treasure Trove scheme. He said she was to do as she liked, it was all one to him if she hadn't enough faith in him to let him invest it for her. So Mrs Burroughs got into her Scimitar at two and reached the Anglian-Victoria at five past. The doors were still shut. Having money of her own and not just being dependent on her husband's money had made her feel quite important, a person to be reckoned with, and she was annoyed. She banged on the doors, but no one came and it was too wet to stand out there. She sat in the Scimitar for five minutes and when the doors still didn't open she got out again and looked through the window. The window was frosted, but on this, in clear glass, was the emblem of the Anglian-Victoria, an A and a V with vine leaves entwining them and a crown on top. Mrs Burroughs looked through one of the arms of the V and saw the tills emptied and thrown on the floor. She drove off as fast as she could to the police house two hundred yards down the village street, feeling very excited and enjoying herself enormously.

By this time the red Vauxhall had passed through Childon on its way to Stantwich. Its driver was a young man called Peter Johns who was taking his mother to visit her sister in Stantwich General Hospital. They met a police car with its blue lamp on and its siren blaring, indeed they came closer to colliding with it than they had done with the mini-van, and these two near-misses afforded them a subject for conversation all the way to the hospital.

At ten to three the police called on Mrs Elizabeth Culver to tell her the bank had been robbed and her daughter was missing. Mrs Culver said it was kind of them to come and tell her so promptly, and they said they would fetch her husband who was a factory foreman on the Stantwich industrial estate. She went upstairs and put back into her wardrobe the dress she had been going to wear that evening, and then she phoned the Toll House Hotel to tell them to cancel the arrangements for the silver wedding party. She meant to phone her sisters too and her brother and the woman who, twenty-five years before, had been her bridesmaid, but she found she was unable to do this. Her husband came in half an hour later and found her sitting on the bed, staring silently at the wardrobe, tears streaming down her face.

Pamela Groombridge was ironing Alan's shirts and intermittently discussing with her father why the phone hadn't been answered when she rang the bank at twenty to two and two o'clock and again at three. In between discussing this she was thinking about an article she had read telling you how to put coloured transfers on ceramic tiles.

Wilfred Summitt was drinking tea. He said that he expected Alan had been out for his dinner.

'He never goes out,' said Pam. 'You know that, you were sitting here when I was cutting his sandwiches. Anyway, that girl would be there, that Joyce.'

'The phone's gone phut,' said Pop. 'That's what it is, the phone's out of order. It's on account of the lines being overloaded. If I had my way, only responsible ratepayers over thirty'd be allowed to have phones.'

'I don't know. I think it's funny. I'll wait till half-past and then I'll try it again.'

Pop said to mark his words, the phone was out of order, gone phut, kaput, which wouldn't happen if the army took over, and what was wanted was Winston Churchill to come back to life and Field Marshal Montgomery to help him, good old Monty, under the Queen of course, under Her Majesty. Or it just could be the rain, coming down cats and dogs it was, coming down like stair-rods. Pam didn't answer him. She was wondering if the colour on those transfers would be permanent or if it would come off when you washed them. She would like to try them in her own bathroom, but not if the colour came off, no thanks, that would look worse than plain white.

The doorbell rang.

'I hope that's not Linda Kitson,' said Pam. 'I don't want to have to stop and get nattering to her.'

She went to the door, and the policeman and the policewoman told her the bank had been robbed and it seemed that the robbers had taken her husband and Joyce Culver with them.

'Oh, God, oh, God, oh, God,' said Pam, and she went on saying it and sometimes screaming it while the policeman fetched Wendy Heysham and the policewoman made tea. Pam knocked over the tea and took the duty-free Bristol Cream out of the sideboard and poured a whole tumblerful and drank it at a gulp.

They fetched Christopher from the estate agent's and when he came in Pam was half-drunk and banging her fists on her knees and shouting, 'Oh, God, oh, God.' Neither the policewoman nor Wendy Heysham could do anything with her. Christopher gave her another tumblerful of sherry in the hope it would shut her up, while Wilfred Summitt marched up and down, declaiming that hanging was too good for them, pole-axing was too good for them. After the electric chair, the pole-axe was his favourite lethal instrument. He would pole-axe them without a trial, he would.

Pam drank the second glass of sherry and passed out.

Wiser than those who had made his escape possible, Alan avoided the narrow lanes. He met few cars, overtook a tractor and a bus. The rain was falling too heavily for him to see the faces of people in other vehicles, so he supposed they would not be able to see his. There wasn't much petrol in the tank, only about enough to get him down into north Essex, and of course it wouldn't do to stop at a petrol station.

His body was still doing all the work, and that level of consciousness which deals only with practical matters. He couldn't yet think of what he had done, it was too enormous, and he didn't want to. He concentrated on the road and the heavy rain. At the Hadleigh turn he came out on to the A12 and headed for Colchester. The petrol gauge showed that his fuel was getting dangerously low, but in ten minutes he was on the Colchester bypass. He turned left at the North Hill roundabout and drove up North Hill. There was a car park off to the left here behind St Runwald's Street. He put the car in the car park which was unattended, took out his sandwiches, locked the car and dropped the sandwiches in a litter bin. Now what? Once they had found his car, they would ask at the station and the booking office clerk would remember him and remember that he had passed through alone. So he made for the bus station instead where he caught a bus to Marks Tey. There he boarded a stopping train to London. His coat, which was of the kind that is known as showerproof and anyway was very old, had let the rain right through to his suit. The money had got damp. As soon as he had got to wherever he was going, he would spread the notes out and dry them.

There were only a few other people in the long carriage, a woman with two small boys, a young man. The young man looked much the same as any other dark-haired boy of twenty with a beard, but as soon as Alan saw him he remembered where he had heard that ugly Suffolk-cockney accent before. Indeed, so great was the resemblance that he found himself glancing at the boy's hands which lay slackly on his knees. But of course the hands were whole, there was no mutilation of the right forefinger, no distortion of the nail.

The first time he had heard that voice it had asked him for twenty five-pence pieces for a pound note. He had pushed the coins across the counter, looked at the young bearded face, thought, Am I being offhand, discourteous, because he's *young*? So he had put the coins into a bag and for a brief instant, but long enough to register, seen the deformed finger close over it and scoop it into the palm of the hand.

Suppose he had remembered sooner, this clue the police would seize on, would it have stopped him? He thought not. And now? Now he was in it as much as the man with the beard, the strange voice, the walnut fingernail.

Some sort of meeting was in progress in the village hall at Capel St Paul, and among the cars parked in puddles on the village green were two Ford Escorts, a yellow and a silver-blue. The fifth key that Marty tried from his bunch unlocked the yellow one, but when he switched on the ignition he found there was only about a gallon of petrol in the tank. He gave that up and tried the silver-blue one. The tenth key fitted. The pointer on the gauge showed the tank nearly full. The tank of a Ford Escort holds about six gallons, so that would be all right. He drove off quickly, correctly guessing – wasn't he a country lad himself? – that the meeting had begun at two and would go on till four.

The van he had parked fifty yards up the road. They made Joyce get out at gunpoint and get into the Ford, and Marty drove the van down a lane and left it under some bushes at the side of a wood. There was about as much chance of anyone seeing them on a wet March afternoon in Capel St Paul as there would have been on the moon. Marty felt rather pleased with himself, his nervousness for a while allayed.

'We can't leave her tied up when we get on the A12,' he said. 'There's windows in the back of this motor. Right?'

'I do have eyes,' said Nigel, and he climbed over the seat and undid Joyce's hands and took the gags off her mouth and her eyes. Her face was stiff and marked with weals where the stockings had bitten into her flesh, but she swore at Nigel and she actually spat at him, something she had never in her life done to anyone before. He stuck the gun against her ribs and wiped the spittle off his cheek.

'You wouldn't shoot me,' said Joyce. 'You wouldn't dare.'

'You ever heard the saying that you might as well be hung for a sheep as a lamb? If we get caught we go inside for life anyway on account of we've killed Groombridge. That's murder.'

'Get it, do you?' said Marty. 'They couldn't do any more to us if we'd killed a hundred people, so we're not going to jib at you, are we?'

Joyce said nothing.

'What's your name?' said Nigel.

Joyce said nothing.

'OK, Miss J. M. Culver, be like that, Jane, Jenny or whatever. I can't introduce us,' Nigel said loudly to make sure Marty got the message, 'for obvious reasons.'

'Mr Groombridge's got a wife and two children,' said Joyce.

'Tough tit,' said Nigel. 'We'd have picked a bachelor if we'd known. If you gob at me again I'll give you a bash round the face you won't forget.'

They turned on to the A12 at twenty-five past two, following the same route Alan Groombridge had taken twenty minutes before. There was little traffic, the rain was torrential, and Marty drove circumspectly, neither too fast nor too slowly, entering the fast lane only to overtake. By the time the police had set up one of their checkpoints on the Colchester bypass, stopping all cars and heavier vehicles, the Ford Escort was passing Witham, heading for Chelmsford.

Joyce said, 'If you put me out at Chelmsford I promise I won't say a thing. I'll hang about in Chelmsford and get something to eat, you can give me five pounds of what you've got there, and I won't go to the police till the evening. I'll tell them I lost my memory.'

'You've only got one shoe,' said Marty.

'You can put me down outside a shoe shop. I'll tell the police you had masks on and you blindfolded me. I'll tell them . . .' the greatest disguise Joyce could think of '. . . you were old!'

'Forget it,' said Nigel. 'You say you would but you wouldn't. They'd get it out of you. Make up your mind to it, you come with us.'

The first of the rush hour traffic was leaving London as they came into it. This time Marty got on to the North Circular Road at Woodford, and they weren't much held up till they came to Finchley. From there on it was crawling all the way, and Marty, who had stood up to the ordeal better than Nigel, now felt his nerves getting the better of him. Part of the trouble was that in the driving mirror he kept his eye as much on those two in the back of the car as on the traffic behind. Of course it was all a load of rubbish about Nigel killing that bank manager, he couldn't have done that, and he wouldn't do anything to the girl either if she did anything to attract the attention of other drivers It was only a question of whether the girl knew it. She didn't seem to. Most of the time she was hunched in the corner behind him, her head hanging. Maybe she thought other people would be indifferent, pass by on the other side like that bit they taught you in Sunday School, but Marty knew that wasn't so from the time when a woman had grabbed him and he'd only just escaped the store detective.

He began to do silly things like cutting in and making other drivers hoot, and once he actually touched the rear bumper of the car in front with the front bumper of the Escort. Luckily for them, the car he touched had bumpers of rubber composition and its driver was easy-going, doing no more than call out of his window that there was no harm done. But it creased Marty up all the same, and by the time they got to Brent Cross his hands were jerking up and down on the steering wheel and he had stalled out twice because he couldn't control his clutch foot properly.

Still, now they were nearly home. At Staples Corner he turned down the Edgware Road, and by ten to five they were outside the house in Cricklewood, the Escort parked among the hundred or so other cars that lined the street on both sides.

Nigel didn't feel sympathy, but he could see Marty was spent, washed up. So he took the gun and pushed it into Joyce's back and made her walk in front of him with Marty by her side, his arm trailing over her shoulder like a lover's. On the stairs they met Bridey, the Irish girl who had the room next to Marty's, on her way to work as barmaid in the Rose of Killarney, but she took no notice of them beyond saying an offhand hallo. She had often seen Nigel there before and she was used to Marty bringing girls in. If he had brought a girl's corpse in, carrying it in his arms, she might have wondered about it for a few minutes, but she wouldn't have done anything, she wouldn't have gone to the police. Two of her brothers had fringe connections with the IRA and she had helped overturn a car when they had carried the hunger strike martyr's body down from the Crown to the Sacred Heart. She and her whole family avoided the police.

Marty's front door had a Yale lock on it and another, older, lock with a big iron key. They pushed Joyce into the room and Nigel turned the iron key. Marty fell on the mattress, face-downwards, but Joyce just stood, looking about her at the dirt and disorder, and bringing her hands together to clasp them over her chest.

'Next we get shot of the vehicle,' said Nigel.

Marty didn't say anything, Nigel kicked at the mattress and lit the wick of the oil heater – it was very cold – and then he said it again. 'We have to get shot of the car.'

Marty groaned. 'Who's going to find it down there?'

'The fuzz. You have to get yourself together and drive it some place and dump it. Right?'

'I'm knackered.' Marty heaved himself up and pushed a pile of dirty clothes on to the floor. 'I got to have a drink.'

'Yeah, right, later, when we've got that car off our backs.'

'Christ,' said Marty, 'we've got four grand in that bag and I can't have a fucking drink.'

Nigel gritted his teeth at that. He couldn't understand why there hadn't been seven like that guy Purford said. But he managed, for Jane or Jenny's benefit, a mid-Atlantic drawl. 'I'll drive it. You stay here with her. We'll tie her up again, put her in the kitchen. You'll go to sleep, I know you, and if she gets screeching the old git next door'll freak.'

'No,' said Joyce.

'Was I asking you? You do as you're told, Janey.'

They got hold of Joyce and gagged her again and tied her hands behind her and tied her feet. Marty took off her shoe to stop her making noises with her feet and shut the kitchen door on her. She made noises, though not for long.

The rain had stopped and the slate-grey sky was barred with long streaks of orange. Nigel and Marty got as far away from the kitchen door as they could and talked in fierce whispers. When the traffic slackened Nigel would take the car and dispose of it. They looked longingly at Marty's radio, but they dared not switch it on.

7

For a couple of hours the police suspected Alan Groombridge. No one had seen the raiders enter the bank. They set up road blocks just the same and informed the Groombridge and Culver next-of-kin. But they were suspicious. According to his son and his father-in-law, Groombridge never went out for lunch, and the licensee of the Childon Arms told them he had never been in there. At first they played with the possibility that he and the girl were in it together, and had gone off together in his car. The presence of Joyce's shoe made that unlikely. Besides, this theory presupposed an attachment between them which Joyce's father and Groombridge's son derided. Groombridge never went out in the evenings without his wife, and Joyce spent all hers with Stephen Hallam.

A girl so devoted to her family as Joyce would never have chosen this particular day for such an enterprise. But had Groombridge taken the money, overturned the tills, left the safe open, and abducted the girl by force? These were ideas about which a detective inspector and a sergeant hazily speculated while questioning Childon residents. They were soon to abandon them for the more dismaying truth.

By five they were back where they had started, back to a raid and a double kidnapping. A lot of things happened at five. Peter Johns, driver of the red Vauxhall, heard about it on the radio and went to the police to describe the white mini-van with which he had nearly collided. Neither he nor his mother could describe the driver or his companion, but Mrs Johns had something to contribute. As the van edged past the Vauxhall, she thought she had heard a sound from the back of the van like someone drumming a heel on the floor. A single clack-clack-clack, Mrs Johns said, as of one shoe drumming, not two.

The next person to bring them information was the driver of a tractor who remembered meeting a Morris Eleven Hundred. The tractor man, who had a vivid imagination, said the driver had looked terrified and there had certainly been someone sitting beside him, no doubt about it, and his driving had been wild and erratic. There had been three bank robbers then, the police concluded, two to drive the van with Joyce in it, the third in Alan Groombridge's car, compelling him to drive. The loss of the silver-blue Ford Escort was reported by its owner, a Mrs Beech.

By then Nigel Thaxby and Marty Foster and Joyce Culver were in Cricklewood and Alan Groombridge was in the Maharajah Hotel in the Shepherd's Bush Road.

Literature had taught him that there were all sorts of cheap hotels and houses of call and disreputable lodging places in the vicinity of Paddington Station, so he went there first on the Metropolitan Line out of Liverpool Street. But times had changed, the hotels were all respectable and filled up already with foreign tourists and quite expensive. The reception clerk in one of them recommended him to Mr Azziz (who happened to be his cousin) and Alan liked the name, feeling it was right for him. It reminded him of *A Passage to India* and seemed a good omen.

Staying in hotels had not played an important part in his life. Five years before, when Mrs Summitt had died, she had left Pam two hundred pounds and they had spent it on a proper holiday, staying at an hotel in Torquay. Luggage they had had, especially Pam and Jillian, an immense amount of it, and he wondered about his own lack of even a suitcase. He had read that hotel-keepers are particular about that sort of thing.

The Maharajah was a tall late-nineteenth-century house

built of brown brick with its name on it in blue neon, the first H and the J being missing. Yes, Mr Azziz had a single room for the gentleman, Mr Forster, was it? Four pounds fifty a night, and pay in advance if he'd be so kind. Alan need not have worried about his lack of luggage because Mr Azziz, who was only after a fast buck, wouldn't have cared what he lacked or what he had done, so long as he paid in advance and didn't break the place up.

Alan was shown to a dirty little room on the second floor where there was no carpet or central heating or washbasin, but there was a sink with a cold tap, a gas ring and kettle and cups and saucers, and a gas fire with a slot meter. He locked himself in and emptied his bulging pockets. The sight of the money made his head swim. He closed his eyes and put his head on to his knees because he was afraid he would faint. When he opened his eyes the money was still there. It was real. He spread it out to dry it, and he hung his raincoat over the back of a chair and kicked off his wet shoes and looked at the money. Nearest to him lay the portrait of Florence Nightingale which he had torn in half and mended with Sellotape.

Outside the window the sky was like orangeade in a dirty glass. The noise was fearful, the roar and throb and grind and screeching of rush traffic going round Shepherd's Bush Green and into Chiswick and up to Harlesden and over to Acton and down to Hammersmith. The house shook. He lay on the bed, tossed about like someone at the top of a tree in a gale. He would never sleep, it was impossible that he would ever sleep again. He must think now about what he had done and why and what he was going to do next. The madness was receding, leaving him paralysed with fear and a sensation of being incapable of coping with anything. He must think, he must act, he must decide. Grinding himself to a pitch of thinking, he shut his eyes again and fell at once into a deep sleep.

Nigel delayed till half-past six, waiting for the traffic to ease up a bit. As far as he was concerned, when you drove a car your right foot was for the accelerator and the brake and your left one for nothing. He got into the Escort and started it and it leapt forward and stalled, nearly hitting the Range Rover in front of it because Marty had left it in bottom gear. Nigel tried again and more or less got it right, though the gears made horrible noises. He moved out into the traffic, feeling sick. But there was no time for that sort of thing because it was a full-time job ramming his left foot up and down and doing exercises with his left hand. He didn't know where he was aiming for and it wouldn't have been much use if he had. His knowledge of London was sparse. He could get from Notting Hill to Oxford Street and from Notting Hill to Cricklewood on buses, and that was about all.

The traffic daunted him. He could see himself crashing the car and having to abandon it and run, so he turned it into a side road in Willesden and sat in it for what seemed like hours, watching the main road until there weren't quite so many cars and buses going past. It hadn't been hours at all, it was still only a quarter past seven. He had some idea where he was when he found himself careering uncertainly down Ladbroke Grove, and after that signs for south of the river began coming up. He would take it over one of the bridges and dump it in south London.

He was scared stiff. He wished he had some way of knowing what was going on and how much the police had found out. The way to have found out was from Marty's radio which the girl would have heard, and heard too that Groombridge was alive. Luckily, he'd managed to whisper to Marty not to switch it on. He was so thick, that one, you never knew what he'd do next.

The manual gear shift was getting easier to handle. He tried breathing deeply to calm himself, and up to a point it worked. What he really ought to do was hide the car somewhere where it wouldn't be found for weeks. He knew he was a conspicuous person, being six feet tall and with bright fair hair and regular features, not little and dark and ordinary like Marty. People wouldn't be able to remember Marty but they'd remember him.

He turned right out of Ladbroke Grove and drove down Holland Park Avenue to Shepherd's Bush and along the Shepherd's Bush Road, thus passing the Maharajah Hotel and forming one of the constituents of the noise that throbbed in Alan Groombridge's sleeping brain. On to Hammersmith and over Putney Bridge. There were still about two gallons in the tank. In Wandsworth he put the car down an alley which was bounded by factory walls and where there was no one to see him. It was a relief to get out of it, though he knew he couldn't just leave it there. He had grabbed a handful of notes out of the carrier. In these circumstances, Marty would have wanted a drink, but stress had made Nigel ravenously hungry. There was a Greek café just down the street. He went in and ordered himself a meal of kebab and taramasalata.

He might just as easily have chosen the fish and chip place or the Hong Kong Dragon, but he chose the Greek café and it gave him an idea. Beginning on his kebab, Nigel glanced at a poster on the café wall, a coloured photograph of Heraklion. This reminded him that before he had worked round to the subject of a loan, he had listened with half an ear to his mother's usual gossip about her friends. This had included the information that the Boltons were going off for a month to Heraklion. Wherever that might be, Nigel thought, Greece somewhere. Dr Bolton, now retired, and his Greek wife, whom he was supposed to (or had once been supposed to) call Uncle Bob and Auntie Helena, lived in a house near Epping Forest. He had been there once, about seven years before, and now he recalled that Dr Bolton kept his car in a garage, a sort of shed really, at the bottom of his garden. An isolated sort of place. The car would now be in the airport car park, for his mother had said they were going last Saturday. Would the garage be locked? Nigel tried to remember if there had been a lock on the door and thought there hadn't been, though he couldn't be certain after so long. If there was and he couldn't use the garage, he would push the car into one of the forest ponds. Thinking about the Boltons brought back to him that visit and how he, aged fourteen, had listened avidly to Dr Bolton's account of a stolen car that had been dumped in a pond and not found for weeks.

He left the café at nine and returned cautiously to the alley. The Ford Escort was still there and no other car was. He got quickly into the car and drove off, this time crossing the river by Wandsworth Bridge.

It took him nearly an hour to get out to Woodford, and he had some very bad moments when a police car seemed to be following him after the lights at Blackhorse Road. But the police car turned off and at last he was approaching the

Boltons' house which was down a sort of lane off the Epping New Road. The place was as remote and lonely as he remembered it, but right outside the garage, on the miserable little bit of pavement that dwindled away into a path a few yards on, four men were digging a hole. They worked by the light of lamps run from a generator in a Gas Board van parked close by. Nigel thought he had better back the car out and pretend to be using the entrance to the lane only as a place for turning. It was only the second time he had got into reverse gear, and he bungled it, getting into first instead and nearly hitting the Gas Board van. But he tried again and managed a reasonable three-point turn, observing exultantly that there was no lock on the garage door and no padlock either. But he couldn't park on the Epping New Road itself which was likely, he thought, to be a favourite venue for traffic control cars.

He drove a bit further, stuck the Escort under some bushes off the Loughton Road, and went into a phone box to phone Marty.

The receiver was handed to Marty by the pale red-haired girl who looked as if she were permanently kept shut up in the dark. She passed it to him without a word. He didn't say anything to Nigel except yes and no and all right and see you, and then he went back to do as he was told and untie Joyce.

She was cramped and cold and stiff, and for the first time her spirit was broken. She said feebly, 'I want to go to the toilet.'

'OK, if you must,' said Marty, not guessing or even wondering what it had cost her to lie out there for hours, controlling her bladder at all costs, hoping to die before she disgraced herself in that way.

He went out first, making sure there was no one there, and brandishing the gun. He stood on the landing while she was in the lavatory. Bridey was out, and no light showed under Mr Green's door. He always went to bed at eight-thirty, besides being deaf as a post. Marty took Joyce back and locked the door again with the big iron key which he pocketed. Joyce sat on the mattress, rubbing her wrists and her ankles. He would have liked a cup of coffee, would have liked one hours ago, but something in him had baulked at making coffee for himself in front of a bound and gagged girl. Nor could he make it now and keep her covered with the gun. So he fetched in a half-full bottle of milk and poured it into two cups.

'Keep your filthy milk,' Joyce mumbled.

'Be like that.' Marty drank his and reached for the other cup.

'No, you don't,' said Joyce, and swigged hers down. 'When are you going to let me go?'

'Tomorrow,' said Marty.

Joyce considered this. She looked around her. 'Where am I supposed to sleep?'

'How about on here with me?'

The remark and the circumstances would immediately have recalled to Alan Groombridge's mind Faulkner's *Sanctuary* or even *No Orchids for Miss Blandish*, but in fact Marty had said what he had out of bravado. Being twenty-one and healthy, he naturally fancied pretty well every girl he saw, and in a different situation he would certainly have fancied big-busted long-legged Joyce. But he had never felt less sexy in his adult life, and he had almost reached a point where, if she had touched him, he would have screamed. Every sound in the house, every creak of stair and click of door, made him think it was the police coming. The sight of the unusable radio tormented him. Joyce, however, was resolved to sell her honour dear. She summoned up her last shreds of scorn, told him he had to be joking, she was engaged to someone twice his size who'd lay him out as soon as look at him, and she'd sleep on the sofa, thanks very much. Marty let her take two of the four pillows off his bed, watched her sniff them and make a face, and grab for herself his thickest blanket.

She lay down, fully clothed, covered herself up and turned her face to the big greasy back of the sofa. Under the blanket she eased herself out of her skirt and her jumper, but kept her blouse and her slip on. Marty sat up, holding the gun and wishing there was some wine.

'Put the light out,' said Joyce.

'Who're you giving orders to? You can get stuffed.'

He was rather pleased when Joyce began to cry. She was deeply ashamed of herself but she couldn't help it. She was thinking about poor Mr Groombridge and about her mother and father not having their party, and about Stephen. It was much to her credit that she thought about herself hardly at all. But those others, poor Mum and Dad, Stephen going to announce their engagement at the Toll House that night, Mr Groombridge's poor wife, so devoted to him and ringing him at the bank every day. Joyce sobbed loudly, giving herself over to the noblest of griefs, that which is expended for others. Marty had been pleased at first because it showed his power over her, but now he was uneasy. It upset him, he'd never liked seeing birds cry.

'You'll be OK,' he said. 'Belt up, can't you? We won't hurt you if you do what we say. Honest. Get yourself together, can't you?'

Joyce couldn't. Marty switched the light off, but the room didn't get dark, never got dark, because of the yellow lamps outside. He got into bed and put the gun under the pillow and stuffed his fingers in his ears. He felt like crying himself. What the hell was Nigel doing? Suppose he didn't come back? The room vibrated with Joyce's crying. It was worse than the traffic when the lorries and the buses went by. Then it subsided, it stopped and there was silence. Joyce had cried herself to sleep. Marty thought the silence worse than the noise. He was terribly hungry, he craved for a drink, and he hadn't been to bed at this hour since he was fifteen.

At the point when he had almost decided to give up, to get out of there and run away somewhere, leaving the money to Joyce, there came a tapping at the door. He jumped out of his skin and his heart gave a great lurch. But the tap came again and with it a harsh tired whisper. It was only Nigel, Nigel at last.

Joyce didn't stir but he kept his voice very low.

'Had to hang about till the goddamned gasmen went. The car's in the garage. I walked to Chingford and got a bus. Christ!'

Nigel dropped the bunch of Ford keys into the carrier bag with the money. He found a bit of string in the kitchen and threaded it through the big iron key and hung it round his neck. They turned off the oil heater. They put the gun under the pillows and got into bed. It was just after midnight, the end of the longest day of their lives.

8

When Alan woke up he didn't know where he was. The room was full of orange light. Great God (as Lord Byron had remarked the morning after his wedding, the sun shining through his red bed curtains) I am surely in hell! Then he remembered. It all came back to him, as Joyce would have said. The time, according to his watch, was five in the morning, and the light came from street lamps penetrating a tangerine-coloured blind which he must have pulled down on the previous evening. He had slept for eleven hours. The money, now dry and crinkly, glimmered in the golden light. Great God, I am surely in hell . . .

He got out of bed and went into the passage and found the bathroom. There was a notice inside his bedroom door which said in strange English: *The Management take no responsibilities for valuable left in rooms at owners risks.* He put the money back in his raincoat pockets, afraid now of walking about with his pockets bulging like that. All night he had slept in his clothes, and his trousers were as crumpled as the notes, so he took them off and put them under the mattress, which was a way of pressing trousers advocated by Wilfred Summitt. He took off the rest of his clothes and got back into bed, listening to the noise outside that had begun again. The noise seemed to him symptomatic of the uproar which must be going on over his disappearance and Joyce's and the loss of the money, the whole world up in arms.

It struck him fearfully that, once Joyce was set free or rescued, she would tell the police he hadn't been in the bank when the men came. He thought about that for a while, sweating in the cold room. She would tell them, and they would begin tracing his movements from the car to the bus station, the bus to the train. He saw himself as standing out in all those crowds like a leper or a freak or – how had Kipling put it? – a mustard plaster in a coal cellar. But she might not know. It all depended on whether they had blindfolded her and also on how many of them there had been. If she had seen his car still in the yard, and then they had blindfolded her and put her in their car or van for a while before driving away . . . He clung on to that hope, and he thought guiltily of Pam and his children. In her way, Pam had been a good wife to him. It seemed to him certain that, whatever came of this, he would never live with her again, never again share a bed with her or go shopping with her to Stantwich or yield to her for the sake of peace. That was past and the bank was past. The future was liberty or the inside of a jail.

At seven he got up and, wearing his raincoat as a dressing gown, went to have a bath. The water was only lukewarm because, although he had three thousand pounds in his pockets, he hadn't got a ten-pence piece for the meter. Shivering, he put his clothes on. The trousers didn't look too bad. He packed the money as flat as he could, putting some of it into his jacket pockets, some into his trouser pockets, and the rest in the breast pocket of his jacket. It made him look fatter than he was. Mr Azziz didn't provide breakfast or, indeed, any meals, so he went out to find a place where he could eat.

Immediately he was in the street, he felt a craven fear. He must be a marked man, he thought, his face better known than a royal prince's or a pop star's. It didn't occur to him then that it had never been a habit in the Groombridge or Summitt families to sit for studio portraits or go in for ambitious amateur photography, and therefore no large recognizable image of his face could exist. By some magic or some feat of science, it would be brought to the public view. He slunk into a newsagent's, trying to see without being seen, but the tall black headlines leapt at him. He stood looking at a counter full of chocolate bars until he dared to face those headlines again.

It was Joyce's portrait, not his own, that met his eyes, Joyce photographed by Stephen Hallam to seem almost beautiful. *Bank Girl Kidnap*, said one paper; another, *Manager and Girl Kidnapped in Bank Raid*. He picked up both papers in hands that shook and proffered a pound note. The man behind the counter asked him if he had anything smaller. Alan shook his head, he couldn't speak.

He had forgotten about breakfast and wondered how he

could ever have thought of it. He sat on a bench on Shepherd's Bush Green and forced himself to look at those papers, though his instinct, now he had bought them, was to throw them away and run away from them himself. But he took a deep breath and forced his eyes on to those headlines and that smaller type.

Before he could find a picture of himself, he had to look on the inside pages. They had put it there, he thought, because it was such a poor likeness, useless for purposes of identification, and adding no character to the account. Christopher had taken the snapshot of himself and Pam and Wilfred Summitt in the garden of the house in Hillcrest. Enlarged, and enlarged only to about an inch in depth, Alan's face was a muzzy grinning mask. It might equally well have been Constable Rogers or P. Richardson standing there beside the pampas grass.

The other newspaper had the same picture. Were there any others in existence? More vague snapshots, he thought. At his wedding, that shotgun affair, gloomy with disgrace, there had been no photographers. He became aware that the paralysis of terror was easing. It was sliding from him as from a man healed and made limber again. He saw the mist and the pale sun, the grass, other people, felt the renewal of hunger and thirst. If he couldn't be recognized, identified, he had little to fear. The relief of it, the slow easing that was now quickening and acquiring a sort of excitement, drove away any desire to read any more of the newspaper accounts. He forgot Joyce, who even now might be safe, might be at home once more with only a vague memory of events. He was safe and free, and he had got what he wanted.

A cup of tea and eggs and toast increased his sense of well-being. The papers he dropped thankfully into a bin. After a few minutes' exploration, he found the tube station and got a train to Oxford Circus. Oxford Street, he knew, was the place to buy clothes. Every Englishman, no matter how sheltered the life he has led, knows that. He bought two pairs of jeans, four tee-shirts, some socks and underpants and a windcheater, two sweaters and a pair of comfortable half-boots. Jeans had never been permitted him in the past, for Pam said they were only for the young, all right for Christopher but ridiculous on a man of his age. He told himself he was buying them as a disguise, but he knew it wasn't only that. It was to recapture – or to discover, for you cannot recapture what you have never had – his youth.

He came out of the shop wearing his new clothes, and this transformation was another step towards ridding him of the fear of pursuit. People, even policemen, passed him without a second glance. Next he bought a suitcase, and in a public lavatory deep below the street, he filled it with his working suit and that money-loaded raincoat.

The case was too cumbersome to carry about for long. No ardent reader of fiction could ever be in doubt about where temporarily to rid himself of it. He caught a train to Charing Cross, and there deposited the case in a left-luggage locker. At last he and the money were separated. Walking away, with only his wallet filled as he had so often filled it during those secret indulgences in his office, he felt a lightness in his step as if, along with the money, he had disburdened himself of culpability. So he made his way up to Trafalgar Square. He went into the National Gallery and the National Portrait Gallery and looked at the theatres in St Martin's Lane and the Charing Cross Road, and had a large lunch with wine. Tonight he would go to the theatre. In all his life he had never really been to the theatre except once or twice to Stantwich Rep and to pantomimes in London when the children were younger. He bought himself a ticket for the front row of the stalls, row A and right in the middle, for Marlowe's *Dr Faustus*.

Next to the theatre was a flat agency. It reminded him that he would need somewhere to live, he wasn't going to stay at the Maharajah longer than he had to. But it wouldn't be a flat. A few seconds spent studying the contents of the agency's window told him anything of that nature would be beyond his means. But a room at sixteen to twenty pounds a week, that he could manage.

The girl inside gave him two addresses. One was in Maida Vale and the other in Paddington. Before he could locate either of them, Alan had to buy himself a London guide. He went to the Paddington address first because the room to let there was cheaper.

The landlord came to the door with an evening paper

in his hand. Alan saw that he and Joyce were still the lead story, and his own face was there again, magnified to a featureless blur. The sight of it revived his anxiety, but the landlord put the paper down on a table and invited him in.

Alan would have taken the room, though it was sparsely furnished and comfortless. At any rate, it would be his to improve as he chose, and it was better than the Maharajah. The landlord too seemed happy to accept him as a tenant so long as he understood he had to pay a month's rent in advance and a deposit. Alan had got out his wallet and was preparing to sign the agreement as A. J. Forster when the landlord said:

'I take it you can let me have a bank reference?'

The blood rushed into Alan's face.

'It's usual,' said the landlord. 'I've got to protect myself.'

'I was going to pay you in cash.'

'Maybe, but I'll still want a reference. How about your employer or the people where you're living now? Haven't you got a bank?'

In the circumstances, the question held a terrible irony. Alan didn't know what to say except that he had changed his mind, and he got out of the house as fast as he could, certain the landlord thought him a criminal, as indeed he was. No one knew more than he about opening bank accounts. It was impossible for him to open one, he had no name, no address, no occupation and no past. Suddenly he felt frightened, out there in the alien street with no identity, no possessions, and he saw his act as not so much an enormity as an incredible folly. In all those months of playing with the banknotes, he had never considered the practicalities of an existence with them illicitly in his possession. Because then it had been a dream and now it was reality.

He could go on living, he supposed, at the Maharajah. But could he? At four pounds fifty a night, that little hole with its sink and its gas ring was going to cost him as much as one of the flats he had seen on offer in the agency window. He couldn't go on staying there, yet he wouldn't be able to find anywhere else because it was 'usual' to ask for a bank reference.

Occasionally in the past he had received letters asking for such a reference, and his replies had been discreet, in accordance with the bank's policy of never divulging to any outsider the state of a customer's account. He had merely written that, yes, so-and-so banked at his branch of the Anglian-Victoria, and that apparently had been satisfactory. He felt sick at the thought of where his own account was – with the Childon sub-branch and in a name that today was familiar to every newspaper reader.

An idea came to him of returning home. It wasn't too late to go back if he really wanted to. He could say they had taken him and had let him go. He had been blindfolded all the time, so he hadn't seen their faces or where they had taken him. The shock had been so great that he couldn't remember much, only that he had saved some of the bank's money which he had deposited in a safe place. Perhaps it would be better not to mention the money at all. Why should they suspect him if he gave himself up now?

It was a quarter past three. It was not on his watch but on a clock on a wall ahead of him that he saw the time. And beside the clock, on a sheet of frosted glass, were etched the A and the V, the vine leaves and the crown, that were the emblems of the Anglian-Victoria Bank. The Anglian-Victoria, Paddington Station Branch. Alan stood outside, wondering what would happen if he went in and told the manager who he was.

He went into the bank. Customers were waiting in a queue behind a railing until a green light came on to tell them a till was free. A tremendous impulse took hold of him to announce that he was Alan Groombridge. If he did that now, in a few days' time he would be back behind his own till, driving his car, listening to Pam talking about the cost of living, to Pop quarrelling with Christopher, reading in the evenings in his own warm house. He set his teeth and clenched his hands to stop himself yielding to that impulse, though he still stood there at the end of the queue.

Steadily the green lights came on, and one customer moved to a till, then another. Alan stayed in the queue and shifted with it as it passed a row of tables spread with green blotters. A man was sitting at one of the tables, making an entry in his paying-in book. Alan watched him, envying him his legitimate possession of it.

The time was half-past three, and the security man moved to the door to prevent any late-comer from entering. Alan began framing words in his mind, how he had lost his memory, how the sight of that emblem had recalled to him who he was. But his clothes? How could he explain his new clothes?

Looking down at those jeans brought his eyes again to the man at the table. The paying-in book was open for anyone to see that two hundred and fifty pounds was about to be paid in, though Paul Browning hadn't been so imprudent as actually to place notes or cheques on it. Alan knew he was called Paul Browning because that was the name he had just written on a cheque book request form. And now he added under it, in the same block capitals, his address: 15 Exmoor Gardens, London NW2.

As a green light came up for the woman immediately in front of Alan in the queue, Paul Browning joined it to stand behind him. With a muttered 'Excuse me', Alan turned and made for the door.

He had found a bank reference and an identity, and with the discovery he burned the last fragile boat that could have taken him back. The security man let him out politely.

9

Joyce woke up first. With sleep, her confidence and her courage had come back. The fact that the others – those two pigs, as she called them to herself – still slept on, made her despise more than fear them. Fancy sleeping like that when you'd done a bank robbery and kidnapped someone! They must want their heads tested. But while she despised them, she also felt easier with them than she would have done had they been forty or fifty. Disgusting and low as they were, they were nevertheless young, they belonged with her in the great universal club of youth.

She got up and put on her clothes. She went into the

kitchen and washed her hands and face under the cold tap, a good cold splash like she always had in the mornings, though she usually had a bath first. Pity she couldn't clean her teeth. What was there to eat? No good waiting for those pigs to provide something. Like the low people they were, they had no fridge, but there was an unopened packet of back bacon on a shelf of that bookcase thing, and some eggs in a box and lots of tins of baked beans. Joyce had a good look at the bacon packet. It might be a year old, for all she knew, you never could tell with people like that. But, no. *Sell by March 15*, it said. She put the kettle on, and Flora margarine into a frying pan, and lit all the other gas burners and the oven to warm herself up.

The misery of Mum and Dad and Stephen she had got into better perspective. She wasn't dead, was she? Stephen would value her all the more when she turned up alive and kicking. They were going to let her go today. She wondered how and where, and she thought it would be rather fun telling it all to the police and maybe the newspapers.

The roaring of the gas woke Marty and he saw Joyce wasn't on the sofa. He called out, 'Christ!' and Joyce came in to stand insolently in the doorway. There are some people who wake up and orientate themselves very quickly in the mornings, and there are others who droop about, half-asleep, for quite a long time. Joyce belonged in the first category and Marty in the second. He groaned and fumbled for the gun.

'For all you know,' said Joyce, 'I might have a couple of detectives out here with me, waiting to arrest you.'

She made a big pot of strong tea and found a packet of extended life milk. Nasty stuff, but better than nothing. She heard Marty starting to get up and she kept her head averted. He might be stark naked for all she could tell, which was all right when it was Stephen or one of her brothers coming out of the bathroom, but not that pig. However, he was wearing blue pants with mauve bindings, and by the time he had come into the kitchen he had pulled on jeans and a shirt.

'Give us a cup of tea.'

'Get it yourself,' said Joyce. 'You can take me to the toilet first.'

She was a full five minutes in there, doing it on purpose,

Marty thought. He was on tenterhooks lest Bridey came out or old Green. But there was no one. The lavatory flushed and Joyce walked back, not looking at him. She passed Nigel who was sitting on the mattress with his head in his hands, and went straight to the sink to wash her hands. All the bacon in the pan, two eggs and a saucepanful of baked beans went on to the plate she had heated for herself. She sat down at the kitchen table and began to eat.

Nigel was obliged to pour tea for both of them and start cooking more bacon. He did it clumsily because he too was a slow waker. 'One of us'll have to go out,' he said, 'and get a paper and more food.'

'And some booze, for Christ's sake,' said Marty.

'How about me going?' said Joyce pertly.

'Be your age,' said Nigel, and to Marty, 'You can go. I'll be better keeping an eye on her.'

Joyce ate fastidiously, trying not to show how famished she was. 'When are you going to let me go?'

'Tomorrow,' said Marty.

'You said that yesterday.'

'Then he shouldn't have,' snapped Nigel. 'You stay here. Get it? You stay here till I'm good and ready.'

Joyce had believed Marty. She felt a little terrible tremor, but she said with boldness, 'If he's going out he can get me a pair of shoes.'

'You what? That'd be marvellous, that would, me getting a pair of girl's shoes when they know you've lost one.'

'Get her a pair of flip-flops or sandals or something. You can go to Marks in Kilburn. She'll only get a hole in her tights and then we'll have to buy goddamned tights.'

'And a toothbrush,' said Joyce.

Marty pointed to a pot, encrusted with blackened soap, in which reposed a toothbrush with splayed brown tufts.

'Me use that?' said Joyce indignantly. She thought of the nastiest infection she could, of one she'd seen written on the wall in the Ladies' on Stantwich Station. 'I'd get crabs.'

Nigel couldn't help grinning at that. They ate their breakfast and Marty went off, leaving Nigel with the gun.

Joyce wasn't used to being idle, and she had never been in such a nasty dirty place before. She announced, without asking Nigel's permission, that she intended to clean up the kitchen.

Marty would have been quite pleased. He didn't clean the kitchen himself because he was too lazy to do so, not because he disapproved of cleaning. Nigel did. He had left home partly because his parents were always cleaning something. He sat on the mattress and watched Joyce scrubbing away, and for the first time he felt some emotion towards her move in him. Until then he had thought of her as an object or a nuisance. Now what he felt was anger. He was profoundly disturbed by what she was doing, it brought up old half-forgotten feelings and unhappy scenes, and he kept the gun trained on her, although her back was turned and she couldn't see it.

About an hour later Marty tapped at the door, giving the four little raps that was their signal to each other. He threw a pair of rubber-thonged sandals on to the floor and dropped the shopping bag. His face was white and pinched.

'Where's Joyce?'

'That's her name, is it? In the kitchen, spring-cleaning. What's freaking you?'

Marty began taking a newspaper folded small out of his jacket pocket. 'No,' said Nigel. 'Outside.' They went out on to the landing and Nigel locked the door behind them. He spread out a copy of the same newspaper Alan Groombridge had read some hours before. 'I don't get it,' he said. 'What does it mean? We never even saw the guy.'

'D'you reckon it's some sort of trick?'

'I don't know. What would be the point? And why do they say seven thousand when there was only four?'

Marty shook his head. 'Maybe the guy did see us and got scared and went off somewhere and lost his memory.' He voiced a fear that had been tormenting him. 'Look, what you said to the girl about killing him – that wasn't true, was it?'

Nigel looked hard at him and then at the gun. 'How could it be?' he said slowly. 'The trigger doesn't even move.'

'Yeah, I meant – well, you could have hit him over the head, I don't know.'

'I never saw him, he wasn't there. Now you tear up that

paper and put the bits down the bog. She's got to go on thinking we've killed Groombridge and we've got to get out of here and get her out. Right?'

'Right,' said Marty.

Joyce finished cleaning the kitchen and then she cleaned her teeth with the toothbrush Marty had bought. She had to use soap for this, and she had heard that cleaning your teeth with soap turned them yellow, but perhaps that was only if you went on doing it for a long time. And she wasn't going to be there for a long time because tomorrow they were going to let her go.

Nigel sharply refused to allow her to go down to the bathroom, so she washed herself in the kitchen with a chair pushed hard against the door. Her mother used to make a joke about this fashion of getting oneself clean, saying that one washed down as far as possible and up as far as possible, but what happened to poor possible? Thinking of Mum brought tears to Joyce's eyes, but she scrubbed them away and scrubbed poor possible so hard that it gave her a reason for crying. After that she washed for herself to wear tomorrow the least disreputable of Marty's tee-shirts from the pile on the bed. She wasn't going to confront the police and be reunited with her family in a dirty dishevelled state, not she.

Marty went out again at seven and came back with whisky and wine and Chinese takeaway for the three of them. Joyce ate hers in the kitchen, at the table. The boys had theirs sitting on the living room floor. The place was close and fuggy and smelly from the oil heater and the oven which had been on all day, and condensation trickled down the inside of the windows. When she had finished eating, Joyce walked in and looked at Nigel and Marty. The gun was on the floor beside the plastic pack with chow mein in it. They didn't use plates, pigs that they were, thought Joyce.

She had never been the sort of person who avoids issues because it is better not to know for certain. She would rather know.

'You're going to let me go tomorrow,' she said.

'Who said?' Nigel put his hand over the gun. He forgot to be a mid-Atlantic-cum-sixties-hippy-drop-out and spoke, to Marty's reluctant admiration, in the authoritative public school tone of his forebears. 'There's no question of your leaving here tomorrow. You'd go straight to the police and describe us and describe this place. We took you with us to avoid that happening and the situation hasn't changed.' He remembered then and added, with a nasal intonation, 'No way.'

'But the situation won't change,' said Joyce.

'I could kill you, couldn't I? Couldn't I?' He watched her stiffen and then very slightly recoil. It pleased him. 'You be a good girl,' he said, 'and do what we say and stop asking goddamned silly questions, and I'll think of a way to work it for the lot of us. I just need a bit of hush. Right?'

'Have a drop of Scotch,' said Marty who was cheered and made affable by about a quarter of a pint of it. Joyce wouldn't. Nor would she accept any of the Yugoslav Riesling that Nigel was drinking. If the situation hadn't changed and wasn't going to change, she would have to think of ways to change it. The first duty of a prisoner is to escape. Her uncle who had been a prisoner of war always said that, though he had never succeeded in escaping from the *Stalag Luft* in which for four years he had been incarcerated. She had never thought of escaping before because she had believed they would release her, but she thought about it now.

When they had settled down for the night and the boys were asleep, Marty snoring more loudly than her father did – Joyce had formerly thought young people never snored – she got up off the sofa and tip-toed into the kitchen. Earlier in the day she had found a ball-point pen while scraping out thick greasy dirt from under the sink, and she had left it on the draining board, not supposing then that she would have any use for it. She hadn't much faith in this pen which had probably been there for years, perhaps before the time of the present tenant. But once she had wiped the tip of it carefully on the now clean dish-cloth and scribbled a bit on the edge of a matchbox to make the ink flow, she found it wrote quite satisfactorily. Enough light came in from outside to make writing, if not reading, possible. Like Alan Groombridge, Joyce found the constant blaze of light shining in from street lamps throughout the night very strange, but it had its uses. She sat at the table and wrote on a smoothed-out piece of the paper bag in which the sandals had been:

They have killed Mr Groombridge. They are keeping me in a room in London. She crossed out *London* and wrote *in this street. I do not know the name of the street or the number of the house. There are two of them. They are young, about 20. One of them is little and dark. The first finger on his right hand has been injured. The nail is twisted. The other one is tall and fair. Please get me out. They are dangerous. They have a gun. Signed, Joyce Marilyn Culver.*

Joyce thought she would wrap her message round the piece of pumice stone from the draining board and drop it out of the window. But she couldn't open the window, though neither of the boys seemed to hear her struggling with it. Never mind, the lavatory window opened and she would throw it out of there in the morning. So for the time being she put the note in that traditional repository favoured by all heroines in distress, her bosom. She put it into the cleft between her breasts, and went back to the sofa. But first she favoured her captors with a look of contempt. If she had been in their place, she thought, she would have insisted on staying awake while her partner slept, and only sleeping while he stayed awake to watch. Look where getting drunk and passing out had got them! But in the yellow light the string with the key on it showed round the dark one's neck, and the black barrel of the gun gleamed dully against the fair one's slack hand.

At nine she was up and washed and dressed and shaking Marty who woke with a blinding headache and much hung over.

'Go away. Leave me alone,' said Marty, and he buried his face in the dirty pillow.

'If you don't get up and take me to the toilet I'll bang and bang at that door with a chair. I'll break the window.'

'Do that and you're dead,' said Nigel, elbowing Marty out of the way and fishing out the gun. He had gone to bed fully clothed, and it was out of distaste for the smell of him that Joyce looked in the other direction. Nigel took her out on to the landing and leaned against the wall, seeing stars and feeling as if an army of goblins in hobnailed boots were forming fours inside his head. He mustn't drink like that again, it was crazy. He wasn't hooked on the stuff like that little brain, was he? He didn't even really like it.

Joyce had her message wrapped round the pumice stone. She stood on the lavatory seat, wishing she could see something of what lay outside and below the window, but it was only a frosted fanlight that opened and this above her head, though not above the reach of her hand. The pumice dropped, and she trembled lest it make a bang which the fair one might hear when it touched the ground. She pulled the flush hard to drown any other sound.

The other one glowered at her when they were back in the room. 'What d'you think you're doing, wearing my tee-shirt?'

'I've got to change my clothes, haven't I? I'm not going to stay in the same thing day after day like you lot. I was brought up to keep myself nice. You want to take all that lot round the launderette. What's the good of me cleaning the place up when it just pongs of dirty clothes?'

Neither of them answered her. Marty took the radio to the lavatory with him, but he couldn't get anything out of it except pop music. Then he went off shopping without waiting for Nigel's command. The open air comforted him. He was a country boy and used to spending most of his time outside; all his jobs but the parcel-packing one had been outdoor jobs, and even when living on the dole he had spent hours wandering about London each day and walking on Hampstead Heath. He couldn't stand being shut up, scared as he was each time he saw a policeman or a police car. Nigel, on the other hand, liked being indoors, he didn't suffer from claustrophobia. He liked dirty little rooms with shut windows where he could loaf about and dream grandiose Nietzschian dreams of himself as the Superman with many little brains and stupid women to cringe and do his bidding. The stupid woman was cleaning again, the living room this time. Let her get on with it if that was all she was fit for.

On her knees, washing the skirting board, Joyce said, 'Have you thought yet? Have you thought when I'm going to get out of here?'

'Look,' said Nigel, 'we're looking after you OK, aren't

we? You're getting your nosh, aren't you? And you can drink as much liquor as you want, only you don't want. I know this pad isn't amazing, but it's not that bad. You aren't getting ill-treated.'

'You must be joking. When are you going to let me go?'

'Can't you say anything else but when are you going to get out of here?'

'Yes,' said Joyce. 'What's your name?'

'Robert Redford,' said Nigel, who had been told he resembled this actor in his earliest films.

'When am I going to get out of here, Robert?'

'When I'm ready, Joyce. When my friend and I see our opportunity to get ourselves safely out of the country and don't have to worry about you giving the police a lot of damaging information.'

Joyce stood up. 'Why don't you talk like that all the time?' she said with an ingenuous look. 'It sounds ever so nice. You could have a really posh accent if you liked.'

'Oh, piss off, will you?' said Nigel, losing his temper. 'Just piss off and give me a bit of hush.'

Joyce smiled. She had never read Dr Edith Bone's account of how, when condemned in Hungary to seven years' solitary confinement, she never missed a chance to needle and provoke her guards, while never in the slightest degree co-operating with them. She had not read it, but she was employing the same tactics herself.

10

The police were told of a silver-blue Ford Escort seen on the evening of Monday, 4 March, in the Epping New Road. Their informant was one of the gang of gasmen who had been working on a faulty main outside Dr Bolton's house, and the car he had seen had in fact been Mrs Beech's car and its driver Nigel Thaxby. But when the police had searched Epping Forest for the car and dragged one of the gravel pit ponds, they abandoned that line of enquiry in favour of a more hopeful one involving the departure of a silver-blue Escort from Dover by the ferry to Calais on Monday night. This car, according to witnesses, had been driven by a middle-aged man with a younger man beside him and a man and a girl in the back. The man in the back seemed to have been asleep, but might have been unconscious or drugged. No one had observed the registration plates.

Alan Groombridge's car was found in the car park in Colchester. His fingerprints were on its interior and so were those of his wife. There were several other sets of fingerprints, and these came from the hands of a Stoke Mill farm worker to whom Alan had given a lift home on the previous Tuesday. But the police didn't know this, and it didn't occur to the farm worker to tell them. By that time they had questioned Christopher and Jillian Groombridge about their friends and anyone to whom they might have talked and given information about the Childon branch of the Anglian-Victoria Bank.

At first it seemed likely that the leak had come from Christopher, he being male and the elder. But it was soon clear that Christopher had never shown the slightest interest in any of the bank's arrangements, was ignorant as to how much was kept in the safe, and hadn't those sort of friends anyway. All his friends were just like himself, law-abiding, prosperous, salesmen or belonging to fringe professions like his own, well-dressed, affluent, living at home in order the better to live it up. They regarded crime as not so much immoral as 'a mug's game'. As for Jillian, she made an impression on them of naïve innocence. All her time away from home, she said, had been spent with Sharon and Bridget, and Sharon and Bridget backed her up. They wouldn't, in any case, have been able to give the name of John Purford because they didn't know it. Perhaps there had been no leak, for nothing need have been divulged which local men couldn't have found out for themselves. On the other hand, the mini-van, located soon after Mrs Beech's complaint, had been hired in Croydon by a man with a big black beard who spoke, according to the Relyacar Rentals girl, with a north country accent. So the police, having turned Stantwich and Colchester and quite a large area of south London upside down, turned their attention towards Humberside and Cleveland.

Wilfred Summitt and Mrs Elizabeth Culver appeared on television, but neither put up satisfactory performances. Mrs Culver broke down and cried as soon as the first question was put to her, and Pop, seeing this as an opportunity to air his new dogmas, launched into a manifesto which opened with an appeal for mass public executions. He went on talking for a while after he had been cut off in mid-sentence, not realizing he was no longer on view.

Looking for somewhere to live, Alan left the suitcase in a locker at Paddington Station. At the theatre he had put it under his seat where it annoyed no one because he was sitting in the front row. He had enjoyed *Faustus*, identifying with its protagonist. He too had sold his soul for the kingdoms of the earth – and, incidentally, for three thousand pounds. See, see where Christ's blood streams in the firmament! He had felt a bit like that himself, looking at the sunset while earlier he was walking in Kensington Gardens. Would he also find his Helen to make him immortal with a kiss? At that thought he blushed in the dark theatre, and blushed again, thinking of it, as he walked from Paddington Station down towards the Bayswater Road.

Notting Hill, he had decided, must be his future place of abode, not because he had ever been there or knew anything about it, but because Wilfred Summitt said that wild horses wouldn't drag him to Notting Hill. He hadn't been there either, but he talked about it as a sort of Sodom and Gomorrah. There had been race riots there in the fifties and some more a couple of years back, which was enough to make Pop see it as a sinful slum where everyone was smashed out of their minds on hashish, and black people stuck knives in you. Alan went to two agencies in Notting Hill and was given quite a lot of hopeful-looking addresses. He went to three of them before lunch.

It was an unpleasant shock to discover that London landlords call a room ten feet by twelve with a sink and cooker in one corner, a flatlet. He could hardly believe in the serious, let alone honest, intent behind calling two knives and two forks and two spoons from Woolworth's 'fully equipped with cutlery' or an old three-piece suite in stretch nylon covers 'immaculate furnishings'. Having eaten his lunch in a pub – going into pubs was a lovely new experience – he bought an evening paper and a transistor radio, and read the paper sitting on a seat in Kensington Gardens. It told him that the Anglian-Victoria Bank was offering a reward of twenty thousand pounds for information leading to the arrest of the bank robbers and the safe return of himself and Joyce. A girl came and sat beside him and began feeding pigeons and sparrows with bits of stale cake. She was so much like his fantasy girl, with a long slender neck and fine delicate hands and black hair as smooth and straight as a skein of silk, that he couldn't keep from staring at her.

The second time she caught his eye, she smiled and said it was a shame the way the pigeons drove the smaller birds away and got all the best bits, but what could you do? They also had to live.

Her voice was strong and rich and assured. He felt shy of her because of her resemblance to the fantasy girl, and because of that too he was aware of an unfamiliar stirring of desire. Was she his Helen? He answered her hesitantly and then, since she had begun it, she had spoken to him first, and anyway he had a good reason for his question, he asked her if she lived nearby.

'In Pembroke Villas,' she said. 'I work in an antique shop, the Pembroke Market.'

He said hastily, not wanting her to get the wrong idea – though would it be the wrong idea? – 'I asked because I'm looking for a place to live. Just a room.'

She interrupted him before he could explain how disillusioned he had been. 'It's got much more difficult in the past couple of years. A good way used to be to buy the evening papers as soon as they come on the streets and phone places straightaway.'

'I haven't tried that,' he said, thinking of how difficult it would be, using pay phones and getting enough change, and more and more nights at the Maharajah, and thinking too how exciting and frightening it would be to live in the same house as she.

'You sometimes see ads in newsagents' windows,' she said. 'They have them in the window of the place next to the market.'

Was it an invitation? She had got up and was smiling encouragingly at him. For the first time he noticed how beautifully dressed she was, just the way his private black-haired girl had been dressed in those dreams of his. The cover of *Vogue*, which he had seen in Stantwich paper shops but which Pam couldn't afford to buy – coffee-coloured suede suit, long silk scarf, stitched leather gloves and nut-brown boots as shiny as glass.

'May I walk back with you?' he said.

'Well, of course.'

It was quite a long way. She talked about the difficulty of getting accommodation and told anecdotes of the experiences of friends of hers, how they had found flats by this means or that, their brushes with landlords and rent tribunals. She herself owned a floor of the house in which she lived. He gathered that her father was well-off and had bought it for her. Her easy manner put him at his ease, and he thought how wonderful it was to talk again, to have found, however briefly, a companion. Must their companionship be brief?

Outside the Pembroke Market she left him.

'If you're passing,' she said, 'come in and let me know how you've got on.' Her smile was bold and inviting, yet not brazen. He wouldn't have cared if it had been. He thought, he was sure, she was waiting for him to ask if he could see her before that, if he could see her that evening. But paralysis overcame him. He could be wrong. How was he to know? How did one ever tell? She might simply be being helpful and friendly, and from any overture he made turn on her heel in disgust.

So he just said, 'Of course I will, you've been very kind,' and watched her walk away, fancying he had seen disappointment in her face.

There were no ads for accommodation in the newsagent's window, only cards put there by people who wanted rooms or had prams and pianos and kittens for sale, and an unbelievable one from a girl offering massage and 'very strict' French lessons. As he was turning away, the back of the case in which the cards were was suddenly opened inwards and a hand appeared. When he looked back, he saw that a new card had been affixed. Doubtfully – because what sort of an inhabitable room could you get for ten pounds a week? – he read it: 22 Montcalm Gardens, W11. He looked up Montcalm Gardens in his London guide, and found that it turned off Ladbroke Grove at what he was already learning to think of as the 'nice' end. A boy of about twenty was looking over his shoulder. Alan thought he too must be looking for a room, and if that was so he knew who was going to get there first. The room might be all right, it was bound to be better than the Maharajah. His legs were weary, so he did another first time thing and, copying gestures he had seen successfully performed by others, he hailed and acquired a taxi.

The name on the card had been Engstrand and it had immediately brought to Alan's mind old man Jacob and Regina in Ibsen's *Ghosts*. One branch of the Forsyte family had lived in Ladbroke Grove. Such literary associations were pleasant to think of. He himself was like a character in a book on the threshold of adventure and perhaps of love.

In Montcalm Gardens two long terraces of tall early Victorian houses eyed each other austerely across a straight wide roadway. The street was treeless, though thready branches of planes could be seen at the far end of it. It had an air of dowdy, but not at all shabby, grandeur. There were little balconies on the houses with railings whose supports were like the legs of Chippendale chairs, and each house had, at the top of a flight of steps, a porch composed of pilasters and a narrow flat roof. The first thing he noticed about number 22 was how clean and sparkling its windows were, and that inside the one nearest the porch stood surely a hundred narcissi in a big copper bowl.

The door was opened to him by a woman he supposed must be Mrs Engstrand. She looked enquiringly at him, her head a little on one side.

'I saw your advertisement . . .' he began.

'Already? I only put it in half an hour ago. I've just got back.'

'They were putting it in when I saw it.'

'Well, you mustn't stand there. Do come in.' Her voice was both vague and intense, an educated voice which he wouldn't have expected from the look of her. She wore no make-up on her pale small face that seemed to peep out from, to be engulfed by, a mass of thick brown curly hair. Had she really been out, dressed like that, in denims with frayed hems and a sweater with a hole at one elbow? She looked about thirty, maybe more.

He went in, and she closed the door behind him. 'I'm afraid the room's in the basement,' she said. 'I'm telling you that now in case you've got any sort of thing against basements.'

'I don't think so,' said Alan. From what he could see of the hall, and, through an open door, of the interior of a room, the house was very beautifully, indeed luxuriously, furnished. There were those things in evidence that make for an archetype of domestic beauty: old carefully polished furniture, precious ornaments, pictures in thin silver frames, a Chinese lacquer screen, chairs covered in wild silk, long and oval mirrors, more spring flowers in shallow bowls. And there was exquisite cleanliness. What would he be offered here for ten pounds a week? A cupboard under the stairs?

Downstairs in the basement was a kind of hall, with white walls and carpeted in red haircord. He waited to be shown the cupboard. She opened a door and he saw instead something like that which he had expected to see at the first house he had visited, before he was disillusioned.

She said, 'It's big, at any rate, and it really isn't very dark. The kitchen's through there. Tenants have the use of the garden. I'm afraid anyone who took this room would have to share the bathroom with Mr Locksley, but he's very very nice. He's got the front room.'

This one was large with French windows. One wall was hung all over with shelves, and the shelves were full of books. The furniture wasn't of the standard of upstairs, but it was good Victorian furniture, and on the floor was the same haircord as in the passage. It looked new, as if no one had ever walked on it. He looked out of the window at a lawn and daffodils and two little birch trees and a peaked black brick wall, overgrown with ivy.

'That's the chapel of a convent. There are lots of convents round here. It's Cardinal Manning country. The Oblates of St Charles, you know.'

He said, 'Like in that essay by Lytton Strachey.'

'Oh, have you read *that*?' He turned round and saw that her intense birdlike little face was glowing. 'Isn't it lovely?' she said. 'I read it once every year. *Eminent Victorians* is up there on the top shelf. Oh, do you mind the books? They're nearly all novels, you see, and there isn't anywhere else for them because my father-in-law can't bear novels.'

He was bewildered. 'Why not?'

'He says that fiction causes most of our troubles because it teaches us to fantasize and lead vicarious lives instead of coming to terms with reality. He's Ambrose Engstrand, you know.'

Alan didn't know. He had never heard of Ambrose Engstrand. Did she mean he could have the room? 'I can give you a bank reference,' he said. 'Will that do?'

'I *hate* having to ask for one at all,' she said earnestly. 'It seems so awfully rude. But Ambrose said I must. As far as I'm concerned, anyone who likes *Eminent Victorians* is all right. But it's Ambrose's house and I do have to do what he says.'

'My name is Browning,' Alan said. 'Paul Browning. Fifteen, Exmoor Gardens, NW2 – that's my present address. My bank's the Anglian-Victoria, Paddington Station Branch.' He hesitated. 'D'you think I could move in this week?'

'Move in today if you like.' She pushed back her thick massy hair with both hands, smiled at his amazement. 'I didn't mean I was really going to write to that bank. I shall just let Ambrose think I have. Caesar – that's Mr Locksley – hasn't even got a bank. Banks don't mean anything. I've proved that because he always pays his rent on the dot, and I knew he'd be lovely because he knows all Shakespeare's sonnets by heart. Can you believe it?'

His head swimming, Alan said he was very grateful and thank you very much, and he'd move in that evening. He went back to Paddington Station and fetched the suitcase and went into a café to have a cup of tea. He was Paul Browning, late of North-west Two (wherever that might be) now of Montcalm Gardens, Notting Hill. It was by this name that he would introduce himself to the black-haired girl tomorrow when he went to the Pembroke Market to tell her what had happened. Tomorrow, though, not today. Quite enough had happened today. He needed peace and quiet to collect his thoughts and make himself a design for living.

11

Joyce Culver's father offered his house, or the price that house would fetch when sold, for the safe return of his daughter. It was all he had.

Marty and Nigel saw it in the paper.

'What's the good of a house or the bread it'll fetch,' said Nigel, 'if you're inside?'

'We could make him promise not to tell the fuzz. And then he could sell the place and give us the money.'

'Yeah? And just why would he do that thing once he'd got her back? Be your age.'

They were talking in low voices on the landing. Joyce was in the lavatory, dropping another note out of the window, this time wrapped round the metal lid of a glass jar. Even in a normal dwelling house, and Marty's place was far from that, it is difficult to find an object which is at the same time heavy enough to drop, unbreakable and small enough to conceal on one's person. She couldn't see where it fell. She didn't know that under the window was an area containing five dustbins, and that Brent Council refuse collectors had already thrown the pumice stone and the paper round it into the crushing machine at the back of their truck. One of the dustbin lids had blown off, and Joyce's second note dropped into the bin on top of a parcel of potato peelings deposited there by Bridey on the previous night.

'When am I going to get out of here?' said Joyce, emerging.

'Keep your voice down.' Nigel was aghast, in spite of the absence of Bridey and the deafness of Mr Green.

'When am I going to get out of here!' yelled Joyce at the top of her voice.

Marty clapped his hand over her mouth and manhandled her back into the room. She felt the gun thrust against her ribs, but she was beginning to have her doubts about the gun, she was beginning to get ideas about that.

'If you do that again,' said Marty, 'you can pee in a pot in the kitchen.'

'Charming,' said Joyce. 'I suppose that's what you're used to, I suppose that's what goes on in whatever home you come from. Or pig-sty, as I should call it. Got an Elsan in a hut at the end of your garden, have you? I shouldn't be at all surprised.'

She held up her head and glared at him. Marty was beginning to hate her, for the shot had gone home. She had precisely described the sanitary arrangements in his father's cottage. It was Thursday, and they had been shut up in here since Monday night. Why shouldn't they just get out and leave her here? They could tie her up and tie her to the gas stove or something so she couldn't move. And then when they'd got safe away they could phone the police, make one of those anonymous calls and tell them where she was. He thought that would work. It was Nigel, whispering out there on the landing or when Joyce was washing – she was always washing – who said it wasn't on. Where could they go, he said, where the call couldn't be traced from? Once give them this address, anyway, and they'd know who Marty was and very soon who Nigel was. They might just as well go and give themselves up now. Nigel had said he had a plan, though he didn't say what it was, and Marty thought the plan must be all hot air and Nigel didn't know what to do any more than he did.

His only consolation was that he could have an unlimited amount to drink. Yesterday he had drunk more than half a bottle of whisky and today he was going to finish it and start on the next one. He couldn't understand why Nigel had begun being nice to Joyce, buttering her up and flattering her. What was the point when it was obvious the only way was to put the fear of God into her? Nigel had got him to buy her *Woman* and *Nineteen* and made him take the sheets and pillowcases to the launderette on the corner. Nigel, who liked dirt and used to say being clean was bourgeois! He poured himself a cupful of whisky.

'You can get me some wool and some needles next time you go out,' said Joyce. 'I need a bit of knitting to pass the time.'

'I'm not your slave.'

'Do as she says,' said Nigel. 'Why not if it keeps her happy?'

The room was spotlessly clean. Joyce had even washed the curtains, and Nigel, with the aid of sign language and a pencil and paper, had borrowed an iron from Mr Green so that she could iron them and iron her own freshly washed blouse. Marty thought he must be off his head, that wasn't the way to break her spirit. He glowered at her resentfully. She looked as if she were just about to set off for work in a job where one's appearance counted for a lot.

Two hours earlier she had washed her hair. She had on a crisp neat blouse and a creaseless skirt, and now she was filing her nails. That was another thing Nigel had got him to fetch in, a nail file, and he'd said something about mascara. But Marty had jibbed at that. He wasn't buying bloody silly mascara, no way.

Nigel didn't say much all that day. He was thinking. Marty made him sick with his silly ideas and the way, most of the time, he was smashed out of his mind on whisky. He ought to be able to see they couldn't get shot of Joyce. Where they went she must go. Only he knew they couldn't take her out into the street with them, couldn't steal another car while she was with them. Yet she must be with them, and the only way she could be was if she could somehow be made to be on their side. It was with some vague yet definite aim of getting her on his side that Nigel had started being nice to her. That was why he made Marty buy things for her and praised her appearance and the cleanliness of the place – though he hated it – and why, that evening, he got Marty to fetch in three great hunks of T-bone because Joyce said she liked steak.

There had been robberies, he thought, in which hostages had been so brain-washed by their captors that they had gone over to the kidnappers' side and had even assisted in subsequent raids. Nigel didn't want to do any Symbionese Liberation Army stuff, he had no doctrines with which to indoctrinate anyone, but there must be other ways. By Friday morning he had thought of another way.

He lay on the mattress in the yellow light that was the same at dawn as at midnight, shifting his body away from Marty who snored and smelt of sweat and whisky, and looking at the plump pale curve of Joyce's cheek and her smooth pink eyelids closed in sleep. He got up and went into the kitchen and looked at himself in Marty's bit of broken mirror over the sink. Beautiful blue eyes looked back at him, a straight nose, a mobile delicately cut mouth. Any polone'd go for me in a big way, thought Nigel, and then he remembered he mustn't use that word and why he mustn't, and he was flooded with fear.

Marty went out and brought back brown knitting wool and two pairs of needles and some proper toilet soap and toothpaste – and two more bottles of whisky. They didn't bother to count the money or ration it or note what they had spent. Marty just grabbed a handful of notes from the carrier each time he left. He bought expensive food and things for Joyce and, in Nigel's opinion, quantities of rubbish for himself, pornography from the Adult Book Exchange and proper glasses to put his whisky in and, now he could afford to smoke again, cartons of strong king-size cigarettes. And he stayed out longer and longer each day. Skiving off his duties, leaving him to guard Joyce, thought Nigel. It maddened him to see Marty sitting there, making them all cough with the smoke from his cigarettes, and gloating over those filthy magazines. He found he was embarrassed for Joyce when Marty looked at those pictures in front of her, but he didn't know why he should be, why he should care.

Joyce scarcely noticed and didn't care at all. She had the attitude of most women to pornography, that it was disgusting and boring and its lure beyond her comprehension. She was having interesting ideas about the gun. One of them was that it wasn't loaded, and the other that it wasn't a real gun. She had written on all her notes – there was a third one tucked inside her bra – that they had killed Alan Groombridge, but now she wondered if this were true. She only had their word for it, and you couldn't believe a word they said. It might be a toy gun. She had read that robbers used toy guns because of the difficulty of getting real ones. It would be just like them to play about with a toy gun. If she could get her hands on that gun and find out that it was only a toy or not loaded, she would be free. She might not be able to unlock the door because the key was on a string round Nigel's neck, but she would be able to run when they took her to the lavatory, or break one of the windows at night and scream.

But how was she ever going to get hold of the gun? They kept it under their pillows at night, and though Marty was a heavy sleeper, Nigel wasn't. Or Robert, as she thought of him, and the dark one, as she thought of Marty. Sometimes she had awakened in the night and looked at them, and Robert had stirred and looked back at her. That was unnerving. Maybe one night, if the police didn't come and no one found her notes, Robert would get drunk too and she would have her chance. She had stopped thinking much about Mum and Dad and Stephen, for when she did so she couldn't keep from crying. And she wasn't going to cry, not even at night, not in front of them. She thought instead about the gun and ways of getting hold of it, for she had as little faith in any plan Robert might concoct as the dark one had. They would keep her there for ever unless she escaped.

They ate smoked trout and Greek takeaway and cream trifle from Marks and Spencer's on Friday night, and Marty drank half a bottle of Teacher's. Everything was bought ready-cooked because Marty and Nigel couldn't cook and Joyce wouldn't cook for them. Joyce sat on the sofa with her feet up to stop either of them sitting there too. She had already completed about six inches of the front of her jumper, and she knitted away resolutely.

'The fact is,' she said, 'you don't know what to do with me, do you? You got yourselves in a right mess when you brought me here and now you don't know how to get out of it. My God, I could rob a bank single-handed better than the two of you did. No more than a pair of babes in arms you are.'

Nigel kept his temper and even smiled. He could look pleasantly little-boyish when he smiled. 'Maybe you've got something there, my love. We made a mistake about that. We all make mistakes.'

'I don't,' said Joyce arrogantly. 'If you do what's right and keep to the law and face up to your responsibilities and get steady jobs you don't make mistakes.'

'Shut up!' screamed Marty. 'Shut your trap, you bitch! Who d'you think you are, giving us that load of shit? You want to remember you're our prisoner.'

Joyce smiled at him slowly. She made one of the few profound statements she was ever to utter.

'Oh, no,' she said. 'I'm not your prisoner. You're mine.'

12

The man called Locksley came home while Alan was putting his clothes away and stowing the money in one of the drawers of a Victorian mahogany tallboy. The door of the next room closed quietly, and for about an hour there penetrated through the wall soft music of the kind Alan thought was called baroque. He liked it and was rather sorry when it stopped and Locksley went out again.

The house was quiet now, the only sound the distant one of traffic in Ladbroke Grove. This surprised him. Since his landlady had a father-in-law, she must also surely have a husband and very likely, at her age, small children. But Alan felt that he was now alone in the house, though this couldn't be so as, through the French window, he could see light from upstairs shining on the lawn. The two radiators in his room had come on at six, and it was pleasantly warm, but there didn't seem to be any hot water or anything to provide it. After looking in vain for some switch or meter, he went upstairs to find Mrs Engstrand.

He knocked on the door of the room from which the light was coming. She opened it herself and there was no one with her. She was still wearing the jeans and the sweater, not the long evening skirt he had somehow expected.

'I'm terribly sorry. There's an immersion heater in that cupboard outside your door and you share it with Caesar. I expect he's switched it off. I must tell him to leave it on *all* the time now you've come. I'll come down with you and show you.'

He only caught a glimpse of the interior of the room, but that was enough. A dark carpet, straw-coloured satin curtains, silk papered walls, Chinese porcelain, framed photographs of a handsome elderly man and an even handsomer young one.

'Caesar's very considerate.' She showed him the heater and the switch. 'He's always trying to save me money but it really isn't necessary. I pay the bills for this part of the house, you see, so Ambrose won't ever see them.'

He didn't understand what she meant and he was too shy to enquire. Shyness stopped him asking her in for a drink, though he had drinks, having stocked up with brandy and vodka and gin on his way there. The bottles looked good on top of the tallboy. Maybe when the husband turned up, young Engstrand, he'd invite the two of them and this Caesar and the black-haired girl. It would give him an excuse for asking her.

That night and again in the morning he listened to his radio. There was nothing about Joyce or himself, for no news is not good news as far as the media are concerned. He bought a paper in which the front page headlines were *Pay Claim Fiasco* and *Wife-swapping Led to Murder*. Down in the bottom left-hand corner was a paragraph about Joyce's father offering his house for the return of his daughter. Alan wondered what the police and the bank would do if Joyce turned up safe and told them she had been alone in the bank when the two men came, that there had been only two men, and only four thousand in the safe and the tills. It was very likely that she would tell them that. He asked himself if, by wondering this, he meant that he didn't want her to turn up safe. The idea was uncomfortable and disturbing, so he put it out of his head and walked to the back of this rather superior newsagent's-cum-stationer's to where there were racks of paperbacks. There was no need to buy any books as his room was like a little library, but he had long ago got into the habit of always looking at the wares in bookshops, and why break such a good habit as that?

It wasn't really coincidence that among the books on the shelf labelled Philosophy and Popular Science he came upon the name of Ambrose Engstrand. Probably the man's works were in most bookshops but he had never had occasion to notice them before.

He took down *The Glory of the Real* and read on the back of its jacket that its author was a philosopher and psychologist. He had degrees that filled up a whole line of type, had held a chair of philosophy at some northern university, and made his home, when he was not travelling, in West London. His other works included *Neo-Empiricism* and *Dream, the Opiate*.

Alan read the first page of the introduction. 'In modern times, though not throughout history, the dream has been all. Think of the contexts in which we use this word. "The girl of my dreams", "It was like a dream", "In my wildest dreams". The real has been discarded by mankind as ugly and untenable, to be shunned and scorned in favour of a shadow land of fantasy.' A few pages further on he found: 'How has this come about? The cause is not hard to find. Society was not always sick, not always chasing mirages and creating chimeras. Before the advent of the novel, in roughly 1740, when vicarious living was first presented to man as a way of life, and fiction took the lid from the Pandora's Box of fantasy, man had come to terms with reality, lived it and loved it.' Alan put the book back. One pound thirty seemed a lot to pay for it, especially as – he smiled to himself – there were a lot of novels in Montcalm Gardens he hadn't yet read.

But it was certain that he had sold his soul and run away in order to find what this Engstrand called the real, so he had better begin by going to the Pembroke Market. The black-haired girl wasn't there, she was taking the day off, and Alan didn't dare ask the man who spoke to him for the number of her house. But he learned that her name was Rose. Tomorrow he would come back and see Rose and find the courage to ask her out with him on Saturday night. Saturday night was for going out, he thought, not yet understanding that for him now every night was a Saturday.

The rest of the day he spent at the Hayward Gallery, going on a river trip to Greenwich and at a cinema in the West End where he saw a Fassbinder film which, though intellectual and obscure, would have made Wilfred Summitt's scanty hair stand on end. There was nothing in the evening paper about Joyce, only *New Moves in Pay Claim* and *Sabena Jet Hi-jacked.* He had been in his room ten minutes when there came a knock at his door.

A man of about thirty with red hair and the kind of waxen complexion that sometimes goes with this colouring stood outside.

'Locksley. I thought I'd come and say hallo.'

Alan nearly said his name was Groombridge. He remembered just in time. 'Paul Browning. Come in.'

The man came in and looked round. 'Bit of luck for both

of us,' he said, 'finding this place. By the way, they call me Caesar. Or I should say I call me Caesar. What they called me was Cecil. I had the name part in Julius Caesar at school and I sort of adopted it.'

'Do you really know all Shakespeare's sonnets by heart?'

'Una tell you that, did she?' Caesar grinned. 'I'm not clever, I've just got a good memory. She's a lovely lady, Una, but she's crazy. She told me she let you have this place because you'd read some essay about Cardinal Manning. Feel like coming up the Elgin or KPH or somewhere for a slow one?'

'A slow one?' said Alan.

'Well, it won't be a quick one, will it? No point in euphemisms. We have to face the real, as Ambrose would say. D'you mind if we take Una?'

Alan said he didn't mind, but what about her husband coming home? Caesar gave him a sidelong look and said there was no fear of that, thank God. However, he came back to say she couldn't come because she had to wait in for a phone call from Djakarta, so they went to the Kensington Park Hotel on their own.

'Did you mean there isn't a husband?' said Alan when Caesar had bought them two pints of bitter. It was a strange experience for him who had never been 'out with the boys' in his life or even into pubs much except with Pam on holiday. 'Is she a widow?'

Caesar shook his head. 'The beautiful Stewart's alive and kicking somewhere out in the West Indies with his new lady. I got it all from Annie, that's my girl friend. She used to know this Stewart when he was the heart throb of Hampstead. Una's about the loneliest person I know. She's a waif. But what's to be done? I'd do something about it myself, only I've got Annie.'

'There must be unattached men about,' said Alan.

'Not so many. Una's thirty-two. She's OK to look at but she's not amazing, is she? Most guys the right age are married or involved. She doesn't go out much, she never meets anyone. You wouldn't care to take an interest, I suppose?'

Alan blushed and hoped it didn't show in the pub's murky light. He thought of Rose, her inviting smile, her elegance, the girl of his dreams soon to come true. To turn

Una down, he chose what he thought was the correct expression. 'I don't find her attractive.'

'Pity. The fact is, she ought to get away from Ambrose. Of course he's saved her. He's probably saved her sanity and her life, but all that dynamic personality – it's like Trilby and Svengali.'

'Why does she live in his house?'

'She was married to this Stewart who's quite something in the looks line. I've seen photos. I tell you, if I wasn't hetero up to my eyebrows, he'd turn *me* on. He and Una had a flat in Hampstead but he was always going off with other ladies. Couldn't resist them, Annie says, and they never left him alone. Una got so she couldn't stand it any more and they split up. They had this kid, Lucy her name was. She was two. Stewart used to have her at the weekends.'

'Was?' Alan interrupted. 'You mean she's dead?'

'Stewart took her to his current lady's flat for the weekend. Slum, I should say. He and the lady went out for a slow one and while they were out Lucy overturned an oil heater and her nightdress caught fire.'

'That's horrible.'

'Yes. Una was ill for months. The beautiful Stewart took himself off after the coroner had laid into him at the inquest. He shut himself up in a cottage his mother had left him on Dartmoor. And that's where Ambrose came in. He fetched Una back here and looked after her. He was writing his *magnum opus* at the time, *Neo-Empiricism*. That's what he calls himself, a Neo-Empiricist. But he dropped that for months and gave himself over to helping her. That was three years ago. And ever since then she's lived here and kept house for him, and before he went off to Java in January he had the basement converted and redecorated and said she was to let it and have the rents for her income. He said it would teach her to assume responsibility and reface reality.'

'What happened to Stewart Engstrand?'

'He turned up after a bit, wanted Una to go back to him. But she wouldn't, and Ambrose said he'd only be retreating into a mother-dream, whereas what he needed was to work experientially through the reality of his exceptional looks and his sexuality. So he worked through them by taking up with a new lady who's rich and who carried him off to her house in Trinidad. Another beer? Or would you rather have something shorter and stronger?'

'My turn,' said Alan awkwardly, not knowing if this was etiquette when Caesar had invited him out. But it seemed to be, Caesar didn't demur, and Alan knew that he was learning and making friends and working experientially through the reality of what he had chosen back there in Childon with the money in his hands.

Rose was there in the Pembroke Market on Friday. She had wound her long hair about her head in coils and put on a long black dress with silver ornaments. She looked remote and mysterious and seductive. He had his speech prepared, he had been rehearsing it all the way from Montcalm Gardens.

'I said I'd come in and tell you how I got on. I found a place from looking in that window, and it's ideal. But for you I'd never have thought of looking. I'm so grateful. If you're free tomorrow night, if you're not busy or anything, I wondered if I could – well, if we could go out somewhere. You've been so kind.'

She said with raised eyebrows, 'You want to take me out because I was kind?'

'I didn't just mean that.' She had embarrassed him, and embarrassment made his voice tremble. But he was inspired to say, afraid of his own boldness, 'No one would think of you like that, no one who had seen you.'

She smiled. 'Ah,' she said, 'that's better.' Her eyes devoured him. He turned his own away, but he seemed beyond blushing.

In as casual a manner as he could muster, he said, 'Dinner perhaps and a theatre? Could I fix something and – and phone you?'

'I'll be in the shop all day tomorrow,' she said. 'Do phone any time.' It was strange and fascinating the way those simple words seemed to imply and promise so much. It was her voice, he supposed, and her cool poise and the swan-like way she had of moving her head. She gave a light throaty giggle. 'Haven't you forgotten something?'

'Have I?' He was afraid all the time of committing solecisms. What had he done now?

'Your name,' she said.

He told her it was Paul Browning. Some hours had passed before he began to get cold feet, and by then he had booked a table in a restaurant whose phone number he had got from a advertisement in the eve ning paper. He stood outside a theatre, screwing up his courage to go in and buy two stalls for himself and Rose.

13

Like Alan Groombridge, Nigel lived in a world of dreams. The only thing he liked about Marty's magazines were the advertisements which showed young men of his own age and no better-looking, posing with dark glasses on in front of Lotus sports cars, or lounging in penthouses with balloon glasses of brandy in their hands. He saw himself in such a place with Joyce as his slave, waiting on him. He would make her kneel in front of him when she brought him his food, and if it wasn't to his liking he would kick her. She would know of every crime he committed – by that time he would be the European emperor of crime – but she would keep his secrets fanatically, for she worshipped him and received his blows and his insults with a dog-like devotion. They would live in Monaco, he thought, or perhaps in Rome, and there would be other women in his life, models and film stars to whom he gave the best part of his attention while Joyce stayed at home or was sent, with a flick of his fingers, to her own room. But occasionally, when he could spare the time, he would talk to her of his beginnings, remind her of how she had once defied him in a squalid little room in North London, until, with brilliant foresight, he had stooped to her and bound her to him and made her his for ever. And she would kneel at his feet, thanking him for his condescension, begging for a rare touch, a precious kiss. He would laugh at that, kicking her away. Had she forgotten that once she had talked of betraying him?

Reality was shot through with doubt. His sexual experience had been very limited. At his public school he had had encounters with other boys which had been nasty, brutish and short, though a slight improvement on masturbation. When he left he found he was very attractive to girls, but he wasn't successful with them. The better-looking they were the more they frightened him. Confronted by youth and beauty, he was paralysed. His father sent him to a psychiatrist – not, of course, because of his failure with the girls which Dr Thaxby knew nothing about. He sent him to find out why his son couldn't get a degree or a job like other people. The psychiatrist was unable to discover why not, and this wasn't surprising as he mostly asked Nigel questions about his feelings towards his mother. Nigel said he hated his mother, which wasn't true but he knew it was the kind of thing psychiatrists like to hear. The psychiatrist never told Nigel any of his findings or diagnosed anything, and Nigel stopped going to him after about five sessions. He had himself come to the conclusion that all he needed to make him a success and everything come right was an older and perhaps rather unattractive woman to show him the way. He found older women easier to be with than girls. They frightened him less because he could despise them and feel they must be grateful to him.

Joyce, however, wasn't an older woman. He thought she was probably younger than he. But there was no question of her looks scaring him into impotence. With her big round eyes and thick lips and nose like a small pudgy cake, she was ugly and coarse. And he despised her already. Though he affected to be contemptuous of gracious living and cut-glass and silver and well-laid tables and professional people and dinner in the evening and university degrees, his upbringing had left on him an ineradicable mark. He was a snob at heart. Joyce was distasteful to him because she came from the working class. But he wasn't afraid of her, and as he thought of what he would gain, freedom and escape and her silence, he became less afraid of himself.

On Saturday morning he brought in coffee, a cup for her and one for himself. Marty had stopped drinking anything but whisky and wine.

'What's that you're knitting, Joyce?'

'A jumper.'

'Is there a picture of it?'

She turned the page of the magazine and showed him a coloured photograph of a beautiful but flat-chested and skeletal girl in a voluminous sweater. She didn't say anything but flicked the page over after allowing him a five-second glimpse.

'You'll look great in that,' said Nigel. 'You've got a super figure.'

'Mmm,' said Joyce. She wasn't flattered. Every boy she had ever been out with had told her that, and anyway she had known it herself since she was twelve. We long to be praised for the beauties we don't have, and Joyce had started to love Stephen when he said she had wonderful eyes.

'I want you to go out tonight,' said Nigel to Marty while Joyce was in the lavatory.

'You what?'

'Leave me alone with her.'

'That's brilliant, that is,' said Marty. 'I hang about out in the cold while you make it with the girl. No way. No way at all.'

'Think about it if you know how to do that thing. Just think if that isn't the only way to get us out of here. And you don't have to hang about in the cold. You can go see a movie.'

Marty did think about it, and he saw it made sense. But he saw it grudgingly, for if anyone was going to make it with Joyce it ought to be himself. For the *machismo*, if he had known the word, rather than from inclination, but still it ought to be he. Not that he had any ideas of securing Joyce's silence by such methods. He was a realist whose ideas of a sex-life were a bit of fun with easy pick-ups until he was about thirty when he would settle down with some steady and get married and live in a semi-detached. Still, if Nigel thought he could get them out that way, let Nigel get on with it. So at six he fetched them all some doner kebab and stuffed vine leaves, drank half a tumbler of neat whisky, and set off to see a film called *Sex Pots on the Boil* at a nasty little cinema down in Camden Town.

'Where's he gone?' said Joyce.

'To see his mother.'

'You mean he's got a mother? Where does she live? Monkey house at the zoo?'

'Look, Joyce, I know he's not the sort of guy you've been

used to. I realize that. He's not my sort either, only frankly, it's taken me a bit of living with him to see that.'

'Well, you don't have to talk about him behind his back. I believe in loyalty, I do. And if you ask me, there's not much to choose between the pair of you.'

They were in the kitchen. Joyce was washing up her own supper plates. Nigel and Marty hadn't used plates, but they had each used a fork and Marty one of his new glasses. Joyce considered leaving the forks and the glass dirty, but it spoiled the look of the place, so she washed them too. For the first time in his life Nigel took a tea cloth in his hands and started to dry dishes. He put the gun down on the top of the oven.

His lie about Marty's mother had given him an idea. Not that mothers, feared, despised, adored, longed-for, were ever far from his thoughts, whatever he might pretend. The reason he had given for Marty's going out had come naturally and inevitably to him. An hour or so before, Marty had brought in the evening paper and Nigel had glanced through it while in the lavatory. *Sabena Hostage Tells of Torture* and *New Moves in Pay Claim*, and on an inside page a few lines about Mrs Culver recovering in hospital after taking an overdose of sleeping pills. Nigel dried the glass clumsily, and with an eye to the main chance, told her what had happened to her mother.

Joyce sat down at the table.

'You're maniacs,' she said. 'You don't care what you do. It'll just about kill my dad if anything happens to her.'

Using the voice he knew she liked to hear, Nigel said, 'I'm sorry, Joyce. We couldn't foresee it was going to turn out this way. Your mother's not dead, she's going to get better.'

'No thanks to you if she does!'

He came up close to her. The heat from the open oven was making him sweat. Joyce was on the point of crying, squeezing up her eyes to keep the tears back. 'Look,' he said, 'if you want to get a message to her, like a letter, I'll see she gets it. I can't say fairer than that, can I? You just write that you're OK and we haven't harmed you and I'll see it gets posted.'

Unconsciously, Joyce quoted a favourite riposte of her mother's. 'The band played "Believe it if you Like".'

'I promise. I like you a lot, Joyce. I really do. I think you're fantastic looking.'

Joyce swallowed. She cleared her throat, pressing her hands against her chest. 'Give me a bit of paper.'

Nigel picked up the gun and went off to find a piece. Apart from toilet paper out in the lavatory, there wasn't any, so he had to tear one of the end-papers off Marty's much-thumbed copy of *Venus in Furs*. The gun went back on top of the oven, and Nigel stood behind Joyce, putting on a tender expression in case she looked round.

She wrote: 'Dear Mum, you will recognize my writing and know I am OK. Don't worry. I will soon be home with you. Give my love to Dad.' She set her teeth, grinding them together. Later she would cry, when they were asleep. 'Your loving daughter, Joyce.'

Nigel put his hand on her shoulder. She was going to shout at him, 'Get off me!' but the gun was so near, within reach if she put out her left arm. There might be no later for crying, but a time for joy and reunion, if she could only keep her head now. She bowed forward across the table. Nigel came round her. He bent over her, put his other hand on her other shoulder so that he was almost embracing her, and said, 'Joyce, love.'

Slowly she lifted her face so that it wasn't far from his. She looked at his cold eyes and his mouth that was soft and parted and going slack. It wouldn't be too disgusting to kiss him, he was good-looking enough. If she had to kiss him, she would. No good making a big thing of it. As for going any further . . . Nigel brought his mouth to hers, and she reached out fast for the gun.

He shouted, 'Christ, you bitch!' and punched the gun out of her hand and it went skidding across the floor. Then he fell on his knees, scrabbling for it. Retreating from him, Joyce backed against the wall, holding her arms crossed over her body. Nigel pointed the gun at her and flicked his head to indicate she was to go into the living room. She went in. She sat down heavily on the mattress, her letter in her hand.

Presently she said in a hoarse throaty voice, 'May as well tear this up.'

'You shouldn't have done that.'

'Wouldn't you have, in my place?'

Nigel didn't answer her. He was thinking fast. It needn't spoil his plan. She had been willing enough to kiss him, she had been dying for it, he could tell that by the soppy look on her face when he'd held her shoulders. It was only natural that getting hold of the gun came first with her, self-preservation came before sex. But there could be a situation where self-preservation didn't come into it, where the last thing either of them would think of was the gun. Attempting that kiss had brought him a surge of real desire. Having her at his mercy and submitting to him and grateful to him had made him desire her.

'I won't let it make any difference,' he said. 'Your letter still goes.'

Joyce was surprised, but she wasn't going to thank him. That soft slack look was again replacing savagery in his face.

'The thing is,' he said, the polite public school boy, 'I thought you really liked me. You see, I've felt like that about you from the first.'

She knew what she had to do now, or not *now* but tomorrow when the dark one next went out. It sickened her to think of it, and how she'd feel when she'd done it she couldn't imagine. Dirty, revolting, like a prostitute. Suppose she had a baby? She had been off the Pill necessarily for a week now. But she'd do it and get the gun and think of consequences later when she was home with her mother and father and Stephen. It had never crossed her mind that in all her life she'd make love with anyone but Stephen. She and Stephen would go on making love every night the way they had been doing until they got to be about forty and were too old for it. But needs must when the devil drives, like her father said. She looked up at the devil with the gun.

'What you wanted to do out there in the kitchen just now,' she said, 'I don't mind. Only not now. I feel funny, it was a shock.'

He said, 'Joyce,' and started to come towards her.

'No. I said not now. Not when he might come back.'

'I'll get rid of him for the whole evening tomorrow.'

'Not tomorrow,' said Joyce, putting off the evil day. 'Monday.'

14

At the theatre Alan had chosen was a much-praised production of one of Shaw's comedies. He had picked it because there wouldn't be any bedroom scenes or sexy dialogue or four-letter words which would have embarrassed him in Rose's company. But when he was at the box office he found that they only had upper circle seats left, and he couldn't take a girl like Rose in the upper circle. All the other theatres round about seemed to be showing the kind of plays he had avoided in choosing *You Never Can Tell*, or Shakespeare which was too heavy or musicals which she might not like.

And then, suddenly, he knew he couldn't face it at all. His cold feet were turning to ice. He couldn't be alone with her in a restaurant, not knowing what to order or how to order or what wine to choose. He couldn't bring her home in the dark, be alone with her in the back of a taxi, after they had seen a play in which people were naked or talked about, or even acted, sex. In the midst of his doubts, a happy thought came to him. When he had gone upstairs to ask Una Engstrand about the water-heater, he had considered inviting her and Caesar Locksley in for drinks on Saturday night. Why not do that? Why not ask her and Caesar and this Annie of his for drinks in his room and ask Rose too? It was a much better idea. Rose would see the home her kindness had secured for him, he wouldn't have to be alone with her until he took her home – perhaps she had a car – and he would have the pleasure of creating an evening so different from those encounters with the Kitsons and the Heyshams, what a party should be with real conversation between people who liked each other and wanted to be together. And it would break the ice between him and Rose, it would make their next meeting easier for him.

Would drinks be enough or ought he to get food? He couldn't cook. He thought of lettuce and sardines and madeira cake, of liver and bacon and sausages. It was hopeless. Drinks alone it would have to be, with some peanuts. Next to the wineshop where he bought Bristol Cream and some vermouth was a newsagent's. The evening paper told him – it preceded Nigel's by twenty-four hours – that the Sabena jet had come down in Cairo, the pay claim negotiations had reached deadlock, and Joyce Culver's mother had been rushed to hospital in a coma. A cloud seemed to pass across him, dulling his happiness and the pale wintry sun. If Mrs Culver died, could anyone say it was his fault? No. If he had given the alarm and the police had chased Joyce's kidnappers, who could tell what would have happened to her? They would have crashed the car or shot her. Everything went to prove that it was better to take no violent action with people like that. You had only to read what was being done in this aircraft hi-jack business. No threats or armed onslaughts like in that Entebbe affair where a woman had died, but submission to the hi-jackers to be followed by peaceful negotiation.

He met Una in the hall. He and Caesar had to use the front door because, long ago, Ambrose had had the basement door blocked up for fear of burglars. Even he, apparently, had some reservations when it came to reality. Una, an indefatigable housewife, was polishing a brass lamp. She had blackened her finger with metal polish.

'I'd love to come,' she said when he told her of his party. 'How sweet of you to ask me. Caesar's gone to Annie's for the weekend. He mostly does. But I'm sure he'll bring her.'

'Does she live in London then?' He had only once been away for the weekend, and that had been to a cousin of Pam's in Skegness, a visit involving days of feverish preparation.

'Harrow or somewhere like that,' said Una. 'Not very far. I'll ask him when he phones tonight, shall I?' She added in her strange vague complex way, 'He's going to phone to find out if he's had a call from someone who knows his number and he wants to talk to but he doesn't know theirs. I'll ask him but I know he'd *love* to.'

She was one of those people whose faces are transformed when they smile. She smiled now, and he thought with a little twinge of real pain for her that she was full of gaiety really, of life and fun and zest, only those qualities had been suppressed and nullified by the loathsome Stewart and the death of her child and perhaps too by the Neo-Empiricist.

'As a matter of fact,' she said, 'it will be very nice to drink some alcohol again. Ambrose doesn't believe in it, you know, because it distorts the consciousness. Oh dear, I don't suppose there's a wineglass in the house.'

'I'll buy some glasses,' said Alan. He went down to his room and put on his radio. There was nothing on the news about Mrs Culver. Some Sabena spokesman and some government minister had said they would do nothing to endanger the lives of the hi-jacked hostages.

That night he dreamed about Joyce. Caesar Locksley asked him if he found her attractive, and the implications of that question frightened him, so he hid from her in a cupboard where there was an immersion heater and lots of bottles of sherry and piles of books by Ambrose Engstrand. It was warm in there and safe, and even when he heard Joyce screaming he didn't come out. Then he saw that the cupboard was really, or had grown into, a large room with many flights of stairs leading up and down and to the left and the right. He climbed one of these staircases and at the top found himself in a great chamber as in a medieval castle, and there fourteen armed knights awaited him with drawn swords.

The dream woke him up and kept him awake for a long time, so that in the morning he overslept. What awakened him then was a woman's voice calling to someone named Paul. 'Paul, Paul!' It was a few minutes before he remembered that Paul was his own name, and understood that it must have been Una Engstrand calling him from outside his room. He thought a tapping had preceded the uttering of that unfamiliar name, but when he opened the door she was no longer there.

It was after half-past nine. While he was dressing he heard from above him the sound of the front door closing. She had gone out. Would she mind if he used her phone? Apparently, Caesar used it. He made himself tea and ate a piece of bread and butter and went upstairs to phone Rose at the Pembroke Market.

It was she who answered. 'Why, hallo!' The last syllable

lingered seductively, a parabola of sound sinking to a sigh. He told her of his alternative plan.

'I thought you were taking me out to dinner.'

He found himself stammering because the voice was no longer enticing. 'I've asked these – these people. You'll like them. There's the man in the next room to me and my – my landlady. You'll be able to see what a nice place this is.'

Very slowly, almost disbelievingly, she said, 'You must be crazy. Or mean. I'm expected to come round and have drinks with your landlady? Thank you, but I've better things to do with my Saturday nights.'

The phone cut and the dialling tone began. He looked at the receiver and, bewildered, was putting it back when the front door opened and Una Engstrand came in.

'I'm sorry,' he said. 'I shouldn't have made a call without asking you. I'll pay for it.'

'Was it to Australia?'

'No, why should it be? It was a local call.'

'Then please don't bother about paying. I said Australia because you couldn't be phoning America, they'd all be asleep.' He looked at her despairingly, understanding her no more than he had understood Rose, yet wishing Rose could have had this warmth, this zany openness. 'Caesar didn't phone till this morning,' she said. 'I knocked on your door and called you but you were asleep. He can't come to your party, he's going to another one with Annie. But I expect you've got lots of other people coming, haven't you?'

'Only you,' he said, 'now.'

'You won't want me on my own.'

He didn't. He thought of phoning Rose back and renewing the invitation to dinner, but he was afraid of her scorn. He had lost her, he would never see her again. What a mess he had made of his first attempt at a social life! Because he had no experience and no idea of how these people organized their lives or of what they expected, he had let himself in for an evening alone with this funny little woman whose tragic life set her apart. His dreams of freedom and fantasies of love had come to this – hours and hours to be spent in the company of someone no more exciting and no better looking than Wendy Heysham.

Una Engstrand was looking at him wistfully, meekly

awaiting rejection. He answered her, knowing there was no help for it.

'Of course I will,' he said.

The day ahead loomed tediously. He went out and walked around the park, now seeing clearly the cause of Rose's resentment and wondering why he was such a fool as not to have foreseen it. He had contemplated a love affair with her, yet he lacked the courage to make even the first moves. Retribution had come to him for even thinking of a love affair while he was married to Pam. The evening paper cheered him, for it told him that Mrs Culver was recovering and that submitting to the hi-jackers' demands had secured the release of all the hostages unharmed, except one man who alleged his neck had been burned with lighted cigarettes. Alan had lunch and went to a matinée of a comedy about people on a desert island. His freedom, so long-desired, had come to solitary walks in the rain and sitting in theatres among coach parties of old women.

Una Engstrand came down at eight-thirty just when he had decided she wasn't going to bother to come after all, that she was no more enticed by this dreary tête-à-tête than he was. She had put on a skirt and tied her hair back with a bit of ribbon, but had otherwise made no concessions to her appearance.

'I would like some vodka, please,' she said, sitting down primly in the middle of his sofa.

'I forgot to buy the glasses!'

'Never mind, we can use tumblers.'

He poured out the vodka, put some tonic in, racked his brains for a topic of conversation. Cars, jobs, the cost of living – instinctively he knew that was all nonsense. No free, real person would ever talk of such things. He said abruptly, 'I saw some of your father-in-law's books in a bookshop.' That wouldn't be news to her. 'What's he doing in Java?'

'I suppose Caesar told you he was in Java. He's very sweet is Caesar, but a *dreadful* gossip. I expect he told you a lot of other things too.' She smiled at him enquiringly. He noticed she had beautiful teeth, very white and even.

She shrugged, raised her glass, said quaintly, 'Here's to you. I hope you'll be happy here.' Suddenly she giggled. 'He's heard there's a tribe or something in Indonesia that doesn't have any folklore or any legends or mythology and doesn't read books. I expect they *can't* read. He wants to meet them and find out if they've got beautiful free minds and understand the meaning of reality. When he comes back he's going to write a book about them. He's got the title already, *The Naked Mind*, and I'm to type it for him.'

He sat down opposite her. The vodka or something was making him feel better. 'You're a typist then?'

'No, I'm not. Oh dear, I'm supposed to be learning while he's away, I'm supposed to be doing a course. And I did start, but they made me have a cover over the keys and it gave me claustrophobia. Caesar says that's crazy. Can you understand it?'

Her expression was such a comical mixture of merriment and rue that Alan couldn't help himself, he burst out laughing. That made her laugh too. He realized he hadn't laughed aloud like this since he ran away from Childon, and perhaps for a long time before that. Why did he have this strange feeling that laughter with her too had fallen into disuse? Because he knew her history? Or from another, somehow telepathic cause? The thought stopped his laughter, and by infection hers, but her small flying-fox face stayed alight.

'It doesn't really matter,' she said. 'Ambrose thinks I'm hopeless, anyway. He'll just say he's very disappointed and that'll be that. But I mustn't keep on talking about him – Ambrose says this and Ambrose says that. It's because I'm with him so much. Tell me about you.'

Until then he had had to tell remarkably few lies. Neither Rose nor Caesar had asked him about himself, and he had hardly spoken to anyone else. He had lied only about his name and address. Rather quickly and with uncertainty, he told her he had been an accountant but had left his job. The next bit was true, or almost. 'I've left my wife. I just walked out last weekend.'

'A permanent break?' she said.

'I shall never go back!'

'And that's all you brought with you? A suitcase?'

'That's all.' Involuntarily, he glanced at the tallboy where the money was.

'Just like me,' she said. 'I haven't anything of my own

either, only a few clothes and books. But I wouldn't need them here. There's everything you can think of in this house and lots of things twice over. You name something, the most way-out thing you can think of. I bet Ambrose has got it.'

'Wineglasses.'

She laughed. 'I asked for that.'

'Before you came here,' he said carefully, 'you must have had things.'

The sudden sharpening of her features, as if she had winced, distressed him. He was enjoying her company so much – so surprisingly and wonderfully – that he dreaded breaking the rapport between them. But she recovered herself, speaking lightly. 'Stewart, that's my husband, kept the lot. Poor dear, he needs to know he's got things even if he can't use them. Ambrose says it's the outward sign of his insecurity and it's got to be worked through.'

Alan burst out, knowing he shouldn't, 'Your father-in-law is worse than mine! He's a monster.'

Again she laughed, with delight. She held out her glass. 'More, please. It's delicious. I *am* having a nice time. I suppose he is rather awful, but if I say so people think it's me that is because everyone thinks he's wonderful. Except you.' She nodded sagely. 'I like that.'

In that moment he fell in love with her, though it was some hours before he realized it.

15

Una stayed till eleven, Fitton's Piece Cinderella hour. But she didn't ask him whatever time it was or cry out that, Good heavens, she had no idea it was so late. After she had gone, he tidied up the room and washed the glasses, thinking how glad he was that Caesar and his girl friend hadn't been there. He was even more glad Rose hadn't been there. Una had talked about the books she had read, which were much the same as the books he had read, and he had never before talked on this subject with anyone. There was something heady, more intoxicating than the vodka he had been drinking, about being with someone who talked about a character in a book or the author's style with an intensity he had previously known lavished only over saving money and the cost of living. What would Rose have talked about? During the hours with Una, Rose had slipped back into, been engulfed by, the fantasy image from which she had come. He could hardly believe that he had ever met her or that she had been real at all. But he went over and over in his mind the things Una had said and the things he had said to her, and he thought of things he wished he had said. It didn't matter, there would be more times. He had made a friend to whom he could talk.

Before he went to bed he looked at himself carefully in the mirror. He wanted to see what sort of a man she had seen. His hair wasn't greased down any more, so that it looked more like hair and less like a leather cap, and his face was – well, not exactly brown but healthily coloured. He who had never got a tan while living in the country, had got one in a week of walking round London. His belly didn't sag quite so much. He looked thirty-eight, he thought, instead of going on for fifty. That was what she had seen. And he? He conjured her up vividly, she might still have been sitting there, her small face so vital when she laughed, her eyes so bright, the curly hair escaping from the ribbon until, by the time she left, it had massed once more about her thin cheeks. Tomorrow he'd go upstairs and find her and take her out to lunch. The idea of taking her out and ordering food and wine didn't frighten him a bit. But he was very tired now. He got into bed and fell immediately asleep.

At about three he woke up. The vodka had given him a raging thirst, so he went into the kitchen and drank a pint of water. After that it would have been natural to go back to bed and sleep till, say, seven, but he felt wide awake and entirely refreshed and tremendously happy. It was years since he had felt happy. Had he ever? When he was a child, yes, and when Jillian was born because she was the child he had wanted, and in a strange way when he was driving off with the money. But he hadn't felt like this. This feeling was quite new. He wanted to go out and rush up and down Montcalm Gardens, shouting that he was free and happy and had found the meaning of life. A great joy possessed him. Energy seemed to flow through his body and out at his fingertips. He wanted to tell someone who would understand, and he knew it was Una he wanted to tell.

So this was being in love, this was what it was like. He laughed out loud. He turned on the cold tap and ran his hands under it, he splashed cold water over his face. The room was freezing because the heating went off at eleven, but he was hot, glowing with heat and actually sweating. He fell on to the bed and pulled the sheet over him and thought about Una up there asleep somewhere in the house. Or was she awake too, thinking about him? He thought about her for an hour, re-living their conversation and then fantasizing that he and she lived together in a house like this one and were happy all the time, every minute of the day and night. The fantasy drifted off into a dream of that, a long protracted dream that broke and dissolved and began again in new aspects, until it ended in horror. It ended with his hearing Una scream. He had to run up many staircases and through many rooms to find where the screams were coming from and to find her. At last he came upon her and she was dead, burnt to death with charred banknotes lying all around her. But when he took her body in his arms and looked into her face, he saw that it was not Una he held. It was Joyce.

The cold of morning pierced through the thin sheet, and he awoke shivering, his legs numb. All the euphoria of the night was gone. He had no idea of how one went a-courting. It would be as difficult to speak of love to Una as it would have been to Rose, more difficult because he was in love with her – that was unchanged – while for Rose he had felt only the itch of lust. He was alone in the house with Una, he must be, and thinking of it terrified him. Inviting her out to lunch was impossible, making any sort of overtures to her was unthinkable. He was married, and she knew it. He had a notion, gathered more from Pam's philosophy than from novels, that if you told a woman you loved her and she didn't love you, she would slap your face. Especially if you were married and she was married. It was apparently, for no reason he could think of, in some circumstances an insult to tell a woman you loved her.

He dressed and went out, thinking he would collapse or weep if he were to meet Una in the hall, but he didn't meet her.

Ex-priest Marries Stripper and *Torture 'Hotly' Denied* said the Sunday papers. They were searching potholes in Derbyshire for the bodies of himself and Joyce. The silver-blue Ford Escort, last observed at Dover, had turned up in Turkey, its passengers blamelessly on their way to an ashram in India. Alan had a cup of coffee and a sandwich which made him feel sick. He noticed, after quite a long while, that it was a nice day. They were back to the kind of weather of the week before he ran away, just like spring, as Joyce had said. The sun on his face was warm and kind. If he went into the park or Kensington Gardens he might meet Rose, so he made for the nearest tube station, which was Notting Hill, and bought a ticket to Hampstead.

Una had lived in Hampstead. He didn't remember that until he got there. He walked about Hampstead, wondering if she had lived in this street or that, and if she had walked daily where he now was walking. He found the Heath by the simple expedient of following Heath Street until he got to it. All London lay below him, and, standing on the slope beside the Spaniards Road, he looked down on it as Dick Whittington had looked down and, in the sunshine, seen the city paved with gold.

His gold lay down there, but it was nothing to him if it couldn't give him Una. He turned abruptly and walked in the opposite direction, through the wood that lies between the Spaniards Road and North End. It wasn't much like Childon Fen. In the woods adjacent to great cities the trees are the same as trees in the deep wild, but at ground level all the plants and most of the grass have been trodden away. A sterile dusty brownness lies underfoot. The air has no moist green sweetness. But on that sunny Sunday morning – it was still morning, he had left so early – the wood seemed to Alan to have a tender bruised beauty, spring renewing it only for further spoliation, and he knew the authors were right when they wrote of what love does, of how it transforms and glorifies and takes the scales from the eye of the beholder.

When he emerged from the wood he had no idea where he was, but he went on walking roughly westward until he came to a large main road. Finchley Road, NW2, he read, and he realized he must be in Paul Browning country. Strange. Paddington was West Two, so he had supposed that North-west Two must be nearby. It was now evident that Paul Browning banked in Paddington not because he lived but because he worked there. Alan took out his London guide, for even though he would never speak to Una again, never be alone with her again, he ought to know the location of his old home.

The street plan showed Exmoor Gardens as part of an estate of houses where the roads had been quaintly constructed in concentric circles, or really, concentric ovals. Each one was named after a range of mountains or hills in the British Isles. It seemed a long way to walk, but Alan didn't know if there was any other means of getting there, and he felt a strange compulsion to see Paul Browning's home. In the event, the walk didn't take so very long.

Most of the houses in Exmoor Gardens were mock-Tudor, but a few were of newer, plainer design, and number 15 was one of these. It was bigger than his own house at Fitton's Piece, but otherwise it was very much like it, red brick and with picture windows and a chimney for show not use, and a clump of pampas grass in the front garden. He stood and looked at it, marvelling that by chance he should have chosen for his fictional past so near a replica of his actual past.

Paul Browning himself was cleaning his car on the garage drive. The front door was open and a child of about eight was running in and out, holding a small distressed-looking puppy on a lead. There was a seat on the opposite side of the road. It had been placed at the entrance to a footpath which presumably linked one of those ovals to another. Alan sat down on the seat and pretended to read his paper while the child galloped the puppy up and down the steps. Paul Browning gave an irritable exclamation. He threw down his soapy cloth and went up to the door and called into the hall:

'Alison! Don't let him do that to the dog.'

There was no answer. Paul Browning caught the boy and admonished him, but quietly and gently, and he picked the puppy up and held it in his arms. A woman came out of the house, blonde, tallish, about thirty-five. Alan couldn't hear what she said but the tone of her voice was protective. He had the impression from the way she put her arm round the boy and smiled at her husband and patted the little dog, that she was the fierce yet tender protector of them all. He folded his paper and got up and walked away down the footpath.

The little scene had made him miserable. He should have had that but he had never had it, and now it was too late to have it with anyone. He felt ridiculously guilty too for taking this man's identity and background, a theft which had turned out to be pointless as well as a kind of slander on Paul Browning who would never have left his wife. Alan asked himself if his other theft had been equally pointless.

The path brought him out at the opposite end to that where he had entered the oval, and his guide showed him that he wasn't far now from Cricklewood Broadway which seemed to be part of the northern end of the Edgware Road. He walked towards it through a district that rapidly grew shabbier, that seemed as if it must inevitably run down into squalor. Yet this never happened. Expecting squalor, he found himself instead in an area that maintained itself well this side of the slummy and the disreputable. The street was wide, lined with the emporiums of car dealers, with betting shops, supermarkets and shops whose windows displayed saris and lengths of oriental silks. On a blackboard outside a pub called the Rose of Killarney a menu was chalked up, offering steak pie and two veg or ham salad or something called a Leprechaun's Lunch. This last appeared to be bread, cheese and pickles, but the thought of asking for it in the blackboard's terms daunted Alan so he ordered the salad and a half of bitter while he waited for it to come.

The girl behind the bar had the pale puffy face and black circles under her eyes of someone reared on potatoes in a Dublin tenement. She drew Alan's bitter and a pint for an Irishman with an accent as strong as her own, then began serving a double whisky to a thin boy with a pinched face whose carrier bag full of groceries was stuffed between Alan's stool and his own. Alan didn't know what made him look down. Perhaps it was that he was still surprised you could go shopping in London on a Sunday, or perhaps he was anxious, in his middle-class respectable way, not to seem to be touching that bag or encroaching upon it. Whatever it was, he looked down, slightly shifting his stool, and saw the boy's hand go down to take a cigarette packet and a box of matches from inside the bag. It was the right hand. The forefinger had been injured in some kind of accident and the nail was cobbled like the kernel of a walnut.

The shock of what he had seen made Alan's stomach turn with a fluttering movement. He looked sharply away, started to eat his salad as smoke from the boy's cigarette drifted across the sliced hardboiled eggs, the vinegary lettuce. Reflected in the glass behind the bar was a smooth gaunt face, tight mouth, biggish nose. The beard could have been shaved off, the hair cut. Alan thought he would know for sure if the boy spoke. He must have spoken already to ask for that whisky, but that was before Alan came in. He watched him pick up the bag, and this time the finger seemed less misshapen. It wasn't the same. The finger that had come under the metal grille and scooped into the palm the bag of coins he remembered as grotesquely warped and twisted, tipped with a carapace more like a claw or a barnacled shell than a human nail.

It was a kind of relief knowing they weren't the same so that he wouldn't have to do anything about it. Do what? He was the last person who could go to the police. The boy left the pub and after a few minutes Alan left too, not following him though, intending never to think of him again. He was suddenly aware that he was tired, he must have walked miles, and he was getting thankfully on to a south-bound bus, when he caught his last glimpse of the boy who was walking down a side street, walking slowly and swinging his carrier as if he had all the time in the world and nothing to go home for.

Alan felt himself in the same situation. For the rest of the day and most of the next he avoided seeing Una. Nearly all the time he kept away from Montcalm Gardens. And he kept away too from north London, from those distant outposts of the Edgware Road when an invented past had bizarrely met an illusion. It was obviously unwise to visit venues, shabby districts and down-at-heel pubs, which suggested crime and criminals to him and where conscience worked on his imagination. He sat in parks, rode on the tops of buses, visited Tussaud's. But he had to go back or settle for being a vagrant. Should he move on to somewhere else? Should he leave London and go on to some provincial city? For years he had longed for love, and now he had found it he wanted lovelessness back again. He came back to his room on Monday evening and sat on the bed, resolving that in a minute, when he had got enough courage, he would go upstairs and tell her he was leaving, he was going back to his wife, to Alison.

From the other side of the wall, in Caesar Locksley's room, he heard her voice.

Not what she said, just her voice. And he was consumed with jealously. Immediately he thought Caesar had been deceiving him and she had been deceiving him, and she was even now in bed with Caesar. He began to walk up and down in a kind of frenzy. They must have heard him in there because someone came to his door and knocked. He wasn't going to answer. He stood at the window with his eyes shut and his hands clenched. The knock came again and Caesar said:

'Paul, are you OK in there?'

He had to go then.

'Annie and I are going to see the Chabrol film at the Gate,' said Caesar. 'Una as well.' He winked at Alan. The wink meant, take her out of herself, get her out of this house. 'Feel like coming too?'

'All right,' said Alan. The relief was tremendous, which was why he had agreed. In the next thirty seconds he realized what he had agreed to, and then he couldn't think at all because he was confronting her. Nor could he look at her or speak. He heard her say:

'It *is* good to see you. I've knocked on your door about fifteen times since Saturday night to thank you and say how nice it was.'

'I was out,' he muttered. He looked at her then, and something inside him, apparently the whole complex labyrinth of his digestive system and his heart and his lungs, rotated full circle and slumped back into their proper niches.

'This is Annie,' said Caesar.

It didn't help that the girl looked quite a lot like Pam and Jillian. The same neat, regular, very English features and peachy skin and small blue eyes. He heard Caesar say she was a nurse, and he could imagine that from her brisk hearty manner, but she brought Pam back to him, her calms and her storms. He felt trapped and ill.

They walked to the cinema. He and Una walked together, in front of the others.

'They say', said Una, 'that if two couples go out together you can tell their social status by the way they pair off. If they're working class the two girls walk together, if they're middle class husband and wife walk together, and if they're upper class each husband walks with the other one's wife.'

'Don't make me out middle class, Una,' said Caesar.

'Ah, but none of us is married to any of the others.'

That made Annie talk about Stewart. She had had a letter from someone who had met him in Port of Spain. Una didn't seem to mind any of this and talked quite uninhibitedly to Annie about Stewart so that the two girls drifted together in the working class way, a pairing which settled in advance the seating arrangement in the cinema. Alan went in first, then Caesar, then Annie, with Una next to her and as far as possible from Alan. The film was in French and very subtle as well, and he didn't bother to read the sub-titles. He followed none of it. In a kind of daze he sat, feeling that he lived from moment to moment, that there was no future and no past, only instants precisely clicking through an infinite present.

Afterwards, they all went for a drink in the Sun in Splendour. Caesar wanted Annie to come home with him for the night, but Annie said Montcalm Gardens was much too far from her hospital and she wanted her sleep, anyway. There was a certain amount of badinage, in which Caesar and both girls took part. Alan had never before heard sexual behaviour so freely and frivolously discussed, and he was embarrassed. He tried to imagine himself and Pam talking like this with the Heyshams, but he couldn't imagine it. And he stopped trying when it became plain that Annie was going, and Caesar taking her home, and that this was happening now.

Una said, after they had left, 'I think Annie was one of

Stewart's ladies, though she won't admit it. I expect he "gave her a whirl". That was the way he always put it when he only took someone around for a week. Poor whirl girls, I used to feel so sorry for them.' She paused and looked at him. 'Let me buy you a drink this time.'

He had an idea women never bought drinks in pubs, that if they tried they wouldn't get served. It surprised him that she got served, and with a smile as if it were nothing out of the way. He couldn't finish the whisky she had brought him. As soon as he felt it on his tongue, he knew that his gorge would rise at a second mouthful. The landlord called time, and he and she were out in the street alone together, walking back to Montcalm Gardens by intricate back ways. It wasn't dark as it would have been in the country, but other-wordly bright with the radiance from the livid lamps. The yellowness was not apparent in the upper air, but only where the light lay like lacquer on the dewy surface of metal and gilded the moist leaves of evergreens.

'The night is shiny,' said Una.

'You mean shin*ing*,' he corrected her stiffly.

She shook her head. 'No. Shakespeare has a soldier say that in *Antony and Cleopatra*. It's my favourite line. The night is shiny. I know exactly what he meant, though I suppose he was talking of moonlight.'

He longed for her with a yearning that made him feel faint, but he could only say stupidly, 'There's no moon tonight.'

She unlocked the front door and switched on lights, and they went together into the fragrant polished hall where the vases were filled with winter jasmine. The sight of it brought back to him the yard at the back of the bank where that same flower grew, and he passed his hand across his brow, though his forehead was hot and dry.

'You're tired,' she said. 'I was going to suggest making coffee, but not if you're too tired.'

He didn't speak but followed her into the kitchen and sat down at the table. It was a room about four times as big as the one at Fitton's Piece. He thought how happy it would make Pam to have a kitchen like that, with two fridges and an enormous deep freeze and a cooker half-way up the wall, and a rotisserie and an infra-red grill. With deft swift movements Una started the percolator and set out cups. She talked to him in her sweet vague way about Ambrose and his books, about the banishment of all Stewart's mother's novels to the basement after her death, flitted on to speak of Stewart's little house on Dartmoor, now empty and neglected. She poured the coffee. She sat down, shaking her hair into a bright curly aureole, and looked at him, waiting for him to contribute.

And then something happened to him which was not unlike that something that had happened when the phone rang in the office and he had had the money in his hands, and he knew he had to act now or never. So he said aloud and desperately, 'Una,' just hearing how her name sounded in his voice.

'What is it?'

'Oh, God,' he said, 'I'll leave, I'll go whenever you say, but I have to tell you. I've fallen in love with you. I love you so much, I can't bear it.' And he swept out his arms across the table and knocked over the cup, and coffee flooded in a stream across the floor.

She gave a little sharp exclamation. Her face went crimson. She fell on her knees with a cloth in her hands and began feverishly mopping up the liquid. He ran down the basement stairs and flung himself into his room and closed the door and locked it.

Up and down the room he walked as he had done earlier. He would never sleep again or eat a meal or even *be*. A kind of rage possessed him, for in the midst of this tempest of emotion, he knew he was having now what he should have had at eighteen, what at eighteen had been denied him. He was having it this way now because he had never had it before. And was he to have it now without its fruition?

Ceasing to pace, he listened to the silence. The light was still on upstairs in the kitchen. He could see it lying in yellow squares on the dark rough lawn. Trembling, he watched the quadrangles of light, thinking that at any moment he might see her delicate profile and her massy hair silhouetted upon them. The light went out and the garden was black.

He imagined her crossing the hall and going up the wide curving staircase to her own room, angry with him perhaps, or shocked, or just glad to be rid of him. He turned off his own light, for he couldn't bear to see any part of himself.

Then he unlocked his door and went out into the pitch-dark, knowing he must find her before she made herself inaccessible to him now and thus for ever.

There was a faint light illuminating the top of the basement stairs. She hadn't yet gone to bed. He began to climb the stairs, having no idea what he would say, thinking he might say nothing but only fall in an agony at her feet. The light from above went out. He felt for the banister ahead of him, and touched instead her extended hand at the light switch. He gasped. They couldn't see each other, but they closed together, his arms encircling her as she held him, and they stood on the stairs in the black dark, silently embraced.

Presently they went down the stairs, crab-wise, awkwardly, clinging to each other. He wouldn't let her put a light on. She opened the door of his room and drew him in, and as it closed they heard Caesar enter the house. Lights came on and Caesar's footsteps sounded softly. Alan held Una in his arms in a breathless hush until all was silent and dark again.

16

Very little food was kept in stock because Marty hadn't got a fridge. The bookcase held a few tins of beans and spaghetti and soup, half a dozen eggs in a box, a packet of bacon, tea bags and a jar of instant coffee, some cheese and a wrapped loaf. They usually had bread and cheese for lunch, and every day Marty went out to buy their dinner. But when it got to five o'clock on Monday he was still fast asleep on the mattress where he had been lying since two. Joyce was in the kitchen, washing her hair.

Nigel shook Marty awake.

'Get yourself together. We want our meal, right? And a bottle of wine. And then you're going to do like a disappearing act. Get it?'

Marty sat up, rubbing his eyes. 'I don't feel too good. I got a hell of a pain in my gut.'

'You're pissed, that's all. You got through a whole god-damned bottle of scotch since last night.' Unconsciously, Nigel used the tones of Dr Thaxby. 'You're an alcoholic and you'll give yourself cirrhosis of the liver. That's worse than cancer. They can operate on you for cancer but not for cirrhosis. You've only got one liver. D'you know that?'

'Leave off, will you? It's not the scotch. That wouldn't give me a pain in my gut, that'd give me a pain in my head. I reckon I got one of them bugs.'

'You're pissed,' said Nigel. 'You need some fresh air.'

Marty groaned and lay down again. 'I can't go out. You go.'

'Christ, the whole point is to leave me alone with her.'

'It'll have to be tomorrow. I'll have a good night's kip and I'll be OK tomorrow.'

So Marty didn't go out, and they had tinned spaghetti and bacon for their supper. Joyce unbent so far as to cook it. She couldn't agree to what she'd agreed to and then refuse to cook his food. Marty stayed guarding Joyce while Nigel went down and had a bath. On the way up again, he encountered old Mr Green in a brown wool dressing gown and carrying a towel. Mr Green smiled at him in rather a shy way, but Nigel took no notice. He flushed Joyce's letter down the lavatory pan.

Marty was holding the gun and looking reasonably alert.

'You see?' said Nigel. 'There's nothing wrong with you so long as you keep off the booze.'

That seemed to be true, for Marty didn't drink any more that evening and on Tuesday he felt almost normal. It was a lovely day to be out in the air. On Nigel's instructions, he bought a cold roast chicken and some prepared salad in cartons and more bread and cheese and a bottle of really good wine that cost him four pounds. He forgot to get more tea and coffee or to replenish their supply of tins, but that didn't matter since, by tomorrow, the three of them would be off somewhere, Nigel and Joyce all set for a honeymoon.

The fact was, though, that neither of them seemed very lover-like. Marty wondered what had happened between them on Saturday. Not much, he thought, but presumably enough for Nigel to be sure he was going to make it. Marty observed their behaviour. Joyce sat knitting all day, not being any nicer to Nigel than she had ever been, and Nigel didn't talk much to her or call her 'sweetheart' or 'love' which were the endearments he would have used in the circumstances. Maybe it was just that they fancied each other so much that they were keeping themselves under control in his presence. He hoped so, and hoped they wouldn't expect him to stay out half the night, for his stomach was hurting him again and he felt as if he had a hangover, though he hadn't touched a drop of scotch for twenty-four hours.

At just after six he went off. It was a fine clear evening, preternaturally warm for the time of year. Or so Marty supposed from the way other people weren't wearing coats, and from seeing a couple of girls walking along in thin blouses with short sleeves. He didn't feel warm himself, although he had a sweater and his leather jacket on. He stood shivering at the bus stop, waiting for the number 16 to come and take him down to the West End.

The two in the room in Cricklewood were self-conscious with each other. Nigel put his arm round Joyce and wondered how it would be if she were thirty-seven or thirty-eight and grateful to him for being such a contrast to her dreary old husband. The fantasy helped, and so did some of Marty's whisky. Joyce said she would have some too, but to put water with it.

They took their glasses into the living room.

'Did you send my letter?' said Joyce.

'Marty took it this morning.'

'So that's his name? Marty.'

Nigel could have bitten his tongue out. But did it matter now?

'You'd better tell me yours, hadn't you?'

Nigel did so. Joyce thought it a nice name, but she wasn't going to say so. She had an obscure feeling that some part of herself would be saved inviolate if, even though she slept with Nigel, she continued to speak to him with cold indifference. The whisky warmed and calmed her. She had never tasted it before. Stephen said it was gin that was the woman's drink, and once or twice she had had a gin and tonic with him in the Childon Arms, but never whisky. Nigel was half-sitting on the gun. It was beside him but not between them. She let Nigel kiss her and managed to kiss him back.

'We may as well eat,' Nigel said, and he took the gun with him to the table. The wine would put the finishing touch to a pleasant muzziness that was overcoming his inhibitions. He liked Joyce's shyness and her ugliness. It meant she wouldn't know whether he acquitted himself well or badly. She ate silently, returning the pressure of his knee under the table. But, God, she was ugly! The only good thing about her was her hair. Her eyelashes were white – no wonder she'd nagged him to get her mascara – and her skin was pale and coarse and her features doughy. In Marty's tee-shirt and pullover she looked shapeless.

He started talking to her about the things he had done, how he had been to university and got a first-class honours degree, but had thrown it all up because this society was rotten, rotten to the core, he didn't want any part of it, no way. So he had gone to live in a commune with other young people with ideals, where they had a vegetarian diet and made their own bread and the girls wove cloth and made pots. It was a free sexuality commune and he had been shared by two girls, a very young one called Samantha and an older one, Sarah.

'Why did you rob a bank then?' said Joyce.

Nigel said it had been a gesture of defiance against this rotten society, and they were going to use the money to start a Raj Neesh community in Scotland.

'What's that when it's at home?'

'It's my religion. It's a marvellous Eastern religion with no rules. You can do what you like.'

'Sounds right up your street,' said Joyce, but she didn't say it unpleasantly, and when she got up to put the plates on the draining board beside Marty's whisky bottles, she let Nigel run his hand down her thigh. Then she sat down closer to him and they drank up the last of the wine. By now it was dark outside, but for the light from the yellow lamps. Nigel drew the curtains, and when Joyce came through from the kitchen he put his arms round her and began kissing her violently and hungrily, pushing her head back and chewing at her face.

She had very little feeling left, just enough to know from the feel of Nigel pressed like iron up against her, that it was going to happen. But she felt no panic or despair, the whisky and the wine had seen to that, and no compulsion to break a window or scream when, for the first time since she had been there, she was left quite alone and free to move. Nigel went out to the lavatory, taking the gun with him. Joyce got on to the mattress and took all her clothes off under the sheet. The third note was still inside her bra. She pushed it into one of the cups and hid the bra on the floor under her pullover. Nigel came back, closing the door on the Yale but not bothering with the other lock. He switched off the light. For a little while he stood there, surprised that the lamps outside lit the room so brightly through the threadbare curtains, as if he hadn't seen that same thing for many nights. Then he stripped off his clothes and pulled back the blankets and the sheet that covered Joyce.

Her head was slightly turned away, the exposed cheek half-covered by her long fair hair. He stared at her in amazement, for he hadn't known any real woman could look like that. Her body was without a flaw, the full breasts smooth and rounded like blown glass, her waist a fragile and slender stem, the bones and muscles of her legs and arms veiled in an extravagant silkiness of plump tissue and white skin. The yellow light lay on her like a patina of gilding, shining in a gold blaze on those roundnesses and leaving the shallow hollows sepia brown. She was like one of the nudes in Marty's magazines, only she was more superb. Nigel had never thought of those as real women, but as contrivances of the pornographer's skill, assisted by the pose and the cunning camera. He looked down on her with appalled wonder, with a sick shrinking awe, while Joyce lay motionless and splendid, her eyes closed.

At last he said, 'Joyce,' and lowered his body on to hers. He too shut his eyes, knowing he should have shut them before or never have pulled back that sheet. He tried to think of Samantha's mother, stringy and thin and thirty-two, of Sarah in her black stockings. With his right hand he felt for the gun, imagining how it would be if he were raping Alan Groombridge's wife at gunpoint. But the damage was done. In the last way he would have thought possible, Joyce had taken away his manhood without moving, without speaking. Now she shifted her body under his and opened her eyes and looked at him.

'I'll be OK in a minute,' said Nigel, his teeth clenched. 'I could use a drink.'

He went out into the kitchen and took a swig out of the whisky bottle. He shut his eyes so that he couldn't see Joyce and tied himself round her, his arms and legs gripping her.

'You're hurting!'

'I'll be OK in a minute. Just give me a minute.'

He rolled off her and turned on his side. His whole body felt cold and slack. He concentrated on fantasies of Joyce as his slave, and on the importance of this act which he must perform to make her so. After a while, after the minutes he had asked her to give him, he turned to her once more to look at her face. If he could just look at her face and forget that wonderful terrifying body . . . She was asleep. Her head buried in her arms, she had fallen into a heavy drunken sleep.

Nigel would have liked to kill her then. He held the gun pressed to the back of her neck. Perhaps he would have killed her if the gun had been loaded and the trigger not stiff and immoveable. But the gun, like himself, was just a copy or a replica. It was as useless as he.

He took it with him into the kitchen and closed the door. Suddenly he was visited by a childhood memory, a vision from some fifteen or sixteen years in the past. He was sitting at the table and his father was spoon-feeding him, forcibly feeding him, while his mother crawled about the floor with a cloth in her hand. His mother was mopping up food that he spilt or spat out, reaching up sometimes to wipe his face with the flannel in her other hand, while his father kept telling him he must eat or he would never grow up, never be a man. The adult Nigel bent his head over the table in Marty's kitchen, as he had bent it over that other one, and began to weep as he had wept then. It was only the thought of Marty coming back and finding him there that stilled his sobs and made him get up again, choking and cursing. Reality was unbearable, he wanted oblivion. He put the mouth of the bottle to his own mouth, closed his lips right round it, and poured a long steady stream of whisky down his throat. There was just time to get back to that mattress and stretch himself out as far as possible from Joyce, before the spirit knocked him out.

*

Marty looked at the shops in Oxford Street, thinking of the clothes he would buy when he was free to buy them. He had never had the money to be a snappy dresser but he would like to be one, to wear tight trousers and velvet jackets and shirts with girls' faces and pop stars' names on them. A couple of passing policemen looked at him, or he fancied they looked at him, so he stopped peering in windows and walked off down Regent Street to Piccadilly Circus.

In the neighbourhood of Leicester Square he visited a couple of amusement arcades and played the fruiters, and then he wandered around Soho. He had always meant to go into one of those strip clubs, and now, when he had wads of money in his pocket, was surely the time. But the pain which had troubled him on Monday was returning. Every few minutes he was getting a twinge in the upper part of his stomach, with cramps which made him break wind and taste bile when the squeezing vice released. He couldn't go into a club and enjoy himself, feeling like that and liable to keep doubling up. It wasn't his appendix, he thought, he'd had that out when he was twelve. Withdrawal symptoms, that's what it was. Alcohol was a drug, and everyone knew that when you came off a drug you got pains and sweats and felt rotten. He should have done it gradually, not cut it off all of a sudden.

How long were those two going to take over it? Nigel hadn't said what time he was to get back, but midnight ought to be OK, for God's sake. He hadn't eaten since breakfast, no wonder he felt so queasy. He'd best get a good steak and some chips and a couple of rolls inside him. The smell in the steak house made his throat rise, and he stumbled out, wondering what would happen if he collapsed in the street and the police picked him up with all that money in his pockets.

He'd feel safer nearer home, so he got into the tube which took him up to Kilburn. Luckily the 32 bus came along at once. Marty got on it, slumped into a downstairs seat and lit a cigarette. The Indian conductor asked him to put it out, and Marty said to go back to the jungle and told him what he could do to himself when there. So they stopped the bus and the big black driver came round and together, to the huge glee of the other passengers, they put Marty off.

He had to walk all the way up Shoot-up Hill and he didn't know how he made it.

But it was too early to go back yet, only a quarter to eleven. Whether his trouble was withdrawal symptoms or a bug, he had to have a drink, and they did say whisky settled the stomach. His father used to say it, the old git, and if anyone knew about booze he should. A couple of doubles, thought Marty, and he'd sleep like a log and wake up all right tomorrow.

The Rose of Killarney was about half-way along the Broadway. Marty walked in a bit unsteadily, wincing with pain as he passed between the tables. Bridey and the licensee were behind the bar.

'Double scotch,' said Marty thickly.

Bridey said to the licensee, 'This fella lives next to me. Will you listen to his manners?'

'OK, Bridey, I'll serve him.'

'In the same house he lives and can't say so much as a civil please. If you ask me, he's had too much already.'

Marty took no notice. He never spoke to her if he could help it, any more than he did to any of these foreigners, immigrants, Jews, spades and whatever. He drank his scotch, belched and asked for another.

'Sorry, son, you've had enough. You heard what the lady said.'

'Lady,' said Marty. 'Bloody Irish slag.'

It was only just eleven, but he was going home anyway. The light in his room was out. He could see that from the street where he had to sit down on a wall, he felt so sick and weak. The stairs were the last phase in his ordeal and they were the worst. Outside his door he thought he'd rather just lie down on the landing floor than go through all the hassle of waking Nigel to let him in. He peered at the keyhole but couldn't see through because the iron key was blocking it. Maybe Nigel hadn't bothered to lock it because things had gone right and there was no longer any need to. He tried the key in the Yale and the door opened.

After the darkness of the landing, the yellow light made him blink. From force of habit he locked the door and hung the string the key was on round his neck. The light lay in irregular patches on the two sleeping faces. Great, thought Marty, he's made it, we'll be out of here tomorrow. Holding his sore stomach, breathing gingerly, he curled up on the sofa and pulled the blanket over him.

Joyce hadn't been aware of his arrival. It was three or four hours later that she awoke with a banging head and a dry mouth. But she came to herself quickly and remembered what her original purpose in going to bed with Nigel had been. She looked at him with feelings of amazement and distaste, and with pity too. Joyce thought she knew all about sex, far more than her mother did, but no one had ever told her that what had happened with Nigel is so usual as to be commonplace, an inhibition that affects all men sometimes and some men quite often. She thought of virile confident Stephen, and she decided Nigel must have some awful disease.

Both her captors were deeply asleep, Marty snoring, Nigel with his right hand tucked under the pillow. Joyce put her clothes on. Then she lay down beside Nigel and put her right hand under the pillow too, feeling the hard warm metal of the gun. Immediately her hand was gripped hard, but not, she thought, because he was aware of what she was after. Rather it was as if he needed a woman's hand to hold in his troubled sleep, as a child may do. With her left hand she slid the gun out and eased her right hand away. Nigel gave a sort of whimper but he didn't wake up.

Taking a deep breath and wishing the thudding in her head would stop, she raised the gun, pointed it at the kitchen wall and tried to squeeze the trigger. It wouldn't move. So it was a toy, as she had hoped and lately had often supposed. She was filled with exultation. It was a toy, as you could tell really by the plasticky look of it, that handle part seemed actually made of plastic, and by the way it said *Made in W. Germany*.

Her future actions seemed simple. She wouldn't try to get the key from Marty, for the two of them could easily overpower her and might hurt her badly. But in the morning, when one of them took her to the lavatory, she would run down the stairs, yelling at the top of her voice.

She decided not to take her clothes off again in case Nigel woke up and started pawing her about. That was a horrible thought when you considered that he was ill or not really a man at all. She came back and looked at him, still sleeping. Wasn't it rather peculiar to make a toy gun with a trigger that wouldn't move? The point with having a toy gun, she knew from her younger brother, was that you could press the trigger and fire caps. She wondered how you put the caps into this one. Perhaps by fiddling with that handle thing at the back? She pushed it but it wouldn't move.

Joyce carried the gun to the kitchen window where the light was brightest. In that light she spotted a funny little knob on the side of the gun, and she pushed at it tentatively with the tip of her finger. It moved easily, sliding forward towards the barrel and revealing a small red spot. Although the handle thing at the back had also moved and dropped forward, no space for the insertion of caps had been revealed. But there wouldn't be any point in putting caps in, thought Joyce, if you couldn't move the trigger. Perhaps it was a real gun that had got broken. She raised it again, smiling to herself because she'd really been a bit of a fool, hadn't she, letting herself be kept a prisoner for a week by two boys with a gun that didn't work? She felt quite ashamed.

Levelling the gun at Nigel made her giggle. She enjoyed the sensation of threatening him, even though he didn't know it, as for days he had threatened her. They'd killed Mr Groombridge with that, had they? Like hell they had. Like this, had they, squeezing a broken trigger that wouldn't move?

Joyce squeezed it, almost wishing they were awake to see her. There was a shattering roar. Her arm flew up, the gun arc-ed across the room, and the bullet tore into the rotten wood of the window frame, lodging there, missing Nigel's ear by an inch.

Joyce screamed.

17

Marty was off the sofa and Nigel off the mattress before the reverberations of the explosion had died away. Nigel seized

Joyce and pulled her down on the bed, his hand over her mouth, and when she went on screaming he stuffed a pillow over her face. Marty knelt on the end of the mattress, holding his head in both hands and staring at the hole the bullet had made in the window frame. In all their heads the noise was still ringing.

'Oh, Christ,' Marty moaned. 'Oh, Christ.'

Nigel pulled the pillow off Joyce and slapped her face with the flat of his hand and the back of his hand.

'You bitch. You stupid bitch.'

She lay face-downwards, sobbing. Nigel crawled over the mattress and reached out and picked up the gun. He pulled a blanket round himself like a shawl and sat hunched up, examining the gun with wonder and astonishment. The room stank of gunpowder. Silence crept into the room, heavier and somehow louder than sound. Marty squatted, taut with fear, waiting for the feet on the stairs, the knock on the door, the sound of the phone down below being lifted, but Nigel only held and turned and looked at the gun.

The German writing on the side of it made sense now. With a thrill of excitement, he read those words again. This was a Bond gun he held in his hands, a Walther PPK. He didn't want to put it down even to pull on his jeans and his sweater, he didn't want ever to let it out of his hands again. He brooded over it with joy, loving it, wondering how he could ever have supposed it a toy or a replica. It was more real than himself. It worked.

'That's quite a weapon,' he said softly.

In other circumstances, Marty would have been quite amused to have fooled Nigel about the gun for so long, and elated to have received his praise. But he was frightened and he was in pain. So he only muttered, ' 'Course it is. I wouldn't pay seventy-five quid for any old crap,' and winced as a twinge in his stomach doubled him up. 'Going to throw up,' he groaned and made for the door.

'Just check what the scene is while you're out there,' said Nigel. He was looking at the small circular red indentation the moving of the safety catch had exposed. Carefully he pushed the catch down again and that thing on the back, which had always puzzled him but which he now knew to be the hammer, dropped down. Now the trigger would hardly move. Nigel looked at Joyce and at the hole in the window frame and he sighed.

Marty vomited for some minutes. Afterwards he felt so weak and faint that he had to sit down on the lavatory seat, but at last he forced himself to get up and stagger down the stairs. His legs felt like bits of wet string. He crept down two flights of stairs, listening. The whole house seemed to be asleep, all the doors were shut and all the lights off except for a faint glimmer under the red-haired girl's front door. Marty hauled himself back up, hanging on to the banisters, his stomach rotating and squeezing.

He lurched across the room to the kitchen and took a long swig from the whisky bottle. Warm and brown and reassuring, it brought him momentary relief so that he was able to stand up properly and draw a deep breath. Nigel, hunched over Joyce, though she was immobile and spent and crying feebly, ordered him to make coffee.

'What did your last slave die of?' said Marty. 'I'm sick and I'm not a bloody woman. She can make it.'

'I'm not letting her out of my sight, no way,' said Nigel. So no one made any coffee, and no one went to sleep again before dawn. Once they heard the siren of a police car, but it was far away up on the North Circular. Marty lay across the foot of the mattress, holding his stomach. By the time the yellow lamps had faded to pinky-vermilion and gone out, by the time a few birds had begun to sing in the dusty planes of the churchyard, they had all fallen asleep in a spreadeagled pile, like casualties on a battlefield.

Bridey went down with a bag of empty cans and bottles before she went to work. The red-haired girl, who had been lying in wait for her, came out.

'Did you hear that funny carry-on in the night?'

'What sort of carry-on?' said Bridey cautiously.

'Well, I don't know,' said the red-haired girl, 'but there was something going on up the top. About half-three. I woke up and I said to my fella, 'I thought I heard a shot,' I said. 'From upstairs,' I said. And then someone came down, walked all the way down and up again.'

Bridey too had heard the shot, and she had heard a scream. For a moment she had thought of doing something about it, get even with that filthy-spoken bit of rubbish, that Marty. But doing something meant the police. Fetching the guards, it meant. No one in Bridey's troubled family history had ever done so treacherous a thing, not even for worthy motives of revenge.

'You were dreaming,' said Bridey.

'That's what my fella said. "You were dreaming," he said. But I don't know. You know you sleep heavy, Bridey, and old Green's deaf as a post. I said to my fella, "You don't reckon we ought to ring the fuzz, do you?" and he said, "Never," he said. "You were dreaming." But I don't know. D'you reckon I ought to have rung the fuzz?'

'Never do that, my love,' said Bridey. 'What's in it for you? Nothing but trouble. Never do that.'

They would never get out now, Nigel thought, they would just have to stick there. For weeks or months, he didn't know how long, maybe until the money ran out. He found he didn't dislike the idea. Not while he had that beautiful effective weapon. He nursed the gun as if it were a cuddly toy or a small affectionate animal, his fear of losing it to Marty, whose possession it was, keeping it always in his hands. If Marty tried to take it from him, he thought he would threaten Marty with it as he threatened Joyce, if necessary kill him. During that night, what with one thing and another, something in Nigel that had always been fragile and brittle had finally split. It was his sanity.

Looking at the gun, passionately admiring it, he thought how they might have to stay in that room for years. Why not? He liked the room, it had begun to be his home. They would have to get things, of course. They could buy a fridge and a TV. The men who brought them up the stairs could be told to leave them on the landing. Joyce would do anything he said now, and there wouldn't be any more snappy back answers from her. He could tell that from one glance at her face. Not threats or privation or uncongenial company or separation from her family had broken her, but the reality of the gun had. That was what it had been made for.

He would have two slaves now, for Marty looked as shaken by what had happened as she did. One to shop and run errands and one to cook and wait on him. He, Nigel, wasn't broken or even shaken. He was on top of the world and king of it.

'We need bread and tea bags and coffee,' he said to Marty, 'and a can of paraffin for the stove.'

'Tomorrow,' said Marty. 'I'm sick.'

'I'd be bloody sick if I boozed the way you do. While you're out you can go buy us a big fridge and a colour TV.'

'Do what? You're crazy.'

'Don't you call me crazy, little brain,' shouted Nigel. 'We've got to stay here, right? Thanks to her, we've got to stay here a long, long time. The three of us can stay here for years, I've got it all worked out. Once we've got a fridge you won't have to go out more than once a week. I don't like it, you going to the same shops over and over, shooting your mouth off to guys in shops, I know you. We'll all stay in here like I said and keep quiet and watch the TV. So you don't blue all our bread on fancy stuff, right? We go careful and we can live here two years, I've got it all worked out.'

'No,' Joyce whimpered. 'No.'

Nigel rounded on her. 'Nobody's asking you, I'm telling you. If I get so much as a squeak out of you, you're dead. A bomb could go off in this place and they wouldn't hear. You know that, don't you? You've had the experience.'

On Thursday morning Marty made a big effort and got as far as the corner shop. He bought a large white loaf and some cheese and two cans of beans, but he forgot the tea bags and the coffee. Carrying the paraffin would have been too much for him, he knew that, so he didn't even bother to take the can. Food didn't interest him, anyway, he couldn't keep a thing on his stomach. He had some whisky and retched. When he came back from the lavatory he said to Nigel:

'My pee's gone brown.'

'So what? You've only got cystitis. You've irritated your bladder with the booze.'

'I'm dead scared,' said Marty. 'You don't know how bad I feel. Christ, I might die. Look at my face, my cheeks are sort of fallen in. Look at my eyes.'

Nigel didn't answer him. He sat cobbling for himself a kind of holster made from a plastic jeans belt of Marty's and a bit of towelling. He sewed it together with Joyce's brown knitting wool while Joyce watched him. He needn't have bothered, for Joyce would have died before she touched that gun again. She had given up her knitting, she had given up doing anything. She just sat or cringed on the sofa in a daze. Nigel was happy. All the time he was doing mental arithmetic, working out how much they would be able to spend on food each week, how much on electricity and gas. The summer was coming, he thought, so they wouldn't need any heat. When the money ran out, he'd make Marty get a job to keep them all.

The next day there was no paraffin left and no tea or butter or milk. The bookcase in the kitchen contained only a spoonful of coffee in the bottom of the jar, half the cheese Marty had bought and most of the bread, two cans of soup and one of beans and three eggs. The warm weather had given place to a chilly white fog, and it was very cold in the room. Nigel put the oven on full and lit all the burners, angry because it would come expensive on the gas bill and upset his calculations. But even he could see Marty was no better, limp as a rag and dozing most of the time. He considered going out himself and leaving Marty with the gun. Joyce wouldn't try anything, all the fight had gone out of her. She was the way he had always wanted her to be, cowed, submissive, trembling, dissolving into tears whenever he spoke to her. She made beans on toast for their supper without a murmur of protest while he stood over her with the gun, and she gobbled her share up like a starving caged animal which has had a lump of refuse thrown to it. No, it wasn't the fear of her escaping that kept him from going. It was the idea of having to relinquish even for ten minutes – he could see from the kitchen window the corner shop, open and brightly lit – the precious possession of the gun.

That evening, while he was thinking about what kind and what size of fridge they should buy, whether they could afford a colour television or should settle for black and white, Joyce spoke to him. It was the first time she had really spoken since she fired the gun.

'Nigel,' she said in a small sad voice.

He looked at her impatiently. Her hair hung lank and her nails were dirty and she had a spot, an ugly eruption, coming out at the corner of her mouth. Marty lay bundled up, with all the blankets they possessed wrapped round him. What a pair, he thought. A good thing they had him to manage them and tell them what to do.

'Yeah?' he said. 'What?'

She put her hands together and bowed her head. 'You said,' she whispered, 'you said we could stay here for years. Nigel, please don't keep me here, *please*. If you let me go I won't say a word, I won't even speak. I'll pretend I've lost my memory, I'll pretend I've lost my voice. They can't make me speak! Please, Nigel. I'll do anything you want, but don't keep me here.'

He had won. His dream of what he might achieve with her had come true. He smiled, raised his eyebrows and lightly shook his head. But he said nothing. Slowly he drew the gun out of its holster and pointed it at her, releasing the safety catch. Joyce rewarded him by shrinking, covering her face with her hands and bursting into tears. In a couple of days, he thought, he'd have her pleading with him to be nice to her, begging him to find her tasks to do for his comfort. He laughed then, remembering all the rudeness and insults he'd had to put up with from her. Without announcing his intention, he switched the light off and stretched out on the mattress beside Marty.

'You smell like a Chink meal,' he said. 'Sweet and sour. Christ!'

Joyce couldn't sleep. She lay staring at the ceiling in despair. With a curious kind of intuition, for she had never known any mad people, she sensed that Nigel was mad. Sooner or later he would kill her and no one would ever know, no one would hear the shot or care if they did, and wounded perhaps, she would lie in that room till she died. The thought of it made her cry loudly, she couldn't help herself. She would never see her mother again or her father and her brothers, or kiss Stephen or be held in his arms. Nigel hissed at her to shut up and give them all a bit of hush, so she cried quietly until the pillow was wet with tears and, exhausted, she drifted off into dreams of home and of sitting with Stephen in the Childon Arms and talking of wedding plans.

Marty's anguished voice woke her. It was still dark.

'Nige,' he said. He hardly ever used Nigel's name or its ugly diminutive. 'Nige, what's happening to me? I went out to the bog and I had to crawl back on my hands and knees. I can't hardly walk. My guts are on fire. My eyes have gone yellow.'

'First your pee, now your eyes. D'you know what the bloody time is?'

'I went down the bathroom, I don't know how I made it. I looked at myself in the mirror. I'm yellow all over, my whole body's gone yellow. I'll have to go see the doc.'

That woke Nigel fully. He lurched out of bed, the gun hanging in its holster against his naked side. He stood over Marty and gripped his shoulders.

'Are you out of your goddamned mind?'

Marty made noises like a beaten puppy. Sweat was streaming down his face. The blankets were wet with sweat, but he was shivering.

'I'll have to,' he said, his teeth chattering. 'I've got to do something.' He met Nigel's cold glittering eyes, and they made him cry out, 'You wouldn't let me die, Nige? Nige, I might die. You wouldn't let me die?'

18

He could hear her talking to Caesar outside the room. She must have gone out to the bathroom. He looked at his watch. Half-past seven. He was embarrassed because Caesar had seen her – dressed in what? The bedspread that he saw was missing? – and he was afraid of Caesar's censure because all his life every friend or acquaintance or relative had appeared to him in the guise of critical authority. She came back and stepped naked out of wrappings of red candlewick, and into his arms.

'What did he say to you?' Alan whispered.

' "Good luck, my darling," ' said Una, and she giggled.

'I love you,' he said. 'You're the only woman I ever made love to apart from my wife.'

'I don't believe it!'

'Why would I say it, then? It's nothing to be proud of.'

'Well, but, Paul, it is *quite* amazing.'

A horrid thought struck him. 'And you?'

'I never made love to any women.'

'You know I don't mean that. Men.'

'Oh, not so many, but more than *that*.'

And a horrider one. 'Not Ambrose?'

'Silly, you are. Ambrose is a celibate. He says that at his age you should have experienced all the sex you need and you must turn your energy to the life of the mind.'

' "Leave me, O Love, that reachest but to dust." '

'Well, I don't think it does. I really think it reacheth to much nicer things than that. You know, it wasn't just incredulity that made me say it was quite amazing.'

He considered. He blushed. 'Honestly?'

'Honestly. But if it's true, what you said, don't you think you need some more practice? Like now?'

That was the best week he had ever known.

He took Una to the theatre and he took her out to dinner. They hired a car. They had to hire it in her name because he was Paul Browning who had left his licence at home in Cricklewood. Driving up into Hertfordshire, they played the lovers' game of looking at houses and discussing whether this one or that one would best suit them to live in for the rest of their lives. He already knew that he wanted to live with her. The idea of even a brief separation was unthinkable. He couldn't keep his eyes off her, and the memory that he had told Caesar he didn't find her attractive was a guilty reproach, though she would never know of it. The word, anyway, was inadequate to describe the effect she had on him. He was glad now that she didn't wear make-up or dress well, for these things would have been an obscuring of herself. More than anything, he liked to watch the play of emotion in her face, that small intense face that screwed itself into deep lines of dismay or surprise, and relaxed to a child's smoothness with delight.

'Paul,' she said gently, 'the lights are green. We can go.'

'I'm sorry. I can't keep from looking at you. I do look at the road while I'm driving.'

When they got home that night and were in his room – she slept with him every night in his room – she asked him about his wife.

'What's her name?'

'Alison,' he said. He had to say that because he was Paul Browning.

'That's nice. You haven't told me if you've got any children.'

He thought of dead Lucy, who had never been mentioned between them. How many children had Paul Browning? In this case there could be no harm in telling the truth. 'I've got two, a boy and a girl. They're more or less grown-up. I was married very young.' Not just to change the subject, but because a greater truth, never before realized, came suddenly to him, 'I was a very bad father,' he said. Of course he had been, a bad father, a bad husband, whose energies went, not into giving love, but to indulging in self-pity. 'They won't miss me.'

Una looked at him with a wistfulness in which there was much trepidation. 'You said you wanted to live with me.'

'So I do! More than anything in the world. I can't imagine life without you now.'

She nodded. 'You can't imagine it but you could live it. Will you tell Alison about me?'

He said lightly, because 'Alison' merely conjured for him an unknown blonde woman in Cricklewood, 'I don't suppose so. What does it matter?'

'I think it matters if you're serious.'

So he took her in his arms and told her his love for her was the most serious thing that had ever happened to him. Alison was nothing, had been nothing for years. He would support her, of course, and do everything that was honourable, but as for seeing her and talking to her, no. He piled lie upon lie and Una believed him and smiled and they were happy.

Or he would have been happy, have enjoyed unalloyed happiness, had it not been for Joyce. The man he had seen in the Rose of Killarney was certainly not the man who had asked him for twenty five-pence pieces for a pound and therefore not one of the men who had raided the bank and kidnapped Joyce. True, they both had mutilated forefingers on their right hands, but those mutilations were quite different, the men were quite different. And yet the sight of that man, or really the sight of that finger, so similiar to the other and so evocative, had reawakened all his conscience about Joyce and all his shame. The bitterness of love unattained had kept that guilt at bay, the happiness of love triumphant had temporarily closed his mind to it, but it was back now, weighing on him by day, prodding him in the night.

'Is Joyce your daughter's name?' Una asked him.

'No. Why?'

'You kept calling that name in the night. You called, "Joyce, it's all right, I'm here." '

'I knew a girl called Joyce once.'

'It was as if you were talking to a frightened child,' said Una.

He should have done something in the Rose of Killarney, he thought, to make the boy speak. It would have been quite easy. He could have asked him where the buses went or the way to the nearest tube station. And then when he had heard the ordinary north London voice he would have known for sure and wouldn't be haunted like this. He understood now why he was haunted. The sight of that finger had brought him fear, disbelief, a need to react against it by pretending to himself that the similarity was an illusion – but it had also brought him hope. Hope that somehow this could open a way to redeeming himself, to vindicating himself for what he had done in leaving Joyce to her fate.

On the Friday morning he locked his door and took out the money and counted it. He could hardly believe that he had got through, in this short time, nearly two hundred pounds. Without really appalling him, the discovery brought home to him how small a sum three thousand pounds actually was. Since finding Una, he was no longer content vaguely to envisage one crowded hour of glorious life with disgrace or death at the end of it. He had known her for a week and he wanted a lifetime with her. He would have to get a job, something that didn't need credentials or qualifications or a National Insurance card. Optimistically, not doubtfully or desperately at all, he thought of taking her away from London and working as a gardener or a decorator or even a window-cleaner.

The doorhandle turned. 'Paul?'

He thrust the money back into the drawer and went to let Una in.

'You'd locked your door.' Her eyes met his in bewildered rejection, and in that look of fear, of distrust, she suddenly seemed to him to represent other women that he had disappointed, that he had failed, Pam and Joyce. Trying to think of an explanation for that locked door, he understood that here was something else which eluded explanation. But she didn't ask. 'I've had a letter from Ambrose,' she said. 'He's coming home on Saturday week.'

Alan nodded. He was rather pleased. Somehow he felt that hope for them lay with Ambrose Engstrand, though he didn't know why or in what form. Perhaps it was only that he thought of the philosopher as prepared to do anything to ensure Una's happiness.

'I don't want to be here when he comes back,' Una said.

'But why not?'

'I don't know. I'm afraid – I'm afraid he'll spoil this.' She moved her hand in an embracing gesture to contain her and himself and the room. 'You don't know him,' she said. 'You don't know how he can probe and question and get hold of things that are beautiful and – well, fragile, and make them mundane. He does it because he thinks it's for the best, but I don't, not always.'

'There's nothing fragile about my feeling for you.'

'What's in that drawer, Paul? What were you doing that you had to lock me out?'

'Nothing,' he said. 'It was force of habit.'

She made no acknowledgement of this. 'I felt,' she said, 'I thought you might have things of your wife's there, of Alison's. Letters, photographs, I don't know.' She gave him a look of fear. Not the kind of fear that is based on imaginings and has in it a counterweight of hope, but settled despair. 'You'll go back to Alison.'

'I'll never do that. Why do you say that?'

'Because you never see her. You never communicate with her.'

'I don't follow that logic.'

'It is logic, Paul. You'd phone her, you'd write to her, you'd go and see her, if you weren't afraid that once you'd seen her you'd go back. With me and Stewart it's different. I haven't seen him for months but he'll turn up, he always does. And we'll talk and discuss things and not care because we're indifferent. You're not indifferent to your wife. You daren't see her or hear her voice.'

'D'you *want* me to see her?'

'Yes. How can I feel I'm important to you if you won't tell her about me? I'm a holiday for you, I'm an adventure you'll look back on and sentimentalize about when you're back with Alison. Isn't it true? Oh God, if you went to see her I'd go mad, I'd be sick with fear you wouldn't come back. But when you did, if you did, I'd know where we were.'

He put his arms round her and kissed her. It was all nonsense to him, a fabric of chimeras based on nothing. Fleetingly he thought of Alison Browning with her husband and her little boy and her puppy and her nice house.

'I'll do anything you want,' he said. 'I'll write to her today.'

'Ambrose,' she murmured, 'would be so angry with me. He'd say I'd no precedent for reasoning the way I do about you and Alison except what I'd got out of books. He'd say we should never conjecture about things we've no experience of.'

'And he'd be so right!' said Alan. 'I said he was a monster, but I'm not so sure. I wish you'd let me meet him.'

'No.'

'All right. I don't meet him and I write to Alison today, now. Will that make you happy, my darling? I'll write my letter and then we'll hire the car again and I'll take you out to Windsor for lunch.'

She smiled at him, thrusting back her hair with both hands. 'The lights are green and we can go?'

'Wherever you want,' he said.

She left him alone to write the letter, and this time he didn't lock the door. He had nothing to hide from her because he really did write a letter beginning 'Dear Alison'. It gave him a curious pleasure to write Una's name and to describe her and explain that he loved her and she loved him. He even addressed the envelope to Mrs Alison Browning, 15 Exmoor Gardens, NW2, in case Una should catch sight of it as he passed through the hall on his way to the post.

His pillar box was a litter bin. He tore the envelope and the letter inside it into pieces and dropped them into the bin, noticing that the last scrap to go was that on which he had written the postal district, North-west Two. Not half a mile away from Alison's house he had seen the boy with the mutilated finger. Suppose he had asked him that question about the buses and the tube and had got an answer and the voice answering had been Suffolk-cockney? What next? What could he have done? Written an anonymous letter to the police, he thought, or, better than that, made an anonymous phone call. They would have acted on that, they wouldn't dare not to. Why hadn't he made the boy speak? It was the obvious thing to have done and it would have been so easy, so easy . . .

Walking back to Montcalm Gardens and Una, he was forced to ask himself something that made him wince. Had he kept silent and fed his incredulity and condemned his over-active imagination because he didn't *want* to know? Because all that talk of redemption and vindication was nonsense. He didn't want to know because he didn't want Joyce found. Because if Joyce were found alive she would immediately tell the police he hadn't been in the bank, he hadn't been kidnapped, and they would hunt for him and find him and take him away from freedom and happiness and Una.

19

'You haven't even got a goddamned doctor,' said Nigel.

But there he was wrong, for Marty had needed a doctor in the days when he had worked. Medical certificates had frequently been required for imaginary gastritis or nervous debility or depression.

' 'Course I have,' said Marty. 'Yid up Chichele.' He clutched his stomach and moaned. 'I got to see him and get some of them antibiotics or whatever.'

Nigel wrapped a blanket round himself and padded out and lit the oven. He contemplated the bookcase; half a dozen slices of stale bread, two cans of soup and three eggs, four bottles of whisky and maybe eighty cigarettes. Having made a face at these last items, he squatted down to warm himself at the open oven. He didn't want Marty coming into contact with any form of official authority, and into this category the doctor would come. On the other hand, the doctor would reassure Marty – Nigel was sure there was nothing really wrong with him – and that ignorant peasant was just the type to start feeling better the minute anyone gave him a pill. Aspirin would cure him, Nigel thought derisively, provided it came in a bottle labelled tetracyclin. He wanted Marty fit again and biddable, his link and go-between with the outside world, but he didn't want him shooting his mouth off to this doctor about not needing a medical certificate, thanks, and his mate he was sharing with who'd look after him and the girl they'd got staying with them and whatever. Above all, he didn't want this doctor remembering that last time he'd seen him Marty had sported a bushy beard like the guy who had hired the van in Croydon.

A groan from the mattress fetched him back into the living room. Joyce was sitting up, looking warily at Marty. Nigel took no notice of her. He said to Marty, not too harshly for him:

'Give it another day and keep off the booze. If your belly's still freaking you tomorrow, I reckon you'll have to go see the doctor. We'll like wait and see.'

They had bread and the last of the cheese for lunch, and a tin of scotch broth and the three eggs for supper. Marty didn't eat anything, but Nigel who wasn't usually a big eater felt ravenous and had two of the eggs himself. The main advantage of getting Marty to the doctor would mean that he could do their shopping on his way back. A lot more cans, thought Nigel hungrily, and a couple of large loaves and milk and butter and some of that Indian takeaway, Vindaloo curry and dhal and rice and lime pickle. He wanted Marty to go to the doctor now, he was almost as keen as Marty himself had been on Thursday night.

He didn't seem keen any more when Nigel woke him at eight in the morning.

'Come on, get dressed,' he said to Marty. 'Have a bit of a wash too if you don't want to gas the guy.'

Marty groaned and rolled over, turning up the now yellow whites of his eyes. 'I don't reckon I've got the strength. I'll just lay here a bit. I'll be better in a day or two.'

'Look, we said if your belly's still freaking you you'd go see the doctor, right? You get down there now and do our shopping on the way back. You can do it at the corner shops, you don't need to go down the Broadway.'

Marty crawled off the mattress and into the kitchen where he ran water over his hands and slopped a little on to his face. The kitchen walls and floor were moving and slanting like in a crazy house at a fair. He took a swig of whisky to steady himself and managed to struggle into his clothes. It didn't help that Joyce, sitting up on the sofa with the blanket cocooned around her, was watching him almost with compassion or as if she were genuinely afraid he might fall down dead any minute.

An icy mist, thick, white and still, greeted him when he opened the front door. It wasn't far to Dr Miskin's, not more than a couple of hundred yards, but it felt more like five miles to Marty who clung to lamp-posts as he staggered along and finally had to sit down on the stone steps of a chapel. There he was found by a policeman on the beat. Marty felt too ill to care about being spoken to by a policeman, and the policeman could see he was ill, not drunk.

'You're not fit to be out in this,' said the policeman.

'On my way to the doc,' said Marty.

'Best place for you. Here, I'll give you a hand.'

So Marty Foster was conducted into Dr Miskin's waiting room on the kindly arm of the law.

Nigel knew Marty would be quite a long time because he hadn't made an appointment. That sort of morning surgery – he knew all about it from the giving if not the receiving end – could well go on till noon, so he didn't get worried. Marty would be back by lunchtime with some food. He was hungry and Joyce kept whimpering that she was hungry, but so what? Nobody got malnutrition because they hadn't eaten for twelve hours.

At one o'clock they shared the can of chicken soup, eating it cold because it was thicker and more filling that way. There was now no food left. Marty was fool enough, Nigel thought, to have taken his prescription to a chemist who closed for lunch. That would be it. He had gone to the chemist at five to one, and now he was having to wait till two when they opened again. Probably wouldn't even have the sense to do the shopping in the meantime.

'Suppose he doesn't come back?' said Joyce.

'You missing him, are you? I didn't know you cared.'

The mist had gone and it was a beautiful clear day, sunshine making the room quite warm. Soon they could stop using any heat, and when the fridge came and the TV . . . Nigel saw himself lounging on the sofa with a long glass of martini and crushed ice in his hand, watching a film in glorious colour, while Joyce washed his clothes and polished his shoes and grilled him a steak. Half-past two. Any time now and that little brain would be back. If he'd had the sense to take a couple of pills straight away, he might be fit enough to get down to the electrical discount shop before it closed.

Nigel told himself he was standing by the window because it was nice to feel a bit of sun for a change. He watched old Green coming back from the Broadway with shopping in a string bag. He saw a figure turning into the street from Chichele Road, and for a minute he thought it was Marty, the jeans, the leather jacket, the pinched bony face and the cropped hair. It wasn't.

'Watching for him won't bring him,' said Joyce who was forcing herself, rather feebly, to knit once more.

'I'm not watching for him.'

'He's been gone nearly seven hours.'

'So what?' Nigel shouted at her. 'Is it any goddamned business of yours? He's got things to get, hasn't he? Him and me, we can't sit about on our arses all day.'

They both jumped at the sound of the phone. Nigel said, 'You come down with me,' pointing the gun, but by the time they were out on the landing the bell had stopped. No one had come up from the lower floors of the house. In the heavy warm silence, Nigel propelled Joyce back into the room and they sat down again. Past three and Marty hadn't come.

'I'm hungry,' Joyce said.

'Shut up.'

Nothing happened for an hour, two hours. Although Nigel had turned off the oven, the heat was growing oppressive, for the room faced west. If the police had got Marty, Nigel thought, they would have been here by now. But he couldn't still be wandering about Cricklewood with a prescription, could he? The knitting fell from Joyce's fingers, and her head went back and she dozed. With a jerk she came to herself again, and seeing that neither Nigel nor the gun were putting up any opposition, she dragged herself over to the mattress and lay down on it. She pulled the covers over her and buried her face.

Nigel stood at the window. It was half-past five and the sun was going down into a red mist. There were a lot of people about, but no Marty. Nigel felt hollow inside, and not just from hunger. He started to pace the room, looking sometimes at Joyce, hating her for sleeping, for not caring what happened. Presently he took advantage of her sleeping to go out to the lavatory.

The phone screamed at him.

He left the door wide open and ran down. Keeping the gun turned on that open door, he picked up the receiver. Pip-pip-pip, then the sound of money going in and, Christ, Marty's voice.

'What the hell goes?' Nigel hissed.

'Nige, I rung before but no one answered. Listen, I'm in the hospital.'

'Jesus.'

'Yeah, listen. I'm really sick, Nige. I got hepa-something, something with my liver. That's why I'm all yellow.'

'Hepatitis.'

'That's him, hepatitis. I passed out in the doc's and they brought me here. God knows how I got it, the doctor don't know, maybe from all that takeaway. They give me the phone trolley to phone you and they want my gear brought in. They want a razor, Nige, and a *toothbrush* and I don't know what. I wouldn't tell them who you was or where and . . .'

'*You've got to get out right now*. You've got to split like this minute. Right?'

'Are you kidding? I can't bloody walk. I got to be in here a week, that's what they say, and you're to bring . . .'

'Shut up! Will you for fuck's sake shut up? You've got to get dressed and get a taxi and come right back here. Can't you get it in your thick head we've got no food?'

Pip-pip-pip.

'I haven't got no more change, Nige.'

Nigel bellowed into the phone, 'Get dressed and get a taxi and come home *now*. If you don't, Christ, I'll get you if it's the last . . .' The phone went dead and the dialling tone started. Nigel closed his eyes. He leant against the bathroom door. Then he trailed upstairs again. Joyce woke up, coming to herself at once as she always did.

'What's happening?'

'Marty got held up. He'll be here in an hour.'

But would he? He always did what he was told, but that was when he was here in this room. Would he when he was miles away in a hospital bed? Nigel realized he didn't even know what hospital, he hadn't asked. He heard the diesel throb of a taxi from the street below several times in the next hour. Joyce washed her face and hands and looked at the empty bookcase and drank some water.

'What's happened to him? He isn't going to come, is he?'

'He'll come.'

Joyce said, 'He was ill. He went to the doctor's. I bet he's in hospital.'

'I told you, he's coming back tonight.'

When it got to ten, Nigel knew for certain that Marty wouldn't come. He came back from the window where he had been standing for an hour, and turning to look at Joyce, he found that her eyes were fixed on him. Her eyes were animal-like and full of panic. He and she were alone together now, each the prisoner of the other. He had never seen her look so frightened, but instead of gratifying him, her fear made him frightened too. He no longer wanted her as his slave, he wanted her dead, but he heard the red-haired girl on the phone and then Bridey coming in, and he only fingered the gun, keeping the safety catch on.

Sunday passed very slowly, beginning and ending in fog with hot spring sunshine in between. Nigel thought Marty would phone in the morning, would be bound to, if only to go in for more bloody silly nonsense about having a toothbrush brought in. And when he did he, Nigel, would find out just what hospital he was in, and then he'd phone for a mini-cab and send it round to fetch Marty out. He couldn't believe that Marty would defy him.

When it got to the middle of the afternoon and Marty hadn't phoned, Nigel's stomach was roaring hunger at him. The bookcase cupboard was bare but for the four bottles of whisky and the eighty cigarettes. For the sake of the nourishment, Nigel drank some whisky in hot water, but it knocked him sideways and he was afraid to repeat the experiment in case he passed out. Most of the time he stood by the window, no longer watching for Marty but eyeing the corner shop which he could see quite clearly and whose interior, with its delicatessen counter and rack of Greek bread and shelves and shelves of cans and jars, he could recall from previous visits. Pointing the gun at Joyce, he forced her to swallow some neat whisky in an attempt to render her unconscious. She obeyed because she was so frightened of the gun. Or, rather, her will obeyed but not her body. She gagged and threw up and collapsed weeping on the mattress.

Nigel had been thinking, when he wasn't simply thinking about the taste and smell and texture of food, of ways to tie her up. He could gag her and tie her hands and feet and then somehow anchor her to the gas stove. 'Somehow' was the word. How? In order to begin he would have to put the gun down. Nevertheless, late in the afternoon, he tried it, seizing her from behind and clamping his hand over her mouth. Joyce fought him, biting and kicking, tearing herself away from him to crouch and cower behind the sofa. Nigel swore at her. She was only a few inches shorter than he and probably as heavy. Without Marty's assistance, he was powerless.

Bridey went out, old Green went out most days. Nigel thought of telling one of them he was ill and getting them to fetch him in some food. But he couldn't cover Joyce with the gun while he was doing so. If he left Joyce she would break the windows, if he took her with him – that didn't bear considering. He could knock her out. Yes, and if he went at it too heavily he'd be left with a sick girl on his hands, too lightly and she'd come to before he got back.

The shop was so near he could easily have struck its windows if he had thrown a stone. His mouth kept filling with saliva and he kept swallowing it down into his empty stomach.

By Monday morning Nigel knew Marty wasn't going to phone or come back. He didn't think he would ever come back now. Even when they let him out of hospital he wouldn't come back. He'd go and hide out with his mother and forget about his share of the money and the two people he'd abandoned.

'What are we going to do for food?' Joyce said.

Nigel was forced to plead with her. It was to be the first of many times. 'Look, I can get us food, if you'll guarantee not to scream or try and get out.'

She looked at him stonily.

'Five minutes while I go down the shop.'

'No,' said Joyce.

'Why don't you fuck off?' Nigel shouted. 'Why don't you starve to death?'

20

Alan happened to be in the hall when the phone rang. Una was in the kitchen, getting their lunch. He picked up the phone and said, Sorry, you've got the wrong number, when a man's voice asked if he was Lloyds Bank. Maybe if he'd been asked if he was the Anglian-Victoria he would have said yes out of force of habit.

'Who was that on the phone?' said Una.

'Alison.'

'Oh.'

'She wants to see me . . .' It was the only excuse he could think of for getting himself up to Cricklewood without Una. Wherever he went she went, and he wanted it that way, only not this time. 'She was quite all right, nice, in fact,' he said with an effort. 'I said I'd go over and see her this afternoon.'

Una, who had been looking a little dismayed, the flow of her vitality checked, suddenly smiled. 'I'm *so* glad, Paul. That makes me feel real. Be kind to her, won't you? Be generous. D'you know, I pity her so much, I feel for her so. I keep thinking how, if it was me, I couldn't bear to lose you.'

'You never will,' he said.

He had dreamed in the night of the boy with the mutilated finger. In the dream he was alone with the boy in the room at the bank where the safe was, and he was desperately trying to make him speak. He was bribing him to speak with offers of banknotes which he removed, wad by wad, from the safe. And the boy was taking the money, stuffing it into his pockets and down the front of his jacket, but all the time remaining silent, staring at him. At last Alan came very close to him to see why he didn't speak, and he saw that the boy couldn't speak, his mouth wouldn't open, for the lips were fused together and cobbled like the kernel of a walnut.

When he awoke and reached for Una to touch her and lie close up against her, the dream and the guilt it carried with it wouldn't go away. He kept telling himself that the boy in the pub couldn't be the same as the boy who had come into the bank and who later had robbed the bank, the coincidence would be too great. Yet when he examined this, he saw that there wasn't so very much of a coincidence at all. In the past three weeks he had wandered all over London. He had been in dozens of pubs and restaurants and cafés and bars. Nearly all the time he had been out and about, exploring and observing. Very likely, if that boy was also a frequenter of pubs and eating places, sooner or later they would have encountered each other. And if the boy turned out to be a different boy, which was the way he wanted it to be, which was what he longed to know for certain, there would be no coincidence at all. It would be just that he was very sensitive to that particular kind of deformity of a finger. What he really wanted was for someone to tell him that the boy was an ordinary decent citizen of Cricklewood, out doing some emergency Sunday morning shopping for his wife or his mother, and when he spoke it would be with a brogue as Irish as that barmaid's.

It was just before the phone rang that the idea came to him of going back to the Rose of Killarney and asking the barmaid if she knew who the boy was. Just possibly she might know because it looked as if the boy lived locally. Surely you wouldn't go a journey to do Sunday morning shopping, would you, when there was bound to be a shop open in your own neighbourhood? Even if she didn't know, he would have tried, he thought. He would have done his best and not have to feel this shame and self-disgust at doing nothing because he was afraid of what might happen if Joyce were found. He should have thought of that, he told himself with bravado, before he hid and left her to her fate and escaped.

It was half-past one when he walked into the Rose of Killarney. There were about a dozen people in the saloon bar, but the boy with the distorted finger wasn't among them. All the way up in the bus Alan had been wondering if he might be, but of course he wouldn't, he'd be at work. Behind the bar was the Irish girl, looking sullen and tired. Alan asked her for a half of bitter and when it came he said hesitantly:

'I don't suppose you happen to know . . .' It seemed to him that she was looking at him with a kind of incredulous disgust. '. . . the name of the young man who was in here last Sunday week?' Was it really as long ago as that? The distance in time seemed to add to the absurdity of the enquiry. 'Early twenties, dark, clean-shaven,' he said. He held up his own right hand, grasping the forefinger in his left. 'His finger . . .' he was beginning when she interrupted him.

'You the police?'

A more self-confident man might have agreed that he was. Alan, trying to think up an excuse for wanting a stranger's name and address, disclaimed any connection with the law and thrust his hand into his pocket, seeking inspiration. All he could produce was a five-pound note, a portrait of the Duke of Wellington.

'He dropped this as he was leaving.'

'You took your time about it,' said the girl.

'I've been away.'

She said quickly, greedily, 'Sure and I'll give it him. Foster's his name, Marty Foster, I know him well.'

The note was snatched from his fingers. He began to insist, 'If you could just tell me . . . ?'

'Don't you trust me, then?'

He shrugged, embarrassed. Several pairs of eyes were fixed on him. He got down off his stool and went out. If the girl knew him well, spoke of him therefore as a frequenter of the pub, he couldn't be Joyce's kidnapper, could he? Alan knew he could, that all that meant nothing. But at least he had the name, Foster, Marty Foster. What he could do now was phone the police and give them Marty Foster's name and describe him. He crossed the road and went into a phone box and looked in the directory. There was no police station listed for Cricklewood. Of course he could phone Scotland Yard. A superstitious fear took hold of him that as soon as he spoke they would know at once where he was and who he was. He came hurriedly out of the phone box and began to walk away in the direction of Exmoor Gardens, towards Alison where he was supposed to be and looking for another phone box in a less exposed and vulnerable place.

By the time he had found it he knew he wasn't going to make that call. It was more important to him that the police shouldn't track him down than that they should be alerted to hunt for a Marty Foster who very likely had no connection at all with the Childon bank robbery. So he continued to walk aimlessly and to think. In the little shopping parade among the ovals named after mountain ranges, he went into a newsagent's and bought an evening paper. As far as he could see, there was nothing in it about Joyce. At three-fifteen he thought he might reasonably go back to Una now, and he retraced his steps to Cricklewood Broadway to wait for a bus going south.

The bus was approaching and he was holding out his hand to it when he saw the girl from the Rose of Killarney. She had come out of a side door of the pub, and crossing the Broadway, walked off down a side street. Alan let the bus go. He thought, maybe she'll go straight to this Foster's home with the money, that's what I'd do, that's what any honest person would do, and then he gave a little dry laugh to himself at what he had said. He followed her across the road, wishing there were more people about, not just the two of them apparently, once the shopping place and the bus routes were left behind. But she didn't look round. She walked with assurance, cutting corners, crossing streets diagonally. Suddenly there were more shops, a launderette, a Greek delicatessen; on the opposite side a church in a churchyard full of plane trees, on this a row of red brick houses, three storeys high. The girl turned in at the gate of one of them.

Alan hurried, but by the time he reached the gate the girl had disappeared. He read the names above the bells and saw that the topmost one was M. Foster. Had Foster himself let her in? Or had it been the mother or wife with whom his imagination had earlier invested the man with the mutilated finger? He crossed the road and stood by the low wall of the churchyard to wait for her. And then? Once she had left, was he also going to ring that bell? Presumably. He hadn't come so far as this to abandon his quest and go tamely home.

Time passed very slowly. He pretended to read the notice board and then really read it for something to do. He walked up the street as far as he could go while keeping the house in sight, and then he walked back again and as far in the other direction. He went into the churchyard and even examined the church which he was sure was of no architectural merit whatsoever. Still the girl hadn't come out, though by now half an hour had gone by.

M. Foster's was the topmost bell. Did that mean he lived on the top floor? It might not mean that he occupied the whole of the top floor. For the first time Alan lifted his eyes to the third storey of the house with its three oblong windows. A young man was standing up against the glass, immobile, flaccid, somehow even from that distance and through that glass giving an impression of a kind of hopeless indolence. But he wasn't Foster. His hair was blond. Alan stopped staring at him and, making up his mind, he went back across the road and rang that bell.

Nobody came down. He rang the bell again, more insistently this time, but he felt sure it wasn't going to be answered. On an impulse he pressed the one below it, B. Flynn.

The last person he expected to see was the barmaid from the Rose of Killarney. Her appearance at the door, not in her outdoor coat but with a cup of tea in one hand and a cigarette in the other, made him feel that he had walked into one of those nightmares – familiar to him these days – in which the irrational is commonplace and identities bizarrely interchangeable.

She said nothing and he had no idea what to say. They stared at each other and as he became aware that she was frightened, that in her look was awe and fear and repulsion, she put her hand into the pocket of her trousers and pulled out the five-pound note.

'Take your money.' She thrust it at him. 'I've done nothing. Will you leave me alone?' Her voice trembled. 'Give it him yourself if that's what you're wanting.'

Alan still couldn't understand, but he questioned, 'He does live here?'

'On the top, next to me. Him and his pal.' She began to retreat, rubbing her hands as if to erase the contamination of that money from them. The cigarette hung from her mouth.

Alan knew she thought he was the police in spite of his denial. She thought he was a policeman playing tricks. 'Listen,' he said. 'How does he talk? Has he got an accent?'

She threw the cigarette end into the street. 'Bloody English like you,' she said, and closed the door.

Una was waiting for him in the hall. The front door had yielded under the pressure of his hand, she had left it on the latch, presumably so that she could the more easily keep running out to see if he was coming.

She rushed up to him. 'You were so long.' She sounded breathless. 'I was worried.'

'It's only just gone five,' he said vaguely.

'Did you have a bad time with Alison?'

He had almost forgotten who Alison was. It seemed ridiculous to him that Una should be concerned about that happy secure woman who had nothing to do with him or her, but he seized on what might have happened that afternoon as an excuse for his preoccupation.

'She was quite reasonable and calm and nice,' he said, and he added, not thinking this time of Paul Browning's wife, 'She thinks I shouldn't have left. She says I've ruined her life.'

Una said nothing. He followed her through the big house to the kitchen where she began to busy herself making tea for him. Her flying-fox face was puckered so that the lines on it seemed to presage the wrinkles of age. He put his arms round her.

'What is it?'

'Did it make you unhappy, seeing Alison?'

'Not a bit. Let's forget her.' He held Una tight, thinking what a bore it was, all this pretence. He was going to have to fabricate so much, interviews with solicitors, financial arrangements. Why had he ever said he was married? Una was herself married, so the question of marriage between them couldn't have arisen. It seemed to him that she must have read at least some part of his thoughts, for she moved a little aside from him and said:

'I heard from Stewart. By the second post.'

She gave him the letter. It was happy and affectionate. Stewart said he had had a call from his father all about her and her new man, and why didn't she and her Paul go and live in the cottage on Dartmoor?

'Could we, please, Paul?'

'I don't know . . .'

'We could just go and see if you liked it. I could write to the woman in the village who looks after it and get her to air it and warm it, and we could be there by the weekend. Ambrose'll be home on Saturday but I'd leave the house *immaculate* for him. He won't mind my not being here, he'll be glad to be rid of me at last. Paul, can we?'

'I'll do whatever you want,' he said. 'You know that.'

He began to drink the tea she had made him. She sat opposite him at the table, her elbows on it, her chin in her hands, her eyes sparkling with anticipation. He smiled back at her and his smile was full of tenderness, yet much as he loved being with her, much as he wanted to share his whole life with her, he wished then that he could briefly be alone. It was impossible. There would be a cruelty in broaching it, he thought, after he had supposedly been all those hours with his wife. But he longed very much for solitude in which to think about what course of action next to take.

Una began talking to him about Dartmoor and the cottage itself. It would be a good place to hide in, he thought, after he had phoned the police and they had rescued Joyce and Joyce had told them the truth about him. They would never look for him in a private house in so remote a place. But before he could phone and certainly before he could leave, he must have more information. He must know for sure that Joyce's kidnapper, the boy whose walnut-nailed finger had scooped up the change and Marty Foster were one and the same.

'Shall we go on Friday?' said Una.

He nodded. It gave him three days.

As their eyes met across the table, his troubled, hers excited, anxious, hopeful, some twenty miles to the south of them John Purford's aircraft was touching down at Gatwick.

21

Nigel and Marty had never thought of counting the notes they had stolen. They would only have done so if the question of dividing it had come up. Soon after he awoke on the morning of Tuesday, 26 March, after he had drunk some warm water, Nigel took the money out, spread it on the kitchen table and counted it. He didn't know how much they had spent but there was over four thousand left – four thousand and fifteen pounds, to be precise. The amount they had taken, therefore, had been somewhat in excess of what he had supposed. He divided it into two equal sums and tied up each of the resultant wads with a black stocking. Then he put them back into the bag with the bunch of Ford Escort keys.

He and Joyce had eaten nothing since the chicken soup at midday on Saturday, and not much for two days before that. Nigel was no longer hungry. Nor did he feel particularly weak or tired, only light-headed. The visions of a future in which he dominated Joyce had been replaced by even more highly coloured ones in which he had Marty at his mercy in some medieval torture chamber. He saw himself in a black cloak and hood, tearing out Marty's fingernails with red-hot pincers. Once he was out of there he was going to get Marty, hunt him if necessary to the ends of the earth, and then he was going to come back and finish Joyce. He didn't know whom he hated most, Joyce or Marty, but he hated them more than he hated his parents. The former had succeeded the latter as responsible for all his troubles.

Since Sunday Joyce had spent most of the time lying on the sofa. She hadn't washed or combed her hair or cleaned her teeth. Dust lay everywhere once more and the bed linen smelt sour. Once she had understood that Marty wasn't coming back, that she was alone with Nigel, that there wasn't going to be anything to eat, she had retreated into a zombie-like apathy, a kind of fugue, from which she was briefly aroused only by the ringing of the doorbell on Monday afternoon. She had wanted to know who it was and had tried to get to the window, but Nigel had caught her and thrown her back, his hand over her mouth. And then they had both faintly heard a bell ringing in the next room and Bridey going downstairs, and she had known to her despair what Nigel had known to his relief, that it had only been some salesman or canvasser at the door.

On the following morning it was nearly twelve before she dragged herself to the kitchen and, having drunk a cup of water, leant back against the sink, her face going white. When she drank water she could always feel the shock of it, teasingly trickling down, trace its whole passage through her intestines. She hadn't looked directly at Nigel, much less spoken to him, since Monday morning, for whenever she allowed her eyes to meet his it only brought on a spasm of hysterical crying. Twice a day perhaps she would go limply towards the door, and Nigel would take this as a signal to escort her to the lavatory. She was weak and broken, a butt for Nigel's occasional violence. She believed that everything had been destroyed in her, for she no longer thought with longing or anguish of Stephen or her parents, or of escape or of keeping herself decent and nice. Aeons seemed to have passed since she had been defiant and bold. She was starving to death, as Nigel had told her to, and she supposed – for this was all she thought of now – that she would grow weaker and weaker and less and less conscious of herself and her surroundings until finally she did die. She walked to the door and waited there until Nigel slouched over to take her outside.

When they were both back in the room, Nigel spoke to her. He spoke her name. She made no answer. He didn't use her name again, it was almost painful to him to bring it out, but said:

'We can't stay here. You said once, you said if we let you go you wouldn't talk to the police.'

Stress and starvation had taken from Nigel's speech that disc jockey drawl and those eclectic idioms, and tones of public school and university re-asserted themselves. Joyce wondered vaguely at the voice which was beautiful and like someone in a serious play on the television, but she hardly took in the sense of the words. Nigel repeated them and went on:

'If you meant that, straight up, we can get out of here.' He looked at her hard, his eyes glittering. 'I'll give you two thousand,' he said, 'to get out of here and go and stop in a hotel for two weeks. Give me two weeks to get out of the country, get clear away. Then you can go home and squeal all you want.'

Joyce absorbed what he had said. She sat in silence, nervously fingering her chin where a patch of acne had developed. After a while she said, 'What about him? What about Marty?'

'Who's Marty?' shouted Nigel.

It was hard for Joyce to speak. When she spoke her mouth filled with saliva and she felt sick, but she did her best.

'What's the good of two thousand to me? I couldn't spend it. I couldn't tell my fiancé. It'd be like Monopoly money, it'd be just paper.'

'You can save it up, can't you? Buy shares with it.' Memories of his father's advice, often derided in the commune, came back to Nigel. 'Buy goddamned bloody National Savings.'

Joyce began to cry. The tears trickled slowly down her face. 'It's not just that. I couldn't take the bank's money. How could I?' She wept, hanging her head. 'I'd be as bad as you.'

With a gasp of rage, Nigel came at her, slapping her face hard, and Joyce fell down on the mattress, shaking with sobs. He turned away from her and went into the kitchen where the money was in the carrier bag. The bunch of car keys was there too, but Nigel had forgotten all about the silver-blue Ford Escort he had hidden in Dr Bolton's garage twenty-two days before.

While still in Crete, Dr and Mrs Bolton had received a telegram announcing that Dr Bolton's mother had died. Old Mrs Bolton had been ninety-two and bedridden, but nevertheless when one's mother dies, whatever the circumstances, one can hardly remain abroad enjoying oneself. Dr

Bolton found the Ford Escort before he had even taken the suitcases out of his own car. He unpacked one of these in order to retrieve, from where it was wrapped round his sandals, the relevant copy of the *Daily Telegraph*. Having checked that his memory wasn't tricking him, he phoned the police.

They were with him in half an hour. Dr and Mrs Bolton were asked to make a list of all the people who knew they had no lock on their garage and also knew they were to be away on holiday.

'Our friends,' said Dr Bolton, 'are not the kind of people who rob banks.'

'I don't doubt that,' said the detective inspector, 'but your friends may know people who know people who are less respectable than they are, or have children who have friends who are not respectable at all.'

Dr Bolton was obliged to agree that this was possible. The list was a very long one and the Thaxbys were only added by Mrs Bolton as an afterthought and not until the Thursday morning. She couldn't remember whether or not she had told Mrs Thaxby. In this case, said the detective inspector, it wasn't a matter of when in doubt leave out, but when in doubt be on the safe side. Mrs Bolton said it was laughable, the Thaxbys of all people. Maybe they had children? said the inspector. Well, one boy, a very nice intelligent responsible sort of young man who was at present a student at the University of Kent.

Which went to show that Nigel's mother had not been strictly honest when recounting her son's activities to her friends.

A few hours after Mrs Bolton had given this vital piece of information to the police, John Purford at last got in touch with them. It wasn't that he was afraid or stalling, but simply that he didn't know the Childon bank robbery had ever taken place. The event had almost slipped his mother's mind. After all, it had been more than three weeks ago, the manager and the girl were sure to be dead, it was a tragedy, God knows, but life has to go on. This was what she said in defence when John saw a little paragraph in the paper about the car being found. He told his partner the whole thing, including the business in the back of the car with Jillian Groombridge. He said it must all be in his head, mustn't it? He had been at school with Marty Foster.

'That's no argument,' said the partner. 'There were folks must have been at school with Hitler, come to that.'

'You think I ought to tell the police?'

'Sure you ought. What have you got to lose? I'll come with you if you want. They won't eat you. They'll be all over you, nice as pie.'

In fact, the police were not particularly nice to John Purford. They thanked him for coming to them, they appreciated that he was able precisely to point out on a street plan the café where he had met Marty Foster and Nigel Something, but they scolded him soundly for giving away information of that kind and asked him, to his horror, if he knew the age of Jillian Groombridge.

They seized upon the fairly unusual christian name of Nigel. A couple on Dr Bolton's list had a son called Nigel. The police went to Elstree. Dr and Mrs Thaxby said their son was in Newcastle. They gave the police the address of the Kensington commune, and there Samantha's mother was interviewed. She also said Nigel was in Newcastle. Marty Foster's father didn't know where his son was, hadn't set eyes on him for two years and didn't want to. The police found Mrs Foster who was living with her lover and her lover's three children in a council house in Hemel Hempstead. She hadn't seen Marty for several months, but when she had last seen him he had been on the dole. Immediately the police set about tracing Marty Foster's address through the files of the Ministry of Social Security.

Nigel got his passport out of the rucksack and read it. Mr N. L. Thaxby; born 15.1.58; Occupation: student; Height: six feet; Eyes: blue. The passport had only been used twice, Nigel not being one of those enterprising and adventurous young people who hitch-hike across Europe or drive vans to India. He thought he'd take a flight to Bolivia or Paraguay or somewhere they couldn't extradite you. He'd have about fifteen hundred pounds left, and once he was there he'd contact some newspaper, the *News of the World* or the *Sunday People*, and sell them his story – for what? Five grand? Ten?

Twice more he had asked Joyce to take two thousand as

the price of silence, and twice more she had refused. This time he went up to her with the gun levelled and watched her flinch and begin to put up her hands to her face. He wondered vaguely if she felt like he did as the result of their long fast, drugged as if with one of those substances that don't stupefy but make the head light and dizzy and change the vision and bend the mind. Certainly, she looked at him as if he were a ghost or a monster. He thought of shooting her there and then and keeping all the money for himself, but it was broad daylight and he could hear Bridey in the next room and, beyond the other wall, old Green's whistling kettle.

'What did you say it for if you didn't mean it? Why did you say you wouldn't talk?' Nigel pushed one of the bundles of money into her face. He rubbed it against her tears. 'That's more than you could earn in a year. Would you rather lie here bleeding to death than have two grand for yourself? Would you?'

She pushed the money away and covered her face, but she didn't speak. Nigel sat down. Standing made him feel a bit faint. He was acutely aware that he was doing it all wrong. He shouldn't be pleading for favours but compelling by force, yet he began to plead and to cajole.

'Look, it doesn't have to be for two weeks, just long enough to let me get out of the country. You can go to a big hotel in the West End. And they'll never find out you've had the money because you can spend it. Don't you realize you can go to a jeweller's and spend the whole lot on a watch or a ring?'

Joyce got up and went to the door. She stood at the door, waiting wordlessly, until Nigel came over and listened and unlocked it. Joyce went into the lavatory. Behind her door Bridey was playing a transistor. Nigel waited tensely, wondering what was the point of a deaf man having a whistling kettle. It was whistling again now. Nigel heard it stop and thought about Mr Green until a clear plan began to form in his mind, and he wondered why he had never considered Mr Green from this aspect before. Nobody ever spoke to him because they couldn't make themselves understood, no matter how loud they shouted, and he hardly ever spoke because he knew the answers he might receive would be meaningless to him. Of course the plan was only a temporary measure and it might not, in any case, work. But it was the only one he could think of in which, if it didn't work, there would be no harm done.

The idea of at last getting something to eat made him hungry again. The saliva rushed, warm and faintly salty, into his mouth. He could revive and perhaps bribe Joyce with food. She came out of the lavatory and he hustled her back into the room. Then he hunted in there and in the kitchen for an envelope, but he had no more luck than Joyce had had when she wanted to write her note, and he had to settle as she had done for a paper bag or, in this case, for part of the wrapping off Marty's cigarette carton. Nigel wrote: 'In bed with flu. Could you get me large white loaf?' Of all the comestibles he could have had, he chose without thinking man's traditional staff of life. He folded the paper round a pound note. Joyce was lying on the sofa face-downwards, but let him only be out of sight for more than a couple of minutes, he thought, let him start down those stairs, and she'd be off there raring to go as if she'd just got a plateful of roast beef inside her. The saliva washed round the cavities and pockets of his mouth. He went out on to the landing and pushed the note under Mr Green's door, having remembered to sign it: M. Foster.

Mr Green went out most days. He had lived for years in one room, so he went out even if he had nothing to buy and although climbing back again up those stairs nearly killed him every time. The note, which suddenly appeared under his door when he was making himself his fifteenth cup of tea of the day, worried him intensely. This wasn't because he even considered not complying with the request in it. He was afraid of young people, especially young males, and he would have done far more than make a special journey to buy a loaf in order to avoid offending the tall fair one or the small dark one, whichever this Foster was. What worried him was not knowing whether his neighbour meant a cut or uncut loaf, and also being entrusted with a pound note which still seemed to Mr Green a large sum of money. But when he had drunk his tea he took his string bag and put on his overcoat and set off.

A young man in a blue jacket caught him up a little way down the road. Asking the way to somewhere, Mr Green supposed. He did what he always did, shook his head and kept on walking, though the young man persisted and was quite hard to shake off. Because the cut loaf was more expensive than the uncut Mr Green didn't buy it. He bought a large white tin loaf, crusty and warm, carefully wrapping it in tissue paper himself, and in the shop next door he bought the *Evening Standard*. This he paid for out of his own money. Then he went for a little walk in his own silence along the noisy Broadway, returning home by a different route and not taking too long about it because it would be wrong and inconsiderate to keep a sick man waiting.

Half-way up the stairs he had to stop and rest. Bridey Flynn, coming home from the Rose of Killarney, caught up with him and passed him, not speaking to him but reading out of curiosity the note which lay spread out on the flat top of the newel post. She disappeared round a bend in the stairs. Mr Green placed the change from the pound note, a fifty-pence piece and two tens and a one, on the note and carefully wrapped the coins up in it. Then he laboriously climbed the rest of the stairs. At the top he put the folded newspaper on the floor outside Marty Foster's door, the loaf on top of the newspaper and the little parcel of coins on top of the loaf. He tapped on the door, but he didn't wait.

Nigel didn't at once go to the door. He thought it was probably old Green who had knocked but he couldn't be positive and he had cause to be nervous. Between the time he had put the note under old Green's door and now, the doorbell had rung several times, in fact half a dozen times. The second time it rang Nigel pushed Joyce up into the corner of the sofa and stuck the barrel of the gun, safety catch off, hard into her chest. She went grey in the face, she didn't make a sound. But Nigel hardly knew how he had borne it, listening to that bell ringing, ringing, down there. He gritted his teeth and tensed all his muscles.

It was about half an hour after that that there was a tap at the door. Nigel was still, though less concentratedly, covering Joyce with the gun. At the knock he jammed it against her neck. When he heard the sound of Mr Green's whistling kettle he went cautiously to the door. He opened it a crack with his left hand, keeping Joyce covered with the gun in his right. There was no one on the landing. Bridey was in the bathroom, he could see the shape of her through the frosted glass in the bathroom door.

The sight of the bread, and the smell of it through its flimsy wrapping, made him feel dizzy. He snatched it up with the newspaper and the package of change and kicked the door shut.

Joyce saw and smelt the bread and gave a sort of cry and came towards him with her hands out. He was still pointing the gun at her. She hardly seemed to notice it.

'Sit down,' said Nigel. 'You'll get your share.'

He didn't bother to cut the loaf, he tore it. It was soft and very light and not quite cold. He gave a hunk to Joyce and sank his teeth into his own hunk. Funny, he had often read about people eating dry bread, people in ancient times mostly or at least a good while ago, and he had wondered how they could. Now he knew. It was starvation which made it palatable. He devoured nearly half the loaf, washing it down with a cup of water with whisky in it. Now his hunger was allayed, the next best thing to bread Mr Green could have bought him was a newspaper. Before he had even finished eating, he was going through that paper page by page.

They had found the Escort in Dr Bolton's garage. Not that they put it that way – 'a shed in Epping Forest'. They'd be on to him now, he thought, via the commune, via that furniture guy, that school friend of Marty's. He turned savagely to Joyce.

'Look, all I ask is you lie low for two goddamned days. That's a thousand quid a day. Just two days and then you can talk all you want.' Inspiration came to Nigel. 'You don't even need to keep the money. If you're that crazy, you can give it back to the bank.'

Joyce didn't answer him. She hunched forward, then doubled up with pain. The new bread was having its effect on a stomach empty for five days. As bad as Marty, as bad as that little brain, thought Nigel, until he too was seized with pains like iron fingers gripping his intestines.

At least it stopped him wanting to eat up all the remaining bread. The worst of the pain passed off after about half an hour. Joyce was lying face-downwards on the mattress, apparently asleep. Nigel looked at her with hatred in which there was something of despair. He thought he would have to give her an ultimatum, she either took the money and promised to keep quiet for a day or he shot her. It was the only way. He couldn't remember, but still he was sure his fingerprints must be somewhere on that Ford Escort, and they'd match them with his prints in the commune, his parents' home, every surface of it, being wiped clean daily, he thought. John Something, the furniture guy, would link him with Marty Foster and then . . . How long had he got? Maybe they were already in Notting Hill now, matching prints. Had Marty ever been to the commune? That was another thing he couldn't remember.

If he was going to South America it wouldn't make much difference whether he shot Joyce or not. He would try to do it when the house was empty but for old Green. And he would like to do it, it would be a positive pleasure. Although he knew the view from the window by heart, could have drawn it accurately or made a plan of it, he nevertheless went to the window and looked out to check on certain aspects of the lie of the land. This house was joined to only one of its neighbours. Nigel eased the window up – the first time it had been opened since Marty's occupancy – and craned his neck out. Joyce didn't stir. He was seeking to confirm that, as he remembered from the time before all this happened and he was free to come and go and roam the streets, no curtains hung at the windows of the second-floor flat next door. This was in the adjoining house. It was as he had thought, the flat was empty and there would be no one on the other side of the kitchen wall to hear a shot. Very likely the people in the lower flats were out at work all day.

He had withdrawn his head and was closing the window when he noticed a man standing on the opposite pavement. Nigel closed the window and fastened the catch. There was something familiar about the man on the pavement, though Nigel couldn't recall where he had seen him before. The man was wearing jeans and a dark pullover and a kind of zipper jacket or anorak, and he had thickish fair-brown hair that wasn't very short but wasn't long either. He looked about thirty-five.

Nigel decided he had never seen him before, but that didn't make him feel any better. The man might have been waiting for someone, but if so it was a strange place to choose, outside a church in a turning off Chichele Road. He could be a policeman, a detective. It could be he who had kept on ringing the bell. Nigel told himself that the man's clothes looked new and his get-up somehow contrived, as if he wasn't used to wearing clothes like that and wasn't quite at ease in them. He made himself turn away and sit down and go through the paper once more.

Ten minutes later when he went back to the window, the man had gone. He heard Bridey's door close and her feet on the stairs as she went off to work.

22

Alan was almost sure he had got the wrong room. The young man with the fair hair, who just now had opened the window and leant out as if he meant to call to his watcher, must be the Green whose name was on the third bell. After the window had closed and the angry-looking face vanished, Alan had crossed the road and pressed that third bell several times, stood there for seconds with his thumb pressed against the push, but no one had come down to answer it.

He walked away and was in the corner shop buying a paper when he saw the girl called Flynn go by. He would talk to her just once more, he thought. The Rose of Killarney was due to open in ten minutes.

This was the second time since Monday that he had come to Cricklewood. He would have come on Wednesday and made it three times, only he couldn't do that to Una, couldn't keep on lying to her. Besides, he thought he had exhausted his powers of invention with Tuesday's inspiration which was that he had to see his solicitor about Alison. Una accepted that without comment. She was busying herself with preparations for their departure on Friday, writing letters, taking Ambrose's best dinner jacket to the cleaners, ordering a newspaper delivery to begin again on Saturday. But Tuesday's sortie did him no good, he was no forrarder.

Although he had spent most of the afternoon watching the house and walking the adjacent streets, he had seen no one, not even the Irish girl, come in or go out.

When he got back he had to tell Una he had been with the solicitor and what the man had said. It was easy for him to say that he would be giving up his share of his house to Alison because there was a good deal of truth in this, and he was rather surprised as well as moved when Una said this was right and generous of him, but how he must feel it, having worked for so many years to acquire it!

'You must think me very weak,' he said.

'No, why? Because you're giving up your home to your wife without a struggle?'

Of course he hadn't meant that, but how could she know? He longed to tell her who he really was. But if he told her he would lose her. He had done too many things for which no one, not even Una, could forgive him; the theft, the betrayal of Joyce, the lies, the deceitfully contrived fabric of his past.

That evening they had gone out with Caesar and Annie, but on the Wednesday they spent the whole day and the evening alone together. They found a cinema which was showing *Dr Zhivago* because Alan had never seen it, and then, appropriately, they had dinner in a Russian restaurant off the Old Brompton Road because Alan had never tasted Russian food. When they got home Ambrose phoned from Singapore where it was nine o'clock in the morning.

'He was sweet,' said Una. 'He said of course he understands and he wants me to be happy, but we must promise to come back and see him for a weekend soon and I said we would.'

Alan thought he would feel better about Joyce once he was in Devon and couldn't sneak out up to Cricklewood in the afternoons, for he knew he was going to sneak out again on Thursday. It was Una who put the idea into his head, who made it seem the only thing to do, when she said she'd buy their tickets and make reservations and then go on to the hairdresser. He could go out after she had gone and get back before she returned. He would definitely get hold of the Irish girl or of Green if Foster didn't answer his bell. It ought to be simple to find out what time Foster came home from work, and then catch him and, on some pretext, speak to him. With pretexts in mind, Alan picked up from the hall table in Montcalm Gardens a brown envelope with *The Occupier* written on it, and which contained electioneering literature for the County Council elections in May. He put it into his pocket. After all, it would hardly matter if Foster opened it in his presence and saw that it was totally inappropriate for someone who lived in Brent rather than Kensington and Chelsea, for by then Alan would have heard his voice.

It was a cool grey day, of which there are more in England than any other kind, days when the sky is overcast with unbroken, unruffled vapour, and there is no gleam of sun or spot of rain. Alan was glad of his windcheater, though there was no wind to cheat, only a sharp nip in the air that lived up to its name and seemed actually to pinch his face.

He began by pressing Foster's bell several times. Then he walked a little before trying again. It was rather a shock to see an old man come out of the house, because he had somehow got it into his head by then that, in spite of the names on the bells, only the Irish girl and the fair-haired young man inhabited the place. The old man was deaf. Alan caught him up a little way down the road and tried to ask him about Foster, but it seemed cruel to persist, a kind of torment, and he felt embarrassed too, though there was no one else about to hear his shouts.

He tried the bell marked Flynn, and because there was no answer to that one either, went back to the Broadway and had a cup of tea in a café. He supposed he must have missed seeing the girl come home because he had been back to the house and tried Green's bell in vain and was now buying his paper when he caught sight of her turning into Chichele Road, plainly on her way out, not her way home. There was a paragraph on an inside page of the *Evening Standard* to the effect that the car stolen in Capel St Paul had been found in Epping Forest. *Kidnap Car in Forest Hideaway*. But the paper contained nothing else about the robbery, its leads being *Man Shot in Casino* and *77 Dead in Iran Earthquake*. He walked along the wide pavement, which had trees growing out of it, until he came to the Rose of Killarney. When it got to five, the Flynn girl herself came out to open the doors.

Bridey had been frightened of the man in the windcheater only for a very short space of time. This was in the seconds which elapsed between her opening the front door to him and her return of the five-pound note. She was no longer afraid, but she wasn't very pleased to see him either. She felt sure he was a policeman. He said good afternoon to her which made her feel it was even earlier than it was and reminded her of the great stretch of time between now and eleven when they would close. Bridey made no answer beyond a nod and walked dispiritedly back behind the bar where she asked him in neutral tones what he would have.

Alan didn't want anything but he asked for a half of bitter just the same. Bridey accepted his offer of a drink and had a gin and tonic. An idea was forming in her mind that, although she would never dream of calling the police or going out of her way to shop anyone to the police, in this case the police had come to her which was a different matter. And she would like to have revenge on Marty Foster for insulting her and showing her up in front of the whole saloon bar. She had never really believed that story of the five-pound note being dropped by Marty as he left the Rose of Killarney. More probably the man in the windcheater was after him for theft or even some kind of violence. Bridey wasn't going to ask what he was wanted for. She listened while the policeman or whatever talked about ringing bells and not getting answers, and about old Green and someone else he seemed to think was called Green – she couldn't follow half of it – and when he had finished she said:

'Marty Foster's got flu.'

Alan said, half to himself, 'That's why he doesn't answer the door,' and to Bridey, 'I suppose he's in bed.' She made no answer. She lit a cigarette and looked at him, gently rocking the liquid in her glass up and down.

'If I come to see him tomorrow,' he said, 'would you let me in?'

'I don't want any trouble now.'

'You've only to let me into the house. I don't mean into his place, I know you can't do that.'

'Well, if I open the door and a fella pushes past me,' said Bridey with a sigh, 'and makes his way up the stairs, it's no blame to me, is it, and me standing no more than five foot two?'

Alan said, 'I'll come in the afternoon. Around four?'

Bridey didn't tell him it was her day off, so she would be home all day and he could have come at ten or noon or in the evening if he'd wanted. She only nodded, thinking that that gave her a long time in which to change her mind, and got off her stool and went round the back out of his sight. Alan was sure she would only come back when more customers came in. He drank up his beer and went to catch the 32 bus.

Una was still out when he came back to Montcalm Gardens. It was nearly six. She walked in at five past with a bottle of wine, Monbazillac which he and she both liked, for their supper. It was quite a long time, while they were eating that supper, in fact, before he realized that she must have been home in his absence. The skirt and jumper she had on were different from what she had worn to go to the station and the hairdresser. But she didn't ask him where he had been, and he volunteered no information. They went downstairs to say good-bye to Caesar, for they would be gone on the five-thirty out of Paddington before he came home on the following day.

'Send me a card,' said Caesar. 'I'll have one with Dartmoor Prison on it. I went and had a look at it once, poor devils working the fields. D'you know what it says over the doors? *Parcere Subjectis*. Spare the captives.'

That made Alan feel they were really going, that and the tickets Una had got. He wished now that he had arranged with the Irish girl to be let into the house in the morning instead of the afternoon, but it was too late to alter it now. And in a way the arrangement was the best possible he could have made, for it meant that he could make his phone call and immediately afterwards leave London. The police would trace the call to a London call box, but by then he would be on his way to Devon. That is, of course, if he made the call at all, if it didn't turn out to be a false trail and Marty Foster quite innocent.

Sitting in his room that night, he told Una that he didn't intend to divorce his wife. He told her because it was true. A dead man cannot divorce. He wanted no more lies, no more leading her into false beliefs.

'I'm still married to Stewart,' she said.

'I shall never be able to divorce her, Una.'

She didn't ask him why not. She said quaintly and very practically, as if she were talking of the relative merits of travelling, say, train or air, first class or second class, 'It's just that if we had children, I should like to be married.'

'You'd like to have children?' he said wonderingly, and then at last, in so many words, she told him about Lucy. In doing so she gave him the ultimate of herself while he, he thought, had given her nothing.

The dream was the first he had had for several nights. He was in a train with two men and each of his hands was manacled to one of theirs. They were Dick Heysham and Ambrose Engstrand. Neither of them spoke to him and he didn't know where they were taking him, but the train dissolved and they were on a bleak and desolate moorland before stone pillars which supported gates, and over the gates was the inscription: *Parcere Subjectis*. The gates opened and they led him in, and a woman came out to receive him. At first he couldn't see her face, but he sensed who she was as one does sense such things in dreams. She was Pam and Jillian and in a way she was Annie too. Until he saw her face. And when he did he saw that she was none of them. She was Joyce, and blood flowed down her body from an open wound in her head.

He struggled out of the dream to find Una gone from his side. He put out his hands, speaking her name, and woke fully to see her standing at the tallboy, opening and emptying the drawers.

It was a reflex to shout. He shouted at her without thinking.

'What are you doing? Why are you going through my things?'

The colour left her face.

'You mustn't touch those things. What are you doing?'

'I was packing for you,' she faltered.

She hadn't reached the drawer where the money was. He sighed, closing his eyes, wondering how long he could keep the money concealed from her when they were living together and had all things in common. She had let the clothes fall from her hands and stood, lost and suffering. He went up to her, held her face, lifting it to his.

'I'm sorry. I was dreaming and I didn't know what I said.'

She clung to him. 'You've never been angry with me before.'

'I'm not angry with you.'

She came back into bed with him and he held her in his arms, knowing that she expected him to make love to her. But he felt restless and rather excited, though not sexually excited, more as if the deed he was set on accomplishing that day would set him free to love Una fully and on every level. And now he saw clearly that if he could show the two men to be the same and act on it, he would undo all the wrong he had done Joyce and himself on the day of the robbery. Ahead of him, once this hurdle was surmounted, seemed to stretch a life of total peace and joy with Una, in which such apparent obstacles as namelessness, joblessness and fast decreasing capital were insignificant pin-pricks.

Nigel and Joyce finished the loaf up on Friday morning. It was another grey day, but this time made gloomy by fog. Nigel wondered if he could get old Green to do more shopping for them – not more bread, certainly. Even a deaf old cretin like him would begin to have his doubts about a sick man on his own, a man with flu, eating a whole large white loaf in a day. He heard Mr Green's kettle and then his footsteps crossing to the lavatory, but he didn't go to the door.

The first thing he had done on getting up was look out of the window for the watcher of the day before. But there was no one there. And Nigel told himself he was getting crazy, hysterical, imagining the police would act like that. The police wouldn't hang about outside, they'd come in. They would have firearms issued. They would evacuate the surrounding houses and call out to him on a loud hailer to throw down his gun and send Joyce out.

The street looked as if it could never be the backdrop to such a drama. Respectable, shabby, London-suburban, it was deserted but for a woman pushing a pram past the church. The man he had seen outside yesterday, Nigel decided, was no more likely to be the police than that woman. As for whoever kept ringing the bell, that could be the electricity meter man. The meter was probably due to be read. But, for all these reassurances, he knew he had to get out.

There was no explaining away the evidence of the newspaper. Nigel thought how helpful his parents would be to the police once they'd been located via the Boltons. They'd shop him without thinking of anything but being what they called good citizens, rack their brains to think where he might be, sift their memories for the names of any friends he had ever had.

'Just keep quiet for twelve hours,' he said to Joyce, 'then you can phone the bank's head office and tell them all you want about me and this place, and hand over the money.' He added, appalled at the thought of it, the waste, 'Jesus!'

Joyce said nothing. She was thinking, as she had been thinking for most of the night, if she could do that with honour. Nigel thought she was being defiant again. Get some food inside her and all the old obstinancy came back.

'I can kill you, you know,' he said. 'Might be simpler when all's said and done. That way I get to like keep all the bread myself.' He showed her the gun, holding it out on his left palm.

Joyce said wearily, 'If I say yes, can we get out of here today?'

The hue and cry for Marty Foster had awakened memories in the mind of a policeman whose beat included Chichele Road. One foggy morning he had found a sick young man crouched on a wall and had helped him into Dr Miskin's where, as he let go of his arm, the young man had whispered to the receptionist, 'Name of Foster, M. Foster.' All this came back to him on Friday and he passed it on to his superiors. Dr Miskin directed them to the hospital in Willesden where Marty was in a ward along with a dozen or so other men.

Marty had been feeling a lot better. Apart from being confined within four walls, he rather liked it in hospital. The nurses were very good-looking jolly girls and Marty spent a good part of every day chatting them up. He missed his cigarettes, though, and he dreadfully missed his alcohol. They had told him he mustn't touch a drop for at least six months.

That he would have a choice about what he did in the next six months Marty was growing confident. He was glad Nige hadn't come in. He didn't want to see Nigel or

Joyce or, come to that, the money ever again. He felt he was well rid of it, and he felt cleansed of it too by removing himself in this way and voluntarily forgoing his share. Marty really felt he had done that, had done it all off his own bat to put the clock back, alter the past and stay the moving finger.

So it was with sick dismay that after lunch on Friday, when they were all back in their beds for the afternoon rest, he raised his head from the pillow to see two undoubted policemen, though in plain clothes, come marching down the ward, preceded by pretty Sister at whom only five minutes before he had been making sheep's eyes. She now looked stern and aghast. Marty thought, though not in those words, how the days of wine and roses were over and the chatting up of the girls, and then they were beside his bed and drawing the screens round it.

The first thing he said to them was a lie. He gave them as his address the first one he had had in London, the squat in Kilburn Park. Then he said he had been with his mother on 4 March, hadn't seen Nigel Thaxby for two months and had never been to Childon in his life. After a while he recanted in part, gave another false address and said that he had lent his flat to Nigel Thaxby whom he believed to have perpetrated the robbery and kidnapping in league with the missing bank manager.

Outside the screens the ward was agog, humming with speculation. Marty was put into a dressing gown and taken to a side room where the interrogation began afresh. He told so many lies then and later that neither the police nor his own counsel were ever quite to believe a word he said, and for this reason his counsel dissuaded him from going into the witness box at his trial.

That Friday afternoon he finally disclosed his true address but by then it had also been given to them by the Ministry of Social Security.

The few clothes Alan possessed went into the suitcase, but he didn't put the money in there. Suppose Una were to ask him at the last moment if he had room in his case for something of hers? Besides, how could he be sure of being alone when he unpacked it? What he should have done was buy a briefcase with a zip-up compartment. He could put the money in the compartment and books and writing paper, that sort of thing, in the main body of the case. For the time being he stuffed the bundles of notes into the pockets of his trousers and his wind-cheater. It bulged and crackled rather, and when Una, off up the road to fetch Ambrose's dinner jacket from the cleaners, came up to kiss him – they always kissed on meeting and parting – he didn't dare hold her close against him as he would have liked to do.

Her going out solved the problem of how to get out himself. It was almost three. He wrote a note: *Una, Something has come up which I must see to. Meet you at Paddington at 5. Love, Paul.* This he left on the hall table with the house keys Una had given him three weeks before.

23

Joyce had given him the answer he wanted, but now he had it Nigel couldn't believe it. He couldn't trust her. He saw himself at the airport going through the place where they checked you for bombs, reaching the gate itself that led you to the aircraft – and a man stepping out in front of him, another laying a hand on his shoulder. If Joyce was merely going to surrender the money to the bank, there would be no compulsion for her to respect her promise to him. She would break it, he thought, as soon as he was out of sight.

He would kill her when the house was empty.

Nigel didn't know who lived on the ground floor, certainly people who were out all day. The red-haired girl and her 'fella' were out a lot. Bridey didn't work every day, but she always went out for some part of the day. Nigel thought it possible that Joyce's body might lie there undiscovered for weeks, but there was a good chance the police would arrive that weekend and break the door down. By then he would be far away, it hardly mattered, and it was good to think of Marty getting the blame and taking the rap, if not for the killing, then for a great deal else.

He listened for Bridey who hadn't gone to work for the

eleven o'clock opening. At three she was still moving about in her room, playing a transistor. Nigel packed his clothes into Samantha's mother's rucksack. He put on his cleanest jeans, the pair Marty had taken to the launderette, and his jacket into the pocket of which went his passport. In the kitchen, over the sink, he removed with Marty's blunt razor the half inch of fuzzy yellow down which had sprouted on his chin and upper lip. Shaved and with his hair combed, he looked quite respectable, the doctor's son, a nice responsible young man, down from his university for the Easter holiday.

Joyce too had dressed herself for going out in as many warm clothes as she could muster, two tee-shirts and a blouse and skirt and pullover. She had put the two thousand pounds along with her knitting into the bag in which Marty had bought the wool for that knitting. She said to Nigel, in a voice and a manner nearer her old voice and manner than he had heard from her for weeks, that she didn't know what a hotel would think of her, arriving without a coat and with rubber flip-flops on her feet. Nigel didn't bother to reply. He knew she wasn't going to get near any hotel. He just wished Bridey would go out.

At three-thirty she did. Nigel heard her go downstairs, and from the window he watched her walk away towards Chichele Road. What about the red-haired girl? He was wondering if he dared take the risk without knowing for sure if the red-haired girl was out of the house, when the phone began to ring. Nigel hated to hear the phone ringing. He always thought it would be the police or his father or Marty to say he was coming home, by ambulance and borne up the stairs on a stretcher by two men.

The phone rang for a long time. No one came up from downstairs to answer it. Nigel felt relieved and free and private. The last peal of the phone bell died away, and as he listened, gratified, to the silence, it was broken by the ringing of the front doorbell.

At Marble Arch Alan had bought a briefcase into which he put the money, having deposited his suitcase in a left-luggage locker at Paddington Station. In the shop window glass he looked with a certain amusement at his own reflection. He had put on his suit because it was easier to wear it than carry it, and his raincoat because it had begun to rain. With the briefcase in his hand, he looked exactly like a bank manager. For a second he felt apprehensive. It would be a fine thing to be recognized now at the eleventh hour. But he knew no one would recognize him. He looked so much younger, happier, more confident. I could be bounded in a nutshell, he quoted to himself, and think myself a king of infinite space, were it not that I have bad dreams . . .

He was a little late getting to Cricklewood, and it was ten past four when he walked up to the house and rang the bell. He rang Marty Foster's bell first because there was a chance he might answer and he didn't want to bother the Flynn girl unnecessarily. However, there was no answer. He tried again and again and then he rang the Flynn girl's bell. Somehow it hadn't crossed his mind there might be no reply to that either, that she could have forgotten her promise or simply be indifferent to her promise and go out. She hadn't exactly promised, he thought with a sinking of the heart.

Of course a taxi could get him from here to Paddington in a quarter of an hour, there was nothing to worry about from that point of view. He stepped back and down and looked up at the windows which looked back at him like so many wall eyes. Maybe the bells weren't working. He couldn't hear any sound of ringing from outside. But the Flynn bell had been working on Monday . . .

Along the street the old deaf man was coming, a string bag in his hand containing some cans and a packet of tea. Alan nodded to him and smiled, and the old man nodded and smiled back in a way that was suspicious and ingratiating at the same time. Slowly he fumbled through layers of clothing to retrieve a key from a waistcoat pocket. He put the string bag down on the step and unlocked the front door.

Knowing it was useless to speak to him but feeling he must say something to excuse his behaviour, Alan muttered vaguely about people who didn't answer bells. He edged past the old man into the passage and, leaving him on the doorstep wiping his feet, began to climb the stairs.

Immediately he heard the bell, the first time it rang, Nigel pointed the gun at Joyce and made her go into the kitchen.

She understood this was because there was someone at the door he feared might be the police, but she didn't reason that therefore he wouldn't dare shoot her. There was something in his face, an animal panic, but the animal was a tiger rather than a rabbit, which made her think he would shoot her before he did anything else. He had taken off the safety catch.

He forced her into a chair and got behind her. Joyce slumped forward, the gun pressing against the nape of her neck. With his left hand Nigel felt about all over the draining board and the top of the bookcase and the drawer under the draining board for the rope. He found it in the drawer and wound it round Joyce as best he could, tying her arms to the back of the chair. When he had got the black stocking off his own bundle of notes, he put the gun down and managed to gag her. By then the doorbell had rung again and was now ringing in Bridey's room. Nigel shut the kitchen door on Joyce and went back into the living room to listen. From downstairs he heard the sound of the front door being softly closed. No more ringing, silence.

Then footsteps sounded on the stairs. Nigel told himself they must belong to old Green. He told himself that for about two seconds because after that he knew that they weren't the footsteps of a stout seventy-five-year-old but of a man in the prime of life. They came on, on, up to the bathroom landing and then up the last flight to the top. There they flagged and seemed to hesitate. Nigel went very softly to the door and put his ear against it, listening to the silence outside and wondering why the man didn't knock at his door.

Alan hadn't knocked because he didn't know which was the right door. There were three to choose from. He knocked first at the door to the room on the side of the house, the detached side. Then he tried the door that faced it because the remaining door must be the one to the front room which was evidently occupied by Green. The old man was coming slowly and heavily up the stairs. Alan stepped aside and attempted some sort of dumb show to indicate whom he wanted, but how do you indicate Foster in sign language? The old man shook his head and unlocked the door at which Alan had last knocked and went inside, closing the door behind him. Alan tried the door to the front room. He waited, sure that he could hear on the other side of it the sound of someone breathing very close by.

Nigel put the gun in its holster underneath his jacket, and then he unlocked the mortice with the big iron key. There was only one man out there. Very probably he knew the room was occupied, so it might be less dangerous to let him in than keep him out. Nigel opened the door.

The man outside was in a suit and raincoat and carrying a briefcase, which Nigel somehow hadn't expected. The face was vaguely familiar, but he immediately dismissed the idea that this might be the man he had seen watching the house. This was – he was convinced of it even before the brown envelope was produced – some canvasser or market researcher.

Alan said: 'I'm looking for a Mr Foster.'

'He's not here.'

'You mean he lives here? In there?'

A nod answered him. 'I understood he was ill . . .' Alan was almost deterred by the look on the handsome young face. It expressed amazement initially, then a growing suspiciousness. But he went on firmly. 'I understand he was at home with the flu.'

At that the face cleared and the shoulders shrugged. Alan felt sure Marty Foster was somewhere in there. He hadn't come so far to give up now, on the threshold of Foster's home. The door was moving slowly, it was about to be shut in his face. Daring, amazed at himself, he set his foot in it like an importunate salesman, said, 'I'd like to come in a minute, if you don't mind,' and entered the room, pushing the other aside, though he was taller and younger than he.

The door closed after him. They looked at each other, Alan Groombridge and Nigel Thaxby, without recognition. Nigel thought, he's not a canvasser, he's not from the hospital – who is he? Alan looked round the room at the tumbled mattress, the scattering of breadcrumbs on the seat of a chair, a plastic bag with knitting needles sticking out of it. Foster might be in whatever room was on the other side of that door.

'I have to see him,' he said. 'It's very important.'

'He's in hospital.'

From behind the door there came a thumping sound, then a whole series of such sounds as of the legs of a chair or table bumping the floor. Alan looked at the door, said coldly:

'Which hospital?'

'I don't know, I can't tell you any more.' Joyce was working herself free of the rope which tied her to the chair, as Nigel had guessed she would. He put himself between Alan and the kitchen door, his hand feeling the holster round the gun. 'You'd better go now. I can't help you.'

It was twenty minutes to five. He was meeting Una at five, he was leaving London – hadn't he done enough? 'I'm going,' Alan said. 'Who's behind that door, then? Your girl friend?'

'That's right.'

Alan shrugged. He began to walk back to the door by which he had entered as Nigel, striding to open it, called back over his shoulder:

'OK, doll, one moment and you can come out.'

Alan froze. He had been pursuing one voice and had found the other – 'Let's see what's in the tills, doll . . .' He turned round slowly, the blood pounding in his head. Nigel was opening the door to the landing. Alan was a yard away from that door, perhaps only a hundred yards away from a phone box. He stopped thinking, speculating, wondering. He took half a dozen paces across that room and flung open the other door.

Joyce had got her arms free and was taking the gag off her mouth. He would hardly have known her, she was so thin and haggard and hollow-eyed. But she knew him. She had recognized the voice of the man she had supposed dead from the moment he first spoke to Nigel. She threw the black stocking on to the floor and came up to him, not speaking, her face all silent supplication.

'Where's the other one, Joyce?' said Alan.

She whispered, 'He went away,' and laid her hands on his arms, her head on his chest.

'Let's go,' he said, and put his arm round her, holding her close, and walked her out the way he had come. Nigel was waiting for them at the door with the gun in his hand.

'Leave go of her,' he said. 'Let go of her and get out, she's nothing to do with you.'

It was the way he said it and, more than that, the words he used that made Alan laugh. Nothing to do with him, Joyce whom his conscience had brought into a bond with him closer than he had ever had with Pam, closer than he had with Una . . . He gave a little dry laugh, looking incredulously at Nigel. Then he took a step forward, pulling Joyce even more tightly against him, sheltering her in the crook of his right arm, and as he heard the roar and her cry out, he flung up his left arm to shield her face and threw her to the ground.

The second bullet and the third struck him high up in the body with no more pain than from two blows of a fist.

24

Nigel grabbed the bundle of notes he had given to Joyce and stuffed it into the carrier with the other one. He had a last swift look round the room and saw the briefcase lying on the floor a little way from Joyce's right foot. He unzipped it a few inches, saw the wads of notes and put the briefcase into his rucksack. Then he opened the door and stepped out.

The noise of the shooting had been tremendous, so loud as to fetch forth Mr Green. Bridey, coming in when she thought the coast would be clear, heard it as she mounted the second flight. Neither of them made any attempt to hinder Nigel who slammed the door behind him and swung down the stairs. In his progress through the vertical tunnel of the house, he passed the red-haired girl who cried out to him:

'What's going on? What's happening?'

He didn't answer her. He ran down the last dozen steps, along the passage and out into the street where, though only five, it was already growing dark from massed rain clouds.

The red-haired girl went upstairs. Bridey and Mr Green looked at her without speaking.

'My God,' said the red-haired girl, 'what was all that

carry-on like shots? That fella what's-his-name, that fair one, he's just gone down like a bat out of hell.'

'Don't ask me,' said Bridey. 'Better ask that pig. He's his pal.'

Mr Green shuffled over to Marty's door. He banged on it with his fist, and then the red-haired girl banged too.

'I don't know what to do. I'd ask my fella only he's not back from work. I reckon I'd better give the fuzz a phone. Can't let it just go on, can we?'

'That's a very serious step to take, a very serious step,' Bridey was saying, when Mr Green looked down at the floor. From under the door, across the wood-grained linoleum, between his slippers, came a thin trickle of blood.

'My godfathers,' said Mr Green. 'Oh, my godfathers.'

The red-haired girl put her hand over her mouth and bolted down to the phone. Bridey shook her head and went off downstairs again. She had decided that discretion, or a busman's holiday in the Rose of Killarney, was the better part of social conscience.

In the room, on the other side of the door, Alan lay holding Joyce in his arms. He felt rather cold and tired and he wasn't finding breathing easy because Joyce's cheek was pressed against his mouth and nose. Nothing would have induced him to make any movement to disturb Joyce who felt so comfortable and relaxed in her sleep. He was quite relaxed himself and very happy, though not sure exactly where he was. It seemed to him that they must be on a beach because he could taste saltiness on his lips and feel wetness with his hands. Yet the place, wherever it was, also had the feeling of being high up and lofty, a vaulted hall. His memory was very clear. He repeated to himself, Alas, said Queen Guenever, now are we mischieved both. Madam, said Sir Lancelot, is there here any armour within your chamber that I might cover my poor body withal? An if there be any give it me, and I shall soon stint their malice, by the grace of God. Truly, said the queen, I have none armour, shield, sword nor spear . . .

He couldn't remember the rest. There was a lot of it but perhaps it wasn't very appropriate, anyway. Something about the queen wanting to be taken and killed in his stead, and Lancelot saying, God defend me from such shame.

Alan smiled at the indignation in that, which he quite understood, and as he smiled his mouth seemed to fill with the saltiness and to overflow, and the pressure on his face and chest became so great that he knew he must try to shift Joyce. She was too heavy for him to move. He was too tired to lift his arms or move his head, too tired to think or remember or breathe. He whispered, 'Let's go to sleep now, Una . . .'

They started breaking the door down, but he didn't hear them. A sergeant and a constable had come over from Willesden Green, supposing at first they had been called out to a domestic disturbance because the red-haired girl had been inarticulate on the phone. The sight of the blood flowing in three narrow separate streams now, altered that. One of the panels in the door had given way when up the stairs appeared two very-top-brass-looking policemen in plain clothes and an officer in uniform. These last knew nothing of the events in the room and on the landing. They were there because Scotland Yard had discovered Marty Foster's address.

The door went down at the next heave. The couple from the ground floor had come up, and the red-haired girl was there, and when they saw what was inside, the women screamed. The sergeant from Willesden Green told them to go away and he jammed the door shut.

The two on the floor lay embraced in their own blood. Joyce's face and hair were covered in blood from a wound in her head, and at first it seemed as if all the blood had come from her and none from the man. The detective superintendent fell on his knees beside them. He was a perceptive person whose job had not blunted his sensitivity, and he looked in wonder at the contentment in the man's face, the mouth that almost smiled. The next time I do fight I'll make death love me, for I'll contend even with his pestilent scythe . . . He felt for a pulse in the girl's wrist. Gently he lifted the man's arm and saw the wound in the upper chest and the wound under the heart, and saw too that of the streams of blood which had pumped out to meet them, two had ceased.

But the pulse under his fingers was strong. Eyelids trembled, a muscle flickered.

'Thank God,' he said, 'for one of them.'

*

There was no blood on Nigel. His heart was beating roughly and his whole body was shaking, but that was only because he had killed someone. He was glad he had killed Joyce, and reflected that he should have done so before. Bridey wouldn't take any notice, old Green didn't count, and the red-haired girl would do no more than ask silly questions of her neighbours. Now he must put all that behind him and get to the airport. By cab? He was quite safe, he thought, but still he didn't want to expose himself to too much scrutiny in Cricklewood Broadway.

On the other hand, it was to his advantage that this was rush-hour and there were lots of people about. Nigel felt very nearly invisible among so many. He began to walk south, keeping as far as he could to the streets which ran parallel to Shoot-up Hill rather than to the main road itself. But there was even less chance of getting a cab there. Once in Kilburn, he emerged into the High Road. All the street lights were on now, it was half-past five, and a thin drizzle had begun. Nigel felt in the carrier for the bunch of Ford Escort keys. If that Marty, that little brain, could rip off a car, so could he. He began to hunt along the side streets.

Nearly half an hour had gone by before he found a Ford Escort that one of his keys would fit. It was a coppery-bronze-coloured car, parked half-way down Brondesbury Villas. Now he had only to get himself on the Harrow Road or the Uxbridge Road for the airport signs to start coming up. The rain was falling steadily, clearing the people off the streets. At first he followed a bus route which he knew quite well, down Kilburn High Road and off to the right past Kilburn Park Station. It was getting on for six-thirty but it might have been midnight for all the people there were about. The traffic was light too. Nigel thought he would get the first flight available. It wouldn't matter where it was going – Amsterdam, Paris, Rome, from any of those places he could get another to South America. His only worry was the gun. They weren't going to let him on any aircraft with a gun, not with all these hi-jackings. Did they have left-luggage places at Heathrow? If they did he'd put it in one, and then, some time, when it was safe and he was rich and had all the guns he wanted, he'd come back and get it and keep it as a souvenir, a memento of his first crime. But he wouldn't go after Marty Foster with it, he wasn't worth the hassle. Besides, thanks to his skiving off, hadn't he, Nigel, pulled off the whole coup on his own and got all the loot for himself?

When he got to the end of Cambridge Road, he wasn't sure whether to go more or less straight on down Walterton Road or to turn left into Shirland Road. Straight on, he thought. So he turned right for the little bit preparatory to taking Walterton Road and pulled up sharply behind a car stopped suddenly on the amber light. Nigel had been sure the driver was going to go on over and not stop, and the front bumper of the Ford Escort was no more than an inch or two from the rear bumper of the other car. Suppose he rolled back when the lights went green?

There was nothing behind him. Nigel shoved the gear into reverse and stamped on the accelerator. The car shot forward with a surprisingly loud crash into the rear of the one in front, and Nigel gave a roar of rage. Once again he had got into the wrong gear by mistake.

In the other car, a lightweight Citroen Diane, were four people, all male and all staring at him out of the rear window and all mouthing things and shaking fists. The driver got out. He was a large heavily built black man of about Nigel's own age. This time Nigel got the gear successfully into reverse and backed fast. The man caught up with him and banged on the window, but Nigel started forward, nearly running him down, and screamed off in bottom gear across lights that had just turned red again, and straight off along Shirland Road into the hinterland of nowhere.

The Diane was following him. Nigel cursed and turned right and then left into a street of houses waiting to be demolished, their windows boarded up and their doors enclosed by sheets of corrugated iron. Why had he come down here? He must get back fast and try to find Kilburn Lane. The Diane was no longer behind him. He turned left again, and it was waiting for him, slung broadside across the narrow empty street where no one lived and only one lamp was lighted. The driver and the other three stood, making a kind of cordon across the street. Nigel stopped.

The driver came over to him, a white boy with him. Nigel wound down his window, there was nothing else for it.

'Look, man, you've caved my trunk in. How about that?'

'Yeah, how about that?' said the other. 'What's with you, anyway, getting the hell out? You've dropped him right in it, you have. That's his old man's vehicle.'

Nigel didn't say a word. He took the gun out of its holster and levelled it at them.

'Jesus,' said the white man.

Nigel burst the car door open and came out at them, stalking them as they retreated. The other two were standing behind the Diane. One of them shouted something and began to run. Nigel panicked. He thought of the money and of help coming and his car trapped by that other car, and he raised the gun and squeezed the trigger. The shot missed the running man and struck the side of the Diane. He fired again, this time into one of the Diane's rear tyres, but now the trigger wouldn't move any more. The jacket had gone back, leaving the barrel exposed, and the gun looked empty, must be empty. He stood, his arms spread, a choking feeling in his throat, and then he dropped the gun in the road and wheeled round back to the car.

The four men had all frozen at the sound of the shot and the splintering metal, even the running man. Now he came slowly back, looking at the useless weapon on the wet tarmac, while the others seemed to drop forward, their arms pendulous, like apes. Nigel pulled open the door of the Ford, but they were on him before he could get into it. The driver's white companion was the first to touch him. He swung his fist and got Nigel under the jaw. Nigel reeled back and slid down the dewed metal of the car, and two of them caught him by the arms.

They dragged him across the pavement and through a cavity in a broken wall where there had once been a gate. There they threw him against the brickwork front of the house and punched his face, and Nigel screamed, 'Please!' and 'Help me!' and lurched sideways across broken glass and corrugated iron. One of them had a heavy piece of metal in his fist, and Nigel felt it hammering his head as he sagged on to the wet grass and the others kicked his ribs. How long they went on he didn't know. Perhaps only until he stopped shouting and cursing them, twisting over and over and trying to protect his bruised body in his hugging arms. Perhaps only until he lost consciousness.

When he regained it he was lying up against the wall, and

he was one pain from head to foot. But there was another and more dreadful all-conquering pain that made his head and his neck red-hot. He moved a bruised cut hand to his neck and felt there, embedded in his flesh, a long stiletto of glass. He gave a whimper of horror.

By some gargantuan effort, he staggered to his feet. He had been lying on a mass of splintered glass. His fingers scrabbled at his neck and pulled out the long bloody sliver. It was the sight of the blood all over him, seeping down his jacket and through into his shirt, that felled him again. He felt the blood pumping from the wound where the glass had been, and he tried to cry out, but the sound came in a thin strangled pipe.

Nigel had forgotten the car and the money and escape and South America. He had forgotten the gun. Everything had gone from his mind except the desire to live. He must find the street and lights and help and someone to stop the red stream leaking life out of his neck.

Round and round in feeble circles he crawled, ploughing the earth with his hands. He found himself saying, mumbling, as Marty had said to him, 'You wouldn't let me die, you wouldn't let me die,' and then, as Joyce had said, 'Please, please . . .'

His progress, half on his hands and knees, half on his belly, brought him on to concrete. The street. He was on the pavement, he was going to make it. So he crawled on, looking for lights, on, on along the hard wet stone as the rain came down.

The stone ended in grass. He tried to avoid the grass, which shouldn't be in the street, which was wrong, a delusion or a mirage of touch. His head blundered into a wooden fence, at the foot of which soft cold things clustered. He lay there. The rain poured on him in cataracts, washing him clean.

Much later, in the small hours, a policeman on the beat found the abandoned car and the gun. Everything was still in the car as Nigel had left it, his rucksack and his carrier, his passport and the stolen money – six thousand, seven hundred and seventy-two pounds. The search for Nigel himself didn't last long, but he was dead before they reached him. He was lying in a back garden, and during that long wet night snails had crept along the strands of his wet golden hair.

25

When the train had gone and Paul hadn't come, Una went back to Montcalm Gardens. Whatever it was that had 'come up' had detained him. They could go by a later train, though they would have no seat reservations. Una decided not to indulge in wild speculations. Ambrose said these were among the most destructive of fantasies, and that one should repeat to oneself when inclined to indulge in them, that most of the things one has worried about have never happened. Besides (he said) it was always fruitless to imagine things outside our own experience. One thing to visualize a car crash or some kind of assault if we have ourselves experienced such a thing, or if one of our friends has, quite another if such imaginings are drawn, as they usually are, from fictional accounts. Una had never known anyone who had been killed in a car crash or mugged or fallen under a train. Her experience of accidents was that her child had been burnt to death.

She made a cup of tea and washed the teacup and tidied the kitchen again. The phone rang, but it was a wrong number. At seven she read the note again. Paul's handwriting wasn't very clear and that five could be an eight. Suppose he had thought the train went at eight-thirty, not five-thirty? He had been so preoccupied and strange these past few days that he might have thought that. Una combed her hair and put on her raincoat, and this time she took a taxi, not a bus, to Paddington. Paul wasn't there.

Although there was a later train, she took her case out of the left-luggage locker where she had left it at five-thirty, because she felt that to do so was to yield to, not tempt, Providence. The curious ways of Providence were such that if you bought an umbrella you got a heatwave for a month, and if you lugged a load of luggage from a station to your home, you were bound to have to take it back again. This thought cheered her, and by the time the taxi was taking her back through the stair-rod rain in the Bayswater Road she had convinced herself that Paul would be waiting for her in Montcalm Gardens with a long story of some tiresome happening that had held him up.

Her first real fear came when she got in and he wasn't there. She went down into the basement and found the bottles he had left outside Caesar's door with a note to Caesar to have them. Caesar hadn't come home, he had gone straight to Annie's. Una poured herself some brandy. It nearly knocked her over because she hadn't eaten since one. They had planned to eat dinner on the train. She tried to obey Ambrose's injunction not to think of imaginary disasters, and told herself that no one gets mugged in the afternoon or falls under trains unless they want to or has a car crash if they don't have a car.

But then her own experience of life showed her what could have happened. Neo-Empiricism, applied by her, showed her what men sometimes did and where men sometimes went after they had left notes and gone out alone. She pushed the thought away. He would phone, and then he would come. She took a piece of cheese out of the fridge and cut a slice off the new loaf she had bought for Ambrose. She tried to eat and she succeeded, but it was like chewing sawdust and then chewing the cud.

At ten she was in his empty room, looking at the tallboy in which there had been papers or letters or photographs he hadn't wanted her to see. It frightened her now that he had left his keys, though what more natural than that he should leave them?

While she had been out that afternoon he must have had a phone call. She knew who would have phoned, perhaps the only person to whom he had given this number. Hadn't she phoned once before to make an appointment? Since that appointment, that visit, Paul had been a changed man. Una went upstairs and sat in the immaculate exquisite drawing room. She picked up the phone to see if it was out of order, but the dialling tone grated at her. Stewart's letter was up on the mantelpiece. She had left it there for Ambrose to read. Now she read it again herself, the bit about hoping she would be happy with her new man.

For a while she sat there, listening to the rain that beat

steadily against the windows and thinking that it was a long time since it had rained like that, a month surely. A month ago she hadn't even known Paul. She got out the phone directory. His name on the page made her shiver. Browning, Paul R. 15 Exmoor Gardens, NW2. She looked hard at his name on the page and touched the phone and paced the length of the room and back again. Then, quickly, she dialled the number. It rang, three times, four times. Just as she thought no one was going to answer, the ringing stopped and a woman's voice said:

'Hallo. Alison Browning.'

'Is Mr Paul Browning there, please?'

'Who is that speaking?'

She had been told, hadn't she? It wouldn't be a revelation. And yet . . . 'I'm a friend of his. Is he there?'

'My husband is in bed, asleep. Do you know what time it is?'

Una put the receiver back. For a while she lay on the floor. Then she went upstairs and got into bed in the room where she hadn't slept for three weeks. Three weeks was no time, nothing, a nice period for an adventure or an interlude. It is anxiety, not sorrow, which banishes sleep, and at last Una slept.

She had never had a newspaper delivered since Ambrose went. Not since Christmas had she heard the sound the thick wad of newsprint made, flopping through the letter box on to the mat. Any sound from the front door would last night have made hope spring, but no longer.

Una went downstairs and picked up the paper. The headlines said, *Joyce Alive* and *Bank Girl Recovers in Hospital*, and there was a big photograph of a girl on a stretcher. But it was the other photograph, of a man in a garden with a woman and an older man, which caught Una's eye because the man looked a little like Paul. But any man, she thought, with wistful eyes and a gentle mouth, would remind her of Paul. It was bound to happen. She went into the drawing room and read the paper to pass the time.

. . . *The nature of Alan Groombridge's wounds have made police believe he died protecting Joyce. She regained consciousness soon after being admitted to hospital. Her head injury is only superficial, says the doctor attending her, and her loss of memory is due to shock. She has no memory of the shooting or of events of the past month in which she and Mr Groombridge were held prisoners in a second-floor rented room in north London . . .*

Una read the rest of it, turned the page, waiting for Ambrose to come.

THE LAKE OF DARKNESS

For Don, again

Nero is an angler in the lake of darkness. . . .

King Lear

1

Scorpio is metaphysics, putrefaction and death, regeneration, passion, lust and violence, insight and profundity; inheritance, loss, occultism, astrology, borrowing and lending, others' possessions. Scorpians are magicians, astrologers, alchemists, surgeons, bondsmen and undertakers. The gem for Scorpio is the snakestone, the plant the cactus; eagles and wolves and scorpions are its creatures, its body part is the genitals, its weapon the Obligatory Pain, and its card in the Tarot is Death.

Finn shared his birthday, November 16, with the Emperor Tiberius. He had been told by a soothsayer, who was a friend of his mother's that she had met in the mental hospital, that he would live to a great age and die by violence.

On the morning of his birthday, his twenty-sixth, one of Kaiafas's children came round with the money in a parcel. He knocked on Finn's door. Someone downstairs must have let him into the house. They didn't know it was his birthday, Finn realized that, it was just a coincidence. He undid the parcel and checked that it contained what it should contain, two thousand five hundred pounds in ten-pound notes. Now it had arrived he had better get on with things, he might as well start now.

It was too early to go up to Lena. She liked to sleep late in the mornings. Not that she would mind his waking her on his birthday, she would like it, she would expect it almost, but he wouldn't just the same. He tucked the money safely away and went downstairs.

Finn was very tall and thin and pale. He was near to being an albino but saved by the watery grey colour which stained the pupils of his eyes. It was remarkable that eyes of such an insipid shade should be so piercing and so bright, like polished silver. His hair, when he was a child, had been white-blond but had now faded to the neutral greyish beige of cardboard. He had a face that was quite ordinary and unmemorable but this was not true of his eyes. Under a longish PVC jacket he wore blue denims, a check Viyella shirt, a black velvet waistcoat, and round his neck one of those long scarves which Greek women wear, black and triangular and sewn along one side with small gold coins. He carried a tool box of laminated blue metal. Finn had a smallish head on a thin, delicate-looking neck and his wrists and ankles and feet were small, but his pale hands were almost preternaturally large with an extravagant span.

His van, a small, pale grey, plain van, was parked in front of the house in Lord Arthur Road. You might call it Kentish Town or Tufnell Park or Lower Holloway. There were some curious houses, mini-Gothic with step gables, fat Victorian red brick, great grey barns with too many bays for grace or comfort, and small, narrow, flat-fronted places, very old, and covered in a skin of pale green peeling plaster. Finn wasn't interested in architecture, he could have lived just as easily in a cave or a hut as in his room. He unlocked the van and got in and drove up past Tufnell Park Station, up Dartmouth Park Hill towards the southernmost part of Hampstead Heath.

It was nine-fifteen. He drove under the bridge at Gospel Oak Station, up into Savernake Road which skirted Parliament Hill Fields, and on the corner of Modena Road he parked the van. From there he could keep the house that Kaiafas owned under observation. He sat at the wheel, watching the three-storey house of plum-coloured brick.

The Frazers were the first to go out. They left together, arm in arm. Next came Mrs Ionides, five minutes afterwards. Finn didn't care about them, they didn't count. He wanted to be sure of Anne Blake who quite often took a day off and had told Finn she 'worked at home'.

However, she emerged from the front door at exactly nine-thirty and set off the way the others had for the station. As a trusted handyman, Finn was in possession of a key to the house in Modena Road and with this he let himself in. His entering as the agent or servant of the landlord was perfectly legitimate, though some of the things he intended to do there were not.

Kaiafas's sister had the ground floor flat and the Frazers the next one up. The Frazers had accepted two thousand pounds from Kaiafas and had agreed to move out at the end of the month. Mrs Ionides would do anything Kaiafas told her and now he had told her she must go back to nurse their aged father in Nicosia. With vacant possession, the house would sell for sixty, maybe seventy thousand pounds. Kaiafas had asked estate agents about that and he had watched prices rising and soaring as houses just like his had been sold. The one next door, identical to his, had fetched sixty in August. The house agent smiled and shook his head and said that had been vacant possession, though, hadn't it? Kaiafas had told Finn all about it, that was how he knew.

He let himself into Mrs Ionides's hall and thence into her living room where one of the window sash cords had broken a day or so ago. He fitted a new sash cord and then he went upstairs to see what could be done about the coping over the bay window that Mrs Frazer said let water in. This occupied him until lunchtime.

He had brought his own lunch with him in an earthenware pot. Not for him the black tea and hamburgers and chips and eggs and processed peas of the workmen's café. In the pot was fruit roughly cut up with bran and yoghurt. Finn ate a piece of dark brown bread and drank the contents of a half-pint can of pineapple juice. Pineapple was not only his favourite fruit but his favourite of all flavours.

After lunch he sat cross-legged on the carpet and began his daily session of meditation. Presently he felt himself levitate until he rose almost up to the ceiling from where he could look through the top of the Frazers' window at the bright green escarpment of Hampstead Heath rising against a cold, sallow, faintly ruffled, sky.

Meditation always refreshed him. He could feel a wonderful sensation of energy streaming down his arms and crackling like electricity out of his fingertips. His aura was probably very strong and bright but he couldn't see auras like Lena and Mrs Gogarty could, so it was no good looking in the glass. He took his tool box and climbed the last remaining flight of stairs. Unlike the Frazers and Mrs Ionides, Anne Blake had given no permission for Kaiafas or his agent or servant to enter her flat that day, but Kaiafas made a point of retaining a key. Finn unlocked Anne Blake's front door, went in and closed it after him. The hall walls were papered in a William Morris design of kingcups and water hawthorn on a blue ground and the carpet was hyacinth blue Wilton. Anne Blake had been living there since before Kaiafas bought the house, ten or twelve years now, and she wouldn't leave even for a bigger bribe than Kaiafas was giving the Frazers. She had told Kaiafas she wouldn't leave for twenty thousand and he couldn't make her and the law was on her side. He could have the flat, she said, over her dead body.

Finn smiled faintly in the dimness of the hall.

He opened the cupboard between the bathroom door and the door of the living room and took out a pair of lightweight aluminium steps. They were so light that a child could have lifted them above his head on one hand. Finn took them into the bathroom.

The bathroom was small, no more than eight feet by six, and over one end of the bath, in the ceiling, was a trapdoor into the loft. But for this trapdoor, Finn would have had to choose some other method. He set up the steps and then he went into the bedroom. Here was the same blue carpet, the walls painted silver-grey. There was no central heating in the house in Modena Road and each tenant had his or her own collection of gas and electric heating appliances. Anne Blake had an electric wall heater in her kitchen, a gas fire in her living room, a portable electric fire in her bedroom and no heating at all in her bathroom. Finn plugged in the portable electric fire, switched it on, and when he saw the two parallel bar elements begin to glow, switched it off again and unplugged it.

He climbed the aluminium steps and pushed up the trapdoor, a torch in his left hand. The loft housed a water tank and a good deal of the sort of discarded equipment which has become unusable but which cannot quite be called rubbish. Finn had been up there before, once when a pipe had frozen and once to get out on to the roof itself, and he had a fair idea of what he would find. He was observant and he had a good memory. He trod carefully on the joists, shining his torch, searching among the corded bundles of the *National Geographic* magazine, the ranks of glass jars, aged Remington typewriter, rolls of carpet cut-offs, flat-iron and trivet, chipped willow pattern dinner plates, until he found what he was looking for. An electric ring.

There was no plug on its lead. It was dirty and the coiled element had some kind of black grease or oil on it. Finn brought it down the steps and set about attaching a 13-amp plug to it. When this was plugged in, however, nothing happened. Never mind. Mending something like that was child's play to him.

The time had come to check up on her. He didn't want her coming home because she was starting a cold or her boss had decided to take the afternoon off. She had been unwise enough to tell him where she worked that time he had been in to mend the pipe, just as she had also told him she always took a bath the minute she got in from work. Finn never forgot information of that sort. He looked up the number in the phone book and dialled it. When he had asked for her and been put through to some extension and asked to hold and at last had heard her voice, he replaced the receiver.

An old, long-disused gas pipe ran up the kitchen from behind the fridge into the loft. This Finn intended to utilize. He cut a section out of it about six inches from the floor. Then he returned to the loft, this time with a 100-watt light bulb on the end of a long lead. He soon found the other end of the gas pipe and proceeded to cut off its sealed end. While he worked he reflected on the cowardice of human beings, their fears, their reserve.

Finn had a sense of humour of a kind, though it was far from that perception of irony and incongruities which usually goes by the name, and he had been amused that Kaiafas, in all their dealings, had never directly told him what he wanted doing. It was left to Finn to understand.

'Feen,' Kaiafas had said, 'I am at my wits' end. I say to her, Madam, I give you five thousand pounds, five thousand, madam, to quit my house. Please, I say, I say please on my knees. What does she say? That it is a pity I ever come away from Cyprus.'

'Well,' said Finn. 'Well, well.' It was a frequent rejoinder with him.

A look of ineffable slyness and greed came into Kaiafas's face. Finn had already guessed what he was after. He had done jobs for Kaiafas and others before, the kind of thing a professional hit-man does in the course of his work, though nothing of this magnitude.

'So I think to myself,' said Kaiafas, 'I make no more offer to you, madam, I give you no five thousand pounds. I give it to my friend Feen instead.'

That had been all. Finn wasn't, in any case, the sort of person to invite confidences. He had merely nodded and said well, well, and Kaiafas had fetched him another pineapple juice, handing over the key to the top flat. And now the first instalment of his fee had come . . .

He had inserted a length of electric flex into the pipe from the loft end, its frayed tips protruding ever so little from the cut-out section behind the fridge but apparent only to a very acute observer. The other end of the flex reached as far as the trapdoor and with a further two yards to spare. Finn was more or less satisfied. Once he might have done the deed without all this paraphernalia of wires and gas pipe and trapdoor, without clumsy manual effort. He looked back wistfully to his early teens, his puberty, now a dozen years past, when his very presence in a house had been enough to begin a wild poltergeist activity. It was with a yearning nostalgia that he remembered it, as another man might recall a juvenile love – bricks flying through windows, pictures falling from the walls, a great stone out of the garden which no one could lift suddenly appearing in the middle of Queenie's living room carpet. The power had gone with the loss of his innocence, or perhaps with the hashish which a boy at school had got him on to. Finn never smoked now, not even tobacco, and he drank no alcohol. It wasn't worth it if you meant to become an adept, a man of power, a master.

He checked that in the electric point behind the fridge there was a spare socket. A certain amount of the black fluffy dirt which always seems to coat the inside of lofts had fallen into the bath. Finn cleaned it with the rags he carried with him until its rose-pink surface looked just as it had done when he arrived. He replaced the aluminium steps in the cupboard and put the electric ring into a plastic carrier bag. It had been a long day's work, for every minute of which Kaiafas was paying him handsomely.

The Frazers would return at any moment. That was of no importance provided Finn was out of Anne Blake's flat. He closed her front door behind him. By now it was dark but Finn put no lights on. One of the skills in which he was training himself was that of seeing more adequately in the dark.

The air was strangely clear for so mild an evening, the yellow and white lights sparkling, dimming a pale and lustreless moon. As Finn started the van he saw Mrs Ionides, dark, squat, dressed as always in black, cross the street and open the gate of the house he had just left. He drove down Dartmouth Park Hill, taking his place patiently in the traffic queueing at the lights by the tube.

The house where Finn lived was a merchant's mansion that had fallen on evil days almost from the first, and the first was a long time ago now. He climbed up through the house, up a wider staircase than the one in Modena Road. Music came from behind doors, and voices and cooking smells and the smell of cannabis smoked in a little white clay pipe. He passed the door of his own room and went on up. At the top he knocked once at the first door and passed, without waiting, into the room.

It was a room, not a flat, though a large one and it had been partitioned off into small sections, living room, bedroom, kitchen. Finn had put up two of the partitions himself. You entered by way of the kitchen which was a miracle of shelving and the stowing of things on top of other things, and of squeezing a quart into a pint pot. In the living room, nine feet by eight, where a thousand little knick-knacks of great worth and beauty to their owner were displayed upon surfaces and walls, where a gas fire burned, where a small green bird sat silent in a cage, was Lena, consulting the pendulum.

'Well,' said Finn, going up to her and taking her free hand. They never kissed. She smiled at him, a sweet vague smile as if she couldn't quite see him or was seeing something beyond him. He sat down beside her.

Finn could do nothing with the pendulum but Lena had great ability with it, just as she had with the divining rod. This was very likely one of the consequences of what those people at the hospital called her schizophrenia. The pendulum was a glass bead suspended on a piece of cotton and when Lena put it above her right hand it revolved clockwise and when she put it above her left hand it revolved widdershins. She had long since asked it to give her signs for yes and no and she had noted these particular oscillations.

The pendulum had just answered yes to some questions which hadn't been revealed to Finn, and Lena sighed.

She was old to be his mother, a thin, transparent creature like a dead leaf, or a shell that has been worn away by the action of the sea. Finn thought sometimes that he could see the light through her. Her eyes were like his but milder, and her hair which had been as fair as his, had reverted to its original whiteness. She dressed herself from the many second-hand clothes shops in which the district abounded, and derived as intense a pleasure from buying in them as a Hampstead woman might in South Molton Street. Mostly she was happy, though there were moments of terror. She believed herself to be a reincarnation of Madame Blavatsky, which the hospital had seized upon as a casebook delusion. Finn thought it was probably true.

'Did you buy anything today?' he said.

She hesitated. Her dawning smile was mischievous. It was as if she had a secret she could no longer keep to herself and she exclaimed with shining eyes, 'It's your birthday!'

Finn nodded.

'Did you think I'd forgotten? I *couldn't*.' She was suddenly shy and she clasped her hands over the pendulum, looking down at them. 'There's something for you in that bag.'

'Well, well,' said Finn.

In the bag was a leather coat, black, long, double-breasted, shabby, scuffed, and lined with rotting silk. Finn put it on.

'Well,' he said. 'Well!' It was like a storm trooper's coat. He fastened the belt. 'Must be the best thing you ever got,' he said.

She was ecstatic with pleasure. 'I'll mend the lining for you!'

'You've had a busy day,' he said. The coat was too big for the room. With every movement he made he was in danger of knocking over little glass vases, Toby jugs, china dogs, pebbles, shells and bunches of dried flowers in chutney jars. He took the coat off carefully, with reverence almost, to please Lena. The green bird began to sing, shrill and sweet, pretending it was a canary. 'What did you do this afternoon?'

'Mrs Urban came.'

'Well!'

'She came in her new car, a green one. The kind of green that has silver all mixed up in it.'

Finn nodded. He knew what she meant.

'She brought me those chocolates and she stayed for tea. She made the tea. Last time she came was before you put up the wall and made my bedroom.'

'Did she like it?'

'Oh, yes!' Her eyes were full of love, shining with it. 'She *loved* it. She said it was so compact.'

'Well, well,' said Finn, and then he said, 'Ask the pendulum something for me. Ask it if I'm going to have a good year.'

Lena held up the string. She addressed the pendulum in a whisper, like someone talking to a child in a dark room. The glass bead began to swing, then to revolve clockwise at high speed.

'Look!' Lena cried. 'Look at that! Look what a wonderful year you'll have. Your twenty-seventh, three times three times three. The pendulum never lies.'

2

On the broad gravelled frontage of the Urbans' house, were drawn up the Urbans' three cars, the black Rover, the metallic green Vauxhall and the white Triumph. In the drawing room sat the Urbans, drinking sherry, oloroso for Margaret, amontillado for Walter and Tio Pepe for Martin. There was something of the Three Bears about them, though Baby Bear, in the shape of twenty-eight-year-old Martin, was no longer a resident of Copley Avenue, Alexandra Park, and Goldilocks had yet to appear.

Invariably on Thursday evenings Martin was there for dinner. He went home with his father from the office just round the corner. They had the sherry, two glasses each, for they were creatures of habit, and had dinner and watched television while Mrs Urban did her patchwork. Since she had taken it up the year before as menopausal therapy, she seemed to be perpetually accompanied by clusters of small floral hexagons. Patchwork was beginning to take over the house in Copley Avenue, chiefly in the form of cushion covers and bedspreads. She stitched away calmly, or with suppressed energy, and her son found himself watching her while his father discoursed with animation on a favourite subject of his, Capital Transfer Tax.

Martin had a piece of news to impart. Though in possession of it for some days, he had postponed telling it and his feelings about it were now mixed. Natural elation was mingled with unease and caution. He even felt very slightly sick as one does before an examination or an important interview.

Margaret Urban held out her glass for a refill. She was a big, statuesque, heavy-browed woman who resembled Leighton's painting of Clytemnestra. When she had sipped her sherry, she snipped off a piece of thread and held up for the inspection of her husband and son a long strip of joined-together red and purple hexagons. This had the effect of temporarily silencing Walter Urban, and Martin, murmuring that that was a new colour combination, he hadn't seen anything like that before, prepared his opening words. He rehearsed them under his breath as his mother, with the artist's sigh of dissatisfaction, rolled up the patchwork, jumped rather heavily to her feet and made for the door, bent on attending to her casserole.

'Mother,' said Martin, 'wait here a minute. I've got something to tell you both.'

Now that the time had come, he brought it out baldly, perhaps clumsily. They looked at him in silence, a calm, slightly stunned silence into which gratification gradually crept. Mrs Urban took her hand from the door and came slowly back, her eyebrows rising and disappearing into her thick, blue-rinsed fringe.

Martin laughed awkwardly. 'I can't quite believe it myself yet.'

'I thought you were going to tell us you were getting married,' said his mother.

'Married? Me? Whatever made you think that?'

'Oh, I don't know, it's the sort of thing one does think of. We didn't even know you did the football pools, did we, Walter? Exactly how much did you say you'd won?'

'A hundred and four thousand, seven hundred and fifty-four pounds, forty-six pence.'

'A hundred and four thousand pounds! I mean, you can't have been doing the pools very long, you weren't doing them when you lived here.'

'I've been doing them for five weeks,' said Martin.

'And you've won a hundred and four thousand pounds! Well, a hundred and five really. Don't you think that's absolutely amazing, Walter?'

A slow smile was spreading itself across Walter Urban's handsome, though somewhat labrador-like, face. He loved money; not so much the possession of it as the juggling with it, the consideration of how to make it multiply, how (with subtle and refined legality) to keep it from the coffers of the Inland Revenue, and he loved the pure beauty of it as an abstraction on paper rather than as notes in a wallet. The smile grew to beaming proportions.

'I think this calls for some sort of congratulation, Martin. Yes, many congratulations. What a dark horse you are! Even these days a hundred thousand is a large sum of money, a very *respectable* sum of money. We've still got that bottle of Piper-Heidsieck from our anniversary, Margaret. Shall we open it? Wins of this kind are free of tax, of course, but we shall have to think carefully about investing it so that you don't pay all your interest away to the Inland Revenue. Still, if a couple of accountants can't work it out, who can?'

'Go and get the champagne, Walter.'

'Whatever you do, don't think of paying off the mortgage on your flat. Remember that the tax relief on the interest on your mortgage repayments is a concession of HM Government, of which a single man in your position would be mad not to take advantage.'

'He won't keep that flat on, he'll buy himself a house.'

'He could become an underwriting member of Lloyd's.'

'There's no reason why he shouldn't buy a country cottage *and* keep the flat.'

'He could buy a house and have the maximum twenty-five thousand mortgage . . .'

'Do go and get the champagne, Walter. What *are* you going to do with it, dear? Have you made any plans?'

Martin had. They weren't the kind of plans he considered it would be politic to divulge at the moment, so he said nothing about them. The champagne was brought in. Eventually they sat down to the casserole, the inevitably overdone potatoes and a Black Forest cake. Martin offered his parents ten thousand pounds which they graciously, but immediately, refused.

'We wouldn't dream of taking your money,' said his father. 'Believe me, if you're lucky enough these days to get your handson a tax-free capital sum you hang on to it like grim death.'

'You don't fancy a world cruise or anything?'

'Oh, no, thank you, dear, there really isn't anything we want. I suppose you'd really rather we didn't tell anyone about it, wouldn't you?'

'I wasn't thinking of telling anyone but you.' Martin observed his mother's look of immense gratification, and this, as much as anything, prevented him from adding that there was one other person he felt obliged to tell. Instead he said, 'I'd rather keep it a secret.'

'Of course you would,' said Walter. 'Mum's the word. You don't want begging letters. The great thing will be to live as if nothing whatsoever out of the way had happened.'

Martin made no reply to this. His parents continued to treat him as if he had earned the hundred and four thousand pounds by the expending of tremendous effort or by natural genius, instead of the merest chance. He wished they had felt able to accept a present of some of it. It would somewhat have eased his conscience and helped him over the guilt he always felt on Thursday nights when he had to say good-bye to his mother and go home. She was still, after nine months, inclined to ask plaintively if by now rhetorically, why he had seen fit to move out of Copley Avenue and go far away to a flat on Highgate Hill.

Into this flat, 7 Cromwell Court, Cholmeley Lane, he now let himself with the feeling of deep satisfaction and contentment he always had when he entered it. There was a pleasant smell, a mixture, light and clean, of new textiles, furniture polish and herbal bath essence. He kept all the interior doors open – the rooms were impeccably neat – so that when you walked through the front door the impression was rather as of entering the centrefold of a colour supplement or *House and Garden*. Or so he secretly hoped, for he kept such thoughts about his flat to himself, and when showing it to a newcomer merely led him through the living room to exhibit from the picture window the view of London lying in a great well below. If the visitor chose to comment on the caramel Wilton, the coffee table of glass set in a brass and steel frame, the Swedish crystal or the framed prints of paintings from the Yugoslav naïve school, he would look modestly pleased but that was all. He felt too deeply about his home publicly to enthuse, and along with his gratitude to goodness knows whom, a certain fear about tempting Providence. There were times when he dreamed of its all being snatched away from him and of his being permanently back in Copley Avenue.

He switched on the two table lamps which had white shades and bases made from blue and white ginger jars. The armchairs were of rattan with padded seats and the sofa, or French bed as the furniture shop man had called it, was really only a divan with two bolsters at the back and two at the sides. Now he had won that large sum of money he would be able to replace these with a proper suite, perhaps one in golden-brown hide.

From the coffee table, between the ashtray with the Greek key design round its rim and the crystal egg etched with the goat for Capricorn – his birth sign – he picked up and studied the list he had made on the previous evening. On it were four names: Suma Bhavnani, Miss Watson, Mr Deepdene, Mr Cochrane's sister-in-law. Martin inserted a question mark after this last, he wasn't sure of her eligibility for his purpose, and besides he must find out what her name was. Some doubt also attached to Mr Deepdene. But about Suma Bhavnani he was quite sure. He would call on the Bhavnanis tomorrow, he would call on them after he had seen Tim Sage.

Martin went over to the window. The temples and towers of London hung black and glittering from the sky like the backdrop to some stage extravaganza. He pulled the cord that drew together the long dark green velvet curtains and shut it out. Tim Sage. For days, ever since, in fact, he had heard that he was to benefit from a fifth share in the Littlewoods' Pool first dividend, he had avoided thinking about Tim Sage, but he was going to have to think about him now because tomorrow Tim was coming into the office to talk about his income tax. It would be the first time he had seen

Tim for a fortnight and before three tomorrow he had to decide what to do.

What to do? He had suppressed that remark to his mother about being obliged to tell one other person, but that was because he had been unwilling to hurt her, not because he was in doubt as to the right way to act. As soon as he allowed himself to think of Tim he knew without a doubt that Tim must be told. Indeed, Tim ought to have been told already. Martin's gaze travelled speculatively over towards the gleaming dark green telephone. He ought to phone Tim now and tell him.

Martin's father always said that one should never make a phone call after ten-thirty at night or before nine in the morning – except, that is, in cases of emergency. This was hardly an emergency and it was ten to eleven. Besides, Martin felt strange about phoning Tim at home. He had never done so. From Tim's own veiled accounts, his home was a strange one, not to mention his domestic arrangements, and who, anyway, would answer the phone? Tim didn't live in a place like this where everything was open and above-board as well as immaculate in a more literal sense.

He turned his back on the phone and switched off the ginger-jar lamps. On second thoughts he helped himself to a small whisky from the glass, brass and steel cabinet. It would be silly to phone Tim now when he was going to see him tomorrow. As he drank his whisky he reflected that, of course, it was because he was going to see Tim tomorrow that he hadn't troubled to phone him before.

Martin was a well set-up, healthy man of medium height with rather too broad shoulders. In an overcoat he looked burly and older than his age. He had a big square forehead and a strong square chin but otherwise his features were shapely and refined, his nose being short and straight and his mouth the kind that is sometimes called chiselled. His dark brown curly hair was already beginning to recede in an M-shape from that broad and prominent forehead. He had greeny-blue eyes, a curious shade, very bright and clear, and even white teeth for the attainment of whose regularity Walter Urban had paid large sums to orthodontists in Martin's early teens.

Following in his father's footsteps, he always wore a suit to work. To wash the dishes he put on an apron. Martin wouldn't have worn an ordinary apron, that would have been ridiculous, but the joke kind made of oilcloth was trendy and amusing and perfectly suitable for men. His mother had given him this one which was orange and brown and represented a gigantic facsimile of a Lea and Perrins Worcester Sauce label. He changed the sheets on his bed, a regular Friday morning task, but he did no other housework because Mr Cochrane was due at half-past eight.

That his cleaner was a mister and not a missus was due to the Sex Discrimination Act. When Martin put his advertisement in the *North London Post* he had been obliged by law not to state that he required female help, and when Mr Cochrane turned up, similarly obliged not to reject him. He was lucky to get anyone at all, as his mother pointed out.

Mr Cochrane usually arrived just after the postman and before the newspaper delivery, but this morning the newsboy must have been early – it was unthinkable for Mr Cochrane to be late – and Martin had already glanced at the front pages of the *Post* and the *Daily Telegraph* before his help rang the doorbell. Always at this moment he wished that he was about to admit a large motherly charwoman, an old-fashioned biddable creature who, if she didn't exactly call him sir, yet might treat him with respect and show some consideration for his wishes. He had read about such people in books. However, it was pointless to indulge in day-dreaming with Mr Cochrane outside the door and likely to appear outside the door every Friday for the next ten years. He liked his jobs, of which he had several, in Cromwell Court.

Martin let him in.

Mr Cochrane was about five feet two and spare and wiry with a little scrap of dust-coloured hair fringing a bald pate. His face was exactly like a skull with lampshade material stretched tightly over it and ornamented with a pair of bifocals. He carried the cleaning gear that he didn't trust his employers to provide, about with him in a small valise.

'Morning, Martin.'

Martin said good morning. He no longer called Mr Cochrane anything. He had begun by calling him Mr Cochrane and had been called Martin in return, whereupon he asked his christian name which Mr Cochrane, flying into one of his sudden rages, had refused to give. It was about this time that a neighbour and fellow-employer told him of his own experience. He had suggested that Mr Cochrane call him by his surname and style, to which he had received the reply that it was a disgrace in this day and age to expect an elderly man, a man nearly old enough to be his grandfather, to call him Mr, it was sheer fascism, as if he, Mr Cochrane, hadn't done enough kowtowing all his miserable downtrodden life. He had been, apparently, a manservant to some more or less aristocratic person in Belgravia. A butler, said one of Martin's neighbours who also employed him, but this Martin didn't believe, for to him butlers were less real a bygone race than dodos.

As a cleaner, he was wonderful. That was why Martin, and presumably the others, kept him on in spite of the familiarity of address and the rages. He cleaned and polished and scrubbed and did ironing all at high speed. Martin watched him open his suitcase and take out of it the khaki canvas coat – like an ironmonger's – he wore for work, the silver-cleaning cloths and the aerosol can of spray polish.

'How's your sister-in-law?' said Martin.

Mr Cochrane, wearing red rubber gloves, had been taking the top of the stove apart. 'She'll never be better till she gets another place, Martin. The blacks were bad enough and now they've got the pneumatic drills.' He was a ferocious racist. 'She'll never be better stuck up there, Martin, so you may as well save yourself the trouble of enquiring. Three hours' pneumatic drills in the mornings she gets and three hours in the afternoons. The men themselves can't keep it up more than three hours and that tells you something. But it's no use moaning, is it, Martin? I say that to her, I say to her, what's the good of moaning at me? I can't do nothing, I'm only a servant.'

'What's her name?'

'Whose name?' said Mr Cochrane, wheeling round from the sink in the sudden galvanic way he had. 'You're always wanting to know folks' names. My sister-in-law's name?

What d'you want to know that for? It's Mrs Cochrane of course, naturally it is, what else would it be?'

Martin forbore to ask the address. He thought that, from Mr Cochrane's persistent descriptions of the North Kensington block of flats and its geographical location, he could discover it for himself. If he still wanted to. Ten minutes in his cleaner's company only made him feel there must be many far more deserving candidates for his bounty than the Cochrane family – Suma Bhavnani, Miss Watson, Mr Deepdene. He pocketed the list lest Mr Cochrane should find it and pore over it paranoidly.

As usual he left for work at ten past nine, taking the route by way of the Archway and Hornsey Lane. Sometimes, for the sake of variety, he drove up to Highgate Village and down Southwood Lane across the Archway Road into Wood Lane. And once or twice, on beautiful summer mornings, he had walked to work as he had done on the day he met Tim in the wood.

The offices of Urban, Wedmore, Mackenzie and Company, Chartered Accountants, were in Park Road, in the block between Etheldene Avenue and Cranley Gardens. Walter Urban was the expert on matters relevant to the Inland Revenue, Clive Wedmore the investment specialist, while Gordon Tytherton had all the complexities of the Value Added Tax at his fingers' ends. Martin didn't specialize, he called himself the general dog's-body and his room was the smallest.

He knew he would keep at this job for the rest of his life, yet his heart wasn't in it. Although he had tried, he had never been able to summon up that enthusiasm for manipulating cash in the abstract which his father had, or even to understand the fascination which the stock market exerted over Clive Wedmore. Perhaps he should have chosen some other profession, though the leanings and longings he had had while still at school had been hopelessly impractical – novelist, explorer, film cameraman. They were not to be seriously considered. Accountancy had chosen him from the first, not he it. Sometimes he thought he had passively let himself be chosen because he couldn't bear to disappoint his father.

And the safety of it, the security, the respectability, satisfied him. He wouldn't have cared for a job or a life sty such as Tim's. He was proud of the years of study which lay behind him, of the knowledge acquired, and always determined not to let a lack of enthusiasm lead to omissions or oversights. And he liked the room he had here which looked out across the tree tops to Alexandra Park, the park and the trees which he had known as a child.

Martin had no clients to see that morning and no phone calls to make or receive. He spent nearly three hours unravelling the zany and haphazard accounts of a builder who had been in business for fifteen years without paying a penny of income tax. Walter looked in to beam on him. The news of the pools win was making him behave towards his son much the way he had done when Martin got his A-levels and then his degree. After he had gone, Martin asked Caroline, who was their receptionist and whom Gordon and he shared as secretary, to bring in Mr Sage's file.

He opened it without really looking at the statements and notices of coding and Tim's own accounts which lay inside. In just over two hours' time Tim would be sitting there opposite him. And he hadn't made up his mind what to do. That firm decision of last night had been – well, not reversed, but certainly weakened by the sight of the *North London Post*. He had to decide, and within the next couple of hours.

Martin usually had lunch in one of the local pubs or, once a week, at a Greek place in Muswell Hill with Gordon Tytherton. Today, however, he drove alone up to the Woodman. It seemed the right and appropriate place in which to be for the solving of this particular problem.

It was far too cold, of course, and far too late in the year to take his sandwiches and lager out into the Woodman's garden. There, in summer, one was made very aware, in spite of the thunderous proximity of the trunk road roaring northwards, of the two woods that nestled behind these divergent streets. To the north was Highgate Wood, to the east Queen's Wood where, walking under the pale green beech leaves, he and Tim had encountered each other on a May morning. Now, in November, those groves appeared merely as throngs of innumerable grey boughs, dense, chill and uninviting.

But Tim . . . Was he going to tell Tim or was he not? Didn't he have a duty to tell him, a moral obligation? For without Tim he certainly wouldn't have won the hundred and four thousand pounds, he wouldn't have done the pools at all.

3

Martin had first known Tim Sage at the London School of Economics. They had been friendly acquaintances, no more, and Tim had left after a year. Martin hadn't seen him again until that morning in Queen's Wood, eight years later.

It was the kind of morning, misty and blue and gold and promising heat to come, when the northern reaches of London look as if Turner has painted them. It was the kind of morning when one leaves the car at home. Martin had walked over Jackson's Lane and into Shepherd's Hill, entering the wood by the path from Priory Gardens. The wood was full of squirrels scampering, its green silence pierced occasionally by the cry of a jay. Underfoot were generations of brown beech leaves and above him the new ones, freshly unfolded, like pieces of crumpled green silk. It had been a strange experience, even rather dramatic, walking along the path and seeing Tim appear in the distance, over the brow of the hill, the idea that it might be Tim gradually deepening to certainty. When they were fifty yards apart Tim had run up to him, stopping sharply like a reined-in horse.

'It has to be Dr Livingstone!'

Why not? Journalist meets explorer in a wood . . .

It was odd the amount of emotion there seemed to be generated in that moment and the intensity of pleasure each felt. They might have been brothers, long separated. Was it because the meeting took place on a summer's morning and under the greenwood tree? Was it the unlikelihood of the wood as a meeting place? Martin had never quite been able to understand why this chance encounter had brought him a sensation of instant happiness and hope and why there had come with it a prevision of lifelon friendship. It was almost as if what he and Tim had experienced for each other, spontaneously and simultaneously, had been love.

But with the utterance of that word to himself Martin had felt both excited and very frightened. Before parting from him, Tim had briefly put an arm round his shoulder, lightly clapping and then gripping his shoulder, the sort of thing a man may do to another man in comradely fashion but which no man had ever done to him before. It left him feeling confused and shaken and two days later, when Tim phoned, it took him a few seconds to find his normal voice.

Tim had only wanted to know if he could consult him as an accountant. He was worried about the tax he had to pay on his freelance earnings. Martin agreed at once, he couldn't help himself, though he had mental reservations.

It was a maxim of Walter Urban's that one man cannot tell if another is attractive. He can only judge in respect of the opposite sex. Martin thought about this and it troubled him. In his case now it wasn't true, and what kind of a man did that make him?

Tim was very handsome, beautiful even, except that that wasn't a word one could use about a man. He had an actor's beauty, dashing, rather flamboyant. One could imagine him as a duellist. His hair was black, short by current standards (though not so short as Martin's), and his eyes a vivid sea-blue. There was something Slavonic about his high cheekbones and strong jaw and lips that were full like a woman's. He was tall and very thin and his long thin hands were stained leather-coloured down the forefingers from nicotine. He had been smoking in the wood and he lit a Gauloise the moment he entered Martin's office.

Tim's affairs were in considerably less of a muddle than Martin was accustomed to with new clients. It impressed him that, as he studied the columns of figures, Tim was able to repeat them perfectly accurately out of his head. He had a photographic memory. Martin promised to arrange things so as to save him money and Tim had been very gratified.

Were they going to see each other again, though? Were they going to meet socially? Apparently, they were. Martin could no longer remember whether it was he who had phoned Tim or the other way about. But the upshot had been a pub lunch together, then a drink together one Friday evening, encounters at which Martin had been uneasy and nervous, though extraordinarily happy as well, with a curious tremulous euphoria.

After that Tim had become a fairly frequent visitor at the flat in Cromwell Court, but what Martin had dreaded during their first few meetings had never happened. Tim had never touched him again beyond shaking his hand, never tried to take him in his arms as had sometimes seemed so likely, so imminent, just before their partings. Yet Tim must be homosexual, for what other explanation could there be for his obvious fondness for him, Martin? What else could explain why he continued to find Tim so attractive? For he did find him attractive. He had wrenched this confession out of himself. Normal men probably did find certain homosexuals attractive if they were honest with themselves. Martin was sure he had read that somewhere, in a book about the psychology of sex probably. The fact was that he liked watching Tim, listening to the sound of his deep yet light voice, as one might like watching and listening to a woman.

It came to him at last that what he really wanted was to *fight* Tim, to engage with him, that is, in some kind of wrestling match. Of course it was quite absurd. He had never done any wrestling and he was sure Tim hadn't. But he thought a lot about it, more, he knew, than was good for him, and such a wrestling figured sometimes in his dreams. It was part of these fantasies that in real life he should actually provoke Tim to a fight, and that might not be so difficult for, in spite of his affection for Tim, he knew he wasn't really a nice person. Long before the wrestling fantasy began, he had seen in Tim signs of ruthlessness, egot ism and cupidity.

Tim lived in Stroud Green. To this address Martin sent business letters but he had never phoned Tim o private number and he had never been there. This for want of being asked. It was the way Tim had loo the tone he had used when asking which had set M determinedly against ever visiting those rooms half a house or whatever it was. Tim had said t see his 'ménage', smiling and raising his some eyebrows, and at once Martin had understood. Tim was living with a man. Martin had never actually been in company with two men living together in a sexual relationship but he could more or less imagine it and the fearful embarrassment he would feel in such a situation.

He had returned a polite refusal – he always had an excuse ready – and after a time Tim seemed to understand, for there were no more invitations. But had he really understood? Martin hoped Tim hadn't thought he wouldn't come because he disliked the idea of slumming down in Stroud Green.

Tim seemed impressed by the flat in Cromwell Court. At any rate, he listened and admired when Martin showed him some new item he had bought and he enjoyed sitting on Martin's balcony on summer evenings, drinking beer and admiring the view. Martin, like his father, often mixed business with relaxation, and it was on one of these evenings when Tim had expressed his envy of those who own their homes, that he suggested he too should buy a flat. He should do so as much for the tax relief on a mortgage as for security.

'With your income and the increasing income you're getting from these short stories, I'd say you can't afford not to.'

'My income, as you call it,' said Tim, lighting his twentieth cigarette of the evening, 'is the lowest rate the NUJ allows the *Post* to pay me. *You* know what my income is, my dear, and I haven't got a penny capital.' Martin almost shivered when Tim called him 'my dear'. 'The only way I'd ever get the money to put down on a house is if I won the pools.'

'You'll have to do them first,' said Martin.

The blue eyes that could sometimes flame were lazy [illegible]d casual. 'Oh, I do them. I've been doing them for ten [illegible]s.'

[illegible]at had surprised Martin. He had supposed doing foot[illegible]ools to be an exclusively working class habit. He was [illegible]ore surprised to find himself agreeing to do them [illegible]to have a go, what had he to lose?

[illegible]n't know how to start.'

[illegible]est old Livingstone,' said Tim, who sometimes [illegible]m in this way, 'leave it to me. I'll work out a forecast for you. I'll send you a coupon and a copy and all you've got to do is copy the same one every week and send it off.'

Of course he had had no intention of copying it out and sending it off. But it had come and he had done so. Why? Perhaps it seemed unkind and ungrateful to Tim not to. Martin supposed he had been to a great deal of trouble to work out that curious pattern on the chequered coupon, a pattern which he found himself religiously copying out each successive week.

Five times he had filled in and sent off that coupon, and the fifth time he had won a hundred and four thousand pounds. He had won it on the permutation Tim had made for him. Tim, therefore, was something more than indirectly responsible for his having won it. Shouldn't he then have gone straight to the phone as soon as the news came to him, to tell Tim?

Martin drove back to Park Road by way of Wood Lane. The wood was a crouching grey mass on either side of the road, crusted underfoot with brown leaves. If he had taken the car that morning in May or if he had walked along Wood Vale instead of Shepherd's Hill or if he had been five minutes earlier or five minutes later, he would never have met Tim and therefore never have won that huge sum of money. In an hour's time he would once more be confronting Tim. Tim was coming at three.

The purpose of his visit was to bring his tax return for the previous financial year and the fees statements from the various magazines which had used his stories. It wouldn't have crossed Martin's mind to keep the news of his win from Tim if Tim hadn't been a journalist. Once tell Tim and the story of his acquisition of wealth would be all over the front page of next week's *North London Post*. Suppose he asked Tim not to use it? It was possible Tim might agree not to, but Martin didn't think it likely. Or, rather, he thought Tim would give a sort of half-hearted undertaking and then drop a hint to another reporter. And this story would be even better when he began on his philanthropy . . .

Martin thought deeply about any major action he took, and about a good many minor ones too. He meant to conduct his life on a set of good solid principles. To perform every action as if it might form the basis of a social law, th was his doctrine, though he couldn't of course always live up to it. Plainly, he ought to tell Tim. He owed Tim thanks, and no consideration that publicity would make life uncomfortable for him for a few weeks should be allowed to stop him. Suppose he received a few begging letters and phone calls? He could weather that. *He must tell Tim*. And perhaps also – a new idea so alarmed him that he was obliged to stop scrutinizing Mrs Barbara Baer's investments and lay the file down – *offer* him something. It might be incumbent on him to offer Tim some of the money.

Tim received the lowest possible salary the National Union of Journalists permitted his employers to pay him. He couldn't buy a house because he had no capital. Ten thousand pounds would furnish a deposit for Tim to put down on a house, and ten thousand, Martin thought, was the sum he ought to give him, a kind of ten per cent commission. He found the idea not at all pleasing. Tim wasn't a deserving case like Miss Watson or Mrs Cochrane. He was young and strong, he didn't *have* to stay working on that local rag. At the back of Martin's mind was the thought that if Tim wanted to get capital he shouldn't smoke so much. He had an idea too that Tim was a fritterer. It would be awful to give Tim ten thousand pounds and then find he hadn't used it to get a home for himself but had simply frittered it away.

Martin continued to present the two sides of this question to himself until three-fifteen. Tim was late. His inner discussion had led to nothing much, though the notion of telling Tim had come to seem rash almost to the point of immorality. At twenty past three, Caroline put her pale red Afro round the door.

'Mr Sage is here, Martin.'

He got up and came round the desk, thinking that if Tim asked, if he so much as mentioned the football pools, he would tell him. But otherwise, perhaps not.

Tim was never even remotely well-dressed. Today he was wearing a pair of black cord jeans, a dirty roll-neck sweater that had presumably once been white, and a faded denim jacket with one of its buttons missing. Such clothes suited his piratical looks. He lit a Gauloise the moment he came into the room, before he spoke.

'Sorry I'm late. A court case that rather dragged on.'

'A story in it?' said Martin, using what he hoped was the right terminology.

Tim shrugged. His shoulders were very thin, and his hands and his narrow, flat teenager's loins. He looked hard like an athlete until he coughed his smoker's cough. The only soft fleshy thing about him was his full red mouth. He sat down on the arm of the chair and said, 'Humanity treads ever on a thin crust over terrific abysses.'

Martin nodded. He was struck by what Tim had said. That was exactly how he had felt that morning while recalling all the chances there had been against the meeting in the wood happening at all. 'Is that a quotation?'

'Arnold Bennett.'

'Humanity treads ever on a thin crust over terrific abysses . . .' Of course there weren't inevitably abysses, sometimes only shallow ditches, Martin thought. Novelists were very prone to exaggeration. 'Let's have a look at all this bumf then, shall we?' he said.

'I've had a demand for nearly five hundred pounds tax. That can't be right, can it?'

Martin got out Tim's file. He had a look at the demand. Tim wanted to know if he could get an allowance for the use of his car and if a library subscription he had taken out was tax-free. Martin said no to the car and yes to the subscription and asked Tim some questions and said he would lodge an appeal with the inspector against the five hundred demand. There wasn't really anything more to say, as far as business went. Tim was on his second cigarette.

'And how's life been treating you, love?' said Tim.

'All right,' said Martin carefully. It was coming now. He felt nervous, he couldn't imagine saying it, couldn't bear to think of Tim's initial disbelief, his dawning wonder, his gleeful congratulations. He said in a tone that sounded in his own head artificially bright, 'I had that carpet laid in the flat, the one I told you I thought I'd have.'

'Fantastic.'

Martin felt himself redden. But Tim's expression was quite serious, even interested and kind. 'Oh, well,' he said, 'I don't lead a very exciting life, you know.'

'Who does?' said Tim. He sat silent for a moment. It

seemed to Martin that his silence was *expectant*. Then he stubbed out his cigarette and got up. Martin found that he had been holding his breath and he let it out in what sounded like a sigh. Tim looked at him. 'Well, I mustn't keep you. I'm having a party tomorrow week, Saturday the twenty-fifth. Any chance you might be free?'

This caught Martin unprepared. 'A party?'

'Yes, *you* know,' said Tim, 'a social gathering or entertainment, a group of people gathered together in a private house for merry-making, eating and drinking et cetera. A feast. A celebration. In this case we shall be celebrating my thirtieth birthday, thirty misspent years, my Livingstone. Do come.'

'All right. I mean, of course I will, I'd like to.'

'The place is unsavoury but the food won't be. About seven?'

Martin felt a lightness and a relief after Tim had gone. He hadn't asked. He hadn't so much as mentioned football or gambling, let alone the pools, and he had hardly mentioned money. Probably he had forgotten ever having introduced Martin to the pools. How absurd I've been, thought Martin, telling myself he would be bound to ask and I would be bound to reward him. As if I could give money to Tim, as if I could ever offer it. All the time Tim had been there he had felt as if he were walking on that fragile crust over that chasm and yet he hadn't really, the ice had been inches thick and perfectly safe to skate on.

Caroline came in with a request from Clive Wedmore for the Save as You Earn literature he had lent Martin the day before.

'Mr Sage is very attractive, isn't he?' said Caroline. 'He reminds me of Nureyev, only younger.'

He wouldn't be much good to you, my dear, were the words that sprang immediately into Martin's head. The vulgarity of this thought was enough to make him blush for the second time that afternoon. 'Be a good girl and take that ashtray away, would you?'

'It smells like being in France.'

She bore the ashtray away, sniffing it appreciatively as if it had been a rose. Martin wrestled with the builder's tax for another hour or so and then he set off down Priory Road to the tobacconist and newsagent's kept by the Bhavnanis.

He felt rather excited. He tried to put himself in Mrs Bhavnani's shoes, imagining how she was going to feel in five minutes' time when she understood that someone cared, that someone was going to give her son life and health and a future. Possibly she would cry. Martin indulged in a full-blown fantasy of what would happen when he made his offer, only breaking off when he remembered that one should do good by stealth and so that the right hand knoweth not what the left hand doeth.

It was an old-fashioned little shop. When he opened the door a bell rang and from the back regions appeared Mrs Bhavnani in a green sari with a bright blue knitted cardigan over it. Her face looked dark and wizened and full of shadows in contrast to these gay colours, and when Martin said he wanted to speak to her privately it grew grim. She turned the sign on the shop door to *Closed*. Martin stammered a little when he explained to her why he had come. She listened in silence.

'You are a doctor to operate on Suma?' she said.

'No, no, certainly not. It's just that – well, my mother told me about him and what I'm saying is that if it's a fact you can get this operation on his heart done in Sydney – well, I could help pay for things.'

'It will cost a lot.'

'Yes, I know that. I mean, *I* could pay. I *will* pay. I'd like you to let me pay for you and him to fly to Sydney and for your accommodation there and for the operation, that's what I mean.'

She looked at him, then lowered her eyes and stood passively before him. He knew she didn't understand. Was her husband in? No, not at present. Martin asked the name of their doctor.

'Dr Ghopal,' she said, 'at Crouch End.' The dark mournful eyes were lifted once more and Mrs Bhavnani said, as if he were some importunate intruder, as if that munificence had never been offered, 'You must go now, the shop is closed, I am sorry.'

Martin couldn't help laughing to himself, and at himself, once he was out in the street. So much for the philanthropist's reward. Of course it would have been far more sensibl and businesslike to have got Dr Ghopal's name in the fir place and to have written to him rather than make tl romantic direct approach. He would write to him tonight. He would also, he thought as he began to drive home, make the preliminary manoeuvres in his project for using half the money. Suma Bhavnani was merely a sideline. The really serious business was his scheme for giving away fifty thousand pounds.

He could concentrate on that, now that Tim Sage was off his conscience.

4

Dear Miss Watson,

I don't know if you will remember me. We met last Christmas at the house of my aunt, Mrs Bennett. I have since then been told that you have a housing problem and that when your employer goes to live abroad next year, you expect to be without a home. The purpose of this letter is to ask if I can help you. I would be prepared to advance you any reasonable sum for the purchase of a small house or flat, preferably not in London or the Home Counties. You could, if you would rather, regard this sum as a long-term loan, the property eventually to revert to me by will. I should then be able to look on this money in the light of an investment. However, please believe that my interest is solely in helping you solve this problem and I hope that you will allow me to be of assistance.

Your sincerely,

Martin W. Urban.

Dear Mr Deepdene,

You will not have heard of me, but I am a friend of the Tremletts who, I believe, are friends of yours. Norman Tremlett has explained to me that the local authority which is your landlord intends to pull down the block of flats in which you are at present living and to re-house you in a flat which will be of inadequate size to accommodate your furniture, books, etc. The purpose of this letter is to ask if I can be of any help to you. I would be prepared to advance you any reasonable sum for the purchase of a small house or flat preferably not in London or the Home Counties.

If you would care to get in touch with me as soon as possible we might meet and discuss this, whether you feel you can accept the money as a gift or would prefer to think of it as a lifetime loan, whether you feel able to consider living outside London, and so on.

Yours sincerely,
Martin W. Urban.

Dear Mrs Cochrane,

You may have heard of me through your brother-in-law. He has told me that you are suffering considerable hardship owing to your housing conditions and are anxious to move. The purpose of this letter . . .

Martin had found these letters very difficult to write. He abandoned temporarily the one to Mrs Cochrane because he still hadn't found out her address. Dr Ghopal must have had his letter by now, though he hadn't yet replied to it. It was pleasant to think of the incredulous delight of those two elderly people when the post came on Monday morning. They would understand without resentment, wouldn't they, what he meant by asking them to choose homes away from London? If he was to benefit four or five people he couldn't rise to London property prices. He posted the letters on his way to have his usual Saturday lunchtime drink with Norman Tremlett in the Flask.

Dr Ghopal phoned him at the office on Monday morning. He would be seeing Mrs Bhavnani that day and then he hoped to be in touch with the great heart surgeon in Australia. The accented voice that always sounds Welsh to English ears cracked a little as Dr Ghopal said how moved he had been by Mr Urban's more than generous offer. Martin couldn't help feeling gratified. His mother had said Suma was reputedly good at his school work. Suppose, as a result of his, Martin's, timely intervention, the boy should grow up himself to be a famous surgeon or a musician of genius or a second Tagore?

Gordon Tytherton came in in the middle of this daydream to say that he and his wife had a spare dress circle seat for 'Evita' on Saturday night and would Martin like it and to come with them? Martin accepted with alacrity.

He passed the rest of the day on the crest of a wave and it was some time before it occurred to him that perhaps he ought to have asked for Dr Ghopal's discretion in the matter of the source of the money. Still, you could hardly imagine a doctor, a general practitioner, telling the press a thing like that. He thought very little more about it until Thursday when, as he came in from lunch, Caroline told him Mr Sage had phoned and would call back.

Had Tim found out, maybe from the Bhavnanis? Not that Martin had said anything about the source of his wealth to Dr Ghopal, but Tim was no fool. Tim would put two and two together. If Tim wanted a story for the *Post* tomorrow this would be just about his deadline, Martin calculated. He pictured the headlines in thirty-six point across the front page . . .

'If he does call back, tell him I'm not available, will you?'

'What, even though you're really here?'

'I'll be too busy to talk to him this afternoon.'

Caroline shrugged and pouted her shiny, blackberry-painted mouth. 'OK, if that's the way you want it. He's got a lovely voice on the phone, just like Alastair Burnet.'

Whether Tim had phoned again Martin didn't bother to enquire. It would now, in any case, be too late for this week's *Post*. He went alone to the house in Copley Avenue, his father having an engagement with a client in Hampstead, and on an impulse told his mother about his fifty thousand pound charity and his offer to Suma Bhavnani. She listened, drinking oloroso, and Martin could see that she was torn between admiration for his magnanimity and a natural maternal desire to see him spend the whole hundred and four thousand on a house for himself.

'I suppose I shouldn't ask why,' she said.

It would have been embarrassing to give his reasons, that life had been extraordinarily kind to him, that he felt he owed the world a living and a debt to the Fates. He didn't answer, he smiled and lifted his shoulders.

'What does Dad say?'

'I haven't told him – yet.'

They exchanged a glance of veiled complicity, a glance which implied that while they could they would keep this, to him highly disconcerting, information from Walter

Urban. Martin refilled their sherry glasses. Later, after they had eaten, Mrs Urban said:

'You know, when you said what you were going to spend that money on I couldn't help thinking of Mrs Finn.'

'Who's Mrs Finn?'

'Oh, *Martin*. You remember Mrs Finn. She was my cleaner. It must have been – oh, while you were still at school, when you were a teenager. A very thin, fair woman, looked as if a puff of wind would blow her away. You must remember.'

'Vaguely.'

'I've made a point of keeping in touch with her. I go there regularly. She lives in such a dreadful place, it would break your heart. A room smaller than this one divided into *three*, and where the bathroom is, goodness knows. I was dying to spend a penny last time I was there but I didn't dare ask, there are such strange people in the house, it's a real warren. There's a son who's a bit backward, I think, and he's got a room downstairs. He's a plumber or a builder's labourer or something. Of course, Mrs Finn herself has had mental trouble. The misery and squalor they live in, you can hardly imagine it.'

There was a good deal more of this and Martin put on a show of listening attentively but he felt that, since Mrs Finn had a son whose responsibility she was, she hardly qualified for his bounty. Besides, he had two elderly women on his list already. Wouldn't it be better to complete it with perhaps a young couple and a baby?

It surprised him that he hadn't yet heard from either Miss Watson or Mr Deepdene. There was nothing from them in the morning. Mr Cochrane and the newspapers arrived simultaneously and Martin leafed quickly through the *North London Post*, looking for a story about Suma Bhavnani or, worse, about Suma Bhavnani in connection with himself.

'I said it was a nice morning, Martin,' said Mr Cochrane severely, putting on his ironmonger's coat. 'I said it was considerably warmer than it has been of late. I suppose you don't think it's worth answering the pleasantries of a mere servant.' His eyes bulged dangerously in their bony sockets.

'I'm sorry,' Martin said. The newspaper made no mention

of the Bhavnanis or himself. Its front page was devoted to the murder of a girl in Kilburn, a story which carried Tim's by-line. 'It *is* a nice day. You're quite right, it's a lovely day.' He saw that he had just managed to deflect Mr Cochrane's incipient rage. It was like looking at some kind of meter on which, when oil or water is poured into the appropriate orifice, a needle oscillates, wavers and finally sinks away from danger level. 'How's your sister-in-law?'

'Much the same, Martin, much the same.' Mr Cochrane, applying silver polish to the tea and coffee spoons, seemed to brood with suspicion on this question. When Martin came back with his overcoat on he said sharply, 'I don't know what accounts for your interest, Martin. She's not a nubile young lady, you know, she's not one of your pin-up girls. Just a poor old woman who went out into service when she was fourteen. You wouldn't trouble to pass the time of day with the likes of her, Martin.'

If it hadn't been for the fact that he knew that Mr Cochrane, by the time he left at noon, would have made the flat more immaculate than even the house in Copley Avenue, would have ironed with exquisite finesse seven shirts, cleaned three picture windows and polished a whole canteen of cutlery, Martin would have booted him out on the spot. He only sighed and said he was off now.

'Good-bye, Martin,' said Mr Cochrane in the tones of a headmaster taking end-of-term farewell of a pupil whose conduct has been idle, slovenly, violent and rude.

It was rare for Mr Cochrane to leave him messages but if he did his notes were in the same disapproving and admonitory style as his conversation. Martin found one waiting for him when he came home just before six.

Dear Martin,

A Mr Sage phoned 2 mins after you left. I said I was only the cleaner and could not account for you going off so early like that.

W. Cochrane.

Martin screwed the note up and threw it into the emptied, and apparently actually polished, wastepaper bin. As it struck with a faint clang the side of this, in fact, metal container the phone began to ring. Martin answered it cautiously.

'How elusive you are,' said Tim's voice. 'You have quite an army of retainers to protect you from the press.'

'Not really,' said Martin rather nervously. 'And what can I – er, do for the press now it's found me?'

Tim didn't answer that directly. There was a silence in which Martin guessed he must be lighting a cigarette. He braced himself for the question and was very taken aback when Tim said, 'Just to remind you you're coming over here tomorrow night, love.'

Martin had forgotten all about the party. It had gone so far out of his head that he had accepted Gordon's invitation to the theatre. Suddenly he realized how much he hated, and had always hated, Tim calling him 'love'. It was much worse than 'my dear'. 'I'm sorry,' he said. 'I'm afraid I can't. I've arranged to do something else.'

'You might have let me know,' said Tim.

Martin said it again. 'I'm sorry,' and then, rather defensively, 'I didn't think it was necessary for that sort of party.'

If it were possible to hear someone's eyebrows go up, Martin felt he would have heard Tim's then. 'But what sort of party, Martin?' the drawly, now censorious, voice said. 'This is going to be a dinner party. Surely you understood that when I said to come at seven? Just eight of us for dinner.' There was a long, and to Martin awful, pause. 'It was to be rather a special celebration.'

'I'm sure my not being there won't spoil the evening.'

'On the contrary,' said Tim, now very cold. 'We shall be desolate.'

The receiver went down. No one had ever hung up on Martin before. He felt unfairly persecuted. Of course he had always refused in the past to go to Tim's but this time, if it had been made plain to him from the first that this wasn't going to be a noisy drunken get-together in uncomfortable darkened rooms, he wouldn't have forgotten about it and he would have gone. If Tim was asking him to dinner, why hadn't he told him so when he had invited him last Friday? Martin felt a sudden, almost fierce, dislike of Tim. When he heard from the tax inspector he would write him a formal letter, not phone this time. He had had quite enough of Tim for the time being. Let a few weeks go by, then maybe at Christmas he'd give him a ring.

But that night he dreamed of Tim for the first time for many weeks. They were in the house in Stroud Green which Martin, in waking reality, had never visited. Tim had spoken of it as unsavoury and in the dream it was more than that, Dickensian in its grotesque squalor, a series of junk-crowded rat-holes that smelt of rot. He and Tim were arguing about something, he hardly knew what, and each was provoking the other to anger, he by a kind of contrived pomposity, Tim by being outrageously camp. At last Martin could stand it no longer and he lunged out at Tim, but Tim parried the blow and together, clutching each other, they fell on to a deep, red, dusty, velvet settee that filled half the room. There, though still locked together, elbows hooked round each other's necks, it was impossible to continue struggling, for the red velvet which had become damp and somehow soggy, exerted an effect of sucking and seemed to draw them into its depths. Or to draw Martin into its depths. Tim was no longer there, the red velvet was Tim's mouth, and Martin was being drawn down his throat in a long devouring kiss.

It was the kind of dream from which one awakens abruptly and to a kind of rueful embarrassment. Fortunately, it was half-past eight when Martin awoke as he could hardly have remained comfortably in bed after visions of that sort. Once recovered, he saw the day floating invitingly before him, a rather-better-than-usual Saturday. It was warmish, a damp, misty November day with the sun like a little puddle of molten silver up there over the dome and cupolas of St Joseph's, jade green and gleaming in that sun's pale glow.

By lunchtime the mist had melted and the sun brightened and Martin wondered whether to walk to the Flask for his drink with Norman Tremlett. It took him about a quarter of an hour to walk there, two or three minutes to drive – but walking there meant walking back too. He often thought of that in the weeks to come, that if he had decided to walk he wouldn't have been there when the doorbell rang and he would never have met Francesca. Why hadn't he? There had been no reason but laziness. A spurt of energy had prompted the walk that led to his meeting Tim, laziness had cancelled the walk which would have prevented the meeting with Francesca. He felt there must be some significance in this, though he was never able to say what it was.

He thought his caller must be Miss Watson. She had never called on him before, but he had never offered to buy her a home before, and he was convinced it must be she. He opened the door, a kindly and welcoming smile already on his lips.

Outside stood a boy holding a bunch of enormous bright yellow incurved chrysanthemums. The boy had thick smooth black eyebrows and big dark brown eyes and very pink cheeks. He was wearing jeans and a kind of tunic of dark blue cotton or canvas and a close-fitting woolly cap that covered all his hair.

He said, 'Mr Urban?' in a voice that sounded to Martin very like a woman's.

'Yes, that's right,' said Martin, 'but those can't be for me.'

'You are Mr Martin W. Urban and this is 12 Cromwell Court, Cholmeley Lane, Highgate?'

'Yes, of course, but I still can't . . .'

'They certainly are for you, Mr Urban.' The woolly cap was suddenly snatched off to release a mass of long glossy wavy hair. The hair was dark brown and nearly two feet long and its owner was definitely a woman, a girl of perhaps twenty. She had a rather earnest voice and she spoke slowly. 'It's really warm today, isn't it? I don't know why I put this on. Look, you can see on the label they're for you.'

He forced himself to stop staring at her hair. 'Please come in, I didn't mean to keep you standing there.' She came in rather shyly, it seemed to him, hesitated between the open doorways, not knowing which to enter. 'In here,' he said. 'People don't send flowers to men unless they're ill, do they?'

She laughed. In here, where the big window made it very light, he was a little taken aback to see how pretty she was. She was tallish and very slim and delicately made and with a beautiful high colour in her face, a rose-crimson that deepened with her laughter. How awful if he had betrayed to her that at first he had taken her for a boy! It was her slimness, those strongly marked eyebrows, her earnest look, the boyishness, in fact, about her which only made her more attractive as a woman. He was suddenly aware of the strong, aggressive, bitter scent of the chrysanthemums.

'Is there a card with them?' He took the flowers from her and found the card, wired on to the bunch of coarse damp stems. The message on it was printed, the signature an indecipherable scrawl. ' "Thanks for everything," ' he read aloud, ' "I will never forget what you have done".'

'The name is just a squiggle. I expect whoever it is came into the shop and wrote that themselves.' She looked distressed. 'Could it be Ramsey or Bawsey? No? I could try and check if you like.'

He was standing by the window and he could see the van she had come in parked on the drive-in to the flats. It was a dark blue van lettered on its side in pink: Floreal, 416 Archway Road, N6.

'Is that your shop on the corner of the Muswell Hill Road? I pass it every day on my way to and from work.'

'On weekdays we don't close till six. You could call in on Monday.'

'Or I could phone,' said Martin. It would be difficult to park the car, one of the worst places he could think of. Was it his imagination that the girl looked slightly hurt? You're twenty-eight, he told himself, and you're fussing like some old pensioner about where you're going to park a car two days hence. He could put it in Hillside Gardens, couldn't he? He could walk a hundred yards. 'I'll come in about half-past five on Monday,' he said.

From the window he watched her drive away. The mist had gone and the puddle of sun and the sky had become leaden. It was twenty-five to one. Martin put on his jacket and went off to the Flask to meet Norman Tremlett. When he got back the first thing he had to do was put those flowers in water. He didn't know anyone called Ramsey or Bawsey or anything like that, he didn't think he knew anyone who would send him flowers.

There were far too many chrysanthemums for one vase, there were too many for two. He had to use a water jug as well as the Swedish crystal vase and the Copenhagen china jar with the spray of brown catkins on a blue ground. Fleetingly, he thought of not putting them into water at all but of taking them with him as a gift for Alice Tytherton. And have Alice think he had chosen them? It seemed awful to say so but they were very ugly flowers. Martin had always believed that flowers were beautiful, all flowers as by definition, and his feeling about these slightly shocked him. But it was no use pretending. They were very ugly, hideous, more like vegetables than flowers really, like a variety of artichoke. You could imagine them cooked and served up with butter sauce.

He began putting them into water and in doing so looked again at the card. Not Ramsey – but, yes, surely, Bhavnani! What more likely than that Mrs Bhavnani should send him flowers as a token of her gratitude. As an Indian she wouldn't know it wasn't the custom in England to send flowers to men, and she might see flowers with different eyes too. The eye of an oriental might not see these great spherical blooms as monstrous and coarse. But if she were the sender, it was an oddly colloquial message she had sent: 'Thanks for everything. I will never forget what you have done.' And why would she come all the way to the Archway Road when there was a flower shop in the same block as her own in Hornsey? It was just as likely that Miss Watson who lived in Highgate, in Hurst Avenue, was the mysterious donor.

His living room was transformed, and somehow made absurd, by an embarrassment of chrysanthemums, chrome yellow, incurved, smelling like bitter aloes. All the time he was arranging them Martin had been searching his memory for what incident in the past that scent brought back to him. Suddenly he knew. A dozen years ago and chrysanthemums arriving for his mother from some friend or recent guest. Those chrysanthemums had been fragile-looking, pale pink with frondy petals, but the smell of them had been the same as these. And what Martin remembered was going into the drawing room where a pale frail woman called Mrs Finn was crying bitterly because she had dropped and smashed a cut-glass vase. The pink flowers lay about in little pools of water and Mrs Finn wept as if it were her heart and not a vase which had broken.

The extraordinary things one remembers, thought Martin, and evoked by so little. He could still see Mrs Finn as she had been that afternoon, weeping over the broken glass or perhaps over her own cut finger from which the blood fell in large dark red drops.

5

His window gave on to the back of a house in Somerset Grove. There were strips of untended garden between and tumbledown sheds and even a greenhouse in which all the glass was broken. But unless he looked down all he could see was the yellow brick back of the other house, its rusty fire-escape and its bay windows. In one of these bays a woman stood ironing.

Finn stared at her, exercising his powers on her, trying to bend her to his will. He bore her no malice, he didn't know her, but he willed her just slightly to burn her finger on the iron. Pressing his body against the glass, he concentrated on her, piercing her with his eyes and his thought. He wanted her to feel it in her head, to stagger, bemused, and graze her trembling hand with the burning triangle.

The iron continued to move in steady, sweeping strokes. Once she glanced up but she didn't see him. All magicians long to discover the secret of making themselves invisible, and Finn wondered if he had found it. He stared on, forcing his eyes not to blink, breathing very deeply and very slowly. The woman had set the iron up on end now and was folding a rectangle of something white. He could have sworn she brushed the tip of the iron with her hand, but she didn't wince. And now, suddenly, she was staring back at him with indignation, looking at him full in the face. If he had been invisible he was no longer. He saw her move the ironing board away from the window to another part of the room and he turned back to what he had been doing before, screwing the cover back on the hotplate.

His room was on the second floor. It contained a single mattress, a three-legged stool and a bookcase. There had once been more furniture but gradually, as he mastered himself and his energies increased, he had disposed of it piece by piece. He hung his clothes from hooks on the wall. No curtains hung at the window and there was no carpet on the floor. Finn had painted the ceiling and the walls a pure, radiant white.

He had no means of cooking anything but he seldom ate anything cooked. On the floor stood a stack of cans of pineapple and pineapple juice and in the bookcase were the works of Aleister Crowley, *Meetings with Remarkable Men* and *Beelzebub's Tales to his Grandson* by Gurdjieff, Ouspensky's *A New Model of the Universe*, and *The Secret Doctrine* of Helena Blavatsky. Finn had picked them up in second-hand bookshops in the Archway Road.

As he was coiling the flex round the hotplate and putting it into a carrier bag, Finn heard Lena pass his door and go on up the stairs. She had been out all the morning at a shop in Junction Road called Second Chance, spending two ten-pound notes Finn had given her from the initial Anne Blake payment. Her movements were uneasy. He could tell by ear alone, by the sound of her feet on the stairs, her footsteps pattering across the landing, whether she was happy or afraid or whether there was a bad time coming. There hadn't been a bad time for nearly two years now. Finn looked on her strangeness quite differently from the way most people did, but the bad times were another matter, the bad times had been brought into being by himself.

He took off the white cotton robe he wore for studying or meditating or just being in his room and hung it on one of the hooks. Finn had no mirror in which to see his long body, hard and white and thin as a root. The clothes he put on, jeans, a collarless grandad shirt, the velvet waistcoat and the scarf with the coins on, had all been acquired by Lena, as had the pearl-handled cut-throat razor with which he now began to shave. He could see his face reflected in the window pane which, if he stood back a little, the opposing brick wall made into a passable looking glass. Nevertheless, he cut himself. Finn, with no pigment anywhere except in those water-grey pupils, sometimes thought it strange his blood should be as red as other people's.

Lena's tiny living room was draped all over with her purchases, a mauve silk dress with a fringe round the hem, a man's grey morning coat, a bunch of scarves, a pair of lace-up can-can girl's boots, and several little skirts and jumpers. The budgerigar, temporarily manumitted, surveyed all this array from its perch on an *art nouveau* lamp standard. In a day or two Lena would sell all these clothes to another shop, retaining perhaps one garment. She nearly always lost by these transactions but sometimes she made a tiny profit. When she saw Finn she recoiled from him, alarmed, inordinately distressed as always by even a pin-head drop of blood.

'You've been cut!' As if it had been done to him by someone else.

'Well, well,' said Finn, 'so I have. Let's cover it up, shall we?'

She gave him a lump of cotton wool that might have come out of a pill bottle or been the bedding of a ring. Finn stuck it on his chin. It smelt, like Lena's clothes, of camphor. She had brought in with her, he saw to his annoyance, a local paper, the *Post*, and he knew at once the cause of her uneasiness. Her eyes followed his.

'There's been a girl murdered in Kilburn.'

He opened his mouth to speak, guessing what was to come. She came up even closer to him, laid her finger on his lips, and said in a hesitant, fearful voice:

'Did you do it?'

'Come *on*,' said Finn. 'Of course I didn't.' The bird flew down and clung to the hem of the mauve dress, pecking at its fringe.

'I woke up in the night and I was so afraid. Your aura had been all dark yesterday, a dark reddish brown. I asked the pendulum and it said to go down and see if you were there, so I went down and listened outside your door. I listened for hours but you weren't there.'

'Give it here,' said Finn. He took the paper gently from her. 'She wasn't killed in the night, see? She wasn't killed yesterday. Look, you read it. She was killed last Wednesday week, the fifteenth.'

Lena nodded, clutching on to his arm with both hands as a person in danger of drowning clutches on to a spar. The bird pecked little mauve beads off the dress and scattered them on the floor.

'You know where we were that Wednesday, don't you?

The day before my birthday it was. All afternoon and all evening we were in here with Mrs Gogarty, doing planchette. You and me and Mrs Gogarty, OK? Panic over?'

Ever since the Queenie business, which had also marked the onset of her trouble, Lena supposed every murder committed north of Regent's Park and south of Barnet to have been perpetrated by her son. Had supposed it, at any rate, until Finn proved it otherwise or someone else was convicted of the crime. From time to time there came upon her flashes of terror in which she feared his arrest for murders committed years ago in Harringay or Harlesden. It was for this reason, among others, that Finn intended to make his present enterprise appear as an accident. Had he known what he was doing in those far-off days, had he not been so young, he would have done the same by Queenie and thus saved poor Lena from an extra anguish.

'Panic over?' he said again.

She nodded, smiling happily. One day she might forget, he thought, when he took her with him to India and they lived in the light of the ancient wisdom. She had begun rummaging through the day's horde of treasures, the budgerigar perched on her shoulder. A cushion, falling out, was caught between an octagonal table and a wicker box. Few objects could fall uninterruptedly to the floor in Lena's flat. She surfaced, grasping something yellow and woollen.

'For you,' she said. 'It's your size and it's your favourite colour.' And she added, like any mother who fears her gift won't be appreciated as it should be, 'It wasn't cheap!'

Finn took off his waiscoat and pulled on the yellow sweater. It had a polo neck. He got up and looked at himself in Lena's oval mirror with the blue velvet frame. The sleeves were a bit short and under the left arm was a pale green darn but that only showed when he lifted his arm up.

'Well, well,' said Finn.

'It does suit you.'

'I'll wear it to go out in.'

He left her noting down her new stock in the book she kept for this purpose. Finn had once seen this book. When Lena couldn't describe a garment she drew it. He went down into his own room and collected his tool box and the hotplate in its carrier and his PVC jacket. It was just gone two. He went in the van but not all the way, leaving it parked in a turning off Gordonhouse Road at the Highgate end.

Finn had waited to do the deed until after the departure of the Frazers. They had moved out the previous Friday. Sofia Ionides always spent Monday evening baby-sitting for her brother and his wife in Hampstead Garden Suburb. Finn didn't mind being seen entering the house in Modena Road, but he would have preferred not to be seen leaving it. By then, however, it would be dark. What most pleased him was the turn for the worse that the weather had taken. From Saturday afternoon it had grown steadily colder, there had been frost this morning, and as he drove up Dartmouth Park Hill a thin snow had dashed against the windscreen. If the weather had stayed as warm as it had been on Saturday morning he might have had to postpone his arrangements.

Anne Blake's flat was clean and tidy and very cold. One day, Finn thought, when he had developed his theta rhythms, he might be able to generate his own bodily heat, but that day was not yet. It would be unwise to use any of Anne Blake's heating appliances, he must just endure it. He attached a 13-amp plug to the flex which protruded from the gas pipe behind the fridge and plugged it in to the point next to the fridge point. Then he put up the steps and climbed into the loft, carrying the hotplate. Up there it was even colder. Finn joined the flex on the hotplate to the flex, some five or six yards of it, that came out of the gas pipe. Down the steps again to test if it worked. It did.

Watching the coiled element on the electric hotplate begin to glow red, Finn checked over his plan for the perfect accident. She would come in at six, turn on the heaters, including the electric fire in her bedroom, maybe have a drink of some sort, then her bath. She might bring the electric fire into the bathroom or she might not, it mattered very little either way. Finn would be lying up in the loft on the joists between the trapdoor and the water tank. When he heard her in the bath he would lift up the trapdoor and drop the hotplate down into the water. Electrocution would take place instantaneously. The hotplate he would then dry and replace among the glass jars and the *National Geographic* magazines. Once more broken and unusable, what more suitable place for it? When all the arrangements of flex and plug had been dismantled, nothing remained but to plug Anne Blake's bedroom electric fire into the bathroom point, switch it on and toss it into the bath water. Accidental death, misadventure, the fire had very obviously (a complaisant coroner would say) slipped off the tiled shelf at the end of the bath.

Finn felt no compunction over what he was about to do. There was no death. He would simply be sending Anne Blake on into the next cycle of her being, and perhaps into a fleshly house of greater beauty. Not for her, this time, the human lot of growing old and feeble, but a quick passage into the void before giving her first cry as a new-born child. Strange to think that Queenie too was a child somewhere now, unless instead her unenlightened soul still wandered aimlessly out there in the dark spaces.

Clambering across the loft, he peered out through a gap between roof strut and tile to watch the fluttering snow. In the wind on the top of Parliament Hill grey trees waved their thin branches as if to ward off the cloudy blizzard. The sky was the hard shiny grey of new steel.

It was because he was at the extreme edge of the roof, lying down to look under the eaves, that he was able to hear nothing in the depths of the house below him. Soft-soled shoes treading the carpeted stairs made sounds too low to reach him. He heard nothing at all until there came the scrabbling of a key in the front door lock.

Finn might just have managed to pull the steps up in time and close the trapdoor but he wouldn't have been able to push the fridge back against the kitchen wall or remove his open toolbox from the middle of the kitchen floor. She had come home more than two hours early. He came across the loft and looked down through the aperture in the ceiling as Anne Blake opened the bathroom door and stood looking up, startled and annoyed. There were snowflakes on her bushy dark grey hair.

'What on earth are you doing up there, Mr Finn?'

'Lagging the pipes,' said Finn. 'We're in for a freeze-up.'

'I didn't know you had a key, it's the first I've heard of it.'

Finn didn't answer, he never went in for pointless explanations. What now? She would never have her bath with him up there, otherwise he might have proceeded as planned. He must try again tomorrow. Nevertheless, it wouldn't be quite safe to leave that mysterious lead proceeding from the gas pipe still plugged in. Finn descended. He wrenched off the plug, went back into the loft and disconnected the hotplate. It would be a good idea actually to lag those pipes, an excuse for being in the roof again tomorrow. He would go down and tell her he would return tomorrow with fibreglass wrap for the pipes.

Finn put the hotplate with the iron and trivet, packed up his tool box and came down the steps, pulling the trapdoor closed behind him. He was sitting on the side of the bath, about to close the lid of the box when, across the blue and yellow papered hall, through the open doorway to the bedroom, he saw Anne Blake crouched down, her back to him, as she struggled to pull open the lowest drawer of a tallboy. Lying on the top shelf of the box was the largest and heaviest of his hammers. How easy it would be now! In just such a manner had he struck Queenie down.

He shut the box, slipping the hammer into his right-hand pocket. Then the box was on the bathroom floor and Finn was moving swiftly across the blue carpet towards her.

6

She was on her feet, clutching to her the two or three garments she had been groping for in the drawer, before Finn had so much as entered the bedroom. He stood still on the threshold and she seemed to find nothing untoward in his looks or his behaviour. She said rather ungraciously:

'Have you finished whatever you were doing up there?'

Finn nodded, fixing her with his pale eyes. He knew she was uneasy in his presence, but there was nothing new in that, most people were. Quite alone in the house with him for the first time, she was probably afraid of rape. Finn smiled inwardly. He wasn't much interested in sex. It was more than a year since he had had anything to do with a woman in that way, and then it had been very sporadically.

He put the steps away and got into his jacket. It was still only four-thirty, but twilight. Anne Blake had turned some lights on and gone into the kitchen. The gas fire, just lighted, burnt blue in the living room grate. Finn still had the hammer in the pocket of his jeans. He went into the kitchen to tell Anne Blake about coming back tomorrow with the fibreglass and while she talked to him, asking him what right Kaiafas had to a key to her flat and scolding him about knocking over something when he moved her fridge, he closed his hand round the hammer handle and thought, how easy, how easy . . . And how easily too he would be found out and caught afterwards, not to mention Lena's terror.

She forgot to ask him to relinquish the key or perhaps she thought he had better keep it since he was coming back the next day. It was still snowing when he got down to the street, but the snowflakes were now the big clotted kind that melt and disperse as soon as they touch a solid surface. Finn walked along Mansfield Road and under the railway bridge at Gospel Oak and got into the van.

Immediately, it seemed, he had closed the door, the blizzard began. The wipers on his windscreen weren't what they had been and Finn decided to stay put until the snow stopped. It flopped on to the roof and windows of the van and streamed as water down its sides.

After about twenty minutes the snow had almost ceased but there was a big build-up of rush-hour traffic headed for Highgate West Hill. Finn couldn't stay parked where he was and he couldn't turn round, so he started the van and drove back the way he had walked. It was dark now but the street lamps were all on, and as he passed the end of Modena Road he saw Anne Blake leaving the house, holding a pagoda-shaped umbrella in one hand and a plastic carrier in the other. She turned in the direction of Hampstead Heath.

Finn turned right at the next turning into Shirlock Road and came out into Savernake Road by the great porridge-coloured pile of All Hallows' Church. Anne Blake had just reached the corner of Modena Road and Savernake Road and was now crossing the road towards the footbridge. Finn parked the van among all the other parked cars and vans. The snow had changed to a thin sleety rain.

It was very dark, though not yet half-past five. Finn supposed that Anne Blake had gone to call on some friend who lived on the other side of the railway line in Nassington Road maybe or Parliament Hill. She wouldn't go shopping that way. Besides, the carrier had looked full. He debated whether to go back into the house in her absence. She would very likely be absent for a couple of hours.

He wondered if she had had her bath. There had been quite enough time for her to have had it, but would she go out into the cold immediately after having had it? She might intend to have it immediately she got in. It would only take him a few minutes, say ten, to reconnect those plugs. But if she had already had her bath he might find himself stuck up there in the loft all night.

Perhaps a dozen people, coming singly or in pairs, had appeared from the approach to the footbridge while he sat there. Its only use really was to take one on to the Heath or into the streets to the east of South End Road. No one living here would use Hampstead Heath station when Gospel Oak was just as near. She hadn't gone to the station.

At last Finn got out of the van, crossed the road and let himself once more into the house in Modena Road. The rain had begun lashing down by the time he got there. He went upstairs without turning any lights on, and at the top, he entered Anne Blake's flat in darkness. A street lamp lit the living room and so, with a richer orange glow, did the gas fire which she had left on. She wouldn't have done that, Finn thought, if she had intended to be out for long.

He went into the bathroom and ran his hand along the inside of the bath. It was wet and so was one of the towels that hung on the chromium towel rail. There was no point in his remaining. He padded softly, although there was no one to hear him, across to the bedroom window. The rain was now coming down in the kind of deluge that no one would venture out in unless he had to. Finn had to.

He opened one of the doors of Anne Blake's wardrobe. Inside, among her clothes, were two or three garments still sheathed in the thin polythene covers in which they had come back from the dry-cleaners. Finn selected one of these, slipped it off the hanger, and the long black evening dress it covered, and pulled it over his head, splitting its sides open a little way down for his arms to go through. It made a kind of protective tunic, impervious and transparent.

The rain began to let up a little as he came up to Savernake Road. There was no one about. He felt drawn by the Heath, by its wide green emptiness, and he walked up the steps and on to the footbridge. A single lamp, raised up high, illumined the bridge, but you couldn't see the railway line, the walls were built up too high for that. To prevent suicides, thought Finn. He gazed across the smooth slope of Parliament Hill Fields to Highgate on the horizon, the emerald domes of St Joseph's gleaming colourless and pearly against a sky which the glow of London made velvety and reddish. The backs of the houses in Tanza Road were as if punctured all over with lights but the glittering screen of rain prevented much of that light from being shed on the path. It seemed to Finn that the whole area to the left of the footbridge and immediately above the railway embankment was extraordinarily dark. He could barely see where the turf ended and Nassington Road began.

He came down the steps on the Parliament Hill side of the bridge. A train rattled underneath as he passed. The rain was running in streams down his plastic covering, though now it was lightening again, setting in evidently for a night of torrents with short drizzly remissions. In the dark hollow where the path ran under the trees to link with the end of Nassington Road, Finn picked his way between the puddles. Now he could see why it was so dark. The lamp at the end of Nassington Road had gone out or never come on.

Finn liked the solitude and the silence. The train and its noise had long gone down the deep cutting to Gospel Oak. No one was venturing out into the rain. A strange tall figure in a shining glassy robe, Finn stood under the trees viewing the grey and rain-washed plain, feeling one with the elements, a man of power, a conqueror.

Someone was coming down Nassington Road, he could just hear the footfalls, though they were deadened by the wetness of the pavement. He stepped a little aside, behind the trunk of a tree. He could see her clearly now, passing under the last lighted lamp, the pagoda umbrella up, the carrier in her other hand empty or nearly so. She had waited to leave for home until the rain lifted a little. He could tell she was nervous because the lamp was out. She looked to the left past where he was standing and to the right, towards the bridge, and then she came on into the lake of darkness.

Finn no more intended to move forward and strike than he had intended to move forward and strike Queenie. It happened, that was all. It happened without his volition or his desire in the same way, perhaps, as the stone had moved and the pictures fallen. At one moment he was standing, watching with those night-seeing eyes of his, at the next the hammer was in his hand and he had fallen upon her. Queenie had made terrible sounds. Anne Blake made none but a throaty gasp, falling forward from the knees as he struck her again and again, now using the wide, flat side of the hammer.

In the dark he couldn't tell which of that dark fluid that spread everywhere was water and which blood. He pulled her away from the path and round the side of the nearest tree. There was no pulse, she was dead. Already she had passed into the unknown and was in possession of what was beyond. He almost envied her.

There was no Lena this time to come in and witness what he had done. He must keep this from Lena, wash himself clean of all the blood that so terrified her, deny her newspapers. Finn picked up Anne Blake's umbrella and furled it. He felt inside the carrier and found there a small suede handbag in which he found twenty-six pounds in notes, a cheque book and two credit cards. He took these and the money with him.

In the light on the bridge he could tell blood from water by running his fingers down his body and then holding up his hands. The lamplight robbed everything of colour, but the fluid was dark that ran from his hands. Someone was coming from the Parliament Hill side. Whoever it was had passed Anne Blake's body. Finn took refuge at the foot of the switchback slope that was designed for those who didn't want to or couldn't use stairs. Footsteps passed across the bridge and went on towards Savernake Road. The rain had returned now to all the force of its former intensity.

Finn stepped out into it and let it wash him clean.

He also washed the hammer in the rain. Once back in the van, he stripped off his plastic tunic and rolled it up into a ball. Underneath he was perfectly clean and fairly dry. He replaced his hammer in the tool box and fastened the lid. The gas fire would still be on in Anne Blake's flat, might very likely remain on all night, but it wouldn't burn the house down.

The problem was to get rid of the contents of the handbag, particularly the cheque book and the credit cards. Finn drove home. It was still only seven, the rain falling steadily as if, having at last found a satisfactory rhythm, it meant to stick to it. Because of the rain he put the van away in the garage he rented in Somerset Grove, an old coach house with bits of rotting harness still hanging on the walls.

With Lena was Mrs Gogarty, the friend who had predicted for Finn a violent death in old age. The two of them were intent upon the pendulum. A white and pink baby's shawl with a scalloped edge had been thrown over the birdcage. Mrs Gogarty was as fat as Lena was thin, with abundant hair dyed a stormy dark red.

'Well, well,' said Finn, 'you *are* cosy. Can I have a lend of a pair of scissors?'

Lena, looking in the mauve dress and yards of stole like the appropriate one of the Three Fates, handed him the Woolworth scissors with which she picked and snipped at her daily finds.

'He's a lovely boy, your boy,' said Mrs Gogarty, who made this remark every time the three of them met. 'The picture of devotion.'

Finn managed to palm his mother's reading glasses off the top of a chest of drawers where they nestled among some half-burnt candles and incense sticks and pieces of abalone shell. He went down to his own room where he cut up the notes and the cheque book and the credit cards into very small pieces. The tin from which he had eaten pineapple chunks at lunchtime was now quite dry inside. Finn put the pieces of paper and card into the empty tin and applied a match. It took several more matches to get it going and keep it going, but at last Anne Blake's twenty-six pounds and her Westminster Bank cheque book were reduced to a fine black ash. The American Express and Access cards were less destructible, but they too went black and emitted a strong chemical smell.

Re-entering his mother's room, Finn dropped the glasses and trod on them. This made Mrs Gogarty scream out and jump up and down, jerking her arms, which was what she did whenever anything the slightest bit untoward happened. Lena was too much occupied in calming her down to say anything about the glasses, she diverted her with the pendulum as one diverts a child with a rattle.

Finn promised to get the glasses repaired as soon as he could. He would go into the optician's first thing tomorrow, he said. In the meantime, had she noticed the rain coming in over her gas stove? Better put a bowl there, and the first moment he got he'd be out on that roof.

'Devotion itself,' gasped Mrs Gogarty.

The pendulum rotated, widdershins and swiftly.

7

The snow, which had been falling for most of the afternoon, had changed to rain when Martin drove across the Archway Road and began searching for a place to park. Southwood Lane was hopeless and so was the narrow congested curve of Hillside Gardens. He finally left the car in one of the roads up behind Highgate Police Station and walked back to the cross-roads, wondering if he might be too late to catch Floreal open, although it was only ten to six.

During the weekend he had asked himself several times why he should bother to call at the shop when he was sure it must have been the Bhavnani family who had sent those flowers. Anyway, did it matter particularly who had sent them? Of course, if he knew he could write a note of thanks or phone. Dr Ghopal had phoned the office during the afternoon to say that the great heart specialist was preparing to operate in the week immediately preceding Christmas. No further time should be wasted when a condition like Suma's was in question. Would Martin buy the air tickets himself and arrange an hotel for Mrs Bhavnani? Martin had agreed to do this, but he had felt unable to make enquiries about the flowers, especially as he was going to see the pretty dark-haired girl that evening.

He saw her when he was still on the other side of the road outside the post office. She was taking in boxes of cut flowers and poinsettias in pots from the pavement. He waited for the lights to change and then crossed the street. The shop, which was very small, had a red bulb in one of its hanging lights, and the orangey glow, the mass of fresh damp glistening foliage, the red velvet long-leaved poinsettias, gave to the place a festive air, Christmassy, almost exciting. It was dark and bleak outside. The shop was alight with reds and yellows and jungle greens, and the girl stood in the middle of it, smiling, her arms full of carnations.

'Oh, I was so sure you wouldn't come!'

She checked herself, seeming a little embarrassed. The colour in her cheeks had deepened. It was as if – he couldn't help feeling this – she had actually looked forward to his coming and had then resigned herself to – disappointment? She turned away and began putting the carnations in water. He said in a voice he recognized as typically his, a hearty voice he disliked:

'Did you happen to find out who was the kind person who sent my bouquet?'

It was a little while before she turned round. 'There, that's all done.' She wiped her hands on the brown and white checked apron she wore. 'No, I'm awfully afraid we couldn't. You see, the person who came in didn't give her name. She just wrote that card and paid for the flowers.'

'You wouldn't know if it was an old woman or a young one, I suppose, or if she was – well, white or Indian or what?'

'I'm afraid not. I didn't see her, you see. I *am* so sorry.' She took off her apron, went into the little room at the back and reappeared wearing a red and blue striped coat with a hood. 'If you're worrying about thanking them,' she said, 'I'm sure you needn't. After all, the flowers were to thank *you*, weren't they? For something you'd done. You can't keep on thanking people for thanking you backwards and forwards, the next thing would be they'd have to thank you for your thank-you letter.' She added, the pink once again bright in her cheeks, 'Of course it's nothing to do with me, I don't mean to interfere.'

'No, you're quite right.' He went on quickly, 'If you're going to close the shop now – I mean, if you're leaving, can I give you a lift anywhere? I have my car.'

'Well, you can. Oh, *would* you? But you're going home and I have to go to Hampstead. I always go to see my friend in Hampstead on Monday evenings and you've no idea how awful it is getting from here to Hampstead if you haven't got a car. You have to go on the 210 bus and they either don't come at all or they hunt in packs.'

Martin laughed. 'I'll go and get the car and pick you up in five minutes.' To make it as fast as that he had to run. When he pulled up at the lights she was waiting, scanning the street, looking lost.

'You're very very kind,' she said.

'Not at all. I'm glad I happened to mention it.' He was already aware that she was the kind of girl who makes a man feel manly, protective, endowed with virile power. Sitting beside him, she smelt of the flowers she had been with all day. She pushed back her hood and felt in her hair to release some slide or comb which held it confined, and the dark silky mass fell down over her shoulders like a cape.

At Highgate High Street, waiting in the traffic queue to turn up past the school, he turned to speak to her. She had been talking artlessly, charmingly, about transport difficulties between Highgate and Hampstead, how there ought to be a new tube under the Heath, a station called the Vale of Health. He didn't speak. He was suddenly conscious that she was not pretty but beautiful, perhaps the only truly beautiful person who had ever been in his car or sat beside him. Except, of course, for Tim Sage.

*

She told him her name as they were driving along the Spaniards Road.

'It's Francesca,' she said, pronouncing it in the Italian way. 'Francesca Brown.'

It turned out that the friend, who had a flat in Frognal, wouldn't yet be home from work. Martin suggested a drink in the Hollybush. The rain was lashing against the windows of the car but Martin had an umbrella on the back seat. He put up the umbrella and held it out over her but, to his surprise and slightly to his confusion, she put her arm through his and drew him towards her so that they were both protected from the rain. There weren't yet many people in the bar. As he came back to her, carrying their drinks, he saw her big dark glowing eyes fixed on him and slowly she broke into a somehow joyful smile. His heart seemed to beat faster. It was eight before either of them realized how much time had passed and even then she lingered for another half-hour.

'Would you have dinner with me tomorrow night, Francesca?'

He had parked the car at the top of Frognal in front of the big houses in one of which Annabel had her flat. Francesca hesitated. The look she turned on him was intense, unsmiling, no longer joyful.

'What's the matter?' he said. 'Is something wrong?'

She said carefully, 'No,' and then in a shy voice but as if she couldn't hold the words back, 'We must meet again, I know that.'

'Then tomorrow?'

Her answer was a vehement nod. She got out of the car. 'Call for me at the shop.'

The grey rain, blown by sharp gusts of wind, swallowed her up. It went on raining most of the night. On the radio at breakfast there was an announcement of a murder that had taken place in Hampstead the evening before. Martin shivered a little to think that while he had been sitting and talking with Francesca, a woman had been murdered less than a mile away, her body left lying out in the teeming rain.

He called for Francesca at the shop at a quarter to six. They had drinks at Jack Straw's Castle and then dinner at the Villa Bianca. Francesca didn't smoke, nor drank more than a glass of wine and for an aperitif she had orange juice. When the time came for her to go home she wouldn't let him drive her. They were standing by his car, arguing about it, Martin insisting that he must drive her and she declaring in her earnest fashion that she wouldn't dream of allowing it, when a taxi came along and she had hailed it before he could stop her. The taxi bore her away down Hampstead High Street and turned into Gayton Road which was what it would have done whether her home had been to the north of Hampstead or to the east or even possibly to the west. Tomorrow night, he thought, he would ask her point blank where she lived. Why hadn't he done that already? He felt almost ashamed when he reflected that he had spent most of their time together talking about himself while she had listened with the attention of someone already committed to a passionate interest in the speaker. Of course he wasn't used to that kind of companionship. It was laughable to think of his parents or Gordon or Norman Tremlett hanging breathlessly on his words. But it hadn't been laughable in Francesca. It had been enormously flattering and gratifying and sweet and it had made him feel very protective towards her – and it had distracted him from asking her any questions about her own life. However, he would ask her tomorrow.

Not the shop this time but the foyer of the Prince of Wales Theatre. This was the way he had conducted his previous and rather brief, unsatisfactory relationships with girls, dinner one night, theatre the next, cinema the next, then dinner again. What else was there? Francesca looked so beautiful that he blurted out his feelings once they were in their seats.

'You look absolutely beautiful. I can't stop looking at you.'

She was wearing a softly draped dress of rose-coloured *panne* velvet, and round her neck on a ribbon a tiny pink rosebud. Her hair was piled like a Japanese lady's in mounds and coils, fixed with long tortoiseshell pins. The unaccustomed make-up she wore made her seem a little strange, remote, and violently sexually attractive. She winced a fraction at the compliment.

'Don't, Martin.'

He waited until the play was over and they were walking

towards his car, parked in Lower Regent Street. Then he said gently and with a smile:

'You shouldn't make yourself look like that if you don't like compliments.'

His tone was light but hers serious and almost distressed. 'I know that, Martin! I know I'm a fool. But I couldn't help it, don't you see? I did want you to think I looked nice.'

'Of course. Why shouldn't you?'

'Oh, let's not talk about it,' she said.

When they were driving up Highgate West Hill he said he was going to drive her home and where did she live? If he would drop her here, she said, she would get a taxi. He pulled into Gordonhouse Road by the Greek Orthodox Church, switched off the engine, turned to look at her.

'Have you got a boy friend that you're living with, Francesca?'

'No, of course not. Of course I haven't.' And she added, 'Not a *boy friend*. Not that I'm *living* with.' He was quite unprepared for what she did next. She opened the car door and jumped out. He followed her, but not fast enough, and by the time he reached the corner a taxi carrying her was starting off up the hill.

That night he asked himself if he could possibly, after only three days, be in love, and decided that he couldn't. But he slept badly and could think of nothing and no one but Francesca until he had phoned Floreal at nine-thirty and spoken to her and been told she would see him again in the evening.

They went to a little restaurant she knew at the top of the Finchley Road. He didn't ask her why she had run away and she volunteered no explanation. After the meal he asked her if she would come back to Cromwell Court with him and he would make coffee. And in saying this he felt shy and awkward with her, for invitations of that kind to girls, he supposed, always carried the implication of a sexual denouement. He had had a secret half-ashamed conviction since last night that she might be a virgin.

She agreed to come. The yellow chrysanthemums were still alive, fresh and aggressive as ever, only their leaves having withered.

'They are *immortelles*,' said Francesca.

After half an hour she insisted on leaving. He helped her into her coat, she turned to him, and they were so close that he brought his face to hers and kissed her. Her lips were soft and responsive and her hands just touched his upper arms. He put his arms round her and kissed her passionately, prolonging the kiss until suddenly she broke away, flushed and frightened.

'Darling Francesca, I couldn't help it. Let me take you home.'

'No!'

'Then say you'll see me again tomorrow.'

'Will you come down with me and find a taxi?' said Francesca.

It was a damp rather misty night, the last of November. From every bare twig hung a chain of water drops. They walked out into Highgate Hill. There were plane and chestnut leaves underfoot, slippery and wet and blackened.

'Shall I call for you at the shop tomorrow?' He had hailed the taxi and it was already pulling in towards them. So many of their dramas, he was later to feel, had been associated with taxis. She shook his hand.

'Not tomorrow.'

'When, then? Saturday?'

She gasped, put up her hands to her face. 'Oh, Martin, never!' And then she was gone.

If his car had been at hand he would have followed that taxi. But it was two hundred yards away in the Cromwell Court car park. He walked back, dizzy with panic, with near-terror, that he had lost her. Because of that kiss? Because he had pressurized her about her private life? He was sitting desolate in his living room when the phone rang. The reprieve of her voice made him sink back with a kind of exhaustion.

'I shouldn't have said that, Martin, I didn't mean it. Only you do understand, don't you, that I can't see you this week-end?'

'No, I don't understand but I'll accept it if you say so.'

'And we'll meet next week, we'll meet on – Tuesday. I'll explain everything on Tuesday and it'll be all right. I promise you it'll be all right. Trust me?'

'Of course I trust you, Francesca. If you say it'll be all right I believe you.' He hadn't meant to say it, he hadn't been quite sure until this moment that he felt it, and it should be said for the first time face to face, but, 'I love you,' he said.

'Martin, Martin,' she said and the phone clicked and the dialling tone began.

It was a strange empty feeling knowing he wasn't going to see her for four whole days. Instead, his parents' house tonight to make up for his absence on Thursday, drinks tomorrow with Norman in the Flask, dinner with Adrian and Julie Vowchurch, Sunday a long gloomy void . . . The postman came early, at ten past eight, bringing the phone bill and an envelope addressed in an unfamiliar elderly hand.

The letter inside was signed Millicent Watson. She addressed him as Mr Urban, 'Dear Mr Urban', though he remembered having been introduced to her as Martin and hearing her call him by his christian name. She hadn't quite understood his letter, she wrote. Was he sure he wasn't mistaking her for someone else? If he was under the impression that she was a client of his firm and had investments, this was not so. She couldn't take on the responsibility of owning property. Moreover, she would never be in a position to repay any money which Urban, Wedmore, Mackenzie and Company might advance her. She had never in her life owed anyone a penny and didn't want to begin now. His letter had worried her a lot, she hadn't been able to sleep for worrying.

Martin was reading this in some dismay when Mr Cochrane arrived. He was carrying a six-foot-long cane with a green nylon brush attached to the head of it. This implement, designed for sweeping the ceilings, had once before been brought into the flat, transported very ill-temperedly by Mr Cochrane on the bus from his home in the Seven Sisters Road. Martin had said he would gladly buy a ceiling brush to save his cleaner so much trouble and inconvenience but Mr Cochrane, getting angrier and angrier, had replied that it made him sick to hear people who had never known the meaning of want, talk of throwing money about like water, spending pounds like pence, Martin would want to buy a dustette next, he supposed, or an electric polisher – and so on.

This morning he omitted any greeting. Positively hurling

himself into his ironmonger's coat, he plunged into a rather incoherent account of his sister-in-law's latest dramas – and thereby imparted to Martin information that otherwise would have been hard to get. The green nylon brush rasped and whisked across the ceiling.

'On the verge of total nervous collapse, Martin, according to the doc. He's put her on eight Valium a day – no, I tell a lie – twelve. I was round there at number twenty, up with her half the night, Martin, and I don't mind telling you . . .'

'Number twenty?' hazarded Martin.

'Number twenty, Barnard House. Top of Ladbroke Grove, isn't it? How many times do I have to tell you? Might as well talk to a brick wall. Now mind out or you'll get cobwebs down on that expensive suit. Beautiful, them chrysanths, aren't they? Must have cost a packet. And here today, as you might say, Martin, and tomorrow to be cast into the oven.'

If only that were true, Martin thought, but the yellow chrysanthemums still looked aggressively fresh on Monday morning. On his way to work he posted the now completed letter to Mrs Cochrane. He drove by way of Highgate High Street and Southwood Lane so that he passed the flower shop, but at twenty past nine it wasn't yet open. He waited till ten and then he phoned her at Floreal. The other girl answered, the one who owned the shop. Martin asked to speak to Miss Brown and wondered why he sensed a sort of hesitant pause before the girl said she would fetch Francesca. Again he felt that quickened heart-beat when her voice came soft and serious, faintly apologetic, on the line. Yes, she was going to see him tomorrow, she was looking forward to it, she could hardly wait, only she had to wait, and would he call for her at the shop?

He had lunch with Gordon Tytherton in Muswell Hill. Gordon had invented a new system of taxation. There was, of course, no question of its ever being implemented, it was purely academic, but Gordon was immensely proud of it, being certain that if put to use it would solve all the nation's economic problems. He talked about it all the time. His little short-sighted eyes lit up and occasionally his voice trembled with emotion as might another man's when he spoke of a woman or a work of art. Martin parted from him at the foot of the hill and went into the travel agency where he collected the air tickets for Mrs Bhavnani and Suma. Should he take them to the Bhavnanis' shop or send them? After a protracted inner debate he decided to send them to Dr Ghopal.

Francesca phoned him at twenty-five to ten on Tuesday morning to say she couldn't see him and not to come to the shop.

'It's not possible, Martin, and something awful's happened! Martin, do you see the *Post*?'

He heard it as the post, the mail. 'What post?'

'The local paper, the *North London Post*. I know you do, I saw it when I was in your flat. Martin, promise me you won't look at it when it comes on Friday. Please, Martin. I'll see you on Friday and I'll explain everything.'

After she had rung off he thought how, if she left her job, he would have no means of knowing where to find her, she would be lost to him. He was in love with someone whose life was a total mystery to him, who might live, for all he knew, in Golders Green or Edmonton or Wembley, with her parents, in a hostel, in her own flat. She was like one of those heroines of a fairy story or an Arabian Nights' tale who come from nowhere, who vanish into a void, and who threaten to disappear for ever if their lover attempts to lift the veil that conceals their secrets.

In her absence, the week passed with a dreary plodding slowness. She dominated his thoughts. Why had she asked for his promise not to look at the local paper? He hadn't given it. Had he done so he would have adhered to his promise but he hadn't and she, strangely enough, hadn't insisted. It occurred to him that the truth might be she really wanted him to see the *Post*, half-feared it, half-desired it, because it was to contain some story about herself, flattering to herself. Francesca was very modest and diffident. Could it be that she was shy of his seeing praise of her? She might have been taking part in some contest, he thought, or succeeding with honours in some examination. And he indulged in a little fantasy in which a photograph of Francesca covered the paper's front page with a caption underneath to the effect that this was London's loveliest flower seller.

The postman and Mr Cochrane arrived simultaneously. Mr Cochrane greeted Martin dourly, said nothing about his sister-in-law, got to work at once on the windows with a chamois leather and soapy water. Martin opened the letter with the Battersea postmark. It was from Mr Deepdene. Here was no misapprehension, no paranoia, no getting hold of the wrong end of the stick. Mr Deepdene wrote that he had never known such kindness in all his seventy-four years, he was overwhelmed, it was unbelievable. At first he had thought of refusing Martin's offer, it was too generous, but now it seemed ungrateful, even wrong, to turn it down. He would accept with a full heart. Martin shut himself in his bedroom, away from Mr Cochrane, wrote a rapid note to Mr Deepdene and put into the envelope with it, a cheque for fifteen thousand pounds. Then he wrote to Miss Watson, asking her to phone him at his office so that they might make an appointment to meet.

The sun was shining on the white frosted roofs that hung like a range of glittering alps beneath his window. It was going to be a fine day, it was Friday, tonight he was going to see Francesca. He stood at the bedroom window, looking down at the white roofs, the long shadows, the occasional spire of whiter smoke rising through the bright mist. Coming across the car park was the paper boy with his canvas satchel. Martin turned away from the window and went into the living room where Mr Cochrane was polishing plate glass and the chrysanthemums were as vigorous as ever. He took the vases out into the kitchen. The big yellow blossoms seemed to look reproachfully at him as he thrust them into the waste bin.

'Wicked waste,' said Mr Cochrane, padding up behind him to empty his bowl of water. 'Not a withered petal on the lot of them!'

The two newspapers had just come through the letter box. Martin picked them up and looked at the *Post*. The front page lead, for the second week running, was the Parliament Hill Fields murder. This time it was a report of the inquest on Anne Blake, the heading was *Woman Killed for £26* and the by-line Tim Sage's. Martin went through the paper to try and find what had so upset Francesca in anticipation. The *Post* was a forty-page tabloid so this took some time, but he could find nothing, no photograph, no story. It was still only ten to nine. Watched curiously by Mr Cochrane, Martin began again, working this time more slowly and meticulously.

Because he could no longer bear the scrutiny of pebble eyes through distorting bifocals, he took the paper into the bedroom. There, using a red ballpoint, he went through each page like a proof reader, ticking its lower edge when he had cleared it.

He found what he was looking for on page seven, a mere paragraph in a gossip column called *Finchley Footnotes*.

The coming year will be an exciting one for Mr Russell Brown, 35, whose first book is to be published in the summer. This is an historical novel about the Black Death entitled The Iron Cocoon. *Mr Brown, who is an authority on the fourteenth century, teaches history at a north London polytechnic. He lives with his wife Francesca and two-year-old daughter Lindsay in Fortis Green Lane.*

8

'Since this is going to be our last meeting,' said Martin, 'I should have liked to take you somewhere nice.' He glanced round the Greek taverna in the Archway Road where she had insisted on coming. It smelt of cooking oil, and over the glass-fronted case of raw kebabs trailed the fronds of a plastic tradescantia. 'Still, I don't suppose it matters.' An unpleasant thought, among so many, struck him. 'Where does *he* think you are? Come to that, where did he think you were all last week?'

'He had flu,' she said, 'and the doctor said to take a week off to convalesce, so he went to his parents in Oxford and took Lindsay with him.'

'I can't believe you have a child,' he said miserably, 'a child of two.' The waiter came to their table. Martin ordered lamb kebab, a salad, for both of them. She passed across the table to him something she had taken from her handbag. He looked without enthusiasm, with dismay, at the photograph of a dark-haired, wide-eyed baby girl. 'But where is she? What happens to her when you're at work?' It was as if he doubted the very truth of it, as if by questioning her closely, he might break her down and make her confess that she had lied and the newspaper been wrong.

'In a day nursery. I take her there in the mornings and Russell fetches her. He gets home before me.'

'I looked him up in the phone book,' said Martin. 'I take it he's the H. R. Brown at 54 Fortis Green Lane?'

She hesitated momentarily, then nodded. 'His first name,' she said, 'is Harold, only he prefers his second name and Russell Brown sounds better for an author.'

'And I used to wonder all the time why you wouldn't let me take you home. I thought you might be ashamed of your home or even have an angry father. I thought you couldn't be more than twenty.'

'I'm twenty-six.'

'Oh, don't cry,' said Martin. 'Have some wine. Crying isn't going to help.'

Neither of them could eat much. Francesca picked at her kebab and pushed it away. Her deep brown glowing eyes held a kind of feverish despair and she gave a little sob. Up till then he had felt only anger and bitterness. A pang of pity made him lay his own hand gently on hers. She bit her lip.

'I'm sorry, Martin. I shouldn't have gone out with you last week, but I did want to, I wanted some fun. I'm not going to indulge in a lot of self-pity, but I don't have much fun. And then – then it wasn't just fun any more.' He felt a tremor of delight and terror. Hadn't she just admitted she loved him? 'Russell came home on Friday, and on Monday he said he'd had this phone call from the *Post* about his book. I knew they'd put something in the paper and I knew you'd see it.'

'I suppose you love him, don't you? You're happy, you and Russell and Lindsay and the Black Death?' Wretchedness had brought out a grim wit in him and he smiled a faint ironical smile.

'Let's go,' she said. 'Let's go back to your place, Martin.'

In the car he didn't speak to her. So this is what it's like, he thought, this is what it had been like for all those men he had heard of and read about and even known who had fallen in love with married women. Clandestine meetings, deception, a somehow dirty feeling of being traitorous and corrupt. And at the end of it a bitter parting with ugly recriminations or else divorce and re-marriage in some High Street registrar's office to an experience-ravaged girl with a ready-made family. He knew he was old-fashioned. He had been a schoolboy when the word 'square' was current slang, but even then he had known he was and always would be, square. A thickset square-shouldered man with a square forehead and a square jaw and a square outlook on life. Rectangular, tetragonal, square, conventional, conservative and reactionary. The revolution in morals which had taken place during his adolescence had passed over him and left him as subject to the old order as if he had actually spent a lifetime under its regime. He would have liked to be married to a virgin in church. What he certainly wasn't going to do, he thought as he drove up to Cromwell Court, was have an affair with Francesca, with Mrs Russell Brown, embroil himself in that kind of sordidness and vain excitement and – disgrace. They must part, and at once. He helped her from the car and stood for a moment holding her arm in the raw frosty cold.

The place looked strangely bare without the chrysanthemums, as a room does when it has been stripped of its Christmas decorations. He drew the curtains to shut out the purplish starry sky and the city that lay like a spangled cloth below. Francesca sat on the edge of her chair, watching him move about the room. He remembered that last week he had thought there was something childlike about her. That had been in the days of her supposed innocence and it was all gone now. She was as old as he. Under her eyes were the shadows of tiredness and suffering and her cheeks were pale. He glanced down at her hands which she was twisting in her lap.

'You can put your wedding ring on again tomorrow,' he said bitterly.

She said in a very low voice, not much above a whisper, 'I never wear it.'

'You still haven't told me where he thinks you are.'

'At Annabel's, the girl who lives in Frognal, the one I see on Mondays. Martin, I thought we could – I thought we could sometimes meet on Mondays.'

He went over to the drinks cabinet and poured himself some brandy. He held up the bottle. 'For you?'

'No, I don't want anything. I thought Mondays and – and Saturday afternoons, if you like. Russell always goes to White Hart Lane when Spurs play at home.'

He almost laughed. 'You know all about it, don't you? How many have there been before me?'

She shrank as if he had made to strike her. 'There haven't been any at all.' She had a way of speaking very simply and directly, without artifice. It was partly because of this, that, like him, she had no sharp wit, no gift of repartee, that he had begun to love her. Begun, only begun, he must remember that. Caution, be my friend!

'We aren't going to see each other any more, Francesca. We've only known each other two weeks and that means we can part now without really getting hurt. I think I must have been a bit crazy, the way I went on last week, but there's no harm done, is there? I'm not going to come between husband and wife. We'll forget each other in a little while and I know that's the best thing. I wish you hadn't – well, led me on, but I expect you couldn't help yourself.' Martin came breathlessly to the end of this speech, drank down the rest of his brandy and recalled from an ancient film a phrase he had thought funny at the time. He brought it out facetiously with a bold smile. 'I was just a mad, impetuous fool!'

She looked at him sombrely. 'I shan't forget you,' she said. 'Don't you know I'm in love with you?'

No one had ever made that confession to him before. He felt himself turn pale, the blood recede from his face.

'I think I loved you the day I brought those horrible flowers and you said –' her voice trembled '– that no one sends flowers to men unless they're ill.'

'We're going to say good-bye now, Francesca, and I'm going to put you in a taxi and you're going home to Russell and Lindsay. And in a year's time I'll come and buy some flowers from you and you'll have forgotten who I am.'

He pulled her gently to her feet. She was limp and passive, yet clinging. She subsided clingingly against him so that the whole length of her body was pressed softly to his and her hands tremulously on either side of his face.

'Don't send me away, Martin. I can't bear it.'

He was aware of thinking that this was his last chance to keep clear of the involvement he dreaded. Summon up the strength now and he would be a free man. But he longed also to be loved, not so much for sex as for love. He was aware of that and then of very little more that might be said to belong to the intellect. His open lips were on her open lips and his hands were discovering her. He and she had descended somehow to the cushions of the sofa and her white arm, now bare, was reaching up to turn off the lamp.

Martin hadn't much experience of love-making. There had been a girl at the LSE and a girl he had met at a party at the Vowchurches' and a girl who had picked him up on the beach at Sitges. There had been other girls too, but only with these three had he actually had sexual relations. He had found it, he brought himself to confess, to himself only, disappointing. Something was missing, something that books and plays and other people's experience had led him to expect. Surely there should be more to it than just a blind unthinking need beforehand and afterwards nothing more than the same sense of relief as a sneeze gives or a drink of cold water down a thirsty throat?

With Francesca it wasn't like that. Perhaps it was because he loved her and he hadn't loved those others. It must be that. He had done nothing different and it couldn't have been any great skill or expertise on her part. She had whispered to him that he was the only man apart from Russell. Before Russell there had been no one and for a long time now Russell had scarcely touched her. She was married and she had a child but still she was nearly as innocent as Martin would have had her be.

She slept beside him that night. At eleven she phoned Russell and told him she would be staying the night with Annabel because of the fog. Martin heard the murmur of a man's voice answering her truculently. It was only the second time in his life he had been in bed all night with a woman. On an impulse he told her so and she put her arms round him, holding him close to her.

In the morning he looked once more at that copy of the *Post* with its cover photograph of the path from the railway bridge to Nassington Road and, on the inside, the paragraph about Russell Brown. It seemed a hundred years since he had first read it, had underlined that emotive name and inserted, after a feverish scanning of the phone book, the number of her house in Fortis Green Lane. He put the paper on top of the neat pile of tabloids on the floor of the kitchen cupboard and the *Daily Telegraph* on the pile of broadsheets. Later, walking up the hill with Francesca – she refused to let him drive her – he called into the newsagent's and cancelled the *Post*. Why had he ever bothered to take a local paper? Only, surely, because of knowing Tim Sage.

Martin hadn't expected to see Francesca again that weekend, he didn't even really mind that, but he had somehow taken it for granted that now they would meet every evening. He was very taken aback when she phoned him on Monday morning to say she wouldn't be able to see him that night, Lindsay had a bad cold, and perhaps they could see each other in a week's time. He was obliged to wait, phoning her every day, very aware of that other life she led with a husband and a little child, yet scarcely able to believe in its reality.

Nothing could have brought that reality more forcefully home to him than Lindsay herself. On the first Saturday afternoon Russell went off to football and she was able to get away she brought Lindsay with her.

'Oh, Martin, I'm so sorry. I had to bring her. If I hadn't I couldn't have come myself.'

She was a beautiful little girl, anyone would have thought that. She was dark like her mother but otherwise not much like her, their beauty being of two very distinct kinds. Francesca had a high colour and fine pointed features, hair that waved along its length and curled at its tips, and her eyes were brown. Lindsay's eyes were bright blue, her skin almost olive, her mouth like the bud of a red flower, a camellia or azalea perhaps, from her mother's shop. Because her straight, almost black, hair was precociously long, she looked older than she was. To Martin it seemed for a moment as if the face beside Francesca's smiling apologetic face was that of an aggressive adolescent. And then Francesa was stripping off coat and woolly scarf and it was a baby that emerged, a walking doll not three feet high.

Lindsay ran about examining and handling the Swedish crystal. Martin's heart was in his mouth, but he scolded himself inwardly for turning so young into an old bachelor. If he was like this now, how would he be when he had children of his own, when he and Francesca had children of their own? Lindsay began turning all his books out of the bookcase and throwing them on the floor. It surprised Martin that Francesca kissed him in front of Lindsay and let him hold her hand and sat with her head on his shoulder. It surprised and slightly embarrassed him too, for Lindsay had so far only uttered one sentence, though that frequently and in a calm conversational tone.

'I want to see my Daddy.'

Martin looked at Francesca to see how she took this, but even when Lindsay had repeated it at least ten times Francesca only smiled vaguely and she continued to give Martin butterfly kisses. It's because she doesn't mind Russell knowing, Martin thought and he felt elated, it's because she knows now that her marriage is over.

Then a rather curious thing happened.

Martin had been saying rather gloomily that he supposed they wouldn't be able to meet much over Christmas.

'No, but I've got something nice to tell you, darling.' Francesca's eyes sparkled. 'I'll be able to come and stay the whole New Year weekend with you – if you'd like that.'

'If I'd like it! It's the most wonderful Christmas present you could give me.'

'Russell's taking her to his parents in Cambridge for the weekend.'

Lindsay came over and climbed on her mother's knee and put her hand over her mother's mouth and said:

'We'll go home now.'

Martin said, 'I thought you said his parents lived in Oxford. That week we met, I thought you said he had taken Lindsay to his parents in Oxford.'

Francesca opened her mouth to speak and Lindsay pinched her lips together. 'We'll go home now, we'll go home now,' Lindsay chanted. 'I want to see my Daddy.'

Lifting Lindsay, Francesca stood up. 'I'll have to take her home, Martin, or we could all go for a walk. Oh, don't do that, Lindsay, don't be so *awful.*' She turned on Martin her direct and transparently honest gaze. 'Russell's parents live in Cambridge, Martin. I'm afraid it's you who got it wrong. One always does associate those two places, don't you think? That's why you got confused.'

She wouldn't let him drive them home but insisted on a taxi.

On Saturday, December 16, Mrs Bhavnani and Suma flew to Sydney and Martin, after drinks in the Flask with Norman Tremlett, did his Christmas shopping. He bought six rose bushes for his father, My Choice, Duke of Windsor, Peace, Golden Showers, and Super Star twice, eau de toilette *Rive Gauche* for his mother, a box of handerchiefs embroidered with blue and yellow flowers for Caroline, and for the Vowchurches, who had invited him on Boxing Day, a macramé hanging plant container. Mr Cochrane would get a ten-pound note. There was no one else to buy for, except Francesca.

This was difficult. He had never seen her wear jewellery so presumably she didn't like it. He couldn't buy her clothes when he didn't know her size or perfume since he didn't know her taste. At last he found two cut-glass scent bottles with silver stoppers in an antique shop and paid thirty pounds for them.

On Sunday he had lunch with his parents. Secretly, so that his father shouldn't observe them, his mother showed him the current *North London Post*. The front page lead was headed *Miracle Op for Hornsey Boy* and there was a photograph of Mr and Mrs Bhavnani with Suma, the three of them posed, evidently several years before, in a very Victorian way in a photographer's studio. Mrs Bhavnani, wearing a sari, was sitting in a carved chair with the boy standing at her knees and her husband behind her.

'It's some relative told the paper,' whispered Mrs Urban. 'Look, it says the money was raised by a customer of the shop who wants to remain anonymous.'

Martin saw that the by-line was Tim's. It was a month now since he had seen Tim. Ought he to give him a ring and arrange to see him at Christmas?

He would be going for a drink with Norman Tremlett on Christmas Eve and to supper with Gordon and Alice Tytherton on Christmas night. Christmas was a time when you made a point of seeing your close friends, and Tim had seemed a closer friend than either Norman or the Tythertons. Had seemed. Martin couldn't remember that there had ever, since that encounter in the wood in May, been such a long time go by without their seeing each other. He had read somewhere that we dislike those whom we have injured but that seemed absurd to him. Surely we should dislike those who injure us? Perhaps both were true. Anyway, you couldn't say he had *injured* Tim by not going to his dinner party. No, it was *he* who had taken rightful offence at Tim's sarcasm and reproaches. So what if they had made him come to dislike Tim? Tim was a dangerous companion, anyway, and not likely to get on with Francesca.

Mr Cochrane didn't come on the Friday before Christmas. He phoned, waking Martin up, at five minutes to six in the morning to say his sister-in-law was about to be taken away to what he called a nursing home. He intended to go with her in the ambulance. Martin wondered if this accounted for Mrs Cochrane's failure to reply to his letter. Perhaps. It couldn't, however, explain why Miss Watson hadn't written again or phoned or why he had had no acknowledgement of his cheque from Mr Deepdene.

9

The police came and talked to Finn. He was one of the last people to have seen Anne Blake alive. Her friends in Nassington Road had told them that. Finn said he had left the house in Modena Road at half-past four, soon after she had come in, and had driven straight home. They seemed satisfied, they seemed to believe him. Finn thought how different things might have been if one of the officers, that middle-aged detective sergeant for instance, had happened to have been involved in the investigation into Queenie's death eleven years before. But no one connected the carpenter and electrician of Lord Arthur Road with the fifteen-year-old white-headed boy who had been in the house in Hornsey when another woman was beaten to death. Finn wasn't frightened of the police, anyway. His fear was for his mother.

Lena's reading glasses were ready for her within a week. By that time the Parliament Hill Fields murder had retreated to the inside pages but Finn was afraid of some old copy of a newspaper falling into her hands. Such a one might be stuffed into the toes of a bargain pair of shoes or used to wrap a scented candle. When Lena set off for the shops, made stout by layers of coats and a lagging of stoles, a Korean straw basket in one hand and a greengrocer's net in the other, he watched her with a pang. He couldn't understand the impulse that had made him slaughter Anne Blake out there in the open, when he might so easily have waited till the next day and achieved an accident. How was he going to master others and control destinies when he couldn't yet master himself?

He had waited in daily expectation for the balance of the payment to come, for one of those olive-faced children to appear with a parcel. It was Christmas before that happened. The eldest boy brought the money wrapped in red paper with holly leaves on it and secured with silver sellotape. Finn's pale glazed eyes and skeletal frame in a dirty white robe frightened him, he muttered something about Dad having had 'flu and now pneumonia, and fled.

Finn peeled off the red paper, not much amused by Kaiafas's idea of a joke. Underneath, before he reached the Mr Kipling jam tart box in which the money was packed, was an inner wrapping of newspaper, the *Daily Mirror*, November 28, with a picture of the path and the grove of trees where Anne Blake had died. Finn tore it to pieces and burnt it as he had burnt Anne Blake's money and cheque book and credit cards.

The money was correct, two hundred and fifty ten-pound notes. No one would come robbing him, he was the last person. They were wary of him in the neighbourhood since he had roughed up those squatters for Kaiafas. Kneeling on the floor, tucking the money into a plastic carrier under his mattress, he heard Lena pass his door. She was chattering away, there was someone with her. Mrs Gogarty, maybe, or old Bradley whose daughter-in-law locked him out of the house while she was at work so that he had to take refuge in the library or with Lena. Finn listened, slightly smiling. She had a host of friends, she wasn't like him, she could love people. She had even loved Queenie . . .

Lena had been over forty when Finn was born. She had never supposed she would have a child and her husband was dying of Addison's disease. The baby she named Theodore after the dead man, which he was destined never to be called except by schoolteachers. For Lena he needed no name, speaking to him summoned a special note into her voice, and to Queenie he was always 'dear'. They went to live with Queenie when Finn was six months old.

Lena couldn't live alone with a baby. She wasn't strong or self-reliant. Queenie was her first cousin and also a widow, a State Registered Nurse who owned her own house and was fat and practical and seemingly kind.

Queenie's house was in Middle Grove, Hornsey, one of a row of neat, narrow houses on three floors under a slate roof. Finn would have liked to sleep in Lena's room but Queenie said that was silly and wrong when there were four bedrooms. Lena had a small pension from Theodore Finn's employers but it wasn't enough to live on and keep Finn on, so later she went out cleaning for Mrs Urban in Copley Avenue, leaving the child at home with Queenie. It was Queenie's aim and desire, though without intentional cruelty, without really knowing what she was doing, to win Finn's love and make him prefer her over his mother. She knew she would be a better influence on him. She read to him out of *Thomas the Tank Engine* and gave him banana sandwiches for tea and wheeled him round the shops, and when people said 'your little boy' she didn't contradict them.

Lena observed it all with speechless anguish. There was no fight in her, she could only contemplate the theft of her son in passivity and pain. But there was nothing to contemplate, for Finn was not to be won. He wavered for a while, half-seduced by the reading and the sandwiches, and then he returned quietly to his mother, creeping into her bedroom at night, finding his way in the dark.

When he was thirteen the poltergeists started. Lena, who was psychic, believed that they were spirits but Finn knew better. Sometimes he could feel the energy coursing through his veins like electricity along wires, charging his muscles and raying out through his finger ends. Lena saw his aura for the first time. It was golden-orange like the rising sun. He was aware of his brain waves, of a surplus of power.

One day all the plates in Queenie's china cupboard rattled down off the shelves and a lot of them smashed. Another time a brick came flying through the kitchen window, and in the same hour the framed photograph of Queenie in her Staff Nurse's uniform, wearing her SRN badge, fell down off the wall and the glass cracked.

Queenie said Finn was responsible, he was doing it himself, though even she couldn't explain how he had brought into the house a rockery stone no one could lift an inch off the ground. The poltergeists went away soon after he started smoking the hashish and when they were gone he regretted them bitterly, praying for their return to any god or spirit or seer he came across in his reading. But they had deserted him. He decided to kill Queenie.

There were a number of reasons for this. He was afraid of her mockery and alarmed at her distaste for his pursuits. She had burned a book of his about the Rosicrucians. He also wanted to know how it would feel to have killed, and he saw killing as a fire baptism into the kind of life he wanted to lead and the kind of person he wanted to be. Queenie was the obvious choice for victim, ugly, stupid, unsympathetic, one who had never begun to see the light, a young soul. And she had a house which she had said, over and over again, she would leave to Lena. Brenda, her daughter, who lived in Newcastle, she never saw and got nothing from but a card at Christmas. Finn couldn't understand why his mother wanted a house of her own but she did want one, and Finn thought she had a better right to one than Queenie.

He carried the dream of killing her about with him for two

years, but when he actually did the deed it happened spontaneously, almost by chance. One night Queenie awakened him and Lena, saying she had heard someone in the house downstairs. It was springtime, three in the morning. Finn went down with Queenie. There was no one there, though a window was open and some money, about seven pounds in notes and change, had been taken out of a tin in one of the kitchen cupboards. Queenie was carrying the poker they used for riddling out the slow-burning stove in the living room.

'Give me that,' Finn said.

'What d'you want it for?'

'Just to try something out.'

She handed it to him and turned her back to look for her rings, the wedding band and the engagement ring, which each night she took off and dropped into a glass dish on the mantelpiece. Finn raised the poker and struck her on the back of the head. She made a terrible sound, an unnerving, groaning wail. He struck her again and again until she was silent and lying in a big, huddled, bloody heap. He let the poker fall and turned round slowly and saw Lena standing in the doorway.

Lena was trembling at the sight of the blood. Her teeth were chattering and she kept making little whimpering whistling sounds. But she took hold of him with her shaking hands and made him wash himself, and she took away his pyjama trousers and his vest, which were all he had been wearing, and stuffed them into the stove among the glowing nuggets of coke. She washed the poker herself. She made Finn put on clean pyjamas and get into bed and feign sleep and then she went out and got the people next door to phone the police. When they came Finn was really asleep, he was never even suspected.

It pushed Lena over the edge of sanity. She had been teetering there for long enough. 'Spontaneous schizophrenia' was what Finn heard a doctor say. That was in the hospital where they had taken her after she had been found going into butchers' shops and crying out that they sold human flesh. She went into the shops and then she walked into the Archway Road and lay down in the middle of the road and cried out to the motorists to kill her.

And they hadn't got the house after all. There was no

will, so it went to Brenda who let them go on living there for just six months. Finn never went back to school after Queenie died, and in the depths of the winter after his sixteenth birthday they moved into Lord Arthur Road, she into her top floor warren, he into this room.

He stood inside the door, listening to the ascending steps and to Mr Bradley's thin broken voice croaking over and over, 'God bless your kind heart, my darling, God bless your kind heart.' After a while Finn went down to the street where he phoned Kaiafas at home from the call box on the corner of Somerset Grove. He needed employment, he hadn't done a job of work since patching up the Frazers' bay.

Kaiafas suggested a meeting at Jack Straw's Castle. That was half-way between their homes, he said, and he coughed piteously into the phone. The meeting was for a long way ahead, two days after Christmas, but Finn couldn't argue, for Kaiafas claimed still to be bed-bound.

The air was charged with frost and the melted snow had frozen again when he went off to Hampstead to keep his date with Kaiafas. Lena wasn't yet back from some trip she had gone on with Mrs Gogarty. There was a waxing moon that hung up over Highbury, greenish white in a fuzz of mist, and a fine snow was falling, tiny hard pellets of snow that burned when they touched the skin. Up on the Heath, the highest you could get above London and still be in it, an east wind was blowing and the broken and re-frozen ice on the Whitestone Pond made it look like a shallow quarry of granite.

The saloon bar in Jack Straw's was half empty. Finn sat down to wait for Kaiafas. He wasn't going to buy himself a drink, wasting money for form's sake. There was only one person in there that he knew and then only by sight. This was the *Post* reporter, a dark man as thin as himself with black hair and a red mouth, whom Finn had often seen conducting a one-man investigation into stories of maltreatment and terrorization of tenants in Lord Arthur Road. The reporter hadn't got very far. The people he interviewed didn't think it worth their while to talk to the police, let alone a newspaper.

Finn watched him. He was talking to a pompous-looking fat man, writing something in a notebook, stubbing out a cigarette. Finn concentrated on him and tried by the power of thought to make him light another cigarette. What hadn't worked on the woman with the iron, worked immediately on the reporter. Finn felt pleased with himself. Then Kaiafas came in. Kaiafas had a wrinkled, seamed face like an old leather bag and eyes like muscatels. When out for the evening he always wore pale-coloured suits of some smooth cloth with a glistening sheen to it. Tonight the suit was silvery blue but Kaiafas had a black sheepskin coat over it with a black fur collar into which he huddled his paler-than-usual face.

'What will you drink, Feen?'

'Pineapple juice,' said Finn. 'The Britvic.'

Kaiafas began to talk of Anne Blake as if Finn had had nothing to do with her death, as if indeed he might not know of her death, but he did so with numerous nudges and winks.

'The rent she pay me, Feen, she could afford have a car, but no, she must go walking in these lonesome places, in the dark. So here we have the result.' Kaiafas had a way of wagging a finger at whomsoever might be his companion. 'She have some good furniture. Antiques. Her sister come and take them all away.' He sounded regretful.

'Well, well,' said Finn.

Kaiafas nudged him. 'An ill wind that blows nobody no good, eh?' He chortled a little which made him cough. Finn didn't ask him how he was, it wasn't the kind of question he ever asked of anyone. 'Another one of those pineapples?' said Kaiafas.

Finn nodded.

'With a drop vodka this time, no?'

'No,' said Finn. 'You know I don't drink.'

'So. Now how about you do a nice decorating job for me, Feen? Paint out the house, do the re-wire and put down a nice bit of carpet I got fall off the back of a Pickford's?'

Finn said he would and drank his second pineapple juice. They talked about it for a while and then Finn left. In Lord Arthur Road he parked the van in the same troughs of frozen grey snow from which he had taken it out. As soon as he entered the house, he knew there was something wrong, he could smell it. He went upstairs in the manner of an animal that keeps climbing though it knows there may be a trap or a predator at the top.

Half-way up the flight between his room and Lena's Mrs Gogarty was waiting for him. She was bending over the banisters so that he saw her white moon face searching for him, hovering over the deep stairwell before he reached his own floor. He came on more quickly and Mrs Gogarty clutched him, holding fistfuls of his clothes. Her face worked, her voice was a croak and she could hardly speak. Mrs Gogarty was afraid of almost everything the natural world held, of enclosed places and open spaces, of spiders and mice and cats, of crowds, of loneliness, of sudden noise, of silence, but she was rather less afraid of insanity than most people are. She had seen so much of it. As they came to the door of Lena's room he managed to get the story out of her.

She and Lena had been to a sale-and-exchange clothes market in Hampstead, in Fleet Road, and coming away from it to catch a bus, had seen a notice attached to a lamp-post which had frightened Lena. Finn wanted to know what sort of notice and Mrs Gogarty could only say over and over, 'The murder, the murder,' but that was enough to make all clear to him. Lena had seen one of the police notices enquiring for information leading to the arrest of the Parliament Hill Fields murderer. No doubt they were posted up all over the area between Hampstead Heath and Gospel Oak stations.

'What happened?' he whispered.

'She shouted out you'd done it. Him? I said, your lovely boy? But words are wind. There weren't so many people, thank God. A taxi came, I got a taxi, but I don't know how I got her in it. I had to hold on to her in the taxi. She's little but she's strong when she's like that.'

'Where is she now?'

'In there,' said Mrs Gogarty, trembling. 'Crouched down like a tiger. She said you'd done the murder and then she said not to send her away. I knew what that meant, I promised not *that*.'

Finn said, 'Wait a minute,' and went down and into his own room. From the back of the bookshelf, behind *Beelzebub's Tales*, he took a glass jar that contained his hypodermic and his ampoules of chlorpromazine. Give her a big dose, fifty milligrams – or seventy-five? Finn had no friends but he had acquaintances who could get him anything. Mrs

Gogarty was still outside Lena's door, her face quivering and tears now shining in the corners of her not quite symmetrical blue eyes.

Finn opened the door and walked across the tiny kitchen. He stood in the doorway of the partition he had made. Lena was crouched in the armchair under the budgerigar's cage, her legs flexed under her, her hands up to her head. When she saw Finn she sprang. She sprang at him and at his throat, holding on to his neck and pressing her thumbs in.

Mrs Gogarty gave a little cry and shut the door and subsided against it like a flung cushion. Finn staggered under his mother's stranglehold. He got his hands under her fingers which had become like steel clasps and he forced her arms down and held her turned from him, one hand holding her wrists, the other arm hooked under her jaw. She was champing now, grinding her teeth, murmuring meaninglessly, 'Take me home, I want to go home.' Finn didn't dare let her go. He knew she would attack him again, for she no longer knew who she was or he was or where they were. He said to Mrs Gogarty:

'You do it.'

She came fearfully to take the syringe, but she had seen it done often enough before, had had it done to herself. Finn could have used a straitjacket but he balked at anything of the sort. He held her until the drug made her limp and then he lifted her up and laid her on the bed in the diminutive bedroom.

'The picture of devotion,' mumbled Mrs Gogarty. 'The very picture.'

'Can you get home on your own OK?'

The big white face quivered in a nod.

'Won't mind the dark?'

'It's been dark,' she said, 'since four,' and she held up for his inspection an amulet she wore round her neck. It wasn't on account of marauders or the glassy pavements that the dark menaced her.

Finn covered Lena up and stayed with her through the night. Before dawn he gave her another injection and she lay quiet and almost without breath as if she were already dead. He didn't know what a doctor would have given her and he wasn't going to call one. A doctor would want to have Lena committed and he wasn't having that, besides listening curiously to her ravings about murder.

These began again in the morning. It was far too late for Finn to produce any trumped-up proofs to exonerate himself. She didn't know him. He wasn't her son but the fiend who had killed Queenie and who had killed since then a hundred women. She screamed so loudly that one of the people from downstairs came up and said he was calling the police if it didn't stop.

Finn got hot milk with phenobarbitone in it down her throat. Because it didn't work at once he forced brandy into her. He was terrified he might overdo it and kill her, but he had to silence those cries. They had been through so much together, he and she, fighting the world, exploring the unseen, approaching strange spiritual agents. She cried herself to sleep and he sat beside her, looking inscrutably at that pale twisted face, holding her big veined hand in his big hand, the nearest he had ever got to tenderness with a living creature.

On the Sunday she walked round and round the room, feeling up the walls with her fingertips as if she were blind, lifting every ornament and feeling it and sniffing it. When she was asleep he took the bird and birdcage down to his room. She would kill the bird, twist it to death in her strong hands as she had the last one, and then break her heart over its death. He gave her phenobarbitone every day until her eyes focussed again and rested on him and a voice that was more or less normal came out of her cracked and swollen lips.

'Don't let them take me away.'

'Come on,' said Finn. 'Would I?'

She cried and she couldn't stop. She cried for hours, tossing this way and that, burying her face in her hands, throwing her head back and forward, crying until it seemed that all the madness had been washed away in tears.

10

'Three cheers for the Three Musketeers!' said Norman Tremlett, waving and slightly spilling his gin and tonic.

He had said this every Christmas for the past ten years and probably would say it every Christmas for the rest of his life if given the opportunity. He referred, of course, to himself, Martin and Adrian Vowchurch. Adrian smiled his thin, tolerant, resigned smile at Norman and handed him a dish of Japanese rice crackers. Although these had been available as cocktail snacks almost as long as Martin (and therefore Norman too) could remember, Norman affected to find them an extremely *avant-garde* novelty, examined them clownishly and expressed as his opinion that they were really made out of insects. Everyone knew the Japanese ate insects. His own father had been offered chocolate-covered ants while in Tokyo on a business trip.

Norman always behaved like this at parties. Nobody minded because he was basically so kind and good-natured. He and Adrian and Martin had been at school together and each, in his particular field, had later entered his father's firm. Norman was a surveyor and Adrian a solicitor. Norman, as well as his Three Musketeers joke, sometimes called them the Triumvirate. It gave Martin considerable deep pleasure and a feeling of power to think that his closest friends were his solicitor and his surveyor and he was sure they felt the same about him being their accountant. He handled the Tremlett and Vowchurch financial affairs and when he had bought his flat, Norman had made the preliminary survey and Adrian had handled the conveyance.

Of the three of them only Adrian had so far married. Because of Francesca, Martin felt closer to him this year than he had done for a long time. Adrian had married a girl with a lot of family money and they lived in a smart little house in Barnsbury. They gave the sort of parties Martin liked, not too many people and nearly all people one knew, proper drinks not plonk, not a buffet meal but a real one with courses. There wasn't any loud music or dancing and the guests stood around in groups talking. Martin couldn't help thinking that Tim would probably be having a Christmas party and that it would be very different from this one, dark, noisy and with goings-on it was better not to think of. Finding himself briefly alone with Adrian, Martin said on an impulse:

'There's a girl I'd like to bring to meet you and Julie – next time you have a party.'

'That'll be for Julie's birthday in March,' his thin face taking on the sharp intense look it did when he was pleased. 'It's serious?'

'About as serious as could be.' Martin looked over his shoulder. 'She has to get a divorce, she'll want to . . .' He was breaking their rule about never consulting each other on social occasions. 'Well, I'll get her to come along and see you, shall I?'

Adrian said very sympathetically, 'Anything I can do to help, you know that. And Martin – congratulations, I'm awfully glad.'

Congratulations seemed a bit premature. They had only known each other for a month. But he was sure, he was certain that no one else would ever suit him as Francesca did. And if, before he could get her entirely as his own, there had to be a divorce and sordidness and haggling over property and maybe trouble with his family, well – he must go through it and endure it, knowing it was all worth while with Francesca at the end of it.

Russell was to take Lindsay to Cambridge by train on Friday evening, having first collected her from the nursery. Martin was going to pick Francesca up at the shop. He had wondered several times why he had queried her saying that Russell's parents lived in Cambridge. Of course she must know where her own parents-in-law lived. It must have sounded to her as if he doubted her, as if he thought she had been lying. When he phoned her at the shop he apologized for what he had said, he couldn't imagine why he had thought they lived in Oxford, he didn't want her to think he was accusing her of any sort of deception. Francesca only laughed and said she had forgotten all about it, she hadn't been in the least upset.

The weather had been growing steadily colder since Christmas, it had snowed and thawed and frozen. Mr Cochrane, wearing a fur hat that made him look like a bespectacled Brezhnev, arrived late for him, at twenty-five to nine, announcing bitterly that he had fallen over on the ice and thought he had broken his arm. However, since he had intercepted the postman and was holding a letter in his right hand and his attaché case in his left, Martin decided he must be exaggerating. Mr Cochrane made a sling for his arm out of his woolly scarf. He didn't mention his sister-in-law beyond uttering the single word 'Terrible!' when Martin asked after her. He made a disgusted reconnaissance of the flat, running his fingers through dust on the woodwork and muttering that some folks were useless when they had to look after themselves. Martin took no notice. He was reading the letter.

Dear Mr Urban,
I am very sad to have to tell you that my father died on December 11. He seemed quite well and in good spirits the previous evening but was found dead in his armchair when the home help came in at nine. Apparently he had just been going through his post and your cheque was found beside him. I am at a loss to know why you should have sent my father a cheque for what seems an enormous sum to me, but I am returning it with apologies for not having sent it back sooner.
Yours sincerely,
Judith Lewis.

Martin was horrified. Had he, in effect, killed poor Mr Deepdene with kindness? It rather looked like it. Mr Deepdene had been seventy-four and perhaps his heart hadn't been very sound, and although he had known the money was coming, the actual arrival of the cheque would be a different matter from hopeful, perhaps doubtful, anticipation of it. Martin imagined him opening the envelope, taking out the brief one-line note, then the cheque, and his aged, tired heart suddenly – what exactly *did* happen in a heart attack? Well, whatever it was, his heart failing and stopping with the wonderful, unbelievable shock of it, his body falling back into the armchair, the cheque fluttering from his lifeless hand . . .

'You want to mind how you go on that ice, Martin,' shouted Mr Cochrane above the vacuum cleaner. 'You want to watch your step, it's very treacherous, look at my arm. I reckon I've dislocated something, put something out, so don't be surprised if I don't turn up next week, Martin.'

The death of Mr Deepdene troubled Martin for most of the day. A client, an up-and-coming country singer, took him out to lunch but he didn't really enjoy himself and he didn't feel he was being very lucid as he tried to explain, over coffee, why the cost of setting up a music room in the singer's Hampstead home might be tax deductible while a swimming pool certainly would not be. He kept imagining Mr Deepdene, whom he saw as small and bent and frail, reading the sum delineated on that cheque and then the pain thundering up his arm and his chest.

Was he wrong to do what he was doing or attempting to do? Was he playing God without the wisdom and experience essential to a god? All he had done with his philanthropy so far, it seemed to him, was to frighten an old woman into insomnia and shock an old man to death. There was, of course, Suma Bhavnani, but for all he knew Suma Bhavnani might have died on the operating table. Yet surely his project was so simple, just to provide homes for a handful of needy people who suffered particularly from London's housing shortage. He wrote a letter of sympathy to Judith Lewis and that made him feel better – or perhaps it was knowing that in an hour he would be with Francesca which made him feel better. Mr Deepdene, after all, might well have had a heart attack whether he had sent him a cheque or not. He was old, past his three score and ten, and it was what people called a lovely way to go, dying like that in the midst of life . . .

Floreal was glowing with flame-coloured light, its window banked with pots of pink cyclamen. Francesca came out to him, wearing the rose velvet dress. She must have just changed, after the other girl had gone, especially for him. If it could be said that Martin disliked anything at all about Francesca, it was her clothes. Most of the time she wore jeans, flounced skirts with hems that dipped, shapeless tunics, 'antique' blouses, shawls, big loose cardigans, scarves with fringes. She dressed like the hippies used to, a pair of scuffed seven-league boots poking out under a skirt of wilted flower-sprigged cotton. These things couldn't spoil her beauty, they merely disguised it. But in the pink velvet her beauty was enhanced, you could see the fragile wand-like shape of her, her tiny waist, her long legs, and the rose colour was exactly that of her cheeks. She put her arms round him and kissed him with tenderness.

As soon as they were in the flat he gave her her Christmas present. The cut-glass bottles with the silver stoppers had come to seem inadequate somehow, so after lunch with the country singer he had bought some *Ma Griffe* cologne with which to fill them. It was odd, but although she admired the bottles and said they were pretty, beautiful really, she'd never seen anything so delicate, he sensed that she was disappointed. He asked her directly but she said no, not a bit, it was just that she hadn't got anything for him and she felt bad about that.

After they had had dinner – steaks which he grilled and a salad which she made – he asked her if Russell would expect her to phone him but she said she and Russell had had a violent quarrel and weren't on speaking terms.

'It was about you, Martin. I told him I was in love with someone else.'

Martin held her hands. She came closer to him on the sofa and laid her head on his shoulder. 'You're going to leave him and get a divorce and marry me, aren't you?'

'I want to, I don't know . . .'

'There's nothing to stop you. I love you and you say you love me . . .'

'I do love you, Martin!'

'You could stay here. We could go up there tomorrow and fetch your things and you need never go back there again.'

She said nothing but put her arms round him. Later, in the bedroom, he watched her undress. She seemed to have no self-consciousness about this, no false modesty, and no desire provocatively to show off. She undressed rather slowly and concentratedly, like a young child. Her body was extraordinarily white for someone with such dark hair and eyes, her waist a narrow stem, her ankles and feet finely turned. She managed to be extravagantly thin, yet curvy and without angularity. He thought of fairy girls in Arthur Rackham drawings – and then, laying her clothes on a chair, she turned her left side to him.

Her upper arm was badly bruised and there was a kind of red contusion on her forearm. But that was as nothing to the bruising on her hip, black and blue and swollen, and all down the side of her thigh to her knee.

'Francesca . . . !'

He could tell she wished he hadn't seen. She tried ineffectively to cover her body with her arms.

'How on earth did that happen to you?' The explanation would never have occurred to him, he had never lived in that sort of world, if he hadn't seen the ashamed misery in her eyes and remembered what she had said about a quarrel. 'You don't mean that Russell . . . ?'

She nodded. 'It's not the first time. But this – this was the worst.'

He took her very gently in his arms and held the bruised body close to his. 'You must come to me,' he murmured. 'You must leave him, you must never go back.'

But on the following day she wouldn't let him fetch her things from the house in Fortis Green Lane. At the end of the weekend she must go home again as they had arranged, she must be home before Russell and Lindsay returned. Martin didn't persist. The last thing he wanted was to spoil the three precious days they had together. On Saturday afternoon they went shopping in Hampstead. Martin had never before been round dress shops with a woman and he found it boring and alarming, both at the same time. Francesca admired extravagantly a coat and dress in grey suede, a pair of tapered pants in cream leather and a dress that seemed quite impractical to Martin, being made of transparent knife-pleated beige chiffon. Francesca didn't notice prices, he knew that, she was naïve about that sort of thing, like a child in a toyshop. It crossed his mind to buy her the coat and dress but then he saw it was three hundred pounds and he didn't have that much in his current account. Besides, what would Russell say – what would Russell *do* – if she brought something like that home with her? In the end, because she looked so wistful, he asked her to let him buy her the little short-sleeved jumper which was the latest thing to catch her fancy. Martin thought fifteen pounds a ridiculous amount to pay for it, but that didn't matter if it made Francesca happy.

They went to the theatre and then to supper at Inigo Jones. Norman Tremlett called in unexpectedly in the morning at about ten-thirty. Francesca had only just got up and she came out of the bathroom in her dressing gown. It was very obvious she had nothing on underneath it. Martin saw with a good deal of pride and pleasure that Norman's eyes were going round in excited circles like a dog's following the movements of a fly. He stayed for coffee. Francesca didn't bother to go and dress. She was quite innocent of the sensation she was causing and sat there talking earnestly about the play they had seen as if Norman were her brother or she wearing a tweed suit and a pair of brogues.

'You're a dark horse,' Norman whispered admiringly as Martin saw him out. 'I never would have thought it of you. D'you often do this sort of thing?'

Deep down, Martin rather loved being treated as a Casanova. But it wasn't right to allow it, it was a reflection on Francesca, on her – well, virtue, if that term still had any meaning today.

'We're going to be married.'

'Are you? Are you really? That's perfectly splendid.' Norman hesitated on the doorstep. 'At the wedding,' he said, 'I suppose – I suppose you'll have Adrian for your best man?'

Martin laughed. 'It won't be that sort of wedding.'

'I see. Right. That's fine. Only if you do need any – well, anyone, you know what I mean – well, you know where to come.'

On New Year's Day, Francesca wore the jumper he had bought her. It showed up the bruises on her arm and she wrapped herself in one of her shawls. At four o'clock she said she ought to go. She would pack her things and go and get a taxi in Highgate High Street. Russell and Lindsay would be home by six at the latest.

'Of course I'm going to drive you home, Francesca.'

'Darling Martin, there's no need, really, there isn't. It's been snowing again and it's bound to freeze tonight and you might have a skid. You don't want to damage your nice car.'

'The taxi might skid and damage nice you. Anyway, I insist on taking you, I'm not going to be put off this time. Russell won't be there to see us arrive if that's what worries you. I'm going to drive you home and if you try to stop me I shall just put you in the car by force. Right?'

'Yes, Martin, of course. I won't argue any more. You're so sweet and kind to me and I'm a horrid ungrateful girl.'

'No, you're not,' he said. 'You're an angel and I love you.'

He had never thought much about the house she lived in but now that he was going to see it, he felt the stirrings of curiosity. He had probably driven along Fortis Green Lane in the past but he couldn't recall it. It was Finchley really, that area, borders of Muswell Hill. While Francesca was packing her case he looked it up in the London Atlas. There was no telling from that whether the district was seedy terraces, luxury suburban or given over to council housing. She came out and he helped her into the blue and red striped coat with the hood.

'If I'd known it was going to be so cold,' she said, 'I'd have brought my fur.' She gave him one of her serious, very young, smiles. 'I've got an old fur coat that was my grandmother's.'

'When we're married I'll buy you a mink. It'll be my wedding present to you.'

He drove up North Hill and into Finchley High Road. Fortis Green Lane ran out of Fortis Green Road towards Colney Hatch Lane. Francesca didn't issue directions, she wasn't that sort of woman. He got the impression, when she was with him, that she was content to let him organize things and steer her life his way. She wasn't so much passive as gracefully yielding. He took a left turn out of Fortis Green Road and they were in the street where she lived.

By now it was growing towards dusk and what daylight remained was clear and blue. Mustard yellow lamps, true opposite in the spectrum to that blue, were coming on in Fortis Green Lane. It was a long wide winding road, disproportionately wide for the small squat houses which lined it. Here and there was a short Victorian terrace, red brick and three storeys high, but the small low houses predominated and eventually took over altogether. They stood in blocks of four, some of brown stucco, some of very pale anaemic-looking brick with small metal-framed windows and shallow pantiled roofs. In their front gardens snow lay on the grass. They weren't bad houses, they weren't slums, but Martin thought he would go to any lengths to avoid living in such a place. He had always, in his heart, despised people who did. Couldn't Russell Brown, who was thirty-five years old and no slouch apparently, a teacher and a writer, have done better for his wife than this? Poor Francesca . . .

Number 54 was the end house of a block, which meant it had a side entrance. It stood on the corner of a side road depressingly called Hill Avenue in which were similar houses stretching away to be lost in the twilight. Their roofs were so low that over the tops of them you could see the branches of trees which Martin guessed must be in Coldfall Wood. He got out of the car and helped Francesca out. There were no lights on in her house. Her husband and child hadn't yet returned. Carrying her suitcase, Martin began to unlatch the small white wrought iron gate.

'You mustn't come in, darling.' She had taken his arm and was looking nervously up into his face.

'Would it matter so much if Russell and I were to meet? We're sure to some day. I'm sure he wouldn't do anything to me.'

'No, but he might do something to me later.'

The truth of this was evident. He had seen the bruises. It wasn't much of a disappointment not seeing the inside of her house. Compared with what he felt about parting from her, not to see her again for perhaps a whole week, it was nothing. He didn't think she would kiss him good-bye with the chance of some neighbour seeing, but she did. Out there in the street she put her arms round his neck and kissed him on the mouth, clinging to him for a moment. But Francesca was like that, too innocent to be aware of the cruelty and malice in other people's hearts.

He got back into the car. She stood there, waving to him, her small bright face made pale by the lamplight, her beautiful hair tucked inside her hood. He turned the car to go back the way he had come and when he looked round again she was gone.

11

Although Martin had confided to Francesca most of what had happened to him in the past, his present circumstances and his hopes for the future, he hadn't said anything about the pools win. He didn't quite know why he hadn't. Perhaps it was because she was still living with her husband. He had a vague half-formed idea of Russell Brown as a thorough-going villain, in spite of his education and his talents. Suppose Francesca told Russell that the man she was in love with had won a hundred thousand pounds on a football pool? If he knew that, Russell might try to extort money from him. Martin thought he would only tell Francesca after she had left Russell and was living here with him in Cromwell Court.

After that weekend he didn't see her again, as he had feared, until the following Monday. On the afternoon of that day Dr Ghopal phoned to say that the operation on Suma Bhavnani had taken place on January 5 and been a complete success. This news had a tonic effect on Martin. Playing God was possible, after all. At lunchtime he had had a sandwich in the Victoria Stakes with Caroline and she had regaled him with a long sad tale about a young couple who were friends of hers and who were paying sixty per cent of their joint wages for the rent of a furnished flat. They had no children and the girl couldn't have children so they wouldn't get a council place, said Caroline, for five years, if then. The furnished flat was four draughty rooms in Friern Barnet. By telling a few white lies about knowing someone who knew someone who might possibly have an unfurnished flat to let in April, Martin managed to get these people's name and address out of Caroline. That night, after he had taken Francesca to dine at the Cellier du Midi and sent her home to Russell in a taxi, he added this new name to his list. It now read: Miss Watson, Mr Deepdene, Mrs Cochrane, Mrs Finn? Richard and Sarah Gibson. He crossed off Mr Deepdene's name, put a question mark after Mrs Cochrane's. Then he composed a letter to the Gibsons, beginning by mentioning the connection through Caroline Arnold and going on to ask if they would care to meet him one evening in the coming week to discuss accommodation he might be able to offer them. It obviously wasn't a good idea baldly to state in the preliminary letter that he was dispensing money in large quantities. Look what an effect that had had on Miss Watson and Mr Deepdene. Better meet and talk about it face to face, which was perhaps what he ought to have done and could still do with Miss Watson.

He hadn't said any more to Francesca about leaving Russell. He had hoped she would say something. Perhaps she hadn't liked to, she was such a self-effacing girl. Next time he saw her, he would insist on their making definite plans. He went about the flat, thinking what it would be like when she was there all the time. He would buy a three-piece suite, of course, and put that cane stuff in the bedroom. Or they could go out on the balcony, they would be an improvement on his two shabby deckchairs. The bathroom ought to be re-carpeted. Francesca would like that, a white carpet with a long pile. And maybe he should buy a wardrobe – the cupboard was full of his own clothes – and a dressing table.

Mr Cochrane would probably make a terrific fuss once he found out Martin was living with a woman. Martin could just imagine his face and his comments. They could always pretend to be married or, come to that, Mr Cochrane could be told to go and Francesca do the housework. Martin didn't want her to work in that flower shop or anywhere else once she had left Russell.

It could only have been a couple of hours after he got Martin's letter that Richard Gibson phoned. He was forthright and he sounded suspicious.

'Look, Mr Urban, Sarah and I have been badly let down about this sort of thing before. If you're really making us a firm offer, that's fine and I'm grateful, but if it's just a possibility or someone else is likely to step in and get the place over our heads – well, we'd rather not know. And I'd better tell you here and now, we can't pay key money or a premium or anything, we haven't got it.'

Martin said the offer was firm and there was no question of key money but he'd rather talk about it when they met. Richard Gibson said any evening in the following week would suit him and the sooner the better, so Martin agreed to go up to Friern Barnet on Monday.

He got back early from the Flask on Saturday because Francesca was coming at two. She got there at five past, wearing the jumper he had bought her and smelling of *Ma Griffe*. He began at once to tell her of his plans for the flat when she came to live with him. When was she going to tell Russell? When would she leave? He supposed that she would want to bring a lot of her other possessions as well as clothes and they would have to . . .

'I can't come and live *here*, Martin.'

She spoke in a small nervous voice and she had begun to twist her hands together in her lap. He stared at her.

'What do you mean, Francesca?'

'I've thought about it a lot, I feel awful about it. But it's not possible. How could we live here? It wouldn't be big enough.'

'Not big enough?' He felt stunned. He repeated her words stupidly. 'What do you mean, not big enough? Nearly all the people in the other flats here are married couples. There's this huge room and a bedroom and a big kitchen and a bathroom. What more do you want?'

'It's not what I want, Martin, you know that. It's Lindsay. Where would we put Lindsay?'

He must have been a fool or totally obtuse, he thought, but it hadn't occurred to him that she would be bringing the child with her. To him, Lindsay was a part of Russell, or rather, she and Russell were part of the life lived in Fortis Green Lane. In leaving it behind, Francesca would be leaving behind all that belonged to it, walls, furniture, husband, child. But of course it couldn't be like that, he ought to have known. He ought to have known vicariously, if not from experience, that a mother doesn't desert her two-year-old child. Lindsay would become his child now. The idea was very disturbing. He lifted his eyes to meet Francesca's mournful eyes.

She would never know what an effort it cost him to say what he did. 'She can sleep in here or have a bed in our room.'

'Oh, dear, you do make it hard for me. Darling Martin, don't you see it wouldn't be right for the three of us to be living all crowded together like that.' It was hard to tell when Francesca was blushing, her cheeks were always so pink. 'She'd – she'd see us in bed together.'

'She sees you and Russell in bed together now.'

'He's her father. I can't take my little daughter away from her father and her home and her own room and bring her here where she'll have to sleep in a living room or on a couch or something.' Her lips trembled. When he put out his arms to her she laid her head against his shoulder and held on to him hard. 'Oh, Martin, you do understand?'

'I'll try to, darling. But what alternative do we have? There isn't anywhere else.'

His pride was bruised by her rejection of his home and he thought of the little box she lived in. After she had gone he began to feel angry with her. Did she expect him to leave the flat he was fond of and buy a house or something just to accommodate the child she had had by another man? This thought was immediately succeeded by another, that it was his Francesca, his love, that he was using those harsh words about. They would find a way, of course they would. Once Francesca had told Russell she wanted a divorce it might be that he would leave. Surely that was what husbands usually did? Martin wondered if he could possibly bring himself, say for a couple of days each week, to live in the house in Fortis Green Lane.

He got to Friern Barnet at the appointed time of eight on Monday evening. The flat was as nasty as Caroline had led him to believe, with bare, stained floorboards, the walls marked all over where other people's posters and pictures had hung. It was furnished partly with Woolworth chipboard and plastic and partly with pre-First World War pitch pine. The Gibsons gave him Nescafé and kept saying how surprised they were that he was young. Sarah Gibson was pale and rather big and dark-haired with a face like Elizabeth Barrett Browning, and her husband was fair and upright and looked like a Guards officer, though in fact he turned out to be a hospital porter on thirty-seven pounds a week.

When Martin told them – he found it very difficult to do this, he even began to stammer – that his intent was to give them money to buy a flat, they refused to believe him.

'But why?' Sarah Gibson kept saying. 'You don't know us. Why should you want to give us money?'

Martin said that he had 'come into' a fortune, which was strictly true. He explained his motives. He even described his experiences with Miss Watson and Mr Deepdene. He had wanted to find a young couple, he said.

'OK, that's fine for you, but what about us? We'd be under an obligation to you all our lives, we'd be sort of tied to you. Anyway, you must want something out of it.'

Martin felt helpless. He couldn't think of any more to say and he wished he hadn't come. Then Richard Gibson said:

'If you're really serious, we'd borrow it from you. I mean, we're both teachers only we can't get jobs. We'd borrow it from you and when we get proper jobs we'd start paying it back like a mortgage.'

That wasn't what Martin had wanted but it was the only arrangement the Gibsons would agree to. He said he would have to do it through a friend of his who was a solicitor. His friend, Adrian Vowchurch, would draw up an agreement for an interest-free loan and he would be in touch with Richard Gibson in a day or two. Sarah Gibson sat staring at him, bewildered and frowning.

Her husband, seeing Martin out, said, 'I honestly don't expect to see you or hear from you again. You see, I don't believe you, I can't.'

'Time will show,' said Martin.

He felt angry. Not so much with the Gibsons as with the world, society, civilization, so-called, which must be in a pretty terrible state if you couldn't perform an act of altruism without people thinking you were mad. Sarah Gibson had thought he was schizophrenic, he had seen it in her eyes. He drove down across the North Circular Road and into Colney Hatch Lane, passing very near to Francesca's home. But Francesca wouldn't be there now, it was Monday and she had gone to Annabel's, she had told him so on aturday.

How much he would love to see her now! Maybe the time d come for him to tell her about the money and how ad come by it, or if not that, it would simply be lovely to be with her and talk to her. He was aware of something he never remembered knowing before he had met her – loneliness. It was nearly nine o'clock. Why shouldn't he go to Annabel's place in Frognal and pick her up and drive her home? He didn't know Annabel's surname but he knew the house she lived in. He had parked outside its gate after their second meeting to say good-bye to Francesca. Would she mind his calling for her? He didn't think so. She had met Norman Tremlett at his flat, now it was time for him to begin meeting her friends.

For all his convincing arguments, he felt apprehensive as he drove across Hampstead Lane. Annabel knew of his existence, he told himself, even Russell knew of it. He wasn't doing anything clandestine or dishonourable, he was simply calling at a friend's house for the woman who was going to be his wife. Young men all over London were doing the same. He drove down past the Whitestone Pond into Branch Hill. A little snow still lay in patches on the brown turf of Judge's Walk. There was mist in the air, a damp icy breath. He drew the car into the kerb at the top of Frognal and crossed the road. As soon as he was alone with Francesca he would tell her he intended to put the flat on the market and buy a house for the three of them. Would she consent to live in Cromwell Court with him until he could do that?

The house outside which he had parked that night in November was large, almost a mansion, with a front garden full of leafless shrubs and small grey alpine plants dripping over steps and the rims of urns. It appeared to be divided into three flats and Martin was rather taken aback to find that there were no names but only numbers to the bells. He had taken very little notice of the house on that previous occasion but now, looking up at its brown bricks and half-timbering, red shingles and red tiles, seemingly numberless windows of both plain and stained glass, he wondered how any young girl on her own, a friend and contemporary o Francesca's could afford to live in a place like this. The because the top storey seemed the smallest and the le grand, he rang the top bell.

After about a minute a woman opened the door. She probably forty, a good-looking blonde, very well-d but for her footwear which was a fluffy pair of be slippers. Martin apologized for disturbing her. Could she tell him in which of the flats someone with the christian name of Annabel lived? He was calling for his fiancée who was a friend of hers. Martin balked a little at calling someone else's wife his fiancée, yet it had the required respectable ring to it.

'Annabel?' said the woman. 'There isn't anyone called that here.'

'There must be. A young girl living on her own.'

'There's myself and my two sons, we have the top floor. Mr and Mrs Cameron have the middle flat. They're elderly and they haven't any children. The ground floor's occupied by Sir John and Lady Bidmead – the painter, you've probably heard of him – and it's them the house belongs to, they own it. I've known them for twenty years and they certainly don't have a daughter.'

It had occurred to Martin while she was speaking that Francesca hadn't actually pointed to this house and said Annabel lived there. It was possible she had meant the house next door. He went next door, a slightly smaller place, semi-detached. An elderly man answered his ring. The owner of the house was a Mrs Frere who occupied the whole of it and whom he referred to as the employer of himself and his wife. Martin called at two more houses but at neither had Annabel been heard of.

The astonishment he felt softened the edge of his disappointment at not seeing Francesca. He tried to remember what had happened on the evening of November 27. She had got out of the car, turned back to say to him, 'Call for me at the shop,' and then disappeared in the heavy rain. It had been pouring with rain and he hadn't been able to see much but he knew she had asked him to park here, had said that Annabel lived just here.

Was Annabel an invention then? Had Francesca made her up? There came into his mind the confusion over here Russell's parents lived. She had said Oxford that first ne, he knew she had. He went up into the flat and with- putting a lamp on, sat at the window, looking down London. He saw spangled towers drowning in mist, he hem, yet he saw nothing. He closed his eyes. Annabel eation to be presented to Russell for an alibi was feas- but to *him*? What motive could she possibly have had? Perhaps she lived a fantasy life in a fantasy world, he had heard of people like that. Perhaps none of the people she had told him about existed – but that wasn't true, of course they did. Russell got his name in the papers and there was no doubting the fact of Lindsay. He put the lights on and drew the curtains and poured himself a whisky. What was the matter with him that he doubted her like this and questioned the very foundations of her being? She had small fantasies, that was all. She slightly distorted the truth as some people did to make themselves appear more interesting. That night in November she had told him she had a friend living in an exclusive part of Hampstead to impress him, and later she couldn't go back on what she had said. Russell's parents very likely lived in Reading or Newmarket but the two great universities had come into her head as more glamorous and intriguing.

He lay awake most of the night, thinking about her and wondering and sometimes feeling rather sick.

Lately he had been in the habit of phoning her every day, but he let the next day and the next go by without speaking to her. Francesca didn't work on Thursdays. She had told him she spent her Thursdays shopping and cleaning the house and taking Lindsay out. Perhaps she did. He wondered if anything she had told him was true. He went to dinner with his parents, the usual Thursday night Three Bears get-together. His mother said a neighbour of hers had seen him shopping in Hampstead with a very pretty dark girl, but Martin shook his head and said she was mistaking him for someone else.

In the morning he phoned Adrian Vowchurch and explained the arrangement he had come to with Richard Gibson. Adrian gave no sign of surprise at hearing that Marti
had fifteen thousand pounds to lend or that he proposed
lend it free of interest. Martin had an appointment wit
client at eleven. It was while he was talking to this man
Francesca phoned. He had to promise to call her ba
half an hour, and for that half-hour endeavour to qu
excitement and his fear while he explained to th
how, if he would spend a minimum of thirty days
country on business each year, he might get a pro

his income free of tax. When he was alone his hand actually trembled as he picked up the receiver.

The explanation of the Annabel affair was so simple and obvious that he cursed himself for doubting her and for his three days of self-torture.

'Darling, Annabel moved away just after Christmas. She lives in Mill Hill now.'

'But they hadn't even heard of her in any of those houses I called at.'

Her voice was soft and sweetly indulgent. 'Now you called at the house where the old lady lives?'

'I just said so, and at the next two down.'

'But you didn't call at the fourth down?'

'Is *that* where she lives?'

'Lived, Martin,' said Francesca. 'Oh, Martin, did you really think I'd been lying to you and deceiving you? Don't you trust me at all?'

'It's because we're not really together,' he said. 'It's because I hardly ever see you. Days and days go by and I on't see you. It makes me wonder all the time about what you're doing and your other life. Francesca, if I put my flat up for sale and buy a house for you and me and Lindsay, would you come and live with me just till the sale went through?'

'Martin, darling . . .'

'Well, would you? It needn't be for more than three months and then we could all go and live in the house. Say you will.'

'Let's not talk about it on the phone, Martin. I'm wanted in the shop, anyway.'

He would have sent her flowers but that would have been coals to Newcastle, corn in Egypt. Instead, he took her a box of hand-made chocolates when he went to call for her at the shop on Monday. He parked the car in Hillside Gar-ens at a quarter to six and walked down through the cold isty dark to the shop. The grey fog in which its orange t gleamed fuzzily gave it the mysterious look of an en-ted cavern. Francesca wasn't alone. Lindsay was with erched up on the counter and occupied in pulling the off a head of pampas grass.

nursery was closed,' Francesca said. 'Their heat-ken down. I thought of phoning you – but I did e you even if it couldn't be for long.'

He held her in his arms. 'You've had a hard day. Come to me and you needn't work, you can be at home with Lindsay all the time. I'll buy us a house.'

'Listen,' she said, 'I had a long talk with Russell. He says he'll divorce me after two years' separation but the trouble is Lindsay. Russell adores her, you have to understand that. And he says – he says –' her lips trembled and she had difficulty in bringing out her next words, '– he says that if I – take her to live with you – he'll ask the divorce judge for custody of – of her – and – and – he'd get it!'

'Francesca, I think that's nonsense. Why would he?'

'He knows about these things, Martin. He's studied the law.'

'I thought he was a history teacher.'

'Well, of course he is but he's studied the law as well. He says he's been as much a mother to Lindsay as I have, fetching her from the nursery and getting her tea and putting her to bed, and he says the judge would see he could look after her on his own, like he often has, and he'd be leading a moral life while I'd be taking her to live in two rooms with my lover!'

Lindsay threw the pampas grass on to the floor and began whimpering. Francesca started to say more about what Russell would do if she took his child to live under Martin's roof, but Lindsay stamped across the counter and pinched her mother's lips together. She said to Martin, though not in a friendly way:

'We're going home in a taxi.'

'Francesca, let me drive you home. You'll never get a taxi out there and the fog's getting thicker.'

'Really, no, Martin.' Francesca struggled and mumbled like Papageno with his padlock. 'Stop it, Lindsay, I'll put you on the floor.'

'But why won't you let me drive you? We'll be there in ten minutes.' Martin hesitated. 'Anyway, think of me, it would give me ten minutes of your company.'

'I want to see my Daddy,' said Lindsay.

'Is it Russell seeing me that worries you? I promise to drop you a hundred yards from the house. How's that?'

'All right, Martin,' said Francesca in the sweet meek voice he loved. 'You drive us home. I don't meant to be ungrateful, it's very very kind of you.'

12

The drive took much longer than ten minutes because of the dense fog. The sky itself, smoky, choking, gloomy white, seemed to have fallen through the dark on to the upper reaches of Highgate. Each car was guided by the tail lights of the one in front, lights that looked as if their feeble glow came through cloudy water.

Lindsay sat on Francesca's knee, helping herself to chocolates out of the box Martin had brought. She liked most of the flavours but not the violet cream or liqueur cherry and when she had taken a bite out of these she pushed the remains into Francesca's mouth. Silver paper went all over the floor of Martin's nice clean car.

Francesca could see Martin was offended at this cavalier treatment of his present but she didn't care about that. He didn't like Lindsay and he showed it, and to Francesca this was so monstrous that whenever she felt like giving the whole business up and just getting out or telling the truth, she thought of how he looked at and spoke to Lindsay and she hardened her heart and went on. He was looking at her like that, now, while they were stopped at a red traffic light. It was the kind of look a polite host gives to a guest's uninvited dog.

'You see, Martin, she'd soon make a mess of your lovely tidy flat.'

'Maybe, but things would be different if we had a house. We could have a big kitchen and a playroom, we'd have a garden. Look, I can see that's valid, what you said about it not being right to let your child sleep on a couch in the living room. So suppose I put the flat on the market tomorrow and start to look for a house for the three of us and you stay with Russell just until the house is ready to move into. How does that sound?'

'I don't know, Martin.'

'Well, darling, will you think about it? Will you, please,

because I ask you and I want it so much? You see, I don't know what else to suggest. You do *want* to come and live with me, don't you?'

It was so cold and foggy and she had a long awkward journey ahead of her. She hadn't the nerve to say no. She touched his arm and smiled.

'Well, then. You won't live with me at the flat and you won't come and stay there with me till we can get a house, so I'm asking you to think about this idea. Will you think about it, darling?'

'I really don't think I'll ever . . .' Francesca started to say when Lindsay clamped a chocolate-smeary hand over her mouth. She didn't have to finish because Martin was parking the car. They had arrived.

She put Lindsay out on to the pavement and got out herself. It was very cold and wet out there, rain penetrating the fog in large icy drops. Martin wanted her to kiss him so she put her head back in through the window and held up to him red lips that a raindrop had already splashed.

'I'll phone you in the morning, Francesca.'

'Yes, do,' said Francesca vaguely. She was holding on to Lindsay with one hand and clasping the chocolate box against herself with the other. Lindsay was pulling and stamping.

'And you'll have come to a decision? You'll decide it's yes, won't you?'

Francesca had more or less forgotten what she was meant to be deciding. Again she said she didn't know but she managed a radiant smile, keeping her options open. Martin drove off waving, though with that hurt look on his face which so exasperated her.

When the car was out of sight she started to walk along Fortis Green Lane in the opposite direction to that which Martin had followed. He had put them down outside number 26 and when they reached 54, Francesca stopped for a moment and looked curiously at the house. It was unlit. On its doorstep was a bottle of milk with a cover over it to stop birds pecking at the cream.

'Mummy carry,' said Lindsay.

'Must I?'

'Must. Lindsay carry sweeties.'

'That's an offer I can't refuse.'

Francesca picked her up and Lindsay gave her a wet sticky kiss on the cheek and waved the chocolate box about. Perhaps it would be a good idea to turn up Hill Avenue? Francesca rejected it and tramped on. The pavement was coated with greyish-black, soupy, liquid mud that splashed up her legs. She realized what she had thought was rain was in fact condensed fog dripping from the tall bushes in front gardens. She felt like one of those women who abound in Victorian fiction, women who are discovered at the beginning of a chapter wandering over heaths or stumbling along city streets at night and in the most inclement weather with a child in their arms. Very likely she looked like one of them too in her lace-up boots and long skirt and woolly shawl wound round her head and her grandmother's old fur coat, spiky and dewed with drops of fog. In spite of the cold and the heavy weight of the little girl and her own tiredness, Francesca suddenly laughed out loud.

'Not funny,' said Lindsay crossly.

'No, it isn't, you're quite right, it isn't a bit funny. You'll find out when you're grown-up that we don't always laugh just because things are funny. There are other reasons. I must be mad. Why did I let him bring us up here, Lindsay? I suppose I was so utterly pissed-off with seeing that look on his face. One thing I do know, I'm not going to see him any more, I'm not going on with it, this is the end, this is it. And Daddy can go – go jump in a pond!'

'Lindsay wants Daddy.'

'Yes, well, he won't get home till after we do even at this rate, so shut up. I want my Daddy I want my Daddy, you're a real pain sometimes.'

'I want my Daddy,' said Lindsay. She screwed up a chocolate paper and threw it into someone's garden.

'We're going to have a bus ride first. You'll like that, you never go on buses. Come on, hoist up a bit. Can't you sort of sit on my hip?'

Lindsay replied by dropping the box and pinching Francesca's lips together. Francesca picked up the box which was now much splashed with mud and growled through Lindsay's fingers and pretended to bite. Lindsay screamed with laughter, took her hand away an inch and clamped it back again.

'Come on, you crazy kid, we'll freeze to death.'

By now they had come out into Coppetts Road and Francesca was looking about her for bus stops when a taxi, which had perhaps dropped an inmate or a visitor, came out of the gates of Coppetts Wood Hospital with its light on. The driver didn't seem to know the whereabouts of Samphire Road, N4, even when Francesca said it wasn't far from Crouch Hill station, but he agreed to let her direct him. Lindsay started screaming that she'd been promised a bus, she wanted a bus, and she made so much noise that Francesca could tell, by the back of his neck, that the driver was wincing. She stuffed Lindsay with more chocolate to shut her up and then they played the growl and snap game most of the way home. The fare was two pounds which Francesca could ill afford.

The pavements here were even stickier and more slippery than in Finchley. It was a depressed, semi-derelict region to which the taxi had brought them, a place where whole ranks of streets had been demolished to make way for new council building. Acres of muddy ground stood bare between half-dismantled ruins, and some of the streets had become mere narrow lanes running between temporary fences ten feet high. Even in the driest weather the roadways were muddy, smeared with clay from the tyres of tractors and lorries. There was an air of impermanence, of dull, unhopeful expectancy, as of the squalid old giving place to a not much more inviting new.

But Samphire Road was sufficiently on the borders of this resurgent neighbourhood for it and the streets which joined it and ran parallel to it, to be left alone. Samphire Road, with its rampart-like houses of cardboard-coloured brick, its grave-sized front gardens, its ostentatious treelessness, was to be allowed to live out its century undisturbed and survive until at least 1995. Sulphur-coloured lamplight turned the fog into just such a pea-souper as Samphire Road had known in its youth.

Francesca unlocked the front door of number 22, painted, some years before, the shade of raw calves' liver, and let herself and Lindsay through an inner door into th hall of the ground floor flat. Inside it was as cold as only old house can be which has no central heating, which been empty for ten hours, and when the month is Janu It was damp as well as cold, with a damp to make cringe. Francesca put lights on and humped Lindsay into the kitchen where she lit the gas oven and switched on an electric wall heater. Breakfast dishes were still stacked in the sink. She unwrapped Lindsay's layers of clothes and then her own layers, spreading her fur coat over the back of a chair to dry. The two of them squatted down in front of the open oven and held out their hands to the pale bluish-mauve flames.

After a while Lindsay said her feet were cold, so Francesca went to look for her furry slippers. In the hall it was as cold as out in the street. There were only two other rooms in the flat, the front room where there were two armchairs and a dining table and a piano and a sofa that converted into a double bed, and the bedroom at the back where Lindsay slept. Francesca drew the curtains across the huge, draughty, stained-glass french windows and lit the gas fire. The gas fire had to be on for at least an hour before she could put Lindsay to bed in that ice box. The slippers were nowhere to be seen, so Francesca went into the other room (known as the sitting room but where no one could have borne to sit between November and April) and found the slippers under the piano. The bed wasn't made. It hadn't been made for several days and it hadn't been used as a sofa more than half a dozen times since Lindsay was born.

Lindsay said, 'Where's my Daddy?'

'Gone to some meeting about historic Hornsey.'

'I'm not going to bed till my Daddy comes.'

'OK, you don't have to.' Francesca made her scrambled eggs and buttered fingers of brown bread. She sat at the table drinking tea while Lindsay plastered chocolate spread on bread and biscuits and even on to a piece of Swiss roll. Lindsay adored chocolate spread, they had had to take sandwiches of it for their lunch. Francesca wiped it off Lindsay's chin and the tablecloth and the wall where a blob of it had landed. She was thinking about Martin. It was like eaven being in the flat in Cromwell Court and in that arm car and eating in the Villa Bianca. She loved comfort d luxury and longed wistfully after them, perhaps, she ught, because she had never known them, had been too living to look for them before. That weekend with n had shaken her, the warmth and ease, so that, in spite of the boredom, she had actually thought of becoming the girl he thought she was. Not just sweet and obedient and passive and clinging and Victorian, but the girl who was going to get a divorce and marry Martin and live with him for ever . . .

'There's my Daddy,' said Lindsay.

The front door banged and there was a sound of feet being wiped on the doormat. Francesca didn't get up and though Lindsay did, bouncing off her chair, she wasn't going to venture into that freezing passage, not even to greet her long-awaited father. He opened the kitchen door and came in, throwing back a lock of wet hair out of his eyes.

'Hi,' said Francesca.

'Hi.' He picked up the little girl, held her in the air, then hugged her to him. 'And how's my sweetheart? How did you get on in Mummy's shop? I bet they made you manageress.' He sang to the tune of the Red Flag, 'The working class can kiss my arse, I've got the boss's job at last!'

'Oh, Tim,' said Francesca, 'we've had an awful evening out in the sticks. Wait till you hear!'

13

'So I just don't see the point of carrying on with it,' said Francesca. She and Tim confronted each other across the kitchen table and across the greasy pieces of paper and copy of the *Post* which had wrapped the fish and chips brought in by Tim for their supper. The kitchen was now very warm and smoky, the windows running with condensation. Lindsay had been put to bed ten minutes before. 'Can I have another cigarette, please? I can't smoke when I'm with him, it doesn't go with the image and it nearly kills me, I can tell you.'

Tim gave her a cigarette. He frowned a little, pushing out his red lips, but he spoke quite lightly in his usual faintly ironic drawl. 'Yes, but, honey, why suddenly throw your hand in now? Why *now* when everything is going so extremely well? I mean, even in our wildest fantasies we didn't foresee he'd fall for you quite so heavily. Or has he?' Tim's eyes narrowed. 'Maybe mah honey chile wasn't being strictly truthful when she said Livingstone wanted to marry her.'

'Well, I'm not always absolutely truthful, Tim, you know that. Who is? But I don't tell pointless lies. Oh, dear, I nearly came a cropper over Annabel, though, didn't I?' Francesca giggled and her eyes met Tim's blue eyes and she giggled even more. 'Oh, dear. Now we must be serious. What I mean is, I don't see the point of carrying on with it because it's not getting us anywhere. All it'll do is lose me my job. If he takes to coming into the shop after me I'll have to leave to get away from him. What did we think we'd get out of it, Tim? I can't even remember.'

'Of course you can remember. Money. Prospects. Opportunities.' Tim lit a Gauloise. 'And, incidentally, my little revenge.'

'Isn't it a funny thing? He says he loves me and all that but he doesn't exactly confide in me. He's never said a word about winning the pools and I don't believe he has.'

'You don't believe in your Uncle Tim's total recall? I tell you, if I died and they opened me up they'd find the perm on that pools coupon written on my heart. Of course, there's just the weeniest chance Miss Urban didn't send it in. But if Miss Urban *did* send it in then, sure as fate is fate, she's won herself the first dividend, all or part of, the lucky lucky girl.'

Tim always referred to Martin as Livingstone or, when his camp mood was on him, as Miss Urban. Francesca, for reasons she didn't understand but thought might be sick reasons, found the camp mood almost unbearably sexy. Tim, when he was that way, made her go weak at the knees and she didn't want that happening now, she wanted to be serious.

'Well,' she said, 'when you sent those awful yellow chrysanths, you said to get in his good graces and get him to take me out a bit because he'd got wads of money and hadn't got a girl friend. You said he might let me have the money to start my own florist's or at least give me some big presents. But nothing like that's happened. He just fell right in love with me. He's not even that interested in sex – well, not *very*. I mean, you'd have raped me if I'd gone on with you the way I have with him. But he's in love, it's not just wanting to screw me, it's real love. And the only place it's going to get me is living with him in his flat or some house he wants to buy. And what's the use of that? What's the use of going on with it, Tim, if I only get to where I have to run away and hide to avoid living with him?'

'One would think, wouldn't one,' said Tim thoughtfully, 'that Livingstone would have given you something more by now than those very strange decanters or whatever they are. Five grand is nothing, but nothing, to spend on a ring, say, or a bracelet in these inflationary times. What about furs? An' mah honey chile shiverin' in her ole coonskin.'

'He did say something about a mink,' said Francesca, giggling, 'when we're married.' She groped about under the fish and chip papers. 'He did give me some chocolates tonight only Lindsay's gobbled most of them. Here you are.'

'She's a chip off the old block all right, she's only left the nougats and the coconuts.'

'The latest is he wants to sell his flat and buy a house for him and me and Lindsay, so I suppose he must have money.'

'Now she tells me. Francesca, what d'you think Krishna Bhavnani told me today? That it was Livingstone put up the money for his kid's operation.'

'Are you going to put something about it in the *Post*?'

'If you're quitting, yes. If you're keeping on, no. Just as untruths have been known to appear in the *Post*, so have truths sometimes been suppressed.'

Francesca laughed. She came behind Tim and put her hands round his shoulders and stroked the Nureyev face. 'Tim, I could keep it up a little bit longer, I could see him on Wednesday, if you really think it's worth while. Now I know about the Indian boy, I could have a go at getting a fur coat. Or a ring. We could sell a ring.'

Tim rubbed his face against her hands, making purring noises. 'Did you switch our blanket on?'

He had bought them an electric blanket for Christmas. 'When I took Lindsay to bed,' she said.

'Then why don't you take me to bed and tell me all about the times you've misbehaved yourself with Dr Livingstone?'

'Miss Urban,' said Francesca somewhat breathlessly.

'Mah honey chile should tak' shame talking like dat befo' her Uncle Tim, Lawd God!'

Francesca and Tim had been living together for three years. Tim had moved into the flat in Samphire Road, instead of just spending nights there, when Francesca found she was pregnant with Lindsay. They had never really considered getting married and couldn't have done anyway since Francesca was still married to Russell Brown. After Tim had met Martin Urban in the wood he had several times invited him to Samphire Road but Martin always refused, Tim hadn't known why. He had been wounded by it, Francesca thought, though Tim never showed that he could feel pain. Then had come the Saturday in November when Tim checked his pools and found, as usual, that he had won nothing while the formula he had given Martin must have scooped the first dividend.

It had disturbed Francesca to see Tim waiting for Martin to phone. Her placid happy-go-lucky nature was ruffled by Tim's intense neurotic anxiety. The days had passed and there had been nothing. As taut as a bowstring, Tim had gone to that interview at Urban, Wedmore, Mackenzie and Company, but still Martin hadn't spoken. The worst thing for Tim had been Martin's refusing to come to the party. Getting a party organized at Samphire Road was no mean feat. They had cancelled it at the last minute because there was nothing much to celebrate and no point in opening the champagne.

'I fear,' Tim had said, camping it up, pretending, 'she's keeping it all the darkest because she doesn't want to have to give any to poor me. Though what I've done I never will know, save be friendly and helpful. Maybe I wasn't quite friendly enough, which some girls, you know, can resent.'

Francesca couldn't hazard an opinion on that but she knew Tim had hoped for something from Martin, even a loan to help them buy a place that would be a cut above Samphire Road. He walked up and down shouting that he would be revenged. He would get hold of some of that money by hook or by crook. After that it was a short step for Francesca to go round with the flowers and – hang on hard.

She was a good-tempered easy-going girl and nothing put her out for long. Tim had once told her that one of the things he liked about her was that she had no morals and no guilt. This made playing the part of Martin's Francesca, the moral and guilty Francesca, rather difficult at first, but Tim had instructed her and even set her a course of reading, Victorian and early twentieth-century fiction mainly, with suitable heroines. She had worked hard at moulding herself according to these models and sometimes after meetings with Martin she felt quite tired. She spent a lot of the time in his company silent and apparently raptly listening, while in fact she was concentrating on how to escape in a taxi and get out of being driven up to Finchley. Now she was faced with the additional problem of how to make Martin believe she loved him and wanted to live with him while refusing to submit to any plan for their living together he might make.

Accordingly, the next time he phoned, she said that she would hate to think of him selling his flat in order to buy a house. She knew how much he loved his flat.

'But I'll have to sell it one day, darling. When you're free and we can get married we'll need a house.'

'I'd much rather you waited till then, Martin.'

'Yes, but that doesn't solve the problem of how we're going to live *till* then, does it?'

That lunchtime, Francesca went across the Archway Road and sold the two cut-glass scent bottles for seventeen pounds fifty. All those taxis were making inroads into her resources and if Martin was taking her to dinner at the Mirabelle, as he had promised, on Wednesday she ought to have a new dress. She ought to try and rake up enough to buy the burgundy crêpe that Kate Ross, who owned the flower shop, had for weeks been trying to sell for twenty-five pounds.

Martin had got into the habit of ringing the shop every morning at ten. At two minutes to ten on Wednesday he phoned, sounding excited, and said he had had a wonderful idea which he would tell her about that night. Francesca went into the room at the back and tried on the burgundy crêpe which Kate had brought in with her and got Kate to agree to take twenty-three pounds fifty for it.

It started to snow at about five, great flakes like goose feathers. Kate always went home at half-past because she didn't have a day off or Saturday afternoon. Martin gasped at the sight of Francesca in the dark red dress with her hair piled up and a dark red and white speckled orchid tucked into a curl. He stared at her adoringly. These transports of his, though she knew they were sincere, always irritated Francesca. She preferred a lecherous reaction which was what she had had from Russell Brown and those other men who had preceded Tim and which she had, in his own individual way, most satisfactorily from Tim. But she smiled and looked rather shy and said quietly:

'Do I look nice?'

'Francesca, you look so beautiful, I don't know what to say. I wish I was more articulate, I should like to write poems to you.'

'I just hope I'm going to be warm enough,' said Francesca, her mind on mink coats, but Martin assured her she would be exposed to the open air for no longer than it took to cross the pavement.

'So what's this wonderful idea?' she said when they were in the car. Martin said he wasn't going to tell her until they were eating their dinner.

Francesca had an enormous appetite and a hearty capacity for alcohol. She and Tim were both the sort of very thin people who can eat as much as they like without putting on weight. But she never ate and drank anywhere near as much as she wanted when with Martin, it didn't fit the image. Tonight, however, she was going to start off with *quenelles* of lobster, *quenelles* of anything being among her favourite food. To precede it, a brandy and soda would have gone down well. Francesca asked for a dry sherry.

Martin's shyness and awkwardness increased during the meal. He had become almost tongue-tied by the time Francesca started on her roast pheasant, and although this suited her well enough, she couldn't help speculating as to what it might be about the wonderful idea that was so inhibiting. Then, suddenly, like a man confessing a sin that has long been on his conscience, he began. Fascinated, she watched the slow process of the blush spreading across his face.

'I haven't told anyone this except my parents. In November I won a hundred and four thousand pounds on the football pools. No, don't say anything, let me finish. I decided I'd keep half and give half away. You can imagine my reasons for wanting to do that.'

Francesca couldn't at all but she said nothing. She felt a curious breathless excitement as if she were on the brink of enormous revelations. Yet he was only confirming what Tim had said all along.

'You see, I felt grateful to – well, to fate or God or something for having had such a fortunate sort of life. I made up my mind to help people who were having housing difficulties but I haven't got very far with that, it's much harder than you'd suppose to get people to accept money. All I've managed to do so far really is pay for a boy to have a heart operation.'

'That's not housing difficulties,' said Francesca.

'No, that was to be the one exception. Apart from that, I'm considering my cleaner's sister-in-law who's having a nervous breakdown because of noise in the place where she lives, and I've managed to get a young couple on very low wages to accept a loan.'

He was smiling tentatively at her, leaning forward, waiting for her approval. Francesca looked blankly at him. It occurred to her that he might actually be off his head. But, no, he was just innocent, he didn't know he was born . . . Suppose she were to throw herself on his mercy, tell him who she was and that Tim was her lover and Lindsay's father and that they were doomed to live in worse conditions than maybe any of those people he had talked about? She couldn't do it, it was impossible. He re-filled her wine glass and said:

'So now I've told you. I don't want to have any secrets from you.' As if he'd just confessed to some weird perversion, thought Francesca. 'But the point of telling – well, I've been a complete fool. I've been worrying about buying homes for other people and worrying about where you were going to live when you left Russell, but it never occurred to me till last night that I don't have to sell my flat or get a mortgage. Apart from what I'm going to give away, I've got fifty thousand of my own. I've got my own half-share of the win.'

'So what's the wonderful idea?' said Francesca carefully.

'To buy a flat for you and Lindsay to live in.' He paused but she said nothing. 'I mean, that solves everything, doesn't it? Lindsay can have her own room, Russell can't possibly accuse you of corrupting her, and after two years when you've got your divorce we can sell both flats and buy a house. How does that suit you? I'm not going to make any conditions, Francesca . . .' Martin smiled and reached across the table for her hand, '. . . only I hope I can come and stay sometimes and I'll be the happiest man on earth if you'll choose a flat that isn't far from mine.'

'So we're going house-hunting on Saturday. He's out on Cloud Nine already, planning colour schemes and fussing about something called cubic footage.'

'Miss Urban was always houseproud, she'll make some lucky chap a wonderful wife one of these days. What did you have to eat?'

'Lobster *quenelles*, roast pheasant and roast potatoes and calabresse and *sautéed* mushrooms *and* asparagus, and a sort of chartreuse soufflé with cream.'

'You should have asked for a paper bag and said you wanted to take some home for your aged relative.'

Francesca giggled. She sat on Tim's lap and took the cigarette out of his mouth and put it in her own. 'But, seriously, Tim, what's the future in letting him buy a flat for me to live in? I shan't live in it. But I can't think of any way of getting out of it, short of flatly saying I won't leave my husband.'

'Suppose I said give it just two weeks more? Just till Monday, the twelfth of Feb? If he's going to buy mah honey chile a love nest he's got to furnish it, hasn't he? In these scandalous times five grand is the least, but the leastest, he can expect to spend on furnishings.'

'He said I could have the cane chairs out of his living room.'

'What a miscreant he is!' said Tim. 'Still, you won't stand for that, will you? Not a girl of spirit like you. You'll ask for five thousand to splash about in Heal's.'

'Oh, dear,' said Francesca with an enormous yawn, 'I'll try, I'll do my best, but not a minute more after Feb the twelfth.'

14

Francesca didn't know whether to fix on the first flat they saw so that she could go home early, or pretend to find nothing to please her so that things would have progressed no further by the time her deadline came. In the event she did neither, for as soon as they were really doing something together, conducting practical business, Martin made clear his belief in man as the master. In this, as in all matters on a higher level than that of deciding what she would wear or perhaps what they should eat, he took it for granted he made the decisions, asking for her approval only as a matter of courtesy.

During the two days since their dinner at the Mirabelle he had been in touch with estate agents, had made himself familiar with the specifications of every flat for sale in the area of Highgate and Crouch End, and had already viewed several. This led to his making of a short list and from it a shorter list which by Saturday afternoon had fined down to one. The flat in question wasn't quite as near Cromwell Court as he would have liked but it was in other respects so suitable that he thought they must overlook that small defect.

Francesca hadn't expected to react with either enthusiasm or dislike to the prospect before her. She had expected to be bored. Her feelings on entering the flat surprised her very much. She had never lived anywhere very spacious or elegant or even ordinarily attractive. There had been her parents' mansion flat in Chiswick, big and cold and pervadingly dark brown, a furnished room in Pimlico and a furnished room in Shepherd's Bush, the little house she had shared with Russell, the basement squat she had shared with Russell's supplanter, her three rooms in Stroud Green. Home to Francesca had never been much more than a place to keep out the rain, where there was a table to eat meals off and a bed to go to with someone she liked. But this was another thing. The fourth floor, the penthouse, of Swan Place, Stanhope Avenue, Highgate, was a different matter altogether.

The living room was very large and you went into the dining part of it through an arch. One wall was all of glass. The heating made it too hot for even her thin coat, she could have gone naked. Looking out of the big plate-glass windows on to hilly streets and patches of green and snowy roofs, being led into the pastel blue kitchen and the pastel apricot bathroom, Francesca found herself thinking that she would like to live here, she would like it very much indeed. It was a crying shame that she couldn't, or that the price to pay for doing so was too high, because she would like it – oh, wouldn't she! And Lindsay would like it and probably Tim too, though you could never tell with him. It was just too awful that she could only have it by being stuffy old Martin's kept woman. She wondered how much it cost.

'What do you think?' said Martin in the car.

'It's lovely.'

'I'm glad you like it, darling, because although you'll think me very high-handed and a real male chauvinist pig, I've actually already told the agent I'll have it and I've put down a deposit.'

'What would you have done,' said Francesca curiously, 'if I'd hated it?'

'I knew you wouldn't, I think I know you pretty well by this time.'

'How much is it, Martin?'

'Forty-two thousand pounds.'

Francesca was silenced. She felt quite weak and swimmy in the head at the thought of so much money. Martin said it would be a good investment, house property was the best investment these days, and before they got married he would sell both flats and buy a house. The property market, he had been told, was due for another steep rise in the spring. With luck he ought to make a big profit on both flats.

They went back to Cromwell Court where Martin had got chocolate éclairs and a Battenberg cake in for tea.

Francesca partook heartily of both. It was the most miserable shame she didn't find Martin in the least attractive. If only she fancied him she could have put up with the yawning dullness and the accountant's talk and the pomposity, for the sake of that lovely flat. But she didn't fancy him, not a scrap, which was odd really because, like Tim, he was tall and dark and though not so good-looking, he was younger and cleaner and he didn't permanently stink of Gauloises. Francesca pondered rather regretfully on the anomalies of sexual attraction while Martin lectured her gently on house property and the registration of land and stamp duty and the making of searches and the mysteries of conveyancing.

Francesca ate another chocolate éclair. Martin wasn't the sort of person who would even consider going to bed in the afternoon, he would think it perverse. She let him hold her hand across the spread of sofa cushions.

'I suppose it'll be months and months before you actually own it?' she said.

'Oh, no. I'm paying cash, you see. My friend, Norman Tremlett – you met him here – he'll do a survey for me on Monday. I've already talked to my solicitor, he's another friend, we were all at school together, and he says provided the survey's favourable there's no reason why the contract shouldn't be ready for my signature by February the twelfth, that's Monday week. Then I'd get completion as soon as possible, maybe three weeks, and you could move in.'

Francesca thought how when she and Russell had tried to buy a house, what difficulties and obstacles there had been! The first two they fixed on had been sold over their heads while the building society hesitated over giving Russell a mortgage. Securing the one they had finally lived in took months and months, nearly a year of their hopes being raised and dashed. But they, of course, had had no money and no old boy network. It no longer mattered, it was history, ten years gone, swept away by oceans of water under the bridge. She smiled at Martin.

'What about furniture, darling?'

'I thought of making a separate deal with the owner for the carpets and curtains and the bedroom furniture and the fridge and cooker. He wants to sell. Of course, if there was anything special you wanted we could go shopping together next Saturday.'

Was there any point now in waiting till February 12? None except that she had given Tim an undertaking. Martin seemed to take it for granted that she would now be spending every evening with him. Francesca pointed out that while she was still with Russell she couldn't go out every night and leave him to look after Lindsay. Perhaps she might manage another day in the week as well as Monday . . .

'I want my parents to meet you,' said Martin.

She insisted on going home at six o'clock and he insisted on driving her. This time he didn't drop her a hundred yards away but set her down outside number 54 and there he waited to see her into the house. Francesca stood outside the white iron gate, waving impatiently at him, while he sat in the car, refusing to go till she did. After a few seconds she saw it was useless. She must either make it look as if she were going into that house or else give up the game.

There was a light on in the hall but nowhere else. She unlatched the white gate and walked quickly to the side entrance which was a wooden door set into a six-foot-high fence. It was rather more than dusk and not quite dark. Francesca boldly tried the handle on the wooden door, and when it worked pushed the door open and found herself on a concrete strip of back yard. It would be rather awful, she thought, but rather funny too if someone saw her lurking there and called the police. After a little while she heard Martin's car go, so she opened the wooden door again and got out as fast as she could, running away down the side street on to which the garden of 54 abutted.

It wasn't until her next meeting with him that she learned how Martin had come back to 'see if she was all right'. How, from a car in the street, he could have known whether she was or wasn't he didn't say. But while there, he said, he had seen Russell Brown come out of the house and walk away towards Coldfall Wood.

First of all he told her that he had felt so happy about the new flat and their future that on Sunday he had decided to rush in (as he put it) where angels fear to tread and had actually called on Miss Watson. There in her employer's house in Hurst Avenue he had explained what his letters perhaps hadn't explained and had convinced her of his good intentions. She had agreed, in tears and some bewilderment, to accept ten thousand pounds with which to buy a small terraced house in the Lincolnshire town where her married sister lived.

'So that's twenty-five thousand disposed of. Do you think it would be wrong of me if I only gave away another twenty? You see, I'm going to have rather more expense than I thought with your flat.'

Francesca said with perfect sincerity that she didn't think it would be wrong at all. Every time he talked of giving money away to these people she didn't know and didn't want to know, she had to turn her face away so that he couldn't see her expression of disgust and dismay. She turned her back on him, picking red tulips and blue irises out of the jars on the floor to make a bouquet for his mother.

'And I've got something else to tell you. I've seen Russell.'

She turned round slowly, holding the flowers. He smiled, looking triumphant.

'He only waited for you to come in to go out himself, didn't he? I must say, it gave me a strange feeling to see him. He looks older than he is, don't you think?'

'I don't know, Martin.'

'More than thirty-five, I thought. D'you like those coneyskin coats on men? They're very "in" this year, I could get one.'

'Was Russell wearing his coneyskin then?' said Francesca with care.

'When I saw him I remembered what he'd done to you and I longed to get out of the car and hit him. But of course I didn't, I thought of how upset you'd be. He went off up towards the wood or the North Circular or somewhere.'

'He's got friends in Coppetts Lane,' said Francesca.

They went out to the car with the flowers.

'I've told my parents a bit about you. I'm afraid I've had to stretch the truth a bit. It seemed politic.'

The truth had been stretched so far by now, thought Francesca, it seemed unlikely to snap tonight.

'I've given them to understand you're already living apart from your husband,' said Martin. 'I refer to you as my fiancée.'

'Then I ought to have a ring,' said Francesca.

'I'm afraid you wouldn't wear it any more than you wear Russell's wedding ring. But shall I get you one for when your divorce comes through, so you can wear it to the registrar's office?'

The Urbans were very much what Francesca had expected, except that Walter Urban was younger and better looking. She found him rather attractive and speculated as to what it would be like to go to bed with a man twice one's age. Margaret Urban sat making patchwork of the same sort as that with which the cushions were covered. It looked a tedious and intricate task, putting all those hexagons together evenly. Francesca wondered why she did it, for they seemed to have heaps of money, but she would have liked a skirt for herself made in that sort of patchwork. It was a shame really that she wasn't, whatever the Urbans might think, in the running to get one.

They were like the Three Bears, she thought. She had gone to sit down on the right-hand side of the log fire and been told *sotto voce* by Martin that that was his mother's chair. They drank sherry, oloroso for Mrs Urban, amontillado for Walter and Tio Pepe for Martin. She felt that, like Goldilocks, she should have tried a little bit of each but settled instead for the Tio Pepe too.

Inwardly, she was amused. How dismayed the two senior Urbans must be at the thought of their only son (a boy brought up with the utmost care) marrying a divorced woman with a child. She tried to read some hint of it in their faces and in Mrs Urban's tone when she looked up from her sewing to ask questions about Lindsay. But there was nothing. They were playing safe, humouring Martin, in the hope, no doubt, that if they didn't oppose him he might get over her before any irreversible step was taken. It was just the way she envisaged behaving herself if anything so awful was to happen as Lindsay bringing home an accountant or a solicitor and saying she wanted to marry him.

When they were on their second glasses of sherry, Martin told them about buying the flat in Swan Place.

'For Francesca and Lindsay,' he said.

Where did they suppose she was living now? Francesca wondered. She expected Martin's announcement to be greeted with grave disapproval. In her experience parents never like you spending money, even your own, but she had reckoned without the passion for wise investment which throbs in the heart of every good accountant. Francesca noticed too that Martin's mother took it very coolly. She had a sensitive awareness of women's reactions and she understood that Margaret Urban, mother of an only son, would now be able to convince herself that if her son and his fiancée lived under separate roofs before marriage, they wouldn't sleep together before marriage either.

'A very sound idea,' said Walter, 'buying the place before prices go up again. Of course you'll elect to describe it as your principal residence?'

'It won't be *his* residence at all, Walter,' said Mrs Urban.

Her husband took no notice of this interruption which had made Francesca discreetly smile. 'Because if Swan Place is your secondary residence you won't forget, will you, that you'll be liable for Capital Gains Tax when you sell it.'

'Do you know,' said Martin, 'I *had* forgotten. The tax payable would be a third of my profit, wouldn't it?'

'Thirty per cent,' said Walter.

They talked about tax and tax avoidance all through dinner. Mrs Urban watched them placidly from under her slate-blue fringe but Francesca was so bored she couldn't control her yawns.

On Saturday afternoon they paid another visit to Swan Place and saw the owner, a Mr Butler, and he and Martin went through what Martin called 'negotiating a price' for the carpets and curtains and bits of kitchen equipment and bedroom furniture. Afterwards he took Francesca out to tea at Louis' in Hampstead. He said that they would go and buy any other furniture she might want next weekend, and when she said she could do that on her own, he said he thought he would like to be there too. After all, it would one day be his furniture as well as hers. Francesca didn't much care, she had given up, the long drag was nearly over. She would see him on Monday and say she couldn't leave Russell or contrive to have a tremendous quarrel with him, and that would be that.

When Francesca had eaten as many cream slices and rum babas as she could manage – it was too late in the day to worry about sticking to a Victorian lady's appetite – Martin suggested they go across the road and see the Bunuel film at the Everyman. But Francesca wasn't having that. If Goldie upstairs would keep an ear open for Lindsay she wanted to go round the pub with Tim. So she said she had to get back to Lindsay because Russell was having dinner with his publisher and someone who might be interested in doing *The Iron Cocoon* for television. This was an excuse in which Tim had rehearsed her and she was glad to have an opportunity of using it. Martin, of course, drove her up to Fortis Green Lane. Once more she had to hide in the side entrance. After Monday, she thought, she would never set foot in Finchley again.

February 10, February 11 . . . It would soon be all over. Francesca tried to think of ways of breaking off with Martin that were not too brutal. It was no good discussing this with Tim who would have advised the bald truth, presented as savagely as possible.

Martin walked into the shop at a quarter to six on Monday, February 12. Last time, thought Francesca, last time. She gave him a vague kiss. She hadn't bothered with pink *panne* velvet or burgundy crêpe but was wearing *her* favourite collection of garments, a patchwork skirt, a Hungarian peasant top with a long cardigan over it, and her Olaf's Daughter's boots which were heaven to wear in the shop whatever Martin might think of them.

'I'm awfully sorry, darling, but before we have dinner I've got to go round to my solicitor's and see about this contract. You won't mind, will you?'

Francesca didn't particularly mind. She wouldn't have minded if they had spent the entire evening at his solicitor's. All that interested her was how to pave the way for disappearing permanently from Martin's life. Perhaps it would be best to stage a quarrel over dinner or make use of an idea which had come to her earlier in the day. This was to say that she was pregnant and that it was Russell's child, so she would have to stay with him, wouldn't she? Francesca thought she could really enter into the spirit of this. And it had the great merit of not humiliating or even much disillusioning Martin. Francesca was amoral and greedy but she wasn't entirely heartless. Martin sometimes reminded her of a big kind dog, a Newfoundland perhaps, that one might have to abandon at the Battersea Dogs' Home but which one wouldn't kick in the face. She would try to let him down as lightly as possible, for her sake, she admitted, as well as his. She hated scenes, recriminations, fuss.

Martin introduced her to Adrian Vowchurch as his fiancée. There was a Mrs Vowchurch somewhere, clattering about in the kitchen regions. Francesca sized Adrian up. She didn't like little hatchet-faced men with supercilious eyes and the sort of public school accent so affected as to be a joke. He shook hands with her and said, insincerely she thought, that it gave him really tremendous pleasure to meet her at last. While he and Martin talked more or less incomprehensibly, it was borne in on Francesca that they were there for the express purpose of signing the contract for the purchase of the Swan Place flat. She could see it, or what was probably it, lying on a blotter on a mahogany desk. Adrian saw her looking and said they hoped for completion within a couple of weeks, allowing for searches (whatever that might mean) and would Mrs Brown like to have a look at the contract? Francesca hesitated. It seemed too unkind to let Martin buy the flat when she hadn't the slightest intention of ever living in it. Somehow the purchase of the flat hadn't seemed real until she saw what, in black and white, it involved.

This agreement is made the Twelfth Day of February, Nineteen Hundred and Seventy —, between John Alexander Butler, of Flat 10, Swan Place, Stanhope Avenue, Highgate, in the County of London (Hereinafter called 'the Vendor'), and Mrs Francesca Brown. . . . Martin had given her address as 12 Cromwell Court. It was absurd on the strength of that one weekend, it was rather touching. She read the rest of the first page. He had presumably brought her here to witness his signature. And once that was done and this contract exchanged with Butler's it would be difficult, if not impossible, for him to get out of buying the flat. Even she knew that. What she ought to do was ask him to postpone signing it, and when they were alone tell him the truth.

She found she lacked the courage to do that. She looked up and met the cold, suspicious eyes of Adrian Vowchurch. He didn't like her. It was far more than that, he distrusted her and resented her presence. He gave an infinitesimal shrug and passed a fountain pen to her.

'Can we have your signature then, Mrs Brown – er, Francesca?'

She took the pen.

'Not there,' he said. 'Up here.'

Martin gave a soft indulgent laugh. She didn't quite understand but she signed where Adrian told her to and then Julie Vowchurch, who had come in and given her a tight smile, signed as witness. Francesca felt excited and puzzled and rather frightened. Martin refused the Vowchurches' offer of drinks and they drove up to Hampstead and had dinner at the Cellier du Midi.

'You don't know how relieved I am,' said Martin, 'that I told you about winning that money. We'll never have secrets from each other, shall we?'

'No,' said Francesca, trying furiously to think. She couldn't wait to be home with Tim.

'Now we've got your flat fixed up and the future settled I want to get the other thing settled too. I mean the philanthropy part or charity or whatever you like to call it. So I'm going to have another go at Mrs Cochrane and I really think the last ten thousand had better go to Mrs Finn. Have I told you about her? She used to be our cleaner and she's a bit crazy, poor old creature, and I'll have to reach her through her son. But I'm sure she's a deserving cause . . . Are you all right, darling? You look as if you're off somewhere in a dream.'

'I'm awfully tired. I won't come back with you, if you don't mind. I'll just get a taxi in Heath Street.' His face fell. 'But I could see you tomorrow, if you like.'

'Darling,' he said, 'if that's a promise I shan't mind letting you go.'

Tim was sitting at the kitchen table doing his reporter's expenses, the greatest work of fiction, he sometimes said, since *War and Peace*. He was smoking what smelt like his hundredth Gauloise of the day and drinking retsina out of a bottle. The oven was on and the wall heater and as usual the condensation was running down the walls.

'Oh, Tim,' said Francesca, 'I feel very peculiar, wait till I tell you. Can I have some wine, please, and a cigarette?'

'Have you had a heart-rending renunciation scene?'

'No, listen, Tim, we went to his solicitor and he had this contract thing for buying the flat and I read it and it said something about being between John Alexander Butler and Francesca Brown. And I nearly didn't sign it because it seemed a bit mean and rotten making him pay for something I wasn't going to live in, but you needn't look like that, I did sign it, and . . .'

'Thank Christ,' said Tim, and his sallow face had become even paler, the red mouth and the black brows standing out like paint. 'Think – you're sure it was made just between this Butler guy and you?' She nodded with eagerness. 'And you signed it on your own? Livingstone didn't sign it?'

'No.'

'When you went to see old Urban didn't he say something about Livingstone having to pay Capital Gains Tax on one of his properties if he sold them both?'

'Yes, he sort of reminded Martin about some law about that and he said if Martin owned two flats and sold them both he'd have to pay this tax on one of them. Thirty per cent of his profit, he said. What's he done, Tim? He didn't say anything to me, he didn't mention it after we'd left the solicitor's. And I didn't say anything and I didn't break things off either . . .'

'Break things off?' said Tim. 'You'll see that guy every night till completion if it kills you *and* me. Don't you see what he's doing? He's buying it in your name so that he can avoid giving the government two or three grand in tax. In other words, in a couple of weeks' time, barring acts of God, that forty-two thousand quid luxury apartment will become the exclusive, undisputed, unencumbered property of mah honey chile.'

'Oh, Tim, I really have done it, haven't I? This is better than a ring or a bit of furniture.'

'And revenge will be very sweet,' said Tim.

He put out his arms and she came into them and they hugged each other.

15

It was rare for any post to arrive for Finn or Lena. There would be the electricity and gas bills every quarter and the little pension from Finn's father's firm and at Christmas, a card from Brenda. That was all. Months could pass by without Finn's receiving a single item addressed to himself and it was therefore with the nearest he ever got to astonishment that he picked up the long white envelope from the doormat.

The direction was to T. Finn Esq. and it was typewritten. Finn was on his way to Modena Road where he was papering walls. When he was in the van he took out the letter and read it.

Dear Mr Finn,

I do not think we have ever met, though our mothers are old friends. Perhaps Mrs Finn has mentioned to you that they had tea together a few weeks ago. I expect you will be surprised to hear from me but the fact is that I have a business proposition to put to you and I wonder if we could meet and discuss this. Could you ring me at the above number in the next few days? I shall be there between 9.30 and 5.30.

Yours sincerely,

Martin W. Urban.

Finn started the van and drove off to Parliament Hill Fields. Martin Urban had been wrong in saying they had never met. Finn seldom forgot a thing like that. He remembered Martin clearly as a spotty adolescent when he himself was eleven or twelve. Lena had taken him with her to Copley Avenue because it was the school holidays and Queenie was ill with flu. He had opened a bedroom door and seen Martin sitting at a desk, using a protractor and a set square. The older boy had turned on him a look which Finn, at the time, had taken for outrage and disgust but which later he understood. That look had in fact only been astonishment that Finn had seemed to be attempting to bridge the huge social gulf between them.

What did the grown-up Martin want of him now? If it was true that Mrs Urban had admired the partitioning of Lena's room, it might be that she had talked about it to her son and he was looking for a builder to do a conversion job for him. Finn was more or less willing, provided the money was right and he wasn't hassled about time. The words 'business proposition' seemed to imply something like that. He let himself into the house in Modena Road and walked from room to room, assessing the stage he had reached. Once the paper was up in the ground-floor front room and the hall floor re-tiled, he could be finished and at leisure. But he would see how he got on before making that phone call.

Remembering that look of Martin's all those years ago in Copley Avenue, he was slightly surprised to read that bit about their mothers being old friends. 'A few weeks ago' wasn't exactly accurate either. A few months was more like it; it had been November 16, he recalled, his birthday. Just as well, he reflected, that the woman hadn't been back again during the terrible month, the weeks of Lena's sufferings. No wonder he hadn't yet finished the work for Kaiafas . . .

She had said there were maggots coming out of the walls. That had been at the beginning when she could still see colours and smell smells, the real and the imaginary. After that she could only see in black and white and grey, and had lain crying all night, all day. He had never left her. If she had gone to the hospital they would have put her in the locked ward. He hadn't dared sleep unless she was drugged and out, for she would spring upon him if she thought he was off guard. Twice she had tried to set the place on fire and when he prevented this she burned herself instead. There were still burn scars on both her wrists and in the hollows of her elbows.

But she had come out of it at last. She always did, though Finn was afraid the time might come when she wouldn't. She could hear people's voices again and see colours again and remember who he was. On the day she held his hand and asked him if he had worn her birthday present yet, he knew she was better and he brought the bird back from downstairs. Mrs Gogarty started coming in to give him a break and he got back to work. In the past week Lena had twice been up to Second Chance and this afternoon Mrs Gogarty was taking her to a street market – somewhere in Islington, he thought it was, miles away from Parliament Hill Fields.

Coming back to Lord Arthur Road at six, Finn found them occupied with the Tarot, not telling fortunes this time but studying the pictures on certain cards. Mrs Gogarty had just bought the pack off a stall for seventy-five pence. It appeared that the Hermit and Eight of Cups were missing. Lena gave a strong shiver as she picked up and looked at the Ten of Swords. It showed the body of a man, pinned to the ground by ten sharp blades down the length of his back and lying by the waters of a lake. Finn covered up the card with the pretty Queen of Pentacles and he thought how if ever he killed again, it must look like an accident, it must be taken for an accident, for Lena's sake.

She gave him a tremulous smile and began to produce from a bag for his inspection the things she had bought that day, a man's trilby hat, a pair of wooden elephant bookends, a green china quadruped with its tail missing, half a dozen copies of a magazine called *Slimming Naturally*.

Later on, Mr Beard who kept the fur and suede cleaner's shop in Brecknock Road and who had once tried, with some success, to raise up the spirit of Cornelius Agrippa, was coming round and bringing his Ouija board. Finn felt a quiet relief that things were getting back to normal. While they waited for Mr Beard, Mrs Gogarty set out the Tarot for Finn and foretold an unexpected accession of wealth.

Finn waited for a couple of days before phoning Martin Urban and then he did so from a phone box by Gospel Oak station at ten in the morning.

'You wanted me to ring you. The name's Finn.'

'Oh, yes, good morning. How do you do? Nice of you to phone. I expect you gathered from my letter that I've got a proposition to put to you that's rather to your advantage. It's not something I'd feel like discussing on the phone. Could we – er, meet and have a word, d'you think?'

'If you want,' said Finn.

'A pub? I'll suggest somewhere half-way between our respective homes, shall I? How about the Archway Tavern? If tonight would suit you, we could say eight tonight in the Archway Tavern.'

He rang off without asking Finn how he would recognize him or telling him what he himself looked like. Finn wasn't much bothered by that, he knew he would somehow smell out in the man the studious and superior adolescent of long ago. But for a little while he did wonder why, if Martin Urban only wanted him to divide a room into two or make two rooms into one, he hadn't felt like even hinting at it on the phone.

Mr Bradshaw was spending the evening as well as most of the day with Lena. His daughter-in-law was having an operation for gallstones and he couldn't get into the house till his son came back from the hospital at nine. It was a cold, misty evening with not much traffic about and a few people. Finn wore the yellow pullover and the black scarf with the coins on and Lena's birthday present. He walked into the Archway Tavern at two minutes past eight and stood still just inside the door, looking about him. As he had expected, he knew Martin Urban at once, a tallish, square-built man, becoming burly and looking older than his age. He was sitting at a table, reading the *Evening Standard*, and as Finn's pale piercing eyes fixed him, he lifted his own. Finn walked up to him and he got to his feet.

'Mr Finn?'

Finn nodded.

'How do you do? You're very punctual. It's good of you to come. I've been thinking about it, I didn't give you much notice, did I? I hope that's all right.' Finn didn't say anything. He sat down. 'What will you drink?'

'Pineapple juice,' said Finn.

'*Pineapple juice?* What, just by itself? You're sure that's all right?'

'Just pineapple juice,' said Finn. 'The Britvic.'

He expected Martin Urban to drink beer, he was the sort who always would in pubs, except perhaps for the last drink. But he bought himself a large whisky, at least a double measure, and a small bottle of soda water. Finn supposed he was nervous about something or someone, and that someone was very likely himself. He inspired trepidation in otherwise quite confident people but he didn't know how to put them at their ease and wouldn't have done even if he had known. He sat silent, pouring the thick yellow juice from the bottle into a small squat glass. They hadn't been alone at their table but now the other man who sat there finished his beer, picked up his coat and left.

'And how's your mother these days?'

'She's OK,' said Finn.

Martin Urban turned his chair away from the table and edged it a little nearer to Finn's. 'Cheers,' he said and he drank some of his whisky. 'My mother does see her sometimes, you know. She looks in when she gets a chance.' He waited for a rejoinder to this but none came. 'I think it was November when she last saw her. She thought – well, she was a bit worried about her.'

'Well, well,' said Finn.

'She was always very fond of her, you see. They'd known each other for a long time.' It was apparent to Finn that he was trying to avoid saying that Lena had been Mrs Urban's cleaner, a statement about which Finn wouldn't have cared at all. He swilled the juice round his mouth, savouring it. A particularly good batch, he thought. 'That stuff you're drinking, is it all right?'

Finn nodded. He watched Martin Urban's face flush to a dark brick red. 'I don't want you to think I'm criticizing, finding fault or anything like that. If you don't own your own home these days, or have a council place, it's pretty difficult to find anywhere to live, let alone anywhere decent. And to buy somewhere you don't just have to be earning good money, you need a bit of capital as well. What I'm trying to say is, when my mother told me the way Mrs Finn was living – through no fault of anybody's actually – I thought, well, maybe I could do something to change all that, to sort of benefit you both, because we're all old friends, after all, aren't we?'

Finn finished his drink. He said nothing. He was beginning to be aware that an offer was about to be made to him but for what and in exchange for what he couldn't tell. This man was as shy of approaching the point as Kaiafas was. Reminded of the Cypriot, he seemed to hear a voice saying in another pub, 'I give it to my friend Feen instead', and at that recollection, at certain apparent parallels, he raised his eyes and let them rest on the flushed, square, somewhat embarrassed, face in front of him.

'I hope I haven't offended you.'

Finn shook his head.

'Good. Then I'll come to the point.' Martin Urban looked round to see that they weren't overheard and said in a lower voice, 'I could manage to let you have ten thousand pounds. I'm afraid I can't make it more than that. You'd have to go outside London, of course.'

Finn's gaze fell and rose again. He was overwhelmed by the munificence of this offer. His fame had indeed spread before him, and it wasn't his fame as a plumber and decorator. Yet one to him were fame and shame, he was without vanity. He drank the remains of his pineapple juice and said, 'It's a lot of money.'

'You wouldn't do it for less.'

Finn did a rare thing for him. He smiled. He spoke one word. 'When?'

Martin Urban seemed slightly taken aback. 'When you like. As soon as possible. You're going to accept then?'

'Oh, yes. Why not?'

'Good. That's splendid. I'm very happy you don't feel you have to put up any show of refusal, that sort of thing. It wastes so much time. Let's drink to it, shall we?' He fetched another pineapple juice and a second whisky. Facing Finn again, he seemed to become doubtful and his expression took on its former shade of mystification. 'I have made myself plain? You have understood me?'

Rather impatiently Finn said, 'Sure. You can leave it to me.'

'That's fine. It's just that I thought you might not exactly have known what I meant. Would you like me to send you a cheque?'

'I haven't got a bank account. I'd like cash.'

'*Cash?* My dear chap, that'd make quite a parcel.'

Finn nodded. 'Pad it out a bit with newspaper. You can let me have half now and half later. That way you needn't let me have the rest till you know I've done what you want. Right?'

'I suppose so. Are you going to be able to do it on your own? You know how to go about it?'

'Find someone else then,' said Finn.

'I'm sorry, I didn't mean that. I *have* offended you. Anyway, it's no business of mine how you go about it. I want to think that once I've let you have the money you're on your own, you're free.' Martin Urban swallowed his whisky very rapidly. He wiped his mouth, he sighed. 'But you will – you will do it, won't you?'

'Haven't I said?'

He was far worse than Kaiafas, Finn thought. And now, as if it was any concern of his where Lena lived or what Lena did, he began talking once more about buying her a house, moving her out of Lord Arthur Road.

'You can still get small houses for less than ten thousand in the country towns. If you don't mind going a good distance, there are building firms putting up houses for that. I'd get her to decide where she'd like to live – near some relative maybe – and then you and she could have a Saturday out there, calling on the agents.'

Finn understood it. Martin Urban wanted him out of the way, a long way away, once the deed was done. He didn't understand how ludicrous it was recommending some country town for Lena, Lena would go mad, madder, maddest away from her precious tiny segmented home, the only home she could bear to live in, away too from her friends, from Mrs Gogarty and Mr Bradshaw and Mr Beard. Finn almost felt like telling Martin Urban to shut up, to *think*, to look at reality, but he didn't do this. He sat silent and impassive while the other talked on about surveyors' reports and freeholds and frontages and party walls. For he was understanding more and more. Martin Urban, like Kaiafas, believed that if he talked in this way of mundane, harmless and practical matters he wouldn't quite have to realize the enormity of the deed for which he was to pay those thousands of pounds.

At last he paused for breath and perhaps for some sign of appreciation. Finn got up, nodded to him and left without speaking again. He had been given no further instructions but he didn't doubt that such would be sent to him in due course.

Over the Archway concourse the snow was dancing down in millions of soft plumy flakes that whirled like fireflies in the light from the yellow lamps.

16

The parcel containing the first instalment of the money was brought to Finn by an express delivery service. A man in a green uniform handed it to him at the door. Finn took it upstairs. The house in Lord Arthur Road had its Saturday smell of baked beans and marijuana, as against its weekday smell of stale waste bins and marijuana. Finn had unwrapped the parcel and was counting the money when he heard Lena coming down the stairs. Her footsteps were almost jaunty. Mr Beard was taking her to a meeting of the Tufnell Theosophists. Lena didn't have many men friends so it was an exciting event for her. Finn opened his door.

'Will you be bringing him back with you?'

Smiling a little and bridling, she said she didn't know. She would like to, she would ask him. Her eyes shone. She was wearing the mauve dress with the fringe and over it a red cloak lined in fraying satin. If you half-closed your eyes and looked at her you might fancy you were seeing - not a young girl, never that, but perhaps the ghost of a young girl. She was like a moth from whose wings most of the dust has rubbed away, a faded fluttering moth or a skeleton leaf. She laid her hand on Finn's arm and looked up into his face as if he were the parent and she the child.

'Here,' he said, 'get something for your tea then.' He thrust a bundle of notes, forty, fifty pounds into her hands.

She smelt of camphor, the mistletoe-bough bride who has been resurrected after fifty years in the trunk. Over the banisters he watched her go down, stuffing notes into her dorothy bag, into her cloak pocket, miraculously spilling none. Rich now, young again, sane again, down the dirty pavements to her psychic swain. Finn returned to his room.

Putting the money away with the rest in the bag under his mattress, he reflected once more on Martin Urban's recommendations. At the thought of Lena alone in a small country town, of Lena alone anywhere, he smiled a narrow smile of contempt. For a moment he imagined her removed from Lord Arthur Road, the only place he could remember where she had found fragments of happiness and peace; removed from him and her dear friends and the second-hand shops and her little cosy segmented space. He thought of the terrified feral mania which would overcome her when she smelt the fresh air and felt the wind and had to hunt for sleep, always elusive, in the spacious bedroom of a bungalow.

But Martin Urban, of course, hadn't talked of transferring Lena to the country because he sincerely believed Finn should buy her a house with the money. His talk of prospective house-buying had been the precise equivalent of Kaiafas's references to his homeland and Anne Blake's expressed regret that he had ever left it. They couldn't bring themselves, these squeamish people, to put their desires into plain words. Finn wondered at it. He thought he could simply have said, fixing his water-bright eyes on his listener, 'Kill this woman, this man, for me,' always supposing he was ever in the unlikely situation of wanting anyone else to do anything for him.

Sitting cross-legged on the floor, he opened a large can of pineapple and ate it with some wholemeal bread and a piece of cheese. He was rather surprised that he hadn't yet been told who his victim was to be. He had expected Martin Urban to bring the money himself and in a note or by circumlocutory word of mouth to give him a name and a description. In the middle of the floor, between the mattress and the pineapple can and other remains of his meal, lay the wrappings from the parcel. They lay in a puddle of sunlight cast by the only sunbeam that had managed to insert itself through the Chinese puzzle of brick walls and penetrate the room. Finn had told Martin Urban to wrap the money up in newspaper, and now his eye was caught by the picture on the front page of the copy of the *North London Post* which had been around the notes and under the brown paper covering. He stretched out a long arm, picked up the newspaper and looked more closely at this picture.

He seldom so much as glanced at a newspaper. He had never seen this copy before but he recognized at once the scene of the photograph. It was the path between the railway bridge and the end of Nassington Road by Parliament

Hill Fields. He recognized it because he had been there and because it was there that he had killed Anne Blake – and also because he had seen this photograph in another newspaper, that which Kaiafas had used to wrap *his* payment as a macabre joke.

So Martin Urban knew. Indeed, it must be because Martin Urban knew that he had picked him to do this particular, as yet unspecified, job for him. How did he know? Finn felt a prickling of the skin on his forehead and his upper lip as a little sweat broke. There was no telling how Martin Urban knew, but know he must or why else would he have sent Finn that newspaper with that photograph in it?

The unfamiliar sensation of fear subsided as Finn reflected that Martin Urban would hardly, considering what he was paying for and was about to have done for him, pass his information elsewhere. He shook the newspaper, expecting a note to fall out. He turned the pages slowly, looking for some hint or clue. And there, on page seven, it was.

A paragraph, ringed in red ball-point, with a street number inserted and a name underlined. Finn read the paragraph carefully, committing certain details to memory. Then he put on the yellow pullover and the PVC jacket. This was an occasion for covering his distinctively pale hair with a grey woolly hat and his memorable eyes with dark glasses. Both these items of disguise were acquisitions of Lena's. Finn locked his door and went down to the garage in Somerset Grove.

There he replaced his licence plates with a pair bearing the number TLE 315R. These he had, two years before, removed from a dark brown Lancia which had been left parked in Lord Arthur Road during a day and a night. He had known they would come in useful one day. Slightly disguised and in his slightly disguised van, Finn drove up to Fortis Green Lane and parked a little way down from number 54. It was just on three o'clock.

It was impossible to tell whether the house was at present empty or occupied. The day was chilly, the kind of day that is called raw, with a dirty-looking sky and a damp wind blowing. All the windows in 54 Fortis Green Lane were closed and at the larger of the upstairs windows the curtains were drawn. It was too early to put lights on.

The front garden was composed entirely of turf and concrete, but the concrete predominated. On the strip of it which ran round and was joined on to the walls of the house, was a dustbin with its lid on the ground beside it. The lid lay inverted with its hollow side uppermost and the wind kept it perpetually rocking with a repetitive faint clattering sound. Finn thought that if there was anyone in the house they would eventually come out to pick up the dustbin lid and stop the noise.

Quite a lot of people passed him, young couples, arm-in-arm or hand-in-hand, older people who had been shopping in Finchley High Road. Their faces looked pinched, they walked quickly because of the cold. Nobody took any notice of Finn, reading his newspaper in his plain grey van.

The dustbin lid continued to rock in exactly the same way until five, when a sharper gust of wind caught it and sent it skittering along the concrete to clatter off on to the grass. Still no one came out of the house. Finn gave it another half-hour and then, when he could tell by the continued darkness of the house that it must be empty, he drove home.

Lena was having tea with Mr Beard. There was a net curtain with scalloped edges spread as a cloth on the bamboo table and this was laden with all the things Lena had bought for tea, lattice pastry sausage rolls and anchovy pizza and Viennese whirls and arctic roll and Mr Kipling almond slices. Mr Beard was talking very interestingly about Dr Dee and the Enochian language in which he was instructed by his spirit teachers, so Finn sat down to have a cup of tea with them. Lena kept giving him fond proud smiles, she seemed entirely happy. He tried to listen to Mr Beard's account of Dee's angel but he found himself unable to concentrate. He kept thinking, turning over in his mind, how was he going to do it? How was he going to kill this stranger he hadn't yet seen and make it look like an accident?

The next day he went back to Fortis Green Lane in the morning. The dustbin and its lid had gone. Finn sat in the van, on the opposite side of the wide road this time, and watched people cleaning cars and pruning rose bushes. No one came out of or entered number 54 and the bedroom curtains were still drawn.

It wasn't until Monday evening, though he went back

again on Sunday afternoon and Monday morning, that his watching was rewarded. First, at about a quarter to seven, a tallish man in early middle age appeared from the Finchley High Road direction, unlatched the white gate, walked up the path and let himself into the house. He was wearing a thigh-length coat of a sleek, light brown fur and dark trousers and a dark grey scarf. The appearance of this man rather puzzled Finn who had expected someone younger. He watched lights come on in the hall, then the downstairs front room, then behind the drawn bedroom curtains. The bedroom light went out but the others remained on. After a while Finn went off and had a pineapple juice at the Royal Oak in Sydney Road and then he walked about in Coldfall Wood, in the dark, under the old beech trees with their steely trunks and sighing, rustling boughs. Finn wasn't the kind of person one would much like to meet in a wood in the dark, but there was no one there to meet him.

The lights had gone out in the house when he returned. It was as well for Finn that he was never bored. He sat in the van, on the odd-numbered side of Fortis Green Lane and, putting himself into a trance, projected his astral body to an ashram in the foothills of the Himalayas where it had been before and sometimes conducted conversations with a monk. Such a feat he could now accomplish with ease. The transcending of space was relatively simple. Would he ever accomplish the transcending of time so that he could project himself back into history and forward into the future?

He slept a little after his astral body had come back and awoke angry with himself in case his quarry had passed by while his eyes were shut. But the house still remained dark. Finn thought he would wait there till midnight, the time now being ten to eleven.

While he had been there cars had passed continually, though the traffic had never been heavy. At just seven minutes to eleven, a white Triumph Toledo pulled up outside number 54 and after a little delay a woman got out. She was young and tall with a straight nose and lips curved like the blades of scimitars and hair like a bronze cape in the sulphur light. Finn lowered his window. He expected to see emerge from the car the man in the fur coat but instead he heard the voice of Martin Urban call softly:

'Good night, Francesca.'

That settled for Finn certain questions that had been perplexing him. This was the right place, after all, this was it. He had doubted. He raised his window and watched the woman stand by the gate, then open the gate and walk up one of the concrete strips to a door between the house wall and the boundary fence. She waved to Martin Urban, opened the door and let it close behind her. Finn felt relieved. He watched the white car slowly depart, then gather speed.

As it disappeared into a turning on the right-hand side, his eyes following it, there passed very close to the van's window on the nearside, almost brushing the glass, a brown furriness like the haunch of an animal. Finn turned to look. Russell Brown was crossing the road now, unlatching the white gate, walking up the path. Although the woman must now have been in there for at least a minute no lights had yet come on. Though, since she had entered by the back way, she might have put lights on only in the back regions. Russell Brown unlocked the front door and let himself into the house. Immediately the hall light came on.

Finn switched on his ignition and his sidelights and drove away.

17

It saddened Francesca to have to give in her notice. She had liked working for Kate Ross, being among flowers all day, arranging flowers in the window and in bouquets, delivering flowers and seeing on people's faces the dawning of delighted surprise. Tim had once said that there was something especially flower-like about her and that – he was presumably quoting – her hyacinth hair, her classic face, her naiad airs had brought him home from desperate seas. He had been rather drunk at the time. But there was no help for it, she had to leave. February 24 would be her last day at Floreal and Adrian Vowchurch had promised completion of the purchase of the Swan Place flat two days later.

'You'll be too grand, anyway, to work in a flower shop,' said Tim, and he put his mouth to the soft hollows above her collar bone. Francesca made purring noises. The air in the room was so cold that their breath plumed up from the bed like smoke. 'Why don't you ask Livingstone to buy you a garden centre?'

'That would be pushing it,' said Francesca primly. 'I think I've done marvels actually. I shan't be getting any more out of him because I shan't be seeing him. Not after he's paid for the flat and that Adrian person has done the what-do-you-call-it. He won't know where to find me when I've left Floreal.'

'He'll be able to find you in delectable Swan Place, though perhaps mah clever honey chile won't give him a key?'

From the electric blanket came up waves of heat that made them both sweat, but that morning Francesca had found ice on the inside of the windows. The atmosphere held a bitter and quite tangible dampness. Tim lit a Gauloise and smoked it in the darkness. The glowing tip of it was like a single star in a cold and smoky sky.

'I don't think I'm going to go there at the beginning. I did think of moving in like he expects me to and after I'd been there a few days stage a tremendous irrevocable sort of row with him and say I never wanted to see him again. But I don't think I could, I'm not good at rows. So what I think now is, I'll just stay at home here very quietly for two or three days and then I'll write him a letter. I'll tell him in that what I'd have told him in the row, that it's all over but that I know the flat's mine and I need it and I'm going to live in it. How's that? Shall we go and live in that lovely place, Tim, or shall we sell it and buy another lovely place?'

'That will be for you to say.'

'What's mine is yours, you know. I think of you as my common law husband. Can you have a common law husband if you've already got an uncommon law one?'

Tim laughed. 'I'm wondering what steps, if any, Miss Urban will take when she discovers your *coup*. You'd better not count on keeping the furniture.' He drew on his cigarette and the star glowed brightly. 'I must say I shan't be sorry when mah honey chile isn't deceiving me every night with another woman.'

'You must feel like a ponce,' said Francesca. 'Ponces never seem to mind, do they?'

'The minding, as you call it, fluctuates in direct proportion to the immoral earnings.' He stubbed his cigarette out and turned to her. 'It has nothing to do with the activities. Personally, I hope you're giving Livingstone a good run for his money.'

'Well, yes and no. Oh, Tim, you've got one warm hand and one icy cold one. It's rather nice – it's rather fantastic. . . .'

Francesca brought Martin a large specimen of *Xygocactus truncatus* from the shop. It had come late into flower and now, at the end of February, its flat scalloped stems each bore on its tip a bright pink chandelier-shaped blossom. Martin was childishly, disproportionately, pleased by this gift. He put it on the window sill in the middle of the window with the view over London. It was snowing again, though not settling, and the flakes made a gauzy net between the window and the shining, yellow and white city.

That was Wednesday and Martin let her go home in a cab, but on Thursday she spent the day and stayed the night in Cromwell Court. Martin took the day off and they bought bed linen and towels, a set of saucepans and a French cast-iron frying pan, two table lamps, a Japanese portable colour television and a dinner service in Denbyware. These items they took away with them. The three-piece suite covered in jade-green and ivory velvet, the brass and glass dining table and eight chairs would of course have to be sent. Francesca said she would be bringing her own cutlery and glass. She was bored with shopping for things she doubted she would be allowed to keep.

They had dinner at the Bullock Cart in Heath Street and Martin said he had heard from John Butler that he and his wife would move out of Swan Place first thing Monday morning. He would give the key to the estate agent or if Martin liked he could call in and fetch it himself during the weekend.

'We could collect it on Saturday,' said Francesca who could foresee the difficulties of any other course.

When Mr Cochrane rang the bell at eight-thirty in the morning Francesca opened the door to him. She was wearing the top half of Martin's pyjamas and a pair of blue tights. Martin had come out of the kitchen with the Worcester sauce apron on. His expression was aghast. Mr Cochrane came in without saying anything, his eyes perceiving the flowering cactus, his nostrils quivering at the scent of *Ma Griffe*. He closed the door behind him, said, 'Good morning, madam,' and walked into the kitchen where he put his valise down on the table.

'How's your sister-in-law?' said Martin.

'Home again,' said Mr Cochrane. He looked at Martin through the bifocals, then carefully over the top of them. Then he said, 'Yes, home again, Martin, if you can call it home,' and, carrying a tin of spray polish and two dusters, he went into the living room where he scrutinized the cactus and, lifting up each item and examining it, the sheets and towels and saucepans and lamps they had bought on the previous day. At last he turned to Francesca, his death's head face convulsed into a smile.

'What a blessing to see him leading a normal life, madam. I like a man to *be* a man, if you know what I mean.'

'I know what you mean all right,' said Francesca, giggling.

'Is there anything special you'd like me to do, madam, or shall I carry on as usual?'

'Oh, you carry on as usual,' said Francesca, 'I always do,' and she gave him her best and most radiant smile.

It was her last day at the shop since Kate had said she needn't come in on Saturday morning. Next week, when she had disappeared, would Martin come to the shop and ask Kate about her? It wouldn't really matter what Martin did after Monday, after the deal was completed and the money handed over. Perhaps she should screw up her courage and really move in on Monday afternoon, as Martin thought she was going to, move in, invite him that evening – and tell him the truth, that legally the flat was hers and she intended to live in it without ever seeing him again. She would never summon up that courage. The only way was to do as she had told Tim she would do, disappear, write to him, when he made a fuss let Tim explain to him, finally take possession when it had all blown over. The flat is *yours*, hang on to that, she told herself, it's yours in the law and nothing can shake that.

Martin called for her at ten to six and they went back to Cromwell Court where he cooked the dinner. At about eleven he drove her up to Fortis Green Lane and Francesca was again obliged to take refuge in the back garden of number 54. Tonight the house was in darkness. She stood against the stuccoed wall, listening for the car to go. As it happened, she came out too soon. It hadn't been Martin's car but a small grey van pulling away. Martin was still there, still watching the house – watching for lights to come on?

She told him she had left her key in the house and would have to wake Russell to let her in.

'Please go, darling. I'll be all right.'

Reluctantly, Martin did go. Francesca was actually trembling. She had to sit down on the low wall for a moment. When she got up and turned round to look warily at the house she half-expected to see its occupant glaring at her from an upper window. But there was no one. It was colder tonight than it had been for a week, the sky a dense unclouded purple and the air very clear. She really needed something warmer on than the red and blue striped coat over her corded velvet smock. Each time Martin landed her up here she tried walking in fresh directions to find a taxi, but now she had exhausted them all. So was it to be down to Muswell Hill or across the Finchley High Road? Martin had headed for Muswell Hill . . . Francesca, who wasn't usually very apprehensive or given to improbable fantasies, found herself thinking, suppose his car broke down and I walked past it and he saw me . . . ? Now that her task was so nearly accomplished, she was growing hourly more and more frightened in case anything should happen at the eleventh hour to stop her getting the flat. People said it was virtually impossible to withdraw from such a deal once the contracts were exchanged. He wouldn't have to withdraw, though, he would only have to have a new contract made with his name on it instead of hers.

Nothing must happen. She only had Saturday to get through now. They had agreed not to meet on Sunday, she would be too busy packing. She pulled up the hood of her coat and set off along wide, cold, empty Fortis Green Lane for Finchley High Road. A taxi picked her up just before she reached it.

'I don't usually ever feel nervous about anything, you know,' she said to Tim. 'I suppose anyone can get nervous if there's enough at stake. While I was sort of lurking in that garden I kept thinking how awful it would be if that man came out of his house. I mean, he might have chased me and Martin might have hit him, thinking he was my husband, I imagined the most fearful things.'

Tim laughed. 'The most fearful thing about that would have been the outcome, the loss of our future home. Otherwise I can't imagine anything funnier than Livingstone having a punch-up with a complete stranger in the middle of the night in darkest Finchley.'

Francesca thought about it. Then she laughed too and helped herself to one of Tim's cigarettes. 'What made you pick on that funny house, anyway? What made you pick on that man?'

'Me? I didn't pick on him. I didn't pick on the house. That was your fiancée. Remember? I didn't even know there was anyone called Brown living in Fortis Green Lane. The idea of writing that par for the *Post* was solely to give verisimilitude to your story. People say newspapers are full of lies but they believe everything they read in newspapers just the same. Fortis Green Lane is a long road and Brown is a common name. There may be half a dozen Browns living there for all I know. Livingstone happened to find this one in the phone book.'

With a giggle Francesca said, 'It would be most awfully unfair then if Martin had hit him.'

'You'll have to take good care he doesn't. He truly is that mysterious individual, the innocent bystander.'

There was a heavy frost that night and the roof tops were nearly as white as when they had been covered with snow. Francesca and Tim lay late in bed and Francesca brought Lindsay in with them. They talked about the flat in Swan Place while Lindsay sat on the pillow and braided Francesca's hair into Afro-plaits. Tim said they would probably have to sell the flat and buy one that wasn't i Highgate, it would be so awkward if they ever ran ir Martin. That would be all right, Francesca said, she wo quite like to live up near the Green Belt or out tow Epping Forest, she wasn't wedded to London. Nor t distinguished author of *The Iron Cocoon*, said Tim, an both laughed so much that Lindsay pinched their lips together.

Tim drove her as near as he dared to Cromwell Court. Martin wanted to know what arrangements she had made for Monday. Had she booked a car? Was Lindsay going to the nursery that day or not? Could she manage all her clothes at one journey? And what about Russell? Had she told him there should be a fair division of their property and had he agreed? Francesca answered these questions as best she could while they were on their way to Swan Place to pick up the key from Mr Butler. She felt elated when the key was in her possession. A key gives such a secure feeling of rights and privacy and ownership. Mrs Butler took her round the flat once more and Francesca could hardly contain her excitement. How different it was to view all this, to tread those soft, subtle-shaded carpets, finger stiff silky curtains, feel the warmth, turn on a tap, press a switch, in the knowledge it was going to be all her own!

'Will you ask me to supper on Monday evening?' Martin said.

'Tuesday. Give me just one day to settle in. Lindsay's bound to be difficult, you know.'

'Yes, I suppose so. Tuesday then.' His face wore the hurt look that blurred his features and made it dog-like. 'Adrian hopes to complete by midday on Monday so you can come any time after. I expect the Butlers will still be moving out.'

Francesca didn't see much point in talking about it when she wasn't going to move in at all. She wished she had the nerve to ask Martin what was to be done with the deeds or lease or whatever it was. Deposited in his bank maybe. Not for long, she thought, not for long. Tim would deal with that, she had done her part, she had almost done it. She held Martin's hand in the car, held it on her knee and said, 'Let's not go out to dine, let's have a quiet evening at home on our own.'

18

Most of the time there was nobody in the house but the man was there more often than the woman. This was a reversal, Finn thought, of the usual order of things. He had never seen them together, though he had been to Fortis Green Lane on five evenings now, each time parking in a different place. He had seen the woman twice and the man three times and once he had seen the man with another woman. This didn't trouble him, nor was he perplexed about the relations of these people to each other or that of Martin Urban to them. Emotions, passion, jealousy, desire, even hatred, were beyond or outside his understanding. They bored him, he preferred magic. He longed now to be able to wield practical magic, to conjure his victim out of the house and into his trap.

But he had lost that power even before the death of Queenie. Sitting in the van, watching, he thought of how, in Jack Straw's, he had concentrated on that reporter and made him get out and light a cigarette. Or had he? Such doubt is the enemy of faith and it is faith which moves the mountains.

Come out of the house, he said in his mind to the darkened windows, the closed front door, the indestructible stucco. He said it over and over again like the mantras he repeated for his meditation. He had no idea, and no means of knowing, if the house was empty or not. There might be a light on in the downstairs back room or in the kitchen. He had been there since five, since before the dark came down, but there had been no sign of life from the house and no flicker of light.

It was a cold evening, the air already laying frost in a ve
thin silvery glitter on the tops of fences and the cross-pie
of gates, on twigs and laurel leaves and on the oblique
windows of parked cars. The sulphur light showed
early spring flowers in some gardens, pale or white c

colour buds and bells. Finn didn't know the names of flowers. The frost wasn't heavy enough to whiten the grass much. Inside the van it was cold. Finn wore the yellow pullover and the grey woollen cap and the leather coat and sat reading Crowley's *Confessions*. Back in Lord Arthur Road he had left Lena and Mrs Gogarty indignant because Mr Beard, proposing to raise up for their edification, Abremelin the Mage, meant to do so by indefensible methods. In fact, by the sacrifice of a pigeon, the emanation from whose blood would provide the material for the seer to build a body out of. Pigeons were commoner than flies in Brecknock Road, Mr Beard had said. Lena and Mrs Gogarty shuddered and twittered and sent Mr Beard to Coventry. Finn wished he was back there with them and the innocent pleasures of planchette to which they had retreated, scared by Mr Beard's sophistication.

A light had come on in 54 Fortis Green Lane, a not very strong light as from a sixty-watt bulb, in the hall. It showed through the slit of a window on the right-hand side of the door and through the small diamond-shaped pane of glass in the door itself. No one came out, no one went in. It was ten o'clock. Finn didn't think anything was going to happen tonight. Again it would have to be postponed. That he had taken Martin Urban's money and as yet done nothing to earn it, vaguely oppressed him. But because it was a waste of time sitting there any longer, he drove down to Muswell Hill, to the Green Man, and drank two bottles of Britvic pineapple juice.

Sitting alone at a table, he fixed his thought on a fat man in a checked sports jacket, willing him to get up and go outside to the gents'. After about five minutes of this the fat man did get up and go outside, but a smaller thinner man sitting with him had gone out a moment or so before. Finn didn't know what to think. As he came out into the street he was visited by a premonition so intense as almost to blind him. He felt it like a pain in his head.

Tonight *was* the time for it. If he would only seize his portunity and go back to Fortis Green Lane now all ıld be well. In his mind's eye, as on a screen, he saw the e quite clearly, the light shining through and alongside ront door, the front garden with its alternating turf oncrete. He stared into this vision and silently commanded Martin Urban's enemy to appear. At once this happened and Finn seemed to be staring into a pair of puzzled and dismayed eyes. He got into the van and drove back to Fortis Green Lane as fast as he could go.

There was no need to watch and wait. As in his vision, Martin Urban's enemy was in the front garden, unlatching the white iron gate. But this time there was no meeting of eyes.

Finn hadn't even switched off the engine. He watched the figure in the fur coat close the gate and turn immediately left into the side street. For what purpose would anyone go out alone at this time on a Saturday night? Finn knew it was no good judging by himself. He might go out to commune with the powers of darkness but others lacked that wisdom. They would be more likely to visit some friend, a nocturnal person who had no objection to late callers.

He allowed his quarry two minutes' start and then he followed. Martin Urban's enemy was nowhere to be seen. The street was deserted. Coldfall Wood, grey and still under the indigo sky, lay ahead of him. He turned right along the edge of the wood and then he saw the figure in the fur coat ahead of him, a long way ahead, casting an attenuated black shadow as it passed under a lamp. There was scarcely any other traffic, parked cars everywhere but only one that moved, a sports car that passed him, going towards Finchley.

Finn lagged behind, stopped for a while. When he started again, driving slowly, it wasn't long before he came to a sign that indicated the nearness of the North Circular Road. The houses had stopped. Soon the parked cars had stopped. On either side of the road he had turned into, stretched open land. Not woods, though, or heath or anything that remotely approximated to real countryside except that grass grew on it. It was a vast acreage of tips, of heaps of rubble, dismantled cars, rusty iron, stacks of wood that looked like collapsed huts, the overgrown remains of abandoned allotments. The whole of this wilderness was weirdly but brilliantly lit by lamps on tall stems which coated the sky with a shimmering brownish fog and gave to the ground a loo[illegible] of total desolation.

There was no dwelling of any kind in sight. Finn kn[illegible] that most new approach roads to motorways or trunk r[illegible] look like this, that the land only had this appearance of nightmare violation because heavy construction work had not long since taken place on it. Yet knowing this, he still had the feeling of having entered a different and uncanny world, a place where the ordinary usages of life were suspended and the occult reigned. In it he felt alone, he and the bobbing shadow in the distance ahead. He felt too that he might even be invisible, had perhaps discovered unwittingly the secret of invisibility which since the beginning of time magicians had sought for.

A thrill of power ran through him. The clear brown sky seemed to be meshed all over with a dazzling veil of gold. But for a distant throb there was silence. Finn made the van glide slowly along. On the left-hand side, ahead of the moving figure, the pavement petered out. It would be necessary, inevitable, soon to cross that wide curving roadway, white and gold and glittering at close on midnight.

The head above the fur collar turned to the right, to the left, to the right again. The black shadow dipped into the road. Finn was in second gear. He rammed his foot hard down on the accelerator, changed in one movement up into fourth, and shot towards the shining, moving pillar of fur. Now, at last, he saw the eyes, round, shining, dark with terror. He had to swerve in pursuit, to make sure. A shattering scream rang through the glittering empty air, arms were flung up in a desperate useless defence, and then, when it seemed as if the suddenly huge, screaming animal-like shape must flatten and paste itself against his windscreen, he felt it under the van, the wheels crunching flesh and bone.

Finn reversed over the thing he had crushed and then drove over it once more in bottom gear. There was a lot of blood, dark and colourless as Anne Blake's had been, splashed blots of it on the white road. He made a U-turn and drove back the way he had come up. For a yard or so his tyres left their imprints in blood. He would clean those tyres when he changed the licence plates, before he went home to Lena.

19

As yet the wood showed no signs of greening but it had grown sparkling brown and the beech trunks silver. Their myriad delicate fronds, for twigs was too solid a word, fanned against a mother-of-pearl sky. Martin was inescapably reminded of Tim. He had a feeling, utterly absurd and one to which he wouldn't have dreamt of yielding, that he should park the car here on the winding bit up to Highgate, and go on a pilgrimage through the wood to find the spot where he had met Tim. The dying day – not so different from a day just born – and the coming spring recalled to him the warmth of that encounter and that other curious feeling which he had felt for no one, not even for Francesca, either before or since.

He drove on. The sky was deepening to lavender and the sunset had brushed it with pink and golden strokes. What had Tim been doing in the wood that morning? Strange that he had never asked himself that question before. While he had come in from Priory Gardens and was walking north, Tim seemed to have entered from the Muswell Hill Road as if he had come from the junction where the Woodman was. Martin was approaching this junction now and it occurred to him that he might go into Bloomers and buy Francesca some spring flowers. Of course he had promised not to see her today but he would phone her when he got home and if she really didn't want to see him tonight he would take the flowers to her on his way to work in the morning.

Bloomers, however, was closed and its lights off, though the time was only twenty to six. Martin drove up Southwood Lane and down the High Street to Cromwell Court. No letters had come by the second post. He had written again to Mrs Cochrane on Friday but perhaps it was too soon yet to expect a reply. In the living room, part on a chair and part on the floor, were still stacked the saucepans, the frying pan, the apricot and brown and cream patterned towels, the brown and white sheets and pillowcases, and the Denbyware dinner service. Francesca might be in need of those things.

In the flat on Saturday afternoon he had noted the Butlers' phone number. He dialled it now and got the unobtainable signal. The Post Office presumably hadn't let her keep the old number when they came in today to re-connect the phone. Perhaps you always had to have a new number. Should he now phone Tim? It was three months, more than that, since he had last spoken to Tim. There was nothing really that he would like more tonight since he couldn't be with Francesca, than to spend a couple of hours with Tim. They hadn't even quarrelled. They had parted because of his own absurd guilt over nothing, he had broken their friendship over that money. And it was nearly all gone now, would all be gone when he had settled with Mrs Finn and Mrs Cochrane.

Tim wouldn't be home yet. Martin phoned Adrian Vowchurch and thanked him for getting completion so promptly.

'Francesca move in all right, did she?'

'Oh, yes,' said Martin.

'By the by, I had a message, heaven knows why, that there are two more keys with the agents. OK?'

Martin said it was OK and that he had wondered why there had only been one key. He kept Adrian talking for a while in the hope that he might invite him and Francesca round one evening but Adrian didn't. He said he must fly because he and Julie were going out to dinner with the senior partner and his wife. Martin thought it likely that Francesca would phone once she had got Lindsay to bed and off to sleep. He drank some whisky, he made himself an omelette with four eggs and two rashers of bacon and a lot of mushrooms, and when he had eaten it and washed up it was half-past eight.

The phone rang at nine. It was Norman Tremlett. Norman lived at home with his parents and he wanted to know if Martin would bring Francesca to dinner on the evening of Saturday week. Martin didn't much want to dine with the Tremletts but he felt excited at the idea of having the right to accept for himself and Francesca just as if they were already a married couple, so he said yes, they'd like to.

Just as it had previously been too early, it now seemed too late to phone Tim, too late anyway for them to arrange to meet and go out anywhere that night. He would phone Tim tomorrow or the next day. For the first time since the autumn Martin unlocked the glass door and went out on to the balcony. The night was cool but the sky so unusually clear that you could see the stars, though so tiny and faint that it was as if the gloomy pall of London had pushed them even greater distances into space. Francesca wasn't going to phone tonight. He realized it with resignation but it was silly to feel such intense disappointment. She would be tired after her long day which had started perhaps with a final quarrel with Russell and ended with Lindsay's tantrums, by now she might well be asleep.

The post brought a letter, not from Mrs Cochrane, but from her brother-in-law. The tone was that of Mr Cochrane's notes, clipped and censorious. It began 'Dear Martin' and the gist of it was that he and Mrs Cochrane would come to Cromwell Court that evening, eight o'clock if this was convenient. Martin looked in the phone book to see if Mr Cochrane was on the phone and found, to his surprise, that he was. But when he dialled the number there was no answer. He would have to try again later. This evening he was to dine with Francesca in Swan Place, so of course he couldn't see Mr and Mrs Cochrane.

He drove to work via Shepherd's Hill, thus passing close by Stanhope Avenue but Francesca's windows weren't visible. It was a nuisance having no phone number for her. He had an appointment with a client at eleven which eventually lengthened over lunchtime and it was half-past two before he got back.

Francesca hadn't phoned.

'Are you positive there haven't been any calls for me?'

Caroline, with black-varnished fingernails today and red hair cropped to a crew cut, said that of course she was positive, he ought to know she didn't make mistakes like that.

'OK, well, would you like to get hold of directory enquiries and find if they've got a number for Brown of Flat 10 Swan Place, Stanhope Avenue, Highgate?'

She came back after about five minutes. 'No, they haven't, Martin, and I'm quite *positive*. He was a very nice man at directory enquiries, got a voice just like Terence Stamp.'

So the Post Office hadn't yet got around to fixing Francesca's phone. She was probably waiting in for them which could be why she hadn't phoned him from a call-box. It didn't matter particularly, he would just go straight there on his way from work.

He left at five-thirty sharp. Swan Place was, if anything, more attractive than Cromwell Court. The block was newer and there were lifts and carpet on the stairs. Martin smiled to himself to think he had spent more on Francesca's home than he had on his own. He went up in the lift and rang the bell of number 10.

No one came. He rang again. She was out. What on earth was she doing out now? Wasn't she expecting him? He wondered where she could have gone at this hour when nearly all the shops were closed. Perhaps to tea with some friend who had a child of Lindsay's age? Martin had never heard of any friend of Francesca's apart from Annabel. He hung about outside the door, wishing he had thought of calling in at the estate agent's to collect those other keys. They would be shut now.

He waited nearly half an hour for her. Then he wrote a note on the back of an envelope he found in his pocket and put it through the letter box. The note said to phone him as soon as she got in.

It began to worry him, thinking something might have happened to her. Suppose Russell had asked her to go back and have a talk with him and was preventing her from leaving again? He drank some whisky, not too much because he was sure to have to drive again that evening. There was nothing to eat in the flat apart from bread and cheese and things in tins.

The phone didn't ring but at just before eight the doorbell did. Martin was sure it was Francesca who had thought that if she had to go out into the street to find a call-box she might as well get in a taxi and come straight to him. On the doorstep stood Mr Cochrane and a very small woman in a scarlet coat and black fur pixie hood. He had forgotten all about them.

' 'Evening, Martin. This is Mrs Cochrane, Martin. Rita, this is Martin.'

Mr Cochrane was in casual gear, denim jeans, a Fair Isle pullover and a kind of anorak with fur trimmings. Martin felt bereft of ideas and almost of speech by the sight of them. But there was no help for it. Mr Cochrane hadn't waited to be invited in or asked to sit down. He had gone in, taken his sister-in-law's coat and hat, seated her on the sofa, hung up her coat and his own in the hall cupboard, and was now alternately rubbing his hands and warming them on a radiator.

'Would you like a drink?' Martin said.

'Whisky for me, Martin, and Mrs Cochrane will have a lemonade with a drop of port in it.'

Martin had neither port nor lemonade. Every bottle had to be removed from the drinks cupboard before Mr Cochrane could decide on a substitute. His sister-in-law hadn't opened her mouth. When she was at last given a wine glass containing a mixture of sweet red vermouth and soda she nodded her head very fast and on and on as if she had a spring where her neck should be. Her mouth had set into a pinched, tight and intensely nervous smile.

Mr Cochrane, now sitting on the radiator, launched into a speech. His attitude was one which Martin hadn't met before in his dealings with the objects of his charity. His sister-in-law was prepared to accept Martin's offer – here Mrs Cochrane, who hadn't ceased to smile, began nodding again – provided she was allowed absolute freedom of choice as to where she lived and what kind of dwelling she lived in. Also Martin must understand that one must move with the times, things had changed out of all knowledge in the past few years and you couldn't buy anything worth considering in the London area for less than fifteen thousand pounds. At this point the phone rang and Martin leapt for it. It was a wrong number. Mr Cochrane said that he supposed it was all right to help himself to more scotch, did so, and terminated his speech with words to the effect that now they understood each other and had cleared the air he would start house-hunting in the morning.

Martin felt he only wanted to get rid of them. If it cost him his last five thousand did it so much matter? He realized that that was what it would do, it would all be gone. Deliberately and methodically he half-filled his glass with whisky and drank it at a gulp.

'I'm glad to be of help,' he said. 'It's good we've been able to arrange things so easily.'

The phone rang. It was Norman Tremlett to ask if Martin and Francesca could make it Saturday fortnight instead of Saturday week. Martin said yes and he would call Norman back. Mr Cochrane had got himself into his anorak and his sister-in-law into her coat and pixie hood and was staring piercingly at the stack of saucepans and china and towels and bed linen.

'If I don't see madam on Friday, Martin, you can tell her I mean to commence the spring cleaning. Subject to her approval of course.'

Martin didn't know what to say to this.

'Come along, Rita.'

Martin closed the door on them and finished his whisky. There was only about an inch left in the bottle so he had that too. After the phone had rung the second time he had made up his mind to drive round to Swan Place as soon as the Cochranes had gone. But he couldn't go now, he had drunk too much. He slept heavily and dreamlessly that night, awakening early with a headache.

By a quarter to nine he was ringing Francesca's doorbell. He continued to ring it long after there was no point. Then it occurred to him that she might still be taking Lindsay to the nursery and he wrote her another note, on the back of the bill for the sheets and towels this time, asking her to phone him before lunch.

When it got to twelve, to half-past, and she hadn't phoned he began to feel real anxiety for the first time. He excused himself to Gordon Tytherton with whom he had said he would have lunch, and went back to Swan Place. Francesca was still out. He simply didn't know what to do, and then he remembered the two spare keys. He drove up to Highgate Village and was given the keys without demur by the estate agent's receptionist.

His notes were still on the doormat. That was the first thing he absorbed. The second – though this took some time fully to register – was that no one had occupied the place since the departure of the Butlers. There were the carpets on the floors and the curtains at the windows, the chairs and tables, the fridge and the cooker and an electric kettle, but there was no food in the kitchen, the fridge door still stood open after Mrs Butler's final defrosting, and in the bathroom there was no soap, no toothbrush. Martin went into both bedrooms to find that the beds hadn't been made up. The cupboard in the main bedroom was empty but for five wire coathangers.

For a while he was nonplussed. He sat down in the penthouse living room by the window that was even bigger than his own in Cromwell Court. But almost immediately he jumped up again. The first thing he must do, obviously, was phone her at home in Fortis Green Lane. For some reason, because she was ill or Lindsay was ill or Russell had intervened and used force, she had been prevented from leaving home on Monday.

Rejecting the idea of phone boxes, which he had hardly ever in his life had occasion to use, he drove home to Cromwell Court. There, for the first time, he dialled the number the directory gave for H. R. Brown of 54 Fortis Green Lane, N10. The bell rang unanswered. She couldn't be at home ill. He felt rather sick, with hangover perhaps or hunger. He made himself a cheese sandwich but he couldn't eat it. The idea of taking the afternoon off to look for Francesca didn't cross his mind. He tried the phone again and then he went back to work, remembering a fear that had come to him during the first days of their acquaintance when she had told him nothing of her circumstances or history and had withheld from him her address. He had wondered what he would do if she left her job, for the flower shop had been the only place where he could be sure of finding her.

Floreal was again closed and unlit when he drove past it just before six. He went home and poured himself a stiff brandy because all the whisky was gone. He thought inconsequentially how a week ago he could have afforded cases of whisky without thinking about it, but not now. He had no more money now than on the last occasion he sent in Tim's pools perm.

No one was answering the phone at 54 Fortis Green Lane. He tried it four times between six and seven. Immediately after he put the phone back for the fourth time it rang. Norman Tremlett. Why hadn't he rung back last night as he had promised? Martin dealt with Norman as best he could, trying not to lose his temper at facetious questions about his 'lovely betrothed' and when the 'happy day' was to be. As soon as he could terminate the conversation he did. He grilled the steak he had brought in with him and ate it without enjoyment. The brandy bottle beckoned him, but he knew that if he drank any more he wouldn't dare drive up to Finchley.

He could tell the house was empty before he even got out of the car. What now? Enquire of the neighbours as he had enquired for Annabel? After sitting in the car for an aeon of minutes, after some painful soul-searching, he tried number 52.

A girl of about fifteen came to the door. He might have been speaking to her in Hausa or Aramaic for all her comprehension.

At last she said, 'You what?'

He realized he had asked questions which, in these lawless times, gave rise to deep suspicion. The girl went away to fetch her mother. Martin rehearsed in his mind better ways of eliciting information but they weren't much better. The woman appeared, drying her hands on a tea towel.

'I'm sorry,' Martin began, 'I know you must think this very odd, but I only want to know if Mr and Mrs Brown next door are away. I'm . . .' It wasn't exactly true but what else could he say?' . . . a friend of theirs.'

It was as if he had demanded payment for goods she hadn't bought or even wanted. She gave a humourless, cynical laugh.

'That's not true for a start. There is no Mrs Brown. He's a widower. He's been a widower for all of five years.'

Martin couldn't speak.

Perhaps she sensed that he had had a shock. Her manner softened. 'Look, you could be anybody, couldn't you, for all I know? Such a lot of funny things go on these days. He's not in, you can see that. I haven't seen him since Saturday but that doesn't mean a thing. He keeps himself to himself.'

She had closed the door before Martin was half-way down the path. His hands shook when he got hold of the steering wheel. He flexed them and took deep breaths and tried to blank out his mind. When he tried again his hands were steady. It wasn't more than a couple of miles down to Highgate, though he was slowed up by the rain which had suddenly begun and now was lashing down.

The phone was ringing as he walked into the flat. He thought that if it was Francesca he wouldn't know what to say, he would be able to find no words in which to speak to her, to ask, even to begin. What she had done to him he didn't know, only that it was terrible.

He picked up the phone. There were pips, six of them.

A voice said, 'This is Finn speaking.'

20

'Yes,' Martin said, 'yes?' He had forgotten who Finn was and the flat low voice meant nothing to him.

'I thought I'd have heard from you by now.'

Heard from him . . . Oh, yes. Finn was Mrs Finn's son and Mrs Finn was . . . He was surprised to hear his own voice sounding so normal, so characteristic even. 'You've been successful, have you?'

A short toneless 'Yes'.

Martin was getting used to ingratitude. He no longer cared. 'I'll send the rest round like I did the first lot, OK?'

'In cash again,' said Finn and put the phone down.

It was still only nine o'clock. Martin poured himself some more brandy but he couldn't drink it, the smell of it made him feel sick. Was it possible that the woman in the house next door had been lying? Why should she, except from madness or motiveless malevolence? Francesca didn't live there, had never lived there. But he had seen her go into the house. . . . No, he had never quite seen that. He remembered little things, that insistence on taxis, her refusal ever to invite him into the house. Where was she now?

She must have a home somewhere. She hadn't come to him like some fairy woman out of the sea or from another world. Surely she had loved him . . . ? There must be some motive for the lies she had told him but that motive might not in itself be evil. He tried to think of reasons for it, sitting there in the chair by the window long into the night. At last he drank up the brandy and went to bed. London went on glittering down there as if nothing had happened.

Next day the world had become a different place. The day was cold and wet, a high wind blowing. He awoke to some sense of indefinable misery. A moment later it was no longer indefinable but had settled into the knowledge that Francesca had deceived him.

The wind was blustery and sharp. He saw it blow someone's umbrella inside out as he crossed the Archway Road. The lights weren't on in Floreal but it wasn't yet nine-thirty. Stuck up on the door, on the inside of the glass, was a notice that hadn't been there last week. *Closed till Monday, March 5.* He turned away. Kate Ross could be ill or just taking a holiday. He went back to his car and drove to work.

Kate would be bound to have Francesca's true address. There were a dozen or so people in the phone book called K. Ross but none in Highgate where Kate lived. Or where Francesca had said she lived. Could he believe anything Francesca had told him?

Her parents lived in Chiswick. Her maiden name had been Blanch. But was that true? There was an E. Blanch in a place called Petrarch Court, Barrowgate Gardens, Chiswick. She had said they lived in a flat, an old mansion block. She had said, she had said . . . He dialled the number, tried to resign himself to hearing a voice say she had no daughter, had never even married.

A man answered. He sounded elderly, as if he might be retired.

'I'm trying to get in touch with your daughter, Francesca Brown.'

There was a dense silence. Then, 'I might say I don't have a daughter.'

Martin didn't know what to say. He nearly put the receiver down. But the old voice, very dry now, said, 'I haven't seen Francesca for five years.' There came a crackling chuckle. 'She was never very filial. A cold-hearted girl. I can give you her husband's phone number, though God knows when she left him. She leaves everybody.'

Martin said he would have the number. He wrote it down.

'That's right,' said Mr Blanch. 'Russell Brown's his name but he'll be out now. At work. She hasn't by any chance left *you*, has she?'

The exchange was an East London one, Ilford or Stratford. Had Francesca given him the Fortis Green Lane address because she was ashamed of her real one? He seemed to hear the dry rasping voice again, 'God knows when she left him. She leaves everybody.' There had been a bitter cynical amusement underlying Mr Blanch's words. For the first time Martin felt the absurdity of his position, the humiliation. How was he going to explain to his parents, to Norman and Adrian, that he had bought Francesca a flat and she had left him without even living in it. 'She leaves everybody . . .'

He couldn't think of an excuse for getting out of dinner with his parents. His mother, drinking oloroso, said she had half expected Francesca too, though she supposed that would have meant a baby-sitter for the little girl. Mr Urban leant against the mantelpiece with his amontillado. Martin had three glasses of Tio Pepe, wondering where Francesca was now and who Lindsay's father was and why she had lied to him so that it seemed almost everything she had said was a lie.

'Do you think Francesca would like me to make her a patchwork skirt?' said Mrs Urban.

Martin said he didn't know, which was the answer he would have been obliged to make to any question put to him about Francesca.

'I don't care for them myself,' said his mother, 'but she looks the type to wear them.'

Martin left early, having taken from the bathroom cabinet one of the sleeping pills his mother had for when she went on holiday. He was home by half-past nine. What did he hope to learn, anyway, by phoning Russell Brown? According to her father, 'God knows when' Francesca had left him, years ago, perhaps, he couldn't be Lindsay's father. At last he did try the number that Mr Blanch had given him, but there was no answer. He took the Mogadon tablet and washed it down with brandy and went to bed.

Mr Cochrane, arriving at eight-thirty in the morning, made no reference to the events of Tuesday evening. He had brought Martin's letters up with him, having encountered the postman on the way in. Martin didn't open them, didn't so much as glance at them. He was in no mood for bills or for querulousness from Miss Watson or the Gibsons which he felt those envelopes might contain.

He carried the saucepans and the frying pan, the dinner service, the two lamps, the bed linen and towels into his bedroom and stuffed them into the bottom of the clothes cupboard. They would come in useful one day, he thought with dry anger, for other people's wedding presents.

Mr Cochrane, in his ironmonger's coat, was emptying cupboards and shelves on to the kitchen floor, the first stage of his spring cleaning. On the table were the two piles of newspapers, the broadsheets and the tabloids.

'Beats me what you want all this muck for, Martin,' said Mr Cochrane. 'Hoarding up rubbish like an old woman.'

Martin took no notice. He was looking through the *Posts* for the copy of December 8, the one that had contained the paragraph about Russell Brown. Surely it had been on the top because it was the last one he had ever received, after that he had stopped taking the *Post*. Then he remembered. He must have used it to wrap up Mrs Finn's money. Naturally he had used the paper that was on top of the pile. Mrs Finn. Some time today, he thought, he had better go to the bank and draw out the other five thousand, phone them first, maybe, as he had done last time . . .

He had been at work ten minutes when Adrian Vowchurch phoned. He said it was rather embarrassing (he didn't sound embarrassed) but he simply had to know whether his account for the conveyance was to go to Francesca or to Martin.

Martin hadn't expected an account at all. It was true that Adrian had charged him for the conveyance of his own flat but since then he, Martin, had put in a whole lot of hours sorting out some family trust muddle for Julie and he wouldn't have dreamt of expecting payment for that. He said shortly:

'To me, of course. Who else?'

'My dear old chap, I only asked. Ladies get very uptight these days if their equality isn't respected. Francesca is a property owner now and a ratepayer. It can go to their heads, you know, and you do rather . . .'

'Adrian . . .' he interrupted but he couldn't finish.

'What? I was merely going to say – if merely is the word – that you do rather talk as if her flat was sort of yours. You can't have it both ways, avoid your tax *and* keep a foot in the door.'

The flat was hers. Did she know that? He had never exactly explained this to her but she must know it, she was no fool. If she knew it was hers surely she would come to it. He put his head round his father's door to say he was going out for an hour. Walter Urban was preoccupied with a client's letter. He looked up, irritability making him more than usually dog-faced.

'Extraordinary chap,' he said, tapping the letter. 'Calls himself the chairman of a financial PR company and he doesn't know the first thing about finance. Here he is telling me he's given away – *given*, if you please – ten thousand pounds to his sister to start some sort of business and can he get tax relief on it? He won't find the government giving anything to him, he'll be giving it to them. Hasn't he ever heard of CTT?'

'CTT?' repeated Martin, although he knew perfectly well what those initials stood for.

'Capital Transfer Tax. Wake up, Martin. His sister's not a charity. Why didn't he consult me before he started throwing his money about?'

Martin asked himself why he too hadn't consulted Walter or even consulted his own knowledge. Was it because he hadn't wanted to know and have his noble-hearted schemes spoiled? Just as he hadn't wanted to know of the true relations between Francesca and her husband? Now, in both cases, he was going to have to pay for wilfully shutting his eyes. Almost all his money was gone and he was presumably going to have to pay tax, at least on what he had given Miss Watson and Mrs Cochrane, though perhaps not Mrs Finn since that was cash . . . Was he planning on being dishonest about it as well? He pushed all thought of money out of his mind – did he really care about it at this juncture? – and drove to Swan Place. The flat was just as it had been on Wednesday, empty, waiting, the fridge door open, the carpet marked with circular depressions where furniture legs had stood.

He had wanted to tell Adrian about it but he hadn't been able to. Adrian's voice had been too cool, too mocking and urbane. He thought of those friends of his whose advice he could ask, Norman, the Tythertons . . . They couldn't help him any more than he could help himself, and behind his back, because they were deeply conservative and unshakeably conventional, they would laugh nervously.

Back in the office, he reverted to that paragraph in the *Post*. He could remember perfectly what it had said. Russell Brown was thirty-five, was a teacher in a technical college who had written a book about the fourteenth century and the Black Death, wife Francesca, daughter Lindsay. Martin sighed and dialled the Ilford number Mr Blanch had given him. There was no answer.

Could the *Post* have got it wrong? Could it have been Fortis Green Road or Fortis Green Avenue instead? That wouldn't explain how Francesca had seemed to live, had repeatedly said she lived, in Fortis Green Lane. The *Post* must have some sort of clue to all this and he knew someone who worked on the *Post* . . .

Tim Sage.

Tim might not know the answer but Tim would be able to help him. Journalists always knew how to go about finding elusive addresses and phone numbers, and elusive people, come to that. And it was foolish to think of himself and Tim as enemies. Why did he do that? There had been no quarrel except in his own mind and in his dreams.

He dialled the *Post*'s head office in Wood Green. No, Mr Sage wasn't there but he could try their Child's Hill office. Martin tried Child's Hill and was told Mr Sage hadn't been in all day. It was always hard to get hold of Tim. In the old days – he thought of pre-November as the old days – it was nearly always Tim who had phoned him. A feeling of desolation crept over him. He sat at his desk, unable to work for the first time in as long as he could remember.

It was about an hour later that Caroline came in to say that an Indian family had arrived and were asking for Mr Urban.

'A man and a woman and a little boy and an old man and an old woman who looks just like Mrs Gandhi.'

He stared at her.

'What do they want?'

'You,' said Caroline. 'They've just got back from India today, or some of them have, and they've been in Australia first and they want to see you and thank you for something. That's what they said.'

The Bhavnanis.

For months he had hoped to see them, had longed, though never quite admitting it to himself, for some crumb of gratitude from someone. And now they had come he knew he couldn't face them.

'Take them in to my father,' he said. 'He's called Mr Urban too.' Although it was only four he walked out of the office and drove back to Swan Place where he sat by the window, waiting for Francesca to come, although he knew she wouldn't come.

Samphire Road. Martin found it in the *London Atlas* he kept in the glove compartment of his car. It was Finsbury Park really, North Four. He didn't think he had ever been there or known anyone else who lived there.

If Tim was out he would sit in the car and wait for him. He would wait till midnight if necessary, he had nothing else to do. But he probably wouldn't have to wait like that because the man Tim lived with would be there. Why had he ever worried about having to meet this man, about seeing him and Tim together? He couldn't have cared less now.

It was getting on for six when Martin left Swan Place. If Tim had had an afternoon job he would be home by now, and if he had an evening job it was unlikely he would go out before seven. He and his friend might be eating their evening meal. Martin recalled the big red sofa he had dreamed about, red velvet, sponge-like yet dusty. It embarrassed him even to think of it.

He drove up Crouch End Hill and down Hornsey Rise. The sky was like a thick grey veil which the sunset had torn open to show through the rents radiant flesh colours. He would tell Tim everything, he thought, and the prospect of being able to be open and candid with Tim at last filled him with a joy so intense that his hands actually trembled on the wheel. For a moment he forgot the loss of Francesca and the bitter, growing disillusionment. The secret he had kept from Tim for three months had weighed upon him – how heavily he was only now realizing – and at last, within a few minutes perhaps, he was about to unburden himself. That his purpose in coming here was to question Tim about the paragraph in the *Post* had receded and dimmed in the fierce light of the confession, the money and its source, Francesca, his long silence and coldness, he was going to make. He longed for it as the devout sinner longs for the confessional and the exhausted tormented prisoner for a chance to admit his guilt.

He had entered a desolate wilderness where streets, walled-in wooden barricades, traversed a grassless, treeless, and almost building-less waste. A few new houses, in strange colours of brick, lemon, pasty white, charcoal, rose here and there in straggling lines. The old streets of old brown houses clung to the perimeter like low cliffs surrounding a crater in a desert. Martin found Samphire Road quite easily, even though his map no longer gave a very clear idea of the layout. It was a gorge in the brown cliff with shabby houses which made Martin think of the living quarters in some aged and perhaps abandoned garrison. Compared to it, Fortis Green Lane was paradise.

He walked up broken concrete steps to the liver-coloured front door and pressed the bell marked Sage. Nothing happened for a moment and then a light came on behind the green and yellow glass transom over the door. He was aware now that he could smell Gauloise smoke, as if Tim hadn't long come in.

The door opened and Tim stood there. He wore jeans and an old grey, heavy, stringy sweater that made him look thinner than ever, gaunt almost. His face was very pale, his mouth as red as fresh blood. Had he always been so pale? He took the cigarette out of his mouth and said:

'I thought you'd turn up. It was only a matter of time before you cottoned on.'

Martin stared at him. He didn't know what he meant. Then something so strange happened, so amazing really, that temporarily he forgot all about Tim. The door at the end of the passage opened and a child came running out and towards them. The child was, must be, but couldn't be, Lindsay.

She came to an abrupt halt and looked at Martin. Her look was full of anger and dislike. She threw herself against Tim's legs, holding up her arms. Tim lifted her up and held her against his shoulder, black hair against black hair, sallow velvet skin touching sallow waxen skin. Four blue eyes looked at Martin. He felt the earth move under his feet, the walls tilt, the dark, frowsty, uncarpeted passage rock back and forth and steady itself.

'You'd better come in,' said Tim.

Martin came in and felt the door close behind him. He was unable to speak. He took a few steps down the passage, then turned, shaking, to contemplate again Lindsay and her undoubted father. But Francesca was her undoubted mother . . .

'I don't understand,' he began. 'You and Francesca . . . Where's Francesca?'

Tim put the child down. He leant against the door, his arms folded. 'She's dead. You didn't know? No, I reckon – well, how could you? She was killed last Saturday night, run over, the car didn't stop.'

Lindsay, clinging to his legs, began suddenly to cry.

21

Lindsay's screams seemed to express the grief of both men, Tim's sorrow, Martin's stunned, incredulous dismay. They were both silent, oblivious of the sobs and howls, the stamping feet, the fists beating at Tim's legs. They stared at each other but Martin was the first to let his gaze drop and to turn away. Slowly Tim reached down and picked Lindsay up. She stopped screaming but continued to sob, her arms and legs clamped against him like a starfish.

A door opened upstairs and a woman's voice called:

'Everything OK, Tim? God, she was making a racket.'

Tim went to the foot of the stairs with Lindsay in his arms. 'Could you have her for half an hour, Goldie?'

'Sure, if you want. She'll have to watch telly, though, it's my serial on.'

'Lindsay wants Goldie!' The child scrambled down her father's body and up the stairs on all fours.

'You'd better come in here and have a drink,' said Tim. 'We could both use a drink.'

He led Martin down the passage into the room from which Lindsay had emerged. It was a kitchen, modernized in skimpy patches round the sink area and a unit of cupboards but otherwise dismally old-fashioned with a defunct boiler in one corner and, in the wall facing them, a fireplace whose flue was blocked up with red crêpe paper. The oven was on and so was a wall heater. On the table, which was littered with newspapers and Gauloise packets, were the remains of a meal and a half-empty bottle of Dominic's military gin.

Martin moved as if in a daze. Tim motioned him to one of the small shabby fireside chairs that flanked the wall heater but Martin sat, or sank, into a bentwood chair at the table and put his head in his hands.

'D'you want it neat or with water?'

'Doesn't matter.'

Martin had never before drunk gin without tonic or martini or some other fancy mixer. He had never drunk it warm which this was. It tasted so disgusting that he gave a strong shudder, but the fiery stuff bolstered him. He turned to look at Tim with haggard eyes. Tim was watching him with something that might have been despair or just indifference. When he spoke it was in a cool detached voice, such as a sociologist might use, reporting on failure, misery, defeat.

'I'll tell you what the police told me and fill in the gaps from my own knowledge. After you'd dropped her at that place in Finchley, she went to look for a taxi to take her home. It wasn't the first time, it's not easy to find taxis up there. She walked a long way, nearly up to the North Circular.' Tim paused, resuming in the same flat voice. 'You can't see how anyone could have failed to see her crossing the road, it's so brightly lit. Maybe the guy was drunk or just not looking. Another motorist found her ten minutes afterwards – or that's what they think. She wasn't dead. She died in hospital on Sunday evening.'

Martin said softly, 'She lived all that time . . . ?'

'She wasn't conscious. Have some more gin?'

Tim re-filled their glasses. He lit another cigarette. The only sign of emotion he gave was the way he drew on that cigarette with nervous, greedy gasps.

'Right,' he said. 'Question time.'

The gin was making Martin hot and dizzy and brave. 'Were you *married* to Francesca?'

Tim laughed, a sound that had nothing to do with amusement. 'You know better than that, you're my accountant. Wouldn't I have had to tell you if I'd been married? Francesca was still married to a guy in Ilford. He's called Russell Brown, *he* really is.'

'But that piece in your paper . . .'

'Pieces in the paper are of human origin. They're not messages from some infallible source of truth.' Tim shrugged. 'I made it up, bar the names. You found the house yourself. I didn't tell you she lived at 54 Fortis Green Lane and, incidentally, neither did she. You fabricated it. You made conjecture into truth just as you did when you saw those bruises on Francesca and thought Russell had put them there. In fact, she'd fallen over on the ice like several thousand other people did that day.'

Martin was silent. Then he said slowly, 'Do you mean that it was all a conspiracy between you and Francesca? All of it?' The enormity of what had been done to him was now breaking over Martin in waves. He could feel a pulse drumming in his head. 'You both of you set out to con me, to get . . .' He understood now, '. . . a flat out of me? You were two – criminals who did that?'

'At the beginning,' said Tim, 'Francesca set out only to get money or a piece of jewellery. I knew about your pools win, of course, I've known from the first. You must have forgotten that though I'm not much of a success at things I've got a spectacularly good memory.' He took a gulp of gin and it made him shudder. 'You aren't the soul of generosity, are you? I got nothing and she got nothing until you hit on your bright idea of a tax dodge. By that time, as you accountants might say, she was in for a penny, in for a pound.'

Martin had got to his feet. He swayed and steadied himself. There was one thing still, one last thing. If she had been unfaithful to Russell Brown with Tim, she had been unfaithful to Tim with him. He looked into Tim's eyes and the voice which he meant to be defiant, spitting revelations, came out falteringly.

'She slept with me! Did she ever tell you that?'

Tim had half-risen, his mouth smiling, his eyes dead. He shrugged. 'So? It was hard work. There was no question of mixing pleasure with business.'

Without thought or preparation, Martin hit him. He

doubled his fist and swung and struck Tim on the jaw. Tim let out a grunt and fell back into the chair, but he was up again straight away, leaping on Martin with both hands raised. Martin ducked and struck out again and fell across the table, knocking over the lamp which rolled on to the floor and went out.

The room was dark but for the fierce red glow from the wall heater, so that redness lay on the air and on the furniture and on Tim, backed against the door, a demon, a fallen angel, painted with red light. He came at Martin again, punching to his face, but this time Martin seized him by the shoulders, by his thin hard rib cage. For a moment they remained upright, locked together, struggling, then they tumbled to the floor and rolled, clutching each other, into the deep dark shadows of the floor and across the thick, old, rumpled rug.

Tim was trying to grab his shoulders so as to beat his head against the ground. Martin was stronger. He was bigger and heavier than Tim, and more powerful. He got hold of Tim's wrists and held them behind his back, wrapping him in his arms.

With this success, this subduing of Tim, a tremendous excitement seized him. He was wrestling with Tim, he was doing what he had longed to do in those dreams. And in the pressure of Tim's hard flesh, the friction of his body writhing and turning so that they rolled this way and that, embraced so tightly that each body seemed to penetrate the other and fuse with it, he felt himself charged and stiff with desire. He felt a passion which made his relations with Francesca seem thin and cold.

Whether Tim realized or not he didn't care. He was lost to all caution and all inhibiting restraint. He spoke Tim's name in a hoarse whisper and the struggling slackened. There was a moment in which Martin hardly seemed to breathe and then, because he couldn't help himself, he put his mouth over Tim's and gave him a long, enduring kiss. The release that came with that kiss seemed to take with it the repressive burdens of a lifetime. He rolled away from Tim and lay on his face.

Tim got up first. He did what he would do on the gallows or at an H-bomb early warning. He lit a Gauloise. His mouth quirked up on one side at Martin and he gave a sort of half-wink. Martin was flooded with shame, the burdens of a lifetime were still there. He got to his feet and sat, hunched, in one of the fireside chairs.

'Don't put the light on.'

'OK, not if you don't want.'

'I'm sorry about that. Just now, I mean.' Martin tried not to mumble. He tried to look at Tim through the red gloom, to meet his eyes and speak lucidly. It was nearly impossible. 'I don't know why I did that.'

'It was the military gin. The fact is, it's meant for guardsmen and you know what guardsmen are.'

'I'm not queer, gay, whatever you call it.'

'It was the gin, love,' said Tim.

He had perched himself on the edge of the table. Martin managed to focus on him now, and if he was flushed it didn't show in that light. 'Perhaps I am, though,' he said in a low voice. 'Perhaps I am really and I never knew it. Why have there been so many things I didn't know and couldn't see, Tim?'

' "Humanity treads ever on a thin crust over terrific abysses". I remember I said that to you before all this started. We've both fallen in with a crash, haven't we?'

Martin nodded. He was embarrassed still and ashamed still but a warmth that had nothing to do with the heater was slowly engulfing him. He loved Tim, he knew it now. Nothing that Tim had done to him mattered any more. He said:

'That flat, the one Francesca was going to move into, you can have it, I want you to have it.'

'Is it yours to give, my dear?'

'Well, I . . .' Technically, legally, it wasn't. It was the technical, the legal, aspect which mattered, though.

'It'll be shared between four people, I should think. Francesca had a husband and a child and parents. Lindsay will get some of it and I suppose Russell Brown will get most of it.'

'Tim, I'll give you . . .' What? He had nothing left to give. 'I want to do something. We've both lost Francesca, that ought to bring us together, it ought to . . . What are you smiling at?'

'Your naïvety.'

'I can't see that it's naïve to want to help someone because you feel you owe it to them. Look, I could sell my flat and buy a small house somewhere – well, not so nice, and you could bring Lindsay and come and live there with me and . . . We have to be friends, Tim.'

'Do we, my dear? I've injured you and we dislike those we've injured.' Tim walked across the room and switched on the central light. It was bright, glaring, uncompromising. 'I'm sorry for what I did now, I bitterly regret it, but being sorry doesn't make me like you any more. I wouldn't dream of sharing a house with you and if you offered me money I should refuse it.' He stubbed out his cigarette, coughing a little. 'It's time you went home now. I have to fetch Lindsay and put her to bed.'

Martin got up. He felt as if he had been hit in the face with something cold and wet, a wet glove perhaps.

'Is that all?' he stammered. 'Have we said it all?'

Tim didn't answer. They were out in the icy dank hallway now and from upstairs, distantly, came a wail, 'Lindsay wants Daddy.'

Tim opened the front door. 'The inquest was today. Accidental death. Cremation Monday, three o'clock, Golders Green. A hearty welcome will be extended to all husbands, real, imaginary, future and common law.'

Martin walked down the steps and into the street without looking back. He heard the door close. His head was banging from bewilderment and incredulity and gin.

It was a quarter past seven. He had been with Tim for less than an hour. In those forty-five or fifty minutes his whole life, the past as well as the present and the future, had been changed. It was as if the world had tilted and he been thrown sliding down the slope of it to hang there, breathless, by his hands. Or as if, as Tim said, the thin crust had given way.

His head was hurting him now. He had drunk a lot of that gin, probably a tumblerful. But he didn't feel drunk, only sick and headachey and drained. He was tired as well but he didn't think he would sleep, he felt as if he would never sleep again.

For a long time he sat in the car in Samphire Road. He only drove away because he was afraid Tim might come out and find him still there, and even then he parked again almost immediately, in one of the streets that had been turned into a cul-de-sac by the crater of devastated land.

It was quite dark now and the rubble-covered waste was totally unlighted. The edges of it only were visible, a horizon of black jagged roofs, punctured with points of light, against the crimson-suffused sky. Francesca had lived here, come from here every morning, returned here each night. It seemed to him infinitely strange, something he would never fully understand. She was dead and had been dead for nearly a week now. In her dying she had somehow come back to him, there had been no terrible betrayal. How could Tim know how she had felt? How could Tim tell that for all her early motives she hadn't, at the end, come to prefer the new man to the old?

From taking a vicious pleasure in the fact of her death – he had felt like that when he first began to understand – he found he could now think of her with a pitying tenderness. They would never have been happy together, or not for long, he could see that. He was getting to know himself at last, he thought.

His head wasn't going to get any better just sitting here. If the place had been more attractive – less downright sinister, in fact – he would have gone for a walk, walked to clear his head, for it was a mild evening with that indefinable smell and charge in the air that heralds spring. But he couldn't walk here. He started the car and drove away into Hornsey Rise.

Someone walked across a pedestrian crossing ahead of him. He braked and waited rather longer than usual. He thought of the manner of Francesca's death. Who could do such a thing? Knock someone down and drive away to leave her dying? She had taken a night and a day to die. He shivered uncontrollably. Whoever it was, the police would find him, the police would be relentless . . . Martin reflected that he shouldn't be driving at all, he had had far too much to drink, a lot over the permitted limit. Perhaps Francesca's killer had also been drinking, had sobered up in terror when he saw what he had done, and terror had made him flee. Martin drove home over the Archway, the road in its deep concrete gorge flowing northwards beneath him.

He put the car on the hard-top parking in front of Cromwell Court, parking it between an orange-coloured Volvo and a small grey van. The Volvo belonged to a doctor at the Royal Free who lived on the ground floor. The grey van was probably some tradesman's, though Martin felt obscurely that he had seen it somewhere before, and recently, and in a context he couldn't at the moment recall. It couldn't be of the slightest importance. He walked across the asphalt to the entrance of the block, aware that someone had got out of the van and was also coming in.

But he didn't hold the door open. He let it swing shut and made for the stairs, wishing, not for the first time, that there was a lift here as there was in Swan Place. Should he get Adrian to fight for Swan Place against that family of Francesca's? Was there any chance of success? At least, he thought as he climbed the third flight, he could now tell Adrian and Norman and his parents the melancholy truth, that Francesca was dead.

The soft but regular footsteps which, lower down, he had heard coming behind him he could now hear again. They were coming up to the top. The driver of the grey van must be calling at one of the other three flats on this floor. Martin got to the top and crossed the corridor to his own front door. There, standing on the threshold of his home, he was suddenly and sharply reminded by the memory of himself and Tim embraced in Tim's red-lit kitchen, and of kissing Tim and holding him in his arms. What would become of him if this was what he wanted? What must he look forward to? He released his pent-up breath and put his key into the lock.

As he did so he heard a low cough behind him. It made Martin jump and he wheeled round. Standing about a yard from him, in grey woolly hat, yellow pullover, black velvet waistcoat and a black scarf with coins sewn round it, was Finn. Martin hadn't really noticed before what extraordinary eyes the man had. They were almost silver. The man with the silver eyes . . .

'Well, well,' said Finn. 'I've been waiting long enough.'

He pushed past Martin and into the flat.

22

The flat was warm and very stuffy. For most of the day the sun must have been shining on that big window. It was rare for Finn to be a guest in anyone's home. He could count on the fingers of his large, splayed hands the number of times it had happened: twice at Mr Beard's, once at Mrs Gogarty's, three or four times in girls' rooms.

He stood looking about him. At the structure and the paintwork mainly, he had a business interest in things like that. He took off his woolly hat but kept his gloves on.

Martin Urban was getting a brandy bottle out of a drinks cabinet. You would think he had had enough, he stank of gin. Finn could tell that something had frightened or upset him. His hands trembled and made the bottle chatter against the glass.

'Brandy? There's no whisky but there's vodka and martini and sherry.'

'I don't drink,' said Finn.

The voice sounded both weary and awkward. 'Look, I'm sorry about the money. I've had a lot on my plate and I'm afraid I forgot all about you. I could give you a cheque here and now, only you will insist on cash.'

Finn didn't say anything.

'Sit down, won't you? I'm sorry you've come all the way here for nothing, you should have phoned.' He sat down and drank his brandy at a gulp as if it were medicine. Finn watched him curiously, watched a flush mottle his skin. He wasn't going to sit down. What would be the point?

'I haven't come here for nothing,' he said.

'Well . . .' Into the glass slopped more brandy. 'Not in the sense that you've reminded me. I can get it for you sometime next week. Cash is difficult, you know, that sort of cash. I'll have to phone my bank first, I'll have to . . .'

Finn took a step forward from the position he had taken up by the balcony door. 'You can get it for me Monday morning,' he said. 'And I don't want it sent, not this time.

Put it in your car on the front passenger seat and leave the car in the car park outside the palace.'

'The palace?' repeated Martin Urban, staring at him.

'Alexandra Palace.' Finn was getting impatient. 'Have you got that? Put the money in a carrier on the front seat of your car and leave it there between one and two Monday, OK?'

Martin Urban had flushed a dark crimson. His eyes had become very bright, his features blurred and thickened. He set down his glass and stood up. Very deliberately he said, 'No, it is not OK. It is very much not OK.' He passed a hand over his forehead, and when he took it down Finn saw that his face was working with fury. 'Just who the hell d'you think you are, coming here, barging in here, telling me what I should do with my own money? You haven't got some sort of right to it, you know. You people, you're all the same, you think anyone with a bit more than you've got owes you a living. It's purely out of the kindness of my heart I'm making it possible for your mother to have a decent place to live in. But I'm damned if I'm going to break an important appointment on Monday morning to go to the bank for you or do without my car for an hour. Why should I? Why the hell should I?'

Finn thought the man was going to fall. He watched him get hold of the back of a chair and hang on to it and draw a long breath and seem to get a grip on himself. Enough control, at any rate, to say coldly now, 'You'd better go,' and then, pushing past Finn to unlock the balcony door, 'Excuse me, I must have some air.'

Martin Urban went out on to the balcony. Finn watched him standing there, looking down on London and then up at the clear, faintly starry, purplish sky. After a moment or two he came in again, appearing partially recovered, and stood staring with a curiously pained expression, like a hurt dog, at the big cactus which stood on the window sill, at its pink, waxen flowers. Without turning to Finn, he said:

'I thought I told you to go.'

Finn didn't reply to this rhetorical question. He said, 'I don't want the money sent. Is that understood? I don't want those delivery people knowing.'

'Knowing what, for God's sake?' Martin Urban turned round and said sharply, 'I'm sick of this. I'm tired, I've had a bad day. If it wasn't that I promised and I don't like to break my word I'd tell you you can forget the money. Right, so you can have a cheque or nothing.'

'Well, well,' said Finn. 'Now we know.'

'Indeed we do. And when that's over I think I'll have done quite a favour to you and your mother.' He went to the writing desk, though none too steadily, and fumbled about inside it for a cheque book.

'Haven't I ever done anything for you?' said Finn.

Without looking at him, Martin Urban said, 'Like what? Like making a damned nuisance of yourself. What have you ever done for me?' He began to write the cheque. Finn went up to him, laid a heavy hand on his arm and took the pen away. Martin Urban jumped to his feet, shouted, 'Take your hands off me!'

Finn held him by the upper arms and looked searchingly into his face. The square, flushed, puffy face was resentful and indignant – and utterly bewildered. Finn could read faces – and minds too sometimes.

'You don't know about it,' he said flatly. 'It wasn't in the papers. Well, it's done. Last Saturday.'

Martin Urban struggled to free himself and Finn let him go. 'How dare you touch me! And what the hell are you talking about?'

It was a strange thing but now that he had to do it Finn found it as hard to put the act into words as his clients had done. He looked around him, he cleared his throat.

'Last Saturday,' he said gruffly. 'I did for the girl. Like you wanted.'

Martin Urban stood quite still.

'*What did you say?*'

'You heard.'

'Last Saturday you . . .'

'I did for that girl, like you're paying me for. I've done it and now I want my money.'

The sound he made was a kind of ghastly groan, the like of which Finn had only previously heard from Lena, and he fell back on the sofa, covering his face with his hands. Finn regarded him as he rocked backwards and forwards, pushing his fists into his eyes, beating them against his temples. Finn stepped away and sat down on an upright chair, understanding now that he had made a mistake. Things, details, fell gently into place like the silver balls in Lena's Chinese puzzle dropping into their slots.

'Give me some more of that brandy.'

Finn poured some brandy and pushed the glass at Martin Urban's mouth. The brandy was drained and there was a shuddering and a kind of sob and the thick broken voice said:

'You were – in the car – that – didn't – stop?'

'I've said so.'

'What am I to do? My God, what am I going to do? You thought I'd paid you to do that? What sort of a monster *are* you?' He got up shakily and stood with his hands pressed to his head. 'I loved her,' he said. 'She loved me. We were going to be married. And you . . .'

He turned towards modern man's succour, lifeline, first aid – the phone. He took an uncertain step towards it. Finn calculated how to get there first, take him by surprise, wrench the wires out of the wall. And then? There was only one way to make certain no one was ever told what Martin Urban knew.

Swaying, holding his head, he stood staring hypnotically at Finn. Finn began to get up. Sweat beads had started to prickle his face. Somehow he must get Martin Urban out of here, into a car, away from this place into some lonely place. In order to silence him he must put on an act, make promises, play along. . . . He didn't know how to do these things, he was powerless, bereft of energy, as if a fuse had blown in him and there was no current to power his limbs.

Martin Urban took down his hands and turned away from the phone. The attack he made on Finn was entirely unexpected. One moment he was standing there in the middle of the room, his fists clenched, his arms gradually falling to his sides, the next he had sprung upon Finn, flailing out, using his hands like hammers. Finn toppled backwards. It was the first time in his life he had ever been knocked down by another.

He rolled over on to his front, pressed himself up with a violence that sent the other man staggering back, and leapt like a panther. Martin Urban ducked and stumbled out on to the balcony. London glittered out there like the window of a tourist souvenir shop. Finn stood poised in the doorway, his arms spread, his body quivering. And the man who had given him five thousand pounds from some quixotic altruism Finn couldn't even begin to understand, stood against the low parapet, convulsed, it seemed, with some kind of passionate need for revenge. He leapt forward again, deceived perhaps by Finn's white thinness.

But Finn was there a split second before him, to smash with his right arm harder than he had ever smashed before. And a strange thing happened. Martin Urban raised his arms hugely above his head in some exaggerated defensive gesture. He staggered backwards in an almost comic, tip-toe slow motion, bathed in the shining night air, against the spangled backdrop, staggered, teetered, until the parapet wall that reached lower than the tops of his thighs, was just behind him. Finn could see what would happen and he jumped to catch the man before he fell. He jumped just too late. Martin Urban made contact with the wall, doubled over backwards, and with a low cry, fell.

Forty feet into a pit of blackness. There was a concrete well down there, an area that perhaps gave access to a porter's basement. Finn stood, looking down. No other windows opened, no one appeared, no one had been alerted by the groaning sound the man had made as he starfished to earth. Finn went in and closed and locked the balcony door. He turned off the lights and stood listening for movement in the corridor outside, for doors opening and footsteps. There was nothing.

He had been a fool to lock that door. It must look like suicide. It must look as if Martin Urban had killed himself over the death of the woman he was to have married. Finn unlocked the door again. He didn't touch the brandy glass. A man might well drink brandy before he committed suicide. The irony of it struck Finn, though, as he moved towards the front door of the flat, the irony that now, at this moment, in this place, he was at greater risk through this man's accidental death than he had ever been when he had done murder.

When he was satisfied that all was quiet and still he passed stealthily out of the flat and pulled the front door softly shut behind him. He went downstairs very fast, passing no one, hearing nothing. The van was waiting for him in a deserted car park. And deserted, too, Cromwell Court and its environs would have seemed but for the lights which shone with tranquillity in most of its broad rectangular windows.

Still, it was only a matter of time, of short time, before that body would be found. He must get away, not linger, not yield to the temptation to steal softly around to the other side of the block and peer into that dark well, check what light must go on or which door open to reveal its occupant . . .

He resisted. As he was driving down Dartmouth Park Hill, coming up to the traffic lights at Tufnell Park station, he heard the wail of a siren. But there was nothing to say it was an ambulance summoned for Martin Urban, it could just as well have been a fire engine or a police car. He put the van away in the garage at the corner of Somerset Grove and walked home along the street where the sulphurous light laid a pinchbeck gleam.

The house smelt of cannabis and waste bins. Finn went on up to the top, taking two stairs at a time with his great loping stride. He felt a surge of confidence and contentment. This time it really had been an accident, he could face Lena without dread. And there was no possibility now of anyone suspecting Martin Urban might not have been alone in the flat, not a soul who knew of any connection between himself and Martin Urban. He was sure no one had seen him or would know him if they had. Yet Martin Urban was out of harm's way, silenced, taking the secret of Finn's mistake with him into the dark spaces or losing it in oblivion as he began on a new cycle of life.

The green bird began a shrill twittering when he came into the room. Mrs Gogarty, who had been making forecasts with the aid of the Tarot, got up and threw the shawl over its cage.

'Well, well,' said Finn, 'we *are* cosy.'

He pulled off his gloves and put them in his pocket and took Lena's hand. She was as transparent as an insect tonight and dusty like a moth. Her dull leaden eyes met his silver eyes and she smiled.

'The picture of devotion!' said Mrs Gogarty with admiring sighs. She studied the cards, laid out now for Finn. 'There's a lot of death here . . .' she began.

Over Lena's head Finn gave her a warning look.

'Ah!' She slid the cards together and the Death Card,

Scorpio's death card, death cloaked and riding a pale horse, came out on top. She covered it with the Queen of Wands. In her mechanical gypsy voice she said, 'There's money here, my darling, a lot of money. But wait . . . No, it's not coming your way, you'll have a disappointment.'

The hand that held Lena's grew cold and limp. He bent down, he looked unseeing into the soothsayer's face.

'What? What did you say?'

'A disappointment over money. . . . Why are you looking at me like that?'

Finn saw, not the cards which Mrs Gogarty's hands now covered in fear, not Lena's face, apprehensive, growing stricken, but a cheque that lay on a writing desk, locked up in Martin Urban's flat. The date had been written – had his name?

The women's eyes fearfully upon him, he stood upright yet trembling in that tiny room, listening to the distant sound of a siren crying through the dark, a herald of the one that must cry for him.